The
Oil Patch
Quartet

The
Oil Patch
Quartet

An omnibus of four novels by
JOHN BALLEM

Cormorant Books

Canada Council
for the Arts

Conseil des Arts
du Canada

ONTARIO ARTS COUNCIL
CONSEIL DES ARTS DE L'ONTARIO

The publisher gratefully acknowledges the support of the
Canada Council for the Arts and the Ontario Arts Council
for its publishing program. We acknowledge the financial support
of the Government of Canada through the Book Publishing
Industry Development Program (BPIDP) for our publishing activities.

Printed and bound in Canada

LIBRARY AND ARCHIVES CANADA CATALOGUING IN PUBLICATION

Ballem, John, 1925–
The oil patch quartet : an omnibus of four novels / John Ballem.

Contents: The devil's lighter. — Oilpatch empire. — Death spiral.
— The barons.

ISBN 1-896951-89-9

I. Title.

PS8553.A45O45 2005   C813'.54   C2005-903443-2

Cover design: Marijke Friesen
Cover image: © Comstock Images
Author photo: Grace L. Ballem
Text design: Tannice Goddard
Printer: Marquis Book Printing

CORMORANT BOOKS INC.
215 SPADINA AVENUE, STUDIO 230, TORONTO, ON CANADA M5T 2C7
www.cormorantbooks.com

For Grace.

The Barons

I

"The company pays to move you up here and then you go your own sweet way." Ed Parsons's voice was scathing. "You young punks make me sick!"

Parsons's reaction took Mark totally by surprise. He had expected his resignation to be accepted with cool professionalism, not with an ugly confrontation like this. He got to his feet. "If that's how you feel, I'll reimburse the company for my moving expenses."

"Offer accepted." The general manager smiled a cunning little smile of triumph. "I'll have the personnel department make out the invoice." He turned to the exploration manager and ordered him to go with Mark and stay with him while he cleaned out his desk.

Mark expected that. Oil companies tend to be paranoid about geologists who quit; they know altogether too much about the confidential oil plays the company might be working on. But he had not expected to be accused of cheating the company over his moving expenses. True, it had only been eight months since Permex had transferred him from the Houston head office to its Canadian branch in Calgary, and Parsons obviously felt Mark was taking unfair advantage of the company by quitting so soon. But that hadn't even entered his mind; his only idea had been to strike out on his own and see if he could make a go of it as an independent oil operator.

"Goddamn it," he complained to the exploration manager, Harvey Morrison, as he opened his drawers and spread their contents on the metal top of his desk, "when I was transferred to the Canadian branch I had every intention of staying as long as the company wanted me to, and then going wherever else in the world they sent me, like a loyal little company man. It was only when I saw what was going on up here that I decided I had to have a piece of it. I wasn't trying to take Permex for a free ride, like Ed thinks."

"I know that, and so does Ed, even if he'd never admit it. But he's worked for Permex all his life and it burns his ass when a bright young buck like you leaves. Besides, he'll pick up merit marks in Houston for squeezing that refund out of you."

Mark stared at him. "You really mean that? It was only $800 and change, for Christ's sake!"

"Like they say, it's not the money, it's the principle," replied Harvey sardonically.

Mark waved a hand at the collection of rolled-up maps, graph paper, and other odds and ends that littered the desk. "The only thing that belongs to me is my slide rule, and that's all I'm taking. Okay?"

"Fair enough," agreed the exploration manager. They both knew that nothing would have prevented Mark, had he been so inclined, from making copies of confidential materials and removing them from the building in the days and weeks preceding his resignation. More importantly, they couldn't expunge from his mind the knowledge and ideas he had acquired while in Permex's employ.

"I'm supposed to warn you not to use or disclose anything you learned while you were with us."

"I have no intention of doing so."

"Well, I guess that does it. I'll take you down to personnel for your termination interview and then you'll be on your own." Harvey held out his hand. "Good luck, Mark. I'm sure we'll see each other around the patch."

Mark grinned. "I'll be back pounding on your door with some red hot deals."

"Not if the man upstairs has anything to do with it, you won't."

The termination interview didn't take long. He surrendered his building pass, and was informed that his insurance policy would lapse in thirty days. He was also told that, because he had worked for Permex for a total of only twenty months — a year in Houston and eight months in Calgary — the contributions the company had made to his pension plan had not vested. However, he was entitled to the contributions he had made personally. It tickled Mark that they amounted to something over $800 — enough to pay back the company for his moving expenses.

"This is going to be a real blow to the ladies in the secretarial pool," the personnel clerk sneered as he stamped "Terminated" on Mark's file. "They'll have to find some new stud to get antsy over."

Mark hadn't lived for twenty-six years without being aware of his own good looks. At just under six feet and weighing an even 160 pounds, he had a trim and well-conditioned physique, but it was his profile that drew lingering glances from the opposite sex. His eyes were light brown under eyebrows several shades darker than his reddish brown hair, and his features were just rugged enough to avoid the pretty boy label.

"You plan to audition for the part?" asked Mark, angered by the smirk on the clerk's pasty face.

And then he was on the street. The thought sent a chill of apprehension through him. Maybe he had just made the biggest mistake of his life — exchanging an assured career with a multinational oil company for the high-risk occupation of peddling oil deals. And he didn't have much in the way of a stake, either. Fifteen hundred dollars in the bank and the two-tone Oldsmobile hardtop he had driven up from Houston were about it.

Mark reminded himself that Bill Crawford had done the same thing a year ago and he seemed to be surviving. Bill didn't talk about it, but the story was that Marianne had hysterics when he came home in the middle of the day and announced he had quit his job. If Bill Crawford, with a wife and young family to support, could take the chance, then what was a footloose bachelor like himself worried about? Hell, the oil boom was just starting and he was in on the ground floor.

The diesel's air horn blatted an urgent warning, startling Mark out of his introspective musings. He looked up to see a yard engine bearing down on him, on the same track he was about to cross. Just in time he jumped back and stood stock — still while the shiny new diesel rumbled past, its engineer shaking his fist. The CPR did its best to keep the growing army of oil — company employees from taking a shortcut across the tracks that ran through downtown Calgary, but it was a losing battle.

Chastened, Mark kept a smart lookout as he crossed the rest of the railway marshalling yard. The Olds was parked a block south of the tracks. It felt strange to be walking through the quiet streets that early in the afternoon, while everyone else was still at work. As he drove back to the apartment, he made a determined effort to shake off the vague sense of unease that seemed to have taken up residence somewhere inside his rib cage. He'd have to begin thinking positively, and a good way to start would be to throw a party to celebrate his joining the ranks of independent oilmen. Arranging a party was simply a matter of making a few phone calls and spreading the word. He'd better let Dave Green know first, though. He and Dave shared an apartment in the new Britannia subdivision. The rents were out-of-sight, but it was where all the action was. Dave was a non-stop talker, but he got away with it because he was genuinely funny; he also didn't mind when you tuned him out. He should have been a stand-up comedian; instead, he toiled in the land department of Stanmin Resources. He was at his desk when Mark phoned to tell him about the party they were throwing.

"Terrific. Anybody we know coming?"

"You never know your luck. I thought I'd ask 'The Bod.' It's a celebration, by the way."

"What are we celebrating?"

"The fact that I resigned from Permex today to go out on my own."

"Boy, you sure played that one close to your old Tattersal vest. Okay, I'll get on the hotline and round up some live ones."

The party lost no time in getting into gear. A growing army of secretaries had invaded Calgary in the last few years, providing an inexhaustible supply of willing young companions for the swinging bachelors who had also arrived in the wake of the oil industry. You just had to mix them with copious quantities of booze — every man brought his own bottle — turn up the volume on the record player, and you had an instant party.

Some of the men cornered Mark in the kitchen, wanting to know more about his plans. A few seemed envious of his new-found independence but the majority were sceptical and mildly patronizing, complacent with their own bright futures as professional managers in an ever-expanding industry. Mark answered their questions for a while, then extricated himself to go in search of his date.

Betty MacDonald, "The Bod" as Dave had nicknamed her, didn't attend parties, she starred in them. She was only too aware of her spectacular physical assets and dressed to display them to the best advantage, swelling young breasts almost bursting out of her low-cut bodice. Mark had been dating her for the past few weeks and had yet to make out with her. In fact he had been watching his alcohol intake in the hope that tonight might be the night. As usual she was holding court, not saying much, but ruling with an inviting smile and mind-blowing cleavage. Mark inserted himself into the circle and asked her if she would like to dance. Strangely, he wasn't jealous of the attention she invariably attracted. It had taken only one date for him to discover that she was a bit of a bubblehead and his intentions were strictly physical.

The table had been removed from the dining area to make room for dancing and the small floor was crowded with couples, most of them barely moving as they swayed to the music like mating snakes. Bill and Marianne Crawford were among the few who were actually dancing. Looking at them over Betty's shoulder, Mark was suddenly struck with the thought that, physically at least, Marianne was a smaller version of The Bod. She was shorter by several inches but she had the same voluptuous full-busted figure and, again like The Bod, her facial features had a faint touch of coarseness. As always, Marianne looked discontented and vaguely resentful. It was common knowledge that she hadn't wanted to leave Houston, but had resigned herself to a spell of "foreign service" to further her husband's career. When Bill made the move permanent by leaving Consolidated Oil to set up his own company in Calgary, she made no secret of her unhappiness, something which did not endear her to their circle of friends. Bill caught Mark's eye and grinned amiably. As soon as he walked through the door, he had shaken Mark's hand and congratulated him on going out on his own, telling him that "he'd never look back." This, coming from someone who had also cut the corporate umbilical cord, was just the reassurance that Mark needed.

As the night wore on the sexual temperature climbed. Some couples slipped outside to the parked cars and others fondled each other in the two bedrooms. The Crawfords and the only two other married couples who were present said goodnight to Mark and slipped quietly away.

Betty had excused herself to go to the bathroom and Mark was fixing himself a drink when he saw Roger Farris coming through the open door. Roger was a sort of modern day remittance man who received a monthly allowance from his wealthy family in Montreal as long as he never came within a thousand miles of that city. He had never worked a day in his life, but he was always trying to ingratiate himself with powerful business and professional men by inviting them to the wild parties he threw and fixing them up on the side with willing young ladies. He had someone in tow now and Mark's eyes widened when he saw who it was. Roger had landed a big fish tonight.

Mark had never met Cliff Marsden, but oil industry journals and the financial pages of the *Herald* and other newspapers had made the heavy-featured face, with its built-in sneer, instantly recognizable. The oil tycoon was one of those living legends that were being spawned by the growing oil industry. He owned the first large-diameter oil pipeline in Alberta and was rumoured to have ambitions to become the pipeline czar of Canada. Definitely the sort of man that an ambitious young oilman should get to know. Mark picked his way through swaying couples oblivious of anything but each other, and went to welcome the new arrivals.

He was always uneasy around Roger Farris. The playboy was pleasant enough, indeed most of the time he fawned over people like a too-friendly puppy, but there was a lack of comprehension in his pale blue eyes that was obscurely troubling. Privately, Mark doubted if Roger was playing with a full deck, but there was no doubt the guy had a talent for lining up party girls. Dave always claimed that Roger "got more ass than a toilet seat," but Mark wasn't so sure.

Betty came out of the washroom just as Roger was introducing Mark to the oil baron. Cliff Marsden ignored Mark's outstretched hand and said to Farris in an urgent whisper, "Who's the blonde? I want to meet her."

"She's with me tonight, sir," Mark said evenly. "I'll be happy to introduce you."

"Why don't you do that, sonny?" Cliff Marsden took his elbow and propelled him over to where a circle of admirers was re-forming around Betty. Cliff was smiling, but the curl of his upper lip turned it into a leer and Mark saw her recoil slightly with something like panic in her eyes. She could handle the eager young studs who swarmed around her, but this older man with his reptilian gaze and unmistakable aura of power and wealth was something completely outside her experience. Cliff was asking her to dance when one of the guests hauled Mark off to deal with a girl who had gone hysterical and locked herself in the bathroom.

It took Mark nearly fifteen minutes to sweet-talk the sobbing woman into unlocking the door. Two of her girlfriends led her into the kitchen and began to pump black coffee into her. There was no sign of Betty in the living room. Christ Almighty, had she left with Cliff? It was possible; a lot of women really dug that power and wealth trip. It would make one Mark Hunter look like some kind of a fool, though. He was heading for the makeshift bar in the kitchen when he heard a woman's scream. It came again, and this time he heard his own name. The scream ended abruptly in the middle of a "help" as if a hand had been clamped over her mouth.

Screaming women were nothing new to the parties that Mark's crowd threw, and everyone except Mark seemed to be content to ignore the cry. Mark dashed out of the room and into the hallway where an oil company lawyer interrupted a heavy petting session long enough to mumble that the scream had come from around the corner, adding, "She's stopped, so everything's under control."

Mark rushed past the lawyer and his half-undressed companion and sprinted down to the end of the hallway, almost caroming into the opposite wall as he swung around the corner. Betty was struggling with Cliff Marsden, pounding ineffectually against his shoulder with her fist. Cliff's right hand cupped her chin and twisted her head cruelly sideways as he pressed his open mouth down on hers. The front of her dress was ripped open and her full breasts had popped free of the confining bra. His left hand groped inside her skirt.

Mark grabbed him by the shoulder, spun him around and threw a wild haymaker that found its target with a bone-crushing splat. Another blow split Cliff's lips. Instinctively he brought his hands up and Mark, who was no boxer but was young and fit, pummelled his exposed midsection. Consumed with fury, Mark unloaded another roundhouse right that snapped Cliff's head back. The older man was completely defenceless. Somewhat shocked by the damage he had done, Mark stepped back and watched him crumple to the floor. Betty, her face garishly smeared with lipstick and her bare shoulders bruised with angry red welts, was trying to cover herself with the torn remnants of her dress.

"You all right?" asked Mark, panting from his exertions, and she nodded numbly. One of her friends came up and wrapped a blanket around her. Gradually Mark became aware of the crowd that filled the hallway with excited whispers. A woman was kneeling beside Cliff, feeling the base of his throat for a pulse. Mark was assailed with sudden panic. Was Marsden dead?

Cliff's eyelids flickered and the young woman, whose name Mark couldn't recall but who he now remembered was a nurse, murmured encouraging sounds. She helped Cliff as he groggily struggled to sit up. He gagged suddenly and spat out a mouthful of blood and white fragments of teeth.

"This man should be taken to a hospital," the nurse declared. "That nose has to be set and he's got a couple of broken teeth."

Aghast, Mark protested, "Christ, if you do that, the whole world will know about it. That's the last thing he'd want. Look, he's not going to die, is he?"

"He's not in a life-threatening situation, no," she replied frostily.

"Okay then. I think someone should drive him home and let the family doctor deal with it."

Cliff was fully conscious now and he beckoned to Roger Farris, who bent over to listen to what he was mumbling, then announced, "He wants to be taken to my place. His doctor will come there."

"I'll go with him," the nurse announced in a tone that brooked no denial. She looked from Cliff's battered face to Mark, sniffed, "Men!" and followed her patient, supported by Roger and another young man, to the elevator.

Mark waited until the elevator doors closed behind them, then went to see how Betty was faring. Two of her girlfriends were going to take her home and spend the night with her.

The party was over. The hushed and suddenly sober guests fled into the night without stopping to say goodnight. Cliff Marsden's reputation in business circles was formidable and more than a little sinister, and the ambitious young men had an almost superstitious dread that their careers might be blighted by simply being bystanders at his humiliation. As for Mark Hunter! The guy had better go into hiding.

But Mark wasn't thinking of his own safety, or future. As reaction set in, he began to feel a certain sense of remorse at the way he had beat up on a man old enough to be his father. "I could have handled it in some other way," he admitted to Dave Green. "Maybe I should have just put a hammerlock on the guy. But when I saw what the son of a bitch was doing to Betty, I just started swinging. I couldn't help myself."

"Don't sweat it. You did the right thing," Dave told him. "But you sure picked yourself one hell of a sparring partner!"

Mark, engrossed in his own thoughts, didn't seem to hear him. "You know, that's the first fight I've been in since junior high," he said with a wondering shake of his head.

As usual, a couple of the female guests remained behind to clear up the debris. One of them attacked the mess in the hall, sprinkling salt over the bloodstains and then soaking them with soda water. Mark took over when she started to mop up with paper towels. Straightening up, she pointed to the door of an apartment only a few feet from where the fight had taken place. "You sure have understanding neighbours. They didn't even open the door to see what was going on."

"They know better," drawled Dave Green who was standing in the hallway smoking a cigarette while he watched Mark work. "The last time they stuck their heads out, we invited them to join the party and the old man didn't sober up for two days."

2

"Sign here, and Hunter Oil Limited will have held its first directors' meeting." The lawyer, who had been recommended by Bill Crawford, smiled and held out a fat fountain pen. Mark's answering grin was self-deprecating, but nonetheless he experienced a sense of excitement as he signed the corporate minutes. The lawyer filled in the date, April 29, 1956, signed as secretary of the meeting, and carefully blotted the ink before closing the minute book.

Mark gazed at the name, Hunter Oil Limited, embossed in gold on the black cover. He had given much thought to the name of his new company, considering and discarding numerous possibilities before settling on his own family name. Hunter Oil — it had a nice ring to it.

Mark took out his cheque book. "How much do I owe you, Mr. Martin?"

"Chester, please. Exactly what I quoted you — $200 as my fee, plus disbursements of twenty-six dollars to pay for the corporate seal and minute book."

The law firm's office was a second floor walk-up, over a store that sold automotive equipment. The wooden stairs were littered with dried lumps of mud tracked in by clients seeking the services of the lawyers, accountants, and land agents who had offices there. Mark absently kicked one of the largest lumps and watched it break apart as it rolled down the steps. The lawyer's account was completely reasonable, but at this rate his tiny stake would melt away like the snows of winter.

Out on the sidewalk, he took a moment to orient himself. The cafe where he was to meet Jeff Nelson for lunch was over on 8th Avenue, one block north and three blocks west of where he was standing. It was unseasonably warm for the end of April, and a dry wind blew gritty dust along the streets. At this rate the road bans would be lifted any day now and the drilling rigs would start making hole again.

It was barely noon but already the Crest Cafe was full. Jeff Nelson waved from a booth halfway along a row of windows fronting on 8th Avenue. Edging his way through the crowd waiting to be seated, Mark saw that Jeff was not alone. His companion was a middle-aged man with a red, heavily veined face whom he introduced as Bernie Andrews.

Mark shook hands and slid into the booth, grateful to Jeff for trying to set him up with a useful contact. Jeff, like himself an American import, was a "lease hound," an independent agent hired by oil companies to acquire leases from private landowners. Mark's first assignment in Canada had been to work with Jeff on a small lease play Permex was running north of Redwater. It had been Mark's job to determine which of the land parcels were the most geologically promising and hence worth paying top dollar for. They had worked well together and as soon as Jeff heard that Mark was trying to make it on his own, he had called him up and offered to put him in touch with some small-time promoters who had access to drilling funds.

A matronly waitress plunked down three glasses of water on the formica tabletop. She took their order and went off with a knowing wink at Bernie Andrews. "The liquor laws in this province are right out of the dark ages," he muttered and, shutting his eyes, swallowed half the water. He shuddered, then pulled out a silver flask and filled up the glass until it was a dark brown colour.

"You gentlemen care to indulge?" he asked, holding the flask out of sight under the table. When they both shook their heads he slipped it back in his hip pocket and took a long pull at his drink.

"According to the bush telegraph, you had a little run-in with one of Calgary's leading citizens the other night." Jeff Nelson's eyes were bright with curiosity. "You'd never know you'd been in a fight, but I'm told it will be another week before Cliff Marsden heals up enough to show his face in public."

"It was strictly no contest. I probably shouldn't have hit him, but it was the only way I could stop him. I take it you know what started it?"

"The story is that he was doing his best to get into your girl's pants," replied Jeff. "Nobody's laying any blame on you, Mark. Just the opposite, in fact. They'll love you over at the Petroleum Club — there hasn't been as much excitement since Atlantic No. 3 blew out of control."

"I admire your courage in taking on Cliff Marsden in this town," said Bernie in a tone that implied he thought Mark had taken leave of his senses.

"I had no choice."

"Of course." It was obvious that Bernie would have watched Cliff rape his own mother without lifting a hand. "But we came here to talk a little business." His bloodshot eyes, shrewd behind pouches of fat, studied Mark's face.

"Jeff tells me you used to work in the exploration department at Permex."

"I did. Right up until last week, as a matter of fact."

"Harvey Morrison's got himself some pretty good boys over there." The reek of rye whisky cut through the smell of frying food as Andrews uncorked the flask to pour himself another belt. "They're getting to be known around this town as pretty fair oil finders."

"They know what they're doing all right," Mark agreed. "I take it you're in the oil business, Mr. Andrews?"

"Call me Bernie, for God's sake, boy, and of course I'm in the oil business." Bernie Andrews looked slightly miffed that Mark had found it necessary to ask. "I'm in what I like to think is the creative side of the business. I put the guys with ideas in touch with the money men." He paused to cast a jaundiced look at the Salisbury steak the waitress placed in front of him. "Our mutual friend, Jeff here, seems to feel you and me might be able to do a little business together."

"I certainly hope so," Mark replied fervently. "Let me tell you about this play I have in mind." He began to describe the prospect, one that he had worked up on his own time, and which was in an area of no interest to Permex. He grew less sure of himself as an impatient scowl darkened Bernie Andrews's mottled face. Discouraged by the promoter's obvious lack of interest, Mark cut his sales pitch short.

"Shee-it boy," Bernie drawled, "you're talkin' about a play that's more'n a hundred miles from any kind of a discovery. What the investor wants is a well that's snuggled right up against Leduc or Redwater — them's the magic words what opens up the ol' purse strings. Drilling way the hell and gone out in the boonies like you're talking about just don't have any sex appeal." He pushed away his half-eaten meal and leaned forward. "Permex's shot a lot of seismic around Redwater, and everybody knows they've been picking up leases on the q.t." Jeff Nelson cleared his throat and Bernie gave him an apologetic glance. "I guess I shouldn't be talking like this with you around, Jeff. Hell, for all I know, you could be doing the fieldwork for them. Maybe Mark and me should continue this little discussion after lunch."

The landman was quick to take the hint and excused himself halfway through his coffee. Bernie told him not to worry about the check and Jeff said, "I'll decorate the table then," and left the tip.

Bernie leaned forward, the smell of whisky unpleasantly sour on his breath. "Just a couple of locations is all I need. You just mention a couple of likely spots, and old Bernie'll do all the rest. I'll raise the money to get the leases and drill them up and cut you in for a nice fat royalty share that nobody needs to know about. How about it, boy?"

The hell of it was that it would work. Mark carried in his head the exact legal description of a half-dozen or so parcels of land that Permex regarded as prime drilling prospects. All he had to do was to whisper a couple of them to the man sitting across the table and he would make himself a potful of cash. Of course there was always the chance that Permex would somehow discover what he had done and sue him. But he knew that risk was minimal. There were any number of ways to hide the fact that he was involved, and even if they suspected something, it was unlikely that Permex would do anything about it. The majors were notoriously reluctant to take legal action in these cases; for one thing, it made them look foolish and, worse still, it might give ideas to some of their other employees.

"I'm afraid I can't help you," Mark said after a considerable pause.

"Can't, or won't?" asked Andrews.

"It doesn't matter. The result is the same either way."

The promoter acknowledged defeat with a rueful grin. "Can't blame a guy for trying." He picked up the check and added casually, "I'd take it as a favour if you didn't say anything about this to Harvey Morrison. I sure wouldn't want to get cross-threaded with Permex."

"I won't say a word. To him or anyone else," Mark assured him.

Feeling slightly sheepish, Mark drove slowly past his apartment building, checking every parked car for hired gorillas. So far there had been no reprisals from the Marsden camp but from what Mark had heard of the man, he was almost certain to seek revenge of some sort. He wouldn't be foolish enough to lay an assault charge, since that would mean the whole story would come out and expose him for the creep he was, nor did he have any sons to avenge him. But it would be entirely in keeping with his character to hire a couple of goons to work Mark over.

Having circled the block twice without spotting anything suspicious, Mark parked the Olds around the corner, walked rapidly along the sidewalk and up the shallow steps into the glass-fronted foyer. He used his key to open the mailbox, wondering whether it would explode in his face or if he would find some playful little surprise like a poisonous snake coiled up inside. But there was only a letter from his mother in California and a couple of bills for Dave. It was not until he was inside his apartment and had checked out all the rooms and closets that he began to relax. He tried to convince himself that he was being paranoid, but he knew that his fears were only too rational. The sound of a key scraping in the lock brought the tension flooding back until he saw Dave Green's pale face peering cautiously around the partly opened door.

"Everything's cool," Mark assured him and Dave stepped jauntily into the apartment. "Ah, Mark Hunter — the man whose name is on everyone's lips. The oil patch's giant killer. A legend in his own time!"

"Come off it, Dave."

"You think I'm kidding? I'll have you know my boss took me to lunch at the Pete Club today, something he's never done before. He introduced me all around as your roommate. I'll be dining out on the story for months. Provided I live so long," he added with an apprehensive glance around the apartment.

"Don't flatter yourself. If anyone's the target, it's me, not you."

"True. But bullets have a nasty habit of ricocheting, you know."

Mark dismissed the subject with a wave of his hand and began to dial Betty's number. She should be home from work by now. She had stayed home for a couple of days but she had been determined to report in today.

"How did it go?" he asked after he had identified himself to the girl who answered the phone and Betty came on the line.

"Okay, I guess. Everybody was really nice but they kept looking sideways at me like I had some weird disease or something."

"The price of fame."

"That kind of fame I can do without." She hesitated only briefly when he asked if he could come over. "Yeah, sure, I'd like to see you. Marge is going back to her own place tonight. She's been super but I can hack it on my own now."

Despite her brave words, Betty still looked pretty traumatized when she opened the door of her basement bed-sitting room. "God, I'm sorry, Betty," Mark whispered and kissed her lightly on the lips. "I feel sick about it."

"I don't want you to," she told him emphatically, a little colour suffusing her cheeks. "If you hadn't been there I don't know what would have happened. Nobody — not one damn soul except you — paid any attention to what that bastard was doing to me."

"Everybody was pretty hammered," Mark replied uncomfortably. "They probably didn't realize how serious it was."

"If you say so." Betty was unconvinced. "You know something else that's real crazy? He acted like I had no business putting up a fight. Like I should be flattered that he wanted to screw me. Can you believe it?"

"He probably figured you were one of the girls in Farris's stable. Most of them are pretty obliging. But," Mark added with a grin, "you sure straightened him out on that score."

She responded with a faint smile, but turned her face aside when he bent down to kiss her. "I'm not going to see you again, Mark. At least not for a while."

"For God's sake, why not?"

"It's that crowd you travel with. The way they treat women, I know they don't mean anything by it — they're just having a good time — but they make you feel like you're some kind of a slave girl in a harem, on call whenever they want to party. Besides," she lifted her head to look directly at him, "if I go on seeing you, I'm going to get hurt. And that I don't need."

She had never looked more desirable than she did at that moment. Her vulnerable and withdrawn mood had erased that faint hint of coarseness from her face, and her stunning figure was even more devastating when it wasn't being deliberately flaunted. But he knew there was no way he could change her mind. At least, not tonight. There was nothing for it but to let the old world take a couple of spins.

3

As the days went by with no activity on the Marsden front, that worry gradually faded, only to be replaced by an even more pressing one. What the hell was he going to use for money? Flogging deals was turning out to be a damn sight harder than Mark had figured on. He spent $250 to buy more seismic data on the Big Coulee area and sat for hours at the dinette table in the apartment, refining and massaging the data, growing steadily more excited by the potential of the play as he worked. But it seemed there was a glut of exciting plays on the street. The majors weren't interested; they concentrated on exploring their own vast landholdings, and the independent operators claimed to already have more deals on their plates than they could handle. Of course, if Mark had something hot from his days with Permex ...? When he shook his head, the meetings quickly terminated.

The road bans had been lifted for two weeks when Mark decided he had to play his hole card and get a well-sitting job. He didn't want to; he wanted to spend all his time getting Hunter Oil up and running. But it would be strictly temporary. He would give it up and concentrate on his fledgling oil company as soon as he had replenished his depleted cash reserves.

As Mark had predicted, getting hired to sit a well turned out to be easy. The current flurry of drilling activity had created a big demand for trained geologists to supervise the crucial final stages of a well — analyzing the cuttings to determine what formation they were in, and calling for core samples and drill stem tests. Centaur Resources, a small independent, hired him at the going rate of seventy-five dollars a day to nurse a well in the Stettler area.

Sitting a well meant being on call twenty-four hours a day, so Mark stayed at the wellsite, bunking in the aluminum-sided trailers that made up the drilling camp. The well came in dry, the core so tight there was no point in running a test.

On his first Friday night back in Calgary, Mark phoned Betty, only to be informed by the operator that her number was no longer in service. He called Marge who, after some persuasion, told him Betty had moved to Vancouver and was looking for a secretarial job out there. Deflated, he thanked her and hung up. He was just about to call her back and see if he could coax Betty's Vancouver phone number out of her when the door swung open and Dave Green shouted, "Party time!" The dozen or so guests he had brought along trooped in after him, several of the men brandishing liquor bottles in brown Alberta Liquor Control Board bags. A short, curvaceous blonde spotted Mark and squealed, "You were right, Dave — he is a doll! Can I have him?"

Mark knew that Centaur planned to drill another wildcat near Stettler so he hung around the apartment, waiting for the call to go to the wellsite. When it didn't come, he dropped in to see the president. Walt Davidson was an easygoing, approachable sort of guy but that morning his manner seemed forced as he waved Mark into a chair.

Trying to ease the unexpected tension, Mark said jokingly, "Hey, you can't blame that dry hole on me! I didn't pick the location."

"I know. I did. What can I do for you, Mark?"

"I was kinda hoping you would hire me to sit your well over on section 33. I need the bread, to be honest."

"Gosh, Mark, I've already hired a geologist for that one."

Mark swallowed. Oilmen were a superstitious lot and maybe Walt figured he was some kind of a jinx because of that dry hole. Like beheading the messenger who brings the emperor news of a defeat in battle. "I hope you weren't dissatisfied with my work," he said stiffly.

"Hell no, Mark. Nothing like that. You called the shots just right."

"Well, what is it then? I kinda figured I had the inside track since I was the one who sat the test well." Mark's eyes narrowed suddenly. "Is Cliff Marsden behind this?"

"Not Cliff Marsden." Davidson's good-natured face was troubled. "I guess you got a right to know. It was Permex. They were downright unhappy with me for hiring you. And you know a little guy like me can't afford to have one of the majors down on him. Not with all the land Permex controls."

"I see," was all a thunderstruck Mark could manage. There was simply no logical reason for Ed Parsons to be acting like this, but when you were dealing with the kind of egos that flourish in the oil patch, logic flew out the window.

"Thanks for telling me, Walt," he muttered as he walked toward the door.

It quickly became clear that the word had gone out. Every day Mark scanned the drilling reports in the *Oil Bulletin* for the names of companies too small to have their own geological staffs and called on them to offer his services. There were no takers.

Spending so much time in the apartment was giving Mark a bad case of cabin fever. He tried to use his time productively; he had wrung the Big Coulee data dry, so he began to cast about for other plays that he could use to build up a portfolio. He was at his makeshift desk in the apartment, poring over contour maps, when the telephone call came. The caller identified himself as an executive assistant to Mr. D.R. Cullen, the president of Peerless Petroleum Ltd. Mr. Cullen would like to meet Mr. Hunter and the smooth voice wondered if one-thirty tomorrow would be convenient. Mark hastily assured him it was.

He had heard the stories about Don Cullen, the Calgary oilman who had taken the company he had inherited from his father and built it into an outfit that rivalled some of the majors in size. Cullen was rumoured to stay in bed until eleven, work for a couple of hours and then start the day's drinking. Drunk or not, he had managed to build Peerless into precisely the kind of company that Mark hoped someday to create. And it was said of the feisty Cullen that nothing pleased him more than to thumb his nose at the big boys.

"You've got an appointment to see D.R. Cullen?" For a moment, Dave Green seemed somewhat taken aback; there was even a slight flush on his pale face. Then he eased effortlessly into his familiar raconteur's role. "Have you heard about his latest caper?" he asked, then went on without waiting for Mark's reply. "It was last Thursday night and old D.R., hammered out of his skull as usual, staggered into the Palliser to use the washroom. He must have thought he was home because he took off all his clothes, carefully hung them on a hook, went back out into the lobby and fell asleep stark balls naked on a couch."

Dave paused for effect. "The best part is that the Imperial Order of the Daughters of the Empire were having their annual dinner in the Crystal Ballroom. It was breaking up just as Cullen came out of the washroom, so he had a lobby full of little old ladies as an audience."

"Timing is everything," Mark grinned.

Mark was whistling under his breath as he stuffed the folder containing the Big Coulee materials in his briefcase and left the apartment to keep his appointment. He never got to open the briefcase. For the first fifteen minutes it seemed that the playful Cullen merely wanted to meet the man who had cleaned Cliff Marsden's clock. As members of the oil elite, Cullen and Marsden were well acquainted with each other, and Don Cullen was vastly entertained by his friend's misadventure.

"The son of a bitch will never live this down," he chortled gleefully.

When Mark tried to steer the conversation around to the Big Coulee play, Don frowned and told him the last thing Peerless needed was another drilling prospect. Just drilling up their own lands would keep them busy till hell froze over. And that, he went on, brought him to the purpose of the meeting. He wanted to hire Mark as a senior geologist, and named a figure that was nearly double what Mark had been making with Permex.

Mark sagged with disappointment. Even if he weren't determined to be his own boss, he could never work for this man and be subject to his notorious whims and caprices. Wondering if he was making yet another enemy, Mark politely rejected the offer, explaining that he wanted to try and make it on his own. "That's something you should be able to understand, sir," he added in an inspired afterthought.

That seemed to strike the right note with Cullen who fancied himself a self-made tycoon, and the colour that had begun to mount in his face subsided.

"I'd be happy to work for you on a freelance basis," Mark continued. "Maybe I could do some well-sitting for you."

"We don't use outside consultants," the exploration manager, perpetually hungover from trying to keep up with his employer, interjected in a raspy whisky voice.

Cullen silenced him with an imperious wave of his hand. Hiring the young geologist would really piss old Ed Parsons off and prove once more that Don Cullen didn't give a shit about the multinationals. The boys over at the Pete Club would eat it up.

"You must have had some pretty good exposure to the Devonian formation when you were with Permex?" Don stated it more as a fact than a question.

"You bet," Mark assured him eagerly. "Most of the wells we drilled were targeted for the Devonian."

"Good God, Don, you're not thinking of having him sit the White River wildcat?" The exploration manager was scandalized. "That's a tight hole!"

"So what?" asked Don airily. "We control all the land for miles around." He gave a sudden, impish grin. He was having one of his celebrated hunches. "You're hired, Hunter. I have a feeling you're going to bring us luck."

His grin broadened as he reached under his desk and pressed a button. "Now that we've settled that, how about a drink?"

The panelling on the far wall slid smoothly back to reveal a lavishly appointed bar. Don got up from his desk and marched across the vast expanse of white broadloom with an eager stride. He was tall, at least two inches taller than Mark, and the only outward signs of dissipation were his watery eyes and the puffiness around his jowls. He could have passed for handsome except for a loose, thick-lipped mouth. He was acutely aware of this defect and attempted to disguise it by chewing on an ever-present cigar.

The last thing that Mark wanted was to get in a drinking bout with the man who had just hired him. Especially at two o'clock in the afternoon. On the other hand, if he refused to drink with Don it might trigger one of the tantrums for which the oilman was famous. Dealing with the guy was like walking through a minefield.

"I could sure go for a beer," he said, adding carefully, "And then I'd better start getting my gear together."

Don's lips began to draw together in a pout, but his excitement over the new wildcat and his hunch that Mark was going to bring them luck had put him in an unusually sunny mood. "There's beer in the fridge," he said as he poured himself a double shot of Glenlivet.

This was the oilman's moment of truth — the moment that would determine whether the wildcat well would be a bonanza or a costly failure. Even though Mark had no financial interest in the well and was just a hired hand, a tingling sensation ran up his spine as the barrel of the core bit rose out of the hole. The core man, the specialist in charge of extracting the core, removed the core head, tapped the core with an expert blow of his hammer and laid a five-foot section of rock on the derrick floor. It wasn't merely oil stained, it was positively dripping with the stuff; high-gravity oil was oozing out of all those lovely big vugs. Mark dropped to his knees for a closer look. Talk about porosity! He glanced up at the crew standing in a silent, awestruck circle above him. The toolpush shifted his wad of chewing tobacco from one cheek to another and grunted, "The last time I seen anything like that mother was in the Persian Gulf!"

Mark rose to his feet and ordered another core to be pulled. By the time they had finished coring, they had established a pay thickness of sixty-two feet. The drone of an approaching aircraft sent the crew scurrying to cover the core boxes with tarpaulins. The airplane, a single-engined Cessna, circled slowly around the rig at a height of three hundred feet. Standing on the drill floor, Mark could see a passenger in the rear seat peering down at them through binoculars. "Sorry fellas, you're just a tad late," he muttered under his breath.

He held off running a production test until the scout plane left. They didn't have long to wait; the closest airstrip was more than two hundred miles away and that didn't leave much spare fuel for circling the rig. When the production test was finally run, it indicated the well should produce at an initial daily rate of five hundred barrels a day. Insignificant by Middle East standards, but a real barn-burner in Alberta. Someday, Mark told himself, Hunter Oil Limited would bring in a well like this. He rechecked the gauge on the storage tank before sending a coded message to Calgary. The news would probably send Cullen off on a two-week binge.

4

"Mr. Cullen is very anxious that you understand the reason why we can't hire you to sit any more of our White River wells." The speaker was one of Cullen's two executive assistants, both Harvard MBAS. They were known as the "charm twins" in the oil patch and their role was to protect their alcoholic boss and to insulate him from the unpleasant realities of the outside world. Like this guy was doing now.

"Mr. Cullen has the highest regard for you and your professional abilities," the executive assistant continued smoothly. "But the fact remains that you are an independent operator and not an employee of this company. The White River field is going to be one of our most valuable assets and it has been decided that it would ... ah, not be prudent to have anyone who is not an employee on the site. I am sure you understand."

"I guess so." Mark could have argued that it hadn't seemed to matter when the first all-important wildcat was being drilled, but what was the use? The decision had been made. The management had put pressure on Cullen and he had caved in. Probably figured it wasn't worth the hassle.

"Of course the situation would be completely different if you were to come on staff with us. Mr. Cullen asked me to tell you that the offer he made is still open. You could have a brilliant career with Peerless, you know."

"Tell him thanks, but no thanks. He'll understand. He knows where I'm coming from." Mark stood up. "Well, I guess that does it. Tell Mr. Cullen I wish him every success in White River."

More to put in time than anything else, Mark left the apartment early one morning and drove out to Turner Valley, the site of the first truly big, and for many long years the only, discovery of oil and gas in Alberta. During the thirties, much of the natural gas that was produced along with the oil was simply flared and burnt off to the atmosphere in a brush-covered coulee that became known as the Devil's Half Acre. At night, the light of the flares was easily visible from Calgary, thirty miles away, and in Depression winters, hobos slept beside the flares to keep warm. Although no one realized it at the time, the wasteful flaring of the natural gas had seriously depleted the reservoir energy that moved the oil out of the formation, and production had fallen off sharply over the years. It was part of oil-patch folklore that only half of the huge reservoir had been discovered and that the other half lay tilted and folded thousands of feet underneath.

Mark spent a couple of hours driving around the area, stopping from time to time to take a closer look at the surface geology. Twice he drove along the main street of Turner Valley where the sour stench of hydrogen sulphide from the refinery hung like a pall over the little oil town. As he expected, the contours of the land and the rock formations on the surface offered little in the way of clues as to what might be underneath. Some cataclysmic upheaval might well have taken place eons ago, but it would take a deep and incredibly costly well to provide the answer to the geological riddle. If Hunter Oil ever made it to the big leagues, it might be worth a flyer.

The visit to the field, the sight of the old tin can refinery smack in the middle of town, and even the rotten egg smell of hydrogen sulphide, had done much to restore Mark's spirits. This was real honest-to-God oil-patch country. He checked his gas gauge as he headed back to Calgary and found he had less than a quarter tank. Five miles later he saw an Esso sign and pulled in. He told the pump jockey to fill her up and headed for the washroom. A white sports car, looking oddly out of place, occupied the single service bay. Even with its hood up, he recognized it as a Jaguar XK, but it would take a closer look to tell which model. On his way back to the pump island, he stopped for a second look.

It was as he thought — an XK 120, the original and by far the best-looking of the entire line. A mechanic, grease-covered cap pushed back on his forehead, was staring dubiously down at the engine, which took up every square inch of space under the long hood. He turned his head and started to say something. The girl was partly hidden behind his lanky frame, but Mark liked what he was able to see. The mechanic was telling her that, "them fancy foreign jobs scare the bejesus out of me. There's no way I'm going to touch that engine. I'm sorry, Miss, but that's the way it is."

The girl looked devastated, almost desperate. "But I've just got to be in Calgary by twelve-thirty. It's awfully important."

Hardly believing his good fortune, Mark stepped into the bay and said, "Maybe I can be of some help. I'm on my way to Calgary and I'd be happy to give you a lift."

Startled, the girl peered at him, trying to make him out against the harsh glare of the open doorway. Then she smiled. "You're a lifesaver! Hang on a sec while I get some things from the car."

Reaching across to the Jag's passenger seat, she retrieved her handbag, a headscarf, and a large plastic bag. She blinked as she stepped into the sunlight and hastily lowered the sunglasses perched on top of her head, but not before Mark caught a glimpse of grey-green eyes set off by long, dark lashes. Her dark hair was pulled back from her forehead and held in place by a blue hair ribbon that matched her sweater. She smiled with the easy self-assurance of the socially secure and popular. To Mark, she looked like the homecoming queen at some exclusive college.

"This is super," she said as they pulled away from the pumps. "I have to meet Daddy for lunch at the country club. He's entertaining some VIPs from Japan and he gets absolutely livid if I'm late. Particularly, if it's the fault of the Jag. He does not approve of that car."

"They're beautiful machines, but I hear they can be a trifle temperamental."

"It's the carburettor," she sighed. "Every now and then I think about trading it in for a nice reliable American model and then it behaves like an angel." She looked appreciatively around the interior of the Olds. "I must say, there's nothing shabby about this set of wheels. Now this car my father would approve of."

"But it's nowhere near as exciting as the Jag," he replied, stealing a surreptitious glance at her left hand as she fished for something in her handbag. From the way she chattered on about her father, it was unlikely that she was married, but she could be engaged. The relief he felt when he saw her third finger was ringless made him wonder what was happening to him. She produced a pouch pack of Chesterfields and pushed the cigarette lighter in with her thumb. "Can I light one for you?" she asked and Mark, who seldom indulged, nodded eagerly. He barely restrained himself from kissing her fingers as she placed a lit cigarette between his lips.

She watched him blow out the smoke without inhaling. "I guess you don't like American cigarettes, do you?"

"It's not that. In fact, I'm American myself. It's just that I'm not much of a smoker."

"I go to college in the States. I'm just home for the summer vacation."

"Whereabouts?"

"California. Stanford."

Mark was impressed. "That colours you bright. What are you majoring in?"

"Economics. And if you ask 'home economics?' I'll brain you."

"The thought never crossed my mind," he grinned. "By the way," he added, "I'm Mark. Mark Hunter."

"Oh dear God," she whispered, the smile congealing on her face. "I'm Jane Marsden."

Mark choked back an exclamation. It was a blow, but it might not be fatal. Not if he played it right. He stole a glance at her. She was everything he had ever wanted in a woman. "I'd like to see you again, Jane." He managed to make it sound casual.

"That would be nice, but I'm afraid it's not possible." She was keeping it light and polite too, but there was an air of finality in the way she spoke.

Damn it! It just wasn't fair! "Okay, so I had a run-in with your father. That doesn't mean you and I can't see each other. This is the twentieth century, not the Middle Ages, for Christ's sake!" He pounded the steering wheel in frustration as he saw the closed expression on her face.

"It wouldn't work, Mark," she said quietly. "In the first place, my father wouldn't allow it, and, anyway, I could never forget what you did to him." She took off her sunglasses and looked at him as they waited for a traffic light. "You don't strike me as the bully type, Mark. Why did you do it? Too much to drink?"

Mark stared at her. "Don't you realize ..." A horn blared impatiently behind him as the light changed. He let out the clutch and turned off Macleod Trail onto 50th Street. A few more blocks and they would be at the country club gate. "You must know why I hit him?"

Her lips thinned with distaste. "It was over a girl. I know that much. Daddy says she was leading him on, and then you suddenly came charging in out of the blue and started hitting him. She was your girl, I guess."

"You really believe that was all there was to it?" he asked in exasperation.

"Of course I do. Everybody knows what goes on at the parties your crowd throws."

"Boy, he's really got you brainwashed," Mark said disgustedly. She put her glasses back on and made no reply.

"Let me off at the side door." She started to gather her belongings as they descended the long, treed drive. "I'll go in through the ladies' locker room. What are you doing?" she cried as Mark drove past the clubhouse. "My father is probably here already!"

"I hope he is. I want to talk to him. I'm sure we can work things out like two reasonable people. I've got to see you again. There he is. Over there." Mark pointed to the far side of the parking lot where Cliff Marsden, broken nose still held in place by a white bandage, was standing with four dark-suited Japanese businessmen beside a black Lincoln.

"Mark, don't! You don't know my father. I'm begging you, Mark. Please." Jane reached for the door handle as if to jump out. But Mark was already pulling into a slot beside the Lincoln. Marsden was staring at the blue and white Olds as if he recognized it. He gave an audible gasp when he saw his daughter in the passenger seat.

"Get out of here, Mark. Fast," she hissed as she hastily clambered out. "Hi, Daddy," she cried gaily, bussing her thunderstruck parent on the cheek. "The Jag broke down and this nice man gave me a lift into town."

Cliff Marsden's face had turned purple and inarticulate strangling noises were coming from his throat. To Jane's horror, Mark had gotten out of the car and was walking right up to her father, hand outstretched. "Look, Mr. Marsden, I know we got off to a bad start. I guess we both kinda overreacted. But, we ..."

Cliff worked up a mouthful of saliva and spat in Mark's open palm. "You bastard," he snarled in a voice that shook with rage, "This does it. I'm going to run you out of town! And don't you ever dare come near my daughter again!"

"Don't throw a spaz fit, Father." Jane tried to speak lightly, but the look she gave Mark implored him to leave. The Japanese businessmen stood a respectful distance away, impassively watching the domestic drama. Jane took her father by the arm and he allowed himself to be led a few steps in the direction of the clubhouse.

"See you around, Jane." Mark got behind the wheel of the Olds and started the engine. Cliff spun around and his cold, lizard eyes glared malevolently after Mark as he drove away. Jane gave her father's arm another tug, and he turned on her angrily. "You've got no business driving around with Mark Hunter."

"Be reasonable, Daddy. I had no idea that's who it was until we were halfway here. We were so busy talking it took us a while to get around to names. Now, simmer down and start being nice to your guests. They must be wondering what in the world is going on."

"I bet they are," Cliff snorted. "No self-respecting Japanese would ever have to take this sort of crap from his daughter."

"She's the class act of that family." Dave uncapped a beer and poured it carefully into his favourite mug, the one that had printed on its side: Earth, this is God! I want all you people to clear out before the end of the month. I have a client who's interested in the property. He took a long pull and continued, "And that, plus the fact that she drives the best looking car you ever saw in your life, is all I can tell you about the lady. She doesn't spend much time in Calgary, goes to a school somewhere in the States. So I don't have the form chart on her. Except that she's a knockout. But you already know that."

"She could have stepped out of every daydream I ever had," Mark agreed morosely. "And she turns out to be Cliff Marsden's daughter. The guy's nuts. Threatening to run me out of town, and forbidding me to see her. He must be living in some kind of time warp to think he can get away with crap like that."

"Cliff Marsden knows exactly what time it is. He's bad medicine, Mark. In fact, if you believe some of the stories about him, he qualifies as some sort of junior grade monster. He's one of those people who've been so successful they figure they're above the law."

"Well, he's not going to stop me from seeing her."

"You serious?"

"I've never been more serious in my life."

Dave took another swallow of beer, belched gently, and murmured, "Well, the weatherman has been predicting a long, hot summer."

Mark let two days go by before trying to contact Jane. The Marsdens weren't in the phone book and when he called directory assistance he was told the number was unlisted. At first Mark was afraid he had come to a dead end; then he thought of Bill Crawford. The Crawfords were beginning to travel with the movers and shakers — much to Marianne's discomfiture, Mark gathered. Maybe Bill would have the Marsden number, or could find it out.

"What do we have here?" Bill paused to tap a few careful drops of Tabasco sauce into his tomato juice. "A Calgary version of the Montagues and Capulets?"

Mark remembered enough high school Shakespeare to reply, "Except this time the lovers will live happily ever after. I hope."

"Like that is it? Sounds serious." Bill sighed and put down his empty glass. "When you look around at all the tender young stuff in this town you have to wonder why on earth any man in his right mind would want to tie himself down."

Mark looked at his friend and thought how it must bug the hell out of him to have arrived in a town like Calgary already burdened with a wife and small daughter. Marianne must have been a real blonde bombshell when they were married and she still looked highly beddable, but their marriage seemed to be turning into one of those uncomfortable situations where the wife couldn't, or wouldn't, keep up with her ambitious husband.

The silence had lasted too long. Mark cleared his throat. "I really do want that number, Bill. Can do?"

Bill nodded and said, "Can do. Jane's mother is a member of the Women's League and her number is in the League's address book. Marianne's got a copy."

"Marianne's a member of the Women's League?" Mark didn't quite succeed in hiding his astonishment. "You two are really climbing the social ladder!"

"She's not a member; she was a 'provisional.' And she's just been told she's not going to make it. But, she's still got the address book, so far as I know. I'll look up the number tonight and you can give me a call at the office in the morning. But for Christ's sake, be discreet. If Cliff Marsden ever found out, I'd never cut another deal in this town."

"The Marsden residence." The voice had the rich chocolate flavour of the old South.

Mark, his throat constricted with tension, asked to speak to "Miss Jane."

The maid wanted to know who was calling and Mark muttered something indistinguishable. She hesitated, and he was sure she was going to ask him to repeat his name, but then she murmured, "Just a moment, please, sir."

"Hello. Who's speaking, please?" That voice: so light and clear. A guy could listen to it all his life and never tire of hearing it.

"It's Mark."

Her sharp intake of breath was clearly audible. "Oh, hi, Terry. How are you?"

"You can call me Terry, or anything you like," replied Mark. "Just so long as I get to see you."

"Gosh, Terry, I'd love to, but I'm really busy these days. Take care of yourself." The line went dead.

Frustrated, Mark stared at the receiver that was now humming hollowly at him. Her old man must have been standing right there for her to come out with that "Terry" business. She sounded thoroughly frightened. The phone was beeping angrily at him now, and he dropped it back in its cradle. For the first time, he admitted to himself that he might not see her again. He had never been in this position before, but if a girl absolutely refused to go out with a guy, there wasn't much he could do about it. In this day and age, he couldn't pull a Lancelot by riding up on his white charger and galloping off into the sunset with her.

5

"Goddammit, Mark," Dave Green gave an exasperated sigh, "you're getting on my nerves — moping around the apartment like a lovesick teenager. Snap out of it, man, don't you realize this town is awash with gorgeous young chicks panting to be laid?"

Mark glanced up from the oil journal he was idly thumbing through. "Don't hold yourself back on my account."

"I need you as bait." Dave grinned and got to his feet. "You want a beer?" Mark declined with a shake of his head.

Standing in the kitchen doorway, beer mug in hand, Dave said, "I'm meeting some of my good ole boys for lunch at the Paralyzer tomorrow. Maybe you should come along, Mark. You just might scare up some drilling money, and you'll have a couple of laughs if nothing else."

Dave's good ole boys were a small band of old-time American promoters who scratched out a living on the fringes of the oil industry. By the mid-fifties, Alberta had become a hot spot for oil exploration, and they made sporadic forays into Calgary, putting up at the Palliser Hotel and sitting around the lobby like a bunch of friendly spiders waiting for a nice juicy fly to come along. Dave could bullshit and tell jokes with the best of them and they had made something of a pet of the young petroleum landman, often inviting him for lunch, or a drink after work.

That day, Dave's hosts were Louis LaPierre who operated out of Shreveport, Louisiana and had an endless stock of Cajun stories, and Danny Brewster, who could occasionally tap into some New York money. They welcomed Mark warmly, obviously intrigued to meet the central figure in the season's most talked about scandal. As was their custom, they lingered for a while in the lobby before going into the Rimrock Room for lunch.

Dave watched the parade of oilmen coming through the revolving doors, broad Texas accents floating across the lobby as they greeted each other. "You know something?" he asked of no one in particular. "If a brass band came in here and struck up the Star Spangled Banner, I'd be the only one who wouldn't have to stand up. It doesn't bother me," he added hastily, afraid that he might have offended his hosts. "It's just kind of weird when you think about it. This town might as well be called Houston North."

LaPierre smiled at him like a benevolent toad. "Don't fret yourself, boy. You Canucks will have your day. All we're doing is teaching you the ropes." His smile turned sardonic as he turned a shrewd gaze back to the lobby.

"Place is filling up nicely," he murmured. "Time for ol' Jesse to go into his act." He had barely finished speaking when a bellboy walked through the lobby, singing out, "Call for Mr. Johnson. Call for Mr. Johnson."

"Over here, boy." A tall man with a senatorial head of silver hair rose impressively to his feet. The bellboy told him he could take the call at one of the public phones near the lobby entrance.

"Jesse Johnson at your service," he boomed into the mouthpiece in a voice that could be heard throughout the lobby. "An oil well, you say? What was the name of that company again? Silver Star Petroleums? Hang on a minute while I write that down — Silver Star Petroleums. Got it. How many barrels a day? Say, that's great. I'm much obliged to you, sir. I truly am. That's very encouraging news."

While the two old pros exchanged knowing smiles, several businessmen sidled across to the pay phones and began to dial. Brewster winked at Mark. "They're calling their brokers. That should be good for a couple of points before the market closes. Like the man says, there's one born every minute. Thank the good Lord," he added with a pious glance heavenward.

"I've never heard of this Silver Star company," said Mark. "Do you know anything about it?"

"Only that Jesse will be long on its stock."

"Oh? That's how it works, eh? Still, it sounded like a pretty exciting well."

"You called that one right, boy. It *sounded* like a good well. It's probably as dry as a popcorn fart."

Chuckling to themselves, the two oldtimers led the way into lunch in a high good humour. They were still on the soup course — the clam chowder for which the restaurant was famous — when the room shook with a thundering roar that brought all conversation to a standstill. The Canadian Pacific transcontinental express was pulling into the railway station behind the hotel. When the racket finally subsided and it was once more possible to talk, Dave beckoned a passing waiter and asked, "What time does this hotel get into Vancouver?"

Brewster gave a snort of appreciative laughter. "You know, I really love this old hotel, trains and all. All the oilpatchers from the States stay here. Hell, some of them have been living here ever since Leduc. Come to think of it, the Palliser is the real reason why Calgary ended up being the oil capital of Canada instead of that other place up the road. But there are times when you'd swear them darn trains are going to bust right through your hotel room door."

What Brewster had said about the hotel solved a minor mystery for Mark. All the recent discoveries had been made in the northern part of the province, much closer to Edmonton than to Calgary. Yet all the oil company head offices were located in Calgary. Maybe the explanation was as simple as the fact that Calgary had the advantage of a famous hotel that catered to visiting oilmen. Brewster finished the last of the chowder and put his spoon down. Turning to Mark, he said, "Now, how about a little show and tell, son. Let's hear about some of them red-hot deals of yours."

Mark went through his growing list, and when he had finished, Brewster looked across at his crony. "That last deal — the itty-bitty one — is tailor-made for Otis, don't you agree, Louis?"

"It should fit his pistol all right," drawled LaPierre.

"Big Coulee is really a much better play," Mark pointed out. "The geology is more definitive and there are a number of potential locations, not just one like in Hambro. That one's a rank wildcat, I hope you realize that?"

"That's the way Otis likes them. Little, high-risk one-holers, that's our boy Otis. He's due to make a swing through these parts sometime next week. I'll tell him to get in touch with you about this here Hambro prospect."

The hotel doorman touched his cap and called the two older men by name as they escorted their guests out of the hotel. "Got any hot tips today, Jack?" Brewster asked him as the little group stood on the sidewalk, squinting in the bright afternoon sun.

"I was about to ask you the same question, sir," he replied. A dust-covered black Studebaker pulled up at the curb and he hurried over to help with the luggage.

"Jack must be getting damn close to his first million by now." Brewster remarked offhandedly as he watched the doorman struggle up the steps with two heavy suitcases under each arm. He anticipated Mark's incredulous stare, and when it came, he said, "It's the gospel truth. Big shots like D.R. Cullen and Charles Thompson are in and out of this hotel all the time and they tell Jack he better buy some of this or that stock. It's real insider stuff and he's made a fortune on the market." He held out his hand to Mark. "I reckon you can expect to hear from Otis Turner within the week."

The possibility of finally getting some action was exhilarating, even if the Hambro prospect was the least promising of all his plays. But there was absolutely nothing he could do until he had his meeting with this Otis character and found out whether the funds would be forthcoming. Now that he had nothing but time on his hands, Jane Marsden seemed to have taken up permanent residence in his thoughts. It was her smile he thought of most, white teeth flashing against clear, tanned skin. He took to driving along the secondary highway that led to the opulent Marsden spread south of the city, hoping in vain for a glimpse of the white XK.

The Crawfords invited him over to their split-level bungalow for dinner one night. The household was a scene of almost stupefying domesticity, but there was an uncomfortable feeling of tension in the air. Bill was the perfect host, chatting easily as he mixed the pre-dinner drinks, but the meal itself was surprisingly mediocre; the roast was overdone, while the potatoes were almost raw, and the gravy was a thin gruel. Marianne, flushed, and vainly pushing back the wisps of blonde hair that fell over her forehead, made apologetic noises as she joined them at the table. Mark gamely assured her that he liked his beef well-done. Her speech was hesitant and he wondered uneasily how many drinks she had knocked back while she was in the kitchen. Their son, Billy, who filled the house with his restless energy, played with his model racing car and bragged about how he would one day be a champion race-car driver. Their daughter, Debbie, already at two and a half a consummate flirt, sat in her high chair next to her father, making eyes at Mark.

After dinner, Billy went upstairs to race his cars on the special course he had set up in his room. Debbie sat on Mark's lap and played with his tie while the two men had coffee in the small living room, and Marianne loaded the newly installed dishwasher. Mark had brought the conversation around to the Marsden family. Bill was saying that Cliff was a real football fan and had been on the Stampeder's board of directors for years.

"Probably because it gives him access to the cheerleaders." Mark lifted Debbie, squealing with delight, high in the air.

Bill shot him a look. "You know something? Before now, no one would ever have thought of making that kind of a crack about Cliff. Not until that business of him making a move on your girl. That's really hurt him in this town."

"It was more than a move. The son of a bitch was doing his level best to rape her."

"And now you've got the hots for his daughter, or have you given up on that?"

"Like the admiral said when the ship was torpedoed, I have just begun to fight."

Mark had convinced himself that the reason Jane had gone through her little charade on the phone was because her father must have been in the same room with her. It would be different if he caught her when Marsden wasn't home. On the day after his evening with the Crawfords, he placed a call at four o'clock in the afternoon, reasoning that Marsden would still be at the office. If Jane wasn't there, he would simply say that he would call back later and hang up without giving his name. It was a no-risk proposition but his throat was tight with tension as he dialed. Miraculously, Jane herself answered; that clear, youthful voice couldn't belong to anyone else.

"Jane, Jane, is that you?" Mark was appalled to hear himself babbling.

"Yes." She sounded puzzled and a little uncertain. "Who is this, please?"

"Mark. Mark Hunter. You remember, I gave you a lift when your car broke down."

"And I'm grateful to you. But I don't want you to keep calling me. There's absolutely no point in it."

"I really would like to see you, Jane. I thought we were hitting it off pretty well together on that drive into town."

"That was before I knew who you were. You seem to forget that it was my father you assaulted, a man almost twice your age. I don't want you to call again, Mr. Hunter. I mean that." The click as she hung up had an ominous note of finality.

"Damn, damn, damn!" Shoulders slumped, Mark sat by the silent phone, finally admitting to himself that he would never get off the ground with Jane Marsden. Then the phone suddenly pealed and he made a grab for it, knocking the receiver to the floor. She had changed her mind!

"Mr. Hunter? This is Otis Turner heah. Our mutual friend, Danny Brewster, suggested I should get in touch with you. Mr. Hunter? Are you theah, Mr. Hunter? Is everything all right?"

"Yes. I'm sorry, Mr. Turner. It's just that I was expecting another call."

"I'm right sorry to disturb you at home, but I jes' arrived from Dallas and I wanted to make sure I didn't miss you."

"I'm glad you called, Mr. Turner. I've been looking forward to meeting you."

"Why don't you and me break bread together tomorrow? Can you join me for lunch at the Palliser 'round noon?"

"I'll be there," Mark said enthusiastically.

Otis Turner's cheeks were pink and jowly, well on their way to becoming full-blown dewlaps. He was dressed like a Kentucky colonel in a cream-coloured silk suit and black string tie. An unlit cigar jutted from his mouth. He removed it as he shook hands with Mark.

It wasn't until they were halfway through lunch that Otis finally let the conversation turn to the Hambro play. Prior to that, he regaled Mark with a highly coloured account of the wild and woolly deals that were being put together in Oklahoma. Some new money had shown up in Tulsa and the good ole boys, a few of whose names were vaguely familiar to Mark, were happily dusting off deals that hadn't seen the light of day for years. Listening to him, Mark began to perceive just how incestuous the oil industry really was. Deals were shopped around among the same small group of players — inspected, rejected, haggled over, or farmed out to reduce the risk. Every now and then there would be an injection of new venture capital and the whole process would start all over again.

Otis's last story involved an oilman who got so caught up in the wheeling and dealing that he ended up with the same deal he himself had promoted two weeks earlier but at three times the cost. Otis chuckled so hard at that one that he had to pull a handkerchief out of his sleeve to wipe his eyes. Stuffing it back up his sleeve, he said, "Now tell me about this Hambro play of yours, boy."

Thus prompted, Mark went into his spiel. Otis produced a thin notebook and carefully jotted down the location of the well, the target formation, and Mark's estimate of the cost. But when Mark began to describe the geology he noticed with dismay that Turner had stopped paying attention. The older man's eyes had glazed over and he seemed more interested in the last few bites of his club sandwich than in what Mark was saying.

"I realize it's not the most exciting geological prospect in the world," Mark concluded defensively. "I already told that to Danny Brewster when I talked to him."

Otis lit a cigar, took a precise pull and dispersed the smoke with a wave of his hand. "I like your little deal, son. I surely do."

"I'm glad to hear that. I kinda got the impression that you weren't exactly blown away by the geology."

Otis smiled tolerantly. "My investors don't worry themselves too much over a little detail like geology. It's the tax write-off that appeals to them."

"Oh, I see. And you figure you can sell them on this deal?"

"I have every confidence, m'boy. I'll make a few phone calls when I get back to Dallas and I expect you'll be able to start that ol' bit turning to the right."

6

The blonde was really coming on strong. Tall, with long, silky hair and clear, glowing skin, she was centrefold material. And she had latched onto Mark as soon as he and Dave Green had walked into Roger Farris's apartment. The apartment was right out of Playboy — subdued lighting, mirrored walls, low, oversized couches and chairs, with cushions strewn everywhere. The *pièce de résistance* was the revolving, circular bed with a built-in bar and an elaborate sound system in the padded headboard. Dave Green called the bedroom Farris's "office," but once again Mark wasn't too sure.

As Farris parties went, it was a small, impromptu affair. The youthful playboy had gone to the Pump Room, in the basement of the Petroleum Building, for dinner. Shortly after he arrived, two couples, including the spectacular blonde, were seated at a table next to his. They had brought along a bottle of bourbon and Roger had no trouble in striking up a conversation. They told him they were visiting from San Francisco. As he often did when there was a good-looking woman involved, Roger invited them back to his place for drinks.

"What a pad!" the blonde exclaimed, gazing around the apartment with rapt eyes. She did a little dance step on the polished marble floor, her swirling skirt revealing a flash of smooth, creamy thigh. Impulsively grabbing Roger's arm with both hands, she cried, "This place cries out for a party! Why don't you call some of your friends?"

"No problem," Roger assured her and began to dial. First he telephoned a girl from his stable and peremptorily told her to grab a cab. Then he called Dave and Mark at their apartment a block down the street, and asked them to come over. The wise-cracking Dave Green was an asset to any party, especially when the guests were strangers who hadn't heard his jokes before. Mark hadn't been keen about going but Dave had talked him into it. In fact, old Dave had been giving him a hard time about the way he was mooning over a girl he had only met once and who had made it clear she had no intention of ever seeing him again. Annoyed with himself and with the world in general, Mark was in a reckless, what-the-hell mood as he returned the statuesque blonde's smouldering look.

Standing up for yet another dance with her, Mark realized he'd had a fair bit to drink in the course of the evening. Her fingers stroked the hair on the nape of his neck, sending a delicious shiver down his spine. So what if Jane Marsden wouldn't give him the time of day? She wasn't the only good-looking girl in the world. He held

Michelle even more tightly and she blew gently in his ear.

Pivoting, laughing down at her as she leaned back against his arm in a mock tango, Mark caught a glimpse of her boyfriend sitting on the marble hearth, glowering up at him. All the guy had done all night was sit by himself and sulk.

"Your friend doesn't look all that happy," whispered Mark.

"Jerry? He's a party-pooper from way back. Don't worry about him." Abruptly, Michelle stopped dancing and kissed Mark passionately, her tongue probing deep in his mouth.

"Goddamn it, I don't have to stand for this shit!" The man called Jerry grabbed the blonde's arm and roughly pulled her away. Confronting an alarmed Mark, he snarled, "Now pretty boy, I'm going to teach you not to mess with another man's woman!"

"Don't be ..." Mark started to expostulate, but the stranger's fist drove into his solar plexus, knocking the wind out of him. He grunted as he was hit again just below the ribs. The pain was unbelievable, his body was paralyzed with the shock. Another driving blow to the midsection and Mark began to sag at the knees. From somewhere, he found the strength to throw a feeble punch but his attacker ducked it with the ease of a professional boxer. Off balance, Mark fell forward but his opponent held him up while he pummelled his ribs. Then he shifted his attack to the head, holding Mark by the shoulder with his left hand and hammering him with his right. Through a red haze of pain, Mark realized that he was systematically being taken apart by an expert.

Jesus Christ, the bastard was out to kill Mark! Dave Green had never thrown a punch in his life, but he couldn't just stand there and watch his best friend being destroyed. He screamed at Roger, "We've got to stop him!" But Roger, a strange light in those vacant eyes, shook his head. "Mark's got it coming."

Dave grabbed the other man from San Francisco by the arm and pleaded with him to stop the carnage, but the man shook him off and continued to watch impassively as his companion worked Mark over. Another blow slammed into Mark with a sickening crunch, and Dave, in desperation, seized the poker and began to rain blows on the head and shoulders of the assailant. Staggered, the man called Jerry turned around to face his attacker and Mark collapsed unconscious on the floor. Dave, a wild look in his eyes, held the heavy poker over his head and yelled, "Get out of here, you fucking killer, or I'll break your skull!"

Breathing heavily, the stranger painfully raised his left hand to massage his right shoulder and looked down at Mark lying on the white shag carpet, a crimson stain spreading out from his head. Seemingly satisfied with his night's work, he grabbed the blonde by the wrist and snarled, "C'mon, you bitch. We're getting out of here!" The other couple followed silently after them.

Dave made a reluctant Roger help him half carry, half support Mark down to Roger's car — a white Cadillac convertible parked in front of the apartment block.

Dave felt a touch of malicious pleasure as he saw the bloodstains seeping into the immaculate white upholstery. The Caddy would have to be sent back to the factory to get those stains out.

Dave pushed in the lighter in the armrest and lit a cigarette. Twisting around in his seat to keep an eye on Mark, he muttered, "Thanks for all the help back there, Roger old buddy."

"I was going to do something," the playboy protested unconvincingly. "At the right time."

"In a pig's ass."

Roger drew to a stop at a traffic light, alongside a Plymouth sedan full of rowdy high-school kids. They fell into a hushed silence when they spotted Mark sprawled unconscious and bleeding on the rear seat of the open convertible.

"He lost an argument with his girlfriend," Dave called out as the light changed and they pulled away from the awestruck teenagers.

Two attendants hurried out with a stretcher and trundled Mark into Emergency when they arrived at the Holy Cross Hospital. Dave chain-smoked while they waited for word on Mark's condition. He would have liked to pace up and down the linoleum-covered floor of the hospital lounge but it was crowded with the relatives and friends of other victims of the night's traffic and violence.

"Lovely playmates you found tonight," he remarked conversationally to Roger as he mashed a cigarette into a metal ashtray leaning crookedly on its stand.

"They seemed okay when I met them," replied Roger. "I was hoping to make some time with the blonde, to tell you the truth. But she was on the make for Mark from the moment she first saw him. Thank Christ," he added fervently. "That Jerry character operates on a pretty short fuse. He'll probably come after you. You thought about that?"

"No, he won't," replied Dave. "I bet that charming little foursome will be the hell and gone across the border by morning. Don't you see?" he went on impatiently at Roger's uncomprehending look. "It was a set-up. The guy was a ringer, probably a professional boxer, hired to provoke a fight with Mark and beat the shit out of him."

"You're saying you think Cliff Marsden had something to do with this?"

"Go to the head of the class." Until that moment Dave had been convinced that Roger had been in on the plot, but now he wasn't so sure. A sexy-looking blonde who didn't seem too interested in the man she was with would be irresistible bait for Roger, and he could be counted on to invite her and her friends back to his pad.

"Mr. Green?" The doctor, a young intern in a white gown, stood in the doorway.

Dave jumped to his feet. "How is he, doc?"

"'Doctor,' if you please," he said huffily. "Mr. Hunter is being prepared for surgery. His jaw is fractured and it will have to be wired shut. His nose is broken as well, but we will have to wait for the swelling to go down before we can do anything about that."

"This business of wiring his jaw shut. Does that mean he won't be able to talk?" To the loquacious Dave Green this was a fate too horrible to contemplate.

"He will be able to mumble but it won't be easy to understand. Until he gets used to it, he will find that the best way to communicate will be by writing notes on a pad of paper. In any case, it will only be for a month." A nurse appeared at the doctor's elbow and he excused himself, saying that he was required in Emergency. He told Dave there was no point in his hanging around, since it would be morning before they brought Mark down from the recovery room.

"Come back in the afternoon. By then he'll be conscious enough to know what's going on."

"Mr. Hunter?" The floor nurse ran her finger down a list of names. "He's in 426G. It's those doors down on the right-hand side."

The green-painted door was halfway open. Dave stuck his head around it and saw the broad back of a uniformed policeman sitting between the first two beds. There were four beds in the room: all of them occupied. Mark was in the one closest to the door, the one the policeman was sitting beside. The officer looked up as Dave tiptoed in. "You a friend of Mr. Hunter?"

Dave, his gaze riveted on Mark's battered countenance, nodded wordlessly. Mark's face was puffed and swollen like a black and blue balloon. His eyes were mere slits in a mass of bruised tissue; two rows of stitches made railroad tracks across his cheeks. His neck was completely covered with a white gauze bandage. He tried to grin and Dave caught a gleam of metal in his mouth.

"You didn't happen to be present when the assault took place, Mr. ...?" the policeman inquired hopefully.

"Green. Dave Green. And it was a fist fight. Kinda one-sided, I grant you, but still a fist fight."

The policeman shook his head in wonder. "If you told me the guy used a baseball bat, I'd have believed you. Mr. Hunter," the policeman paused to give Mark a reproachful look, "doesn't seem to want to lay charges."

"I can understand why." Dave caught the gleam of approval in Mark's eyes and continued, "It was a private quarrel. Over a blonde. You know how it is. Besides the guy was from San Francisco and I bet he's back there already."

As soon as he heard the part about San Francisco, the constable closed his notebook and got to his feet. "Seems like I'm just spinning my wheels." He paused at the foot of the bed to look down at Mark. "You want to pick fights, I'd stick with little old ladies."

"Yeah," Dave murmured. "Next time you're tackling a manxome foe, make sure you bring your vorpal blade."

The policeman gave him a strange look, muttered, "Something like that," and left.

Mark was released from the hospital on the afternoon of the third day. His face still resembled something from a cheap horror flick, but he was steady on his feet and he was able to walk unassisted to Dave's car. By now, Dave could understand most of the garbled sounds issuing through Mark's clenched teeth, but Mark had to resort to the scratch pad for the other visitors who dropped in to see him at the hospital and stare in horrified fascination at his damaged face.

Alone in the apartment during the day, Mark felt totally cut off from the outside world. He didn't dare answer the phone when it rang; an unsuspecting caller might think he had a werewolf on the other end of the phone. He was supposed to take his nourishment through a straw, but he soon found it more efficient to simply pour the vanilla and strawberry flavoured concentrate behind his lower lip and use his cheek muscles to force it down his throat. The wire cutters were always at his side. He had been instructed on how to use them if he ever began to choke.

Desperate for something constructive to do during the long, empty hours, Mark hit on the idea of having Dave bring him books on corporate law and finance from the public library. It took some time to get used to the jargon, but he was agreeably surprised at how much he was able to sort out for himself. It would be useful background stuff once he got Hunter Oil Limited off the ground. Provided he ever did, of course. Or would Cliff Marsden attack him on that front, as well? Surely the son of a bitch would be satisfied with the fearful beating that Mark had been given. According to the gossip that Dave came home with, the tycoon's only reply was a smirk whenever someone brought up the subject.

As the days passed, Mark's condition steadily improved. His ribs stopped hurting with every breath he took and the swelling went down enough so that his nose could be set. When the surgeon congratulated him that the bone hadn't splintered, Mark screwed up his courage and scribbled a note asking what he would look like when it was all over. The doctor studied his face for a moment, then asked, "Do you have a recent photo of yourself before this happened?"

When Mark gave an affirmative nod, the surgeon told him that that's what he would look like, except for two small scars under his cheekbones and a thin incision scar on his neck. And the scars would gradually fade until they would be almost unnoticeable. Mark was ecstatic with relief. It was more than he had dared hope for.

When he returned to the apartment he found a long, distraught letter from Betty MacDonald waiting for him. She was on a guilt trip, blaming herself for what had happened and offering to fly back to Calgary to see him. The tone of her letter made it clear that she was his for the taking. Mark had a sudden mental image of that luscious body lying beside him and reached for the phone. She had typed the number of the Vancouver law firm where she worked at the bottom of her letter, and he was halfway through dialing it before he remembered his wired jaw. His speech was gradually improving but it wasn't up to a long-distance telephone call. The receptionist at the law firm would jump right out of her skin at the strangled, gargling sounds coming out of the earpiece. She would probably think she was the victim of some new kind of obscene phone call. The delay gave Mark time to reconsider. The thought of making love to "The Bod" would tempt a saint, but it would also be taking unfair advantage of her feelings of guilt and remorse.

That same evening he wrote her a long letter in reply. He told her that she was totally wrong to blame herself, that they were both victims of Marsden's inflated and perverted ego. Nobly, he refrained from taking her up on her offer to visit him. As he used a moistened Kleenex to seal the envelope, he wondered if he would have been so highminded if he hadn't met Jane Marsden. But that was a dead end. He almost gave in to the temptation to open the letter and add a postscript inviting Betty to come to Calgary.

It was during a conversation with Otis Turner that Mark finally abandoned the use of the notepad. Dave had brought the courtly Texan back to the apartment after work. The oilman was in Calgary to finalize a number of, as he put it, "modest little drilling deals," including Hambro. He watched Mark's increasing frustration as he wrote down questions and answers on the terms of the deal, and finally said, "No need for all that scribblin' boy. I can understand you jes' fine so long as you talk real slow."

The next day Mark drove himself to the outpatients' clinic at the hospital. The surgeon who had set his jaw wanted to examine his progress and fix a date for cutting the outer wires. The clinic was in the same wing as the emergency department, and Mark felt an atavistic *frisson* of fear as he saw the neon Emergency sign, pale in the bright sunlight, over the ambulance entrance. He had just been coming to when they had arrived at the hospital that night and he would never forget the disoriented feeling of helplessness as he was lifted onto a stretcher and rushed down a brightly lit hall with white-coated figures running alongside. But that was in the past and Mark, knowing that he was faced with nothing more painful than a checkup, was buoyant with good cheer as the admitting nurse directed him to a waiting room. He had no way of knowing it, but it was the same depressing chamber where Dave and Roger had waited for news of his condition.

Jane Marsden, looking utterly gorgeous and dashing in riding clothes, was perched on the edge of a chair against the far wall. Her face remained carefully expressionless until she finally realized that this apparition was mumbling her name. When she recognized who it was, her expression changed to one of appalled concern, and Mark, who flattered himself that he was beginning to look halfway human again, was crushed. But never mind that, what the hell was wrong with her? Had she hurt herself in a fall? Maybe broken her back — no, she wouldn't be sitting up if she had.

It took him three tries before she understood that he was asking whether she was all right. "It's not me," she told him. Her expression softened as she added, "But it was kind of you to ask. I was helping out an instructor at Pony Club and one of the pupils took a tumble. I think she was only winded, but I brought her in to make sure she doesn't have a concussion."

While she spoke her eyes never left his face. "I had heard about your ... er, accident ... but I never realized how badly you were hurt. I'm terribly sorry."

"You should see the other guy," Mark told her cheerfully.

It took her a moment to grasp what he said, then, as if unable to help herself, she gave a little grin. Ducking her head to hide it, she spotted the wire cutters in his hand and her eyes widened.

Mark held them up and said lightly, "These are my escape hatch. In case I suddenly start to choke."

"I thought that might be it. You've really had a rough time of it, haven't you?" she paused, then said somewhat breathlessly, "I don't care what people are saying, my father had nothing to do with it. He's not that kind of a person."

Mark thought it best to maintain a tactful silence, but that didn't satisfy her. "You don't believe me, do you?" she demanded fiercely.

"Let's say I can't prove otherwise. Comes to the same thing in the end."

"No it doesn't. Not at all." She frowned, and he wanted to reach out and erase the tiny lines between her eyebrows. "You just made a play for the wrong guy's girl-friend," she added with spirit."

"Touché!" Mark's jaw was beginning to ache.

She saw him wince and murmured contritely, "That doesn't mean I'm not sorry about what happened to you. I am. Truly."

"Sorry enough to have dinner with me?"

She hesitated, and Mark held his breath. Before she could reply, however, a white-coated medical resident came into the lounge. He was holding the hand of a young girl clad in a grass-stained T-shirt, blue jeans, and jodhpur boots. The girl detached herself from him and ran across to Jane who bent down to hug her, gently stroking her hair.

"Wendy has a mild concussion," the intern told Jane. "Nothing serious, but her parents must see that she doesn't fall asleep for any length of time. For the next three nights they'll have to awaken her every two hours. If they can't rouse her they are to call their family doctor immediately."

"I'll tell them," Jane promised.

The intern cast a glance of professional interest at Mark. "Ah, the nurses' favourite patient! Coming along nicely, I see. How are the ribs?"

"Haven't had a twinge for two days," replied Mark, wishing the guy would leave before Jane made her escape.

"Good. Well, Doctor Morton shouldn't be long." The intern sauntered off. Things were usually pretty slack in Emergency during the daytime.

Jane had lingered in order to speak to him. Mark realized that it wasn't her style to take the easy way out. Her eyes, more grey than green in the artificial light, were serious and Mark thought to himself, "Oh, oh, here's where I get told for the last time to get lost and stay lost."

"I won't have dinner with you," she said slowly. Mark, accepting defeat, nodded numbly. It took him a moment to realize she was still talking. He heard her say, "I'll be instructing Pony Club at Borden's Riding Academy tomorrow afternoon. You know where that is?"

"Sure." Mark hadn't the faintest clue where the damn place was, but he'd find out. He didn't want to interrupt when things were beginning to sound so promising.

"I'll be through at four o'clock. If you want to meet me there, we can go somewhere for ..." she paused and looked sympathetically at his wired jaw, "... a milkshake or something."

The thought of drinking a milkshake on top of the liquid concentrate that was his steady diet almost made Mark gag, but he agreed enthusiastically. Hell, he'd happily quaff castor oil if it meant seeing Jane Marsden.

As it turned out, however, the big date didn't live up to Mark's high expectations. To him, it was to be the first step in a romance that would never end. But it soon became depressingly obvious that Jane regarded it as merely a social gesture, a way of expressing sympathy for the injuries he had suffered, and possibly, and maybe unconsciously, an unspoken apology for the treatment he had received at the hands of the Marsden family.

Mark got off on the wrong foot by immediately trying to pin down another rendezvous. At first Jane attempted to politely ignore his importuning but when he persisted, she finally turned to him and said, "Look, Mark, I'm pretty much tied up with someone else. I'm sorry, but there it is."

That was an unexpected blow. Nobody had warned him about that. "You're not engaged or anything, are you?" he blurted.

"No." Jane looked at him with faint alarm.

After that it was downhill all the way. Mark, annoyed with himself and frustrated with his inability to articulate his words properly, fell into something that was close to a sulk, staring morosely into the nauseating depths of his milkshake. He had ordered maple, a flavour he detested, because it was the only one his concentrate didn't come in.

They said goodbye rather formally in the parking lot of the Dairy Queen. She held out her hand and he touched it briefly, before dropping it as though it would sear his flesh. As he turned away to go over to his own car, he caught a glimpse of what could have been laughter in her eyes. It reminded him that this girl had a lively sense of humour; it probably amused the hell out of her watching him make a horse's ass of himself.

7

Since he still wasn't answering the phone, the bank had to mail him written notification that a letter of credit in the amount of $75,000 had been issued in favour of Hunter Oil Limited. Mark stared at the brief notification form with something close to disbelief. Although he and Otis Turner had signed an agreement whereby the latter was to raise the funds to drill the Hambro well, there was something so, well — so bogus — about Turner, that, in his heart, Mark had never thought it would really happen. But there was nothing bogus about the letter of credit. He had the money to drill his first oil well. Hunter Oil Limited was on its way!

By the time Dave Green arrived back at the apartment after work, Mark's euphoria was tempered with apprehension. "As you know, I'm not all that confident about the geology of that play. I could end up blowing the $75,000."

Dave's expression was enigmatic as he replied, "Oh, I imagine old Otis would be pretty philosophical about that."

Despite the fact that he wouldn't use the phone and was too self-conscious about his mumbling to meet with strangers, Mark was able to make all the arrangements to get the well underway.

He purchased a second-hand typewriter and laboriously pecked out a bid letter and mailed it to six drilling companies. He also typed out an application for a drilling licence and Dave took it around to the Oil and Gas Conservation Board during his lunch hour.

Only three of the drilling companies submitted a bid. Times were good and the bids were higher than Mark anticipated. But they were all within his budget and, after much debate with himself, he finally chose the highest bidder. Apex Drilling was the Cadillac of the drilling industry; its rigs were well-maintained and its crews were superbly trained.

The Basal Quartz was their target and the well prognosis Mark had prepared called for it to be reached around the 6,000 foot level. With luck they should be able to punch the well down to that depth in just under three weeks. Mark had arranged things so they would still be some 2,000 feet above the target formation when it was time for the three main wires to be cut. The smaller wires embedded in his gums would have to remain in place for another two weeks, but at least he'd be able to talk clearly and eat real food.

The wire-cutting operation was performed in the oral surgeon's clinic and, while incredibly bloody, did not require a general anaesthetic, so Mark was back in action that same afternoon. The daily drilling reports that the toolpush phoned in from the Hambro location showed steady progress as the rig sliced through the shale like so much butter. When the rock cuttings coming up from the hole showed they were in the Belly River formation, Mark decided to call Otis Turner.

"Of course it doesn't prove anything," Mark, revelling in his ability to speak clearly, said over the long-distance line, "but the fact that the Belly River is there and right on target has to be encouraging. And we encountered a small gas kick when we hit the Belly River. It wasn't worth following up, but at least it shows there are hydrocarbons in the area."

"Looks like you've called it right on the button so far, boy." Otis didn't sound too excited, but, after all, it was just another well to the veteran oilman who had participated in hundreds of them in the course of his career. "When do you expect to hit the Basal Quartz?"

"Next Wednesday. Six days from now," Mark told him. "If God is willing and the creeks don't rise. And provided it's there, of course."

"Yeah. Them old sandbars can fool you. Well, good luck, Mark. I'm goin' to be kinda out-of-pocket for the next week, so give me a call when it's all over."

"Well, okay. If that's what you want." Astounded, Mark put down the phone. How casual could you get? It was bad enough when Otis had told him not to bother sending the daily drilling reports, but not to want to know the final result the minute it was available? Mark reminded himself once again that while this was the first well he had drilled for his own account, it was old hat to Otis.

As Mark had feared from the start, the Hambro well came in dry. As a geologist, it was some comfort to know the formation was present, exactly as he had predicted. But it was too tight to contain any hydrocarbons. The operation was a success, but the patient died. Despite the promoter's seeming indifference, Mark was nervous as he placed the call to break the bad news. No oilman likes a dry hole, no matter how unimportant the well may be.

"Hell, son, you got no call to blame yourself. You called the formation dead on, and you can't do better than that. It ain't your fault that it was tight." If anything, Otis sounded more cheerful than before, back when things still looked promising. "My investors are all big boys. Don't feel bad, son. You've got a lifetime of wildcatting ahead of you and don't forget that one good well makes up for a whole mess of dry holes."

"I've got to hand it to Otis. He took it like a real pro." Mark had just finished telling Dave Green about the dry hole. They were sitting in the dining room of the apartment having a beer before dinner. "In fact he was doing his best to cheer me up."

"They don't call him '150 Points Turner' for nothing."

"Just what the hell is that supposed to mean?" demanded Mark.

"Otis has the quaint habit of selling 150 points of his deals. You ever tried to account for 150 per cent of the production from an oil well? He must have been shitting square bricks when it looked like you were going to hit."

"Why didn't you tell me about this, for Christ's sake?"

"I thought about it," admitted Dave. "Then I figured, "Oh, what the hell?" It was a way to get your well drilled, and if you struck oil, that would have been Otis's problem, not yours. As a matter of fact," Dave added with a grin, "it would have been interesting to see what the fraudulent old fart would have done. You can bet he'd have stick-handled his way out of it somehow."

"Sure he would have. And then he'd brag about it to the other good ole boys." Mark raised his glass in mock salute. "They're a breed apart, those characters. The oil patch wouldn't be the same without them. But once is enough for me. I've got to find some financial backers who play straight up."

Dave swallowed the last of his beer. "By the way, I discovered who Jane goes out with. Like you asked."

"Who is it?"

"Are you ready for this?" Dave paused for effect. "Rhodes Taylor."

"The guy who owns Apex Drilling?"

"The very same. Calgary's most eligible bachelor. Daddy is said to approve."

"He's too old for her."

"He's thirty, which makes him all of four years older than you. Not exactly what you'd call a generation gap. An eminently suitable match, according to the plastic duchess."

"Who in hell is the 'plastic duchess'?"

"Mrs. Cullen. 'Bea' to her friends. D.R.'s wife. They call her the plastic duchess because she's had so many facelifts her doctor has retired and gone to live in Hawaii."

"How come you know her?"

"She thinks I'm funny," replied Dave. "Anyone who's married to old D.R. deserves a few laughs." But Mark was no longer listening. He'd been expecting that Jane's boyfriend would turn out to be some young college kid home for the summer who could be blown out of the water by Mark's worldly charm. But Rhodes Taylor was another matter altogether. The guy was reputed to be worth millions and, worse, he was at the stage in life where he'd be thinking about getting married and starting a family. Except he'd probably think of it as starting a dynasty. Mark wrenched his mind away from this revolting line of thought, to find that Dave was still talking. "You've got one thing going for you," he was saying.

"What's that?" Mark demanded. Maybe Taylor liked boys.

"The guy's a workaholic. If he's not on the long-distance phone, he's on an airplane flying to some meeting or other. My friend, the plastic duchess, wonders where he finds the time to court the delectable Miss Marsden.

8

"There's a football game this weekend, isn't there?" asked Mark. It was Saturday morning and he and Dave were lounging about after breakfast, reading *The Albertan*. The remaining wires had been removed from Mark's gums earlier in the week and he had completely shaken off the effects of the general anaesthetic. It felt great to no longer have a mouthful of metal.

"Yeah. Tomorrow afternoon. The Stampeders versus the Eskimos." Dave lowered his part of the newspaper and looked across the room at Mark. "Why the sudden interest? Football's not your bag." He struck himself a mock blow to the forehead. "Pardon me all to hell for being so slow. You figure Jane might be there and you want her to see how pretty you look. Right?"

"Farthest thing from my mind," replied Mark blandly. "I just thought it would be a pleasant way to spend Sunday afternoon. You have your usual two tickets, I presume?"

"Not so fast, old buddy. I've got plans for those tickets. I've been hanging on to them until I got the phone number of a foxy new secretary in the exploration department. I'm going to give her a call in a few minutes and ask her if she'd like to take in the game."

"Buy her dinner instead."

"Jane's old man attends every home game, you know."

When Mark showed no reaction to this, Dave sighed and returned to the stock market quotations. Both of the penny oil stocks he had bought on hot tips were falling out of bed.

Sitting in the rickety wooden grandstand, Mark looked upon the world and found it good, Rhodes Taylor notwithstanding. The sun was shining and his face had returned to normal. His doctor had been bang on; the only sign of the beating were two small scars below his cheekbones and a hairline incision under his chin. If anything, they added a rather dashing touch to his appearance. At least that was what more than one girl had told him. On the way to Mewata Stadium, Dave had muttered darkly that if Cliff Marsden saw Mark looking like a goddamn movie star once again, he'd hire more goons to work him over. The thought gave Mark pause, but then he dismissed it. He and Marsden were even; surely the pipeline magnate wouldn't risk a criminal charge by setting up another attack.

Mark spent more time trying to spot Jane in the stands than he did watching the play on the field. Dave told him not to bother; if she was there at all she'd be up in the press box with her father. During halftime, Mark wandered from one concession stand to another, hoping to see her in one of the lineups. His search was in vain, but he did run into a number of friends and acquaintances, all of whom were gratifyingly astonished at his restored appearance. A woman, whose trim figure was emphasized, rather than obscured, by her severely tailored suit, marched up to him and scrutinized his face from every angle. It took Mark a few seconds to place her as the nurse who had looked after Cliff Marsden the night of the party.

"You're a very lucky man," she announced finally. "Doctor Morton did a superb job."

"I know. And I'm very grateful to him. But how can you tell? You've only seen the 'after' stage."

"I was on duty in Emergency the night they brought you in."

"Oh. Well, then I'm grateful to you too. I think the guy was out to kill me. I guess an eye for an eye isn't enough for Marsden."

"I know nothing about that. And I would be very careful about making any accusations if I were you." She marched off, taut bum straining against her tight skirt.

Mark shrugged, bought a couple of Cokes — he would never willingly drink another milkshake in his life — and returned to the stands. While the teams were exchanging ends for the final quarter, Dave poked him in the ribs. "Looks like you're going to have company."

God in heaven! Was Marsden sending another squad of thugs to work him over? Alarmed, Mark half rose in his seat, and spotted Jane climbing the stairs. She smiled when she saw him looking at her and his heart turned over.

"Hi," she said a little breathlessly when she reached his row of seats. "Everyone's talking about how wonderful you look and I came over to see for myself."

Probably to make her feel less guilty on her father's account, thought Mark, but he didn't care. It was enough that she was there, talking to him.

"You look great. You really do." There was an odd note to her voice that made Mark stare at her. Maybe he was daydreaming, but he could swear that something — a sudden awareness of each other — passed between them.

"Don't mind me," Dave Green murmured.

Mark turned to him and said, "I keep forgetting that you two don't know each other, do you? Jane, meet Dave Green."

"Hi, Dave. I've heard a lot about you. Everybody says you should be on TV. Doesn't he look super."

"Not nearly as good as the person I planned to bring. For starters, she was a girl."

"Some of us came to watch the game," a voice shouted from two rows up.

"Let's go down below where we can talk," urged Mark.

"Okay. But just for a few minutes."

When another irate voice hollered, "Down in front," they hurried down the grandstand steps and walked back to the food concession area where the vendors were starting to close the shutters on their booths.

"I know I sound like a broken record, but I really want to see you again. And," Mark drew a deep breath and rushed on, "I have a crazy hunch you feel the same way."

Her eyes widened at that and she said softly, almost as if talking to herself, "I'm not denying that. But you can't call me at home. You can reach me at the riding academy most afternoons. Four o'clock is a good time to call."

"Tomorrow afternoon, for instance?"

She nodded, and without giving himself time to think, he bent down and kissed her on the lips. A light, brief kiss, but still a kiss.

"Till tomorrow," he whispered and walked away, leaving her standing there with a startled look on her face. Startled, but not, so far as he could tell, annoyed.

The Eskimos must have scored a touchdown because the stands erupted in groans and catcalls as he climbed back up to rejoin Dave. Mark couldn't have cared less.

Although Jane obviously intended him to call her on the phone, Mark decided to drive out to the stables. On the way he passed the Dairy Queen where they had had their first, unsatisfactory date. Things had improved considerably since then; he could talk like a normal human being once more, and, best of all, there had been that look in Jane's eyes. God; he hoped he wasn't fooling himself on that score.

He parked the Olds at the end of a row of sedans and station wagons. A number of women in their mid- to late-thirties, mothers-cum-chauffeurs of the Pony Club kids, lined the rails to watch the class in progress. Mark remained in the car. From where he sat he had an unobstructed view of Jane, standing in the centre of the ring, watching and calling out encouragement as the young riders trotted their mounts over wooden poles raised a few inches above the ground. A few minutes later she told them to walk their horses on a loose rein for five minutes, then cool them and put them away. When the class was over, she crossed the ring to exchange a few words with the railbird parents. Mark saw her do a double take when she recognized the blue and white Olds at the end of the line. She came over as soon as the women, laden with pails, brushes, and leg bandages, had dutifully followed their children to the barn.

Mark opened the passenger door and she climbed in beside him. Underneath her black-velvet riding cap she was frowning slightly. "I didn't expect you to drive all the way out here. A phone call would have done just as well."

"It's a nice day for a drive in the country," he replied blandly.

"Look, if we're going to see each other," she glanced sideways at him as she spoke and he nodded in enthusiastic agreement, "I'm afraid we'll have to do it on the q.t. I hate to say that because it makes me feel sort of cheap. But if my father were to find out I was seeing you he would be beside himself." To Mark's astonishment and dismay, she actually shivered.

"He might surprise you. Maybe he figures the slate has been wiped clean and all is forgiven."

"Not a hope. And I wish you would stop insinuating that he was responsible for what happened to you." She removed her hard hat and rubbed her forehead. "I don't know about this, Mark," she said with a small sigh. "Maybe the whole scene is going to be just too heavy for us. Perhaps we should forget about seeing each other."

"Don't say that! Don't even think it," implored Mark. "From this moment on, I shall regard your father as a prince among men, more sinned against than sinning."

"You know, for a geologist you sometimes have a funny way of talking."

"It comes from rooming with Dave Green."

"Would it be asking too much for you to ... well, sort of spread the word that you don't blame my father. It might help to stop some people in this town from saying those awful things about him."

"Done. And I will recruit Dave in the same noble cause. Having old motor-mouth talk it up will be more effective than taking an ad in the paper. Now, in what out-of-the-way corner of the world will we meet for dinner?"

She had obviously been thinking about that one, for she replied almost immediately. "There's a restaurant just outside the city limits on the road to Banff. It's called The Bearspaw and only tourists ever seem to go there. I can meet you there at seven-thirty if you like."

While she spoke she kept looking out the side window and as soon as she saw the contingent of Pony Clubbers trooping out of the barn, she opened the door and slipped out. "You better leave now," she said as she closed the door. "I'll see you tonight."

Mark raised the wine bottle but Jane smilingly placed a hand overtop of her glass. With a guilty glance over his shoulder at the manager, standing by the cash register and studiously looking the other way, Mark refilled his own glass and put the bottle back under the table. He could feel the alcohol warming his cheeks and decided that it would be his last drink of the evening. After finally beginning to make some progress with this lady, he had no intention of blowing it by getting himself sloshed. Particularly since her first glass of wine was still half-full.

Looking at her sitting across the table, with her clear skin glowing in the subdued light and her dark-fringed eyes alive with intelligence and humour, Mark knew beyond all doubt that she was what he wanted for the rest of his life. With that certain knowledge came a stark feeling of terror at the thought of having to live his life without her. To her, he probably meant nothing more than a summer romance, a diverting fling between college semesters. One of two summer romances, he reminded himself grimly. He had almost succeeded in forgetting about Rhodes Taylor.

"Is there something the matter?" asked Jane. "You look awfully serious all of a sudden."

Mark snapped out of his reverie. "My mother would say that somebody just walked over my grave."

"Where do your parents live, Mark? Texas?"

"My father was killed in the war. He was a major in the Marine Corps and his amphtrac was blown up by a mine when they hit the beach on the Tarawa Atoll."

Instinctively, Jane reached across and touched his hand. "It must have been a terrific blow."

"It was. I was fourteen at the time and that's not the best age for a boy to lose his father. The only thing that made it bearable was that a lot of the other kids at school were in the same boat. That, and a feeling of patriotic pride. My dad was a war hero and I was proud of him. Still am, as a matter of fact."

"And your mother?"

"She remarried while I was at Texas U. She and her second husband live in California in a little place not far from Carmel."

"Do you see her often?"

"Not very. They travel a lot. He's totally devoted to her. She's very beautiful." He shrugged. "They have a good life."

A good life that doesn't leave much room for a child from a former marriage, thought Jane. But there was no need to feel sorry for this self-confident young man. He wasn't what you would call deprived.

Jane was facing the entrance while Mark had his back to it. "Oh, oh," she muttered under her breath.

"What is it?"

"A girl I know just walked in. With someone who is not her fiancé. She's just spotted us.

"No, I think she's decided to let on she hasn't seen us."

"Are you worried? That she might talk, I mean."

"It's not her I'm worried about. It's the guy with her. He's a football player, and they gossip worse than a pack of old women."

"And your father is closely connected with the team."

"Uh, huh." She gave a slight shrug as if to dismiss the subject, but her expression was troubled. It seemed a little unreal to Mark that a grown woman would be so cut up over what her father might think, but then Cliff Marsden wasn't your average father. Unconsciously, he fingered the scar on the right side of his neck. Jane saw the gesture and winced visibly. Determined not to let the incident spoil the evening, she smiled and asked Mark how his oil company was coming along. Ruefully, he told her about Otis Turner and his 150 point deals.

"I love it!" she laughed when he finished, adding without thinking, "I can hardly wait to tell Dad. He'll ..." She raised her hand to her mouth and murmured, "Except that I won't, will I? Oh, Mark, I hate this!"

"Yeah, I know. Anyway," Mark, not knowing what else to say, went on talking, "what I have to do now is find some risk capital."

Jane had recovered her poise. "I know that Dad from time to time has backed people who wanted to get started in the oil business, but somehow I can't ..." She grinned impishly and left the sentence dangling.

"I can't either." Mark grinned back. He caught the waitress's eye and she came over with the cheque. Outside in the paved parking lot, he looked around and asked, "Hey, where's the Jag?"

"Too conspicuous." She pointed to a dark-blue Ford.

"That's my transportation for tonight."

"Okay. I'll follow you into town. The night is young and you are definitely beautiful."

"I'd rather we said goodnight here. There'll be other times." She held out her hand. "It's been fun. I enjoyed myself."

Smiling, Mark pulled her toward him, his lips seeking hers. She wrenched her hand away and stepped back until she bumped into the car. Her eyes, wide and dilated, stared past his shoulder. Instinctively, Mark hunched his shoulders as if to ward off a blow. Was her father standing there, behind him? Mark looked fearfully over his shoulder. The parking lot was deserted. What had come over her? Whatever it was, she had snapped out of it, for those lovely eyes were focused on him and she was smiling, albeit a little tremulously. With a whispered "Good night," she slipped behind the wheel of the Ford.

"I'll call you," he said.

"Please do. At the stables. But this time, just phone. A lot of the Pony Club mothers are friends of the family."

It was a very puzzled and disturbed Mark who drove back into town. Everything had been perfect until he made that move to kiss her. Maybe it was his fault; maybe that kiss at the football game had led him to presume too much. After all, there was nothing wrong with a girl not wanting to be rushed. Reassured by these thoughts, Mark pressed his foot down on the accelerator and the Olds picked up speed.

9

Mark rubbed eyes smarting with fatigue, sighed, and switched the desk lamp back on. The table was covered with contour maps with their elegant, flowering curves, but it was the squiggly lines of a well log that he was concentrating on. Picking up his slide rule, he rechecked his resistivity and porosity calculations. Rising excitement swept away the cobwebs of fatigue as he finally admitted to himself that he might be on to something. He got to his feet and went out to the kitchenette to pour himself a cup of coffee. It was undrinkable, which was hardly surprising, as it had been sitting on the stove ever since Mark, unable to sleep, had crawled out of bed at four in the morning to return to his logs and maps.

Fortunately, he was alone in the apartment. Dave was out in the field trying to pick up some freehold oil and gas leases for Stanmin. And that was the sum total of what Mark knew about Dave's field trip. To know even the general area where Dave was leasing would be to learn something about Stanmin's exploration plans. It was another of those conflicts of interest that inevitably cropped up whenever people from different parts of the oil patch shared accommodation, or just socialized together. For the same reason, Mark couldn't discuss any of his prospects with Dave, including this one, which was suddenly looking so promising. But Dave's absence had made it possible for Mark to concentrate for hour after hour on the riddle of the Cardium sands.

Mark poured the tar-like coffee into the sink and checked his watch. He still had two hours before it was time to call Jane. He'd better get in some sack time or he wouldn't be capable of forming a coherent sentence when he talked to her. There had been times when he was staring blearily at the maps and logs that the thought that he was doing it for her was what kept him going. Crazy. Nonetheless, he was smiling as he set the alarm and crashed into bed.

"Mr. Cullen, how ..." The oilman, who was obviously in the grip of a ferocious hangover, held up a hand to interrupt Mark.

"I think it's time you called me Don, or D.R. will do. And could you please speak a little lower?"

"I'll whisper," promised Mark with a grin. "I asked for this appointment with you to see if you could give me some advice on how to go about raising drilling money. I mean serious money that will finance an ongoing exploration program."

"I heard about you and Turner." Don started to laugh, then broke off as the hangover clamped down on his head like a vice. "God, I can't stand this," he muttered and tottered on unsteady legs over to the bar. His hands shook as he poured himself a hefty belt of Scotch. He downed half of it in one gulp and the sickly look began to recede from his face.

"The word is that Otis will avoid you like the plague in the future. He's afraid you may be an honest-to-God oil finder."

"I hope he's right. That's what you are."

"Yeah." Pleased, Don took another, smaller swallow of whisky. He was acting much less distracted now. "We're kind of a rare breed."

"I don't belong to that club. Not yet. But I intend to."

Don Cullen's bloodshot eyes had been scrutinizing Mark's face as they talked. "You look great, boy. A lot better than I expected, after the way Cliff Marsden nearly had you killed."

Remembering his promise to Jane, Mark demurred. "I can't be sure it was Marsden."

"It was Marsden, all right. I've known that son of a bitch since he was a boy and it's just like him to hire someone to do his fighting for him." Don put down his empty glass and leaned back in his chair. "It's ancient history now, but Cliff Marsden was one of the worst of the wartime profiteers. Instead of sending the bastard to jail, the fucking federal government gave him a medal — the Order of the British Empire, for Christ's sake. He's probably got those bloody initials tattooed on his arse!"

Intrigued, Mark asked, "Is that how he got his start? War profiteering?"

"For all practical purposes, yes. When the war started he had a little two-bit road construction company — a couple of bulldozers and scrapers. He didn't waste any time in getting his company and himself declared essential to the war effort, which meant he wasn't allowed to enlist. That was fair enough, I guess, but it used to make me want to puke when I was home on leave and he would go on about how badly he wanted to join up. He kept getting bigger and bigger government contracts, mostly for the airfields we were building out here for the Commonwealth Air Training Program."

Don went over to the bar to fix himself another drink, and Mark ventured, "Sounds like he was making a real contribution to the war effort."

"He was. If that had been all there was to it, he would have deserved his bloody medal. But he was gouging the government at every turn, falsifying invoices, charging for work that was never done — huge cost overruns on every project. He got away with it because the important thing was to get the job done and to hell with the cost. That suited our boy Cliff right down to the ground."

"Do you know this for a fact, or is it just a rumour?"

"I don't spread rumours." Don gave his visitor a severe look. "One of my accountants used to work for Marsden Construction until he couldn't take it any more."

"Why didn't he blow the whistle?"

"He tried to. But the government boys didn't want to hear about it. They had devoted a lot of time and effort building Cliff up as a hero of the home front, and I guess they must have figured that exposing him as a racketeer would have been bad for morale. So Cliff got his O.B.E., but people know, and people talk." He paused for another swallow of Scotch. "Cliff's a moody bastard, and I often wonder if that's behind it — knowing that people like myself hold him in contempt for what he did in the war."

"You were in the war yourself?"

Don grunted. "Three years overseas service with the Calgary Highlanders. We saw our share of action."

"My father was killed in the war." Mark went on to tell him how his father had been killed in battle for the Tarawa Atoll.

Don was visibly moved. His eyes were rheumy with unshed tears and he had to clear his throat before he could speak. "Those Marines are one tough outfit. Always the first to hit the beach." He blew his nose noisily. "Well, you didn't come here to reminisce about the war. You want to raise some exploration money, is that it?"

Mark nodded eager assent.

"You're talking risk capital. And that's a mighty scarce commodity."

"I thought I might try to raise some money in Toronto and Montreal."

Don hooted with laughter, this time without wincing. "Raise money in Toronto and Montreal, he says! It does my soul good to talk to you, Mark."

"What's so funny about that? After all it's the same country and there must be pools of capital down there that have to be invested someplace."

"But not in oil and gas, my young friend. Those bastards know fuck all about oil and gas and that's the way they intend to keep it. Even if you went down there with proven reserves in the ground, complete with an evaluation certificate signed by the good Lord Himself, you couldn't raise a nickel. And what you're talking about is drilling wildcats, not borrowing on proven reserves." Don shook his head. "I've been there. Save yourself the airfare."

"Do you have any suggestions? I know it's asking a lot but I'm pretty desperate."

Don put his empty glass down on the desk blotter and looked at Mark as if trying to make up his mind. Then he said, "There's only one place where you might have a chance of raising this kind of venture capital, and that's Texas. Some of the old families have been in the oil business for years and they understand how it works. You just might find someone down there who would be willing to take a flyer with you."

Don glanced at his watch and frowned. "Tell you what, come back here tomorrow at the same time. I'll make a couple of phone calls."

It was obvious that the oilman wanted to get rid of him, probably because he needed another drink and didn't want Mark to know. Mark immediately jumped to his feet. "That's terrific, Don. I really appreciate this."

Don, with a spontaneity that was quite unlike him, punched Mark on the arm and said, "I got a hunch that old 150-points Turner is right about you being an oil finder. And that's what this industry needs. God knows we've got enough corporate bureaucrats and bean counters. We need men who can go out and find oil, or the industry will self-destruct."

Carried away by his own rhetoric, Don opened the office door with a flourish that nearly knocked him off his feet. His secretary, a prim, middle-aged specimen with gold-rimmed glasses, sniffed audibly and announced, "Miss Leigh is here to see you, sir." The way she emphasized the 'sir' left no doubt about her feelings.

"Ah, yes." The oilman seemed flustered. A flashily dressed blonde, somewhere in her twenties, was perched on the arm of the massive, leather armchair. When Don said, "Come in, Miss Leigh," she rose leisurely to her feet, stubbed out her cigarette in an onyx ashtray and strolled across the reception area, hips rolling provocatively. She gave Mark a nakedly challenging look as she passed him.

"I'll see you tomorrow, Mark," Don called out with false heartiness as he closed the door behind the tarty Miss Leigh. The secretary's typewriter sprang to life with a furious clatter, but Mark was positive he heard the snick of a bolt being slid home.

When he related the curious little incident to Dave Green that night, the landman gave a low whistle. "I've heard rumours that Cullen has hookers come round to his office to give him a blow job but I never really believed it. Not until now. His own goddamn office! Is that chutzpah, or is that chutzpah?"

"I'm off to Houston next week," Mark said between bites of his cheeseburger. "To see if I can raise some liquid capital. D.R. Cullen came up with a couple of contacts."

"How much are you looking for?" Jane's straw made a sucking sound as she finished her milkshake. They had taken in an early movie and then dropped into the Dairy Queen for a snack.

"Whatever I can get. What I'd really like would be to find a backer who would stake me for a complete exploration program. Pinning everything on a single rank wildcat isn't the best way to go about finding oil. More often than not, it takes a series of wells to zero in on a reservoir." Discussing his plans with Jane filled Mark with a deep contentment.

That feeling was abruptly shattered as he heard her say, "I'm going to tell my father I'm seeing you. That is, if you intend to ask me out again."

Mark reached across the table for her hand. "Of course I do. But this business of telling your father ..." Mark shook his head. "That does not strike me as a smart move. Not smart at all. Remember how he reacted when I tried to make peace."

"I know. But I also know that I can't go on seeing you behind his back."

"I realize that's not your style. But, Jesus, honey, what if he comes on the heavy parent and forbids you to see me?"

"He won't," she replied confidently. "He'll probably go through the roof, but I'm still his daughter."

He drove her back to where the blue Ford was parked. Holding the driver's door open, he looked down at her and whispered, "It's there, isn't it? The feeling between us."

"I think so. I'm kind of mixed up." She lifted her face to be kissed.

Jane's mother was waiting for her in the front hall as she opened the door from the garage. "What's the matter, Mom?" Jane was alarmed at the stricken look on her mother's face.

"Your father wants to see you. He's in the study."

"What about, Mom?" Jane tried to speak lightly, but her heart was pounding in her chest.

"He knows you've been seeing that Mark Hunter." Eleanor Marsden drew in a long, shuddering breath. "He's beside himself. I'm begging you, Jane, not to do or say anything that will make him worse." Her eyes were wide with fear as she followed her daughter across the huge, sunken living room and down a marble-tiled hallway to the study. Cliff Marsden stood behind his desk, fingers digging into the leather back of a chair as if to keep from lashing out at something. His appearance frightened Jane. Normally, when her father's temper boiled over, as it did all too often, he flushed a purply red. But tonight his face was ashen, drained of blood."

"You wanted to see me, Father?"

"You're damn right I did!" he snarled, infuriated by her outward composure. "Sneaking around behind my back with a prick like Mark Hunter!"

Cliff Marsden had a foul tongue, but it was totally unlike him to use it on his daughter. Shaken, she replied, "I'm sorry you found out before I had a chance to tell you myself. I was going to in the morning."

"You know what that son of a bitch did to me, don't you?" Cliff's voice was a suppressed scream.

"I know he was the one who beat you up, if that's what you mean."

"He did more than that. A hell of a lot more. He made me into a laughing stock — a dirty joke in every club in town. The bastard!" Breathing heavily, Cliff strode over to the bar, poured himself three fingers of Scotch and downed it neat.

"Don't you think it's a little unfair to Rhodes, dear?" Eleanor imposed timidly. Her husband looked as if he was about to tell her to shut up, then thought better of it. "Your mother's right," he said. "You've been going out with Rhodes ever since you came home. How do you think he'll feel when he finds out you've been two-timing him."

"I haven't been two-timing him," Jane retorted with a show of spirit. "Rhodes and I are just good friends."

"Oh?" Abruptly switching tactics, Cliff gave her a beseeching look and said, "Don't do this to me, pet."

Jane had not expected to lose this confrontation. She had anticipated her father's anger and the incriminations, but she had fully expected to prevail in the end. Now she realized that was not the way it was going to be. She couldn't explain it to herself but she knew she was going to submit. "Does it really mean this much to you, Dad?" she asked miserably.

Sensing victory, he replied in a low voice. "It would just about destroy me if you got involved with that guy." He was about to add something about Mark's reputation as a womanizer but realized in time that any criticism of Mark could backfire on him by arousing her protective instincts. "Promise me you won't see Hunter again," he pleaded.

Looking at her father's anguished face and aware that she was probably making a terrible mistake, but not knowing what else to do, Jane blurted, "All right. You win," and fled from the room.

Mark stared in incredulous horror at Jane. She had just informed him that she was not going to see him any more and he knew from the tone of her voice that she meant it.

"We have to stop now before anyone gets hurt," she repeated as if to convince herself.

"It's too late for me," he said harshly.

"I'm sorry. I truly am. But I'm sure you'll recover," she replied with a sad little smile.

"And what about you? There is something between us. You can't deny that."

"I'm not trying to. And I realize it might have developed into something wonderful. But I can handle it if we stop right now. And so can you."

"If you only knew." Mark could no longer bear to look at her. He stared straight ahead through the Ford's windshield and said bitterly, "I don't know how your father got to you, but you can tell him from me that he's revenged himself beyond his wildest dreams."

"Oh, Mark!" Jane began to cry softly to herself as he, still without looking at her, climbed out of the parked car and walked away.

10

The stewardess popped open the door of the DC6-B, letting the hot, humid air flow into the cabin. Mark retrieved his briefcase from under the seat in front of him and joined the line of passengers clumping down the metal stairs to the tarmac. The asphalt, softened by the heat, clung to his shoes, making little sticky noises as he walked toward the terminal.

Waiting for his suitcase to be spewed out through the rubberized baggage door, and feeling his shirt collar beginning to wilt, Mark asked himself yet again why he didn't give up on the Canadian scene and come back here. He didn't have to stay in Canada. He was just beginning to get the hang of this wheeling and dealing business and what he learned would be every bit as useful in the oil patch of the American southwest as in western Canada. And, unlike Calgary, there was nothing in Houston to remind him of Jane. He clamped the lid on that thought, fast.

"You're the fella that Permex sent up to Canada, ain't ya?" Without taking his eyes off Mark, J.C. Lowe ejected a thin stream of tobacco juice from the side of his mouth. Out of the corner of his eye Mark watched it dribble down the lip of the silver spittoon. "Morley Adams," Lowe went on, naming the chairman of Permex, "is a good buddy of mine. He tells me you didn't stay very long with them once you got there."

"That's right. The oil industry is in its infancy up there and I saw an opportunity to get in on the ground floor." Even as he spoke, Mark knew he was just spinning his wheels. Someone at Permex, Ed Parsons most likely, had found out about his fundraising trip to Houston and alerted the old-boy network. And now this ol' boy across the desk from him, with his red suspenders and chewing tobacco, was letting him know where he stood. Still, he might as well go through the motions. He made a tentative gesture at his briefcase. "Would you like to see some of the plays I've worked up?"

"I reckon not, boy. When ol' J.C. puts on the harness with a partner, I like it to be with someone who's goin' to stay hitched for a spell."

"Thank you for your time, sir." Mark stood up, unexpectedly finding himself making a stiff little bow, and headed for the door. Stepping from the lobby of the air-conditioned office building into the street was like going into a steam bath with your clothes on. Mark, seething over the humiliating treatment he had received, scarcely noticed. Underneath his anger was the worrisome thought that if the Permex people had gotten to the second contact that D.R. had given him, his whole trip, which he couldn't really afford, would have been a total waste.

But Claude Defran was the soul of cordiality when Mark called to confirm his appointment. Although the Defran family had lived in Houston for generations, his French ancestry led Claude to affect a certain flamboyance of speech and style that he fondly believed to be Gallic verve. "Claude Defran carries on like he's at the Court of Versailles," Don had told Mark, "but he's a damn good businessman all the same."

"And how is my good friend, D.R.?" Defran asked as he stood aside and indicated Mark should precede him into his office. "Still drinking too much?"

"I'm afraid so." Defran's office was totally unlike the typical oil executive's. Instead of the usual leather armchairs and desk the size of a drilling platform, the spacious chamber was filled with antique furniture. "Louis something or other period," Mark thought to himself, and there was no sign of a desk. Defran led the way across an Oriental carpet, faded over the years to an exquisite rosy pink, and waved Mark into a spindly armchair that looked as if it belonged in a museum. Mark gingerly eased himself into it.

"I keep telling D.R. that he should give up this terrible whisky, which will surely kill him, and drink only red wine, but ..." Defran gave an elaborate shrug and offered Mark a cigarette from an engraved silver box. When Mark declined, he lit one for himself with a table lighter made from a small porcelain vase. The tobacco smelled Turkish and strong. Defran cut a figure that skirted perilously close to caricature. Of average height, he was beginning to thicken around the middle; his dark hair had receded to the midway point of his tanned scalp, and he affected a pencil moustache. He wore a striped, seersucker suit with a burgundy bow tie and matching pocket handkerchief. Now he was smiling encouragingly at his guest.

"I have to tell you, Mr. Hunter ... Mark, then," he amended when Mark protested, "and you must call me Claude. As I was about to say, your timing is most fortuitous. I have been following the exciting things that have been happening up in Canada, and for some time now I have been thinking that perhaps I should find some way to participate. In the oil business, as we both know, one cannot stand still — it's a case of finding more oil to replace that which we produce, or perish."

Mark warmed to his dapper host. Obviously, there was no need to tell Claude Defran what made the oil business tick. He opened his briefcase and spread out some papers on a low, highly polished mahogany table. Claude held up his hand with an apologetic little smile, and said, "Before we talk about specific deals, I would appreciate an overview of the situation up there. The big picture, so to speak."

Mark took a moment to collect his thoughts, then began with the Devonian D-3 reef at Leduc, discovered after years of discouraging dry holes. Imperial Oil alone had drilled 133 dusters and spent $23-million in western Canada before spudding Leduc No. 1. He told Claude about Atlantic No. 3 — another Leduc D-3 well that went wild, spewing enormous quantities of oil over the countryside and eventually setting itself on fire before being brought under control. More than anything else, the spectacular blowout had focused the attention of the world on the potential of the western Canada sedimentary basin. Leduc was followed by other dramatic discoveries, including Pembina, a blanket, oil-bearing sand that stretched for miles. Defran forgot to light his second cigarette when Mark began to talk about Don's White River discovery. There was no need to hold anything back, since Don, with his showman's flair and secure land position, had elected to go public with the information, rather than keeping it confidential for the year that government regulations allowed. Mark paused while a black steward in a white jacket served them coffee.

"Of course," he continued, "there have been a lot of dry holes, as well. I drilled one myself, as a matter of fact," he added with a rueful smile.

"D.R. told me about that. I understand it was a narrow escape for Otis Turner."

"Everybody seems to have known about his 150-point deals except me."

"The oil patch has so many colourful characters that it takes a lifetime to get to know them all. However, I must admit you're off to a good start. Now, would you fill me in on the political climate, please?"

"That's a real plus. It's very stable, and the provincial government is doing everything it can to help develop the oil industry. There's one thing that makes it very different from the situation down here, though. In Canada, it's the government, and not the private citizens, that owns most of the mineral rights."

"How do they lease them out? By auction?"

"Right. They post a parcel of lands and the oil companies submit sealed bids."

"That seems satisfactory. It should make it much easier to assemble a large block of land, rather than having to deal with God-knows-how-many ranchers and farmers, and their countless heirs, which is what we have to do here in Texas."

"It does," Mark agreed. "But there's one big drawback. The majors have managed to acquire huge tracts of land and they can sit on them for years by paying a small annual rental. The only way a new player can get in on the game is to negotiate a farm-out deal with them. Mind you," Mark added, "there are all kinds of land that hasn't been posted yet, but there's no question about the big boys having locked up some of the best potential areas."

"Yes, I can see where that could be a problem." Claude glanced at a gold-filigreed mantel clock. "I took the liberty of making reservations for lunch at the Petroleum Club. I hope you are free to join me?"

"Absolutely. And I really appreciate the time you're making available to me. I know how valuable your time is."

"I find it time very well spent."

As soon as he spotted the ungainly Citroën in the underground parking lot, Mark knew it had to be Claude's car. "My friends tease me about this automobile," Claude remarked complacently as they headed for the Houston Petroleum Club, "but I find it to be very comfortable. The suspension is hydraulic, you know."

Mark smiled. He felt very much at ease with the dapper little oilman. Claude managed to manoeuvre the Citroën into a cramped parking space on the first try. He gave a self-satisfied little grin and said, "After lunch we will bring in my top exploration people and have a look at your plays. If they turn out to be as promising as I am sure they will, then I believe you and I will do business together."

Mark's mood was euphoric as the elevator bore them swiftly up to the premises occupied by the club. With the wealthy and astute Claude Defran backing him, he would be ideally positioned to take advantage of the burgeoning Canadian oil scene.

Houston was dry, but each member of the Petroleum Club had his own private stock of liquor in his locker. Without asking, a black waiter brought a bottle of burgundy to Defran's table. Claude inspected the label and nodded approval. Turning to Mark, he said, "I always have wine with lunch, but if you would prefer something else?"

"Well, I really would like a beer, if it's not too much trouble."

Claude frowned slightly and Mark was afraid he had committed some unforgivable faux pas. Then his host's brow cleared. "I regret I do not keep a supply of beer on hand but that's no problem." He turned to the foursome at an adjoining table and asked, "Okay if I borrow some beer, Charlie?"

"Sure thing, Claude. Help yourself to whatever you need."

Mark couldn't help noticing that Charlie seemed very pleased to be able to do this small favour for Claude. It was also obvious from the way Claude had been greeted by the other oilmen, as he and Mark made their way to the table, that he ranked high in the Houston oil hierarchy.

Claude was very abstemious, taking only one glass of wine with his meal. They went into the lounge for coffee and Claude introduced Mark to some of his fellow oilmen. A couple of the names filled Mark with something close to awe — they were legends in the oil patch, names that had seemed almost god-like to Mark back in the days when he had worked as a rookie geologist for Permex here in Houston.

"Can I see you for a minute, Claude?" The speaker was a big florid-faced man with a wide expanse of white shirt underneath his unbuttoned jacket. He was chewing on an unlit cigar and the thick fingers of his ham-like hand held a snifter of brandy.

"Of course, Morley. Of course!" exclaimed Claude with his typical, effusive courtesy. "But first let me introduce you to a new friend, and I hope, new associate, of mine."

"I know who he is. That's what I want to talk to you about." Trailing a mystified Claude behind him, the florid-faced man led the way to a distant corner of the lounge.

Even though Mark had worked for Permex for nearly two years he had never met Morley Adams — chairmen of the board don't have much contact with lowly young geologists — but as soon as Claude said Morley, Mark made the connection. Now that his memory had been jogged, he could recall seeing that large, round visage adorning the inside front cover of Permex's annual report.

The jig was up. He could read it in Claude's expressive face as Morley Adams harangued him. At first he looked surprised, then he tried to protest but subsided as Adams steamrollered on. He looked angry, then shaken, and finally subdued. When Adams stopped talking, Claude gave a fatalistic little shrug, muttered something, and walked back toward Mark, not meeting his eyes.

Neither man spoke until they were back in the Citroën, purring along a street lined with giant oaks. Cicadas buzzed in the trees, filling the air with a strident, electric hum that was painful to the ear.

"Mr. Adams put the hex on me, didn't he?" Mark rolled up the window to shut out the appalling racket. He lowered it almost immediately as sweat began to break out on his forehead.

Claude nodded miserably. "He told me in no uncertain terms that if I became associated with you in any way, I could kiss goodbye to a farm-in deal I've been trying to wheedle from Permex for almost a year. That deal is awfully important to me, Mark. It involves some of the best prospective lands in the entire state."

"I understand. What I don't understand is why a big outfit like Permex is waging a personal vendetta against a little guy like me. All I did was quit working for them, for Christ's sake!"

"It's not the company. It's men like Morley Adams and Ed Parsons, his manager up in Canada. I've known both of them for years. They enjoy wielding power for power's sake. It's how they get their jollies. As professional managers of public companies with no major shareholders to rein them in, they can pretty much do whatever they like."

After a dejected Mark had collected his briefcase, Claude accompanied him back to the elevators. "You are a true gentleman, Mark," he said as they shook hands. "I hope that at some time in the future, when the Morley Adams and Ed Parsons of this world are put out to pasture, we find ourselves working together."

"I always figured Ed Parsons for a mean son of a bitch." Don Cullen puffed furiously on his cigar, "but I never thought even he would go to these lengths."

"Well, he did. He and his boss really fixed my wagon. They make a lovely pair, those two."

"It's a damn shame. Defran would have made an ideal partner for you." Don looked distastefully at his overheated cigar and laid it down in a gold ashtray shaped like a cowboy hat. "You ever figure Cliff might have been behind this?"

As always when Cliff's name was mentioned, Mark unconsciously fingered the scar on his cheek. "No. I put it down to pure spite on Parson's part. We didn't part on the best of terms when I left Permex."

Don was unconvinced. "Cliff has really got it in for you, son. I'd keep my head up, if I were you."

After his downcast visitor had left, Don sat for a long time alone in his office, pondering his own fortunes. To the world at large, Peerless Petroleum Ltd. was a hugely successful, financially sound enterprise. But the enormously expensive off-shore drilling program in California that Cullen had impetuously committed the company to was threatening to bleed the treasury dry. The banks weren't aware of the full extent of the damage yet, but it wouldn't take long before they started asking some pointed questions. If he was going to do anything, he'd better do it fast, while his credit was still good.

II

"I don't think we should go, Bill." Marianne gave her husband a pleading look. "Roger's parties always seem to end in a big fight with somebody getting hurt."

Bill knew that wasn't the real reason why she didn't want to go. It was her damn insecurity; her sense of inadequacy in social situations. There was no need for it — people were quite willing to take Marianne for what she was — a sexy looking blonde with no intellectual pretensions. This line of thought made Bill look at their daughter, quietly playing on the floor with her dolls. Debbie was going to look exactly like her mother, but even at two and a half she had a focus, a quickness of mind, that Marianne had never possessed. Physically she was her mother's daughter, but mentally she was his. It was the opposite with Billy: he was the spitting image of his father, but his restlessness and impatience when asked to concentrate marked him as his mother's child.

"It's important that we go, dear," he said impatiently. "There will be men there that I want to know better; men who can make deals." He paused, then applied the clincher. "It's our livelihood, you know. It's what puts bread on the table."

It worked, as he had known it would. Ever since he had left the employ of Consolidated Petroleum with its regular paycheques, Marianne lived in terror of their going broke.

"I'll call the sitter," she said, getting up from the couch.

"Oh, hello, Bill." Roger gulped, his Adam's apple worked up and down in his tanned throat. "Hello, Marianne," he added faintly. He remained blocking the doorway for a moment, then shrugged and stood aside, a strange little smile on his handsome, vacant face.

Marianne gasped and grabbed Bill's arm as they stood frozen at the entrance to the living room. A white bedsheet had been strung between two stepladders, hiding the faces of six naked women. Numbers from one to six were painted with lipstick on their abdomens. A group of men, Cliff Marsden among them, stood in front of the display of flesh, joking among themselves as they jotted down notes on their scorecards, trying to match names with the numbers.

One of the men glanced over his shoulder and caught sight of the Crawfords. "Hey, fellas, looks like the club has some new members!"

Cliff's face was a study in naked lust as he stared at Marianne, boldly undressing her with his eyes.

"It's just a harmless little game we play," said Roger as he handed drinks to the stunned Crawfords. Marianne's was dark brown and she downed half of it before Bill could say a word. "I'm better than any of them," she announced in a loud stage whisper.

"Let's get out of here." Bill took her by the elbow, surprised to find her resisting the pressure.

"Don't rush away," Roger said. "The ladies will be getting dressed in a minute, and we'll just have a nice respectable party."

"Marianne, I think we should leave," said Bill in a terse whisper. But his wife merely smiled dreamily and handed her empty glass to Roger for a refill.

With much tittering and nervous chattering, the ladies, now wearing cocktail dresses, streamed back into the living room, accepting drinks from the men, with flirtatious smiles. Marianne was shocked and more than a little titillated to find that she recognized five of the six from her Women's League days. In fact, the two youngest, the attractive brunette wife of a rising young lawyer and the Scandinavian-looking blonde, had been provisionals with her. Of course, they had made the cut and were now full-fledged members of the League. Neither of their husbands were present, which was par for the course; the oil business requires almost constant travel as the price of success. Upwardly mobile executives found themselves spending more time away from their families than with them — a situation that inevitably led to various degrees of domestic stress.

Bill drew his host aside. "What's going on here, Roger? I think I have a pretty good idea, but spell it out for me. I wasn't supposed to bring Marianne, was I?"

"No, you weren't. It's my fault. I didn't make that clear enough. But she doesn't seem to mind," Roger added with a wink and a nod in Marianne's direction. She was chatting with Cliff Marsden, of all people, with an animation that she hadn't shown since they left Houston.

"It's sort of a key club. The women throw their house keys in a basket and the men go home with whoever owns the key they pick. Tonight we also had a little contest for a change of pace. The guy who identified the most bodies wins a night with Sharon. Cliff got 'em all right, which figures. He seems more interested in Marianne, though."

Before Bill could reply, Sharon, the young lawyer's wife, sidled up to him and stroked the sleeve of his jacket. "I hope you win me some night, Bill."

Speechless, Bill stared at her. She laughed, reached up to kiss him lightly on the lips, and slipped away.

"See what can happen, Bill? Maybe you should join the club." Roger paused to glance over again at Marianne who was now talking to two men while a surly-looking Cliff Marsden glared at the competition. "Maybe Marianne would like to, as well. She seems pretty broad-minded."

Bill flattered himself that he was no prude, but he was — there was no other word for it — scandalized. He felt completely out of his depth. "It's too rich for my blood," he muttered, thinking of how he could extricate himself and Marianne with the least fuss. It was just this type of situation that had landed Mark in the hospital.

At first, Marianne didn't want to leave. But the petting was getting heavy and when she saw Astrid, the Scandinavian-looking blonde, fondling her partner's crotch, she shuddered and reached for her purse. Cliff started to protest, but his experience with Mark had taught him caution, and he contented himself with kissing Marianne's hand. The smug look on his face made Bill want to hit him.

Sharon stood in the doorway and waved at the departing Crawfords as they waited for the elevator. "See you both real soon," she called out impishly.

"The hell you will!" Bill gritted as the elevator doors whooshed shut behind them.

"I'm sorry I got you into that," he apologized as he pulled away from the curb in front of Roger's apartment block.

"I didn't mind," she surprised him by saying. "It was kind of exciting in a weird sort of way."

Bill shot his wife a severe look. "That kind of excitement we can do without." His work took him out of town for extended periods and the thought of Marianne taking up with that crowd made his blood run cold. He tried to discard the idea as being unworthy of her, but he was uneasily aware that her sex-kitten looks would guarantee her an acceptance and admiration in that circle that was denied her elsewhere.

As if echoing his thoughts, she murmured, as they were turning into their driveway, "I've got a better figure than any of them, haven't I?"

"Much."

That night she had an orgasm, an increasingly rare occurrence for her.

12

"Come along, darling. Daddy will tuck you in." Cliff Marsden took his daughter's hand and led her toward the stairs.

The child hung back, casting an imploring look at her mother. Laughing, Cliff reached down and gathered her in his arms. "This is our special time, remember? And if you're very good, I'll give you the present I brought."

"Don't get her too excited, dear." Denise Charbonneau put aside her knitting and got to her feet. "I'll come up with you."

"You'll do no such thing. This time of the day belongs to Jennifer and me." Cliff spoke lightly but his icy stare dropped Denise back in her chair as if she had been pushed. She had learned never to cross this enigmatic man, who had fathered her two children and bought her this beautiful split-level bungalow in a fashionable suburb of Montreal.

As Marsden carried Jennifer up the stairs, Denise heard sounds coming from the ground floor bedroom. Jamie always got upset when his father made a fuss over Jennifer. She sighed and walked into the bedroom.

Jamie's bed was really a cage. Smooth steel bars that could be locked in place, extended almost up to the ceiling. They were only used during Cliff's visits. Jamie was holding onto them as he stood on his mattress, rocking back and forth.

His thick lips worked as he mouthed the only words he knew, "BaayBee" and "Mummeee." The doctors had told Denise that he probably derived comfort from making these sounds, and it was true that he repeated them to himself, over and over, but she knew that he also made the correct associations. She was clearly "Mummy" and "baby" was himself, and possibly Jennifer.

"Mummy loves Jamie. Jamie's a good boy." Denise spoke soothingly but was careful not to touch her son. He could be unpredictable at times like this, and he was frighteningly big and powerful for a seven-year-old. It had nearly destroyed Cliff when it became obvious that his newborn son — his only son — had been born with Down's syndrome. Denise was sure that Cliff would have denied being the father, except that those heavy, coarse features were a dreadful parody of his own.

The knowledge that this creature had sprung from his loins was a massive blow to Cliff's ego. Before Jamie was born, he had confided in her that he felt a responsibility to perpetuate his genes. That was probably why she had been able to persuade him to let her get pregnant again. Jennifer had been born perfect and had quickly turned into a dark-eyed little beauty. No wonder her father doted on her. Denise softly closed the bedroom door and went back to the living room to wait for Cliff.

"She really liked her present." Cliff was smiling as he joined her.

"What was it?"

"A little pearl necklace."

"Oh, Cliff, she's too young for that!"

"She liked it. She likes beautiful things." He frowned at the sound of Jamie's moaning, faintly audible through the closed bedroom door. "That boy belongs in an institution."

"Not yet. Please, not yet." Denise's English was almost flawless, but as she defended her son, her slight French accent became more pronounced. "I can handle him."

"He's getting dangerous, and you know it," Cliff snapped, but she forestalled any further discussion by sitting on his lap and raising her lips for a kiss. She was wearing a low-cut dress and, from the way her breasts were pushed up, he knew she had on the lacy lingerie he found so sexy.

"You can tie me up, if you want," she whispered as his mouth closed on hers.

"Where are you going?" Brown eyes wide with alarm, Denise struggled against the soft bonds that held her.

"I'm just going to get myself a drink." Cliff watched her twist and strain against the silk scarves that tied her to the bedposts. The movements of her body as she struggled were almost unbearably sensuous. "I love it when you do that," he murmured, bending over until his tongue found her clitoris. "Don't wear yourself out, my darling," he smiled as he straightened up. "I'll be right back."

But it was almost ten minutes before he returned, without a drink but with an erection. Maybe he had played with himself to get a hard-on, Denise told herself as he entered her. He did that sometimes.

Scant minutes later, Denise rubbed her chafed wrists, and pretended to pout. "I don't like it when you go away and leave me tied up like that."

"That's what makes it exciting. The feeling that I can do what I want with you. Hey, where are you going?" he demanded as she slipped into a nightgown and headed for the door.

"I'm going to get myself a drink," she retorted defiantly. Pausing outside Jennifer's door, she listened intently, but there was no sound. Relieved, she continued down the hall and eased Jamie's door open a crack. The sound of his grunting and gnashing of teeth told her that he was asleep. Sleep was a tortured state for poor Jamie. It was as though his mind, and she was convinced he did have a reasoning mind, was trying to escape from that tragic body. Denise gently closed his door and padded on bare feet toward the kitchen.

13

The non-productive Texas trip had pretty well blown what was left of Mark's stake. He would allow himself another two or three weeks to cut a deal and, if that didn't work, he'd pack it in and go back to the States. Just like Cliff Marsden had predicted. He could picture the supercilious smirk on the tycoon's face. Well, by God, he'd knock on every door in town before he gave him that satisfaction.

Mark had no trouble in setting up appointments; everyone returned his calls and seemed eager to see him. It took several meetings that generated a lot of conversation but no results before it dawned on him that he was being treated as a curiosity. His run-in with the powerful Marsden clan had made him a notorious figure in the oil patch and people wanted to be able to boast that they knew the guy who had punched out Cliff Marsden. But they had no intention of doing business with him.

"I'm washed up in this town," Mark, discouraged after a day of fruitless interviews, told Dave. It was Dave's week to cook and he was in the kitchen, frying sausages for their supper. Dave took a swig from his beer mug and started to say something just as the phone rang. When Mark picked it up, the caller introduced himself as Garth Kennedy and apologized for calling Mark at home, saying that he hadn't been able to track down his office number. Mark told him that was because he didn't have an office, but was working out of the apartment for the time being.

"We'll meet in my office then," Garth replied and gave Mark an address on the fourth floor of a downtown office building. "Nine o'clock in the morning suit you?"

"Well, sure. But can I ask what we're meeting about?"

"You and I are going to cut a deal, that's what it's about. See you at nine."

The uniformed operator slid back the accordion folds of the elevator door and told Mark that Kennedy's office was the last one on his right. Kennedy Developments was printed in black letters on the frosted glass panel. Smaller lettering in the lower left-hand corner invited the world to walk in. A young woman — Mark put her at not much more than twenty — looked up from her typing and smiled. "You must be Mark Hunter. I'll tell Mr. Kennedy you're here." But before she could get up from her desk, the door of the inner office opened and Garth Kennedy came out to shake hands. Garth was plump and soft-looking. He was in shirt sleeves, tie and collar loosened around a size twenty neck. Long strands of sandy hair had been teased into place in a vain attempt to cover his freckled scalp, imparting a comic aspect to his appearance.

"I hear you bin goin' all round town looking for backers," he said as he lowered himself into a desk chair so new its leather creaked. In fact, all the furniture looked brand new. Mark nodded, and Garth went on, "I got a hunch your search may be over. I'm pretty good at finding money, but I don't seem to be any great shakes at finding oil. That's why I figured we should talk."

"What did you have in mind?"

"A partnership. Fifty-fifty right across the board; I furnish the money and you find the oil. How does that grab you?"

"What kind of money are we talking about?"

"I've got a million-dollar line of credit with the bank, for starters. And there's plenty more if we come up with any kind of a track record. I expect, and want, you to check me out, by the way. I'll give you the names of some of the fellows over at Tri-Province you can talk to. Including the president."

The guy was beginning to sound like he was for real. "How do you see this partnership being set up?" asked Mark.

"We'll let the lawyers work out the details. But, basically, it'll be a company that we own fifty-fifty. We can use your company if you like." Mark's eyes narrowed, he didn't much care for the idea of sharing Hunter Oil with anyone. Spotting his reaction, Garth shrugged, "On the whole, it might be better to use a brand new company. Start with a clean slate, so to speak. There's one thing I've learned from bitter experience, though. We've got to have a buy-sell arrangement. To protect both of us."

"Can you spell that one out for me?"

"It's an escape hatch. A company can get tied up worse than a hobbled mule if the two equal shareholders can't agree on how it should be run. I've been through that once and, believe me, it's the most frustrating thing that can happen to a man. With a buy-sell arrangement, either one can offer to sell his shares to the other at a certain price, and the other guy can either sell his shares or buy the other fellow's shares at the same price. It's fair to both parties. But have your lawyer check it out for you. I'll be responsible for his fees, regardless of whether we make a deal or not."

Garth's insistence that everything be checked out was very reassuring to Mark. The president of the Tri-Province Bank confirmed the million-dollar line of credit, and made it clear that Garth could have access to additional funds just by picking up the phone.

"There's nothing unusual in a buy-sell agreement," Chester Martin assured Mark. "It's frequently used in circumstances like this where you have two equal partners. Sometimes it's just a simple right of first refusal if an offer comes long, but this one has a shotgun."

"What's a shotgun?"

"It's right here." The lawyer turned the agreement around so that Mark could read it right side up and tapped a short paragraph at the bottom of the second page.

"Either party can trigger the buy-sell anytime he feels like it. That's okay. But he can also specify the price at which he will buy or sell."

"What's wrong with that?" demanded Mark, not wanting to hear anything that might spoil the deal.

"It works fine under normal circumstances. But where one party has more financial clout than the other — which is the case here, I gather?"

The lawyer looked inquiringly at Mark, who laughed briefly and replied, "Good Lord, yes."

"You can see what might happen," Martin went on. "This Kennedy could make an inflated offer for the shares, one that you couldn't match. That way you would be forced to sell your share of the company."

"Is there a way around it?"

"Yes. I'd be a lot more comfortable if there was a provision for an independent arbitrator to fix the value of the shares, rather than leaving it to the parties themselves."

"Okay. Let me try it on Kennedy."

Garth Kennedy looked dubious when Mark explained the change he wanted. But he said he'd talk it over with his lawyer and have an answer for Mark that afternoon.

"The idea of some outsider telling me what my property is worth gives me heartburn, Mark," said Garth when they reconvened in his office. "I think the deal is fair the way it is. No businessman in his right mind would put an unrealistically high price, knowing the other guy could sell and leave him stuck with a bad bargain. That's pretty effective protection, the way I see it."

"Is this a deal breaker?"

"I'm afraid so," sighed Garth. "I just can't abide some stranger telling me what to do. Sorry, but that's the way it is."

He'd never have another chance like this. The Kennedy money was his ticket to making it big in the oil patch. Mark took a deep breath. "Okay. It stays the way it is." He held out his hand and a beaming Garth took it, saying, "Okay, partner, we got ourselves a deal."

The pieces fell into place with a speed that astonished Mark. It was amazing what could be done when there was no shortage of money. The law firm acting for Garth prepared the paperwork and Chester Martin vetted it. Martin accepted Mark's decision on the buy-sell provision with good grace. He had alerted Mark to the hazard and, if a client chose to accept the risk, there was nothing more a lawyer could do. "Anyway," he told Mark, "if Kennedy does come in with a crazy bid down the road, you'll end up with a nice fat profit."

Mark frowned. He was out to build an oil company, not to pocket a quick profit. But, as Bill Crawford had pointed out, it could work in his favour as well. As operator of the properties, Mark would be in the best position to know what the company was worth.

In less than two weeks Mark was the president of a newly formed company, Central Resources Ltd. He didn't care for the name — he thought it was totally lacking in sex appeal, but Garth liked it. "It has a solid ring to it," he said. "People will think it's been around for generations."

At Garth's suggestion, the new company moved into the same office space he already occupied. "I plan on being a true silent partner," he informed Mark. "In fact, I expect to be away from Calgary most of the time while you get on with the job of finding oil." The new company took a sublease from Kennedy Developments. When Mark signed the document, he was surprised to find that Garth had leased the premises only a few weeks earlier. When he mentioned this, he was told that the lease on Garth's old office had expired the previous month.

The arrangement was ideal from Mark's point of view. He had solid financial backing and a free hand in running the company. That freedom had a sobering effect on him as he agonized over where the company should drill its all-important first well. He sat at his desk for hours, poring over maps whose curving lines he knew by heart, while the young stenographer he had taken over from Kennedy put in her time reading movie magazines and paperback romances. He kept coming back to the Big Coulee play. The only thing that held him back was the total lack of other wells in the area, which meant he would be drilling with no well contract and thus no hard information on what to expect. But he liked the seismic — he had from the first.

Having selected Big Coulee, he then tried to lay off some of the action, without success. Everyone seemed to have their own list of red-hot prospects to be drilled. After the eighth company had rejected his proposal, Mark knew he either had to drill on his own, or move on to another play. Unexpectedly, his silent partner, when he finally tracked him down in Miami, helped him reach a decision by reminding him that he had a considerable war chest at his disposal and inquiring, rather sharply, as to when he was going to start finding some oil. Stung, Mark went looking for a drilling rig as soon as he put down the phone.

Constructing a two-mile lease road into the Big Coulee location was one of the larger cost items involved in drilling the well. Despite its high cost, the rutted and potholed road would have torn the transmission out of an ordinary passenger car, so Mark purchased a GMC pickup truck for field work. The Central Resources sign painted on its door gave him an undeniable feeling of pride, but he found himself wishing it read Hunter Oil instead. He was on his way to the wellsite late one afternoon in the pickup when the white Jag flashed by, a tiny puff of blue smoke coming from its exhaust as Jane shifted into top gear. Instinctively, Mark floored the gas pedal to give pursuit but quickly abandoned the effort. She was heading for the Marsden place and he hadn't a prayer of overtaking her before she turned in the gate. She was driving too fast for the road, dammit.

Mark's thoughts were grim as he drove the remaining hundred miles to the well. The pickup's engine was still not completely broken in, and he forced himself to maintain a sedate fifty miles an hour when he ached to ease the longing for Jane with some high-speed driving. His black mood lifted somewhat when he saw how smoothly things were running at the well. He had been right to wait an extra week for an Apex rig to be released from the well it was drilling. Diesel engines, running in tandem, hummed quietly to themselves as they powered the drilling bit through rock at the gratifying rate of a hundred feet per day. If they maintained this kind of progress, he'd be back at the well in less than a week to supervise the coring and testing.

As it turned out, it was only five days before the toolpush alerted the Calgary office that they expected to reach the target formation within twenty-four hours. Mark left immediately for the wellsite. He would bunk in one of the camp trailers until they found out whether the well was a duster or a gusher. The first indication came with the oil-stained cores, and when they ran the tests, Mark knew he had a commercial oil well. Not a barnburner by any means, but a well that was capable of putting out a respectable seventy-five barrels a day.

The second well, a half-mile to the north, was also productive, although not to the same extent, but the third well, drilled as a stepout to the south, came in dry. With the drilling of an infill well in the quarter section immediately north of the discovery well, Central Resources had itself a nice little oilfield. Now the trick was to build on this initial success and make the company a real player in the oil patch.

Mark's next effort was a Viking oil play near the village of Claymore, some fifty miles northeast of Edmonton. The well discovered hydrocarbons all right, but the wrong kind. Discovering natural gas was worse than a dry hole. At least with a dry hole you could plug it and walk away from it, but the Conservation Board wouldn't let you abandon a natural gas well; the luckless operator had to keep it in a suspended status until the gas could be sold. The trouble was that there was no market for natural gas; you couldn't cart it around in tank trucks like you could with crude oil. Transporting gas required a pipeline and that meant first finding a market and then embarking on the financing and construction of a pipeline system that could cost in the hundreds of millions.

Discovering gas instead of oil was a disappointment to Mark, but he was confident he knew the answer. The discovery well must have encountered the gas cap on top of the oil reservoir. All that was necessary was to move down dip and tap into the oil leg. The drill stem test run on the discovery well indicated that it could flow at rates of up to ten million cubic feet per day, which Mark interpreted as meaning that the gas cap must be very extensive, so he located the second well three miles southeast. He knew he was taking a chance of missing the reservoir altogether but, if that happened, he would move in closer to the discovery well on the third attempt. But, to Mark's dismay, the three-mile stepout turned out to be another gas well, every bit as potentially productive as the first. The geologist in him thrilled to the undeniable fact that he had made a significant discovery of hydrocarbons, but what the hell good was that when you couldn't sell the damn stuff?

Still, Mark couldn't stay away from the geological map of the area. If the trend continued updip of the discovery well, he would have stumbled onto a gas field of truly astronomical proportions. However, Central didn't have the mineral rights tied up that far north. He told himself that the sensible thing would be to forget the whole thing and go back to looking for oil. But leases in the area could be picked up for a song. He thought about calling Garth Kennedy, but decided against it. There was still plenty of money left in the kitty and he could blow twenty-five thousand or so on land acquisition without any qualms. He got in touch with Jeff Nelson and retained the lease hound to pick up leases in the general area of the discovery.

It was essential to move quickly because other oil companies would move in once they learned a lease play was underway, even if they didn't know the reason behind it. Jeff hired two agents and they fanned out across the countryside in a leasing blitz, driving into farmyards and tramping across fields to talk to farmers on their tractors. At the end of ten days, they had succeeded in acquiring virtually all the mineral rights Mark had specified.

The north stepout well encountered gas at the same high production rates and Mark realized he had a giant discovery on his hands — a real elephant, in oil-patch lingo. The only problem was, what was he going to do with it?"

"Rumour has it that you've drilled yourself a bunch of gas wells." Bill Crawford's tone was commiserating. "I had the bad luck of drilling a couple of those myself last winter. My investors were not happy, I can tell you."

"I know what you mean," Mark replied noncommittally. He had heard about the Lost River play that Bill had walked away from after drilling two wildcats and coming up with nothing but gas. But the reserves behind those two wells were just a fart in the wind compared to the Claymore field. Extrapolating from the results of the wells he had drilled so far, Mark figured the reservoir could contain 100 billion cubic feet of gas, probably more. If Claymore were anywhere near a large population centre where the gas could be used to heat homes and as a fuel for industry, it would be an incredible bonanza. But way out there in the boonies, the reserves were worthless. Unless, of course, a way could be found to connect them to a market.

"How lucky can a girl get?" asked the matronly waitress, whose years allowed her to flirt with impunity, as she topped up their coffee. "Having the two handsomest men in Calgary at my table."

"My plastic surgeon thanks you," grinned Mark and she waddled off, chortling to herself. Mark leaned forward. "Whether we like it or not, Bill, there's going to be an awful lot of gas discovered in this province. We can't just let it sit in the ground."

"You're looking a long way down the road, my friend. All the local markets are already tied in to their own gas supply."

"I realize that. I'm talking export. Major export."

"You're also talking major pipeline. And we both know who fancies himself to be the pipeline czar of Canada, don't we?"

Mark grimaced. "Don't remind me. I'd just as soon you didn't tell anyone about this little talk of ours, Bill. Maybe this export thing will never fly, but it makes a lot of sense to me."

"My lips are sealed," Bill assured him. The grey-blue eyes were thoughtful, "You just might be on to something, Mark. There are a lot of people like myself who have gas reserves sitting idle behind pipe, and if you could come up with a way of converting those reserves into cash flow, you could write your own ticket."

They tossed for the luncheon check, and Mark lost. He was standing by the cash register when Jane and her mother walked into the Rimrock Room. While they waited to be seated, Jane glanced idly around. When she saw Mark she gave a little gasp that made her mother glance sharply at her. Mark, having had the advantage of seeing her first, was able to murmur politely, "Hello, Jane. Mrs. Marsden."

Eleanor Marsden looked almost frightened, but Jane had recovered her poise and said coolly, "Hello, Mark. How are you?"

Bill, who had been helping himself to a mint from a dish on the sideboard, came over and both women turned to him eagerly, grateful for the diversion. Then the head waiter bowed obsequiously to the Marsden ladies and the awkward little encounter was over.

"It's none of my business," Bill said offhandedly as they walked across the ornate, high-ceilinged lobby, "but that girl's in love with you."

Before an astonished and elated Mark could reply, he and Bill were hailed by Otis Turner who, followed by the beaming millionaire doorman, had just come in through the revolving door. "I hear great things about what you're doing with Venture," he said, naming Bill's company.

"Things haven't been too bad," replied Bill with a self-deprecating grin.

"Not too bad!" Otis snorted. "You're beginning to sound like a Canadian! From what I hear, you're doin' real fine!" He turned to Mark. "And, young fellah, I hear you can't find nothin' but gas. Maybe you should cut me in on some of your deals."

Mark, still glowing with what Bill had said, grinned. "You better be careful, Mr. Turner. Those wells will go on production one day."

A gleam of amusement flickered in the promoter's eyes and he gazed fondly at the young oilmen. "You two would make one hell of a team, you know that?" He nodded to himself as if reaffirming his own judgment, then picked up his battered briefcase and followed the doorman over to the registration desk.

"You really think that?" asked Mark as they walked north along 1st Street, past the Grain Exchange Building.

"Think what?" asked Bill, whose thoughts had been busy with Mark's ideas about finding a market for the natural gas.

"What you said about Jane."

"That she's in love with you? Sure. It sticks out a mile." Bill's smile was bitter. It was common knowledge that he and Marianne were having their problems, and Mark had heard that Bill had shown up alone at a couple of Roger Farris's parties. He glanced sideways at Mark. "You plan on doing something about it?"

"You know something? I've always had a yen to take up horseback riding."

14

"You ride English or Western?" The young woman behind the scarred wooden desk regarded Mark with open interest.

He grinned at her. "Whichever is easiest. I've never been on a horse in my life. I thought I'd give it a try and see whether I liked it."

"You'll need someone with you. That's $2.50 an hour extra."

"Suits me." Mark handed her a ten-dollar bill and she gave him $2.50 back. "I'll take you out myself. My name's Sue."

"I'm Mark."

"Okay, Mark, let's go find you a horse."

"A nice, gentle horse," added Mark as he followed behind her, admiring the fit of her skin-tight jeans. Her hair, dark honey-blonde streaked by the sun, was braided in a tight ponytail.

"We'll find you a real mellow one," she assured him as she headed for a small corral where four horses, already saddled, were tethered to a rail. She went over to a sorrel gelding and tightened the girth of the Western saddle. "This is Sandy," she informed Mark. "He's been out once already today so he won't give you no trouble."

Like most Western horses, Sandy was fairly small, standing just over fifteen hands at the withers, but that was no comfort to Mark. He was totally preoccupied with the problem of somehow getting himself from the ground up into the saddle. Sue showed him how to put his left foot in the stirrup and push himself up with his right leg. The patient gelding stood without flinching while Mark hopped helplessly on one foot, made a desperate grab at the cantle of the saddle and hauled himself up, his right foot scraping the horse's rump.

"That's great!" enthused Sue as she adjusted the length of his stirrups. "Almost nobody manages to do it the first time like that." She looked up at him, her scrubbed face bare of makeup. "These horses neck-rein. If you want him to turn to the right, just move your hand to the right, and vice versa. If you want to stop, just pull back on the reins." She gave the horse a friendly pat. "Sandy's real good at stopping, aren't you, boy?" She mounted her own horse in one fluid motion.

"I figure the best way to get you started is a little trail ride," Sue said as she led the way out of the yard. "Then if you like it, you can make up your own mind about whether you want to learn English or Western."

"The Pony Club teaches the English style of riding, doesn't it?"

"Yeah. But you're a little long in the tooth for them."

Mark laughed. "I wasn't thinking of that. A friend of mine is a Pony Club instructor out here. I kind of expected to run into her, as a matter of fact."

"What's her name?"

Mark clutched at the reins as the horse stumbled over a loose stone. When the minor panic was over, he said, "Jane Marsden. Know her?"

"Sure I know Jane. But she quit last week. To go back to school, I guess."

"Oh?" So much for his brilliant strategy.

Sue twisted around in her saddle to look at him. "You sound real disappointed. You sure it's the riding you're interested in?"

"Absolutely." And, in fact, Mark was beginning to enjoy himself. Sandy seemed content to plod along behind Sue's horse, and Mark finally summoned up the courage to lift his gaze from the path immediately in front of him and look around at the scenery. In late September, the dark-green of the foothills was splattered with patches of gold and the higher peaks of the distant Rockies were covered with snow. Just before they turned back, Sue put her horse into a trot and told Mark to kick Sandy with both heels. Gingerly, he tapped his heels against the horse's sides, half expecting to be bucked off. Sandy, more from a desire to keep up with the other horse than because of Mark's diffident urging, finally broke into a shambling trot.

"Hang on to the pommel, if you want to," Sue called back over her shoulder, but Mark gamely kept his free hand at his side and let himself bounce in the saddle, feeling as if his insides were being stirred in a blender. "You're doin' real good, Mark," Sue said as the horses dropped back into a walk. Making her horse pivot smartly on his haunches, she said, "We'll walk back to the stables. Even the worst plug in the world would gallop all the way home if you let 'im."

"Whatever you say," replied Mark, relieved that there would be no more bouncing in the saddle. The inside of his knees were rubbed raw and he wasn't sure he would be able to unlock his hip joints when it came time to dismount, but he had really enjoyed the experience. As they neared home, the horses pricked up their ears and stepped out smartly.

"You liked it, didn't you?" grinned Sue as Mark slid off the horse and stood somewhat unsteadily on the ground. "You should sign up for some lessons. I could make a real cowboy out of you in a couple of months."

"I'd like to, but I'm going to have to take a rain check. I expect to be away most of the time for the next few months. But I'll be back as soon as I can free up some time."

"See you around." Sue gave a wistful little smile as she led the horses away.

California. That was the answer. San Francisco was approximately 1,200 miles from the Claymore field. Mark put down the ruler and looked up from the map. The Golden State was growing exponentially; it seemed that every time someone shook the US, people rattled down to California. He was way down on the learning curve

— he didn't even know whether northern California was already supplied with natural gas or even if natural gas could compete with other fuels in the marketplace. But those blanks could be filled in. The important thing was that the northern part of California represented a population centre that looked as if it might be within economic reach of a pipeline from Alberta. Jesus Christ, who did he think he was? Financing and constructing 1,200 miles of large-diameter pipeline was a mega-project — a job for someone with the resources of a Cliff Marsden, not a twenty-six-year-old junior geologist. But he was the one with the gas, not Marsden. Besides, Mark grinned to himself, he would be twenty-seven next week. His expression was thoughtful as he quietly closed the atlas and turned it in at the reference desk of the public library.

At the end of a week's intensive research Mark was much higher up the learning curve. He now knew that San Francisco was supplied with natural gas, a fact which almost stopped him in his tracks until he learned that most of the gas came from the Four Corners field in the San Juan Basin. Because of its central location, gas from Four Corners was in great demand, and Mark had heard the rumours circulating in the oil patch that the prolific field was oversold. As production declined over the next few years, it would be unable to meet all its commitments. He also knew that nothing makes a utility company more edgy than a possible shortage of supply. Norcal Gas and Electric Co. was the giant utility company that serviced both San Francisco and a large part of northern California. Too unsure of himself to go directly to the president, Mark contacted the manager of gas supply who, although he sounded somewhat dubious on the phone, agreed to see him if he came to San Francisco.

"We are always interested in looking at ways to diversify our gas supply," the manager chose his words carefully, as if on the witness stand. "You claim ... er, say that you have reserves in excess of one hundred bcf?"

"At a minimum," Mark replied. "That's enough to deliver one hundred million cubic feet a day for twenty years." A yearning look crossed George MacGregor's face when Mark mentioned twenty years. Mark smiled inwardly; he knew that the reserves life index of Norcal's gas supply was a precarious seven years.

"One hundred million a day would never support a pipeline from Alberta." George MacGregor sounded as if he had just recently heard of the place.

"I realize that. But 300 million would."

"Three hundred million? For twenty years?" George's expression was that of a man who has just had a forbidden glimpse of paradise.

Mark couldn't resist a grin. "That kinda got you where you live, didn't it?" George gave a weak grin in reply and Mark went on, "I think that 300 million is a realistic ballpark figure for the unconnected gas that could be tied into a pipeline. I don't have to tell you that the producers would be happy to find any kind of a market for their shut-in gas." Mark leaned forward to place a single sheet of paper on the manager's walnut desk. "Using the rule of thumb of a construction cost of $10,000 per inch-mile, a daily volume of 300 million cubic feet easily justifies a thirty-inch pipeline."

"A thirty-inch line will carry a lot more than 300 million cubic feet," George observed as he studied the figures.

"More like a billion, fully powered," Mark agreed casually.

George MacGregor put the sheet of paper down and stared at Mark. "Are you saying that kind of volume is possible?" he asked incredulously.

"I think it's entirely feasible. Much to everyone's disappointment, Alberta seems to be turning out to be a gas-prone province. If the producers could see a viable market for gas, there's no doubt in my mind whatsoever but that they would develop the necessary reserves to support the volumes we're talking about."

George leaned back in his swivel chair and lit a Camel. He was too preoccupied to offer one to Mark. He slowly exhaled a thin stream of light blue smoke. "You sure seem to have done your homework," he admitted, almost grudgingly. "The president said he'd like to meet you if I thought there was anything to your proposal." He pushed back his chair. "Excuse me a moment while I see if he's free."

If Harrison Dobbs thought Mark was impossibly young and inexperienced to be talking about building a pipeline to carry gas from Alberta to California, he gave no indication of it. The slender, silver-haired executive, immaculate in a dark suit and silver tie, listened with growing interest as Mark went over the ground he had already covered with MacGregor. When Mark finished, Harrison glanced at his gas supply manager. "I must admit to feeling more than a little remiss in not having thought of Canada as a possible source of supply. Too conditioned to looking to Texas, I guess. But those Texas fields won't last forever, so your visit is timely. Very timely." He played with a silver letter opener while his listeners waited respectfully for him to continue. "One thing troubles me, though. Canada is a sovereign state and the government may not want to see that valuable and irreplaceable resource leave the country."

"That's a possibility, of course," Mark conceded. "But there's so much gas in Alberta, shut in for lack of a market, that I can't see the government standing in the way. I don't know whether you're aware of this, sir, but there's a fair bit of tension up there between the west and what they call central Canada — Ontario and Quebec, where the votes are. If the government stepped in and blocked the export of gas, it would be seen as another slap in the face for the West, which already feels it's getting a raw deal out of Confederation."

"Interesting. You seem to have gained a remarkable insight in the short time you've been up there." The president put down the letter opener. "Do you have any idea how much a project like this would cost?"

"Four hundred million dollars, give or take a few million. The route is a pipeliner's dream — flat, open country for the most part, with easily accessible passes through the mountains and very few major river crossings."

"Four hundred million dollars," Dobbs repeated softly. "A not insignificant amount of capital to raise. I assume you will be looking for partners with financial clout? This project sounds like it would be right up Cliff Marsden's alley, for example. Have you talked to him?"

"No. Nor do I intend to," Mark replied grimly. "We are not on what you might call the best of terms." Damn. The meting had been going so well. Was he forever to be stymied by the looming figure of Cliff Marsden?

Behind his rimless glasses, Harrison Dobbs's eyes were alight with sudden interest. "You're not by any chance the young man who punched Marsden out, are you?"

Mark nodded, wondering if this would shoot down the deal before it got off the ground.

"A man like Cliff Marsden would make a bad enemy," mused Harrison.

"I have already found that out." Unconsciously, Mark fingered the thin scar under his chin. Harrison raised an eyebrow and looked as if he was about to ask another question, but checked himself and murmured, "From what I know of Marsden, he wouldn't take kindly to the idea of someone else building a major pipeline out of Canada. I think he feels that's his turf, where pipelines are concerned."

"He doesn't have the gas. I do."

"There is that, isn't there? I suppose the first thing to do is to verify that the reserves are there. Did you bring anything our consultants could look at?"

"I've got everything they need over in my hotel room — well-logs, test results, seismic actions — the works." As he spoke, Mark realized how vulnerable he was. He didn't mind giving them the geological information on the Claymore field; he was confident he had virtually all the potential land sewed up. However, there was nothing to prevent Norcal from taking his idea and running with it. The Claymore reserves gave him a certain advantage, but there were other gas fields in the province, although none of the size and quality of Claymore. Maybe he should be content to just sell the gas and let someone else worry about building the pipeline. But, dammit, the whole concept was his — he ought to be the one to build that pipeline. And if Cliff Marsden elbowed him out of the way and took over his project — unable to complete the thought, Mark got to his feet and said he would go to his hotel and get the maps and data. And while he was there he would place a call to Chester Martin in Calgary.

At first, the lawyer assumed Mark wanted a confidentiality agreement to protect the geological information before he disclosed it to Norcal. There was a longish pause when he realized what Mark's real concern was. He began to speak just as Mark was about to ask if he was still on the line.

"The only possibility I can see is, in consideration of your showing them the data, to get a commitment from them that, if they decide to import gas from Alberta, they will support your efforts to finance and construct a pipeline. Give me half an hour to collect my thoughts and I might be able to dictate something over the phone."

"I've tried to keep it short and simple," Chester said when he called back. He dictated slowly while Mark copied it down. The document, covering less than two pages, was in the form of a letter addressed to Norcal, and was meant to be countersigned by them.

"It's probably not realistic to expect Norcal to sign an undertaking like that," the lawyer said after Mark had read it back to him. "It would be great if they would, of course, but I really can't see that happening. Maybe your fallback position would be to just put the contents of that letter in your own words and tell them that you expect their support. I don't know how these big utility companies operate, but a handshake deal usually stands up in the oil patch."

"You mean an Oklahoma contract — I'll be a son of a bitch if I don't?" Mark grinned into the mouthpiece. "That may be the way to go. I'll have to make up my mind pretty damn quick because I want to get back over there before they close for the day. Appreciate the help, Chester."

There was a third man in the president's office when Mark, apologizing for keeping them waiting, was ushered in the door by a severe-looking secretary. Harrison introduced him as Dr. Szabo from De Lyall & Morton, an internationally recognized firm of geological consultants. Szabo, a small, bespectacled man in his early sixties, shook hands perfunctorily, his gaze riveted on the bulky briefcase Mark was toting.

The letter agreement Chester had dictated over the phone was folded in Mark's rear pocket. He decided it would remain there. His negotiating instincts told him it might kill the deal if he were to confront the autocratic Dobbs with it. Dismayed to hear his voice crack with nervousness, Mark cleared his throat noisily and said, "Can I take it that if Norcal decides to pursue the idea of acquiring Canadian gas, you will support my efforts to build the pipeline?"

Dobbs glanced at him shrewdly. "It sounds as if you've been talking to a lawyer. That's probably what took you so long. Well," he continued after a pause, "I can understand how you feel. On the other hand, we can't afford to be committed exclusively to someone who hasn't got the necessary stroke to make the project visible. What I am prepared to do is to agree to work with you on the understanding that we're free to go our own way if you can't cut the mustard."

Mark knew it was all he was going to get. "Agreed," he said and held out his hand, seeking to reinforce the bargain. Harrison took it, a knowing glint in his eyes.

Once he had possession of the briefcase, Szabo was eager to be off. Pressed by Harrison, he said that, by working over the weekend, he could have a preliminary report in their hands sometime Monday. "It's hardly worth your while to go back to Calgary," Harrison said pleasantly to Mark. "My wife and I would be happy to have you stay with us."

It was an extremely hospitable gesture and Mark wondered if it was wise to turn it down. Nonetheless, after expressing an appreciation that was obviously sincere, he said that he had planned on renting a car and driving south to take in some of the fabulous scenery.

The fabulous scenery Mark had in mind came equipped with greyhound legs, dark hair flecked with golden highlights and sweeping dark eyelashes. It seemed to Mark that the rented Ford had barely left San Francisco behind before a highway sign was welcoming him to the city of Palo Alto, population 51,676, and the seat of Stanford University. The dashboard clock showed five after ten. It was Friday, so Jane would probably be in class, or maybe working in the library. The way to the university was plainly marked with arrow signs. The low university buildings, quadrangles of buff sandstone in the California mission style, were nestled in the beautiful Santa Clara Valley, with rolling hills barricading the Pacific Ocean to the west.

"I'm not sure how much I should be telling you." The clerk in the administration building frowned and looked up from the index card.

Standing on the other side of the counter, Mark gave her his most engaging grin. "Like I said, I'm a good friend of hers from Calgary." The reference to Calgary seemed to comfort the clerk, the index card verified that Jane was from there, wherever it might be. "I was in San Francisco on business and thought I would pop down here and see her. She'll be glad to see me. Honest she will."

Reluctantly, the clerk capitulated. "Miss Marsden is an economics major and she's registered in Economics 401 which is in session right now." She came out from behind the counter. "I'll show you how to get there. The class will be over at eleven."

Five minutes to go. Standing in the cool shade of the long colonnade, Mark stared at the archway where Jane should appear. His throat was so dry he wasn't sure he would be able to speak. He tried to reassure himself by thinking of what Bill Crawford had said. But what could Bill possibly know of how Jane felt? He heard the sound of voices, then laughter — her laughter. A chattering group of students came through the archway and headed in his direction. Jane, her dark hair held back by a red hair-band, and clutching two loose-leaf ring binders in her arms, was in the front, laughing at something the man beside her had said. He was tall, several inches taller than Mark, and moved with the easy grace of a trained athlete. His interest in Jane was only too obvious.

Mark, feeling like an intruder, stepped out from behind a column and turned to face the oncoming students. "Mark!" The ring binders clattered to the cement floor. A flustered Jane bent to retrieve them, but the young man beside her was faster. "I'll catch up later," she said with a shaky smile as he handed them to her. He gave Mark an unfriendly look as the little group, fairly humming with suppressed excitement, moved on.

"It's good to see you, Mark," Jane said finally, with a polite little smile. She might have been a hostess seeking to make an awkward guest feel at home.

"Look, I'm sorry to barge in on you like this, but I was stuck in San Francisco over the weekend so I thought I would look you up." Mark realized he sounded as gauche as hell, but, like Dave Green said, there was something about this girl that made him behave like a teenager. Her fixed smile was still in place, but she was looking past him, in the same direction as that taken by her fellow students. Her eyes flew back to him when he asked her to go out with him.

"Your father will never know," added Mark, taken aback by the indecision so painfully etched on her face.

"There's no need to bring him into this," she almost snapped, but it worked. "Well," she said slowly, "since you've gone out of your way, I suppose I could see you tonight."

It was a graceless, almost grudging, acceptance, totally unlike her usual style. Maybe she was warning him not to expect anything beyond tonight. Mark pushed the thought aside. For the moment, it was enough that she was actually going out with him. They agreed that he would call for her at six and then she, pleading that she was already late for a class, hurried off.

She seemed a little startled when he informed her they were going to San Francisco for drinks and dinner.

"But there are lots of perfectly good restaurants right here in Palo Alto," she protested.

Mark dismissed her concern with an airy wave of his hand. "San Francisco is only an hour away. I thought you'd enjoy a change of scene."

After dinner at an Italian restaurant, they went to the Top of the Mark for a nightcap and were lucky enough to get a table by the window. Looking down at the lights of the city, Mark felt a rush of excitement. Incredibly, the day might come when it would be the gas, carried by his pipeline, which would fuel this great metropolis. He longed to share his dream with Jane but knew that was out of the question. Mention the word pipeline, and the spectre of her father would join them at the table. There must be something good about that son of a bitch to inspire such loyalty from his daughter. There were men like that — ruthless in their dealings with the outside world, but doting and devoted parents inside the family circle. God only knew how Jane would react if the California pipeline turned into a head-to-head confrontation with Cliff Marsden. If it happened right now, Mark was sure Jane would side with her father, but let the world take a few more spins and who knows? There was something between them; he could see it in her eyes.

She came into his arms willingly enough when he parked in front of her residence and doused the lights. But when his hand strayed to her breast she jerked back, banging her elbow on the dashboard. Chastened by the look of fright in her eyes, but inwardly thrilled that she was inexperienced, Mark mumbled something about not wanting to rush her. She gave a nervous little laugh and lit a cigarette. By now she had learned not to bother offering Mark one. Practically everyone he knew smoked, but he just couldn't seem to get the hang of it. All it did was make his eyes smart when he bent over seismic maps.

"Well, I guess that's it until my next visit to San Francisco," he said casually when she had stubbed out her cigarette. She had already told him that she couldn't see him again that weekend — she had a date for Saturday night, news which Mark, although he knew he was being irrational, received with a sharp stab of jealousy — and that she needed Sunday night to study. He leaned across the seat and kissed her gently on the lips. "Okay?"

"Okay," she whispered.

Mark got the go-ahead from Norcal late Monday afternoon. Dr. Szabo, with the enthusiasm of the true scientist, congratulated him on his magnificent find. "In fact," he told the meeting, "I would put the recoverable reserves as high as 125 billion cubic feet of gas."

Harrison Dobbs and his supply manager exchanged glances. If they could tap into reserves of this magnitude, their supply worries would be a thing of the past. Harrison cleared his throat. "We've also done some preliminary ballparking on the economics. Using your estimate of the construction costs, which we feel is pretty accurate by the way, we could see a price to the producer of fourteen cents per thousand cubic feet of gas."

"Is that in the field or at the outlet of a processing plant?" Mark inquired.

"At the plant outlet."

Mark looked dubious. "That's pretty thin. It might be okay for some sweet gas that requires practically no processing, but my own view is that it will take at least sixteen cents to get the job done."

"If we could convince the California Public Utilities Commission that the higher price was necessary in order to obtain a dependable supply source, they would probably let us pass it on to our customers." Harrison seemed to be thinking out loud. "All right." He stood up and held out his hand. "We'll go with sixteen cents. Why don't you try that on your fellow producers up there and see how you make out? No binding commitments at this stage, of course."

"Wait till I tell you what happened to Ed Parsons, your esteemed former boss, while you were away." Beer mug in hand, Dave Green stood in the doorway of Mark's bedroom.

"Nothing good, I trust." Mark paused in his unpacking and looked expectantly at his roommate.

"Old Ed got caught with his hand in the cookie jar. It seems Jeff Nelson picked up fifty thousand acres of freehold leases in Saskatchewan for twenty-five cents an acre, then his client lost interest and told him to dump them for whatever he could get. Jeff ran into Parsons on the street and Parsons told him he'd take them off his hands for seventy-five cents per acre. It was a sweet deal for both Jeff and his client, and Jeff rushed right over to the Permex office with an armload of leases. Parsons's secretary got all excited and told him to take them away. It wasn't Permex who was buying them, it was Brian Lockhart."

"Jesus," breathed Mark. Lockhart was notorious for his shady deals.

"You can almost guess what happened next," Dave paused for a swallow of beer. "Permex ended up buying the leases from Lockhart for three bucks an acre."

"And Lockhart and Parsons split the difference?"

"It seems old Ed got the lion's share. Ninety per cent to Lockhart's ten."

"How did they find out about it?"

"Your friend Jeff blew the whistle."

"Yeah. I can see that happening. Jeff is a straight arrow."

"Plus the fact that if he hadn't, and then somebody in Permex stumbled across it, he'd be finished as a landman."

"When I think of that sanctimonious bastard giving me a hard time over my moving expenses," Mark muttered, shaking his head. Surprisingly, he felt little elation over his enemy's downfall, but it would be a relief not to have to worry about Parsons trying to thwart him at every turn.

15

Marianne took her time answering the phone. As always it would be for Bill, and he was out of town. But this time it was for her. Even more surprisingly, it was Sharon Livingston who was calling. The young society matron, who had married into one of the old Calgary families, had always snubbed Marianne, but now she was asking Marianne to go out for dinner with her and another "grass widow," Astrid Winslow.

At first, Marianne didn't know what to say. Sharon Livingston, and to a lesser extent, her sidekick, Astrid Winslow, were the crème de la crème of Calgary society. Although the way they were carrying on at that wife-swapping party wasn't exactly high society. Or was it? Maybe that's what society folks did for kicks. Anyway they seemed to be getting away with it because of who they were — or, rather, who Sharon Livingston was. Marianne knew it would really please Bill if she became friends with them. He was so ambitious.

As these thoughts flitted through her mind, Marianne heard herself promising to see if she could find a babysitter. That wouldn't be a problem. Anne Fleming, a high school student who lived just down the street, was always ready to oblige.

"With all our men away all the time, it's up to us to make our own fun." Astrid's narrow, green eyes glittered and her dangling earrings swung to and fro as she nodded her head to emphasize the point.

"Is your Bill away as much as my Allan?" Sharon's fork, holding a piece of steak so rare it was almost bloody, was poised in front of her parted lips. The three of them were having dinner in the Pump Room, and Marianne was fascinated and faintly appalled by the sensuous way Sharon attacked her almost raw meat.

"I don't know how much Allan is away, but it seems Bill is never home. If he's not out in the field supervising some well, he's in New York or Houston trying to raise money." Marianne took a long pull on her drink. Sharon had brought along a bottle of rye and they were mixing it with ginger ale. Marianne would have preferred bourbon, but the Canadian whisky produced the same hazy buzz that masked her ever-present sense of inferiority. She smiled dreamily at her two attractive companions.

"That's the trouble with this damn town." Sharon let a trickle of juice remain for a moment on her chin before wiping it off. "If a man wants to get anywhere, he's got to practically live on an airplane."

"While the cat's away ..." Astrid's green eyes were dancing.

"Are you game for a little adventure, Marianne?" Sharon masticated the last morsel of steak and carefully placed her knife and fork on the wooden platter.

"I guess so." Marianne was suddenly wary, but she didn't want to jeopardize this new-found friendship and the promise it held for the future.

"We're going to have a night on the town." By what seemed to be a tacit agreement, it was Sharon who was doing the talking. She was accustomed to having people do what she wanted. "As soon as we have our dessert and coffee," she continued, "we're going to Hendley's and you're coming with us."

"What's Hendley's?"

"A place where people dance," explained Sharon, enunciating the words carefully as the whisky made itself felt. "Everybody goes stag and you meet the yummiest men. It's perfectly respectable," she added when she saw the frightened look in Marianne's eyes.

"Oh, I couldn't do that." Marianne shrank back in her chair, her eyes fixed on the illuminated Exit sign.

"Of course you can. I bet you love to dance, don't you?"

Marianne nodded, her thoughts flying back to her high school days in Midland, Texas where she was the acknowledged school sweetheart and could cut a rug with the best of them. Those had been wonderful years, maybe, she stifled an alcohol-induced sob, the best years of her life.

"They have a terrific band," Sharon was saying. She reached out and lightly squeezed Marianne's arm. "C'mon Marianne, be a sport. Nobody will ever know. We never use our real names when we go there." She turned to Astrid. "Who are you going to be tonight?"

"Tonight I think I'll be Erica," replied Astrid after a thoughtful pause. "I feel kind of dangerous and lowdown."

"And who would you like to be, Marianne."

"Jackie. I've always wanted to be called Jackie."

Marianne tried to snatch her hand back, but the attendant was too quick for her. She looked at the blue stamp on the back of her hand with something like horror.

Sharon laughed and held out her own hand. "That's just so they know we've paid the admission. Don't worry. It washes off."

Marianne was still staring at her hand. Without her wedding and engagement rings it looked almost obscenely naked, and the stamp of blue ink seemed like the brand of an adulteress. Like the Puritans used to do.

Astrid gave her an impatient push. "C'mon, 'Jackie,' we're holding up the line."

The dance hall was like the inside of a warehouse with an immense dance floor taking up almost all the space. A twelve-piece orchestra occupied a floodlit stage at the far end, and the floor was crowded with jitterbugging couples. The men who were not already dancing, perambulated slowly around the perimeter of the floor, looking for partners.

Standing slightly to the rear, Marianne marvelled at the cool self-assurance of her new-found friends as they turned down one offer to dance after another. It was like they were shopping at a supermarket. Most of the men accepted their dismissal with the same businesslike attitude, but a few who seemed to know the two girls looked surprised and insulted. Their expostulations had no effect and they turned away with an ego-restoring shrug of the shoulders. First Astrid, then Sharon, found partners who measured up, and allowed themselves to be led off to the floor.

Marianne had been coping with the men who swarmed around her by giving small negative shakes of her head while staring fixedly at her two female companions. Deprived of that support, she smiled a nervous acceptance to a good-looking man with a gleam of humour in his brown eyes.

After the first few steps, they smiled at each other, acknowledging their mutual expertise. She followed him effortlessly as he opened up, throwing in intricate new variations of the standard steps. Her skirt swirled above her knees as he spun her around. Flushed and smiling they applauded energetically at the end of the set and stayed on the floor waiting for the music to start up again.

Her partner's name was Ralph — Ralph Robertson, and he told her he was a petroleum engineer employed by Trojan Petroleums. She hesitated when he asked her name, before finally muttering, "Jackie." He shot her an inquiring look, but merely said, "Okay, Jackie, let's dance," as the music began once more.

Marianne was in a state of bliss as she twirled and spun. She was transported back to the days at Midland Central High where she had reigned as the "sweater girl" of the year. Once, as Ralph lifted her in the air, she saw Sharon looking at her with an expression that could only be envy. Imagine, Sharon Livingston envying her!

When the leader announced that the band was taking a half-hour intermission, Ralph asked her if she would like a drink.

"When you say drink, I hope you mean something with alcohol in it?"

"Why, sure." Looking slightly startled by the directness of her reply, he patted his hip pocket. "I've got a mickey of rye." Telling her to wait, he went off to the counter where they sold soft drinks and came back with two bottles of ginger ale, well laced with whisky.

"Let's find a table," he said, handing her one of the bottles. She sucked greedily on the straw and pointed to where Sharon and Astrid were sitting. "We can join my friends."

"Ah, the married ladies from Mount Royal. They always look as if they're slumming when they come here."

"You ... you know them, then?" stammered an alarmed Marianne.

"I don't know them. I know who they are." He smiled, his fingertips lightly touching the inside of her bare arm. "Since you're with them, I take it you're married too."

"That's none of your business."

Ralph shrugged. "It's no big deal. I'm married myself."

"Where's your wife?"

"Home. I'm working late tonight. A guy has to put in a lot of overtime to get ahead in the oil patch." He tugged gently at her arm. "Well, shall we join your friends, or not?"

Feeling as if she were playing a game whose rules had never been explained to her, Marianne led the way over to where Sharon and Astrid were sitting, coolly shaking their heads at the shoals of men who drifted by, asking if they could join them. Marianne introduced Ralph, using her friends' fictitious names. It immediately became apparent that Ralph was very interested in Sharon. She quickly responded to the attention he was paying her; he was, after all, an extremely presentable man. But there was also a little gleam of triumph in her eyes when she looked at Marianne. He was on his feet asking Sharon to dance, as soon as the band returned to the stage.

"He knows who you are," Marianne told Astrid as Ralph and Sharon threaded their way through the crowd to the dance floor.

"Oh? That's interesting." Astrid didn't seem unduly concerned. "That explains the big play for Sharon."

"What do you mean?"

"It's the Livingston name, darling. Men simply can't resist the chance to make out with one of the Livingston women. Don't feel badly, Marianne, I've seen it happen dozens of times."

"I don't feel badly," retorted Marianne. "All I did was dance with the guy." Gratefully, she smiled up at the youth who was bending over, asking her to dance.

By the end of that dance Marianne felt she had had enough for one night. Her head was beginning to ache, partly from the whisky she had drunk but also from the confusion she felt. Too many things were happening too fast. Being with Sharon and Astrid and meeting new men as though she were still single was exciting, almost too exciting. But it also directly contravened all the values she had been brought up with. Not for the first time, Marianne regretted that she had married so young, before she had had a chance to find out what life was all about.

Sharon was understanding when Marianne announced she would grab a cab and go home. Sharon and Ralph Robertson were obviously hitting it off, and her smile was self-satisfied as she purred that she would call Marianne in the morning. Holding Sharon's hand, Ralph waved an amiable goodnight to Marianne, and said, "We'll get together real soon."

Startled, Marianne realized he meant exactly what he said. He planned on getting around to her when it suited his convenience. Who the hell did he think he was, anyway?

Marianne, feeling, as she so often did, that she hadn't lived up to what was expected of her, was convinced that she would never hear from Sharon again. But at eleven o'clock the phone rang and it was Sharon, inviting her to lunch at the Country Club. Lunch with Sharon Livingston at the country club! Now there was something she could tell Bill! Anne Fleming would be at school, but Mrs. Fleming would be glad to give Debbie and Billy their lunch, so that was all right. The Flemings had a toy poodle that the kids really liked.

"You should have stayed. It turned out to be a fun night." Sharon was demure in a little flowered hat with a wisp of veil. The sight of Sharon's hat had thrown Marianne into a panic, wondering if she had committed some terrible faux pas by not wearing one herself. She regained some of her composure when she saw that most of the women in the dining room were hatless.

"Ralph knows who you really are," Marianne whispered while Sharon filled in a chit.

"Yes. So Astrid told me." Like Astrid, Sharon didn't seem overly concerned. "He never let on. Not even after we ... well, you know." Sharon's smile was reminiscent.

"Are you going to see him again?" Despite herself, Marianne was fascinated. This was living dangerously!

"Oh, no." Sharon looked almost shocked at the idea. "That's one of the rules. We never go with the same men twice." Sharon lit a Player's, using a gold Dunhill lighter. "Sometimes they have a hard time accepting that," she added, blue smoke escaping from her mouth along with the words.

"How did Astrid make out?" Marianne was pleased to hear how matter-of-fact she sounded.

"Just fine. She always likes to wait until the last possible minute before committing herself, but all the men come running when she crooks her little finger. And what about you, Marianne? Did you enjoy yourself? You certainly were dancing up a storm for a while."

"It was ..." Marianne paused, searching for the right word, "exciting. I felt really alive. Almost as if I ..." Loyalty to Bill made her stop.

"Were single? I know the feeling. Being married to someone in the oil business is like being a navy wife. You're expected to keep the home fires burning while hubby gallivants all over the world, having himself a high old time. Well, that's not good enough for this girl."

"But your husband is a lawyer, not an oilman."

Sharon shrugged. "All his clients are in the oil patch, so the result is the same."

The lunch hour was coming to a close, and many of the departing ladies made a point of stopping at their table to speak to Sharon. She was graciousness itself, and Marianne marvelled at the difference between the young society matron she was today and the thrill-seeking minx of last night. As Sharon made the introductions,

Marianne recognized more than one "old Calgary" name — families whose forebears had been ranching in the area years before the little prairie settlement on the Bow River was incorporated into a town.

"It's a shame you didn't make the League," murmured Sharon as they were finally left alone with their coffee.

Marianne raised her hand and said something indistinct as if to dismiss the subject, but Sharon pressed on, "I'm going to make it my business to see that you get in next year."

She could do it, too. "That would be nice," said Marianne faintly. Her life was picking up speed at a dizzying rate, and it seemed to be out of her hands. Part of her wanted to retreat to the security of her home and the numbing effect of alcohol, but the "sweater girl" in her cried out for more from life before it was too late.

Bill arrived home that night, enthused about what an improvement the new TCA Viscount turbo props were over the old, lumbering, noisy North Stars that were in service when he had first started making business trips. He was pleased, and more than a little impressed, when Marianne told him about having lunch with Sharon Livingston, and that Sharon had sworn she was going to get her into the Women's League.

The feeling of contentment engendered by Bill's reaction to her excursion into high society and their deep lovemaking that night quickly evaporated the next morning when Bill packed a suitcase before leaving for the office.

Holding Debbie in his arms while Billy played at his feet, he gave Marianne a rueful smile and said, "I'm sorry, hon, but I have to fly to Denver this afternoon."

"When will you be back?" asked Marianne almost listlessly.

"Not until Tuesday at the earliest." Bill kissed his daughter and put her back on her feet. As he crouched town to tousle his son's hair, he looked up at his wife. "I'm trying to farm out some Venture lands to a syndicate down there and there's some hard bargaining to be done."

Anger and frustration simmered in Marianne all morning. She poured herself a drink as she made lunch for herself and the children. Empty glass in hand, she hesitated, then shrugged and poured another to have with their soup and sandwiches. The liquor fuelled her anger and, as soon as she had settled Billy and Debbie down for their afternoon nap, she picked up the phone and dialled Sharon's number.

"My lord and master arrived home last night, screwed me, and took off again this morning. I'm totally fed up."

Marianne's bluntness brought a little gasp from Sharon, then she laughed and said, "They think if they give us a good screwing from time to time that that should keep us happy and being nice, little, supportive wives. Anyway, Marianne, I'm in the same boat as you. Allan has gone off to a think-tank session put on by Regal

Pipelines, the Marsden company. They're big clients of his. It's stag, of course, but they'll find some trouble to get into. Men!" Sharon paused, then went on in a quick rush of words. "I'll give Roger Farris a call. If you give him enough time, he can arrange a party where discretion is guaranteed. Are you game?"

Marianne drew a deep breath, looked around the silent house, and whispered, "I'm game."

16

The blood rushed to Cliff Marsden's head and he held onto the edge of the desk to steady himself. His visitor looked at him in some alarm. "You okay, Cliff?"

Cliff breathed deeply and the room snapped back into focus. He let himself drop heavily back into his swivel chair and pounded the desk in frustration. "That young prick! Who the hell does he think he is?"

Pete Cranshaw shifted uncomfortably in his seat. "I figured you should know, Cliff. Hunter wanted me to keep it strictly confidential, but I thought you'd want to know he was trying to round up a package of gas to ship south."

"You did right, Pete. And I want you to know I appreciate it." At this, Pete visibly relaxed. Cliff Marsden was a heavy hitter; being in his good books could lead to a big payoff some day.

"Okay, Pete, let's have it." The flush had receded from Cliff's face and his narrow eyes were coolly calculating.

"There's not a lot to tell, Cliff. The basic idea is pretty simple. Hunter thinks he's found a market in northern California for something like 300 million cubic feet of gas per day. He figures he can provide about a third of that himself from the Claymore field and he's looking around for the rest. He's talking about sixteen cents at the plant outlet and I reckon he'll get a lot of takers at that price."

"How far along is he with this project?"

"Barely off the ground. He was in San Francisco just last week talking to the gas distribution company there. He claims they're mighty interested."

Cliff grunted assent. "They would be. They've got to find some long-term supplies of gas pretty soon or they'll be out of business." Grudgingly, Cliff admitted to himself that Mark's plan was inspired. He should have thought of it himself, except that, like most oilmen, he was accustomed to thinking of natural gas as an expensive nuisance. But, the race had just started. Hunter was first out of the gate, but so long as he didn't have a binding deal with Norcal, Cliff would soon have him eating his dust.

Cliff showed his goodwill to a flattered Pete Cranshaw by escorting him to the elevators. Back in his office, he instructed his secretary to place a call to Harrison Dobbs. He had met the president of Norcal a couple of years ago when they sat at the same dinner table during a petroleum convention in Denver.

"I was sort of expecting to hear from you." Harrison's voice was cordial.

"You know what I'm calling about, then. You haven't signed anything with Hunter, have you?"

"No. But he does have the Claymore field. Do you have that kind of reserves and deliverability?"

"I can assemble all the supply you need," Cliff assured him blithely, while acknowledging to himself that Claymore gave the detested Hunter a tremendous leverage. "At an attractive price," he added. "I think it would be to our mutual advantage to meet and talk things over. I can fly down whenever it's convenient for you. What about early next week?"

"I'd be happy to see you any time, Cliff. However, we better not make it next week. Young Hunter's due back down here for some further talks on Tuesday. Something tells me that it might not be too smart to have the two of you in town at the same time. Why don't we make it the week after?"

"Suits me," Cliff agreed reluctantly. He was tempted to press for a meeting on Monday, but he realized the delay would give him time to get his act together so he could present Norcal with a complete package. "I am counting on you not to make any kind of a firm deal with Hunter before we talk."

"I owe it to our customers to make the best deal possible, so I will do nothing hasty," purred Harrison unctuously.

Cliff had what he wanted. He buzzed his executive assistant and told him to convene a meeting of department heads in half an hour. He'd throw manpower and talent at this project and come up with a proposal that would impress Norcal right out of their socks. Except, dammit, it couldn't include Claymore. A scowl settled over Cliff's heavy features, unnerving the executive assistant as he came in to report that the meeting was set for three o'clock.

Cliff's dark brooding was interrupted by the sudden ringing of his private phone — the one that only Denise had the number of. She was good about not bothering him, so it had to be something serious. A pulse throbbed in his eardrums as he picked up the phone.

"Oh, Cliff, something terrible has happened!" a distraught Denise sobbed. A flash of hope surged in Cliff's chest. Maybe that unspeakable son of his had managed to get himself killed.

"For Christ's sake, Denise, calm down and tell me what's happened," he barked.

He heard her draw several deep breaths as she fought for control. "You know the Martineaus? They live down the street."

"You know perfectly well I don't know the Martineaus," Cliff snapped impatiently. He took great care never to meet any of Denise's friends or acquaintances. "Get on with it!"

"Oh, Cliff, it's so awful, I don't know what to say."

"Denise, for Christ's sake!"

"The Martineaus have a little girl, Suzette. She's the same age as Jennifer and they play together all the time."

"Jesus, don't tell me Jamie ..."

"It has nothing to do with Jamie." Denise paused, swallowed audibly and went on, "Madeleine Martineau, Suzette's mother, brought Jennifer back a few minutes ago. They were playing over at Suzette's house and her mother said that Jennifer — our Jennifer — had taken Suzette's panties down and was touching her — you know where. And she touches herself there, too, Cliff. I've seen her. Oh, God, Cliff, I don't know what to do."

"It's that damn boy! He's been doing things to Jennifer. This settles it. He's got to go!"

"Jamie had nothing to do with it. I know you can't stand him, Cliff, but you've got to believe that. I think it must be one of the neighbourhood children that is doing this to her."

"That could be," Cliff admitted. It was all clear to him now. He would have to extricate himself from the Montreal connection. The risk of exposure had become too great. And he knew just how to do it. Jamie. Denise would fight like a tigress to keep her son, and he could use that to break up the affair. He would provide for them, of course. His conscience clear, Cliff began to smile as he thought of the pleasure of launching the search for a new mate. His step was unwontedly brisk as he headed for the meeting that would start the campaign to wrest the California pipeline project away from Mark Hunter.

"You're coming down *here*?" Jane was alarmed to hear herself actually squeaking.

"You don't sound very pleased."

"Of course I am, Daddy. It's just that I have this paper to do. I was planning to pull some all-nighters."

"I see." Cliff was disarmed. He was immensely proud of his daughter's academic achievements. "My meeting in San Francisco is not until a week next Tuesday. Surely you'll be finished by then?"

"Absolutely," replied a relieved Jane. "Where will you be staying?"

"At the Fairmont, where I always stay. I'll call you sometime Tuesday."

It'll work out all right, Jane told herself. Mark was going back to Calgary on Sunday and her father would probably fly down in the company Lodestar on Monday. He'd want to get a good night's sleep and be bright-eyed and bushy-tailed, as he liked to say, for his meeting on Tuesday. God, she hated this! Sneaking around behind her father's back, breaking her promise to him. Maybe she shouldn't have agreed to see Mark, but that seemed to be out of her hands. She couldn't resist the chance to be with him, to see once more the way his eyes lit up when he looked at her, the way his lips quirked when something amused him. What would she do if he tried to take them beyond necking? Her mind steered away; even when she deliberately tried to reach a decision, her thoughts refused to take coherent form.

"You've been busy," Harrison Dobbs finished reading the last paragraph and glanced up at Mark. "You're sure you can sign up this gas supply?"

"At sixteen cents per thousand cubic feet, I'm sure."

Harrison sighed and laid Mark's report on his desk. "That may prove to be a bit of a problem. George and I," he looked across the desk to MacGregor who nodded confirmation, "paid an informal call on the chairman of the Utilities Commission last Wednesday. He didn't seem all that charmed, to put it mildly, with what it would cost the California consumer to pay sixteen cents for the gas and then transport it some twelve hundred miles through a brand new pipeline. And he wasn't all that keen on having to rely on foreign-sourced gas. Not keen at all, in fact."

"He has no choice," countered Mark.

"You may be right. Ultimately. But that's some years down the road. Things can change from year to year and the chairman obviously hopes there will be some significant new gas discoveries closer to home."

"The citizens won't be very happy with him if their gas supply is curtailed and they have major brown-outs. Or with you, either."

"I know that only too well. Don't get me wrong, Mark. We want your gas. It's just that it may turn out to be a little more difficult than I had first thought."

Harrison tapped the tip of the letter opener against his thumbnail, then put the opener down on the desk with the air of a man who has come to a decision. "In fairness," he said, "I should tell you that I have been contacted by Cliff Marsden. We have a meeting scheduled for next week. He seems to think he can supply us with gas at a very favourable price. And he is, of course, an experienced pipeliner."

The worst case scenario had happened. Marsden had gotten wind of the pipeline project and was moving in. Mark swallowed hard and fought back. "I know for a fact that he hasn't got anything like the quality of reserves I have in Claymore."

Harrison gave a wintry smile of acknowledgement. The perfect solution would be to have both Claymore and Cliff Marsden. That way he could be sure the pipeline would be built, and he wouldn't have to nursemaid this ambitious young man through all the complicated stages of planning, financing, and constructing a major transmission line. The realization that Mark was saying something brought Harrison out of his fleeting reverie. "I'm sorry, Mark. Would you mind repeating that? I was thinking about all the obstacles that must be overcome before this pipeline can be built. I find the prospect quite daunting, I must confess."

Hearing this, Mark thought that maybe his new inspiration wasn't so red-hot after all. But he pressed on. "I was saying that I'm prepared to offer Norcal partici- pation in the pipeline. Up to fifty per cent, if you want."

At first, Harrison was inclined to dismiss the suggestion out of hand. But pipelines are known as the cash cows of the oil industry, generating a steady flow of revenues as they, impervious to weather conditions, carry their hydrocarbon cargoes, day in, day out, for twelve months of the year. And this pipeline would be regulated, just like Norcal's distribution system, which meant that it would be virtually guaranteed its rate of return. Harrison was well-accustomed to functioning in a regulated environment. Norcal had thrived in it for years. Now that he thought about it, an ownership position in the new pipeline would be a natural extension of Norcal's utility activities. Harrison made up his mind — Norcal would be a full partner in the pipeline regardless of which Canadian group built it. He looked at Mark with new respect — this young man had a habit of coming up with the big, basic concepts. "I have always assumed that we would take a substantial equity position," he said loftily. This was news to MacGregor, and the manager of supply opened his mouth as if to interject, but quickly subsided when the president shot him a warning glance.

The little byplay was not lost on Mark. He was almost positive that Harrison had never even considered the possibility of becoming a joint owner until he had brought it up. That didn't matter. What mattered was that if Norcal came in, the pipeline was as good as built. And he doubted if Marsden would be all that enchanted with the idea of sharing ownership with anyone. He was notorious for being a lone-wolf operator. Feeling he had scored a bit of a coup, Mark stood up to take his leave.

The Jag, in low gear and looking almost dowdy with its canvas top in place, followed a cable car up the precipitous incline of Powell Street to the brow of Nob Hill. The cable car, bell clanging furiously, made it through the light at the intersection with California Street, but Mark just missed it. The rain had slackened and he used the back of his hand to wipe condensation off the windshield. Jane leaned forward to do the same thing to her side. Suddenly she gave a small gasp. "What's the matter?" demanded Mark.

"It's Daddy. Over there in front of the hotel. Beside that limousine. Oh God," Jane moaned, "he'll recognize the car."

"He's not looking this way." Mark peered through the rain-spotted Plexiglas side-window. It was Marsden all right. He was standing by the open trunk of a black Cadillac limousine while the doorman lifted his suitcase out and closed the lid. The light changed and the car behind honked an impatient horn. Mark let in the clutch and got out of there. Fast.

"How come he's down here so early? His meeting's not until next week."

"He does this sometimes — arrives in a city a couple of days before a meeting. He calls them his private days. He says it's the only way he can get away from the pressure of business and have some time to himself."

"Nice work if you can get it," Mark grunted.

"You have no idea the pressure he's under," Jane flared. "He has hundreds of people depending on him for their livelihood."

"Okay. Okay." Mark held up his hand in surrender. "Remember we have already agreed he is a prince among men." He shifted down to second gear as they started the almost vertical descent down Mason Street."

"I'm going home, Mark."

"Home?" Mark stared at her incredulously, nearly missing a red light. "We've got dinner reservations and then we were going to take in a movie."

"I know. And I'm sorry. But I'm going back to the residence. I'll drop you at the St. Francis. Please don't argue, Mark."

Looking at her set face, Mark realized that there was no way of talking her out of it.

When he pulled up in front of his hotel, she managed a wan smile. "You must think I'm all kinds of a fool, Mark. Maybe you should forget about me."

"Don't say that. Don't even think that." He kissed her, alarmed at the rigid set of her shoulders. "Look, I'll phone you later tonight at the residence and we'll talk. Okay?"

She nodded mutely and unsnapped the side window to reach outside and open the door, the Jag not being equipped with such frills as inside door handles.

17

"Do I get the other half now?" asked the brunette.

Cliff nodded and extracted half of a thousand-dollar bill from his wallet. He had given her the first half at the start of the weekend. Trying not to show her relief, she tucked the neatly severed second half in her garter belt. God knew she had earned it, although she was smart enough to keep that thought to herself. He was a pretty kinky guy, but she had to admit that she had gotten a kick out of dining in two of the city's poshest restaurants. A girl in her business didn't get to do that very often.

"Is it all right if I put on the rest of my clothes now?"

He nodded absently, not looking at her. Nor did he speak or turn around when she let herself out, quietly closing the door behind herself. Claymore. Without that field, the economics just weren't there. In order to attach a sufficient gas supply to deliver 300 million cubic feet per day you'd have to criss-cross the whole damn province with a network of gathering lines, picking up a few billion feet of reserves here and a few billion there. The studies his staff had put together — studies he had no intention of letting Dobbs see — showed that the cost of doing this would leave no money to pay the producers for their gas. Throw in Claymore, and the numbers began to sing — showing a handsome return on the pipeline investment with plenty left over to pay the producers. But Claymore belonged to that cocky son of a bitch — just in time he stopped himself from repeating that hated name, even silently to himself.

He could always try to buy Claymore, of course. But Hunter would almost certainly refuse to sell it to him, and if he tried to do it indirectly, he'd still end up making an overnight millionaire out of the young prick. And that, by God, was something he had no intention of doing.

He'd just have to bluff his way through the meeting with Norcal. Instead of the neatly packaged project he had hoped to present, he'd have to do the smoke and mirrors bit. Dobbs wouldn't press him too much at this preliminary stage, but pretty soon he'd expect to see some hard numbers.

Harrison turned out to be much more anxious for facts and figures than Cliff had anticipated. He was too smooth an operator to come right out and say so, but it was clear that he was disappointed with the vague generalities in Cliff's report on the subject of gas supply. It was obvious that he was excited by the prospect of tapping into the Canadian gas reserves; his supply problem must be even more crucial than Cliff had suspected. For the first time, Cliff was convinced that the California pipeline was going to happen. And by God, he was the one who would build it! It would launch him into the international scene, where he belonged.

The company engineers who had flown in from Calgary to assist Cliff with his presentation stared down at the boardroom table as if its polished surface held the answer to the riddle of the universe. Their boss was accustomed to dominating every meeting he condescended to attend — he would not be enjoying the reception he was getting from the Norcal people. It was painfully evident that they had come up short, and some — maybe all of them — could expect to be fired before they got back to Calgary. The worst part was that Cliff Marsden was never content to just fire an employee, he went out of his way to make it difficult for the poor wretch to find another job.

Norcal had laid on an elaborate lunch in the executive dining room. Cliff would have liked to refuse, so that he could vent his rage and humiliation on his unfortunate subordinates, but this was not the time to risk offending Harrison Dobbs. Knowing that they had been granted only a respite and not a reprieve, Marsden's engineers cautiously sipped their drinks and made dispirited conversation with their Norcal counterparts.

Cliff sought comfort in a double martini and wore a forced smile as he chatted with Harrison. The Norcal president was rather entertained by his guest's discomfiture — his personal acquaintance with the man was slight, but everything about him seemed to confirm his reputation as an arrogant bully. He did not envy those poor devils from Marsden's engineering department — they looked absolutely cowed. The professional manager in Dobbs deplored this way of handling staff — it turned them into useless "yes" men.

"That was a very useful discussion this morning." Harrison took a discreet sip of his tonic water. Cliff glared at him, but there was no hint of irony in the president's expression as he went on, "I mean that sincerely, Cliff. It brought out in the clearest possible way how, with Claymore, everything works like a well-oiled machine. Without it, the numbers just don't parse."

"I can make them parse," gritted Cliff.

"I hope so, Cliff." Harrison sounded unconvinced.

"Let me get this straight, Harrison. Are you saying that with Claymore, the project is viable and without Claymore, it's not?"

"That's the way it looks to me. So far, anyway."

"There'll be other fields just as big as Claymore discovered up there."

"Undoubtedly. But when? That's the problem, Cliff. Time is of the essence, as the lawyers like to say."

"Sooner than you might think," replied Cliff with a rising note of excitement. He would find his own Claymore. He had never done much more than dabble in the exploration side of the oil industry; he had been content to make his fortune build-

ing and operating pipelines to carry the oil that others found. That didn't matter —
you could solve any problem if you threw enough dollars at it. But there was no time
to waste — he had to get back to Calgary and start assembling the team that would
find him the reserves he needed.

"Of course I understand, Daddy. Don't worry about it. I'll come see you the next
time you come to San Francisco, or when I come home for the Christmas break."
  "Did you get those papers done in time?"
  "What ... Oh, yes. Barely made the deadline, but I'm pretty happy with them."
  "Coming from you, that means they'll be straight *As*." For the first time, a note of
animation crept into Cliff's voice. "You know how proud I am of you, angel."
  "I'll try not to let you down." Jane remained in the little booth for a few moments
after hanging up. Her relief at not having to see her father made her feel disloyal and
a little ashamed. He was so self-centred that he was almost oblivious to the feelings
of those around him, but he had always been disturbingly perceptive about her and
would have been sure to spot how uneasy and confused she was. To make matters
worse, her preoccupation with Mark was destroying her concentration. If she didn't
get her act together soon, her grades would suffer and she would have let her father
down once again. But that was something within her control. She'd hit the books
starting right now. That would solve the problem of Jimmy as well. He kept asking
her to watch him play basketball or take in a movie, and couldn't understand when
she kept turning him down. But he'd understand about her studies — it wasn't
unusual for star students to become anti-social and reclusive in their final year as
they crammed for the best possible marks.

As the Lodestar droned north, Marsden's engineers waited for the inevitable
dressing down, but the excitement of his new scheme had wiped the morning's
humiliation from their boss's mind. He regarded them with an indifferent gaze as
they sat stiffly in their seats. They were all civil engineers — essential for building
pipelines, but not worth a pinch of coon shit when it came to finding oil and gas.
Especially gas. The first thing he'd do when they got back to Calgary was to find out
what geologist currently had the best track record, and hire him away from wherever
he was working. His lips turned down in a bitter grimace as he realized the name he
was bound to hear most often would be Mark Hunter — that son of a bitch. The
engineers braced themselves when they saw his sour expression, but he remained
wrapped in his own thoughts while the unpressurized Lodestar picked its way
through towering columns of white cumulus.

"I never figured you for a wildcatter, Cliff." Don Cullen swallowed a stiff belt of
Scotch and sighed gustily. "I always thought pipelining was your game."
  "It is. But things are a little slow right now as far as new construction is

concerned." Cliff gave a humourless smile. "After all, I have to find some way of spending all that cash flow."

"Drilling rank wildcats can solve that problem for you, all right," grunted Don with the air of one who knows. "What are you going to do? Set up a new company?"

"Maybe later. For the moment, I'll go with an exploration division of Regal Pipelines."

Don heaved himself out of his chair and walked over to the bar to freshen his drink. It made sense for Cliff to branch out into the exploration end of the business. Regal Pipelines generated a steady stream of revenue that had to be invested somewhere. And he could write off the exploration expenses against income taxes. It was a natural, and if Cliff went at it the right way, he'd make big bucks in the oil patch. Don was flattered that Cliff had come to him for advice — it was further confirmation of his own status in the industry. He'd help him, even though he despised the son of a bitch for his wartime cowardice. In some ways they had a lot in common; they were both the sons of old-time Calgary families and they had known each other since childhood. More importantly, they were both mavericks. And by helping Cliff, he could even the score with that supercilious English bastard, John Frame, who always looked at him with icy disdain and called him a disgusting drunk behind his back. Frame had been sent over from England to establish Triarch Petroleums and get in on the Alberta boom.

"I have the perfect solution for you, Cliff." Don carefully set his full glass down on an end table and lowered himself back into his chair. "A ready-made exploration department. Triarch has assembled a team of three geologists and two geophysicists — the cream of the crop, in my opinion. All you have to do is hire them away from Triarch. Offer to double their salaries and cut them in for an override on anything they discover, and you're in business."

The five earth scientists who had formerly comprised Triarch Petroleums's crack exploration department quickly discovered that, working for Cliff Marsden, they earned every penny of their inflated salaries. He expected results, and he expected them now. The man seemed to have no conception that it could take years of patient research and analysis to mount a large-scale exploration program. Worse, he seemed to expect them to use the information they had obtained while in the employ of Triarch. And he was after gas, of all things. Huge quantities of gas. Another Claymore field. It did no good to explain that Claymore was a once in a lifetime discovery. Their new employer wanted action. In desperation, they purchased all the seismic information that was publicly available and frantically studied it for clues to the possible existence of large underground geological structures. "It's like shooting darts blindfolded," groaned their leader as they drew up a list of possible locations for an impatient Marsden.

When the first well was spudded, a scant three weeks after Cliff had shanghaied the Triarch exploration department, even the normally phlegmatic pipeline tycoon was caught up in the excitement of the high-stake gamble of drilling a wildcat well. He was on hand at the remote wellsite when they reached total depth, and even managed to behave in a reasonably civilized manner when it came in dry. "You can't win 'em all, Bob," he consoled his crestfallen chief geologist as they sought shelter in the dog house from the chill wind.

Emboldened by his boss's unexpectedly sympathetic attitude, the geologist pleaded for time to work up a proper exploration program.

"Time is what we haven't got," Cliff snapped and, to the geologist's horror, ordered the drilling program to be stepped up. "I want you to hire three more rigs and put them to work."

"Jesus, Cliff. This isn't a game of averages, you know. It's not a matter of punching down enough holes and eventually coming up with the big one. It's a science, for Christ's sake!"

"It's not your money we're spending."

"But it's my reputation."

"Your reputation will be made when we find another Claymore." Cliff terminated the conversation by stalking out of the doghouse, slamming its steel door behind him, and leaving his shaken geologist wishing he were back in the rational world of Triarch Petroleums.

Ironically, one of the wells in Cliff's feverish exploration program discovered an oilfield of respectable size. Marsden waved aside the news of the find with an impatient hand and told his dispirited team to get on with the job of finding a giant gas field. Word of Cliff's fruitless quest circulated freely through the oil patch and soon reached the ears of Harrison Dobbs. The utility magnate had been doing a lot of hard, analytical thinking since the possibility of tapping into the vast Canadian gas reserves had been brought to his attention. His concentration was improved by the forecasts of supply and demand prepared by his staff which indicated that he had little more than a year before it became absolutely essential to make a start on the pipeline.

All this thinking had led to two main conclusions: first, that the Claymore field was the essential underpinning of the whole project and, second, that Cliff Marsden was the one to build the pipeline. He liked Mark and detested Marsden, but the reality was — and Harrison was nothing if not a realist — that with the resources of the Marsden organization behind it, building the international pipeline would be a piece of cake. And he could handle egotistical bastards like Marsden. He'd been doing that all his life. On the other hand, if he was forced to rely on Mark to plan, finance, and construct the project, it would be strictly a grassroots operation that might never get off the ground. If that happened, he, Harrison Dobbs, would get the blame when the lights began to dim.

Under normal circumstances it would be simple. Mark, as the owner of the gas, would sell it to Norcal and take his profit from the price of the gas. Marsden — make that Marsden and Norcal — would build the pipeline and make their money by collecting a fee for transporting the gas. That's the way it should be — everyone doing what they did best, and being handsomely rewarded for it. But it wasn't going to be that way. Not this time. Not with the two principal players at each other's throat. Harrison sighed under his breath and went back to thinking. He'd have to play it cool until he came up with something. It was strange, but true, that if you gave things a little time to work themselves out, something usually turned up.

Harrison's relaxed, almost indifferent, attitude troubled Mark on his next visit to San Francisco, making him wonder if Harrison had some alternative plan in mind, possibly an unknown new source within the US itself. US gas was bound to be Harrison's first choice if it were available. As their meeting broke up, he wished Mark the compliments of the season, but only smiled noncommittally when Mark expressed the hope that 1957 would see the start of the pipeline.

Mark was still full of foreboding as he checked out the U-drive, but the foreboding soon changed to anticipation as he took the now familiar road to Palo Alto. Jane had agreed to see him, even though it was less than a week to her first exam. She was thinner by several pounds and there were faint smudges under her eyes, but her mood was upbeat. Most importantly, she seemed unreservedly glad to see him.

Crossing her fingers, she admitted to feeling that she was on top of her courses. Mark perceived that this somehow made her feel less guilt-ridden about seeing him. Their date was brief; she wouldn't even touch a glass of wine and she insisted on being back at the residence by eleven, but for Mark it was enough to see her in good spirits and so much at ease with him. The only strain came when the matter of her Christmas vacation arose. She was going to spend the holidays in Calgary and was adamant that they could not go out together while she was there. With his increasing prominence in the oil patch, Mark was being included in more and more invitation lists, and the thought of bumping into her at some party, maybe with someone like Rhodes Taylor, was a knife in his gut. She obviously had been thinking about it as well, for she suggested that she could come back to Stanford early — a couple of days before New Year's on the pretext of working on her thesis and if he came to San Francisco they could spend New Year's eve together.

Heart hammering with the implications of this, Mark held her close and whispered, "I'll make my airline reservations first thing in the morning!"

They said goodnight at the door of her residence. "Ace those old exams, darling," Mark whispered as he brushed his lips against her eyelashes and then kissed her on the mouth. He sang and hummed snatches of love songs all the way back to the St. Francis.

18

The Calgary cocktail circuit had two delicious pieces of gossip to titillate it over Christmas. First, there was the gratifying fact that the unpopular Cliff Marsden was getting nowhere in his frantic search for gas, but this was quickly being overtaken by the rumour that the mighty Cullen empire was in danger of imminent collapse.

Bill Crawford confirmed this as he and Mark stood chatting at an afternoon open house in an oil company president's Mount Royal home. "Old D.R.'s got himself wedged between a rock and a hard place this time." Bill shook his head. "He joined a consortium of multinationals to bid on some lands off the California coast. Big dollars. Then they proceeded to drill four dry holes in a row. At five million a pop. The word is that the consortium intends to walk away from the whole scene and write it off against their income tax. The problem is that D.R. has no other US income to write it off against, plus the fact that he borrowed the whole amount from the banks."

Mark was surprised by how much the news upset him. Cullen was an incorrigible old reprobate, but there was nothing mean or evil about him. Like there was about Cliff Marsden, for example. Mark glanced out the bay window and saw Marsden's new Lincoln limousine parked right beside the driveway. Pale blue smoke bubbled from its exhaust. Joe Antonelli, Marsden's recently acquired driver, who looked more like a Mafia hit man than a chauffeur, had the heater on to keep himself warm. Carefully not looking in the direction of the fireplace where Jane was chatting easily with some older women, Mark said, "Peerless is one of the very few independent oil companies big enough to have some clout in the industry."

"I agree. And it would be a shame if it went under. But, old D.R. *will* insist on playing with the big boys, and this time it looks as if he's got his tit in the wringer. The way I hear it, he still thinks the area has potential and is trying talk his partners into drilling one more wildcat. Damn! She's spilled her drink!" Bill strode quickly to the side of his wife, who was dabbing ineffectually at a large, dark stain on her skirt. Jane had already taken the nearly empty glass of bourbon and Coke from Marianne and handed it to a waiter who rushed up to help.

"Come on, Marianne," said Bill quietly as he took her by the elbow. "We'll get you home so you can change."

She went meekly enough, an apologetic little smile on her face. Mark felt desperately sorry for Bill, and for Marianne, too, for that matter. She hadn't asked to be dragged up here, thousands of miles away from everything that was familiar to her. Her insistence on drinking bourbon was in itself a small act of defiance. They were a wretchedly unhappy couple and God knew where it would end. Instinctively, he looked across at Jane. Their eyes met and they exchanged a deep commiserating look that said this would never happen to them.

Cliff had been standing on the sidelines, relishing the spectacle Marianne Crawford was making of herself. That son of a bitch Crawford, with his movie star looks and early success, had too damn much going for him. It was good to see him humiliated like this. What Bill didn't know was that his sexy-looking wife was beginning to play around when he was out of town. That precious pair, Sharon and Astrid, were gradually luring her into their fast-living circle. Cliff had heard rumours of a party she had attended at Farris's place where the men wore black masks and the women wore red — and nothing more. If the party had taken place, he hadn't been invited. Nor, so far as he knew, had any of his friends. Funny. But his time would come. Although it better be soon, before the drink messed her up. Licking his lips, Cliff watched her swaying hips as Bill steered her toward the door. He saw her give a playful little waggle of her fingers as she passed Mark. But Hunter wasn't looking at her. He was staring across the room with a besotted look on his face.

Quickly turning his head, Cliff caught the answering look in Jane's eyes before she hastily averted her face. Shit! And he had been congratulating himself that she had lost interest in him! Hunter hadn't been on the scene at all since she arrived home and she never mentioned his name. Stanford! What a blind fool he had been! Hunter had made God alone knew how many trips to San Francisco this fall and it was only an hour's drive to Palo Alto. Cliff gave a strangled cough as the sour bile rose in his throat.

It would be a simple matter to have Hunter tailed the next time he went to San Francisco. Antonelli could set it up with one phone call. But did he really want to know? The thought of Jane in that bastard's arms filled him with a rage so fierce that he feared he might be having some sort of attack. There was a sudden roaring in his ears and his vision was obscured with a red haze. He took a deep breath and the frightening sensations subsided. He helped himself to a drink from the tray of a passing waiter and downed it like a dose of medicine.

He caught Eleanor's apprehensive look and scowled at her, before turning away to talk to some of his male contemporaries.

Shaken by the vicious glare in her father's eyes, Jane forced herself to join in the official chatter that had sprung up to cover Marianne's embarrassing exit, but her thoughts were in turmoil. She and Mark had been doing so well, only to be betrayed by a single, unexpected glance. But even with that, her father couldn't know for sure. He had been wonderful to her all through the holidays, just like always, and that would never have been the case if he had had even the slightest suspicion. Subtle her father was not. And there were three more days for her to get through before it was time for her to go back to school. To meet Mark, actually. Oh God, why did life have to be so complicated?

"You seem awfully down, dear," Eleanor Marsden ventured timidly as the limousine bore them homeward through the early winter dusk. The partition was closed, sealing them off from the sinister-looking chauffeur.

Cliff's scowl deepened, but he replied mildly enough, "It's that damn drilling program. They're starting to call me 'Dry Hole' Marsden."

"I'm so sorry, dear." Eleanor made as if to touch her husband's hand, but desisted when she saw the forbidding set of his heavy-jawed profile. Sitting on the jump seat across from her parents, Jane couldn't decide whether he was being genuine or not. Drilling a string of dry holes would put anyone in a black mood, especially if they, like her father, were desperately searching for gas to support a pipeline project. It could also be a useful cover-up for the rage that would consume him if he suspected something about her and Mark. But if he wanted to blame the discouraging drilling results, that was fine with her.

Thank God she had agreed to attend another house party with Rhodes Taylor that night! That would get her out of the house and away from her father's suspicious gaze. Poor mother would have to bear the brunt of his ill humour, but she would probably solve that in her usual fashion by retiring to her room. Her parents lived a life of armed truce; Jane couldn't recall a single look or gesture of affection ever passing between them. Her father had ruined her mother's life with his callous indifference and now he seemed determined to control hers. Jane was gripped by a sudden, hot anger. He had no right to be so damned self-centred and overbearing. Her anger was quickly replaced with a feeling of alarm. What was happening to her? All her life, even as a schoolgirl, she had stood up for her father, even if sometimes that meant only staring down his detractors with a defiant, contemptuous look.

Rhodes had a new car — a black, Cadillac sedan. "It's you, Rhodes," Jane told him, hiding a smile in the darkness as he led her toward it."

"You really think so?" Pleased, he held the door for her, then went round to the driver's side. "I worry a little that people might think it's too ostentatious. I don't drive it to the office."

No, thought Jane, a shade unkindly, you would use a free company car for that. Poor Rhodes! You'd think with all the money he made that he wouldn't give a damn what people thought. But, socially, he was painfully insecure, giving that nervous little cough of his, and baring his teeth in a false, uneasy smile that seldom reached his eyes. Jane was aware that her own social poise was part of the attraction she held for him. That, and the fact that she was a Marsden. To her increasing dismay, Rhodes had recently been showing signs of becoming altogether too attracted to her. He had once remarked, in his portentous way, about how he was getting on in years — at thirty! — and that maybe it was time he was settling down. Just what the staid

Rhodes had to settle down from left Jane somewhat bemused, but she had forestalled any follow-up on his part by brightly agreeing that he should find himself a nice girl to share his life. He had shot her a startled look and fallen silent.

And yet there was another, unexpected, side to this shy and diffident man — almost a public persona. His company advertised extensively in the newspapers and trade journals and each advertisement contained his photo. The company also employed a full-time public relations man whose principal job was to set up interviews for Taylor with co-operative journalists. Rhodes actually craved publicity, but only on his own terms and when he could be in complete control of the situation.

The party was a young people's holiday get-together hosted by the daughter of a prominent ranching family at their townhouse. It was as "old Calgary" as you could get, and it had never occurred to Jane that Mark would be there. But he was almost the first person she saw, talking to his sidekick, Dave Green. Brenda Lester, the hostess, was laughing at something Dave said but her eyes never left Mark's face. Her animation died away when she saw his reaction to the sight of Jane. She gave a little shrug and walked over to welcome the new arrivals, her guarded expression reflecting the knowledge that men were not turned on by her spare, flat-chested figure and raw-boned features. Ever since high school she had lived with the fact that it was her family's wealth and social position that accounted for such dates as she did have.

Are Mark and I this obvious? Jane asked herself as she returned Brenda's greeting. This is the second time today we've been caught out. For some reason the thought did not displease her.

Rhodes held Brenda's hand in both of his while he went on about how charmed he was to be there and how lovely she looked. That made her blink but when she saw the serious man was completely sincere, she relaxed and smiled warmly back at him. While the two of them were engrossed with each other, Mark touched Jane on the arm and motioned toward the dance floor.

"Your father looked positively homicidal when you left this afternoon," said Mark as they danced.

"He wants Mother and me to believe that it's the lousy luck he's having with his exploration program." Jane bit her lip and looked up at Mark, "Should I have said that? I mean, you being competitors and all."

"It doesn't matter. Everybody knows he's come up with diddly-squat," Mark assured her, encouraged nonetheless to have this direct confirmation of what the street was saying.

Jane still looked a little troubled, but continued, "He suspects something, Mark. I think it was the way we looked at each other when Marianne was putting on that little show this afternoon. But you know what?" She tilted her head to look up at him. "I've just about had it with my dear father's moods and sulks."

"Hallelujah!" Mark held her closer.

The next couple of hours gave Mark a foretaste of what life with Jane would be like. She was carefree, almost abandoned, laughing up at him while they danced on and on. Everyone in the room would know they had something going, but it didn't seem to phase her. It was Mark who, feeling a twinge of guilt, finally suggested that maybe they should find Rhodes.

"Don't worry about him. He's having the time of his life. Look over there by the piano."

Rhodes and Brenda were dancing cheek-to-cheek, drawing apart every now and then to smile at each other with the breathless thrill of discovery. Brenda's plain features were transformed into something close to beauty.

"They've found each other," whispered Jane. "I think it's wonderful! They're absolutely right for each other, when you think about it."

A little flicker of apprehension crossed Brenda's face as Mark and Jane came up to them at the end of the piece. But Rhodes held on to her hand as he greeted them. Jane managed to keep a straight face as he solemnly apologized for neglecting her. "Just don't leave without me," she told him gaily as she took Mark by the hand and led him off."

"Let's grab our coats and sit in the car for a while," she said a little breathlessly, her cheeks touched with a hint of colour. His heart suddenly thumping, Mark followed her along the hall to the bedrooms where the coats were piled. When they were in the car she told him to drive around the corner to get away from the street lights.

This time she didn't flinch when his hand touched her breast. Moaning softly, her mouth open against his, she sat up straight so he could unhook her bra. Almost reverently, Mark cupped the perfect globes in his hands, her nipples hardening as he lightly brushed them with his thumbs. He felt her fingers begin to stroke the inside of his thigh, then she was tugging at his zipper. Almost as if he were a spectator, he watched, with a mixture of delight, incredulity, and dismay, as she took him in her mouth. Then everything else was swept away in a flood of exquisite sensation.

"Did you like that?" she asked gravely, looking up at him with eyes that were strangely unfocussed.

"It was wonderful," he managed to murmur, his mind racing as he tried to come to terms with what had happened. So she was more experienced than he had thought — all that proved was that she was human, and he was no saint himself if it came to that. The way she had suddenly taken charge was vaguely disturbing, but, again, why not?

He smiled down at her upturned face. "You look just like a little girl." He kissed her. "We better get back to the party. I hate the idea of turning you back to Rhodes, but I guess my driving you home wouldn't be such a hot idea?"

"God, no!" That snapped her out of her seeming trance. "Daddy will be waiting up for me, and if he saw you drive into the yard ..." Mark interrupted her by placing his fingers on her mouth. "Okay. I get the picture. But sooner or later, we are going to have to face up to it."

"Not tonight. Not in the mood he's in."

The party was beginning to break up as Mark backed the Olds into their former parking spot. Laughing couples, some of the men unsteady on their feet, lobbed snowballs at each other as they made their way to the cars.

"We're still on for New Year's, right?" asked Mark as they walked hand-in-hand up the lighted path. He held his breath when Jane hesitated before replying, "Yes. I'll be glad to get away if you want the truth. Things haven't been all that great around the house."

It was the first time she had admitted that everything was not perfect in the Marsden household. Mark made no reply beyond squeezing her hand.

Mark wished he could look forward to his San Francisco tryst as just the fulfilment of an incredible sexual fantasy. But it wasn't that simple. He loved Jane and wanted to marry her. Had from the very first time he saw her. But what if she, beneath that wholesome exterior, turned out to be hopelessly promiscuous? Her sucking him off — his mind recoiled at the words — was totally unexpected and completely at variance with her normal behaviour. It was almost as if she became another person. Then the thought of lying with her, of exploring every delicious detail of that breathtaking body, would sweep over him, leaving him dry-mouthed and flushed.

Feeling somewhat tarnished, he purchased several packets of French safes the afternoon he arrived in San Francisco. He also laid in a couple of bottles of champagne. His hotel room with the king-sized bed, lamps softly glowing, champagne cooling on ice and sentimental music wafting from the radio, was the perfect stage for a seduction. He wished it were the first night of their honeymoon.

Beyond making dinner reservations, they had no formal plans for celebrating New Year's Eve. To Mark's profound relief, all of Jane's university friends were still on vacation, which left the two of them on their own. Mark had his own agenda, but it didn't work out that way. Jane greeted him at the door of the residence with a breezy kiss, but moved away when he tried to hold her close.

After a lingering late dinner she insisted they go to Union Square to join the throng welcoming in the New Year. They kissed as the countdown to midnight ended and he shouted above the din, "1957 will be our year, darling!"

"I hope so," she mouthed back, not meeting his eyes. Then she brightened. "Why don't we grab the champagne and drive down to Carmel and walk on the beach?"

And so it was that instead of making love in Mark's luxurious hotel room, they trudged along the rocky beach, littered with bleached tree trunks. Arms around each other's waist, they took swigs from the bottle of Cordon Rouge as they went.

High on the cliff above them, the lone figure of a man shivered in the cold, desperately wanting a cigarette but not daring to light one. He cursed softly and drew his unlined jacket more closely around him as his quarry moved on.

19

"You want the guy wasted?" Joe Antonelli's pockmarked face was expressionless. "Five thou should cover it."

Appalled, yet strangely excited, Cliff stared at his bodyguard. Joe made it sound as ordinary and commonplace as buying a new car. Wouldn't it be something to have that bastard out of his life. "How would it be done?" he asked, almost despite himself.

Joe shrugged. "Hunter would have an accident. A fatal accident. Nobody would ever know any different."

God, it was tempting. But he needed Hunter alive. Cliff had finally decided to call off the frantic drilling program that was going nowhere and was making him the laughing stock of the oil patch. Somehow or other he had to gain control of Claymore, and for that he needed Hunter. Once Claymore was his, Joe's suggestion might deserve a second look.

Joe suddenly cracked a knuckle, the noise sounding like a gunshot in the quiet office. With a start, Cliff realized that he was waiting for an answer. "Thanks, Joe, but I'll pass. Doing away with my business enemies is not my style."

Business enemy my arse, Joe thought, it's the thought of this guy screwing your daughter that's eatin' on you. But all Joe said was, "Let me know if you change your mind, boss."

A strangled groan broke from Cliff's lips when the door closed behind the burly bodyguard. It had taken all his willpower not to let his rage and frustration pour out in a primordial howl. Words from Joe's verbal report pummelled him — "walking on the beach, holding hands like a pair of goddamn teenagers," "laughing — always fuckin' laughing," "laughing and kissing all the fuckin' time." It seemed they weren't lovers, not yet anyway. But they were in love, that was obvious. Jane. His Jane. He was going to lose her. Maybe he had already. Maybe he had never ... The phone gave the cricket chirp that he had grown to detest; he'd have it replaced tomorrow.

It was Bob Alderson, the head of the team he had imported from Triarch. What an expensive fiasco that had turned out to be! He wondered if Cullen had set him up? No, Don had no reason to do that. Alderson was the only one of the Triarch bunch who still had the guts to talk to him, although he usually managed to do it by phone. Alderson was asking for authority to plug and abandon their latest hole.

"Sure. Go right ahead," Cliff's tone was heavily sarcastic. "Why should this one be any different from all the others?"

Slamming down the receiver, he stared with angry, unseeing eyes at a large oil painting of a construction crew laying a pipeline across a fast-flowing river. This latest dry hole only confirmed what he already knew — he would never be able to catch up to Hunter by exploring for gas; the only way was to take Claymore away from him.

"The street has it that Marsden has shut down all his drilling operations." Dave Green poured the beer as if it were vintage wine, tilting the mug to cut down on the foam.

"It's about time he came to his senses. What's the point of having all that high-priced help if you don't listen to them?"

"Marsden treats his staff like mushrooms," Green paused, then explained when Mark lifted an inquiring eyebrow, "You know, keep them in the dark and feed them shit."

Dave was already on his second beer by the time Mark got back to the apartment the following night.

"Marsden not only feeds his employees shit," he muttered with a shake of his head. "He treats them like shit. You know what the son of a bitch did?"

"Nothing would surprise me," Mark replied as he hung his parka in the closet.

"Ran all the Triarch guys off. Got rid of them just like that."

Mark whistled. "He must be dead serious about shutting down his exploration program."

"If he's thrown in the towel that makes you the winner, right?"

"I wish I could believe that," said Mark slowly. "But somehow I can't."

"I have always believed that the adage 'know thy enemy' is as true in business as it is in war," Harrison Dobbs pontificated.

Cliff stirred impatiently in his chair. Had he been summoned — damn summarily summoned — into Harrison's presence just to listen to a lecture on business tactics? So what if Harrison was a guest lecturer at the Harvard Business School, he, Cliff Marsden, had better things to do with his time.

His ill-disguised impatience was not lost on his host. Cliff really was a first-class boor. Young Hunter would be much more pleasant to deal with, but he just didn't have the necessary firepower. Harrison sat even more erect in his chair. "I am correct, am I not, that there is absolutely no chance of you and Hunter joining forces?"

"Me work with that asshole? Never!"

Harrison winced. "A simple 'no' would have sufficed." He paused, then shrugged slightly, and continued, "I have decided that your company is the logical choice to build the pipeline ..."

"Now you're talking!" interjected an elated Cliff.

"Quite." Harrison's smile was wintry. "There are, however, two conditions.

"I'm listening."

"One, Norcal will share in the ownership of the pipeline as a full fifty-per-cent partner."

"I don't have partners."

"There's always a first time. Hunter has already offered full participation, by the way. If you can't live with the idea, we will terminate this conversation here and now. But remember that half a loaf is better than none."

"Another adage?" sneered Cliff. But he had done enough negotiating in his life to know that this time he was outgunned. "All right," he snarled, conceding defeat. "What's your second condition?"

For the first time, Harrison looked a little uneasy; his air of cool detachment seemed to have deserted him. He looked around his baronial office as if to reassure himself that they were alone. "I will be retiring in a few years," he murmured.

A cynical smile twisted Cliff's thick lips. This was the real reason Harrison had selected him over Hunter — so he could cut a side deal for himself. He couldn't do it with Hunter — Hunter didn't have the cash.

Cliff sat back in his chair and listened with an air that was almost philosophical as Harrison outlined his terms. The sanctimonious bastard sure wasn't backward when it came to lining his own pocket. Cliff was to deposit $100,000 in a numbered Swiss bank account immediately on his return to Calgary, "as a gesture of good faith on your part, you understand," and on the day construction of the pipeline began, an additional $900,000 was to be deposited in the same account.

"That's quite a bribe you're asking for," murmured Cliff.

Harrison flinched, as Cliff had known he would, but all he said was, "Call it what you will, but those are my terms. Take it or leave it."

"Oh, you've got a deal. It's just that I find it very reassuring to know that the distinguished and righteous Mr. Dobbs is not above selling himself out. It restores my faith in the human race, if you know what I mean."

"Are you quite finished?" asked Harrison icily.

Cliff, cynical smile still in place, shrugged and said, "Sure. Carry on."

"Very well. The key to Hunter's situation has got to be in his financing. The man came out of nowhere. One day he's a down-at-the-heels geologist, then overnight he's got the wherewithal to launch a substantial exploration program. The first thing we must find out is who is backing him."

It didn't take much digging to find out that Mark had a silent partner. The partner's name was Garth Kennedy and the more Cliff found out about him, the more puzzled he became. The guy seemed to spend most of his time on the Hawaiian island of Maui. He lived with a retired hula dancer in a moderately priced apartment several blocks away from the beach. It was an unusual lifestyle for a man with a substantial interest in the rich Claymore field and whose company was locked in a life or death struggle to build a huge international pipeline project. Maybe he was content to leave the driving to Mark and simply rake in his share of the loot. If so, it had turned out to be a masterly strategy so far, Cliff grudgingly conceded. When Mark lucked into Claymore, the value of his partner's investment would have increased exponentially. But why was the guy living so simply, like some middle-aged widower with a modest pension?

And he had no track record whatsoever in the oil industry, at least as far as Cliff could discover. He seemed to have blown in from nowhere, fixed Mark up with a line of credit at the bank, and then faded into the background like a goddamn chameleon.

Cliff was about to unleash Antonelli's contacts on Kennedy to find out everything there was to know about the man when he checked himself. This was his type of hunting ground — Antonelli's thugs would be lost in the corporate jungle. Mark's company — dammit, he'd have to stop thinking about that bastard by his first name — anyway, Central Resources did its banking at the Tri-Province. He had to think for a moment before he remembered the name of the bank's headman — Tri-Province was a junior bank and Regal Pipelines had never done any business with it. Alf Hindle, that was the name. He'd give old Alf a call and set up a lunch.

The bank manager was almost bursting with self-importance as he followed the headwaiter across the crowded dining room. Having a one-on-one lunch at the Petroleum Club with Cliff Marsden was bound to enhance the bank's status in the city. The bank's board of directors had been ecstatic when they heard that Marsden had invited the head of their Alberta operations to lunch. What a coup it would be if the bank took over some of the Regal Pipelines accounts! They had even arranged a special meeting of the executive committee of the board for two o'clock so Hindle could brief them on what had transpired.

Alf cleared his throat nervously as he sat down across the table from his intimidating host. But Cliff was all solicitude as he filled in the bar and food chits. Alf played it safe by ordering a beer along with a steak sandwich, medium rare. He relaxed as the meal progressed and Cliff continued to exude charm, inquiring about Tri-Province's success in making inroads in the major banks' territory.

Alf sighed and put down his fork. "It hasn't been all that great, to be honest with you, Cliff." Marsden had insisted that the banker call him by his first name and Alf had used it at least a dozen times during the course of the meal. "The big customers — including Regal —" he added with an ingratiating grin, "don't seem to know we exist. I suppose it's a case of their getting whatever they need from the majors, so why look any farther?" He accepted a Havana from Cliff, and the hovering head waiter was immediately at his side, flicking a silver Ronson.

"Yeah, I can see how that could happen," Cliff commiserated. Satisfied that his cigar was burning evenly, he took a tentative puff and said musingly, "Still, you have made some progress. For instance, I know you have the Central Resources account."

"That's true." Alf was instantly on his guard. So that's what the lunch was about. Was Marsden going to ask the bank to call Hunter's loan?

"I understand Central's backer is somewhat of a man of mystery. Do you ever see this Garth Kennedy?"

Feeling as if the ground might give way underneath him at any moment, Alf swallowed and gingerly replied, "I only met him once. Back when the line of credit was being set up." Surely that much was okay, particularly since Marsden already knew the man's name.

"Nobody seems to know anything about the guy," Cliff persisted. "But I suppose his collateral was adequate?"

"It would have to be, wouldn't it?" replied Alf with a tight little smile. "I really can't say any more than that, Cliff. You know how it is with bankers and their clients — just like priests in the confessional."

"Of course. And let me say that I find your attitude very commendable. It's good to see a banker who respects his clients' confidentiality." Cliff pushed back his chair. "Still," he went on as they walked out of the dining room, "I am interested in finding out more about this Garth Kennedy. Think about it. There's no need to tell you that I would be extremely grateful — in a tangible way, of course — for anything you might be able to tell me. Such as," he added casually as they shrugged into their heavy coats, "the identity of Kennedy's mysterious backer."

"I'm afraid that would be going too far," Alf said primly.

So there was someone behind Kennedy! "Tell you what, Alf," said Cliff as they shook hands outside the club. "I'm going to have our pipeline division establish an operating account with your main branch, and we'll see what happens from there."

"Regal is going to set up an account with us!" Alf told his delighted directors. "It's only a small operating account, but it's a start."

"Congratulations, Alf," the chairman beamed. "I confess I am still a little puzzled as to why Marsden sought us out. Do you suppose he's blown so much money on this drilling program that the major banks are cutting back on his credit?"

"That's not it." Alf shook his head decisively. "He's after information. He made it abundantly clear that if I told him who Mark Hunter's real backer was we could expect a big slice of Regal's banking business."

"We couldn't do that," harrumphed Brian Gilbert, the vice-chairman of Tri-Province's board. "It would be highly unethical."

"That's precisely what I told Cliff." Alf could see that the others were impressed by his casual use of Marsden's first name.

"Well," said the chairman in a tone that indicated the discussion had come to an end, "since the two of you hit it off so well, maybe we can look forward to a substantial share of the Marsden business without compromising our integrity."

"There's a Mr. Gilbert here to see you, sir. He doesn't have an appointment and he says he can come back another time if it's inconvenient."

"No, it's okay. I'll see him." Cliff cast an appreciative eye at his shapely secretary as she exited. There was no point in speculating what Brian Gilbert wanted to see him about. Gilbert was a small-time independent operator who lived from deal to deal. His main claim to fame was that, for some unknown reason, the Tri-Province bank had elected him to its board. His interest suddenly quickened, Cliff sprang up from behind his desk to greet his visitor with a welcoming smile. Waving him to a seat, Cliff pressed one of his prized Havanas on his flattered guest.

"What can I do for you, Brian?" Marsden blew a perfect smoke ring and settled back in his chair.

"I understand there's a certain piece of information you'd like to have."

"Are you here on behalf of the bank, or on your own?"

"Strictly on my own, Cliff."

"I see. Well, it's true I would like to know the person who's backing Mark Hunter. I know it's not this Garth Kennedy."

"Kennedy's name is on the loan guarantee, but you're right, Cliff. He's just a man of straw."

"That much I had figured out already." Now Cliff remembered something else about Gilbert. It was rumoured he was a big player at the Las Vegas craps tables. "Are you going to tell me the name of the man behind him?"

"That's valuable information, Cliff."

"I agree. How valuable do you figure it is?"

"I had in mind $100,000." The words came out in a rush.

"That's a lot of money, Brian."

"Anything less wouldn't be any good to me. I'm into the Las Vegas mob for that amount and they don't offer discounts. I've got a week to come up with the cash or they say I'll spend the rest of my life in a wheelchair. It's a hundred grand or no deal, Cliff."

"How do you want it? Cash?"

"Yes." An audible sigh of relief escaped from Brian Gilbert's lips. "How soon can we do this deal, Cliff?"

"I should have the cash by tomorrow. I'll call you at your office and we'll arrange a meet." Spending so much time in Antonelli's company was affecting his vocabulary.

"D.R. Cullen? Are you positive? Why in hell would D.R. do a thing like that?"

"The way I hear it, he took a fancy to young Hunter. Thought he had the potential to be a real oil finder. He turned out to be one hundred per cent right on that score."

"We'll split up at the end of the block," Cliff said as they walked past the sandstone courthouse. "You turn right on 5th. And take this briefcase with you."

"Now we're getting somewhere!" Harrison Dobbs paused as if collecting his thoughts, then went on, "D.R. Cullen. Isn't he involved in some offshore drilling here in California?"

"He's the one."

Cliff wasn't surprised that Harrison knew about D.R.'s participation in the offshore drilling program. Despite its worldwide operations, the oil industry is a remarkably close-knit community and most of its top players are known to each other, even if only by reputation. Besides, as president of Norcal, Harrison would naturally have been following the progress of the drilling program. While the primary target was oil, there was always the chance that the wells would discover gas instead.

The long-distance line hummed quietly as Harrison pondered. "I assume that someone like Cullen would be difficult to make a deal with. He must have enormous resources behind him to be able to participate in the offshore play."

"The rumour here in Calgary is that he's badly overextended."

"Which means he may be vulnerable. Obviously this Cullen is the key to Claymore. Do you know him well enough to approach him, Cliff?"

"I know him all right. We grew up together. But I don't know how he'd react. He's an alcoholic, as you probably know, but he's got a reputation in the industry as being a high-principled son of a bitch." Cliff's voice was tinged with what might have been jealousy, or even regret. Then his innate cynicism reasserted itself as he added, "Depends on how bad he's strapped for cash, I suppose."

"It will probably come down to that, in the end," agreed Harrison. "And if I may say so, I speak from a wealth of experience." He sighed, as if disheartened by the venality of his fellow man. "Anyway, Cullen is our target. Concentrate on him. We are off to a very promising start, Cliff, and I congratulate you."

"Thanks," Cliff said laconically, adding just before he put down the phone, "By the way, Harrison, half of the hundred thousand I paid Gilbert will be deducted from your bonus."

20

The delegation from the Canadian Petroleum Association, Bill Crawford among them, were a few minutes early for their appointment with Cullen's two executive assistants. As they waited in the opulent reception area, they discussed the fine points of the brief they were working up for presentation to the federal government, seeking greater market penetration for western Canadian oil. Cullen's private secretary was typing furiously at her desk outside his closed office door, throwing the typewriter's carriage back with vicious force at the end of each line.

Suddenly the door was wrenched open, and a distraught looking blonde, holding her unbuttoned blouse with one hand and her skirt with the other, stumbled out. "There's something wrong with him," she wailed. "I think he's having some kind of attack."

The visiting oilmen looked at each other, then rushed past the terrified woman into Cullen's office. "Call an ambulance! On the double," Bill shouted over his shoulder at Cullen's secretary.

Don Cullen, his pants and boxer shorts down around his knees, was seated on a long leather couch. His face was ashen and beaded with sweat. "My chest," he croaked, his eyes filled with terror. "It hurts. I can't breathe."

"Take it easy, Don," Bill tried to calm him. "You're going to be okay. The ambulance is on its way. We better get you looking a little more respectable, though."

He and another man gently lifted Cullen a few inches off the couch while two others tugged his clothes back in place and zipped him up. All of them accompanied the stretcher down to street level and, as the ambulance pulled away, Bill turned to his companions. "There's no need for anyone to know what Cullen was doing when he had his attack."

They nodded solemnly, although Jeff Murphy's lips were twitching. Realizing that the story was too good to keep, but wanting to do what he could, Bill implored them once again to think of Cullen and his family and keep their lips zippered.

"That's what Cullen should have done with his fly," Murphy sniggered.

Despite Bill's pleas, the news of Cullen's heart attack and the titillating fact that he had been with a prostitute when it happened, swept through the oil patch in a matter of hours. Cliff Marsden was still at his office when he heard about it. It was Antonelli who told him. The Mafia trained thug was becoming almost a confidant.

"You'll get a charge out of this, boss," Joe said with a rumbling chuckle. "Your friend, D.R. Cullen, had himself a heart attack. In his office." Cliff, feeling all too mortal himself, frowned and started to interrupt. Joe held up a meaty hand. "Wait till you hear the rest of it. He had a broad — a pro — in there giving him a blow job when it happened."

Now Cliff laughed. Laughed so hard he had to remove his glasses to wipe his eyes. Old D.R. had outdone himself this time. His reputation was cinders anyway, but he would never live this down. If he lived. The laughter died in Cliff's throat. "Find out what hospital he's in," he ordered suddenly.

"I already know that," Joe replied. "They took him to the Holy Cross. You plan on sending flowers?"

"We were doing some business together. I need to see him."

"I don't know about that, boss. Ain't they supposed to keep them heart cases quiet?"

"I'll talk to his doctor. I'll tell him that Cullen will be stewing about this deal and it'll be better if I talk to him about it."

"Five minutes, Mr. Marsden. Not a moment longer." The nurse adjusted the screen that separated Cullen's bed from the rest of the intensive care ward and withdrew. Don Cullen, an intravenous tube inserted in his arm, gazed up at his visitor without enthusiasm.

"Sorry that you had this little scare, Don. But I know you'll be out of here in no time."

"I was in the office when it happened. Did you hear that?" Don's voice was a raspy whisper and his bloodshot eyes anxiously scanned Cliff's face.

"Yeah. We all work too hard, Don. We should learn to take some time off and smell the roses." Cliff's reply seemed to satisfy him and some of the strain went out of his face.

"Look, Don, we haven't much time, so I'll come right to the point. I know you're the one who's backing Mark Hunter's play." Cliff paused, then went on when Don said nothing. "I want to buy your interest, Don. Hear me out." Cliff brusquely waved aside Don's attempt to interrupt. "Everybody knows you want to drill another wild-cat off California. Right?"

"It'll vindicate me. Prove I've been right all along." Excitement strengthened Don's voice and he half-raised his head from the pillow. He gave a sharp gasp and let it fall back.

"Don't get over excited, Don, for God's sake." Cliff glanced uneasily over his shoulder at the screen, half expecting to see an irate nurse bearing down on him. "Your partners intend to shut the drilling program down. Right so far?" Cliff didn't wait for an answer but pressed on. "Suppose you had the funds to drill the well as an independent operation and put your partners on penalty. Would you do it?"

"Hell, yes." Beads of sweat were forming on Cullen's brow. "This well would be the payoff. Everything we've learned from the first four holes indicates there's an ocean of oil under that location."

"Maybe there's a way we can both realize our dreams, Don. You get to drill that well and I get to build me an international pipeline."

"I can't do it, Cliff. I can't cross Hunter up like that."

"But think of the well, Don ..." Cliff broke off as the nurse parted the screen and said, "Time's up, Mr. ... Oh, my God, he's coding!" Her finger stabbed a button and she began to thump the unconscious Cullen's chest.

A white-coated resident pulling an oxygen tank on a trolley hurried along the corridor as the chastened and somewhat frightened pipeline tycoon headed for the elevators. Maybe he could make a deal with Don estate.

Don survived the cardiac arrest, although it was a week before his vital signs stabilized enough for him to be released from intensive care, and another week before Cliff was allowed to visit him in his private room. Cliff used the interval of time to investigate the financial affairs of both Peerless Petroleum and Don Cullen personally. Both were teetering precariously on the verge of disaster.

In order to keep his California adventure alive, Cullen had given personal guarantees to the banks that would leave him a pauper if they were called. Cullen had not only bet the company on the California play, he had bet his personal fortune as well. As he analyzed the information he had gleaned from his extensive contacts in banking circles and the oil patch, Cliff marvelled at the lengths Cullen had gone to in order to maintain his reputation as an oil finder.

Don Cullen, wearing a silk bathrobe, was seated in a chair by the window. "Christ, Don, you look better than you have in years!" Cliff exclaimed in genuine astonishment.

"It's this damn hospital regime," Don responded with a wan smile. "You don't happen to have a flask on you, do you?"

"I'm sorry I don't. But I'll bring one next time. So we can drink to our deal."

"There isn't going to be a deal, Cliff. We've been through that."

"It's time you started to think about yourself, Don. And Bea." Cliff caught the flicker in Don's eyes at the mention of his wife. Don and his plastic duchess might not have much use for each other, but putting her financial security at risk must be weighing on his conscience.

"Here's what I'm prepared to do, Don. I want to see the paper that sets out your deal with Hunter and if it holds up, I'm prepared to pay you five million for it. That's a premium price — more than twice what your interest would be worth at the going rate of three cents per mcf in the ground. And that's not all. If the California well comes in dry, I'll purchase an annuity that will give you and Bea one hundred thousand a year for as long as either of you live. We'll have the lawyers fix it up so it's out of reach of your creditors."

"It's tempting, Cliff. Mighty tempting. But I just can't bring myself to shaft a guy like that."

"Your feelings do you credit, Don. But you've got to start thinking about yourself and your family. You've already had a warning that you're not going to live forever. And I know you're way out on a financial limb. Why don't you at least let me have a look at the paper?"

"That look should be worth something, Cliff. Say a hundred thousand. A cheque will be fine."

"You always were a tough negotiator." Cliff reached into an inside breast pocket for his cheque book. Feeling that he was at last making some progress in his war with Hunter, he wrote out the cheque and handed it to Cullen with something close to a flourish.

"Thanks, Cliff. I'll phone Miss Fraser and ask her to make you a copy. She'll call you when it's ready."

"Here's the way it shapes up," the lawyer said after reading the mimeographed document through a second time. "This Garth Kennedy has executed a declaration of trust in favour of D.R. Cullen covering Kennedy's interest in the agreement with Mark Hunter. That agreement is attached as an exhibit to the declaration of trust. The agreement between Kennedy and Hunter has a buy-sell clause that complicates things a bit."

"I already saw that. What about the declaration of trust? Could I buy that from Cullen without triggering that damn clause?"

"I'd want to look into it further, of course," the lawyer said cautiously. "But I think the answer is yes. I don't believe the buy-sell provision comes into play until you get to the agreement between Kennedy and Hunter."

"And under the declaration of trust, Kennedy has to do whatever Cullen tells him. Right?"

"Exactly. The document is perfectly clear on that point. Look at this clause."

Cliff frowned at the legalese. "In plain English, if I took over from Cullen, this guy Kennedy would have to do what I tell him?"

"Yes. Including, of course, the way he votes his shares in Central Resources."

"I trust that I don't have to remind you this is all strictly confidential?"

Looking slightly offended, the lawyer replied, "What is said between a solicitor and his client is always confidential, Cliff. Not to mention protected by privilege."

When Cliff left the law firm's offices he was determined to acquire Cullen's interest under the declaration of trust at any cost.

Once again Cliff was struck by the improvement in Don's appearance. He looked almost healthy.

"I've been thinking over what you said, Cliff. About having some responsibility to get my affairs in order. You're absolutely right. And I figure I don't owe Hunter anything."

"He owes you, Don. You're the reason he's where he is today."

"That's how I figure it, too. Okay, Cliff, she's yours for seven million and you can stick your damn annuity up your arse!"

"Seven million! Jesus Christ, Don, it's not worth anything like that!"

"It is to you. Anyway that's my price." The price of my soul, the unspoken thought flashed through Don's mind. "Take it or leave it."

"That heart attack sure as hell hasn't softened you up any." Cliff studied the oilman's face for a moment, then heaved a resigned sigh and pulled a folded paper from his pocket. "You win, Don. I had the lawyers draw up a little agreement. If we substitute," he paused and shook his head, "seven for five million and scratch out the business about the annuity, it'll do the job."

Don, half-moon glasses perched on the end of his bulbous nose, read the one-and-a-half page agreement carefully. "Short and sweet," he grunted and took Cliff's pen.

"How about a drink to celebrate?" asked Cliff as he tucked his copy of the agreement back in his pocket. "This time I did bring along a flask."

Don hesitated, then shrugged. "I guess I could use one at that." His expression was glum as he raised the glass and his thoughts were of Mark Hunter. Imagine having a son of a bitch like Cliff Marsden for a partner!

"I've got him. I've got Hunter by the balls!" Cliff crowed over the long-distance phone.

"Excellent. Things do seem to be falling into place for us," Harrison applauded. Having seen a copy of the declaration of trust, he was completely familiar with its contents. "Now we crank up our captive trustee and put him in play."

"It seems an awfully long flight for such a short visit, dear," Eleanor Marsden remarked mildly as the DC-7 droned over the Pacific.

"The break will do us good," Cliff assured her brusquely and went back to his perusal of *The Wall Street Journal.*

Almost as soon as they were installed in the palatial pinkness of the Royal Hawaiian, Cliff informed his wife that he was going to make a side trip over to Maui to look at some property he was thinking of investing in. "I'll leave in the morning and be back in time for dinner. You can get in some beach time while I'm gone. But not too much," he added jovially, "we don't want you burnt to a crisp."

Startled by this unwonted solicitude for her welfare, Eleanor smiled vaguely and said, "I'll be perfectly fine, dear. You just go ahead and do your business and don't worry about me."

Garth Kennedy was waiting in the shade of the thatched hut that served as a terminal when Cliff's chartered light Twin touched down. Kennedy had the appearance of a man contentedly going to seed — his broad face was smothered with freckles, and a loose-fitting aloha shirt allowed plenty of room for his expanding waistline. But his expression was anything but carefree. He had heard enough stories about this irascible and unpredictable man who was now his new boss to make him thoroughly uneasy. Even worse was the possibility that his comfortable sinecure might be coming to an end. Garth plastered a broad smile on his face, sucked in his gut as best he could, and held out his hand. Cliff looked as if he would have liked to ignore the gesture, but he finally shook hands after first surreptitiously wiping his own on his pant leg. It angered him that he was self-conscious about his sweaty palms even with someone like this buffoon.

At Cliff's curt suggestion, they walked along the edge of the deserted airstrip for their talk. To Garth's relief, there was no mention of his role being terminated. But it soon became clear that Cliff intended him to work for the monthly stipend he received. With growing dismay, the one-time actor heard Marsden say that he wanted him "on the scene," and was ordering him to return to Calgary. "It's probably best for you to stay at the Palliser. I'll pick up all your expenses, of course. You, Mr. Kennedy, are going to start taking an interest in your company. Now, here's what I have in mind ..."

Cliff arrived back in Honolulu at four o'clock that afternoon. With several hours to kill before he was due back at the hotel, he told the taxi driver to take him to the highest-priced brothel on the island. He might as well sample a dusky Polynesian maiden while he was in the islands.

21

"Mr. Kennedy is here to see you, Mark."

"Mr. Kennedy?" Mark gaped at his secretary, much more efficient and skilled than the one he had inherited from Kennedy Enterprises. "Garth Kennedy? Show him in."

Mark put on a show of enthusiasm as he greeted his partner, but in reality he was anything but pleased. He had become accustomed to calling all the shots for Central Resources without interference and Garth's unexpected arrival reminded him that this rather disreputable-looking individual owned fifty per cent of the voting shares. Garth had put on a lot of weight since Mark had last seen him, his suit jacket gaped open to expose a wide expanse of white shirt straining at its buttons.

"I thought nothing would ever pry you loose from that Polynesian paradise of yours," grinned Mark as they shook hands.

Garth, looking a little abashed, fiddled with his tie, loosely knotted around an unbuttoned collar. "There's such a thing as going too native, I guess. My conscience started to bother me, letting you do all the work while I lay around on the beach."

"Don't give it another thought," urged an alarmed Mark. "Everything's working out just fine the way it is."

"Well, I just don't feel right about it. Why don't you fix me up with an office and a secretary, and old Garth will roll up his sleeves and pitch right in."

"Okay, Garth, why don't we do that?" Mark agreed weakly. Maybe it was just a passing whim on Garth's part. With any luck he would soon realize there was nothing for him to do, and go back to the islands. But the next day Garth, looking somewhat more respectable in a new suit that accommodated his bulk, suggested he should have a title. Mark, knowing he had no choice, agreed and offered to make him vice president.

Garth demurred. "I was thinking more like chairman of the board," he said in his husky voice.

"Jes ... — well, okay. I guess that would be all right."

To Mark's increasing irritation, the new chairman of the board seemed to want to know everything about every aspect of the company. With a little deprecatory cough he bombarded Mark with questions. Despite his country bumpkin "aw shucks" approach, most of Garth's questions were very much to the point. So much so, in fact, that Mark began to wonder if somebody was coaching him. But who? And, more importantly, why?

Mark soon discovered that Garth's energy level dropped off sharply in the afternoon. It was Kennedy's custom to go back to the Palliser for lunch, where he would order up food from room service and wash it down with several belts of rum and Coke.

Mark was so concerned about having Garth on the premises that he was tempted to postpone a planned trip to San Francisco. But he had to keep the pressure on Dobbs who seemed to be in no hurry to close a deal. And it would be his last chance to see Jane before she started the run-up to her final exams. Their long-distance romance seemed to be progressing satisfactorily; he was pretty sure she was in love with him, although the subject of marriage was never mentioned. Nor had there been a repeat of the night she had gone down on him. They got into a lot of heavy breathing stuff but that was as far as it went. The incident lingered in the back of his mind as a troubling aberration on her part.

"Don't give the farm away when you're down there in California." Garth ambled into Mark's office as the latter was snapping shut the larger of his two briefcases. Mark looked at him sharply, trying to read his expression. But Garth's bland face wore its usual amiable grin. Mark shrugged, hefted the two briefcases, and started out the door. Garth detained him with a slight tug of his sleeve. "What I meant was that I wouldn't like to see you sign anything that was binding on the company, Mark."

Furious, Mark wheeled on him. "Listen up, Garth. If I could get Norcal on the dotted line, which I can't, I'd sign in a flash!"

Garth had taken a step backward into Mark's office. "All I meant was that there could be better deals that we should look at."

"There are no better deals. We'll talk this through when I get back."

Mark was still fuming as he drove to the airport. The last thing he needed was to have Kennedy trying to make like a high-powered executive. He could live with that he supposed, but the guy had a fifty per cent vote. Why hadn't he been content to stay in his little grass shack?

Mark debated with himself whether or not to tell Dobbs about the unexpected and unwelcome return of his prodigal partner. He had come to look upon Harrison Dobbs as being in some ways his business mentor and finally decided to unburden himself. Without going into details, and carefully avoiding any reference to Kennedy's doubts about the California market, he described to Dobbs how Kennedy had suddenly returned from his Hawaiian idyll and begun throwing his weight around.

Figuring he had nothing to lose, he added casually, "I sometimes wonder if Marsden isn't putting him up to it."

Harrison shook his head. "I very much doubt that." He looked thoughtfully at Mark, then said with a careful lack of emphasis, "I have reason to believe that Marsden has abandoned any plans to build the California pipeline."

"What? Say, that's great!" A jubilant Mark exclaimed, but his initial enthusiasm quickly evaporated when he saw the enigmatic look on Harrison's face.

"I feel I should remind you, Mark, that while Marsden's removal does clear the way for you, the project itself is still far from certain. The authorities keep reminding me that domestic gas is the preferred alternative."

"Yes, but where are you going to get this domestic gas?"

"As to that, we shall have to wait and see." Harrison's expression was inscrutable.

Despite Harrison's caution, Mark's mood was upbeat as he sped along the highway to Stanford. Marsden was out of the picture! He could scarcely believe it, yet it made sense. Marsden had utterly failed in his attempt to assemble a supply of gas to feed the pipeline. Building the pipeline had become an all-engrossing challenge to Mark. Even more challenging than the search for oil. Making all the pieces fit and convincing people that the project was viable was turning out to be a great deal more exciting than sticking pins in a geological map. And once the pipeline was in place, it would profoundly affect and shape the development of the oil and gas industry in Western Canada. Not to mention the impact it would have on California, where an assured source of supply would allow that golden state to continue its uninhibited growth. Heady stuff, indeed!

Lately, Mark had begun to approach a date with Jane with considerable trepidation. There were depths and facets to her personality that kept him off-balance. He could never be accused of taking her for granted, he told himself with a wry grin. Tonight, he had the sinking feeling that they were strangers from two different worlds. She looked very fetching in her powder-blue sweater and matching hairband, but she also looked, Mark realized with an increasing sense of despondency, every inch the typical co-ed. Nor did it help that the pressure of the upcoming exams made her somewhat distraught and abstracted.

As they said goodnight, Mark tried to reclaim her attention by holding her close and kissing her roughly on the mouth. She responded at first but as his tongue tried to part her lips, she shook her head and looked up at him with that troubled expression that always reminded him of a small child. Wordlessly, he dropped his arms and released her.

"How did things go in Frisco?" Trust Garth not to know that the residents of San Francisco detested the diminutive.

"So, so. The Norcal people are playing it cool."

"They're playing you for a sucker, that's what they're doing. Using Canadian gas to get a better price from the American producers." Garth settled himself in a chair across from Mark's desk and lit a cigar, scratching a kitchen match with his thumbnail. Mark was, for all practical purposes, a non-smoker and the acrid smoke made his eyes burn.

"What American producers? There isn't a spare cubic foot of gas in the entire US That's why Norcal needs us."

Garth waved this aside with a dismissive gesture of a freckled hand. "Hell, them producers can move gas around like they was a pack of magicians. 'Displacement' they call it. I'll supply your contract in California and you supply mine in Oklahoma. By the time they've finished nobody can tell how much gas there really is underneath all the hocus pocus."

Where was he getting this stuff? Anyway, Kennedy was absolutely correct that producers played games with their gas reserves. There were times when it was like the Lord with the loaves and fishes. "What you say is true enough," he agreed. "But Norcal needs gas that their customers can use to heat their homes, not just figures in a reserves estimate."

Garth was unconvinced. "If you think them good ol' boy producers are going to let a market like that get away from them, you're dreaming. And you're also kidding yourself if you think the Canadian government is going to roll over and let all that gas out of the country."

This was worse than Mark had thought. Up until now, he had assumed that Kennedy, however reluctantly, would ultimately go along with what Mark wanted. But what if he got stubborn and dug his heels in?

"Where are you going with all this, Garth?"

"I just don't think you should put all your eggs in the California basket, that's all. Why don't you talk to the boys who are building the TransCanada pipeline? That line will be finished long before your project gets off the drawing board and you won't need the government's okay to export the gas."

Kennedy seemed to be remarkably well-informed, especially for someone who once professed to have only a passing interest in the oil business. Mark leaned back in his swivel chair and patiently explained that TransCanada had already contracted all the gas they need. "And their price is nowhere near as attractive as what we can get from California," he added.

"There you go again, Mark. Making like California was a sure thing, when it ain't. I think you should be looking for a market closer to home."

After Garth left for his liquid lunch, Mark softly pounded his fist on the desk in frustration. To have Marsden out of the picture, and then to be thwarted by a stubborn and misinformed partner. It wasn't going to happen, by God. He wouldn't let it!

"My silent partner has suddenly found his voice."

"And I gather you don't much care for the song he's singing," smiled Chester Martin.

"He's been dropping some pretty broad hints that he might try and scuttle the California project." Mark hitched his chair closer to the lawyer's desk. "What happens if push comes to shove?"

"Stalemate. The classic corporate nightmare."

"That's what I was afraid of. That's why he was so insistent on that buy-sell clause. There are times when that guy is a lot more savvy than he looks."

"Are you thinking of putting your shares to him?"

"Explain to me once again how that works. You called it a shotgun, I remember."

"That's just what it is. A shotgun to your partner's head. You can offer to sell your shares to Kennedy for a specified price. Then he has the option — for sixty days in your agreement, if I remember correctly — to either buy your shares or sell you his for the same price."

"So I can force him to sell me the shares, is that it?"

"Not necessarily. Don't forget it works both ways so there's always the danger that he might buy you out."

"Christ! Talk about being between a rock and a hard place! Got any advice for me, counsellor?"

"Well, it wouldn't do any harm to position yourself so you could make a move if you had to. For example, you should figure out what his shares are worth and line up the necessary financing. What kind of money are we talking about, by the way?"

"Ballparking it: $3-million. But if I put my shares to him at that price, he'd probably grab them and run." Mark frowned. "It's like a life-and-death game of poker. And I never did like card games. Well," he pushed back his chair and got to his feet. "I guess I better talk to some friendly bankers."

But the bankers turned out to be a lot less friendly than Mark had anticipated. He decided against approaching Tri-Province, the company's own bank, and instead concentrated on three of the leading national institutions. He quickly learned that gas in the ground, unconnected to a pipeline and not under contract, was almost worthless as collateral for a loan. The revelation shook Mark, who had grown accustomed to thinking of himself as a wealthy man. Fortunately, the company's few producing oil wells generated enough revenue to meet expenses, including Mark's relatively modest salary. Still it was a shock to discover that Claymore, despite its enormous reserves of natural gas, would be almost totally discounted by the financial world until the gas was connected to a market and sold.

Returning to his office after a particularly discouraging session with a banker who still thought of gas as a nuisance rather than a valuable asset, Mark's spirit lifted when he saw the handwritten envelope on top of his morning mail. The California postmark confirmed that it was from Jane — the first letter he had ever received from her! He picked up the letter opener and carefully, almost reverently, slit the envelope.

Although the results wouldn't be known for two weeks yet, she felt good about her exams. Mark smiled to himself, it would be A+s across the board. Anything less would not satisfy her obsessive drive to excel. His smile turned to a frown as he read on. She was going to stay on at Stanford to help Professor Andrews with some research. Mark had met Professor Andrews briefly during one of his visits and hadn't liked what he saw. The guy was older — he looked to be somewhere in his mid-forties — but he was handsome in a distinguished sort of way that went with the pipe and the tweed jacket with leather elbow patches. He was far too old for her, of course, but it was painfully obvious that his interest in Jane went beyond the purely professorial.

Damn, damn, damn! In six weeks time the summer would be practically over. And he had had such plans. He had been taking riding lessons and, under Sue's tutelage, had become reasonably proficient. He had meant it as a surprise for Jane, but as the lessons progressed and his confidence increased, he found himself enjoying the sport for its own sake. Hell, with the way Jane was dragging her feet about coming home, he would be Olympic calibre by the time she finally did arrive. He winced at a sudden mental picture of Jane and the distinguished professor with their heads close together as they researched some obscure point. Did economics have obscure points? Hell, it was all obscure! Not for the first time, he felt a certain resentment that he was always the one who stood around waiting until it was convenient for her to see him.

He was still holding Jane's letter when he became aware of Garth standing in front of his desk with a thick accordion file in his hands. "You okay, Mark?"

Mark blinked. "I'm fine. What is it? I'm kinda busy."

"Well, this is kinda important. I've looked into it pretty damn carefully and I agree with you that California is the only market that can take our gas at the present time."

"Well, hallelujah! Now we can get on with it!"

"You weren't listening, Mark. Remember I said 'at the present time.' Lookee here." He began to unpack the file and spread the materials on Mark's desk. At first Mark tried to ignore them, but his interest was caught when he saw that for the most part they consisted of reports by consultants with detailed price projections for natural gas. Impressed in spite of himself, Mark asked how in the world Garth had managed to assemble the material.

"Oh, I have my sources," he replied vaguely while he unfolded a sheet of paper covered with numbers. "Here's the bottom line. I had a consultant take an average of seven price forecasts and do a present worth calculation comparing selling the gas two years from now at sixteen cents per mcf, which is your California case, versus leaving it in the ground for six years and selling it at the higher prices that would prevail then."

Garth sounded as if he were repeating words he had memorized, but he seemed to fully grasp the points he was making. The guy either had a lot more oil industry experience than he let on, or he was a quick study with a very good teacher. His voice rang with confidence as his thick finger jabbed at the summary sheet.

"These two columns over here prove that we'd be better off to leave Claymore shut-in for at least six years instead of trying to sell it now. And there's no production within miles of Claymore so it's not as if we're being drained."

Exasperated, Mark exploded, "If you think I'm going to leave that gas in the ground and let someone else grab that California market, you better think again. Look, Garth," he went on in a calmer tone, "in the first place, there's absolutely no guarantee that those prices will be realized — you know what they say about forecasts: the only thing certain about them is that they'll be wrong. Hell, there may not even be a market for new volumes of gas at any price. And we need the revenue from Claymore to build the company and we need it now."

Garth didn't seem to have heard him. He was still peering down at the present worth calculations. "These numbers tell us there's no need to panic about selling the gas, Mark. There's no need for you to be busting your ass while we'd be better off just sitting on our hands."

"Jesus Christ!" A furious Mark got up from behind his desk and stormed out of the office. He had to go somewhere and cool off or he'd end up punching his partner's fatuous face. He gunned the Olds out of the gravelled parking lot with no firm idea where he was headed but quickly decided to go home and change into his riding clothes. A long ride in the country should help him sort things out.

"Things are dead quiet around here today. You want some company?" Sue stood in the doorway of the stable, the bright sunlight revealing a scattering of light freckles across the bridge of her snub nose."

"Sure." Mark would have preferred being alone to do some hard thinking but there was no way he was going to hurt Sue's feelings by turning her down.

Her ponytail bounced as she cantered along the trail ahead of Mark, her trim bottom glued to the saddle. Although it was still only late spring, the day had a feeling of high summer about it. A hot sun blazed down upon the green and golden countryside from an immaculate blue sky. White-faced Herefords looked up from their grazing to gaze with mild, incurious eyes at the two horses loping past. Sue twisted around in the saddle to smile back at Mark, her small breasts pressing against the thin fabric of her shirt. He could feel his arousal stirring.

They stopped to rest the horses in a small clearing inside an aspen grove. Mark kept his back to Sue as he looped the reins around a slender tree trunk but when he straightened up he saw her looking directly at him. Her eyes widened as she saw the bulge in his blue jeans and she smiled mischievously. "Is that for me?"

Then her smile faded and she ran to him with an inarticulate cry, lightly touching his erection. The scrubbed face looked up at him imploringly and she moaned as her muscular little body rubbed against his. "Oh, Mark, I want you! Take me, please. Oh, please. Oh, God, yes!" she shrieked as his hand pressed against her pelvis.

Her shrieks increased as he entered her and then mounted to a wild, groaning crescendo while she writhed ecstatically under him. He quickened his tempo as she began to pant, "I'm coming, Mark! I'm coming! Oh, God!" She gave a full throated, uninhibited yell as they climaxed together.

"I'm sorry I made so much noise, Mark. I just couldn't help myself." Sue plucked a blade of dead grass from her hair and smiled shyly over at him.

"Don't apologize for God's sake! It was incredible. Although there were times when I was afraid we were going to spook the horses!" A shaken Mark realized that he had just experienced the most physically intense sex of his entire life.

"I don't want you feeling guilty about it." Sue rolled over on her side, into a patch of sunlight that made the drops of moisture on her golden pubic hair glitter like diamonds. "It just happened, that's all. I know you're in love with Jane Marsden."

Mark looked at that small, naked body ridged with sharply etched muscles, and knew he simply would not have the willpower to walk away from this incredible sex machine. He got to his feet and began to brush off his shirt.

"Sue?"

She paused in the act of pulling on her jeans and looked up. "Yes, Mark?"

"I want to see you again."

She tucked her shirt into her waistband and lifted her face to be kissed. "Whatever you want, Mark."

22

Garth Kennedy's look was reproachful but Mark was sure he could also detect more than a hint of alarm. "Don't even joke about something like that, boy. You and me is partners."

"I wasn't joking, Garth. You said yourself right at the start that this was what the buy-sell clause was for — to provide an escape hatch when the owners reached an impasse."

"We ain't reached no what-you-call it. We're both trying to do the right thing for the company."

"But we don't agree on what the right thing is. Unless you're coming around to my view that California is the way to go?"

Garth shook his head stubbornly. "No, sir. But that don't matter. You haven't had a peep out of Norcal for weeks, have you?"

"They'll come round," replied Mark with more conviction than he felt. "They need us."

"If they need us so bad, how come they're not knocking our door down?" With this parting shot, Garth stalked out of the office, leaving an elated yet frustrated Mark. Elated because he sensed that the last thing Garth wanted was to have the shares put to him, and frustrated because he didn't have the financial resources to take advantage of the situation.

With so much depending on one stalled project, there was little for Mark to do at the office. He managed to fill in the mornings by studying the drilling reports of two potential oil wells Central was participating in, and by making a few phone calls, but by early afternoon, he was pacing restlessly up and down his office and staring out at the mountains sharply etched on a canvas of blue sky. Borden's stables were out there in the sprawling foothills. Mark stood stock-still for a moment, then spun on his heel and walked rapidly out of the office, not giving himself time to think.

Sue was out with a trail ride, but the manager said they were due back in half an hour. Mark saddled the gelding he usually rode and practised changing leads in the ring. Six riders suddenly appeared on the brow of the hill behind the stables, looking like a posse out of the Old West as they began to descend with Sue in the lead, their hooves stirring up little puffs of dust. She raised her hand in a half-salute as they trooped past the ring in single file.

She hurried over to the ring as soon as the horses were unsaddled and turned loose in a corral. Mark, his throat dry from something more than the dust said, "It was too nice a day to stay in the office. Are you finished for the day, or do you have some more rides to take out?"

"That was my last group. I'll get me a fresh horse."

This time she took a path that led down to a small creek. They forded the shallow stream and walked along an overgrown path that led deeper into the woods, pushing back overhanging branches as they rode. The path angled across a narrow neck of land and came out where the creek doubled back on itself. A dilapidated shack that had once been the clubhouse of an archery club leaned precariously above the bank. A pair of phoebes with a nest on one of the rafters flew distractedly above their heads, shrilling their distinctive cries.

As soon as they had tethered the horses, Sue was in his arms, her hand reaching for his tumescent crotch. The sagging floorboards creaked alarmingly under their feet as she led him into the shack, carpeted with bird droppings. The male phoebe nearly parted Mark's hair as it darted past and flew out a broken window. It perched on a stump just outside the shack, pumping its tail as it scolded the intruders.

"Jesus, Sue." Mark looked around in consternation. But she had taken a key from her jeans pocket and was unlocking a padlock on the far wall. She had to push against it with all her strength but the door opened with a screech of protesting wood. Cretonne curtains had been tacked over the single window whose glass was miraculously unbroken, and the room was furnished with a sofa, end tables and two armchairs. The upholstery was faded but clean.

Three engraved gold and silver belt buckles hung on the wall next to a mirror. Sue saw him eyeing them and pressed herself against him, her hands busy. He unbuttoned her blouse, driven half-wild by the thought of how she would writhe and scream underneath him. Their bodies were slick with sweat in the stuffy little room as they strained toward a climax, her breath coming in great panting gusts and her vagina clamping around him in convulsive spasms.

"The inside of my mouth is so dry I can hardly talk," she croaked as, their passion spent, they lay together on the couch.

"You make love like nobody else in the whole wide world."

She smiled, a little shyly. "I just let it happen, I guess."

What the hell did he think he was playing at? Mark's thoughts were turbulent as he drove back into town. He was in love with Jane and wanted to marry her. Right? He was surprised at how long that one hung in the air before the answer came back. It was yes, but with the troubling and ever-present realization that Jane meant a great deal more to him than he did to her. How would that work out in the long run? Would he not grow restive with having to always adjust to her moods, to having her make decisions without any regard as to how he might feel? When they last talked on the phone two nights ago, she had coolly informed him that the research was going slower than expected and that she would probably stay on campus for an additional two weeks. He felt badly let down, but he had no choice other than to accept it. She wouldn't have paid any attention if he had kicked up a fuss.

Mark was too honest with himself to use this as an excuse for the way he was carrying on with Sue. He was screwing her because she was an incredible piece of ass. Pure sex. Those belt buckles were kind of off-putting, though. He knew what they were — championship buckles awarded to rodeo cowboys. It wasn't too hard to guess how Sue had won those trophies. Did he care? Not really, but it did tend to cool a guy's ardour.

Mark's lips tightened in an involuntary grimace as he was assailed with yet another mental image — this time Jane and the professor were working side-by-side in a cool and lofty library, exchanging smiles of scholastic satisfaction as they uncovered another academic clue. His imagination was working overtime these days — conjuring up cozy little vignettes of Jane and her damn professor together. Always together. Why didn't she come home? A feeling, almost a premonition, that his life was spinning out of control came over Mark.

"It's time for the next move in our little game," Harrison said.

"We must make Hunter put his shares to Kennedy. It's essential that Hunter be the one to take the initiative."

"I know that, for Christ's sake!" Cliff snarled into the mouthpiece. "Do you think I don't know how the damn agreement works? One guy offers to sell his shares at a price and the other party has sixty days to either buy them or sell his own shares at the same price."

"Exactly. There's no call to be upset with me, Cliff. I was merely thinking out loud for my own benefit. If you agree, I propose to bait the trap for our young friend."

"Do that." Still fuming, Cliff hung up. He bitterly resented Dobbs' patronizing attitude, but the patrician executive's co-operation was essential to the defeat of Hunter. So what if it was Dobbs's Machiavellian mind that had devised the master plan. The final victory would belong to Cliff Marsden.

"Mr. Dobbs is on the line, Mark." As he reached for the phone Mark was struck, almost in passing, with how many significant events in a businessman's life began with his secretary telling him that so-and-so was calling.

Dobbs was uncharacteristically direct. "It's time we put the project on the front burner, Mark. How soon can you get down here for a meeting?"

"As soon as I can arrange a flight."

"Good. Let me know when you'll be arriving."

It was mid-afternoon and Garth had his feet up on his desk and seemed to be dozing. He came to attention, however, when Mark told him Dobbs had called and seemed ready to deal.

"You can talk to him, Mark, but no deal," he said, lowering his feet to the floor.

"For Christ's sake, Garth!" swore an exasperated Mark, "why don't you admit this is a fantastic opportunity?"

"At twenty cents per mcf I'll admit it. Not at sixteen."

Dobbs was finally saying exactly what Mark had longed to hear for all those months. While his manager of supply, George MacGregor, nodded his head in emphatic agreement, the president of Norcal was candidly admitting that, after an extensive search, they had been unable to come up with a domestic gas supply that would meet their requirements. "I have discussed this informally with the chairman of the Utilities Commission and he agrees that we have no option. He is still balking at the price but I'm sure he will come around in the end." He paused and looked expectantly at Mark.

"We have ourselves a problem, gentlemen," Mark announced gloomily.

"What do you mean?" demanded Harrison with pretended concern. "You haven't sold the gas to someone else, have you?"

"Nothing like that. It's just that my partner — my equal partner — I told you about him if you remember." Harrison nodded, and Mark continued, "Well, he doesn't think this is the way to go. My lawyer tells me that without his approval, I can't commit the company."

"We need that gas, Mark."

"Can you pay twenty cents and mcf for it?"

"Good God, no!" Harrison and his gas supply manager exchanged a look that was almost despairing. "Look, Mark, there simply has to be a way around this. Can't you make this partner of yours see reason?"

"God knows I've tried," Mark replied absently while a lightbulb went on in his head. If Norcal were this desperate for gas, maybe they would finance a buy-out of Kennedy's interest. Compared to the overall cost of the project the few millions it would take were almost insignificant.

"I do have a buy-sell arrangement with my partner," he said slowly.

"Now we're getting somewhere!" breathed Harrison. "How does it work? I mean, is it a right of first refusal or what?"

"It's the shotgun type."

"Then it's simple! All you have to do is pull the trigger."

"I'm afraid it's not that simple. In the first place I don't have the funds to purchase his shares, and of course there's always the danger that he will decide to buy me out."

"H'mm. I was overlooking that possibility. Do you think there's a real risk of him doing that?"

"Depends on the price, I suppose. And how deep his purse is. As I very quickly found out, the banks aren't prepared to lend money on the security of the shares alone." Mark paused. "For what it's worth, I got the impression that he definitely does not want my shares put to him."

"So you've been looking into this already. What kind of money are we talking about, Mark?"

"Somewhere in the three to four million range, although I sure wouldn't want to sell my shares for that."

"I see. And you can't raise the money yourself, I take it?"

"That's right. But Norcal could always lend it to me."

Harrison smiled and ran his finger along the blade of his letter opener. "I must admit the same thought has been running through my mind. It would have to be approved by my board of directors, of course, and the legal department will want to check out your agreement with your partner. Do you have a copy with you?"

"No. I'll have to have it sent down. Why don't I have my attorney bring it down? That way he'll be on the spot to act for me if we're able to put together a deal."

"Splendid idea. And we'll pick up the tab."

Chester Martin readily agreed to fly down to San Francisco with the agreement. "When you think about it," he said over the phone, "the whole deal makes a lot of sense from everyone's point of view. You get rid of an unco-operative partner and Norcal gets the gas."

As lately had become almost the rule, the excitement of seeing Jane was mixed with an ill-defined unease. Mark slowed the rented convertible almost to a crawl as he drove through the campus. Jane had told him how to get to the residence, kept open for summer students and holdovers like herself, where she was now staying. She was waiting for him and climbed into the car as soon as he drove up and told him to keep on going.

"Hey, don't I get a kiss?" he protested.

She smiled, although to his anxious eye it seemed a little forced. "Wait till we get off the grounds."

Mark turned off at the first side road and leaned across the seat to kiss her. She kept it cool and brief. "My father knows we've been seeing each other. I think he's had us followed. Or rather, I think he's having you followed," she said when they drew apart.

A tingle of fear ran up Mark's spine. "Christ. Are you sure?"

"About being followed? Not absolutely, although from what he said I think we are." To a horrified Mark, she seemed impossibly calm and matter-of-fact. "I am sure about Daddy knowing. He created a horrible scene the day after my graduation." She shivered. "It was frightening. I have never seen him worked up quite like that before."

"You must have stood up to him, since we're here." Mark stole an uneasy glance over his shoulder but the road behind them was clear.

"I did. It was the hardest thing I've ever done in my life. And ..." she hesitated, then said in a rush, "and I told him that if anything happened to you he'd never see me again."

What it must have cost her to finally admit to herself that her father was capable of such action. He squeezed her hand and climbed out to unsnap the cover of the convertible top. He would feel a little less vulnerable with it up.

He drove her back to the residence a little after midnight. "Now that you've found out you can stand up to your father," he said as he switched off the ignition, "why don't we tell him that we're going to get married?"

Jane busied herself with the cigarette lighter. "Let's see how things work out this summer." The smoke from her cigarette curled along the windshield and out a side vent.

"It's summer already," replied Mark as lightly as he could manage. "By the way, when are you coming home?"

"Pretty soon. Another week or so."

"How are you and Professor what's his name getting along?"

"Fine. And his name is Norman Andrews, as you know perfectly well."

"Does he have a family?"

"He and his wife are separated."

Jesus. It was even worse than he had imagined. "Do you ever go out with him?"

"We have dinner together sometimes when we're working. Nothing for you to get excited over."

"I'm not getting excited," lied Mark. "Hell, the guy's old enough to be your father!"

"What's that got to do with anything? Age is all in your mind." Christ. It sounded like she was quoting the guy. Mark's heart sank further when she added, "He thinks I should come back next year for post-graduate work."

She saw the look on his face and touched his cheeks with her fingertips. "I'm sorry, Mark. I've been miserable to you tonight, but I'm sort of mixed up. Will I see you before you go back to Calgary?"

"Of course. But it won't be tomorrow night. Chester Martin is coming down and we've got work to do."

"The lawyer? Does that mean you and Norcal have got a deal?"

"Well, we're making progress. Clearing away some of the underbrush at least."

"Daddy's not going to like that one little bit, but I think it's wonderful." She kissed him quickly and slipped out the passenger door.

So Cliff hadn't bothered to tell his daughter that he had abandoned the California project. Still, there was no reason why he should. It was not the sort of thing you had to go public with. Jane had been in one of her strange, abstracted moods tonight. If only she felt as sure as he did that they were right for each other. But she didn't. But sometimes she did. Or seemed to. He hated the thought of her spending all that time with that Andrews character. Despite what Jane said, the guy was old enough to be her father. But that didn't help. Lots of women fell for the father figure. With a father like Cliff Marsden, you couldn't blame a girl for looking for a substitute father image. Mark was grinning in spite of himself as he turned into the hotel's underground parkade. But the fact was that Jane really loved that obnoxious father of hers.

"I have a problem with the wording of this clause," Chester Martin put down the sheet of paper and glanced over at the attorney from Norcal's legal department. "It seems to commit Mark to offer to sell his shares to Kennedy. I'm sure that was never the intent."

The attorney looked at Dobbs who gave an almost imperceptible nod of assent. "That's my fault. I drafted it that way because I thought that was the deal."

Chester scribbled something on a yellow note pad, ripped off the page and handed it to his counterpart. "This should do the job. It provides that if Mark decides to put his shares, and if Kennedy tenders his, Norcal will provide the necessary financing up to $5-million. Anything over that amount will require the express approval of Norcal."

The Norcal attorney quickly scanned the brief paragraph. "Beautifully clear and to the point. We'll insert it just the way it is." He looked first at his boss and then at Mark. "We still have to fix a time limit for Norcal's obligation to provide the financing. Any ideas, gentlemen?"

"We don't have a lot of time to play with. California needs this gas," Harrison murmured.

"Why don't we work backwards from our time frame for the pipeline project," suggested Mark. "If we're to get the line built in time to meet your requirements, we'll need to have firm contracts for the gas supply signed by not later than the end of September. Right?"

Harrison did a little mental arithmetic, then nodded agreement.

"Okay," continued Mark, "that means we'll have to get Kennedy out of the picture by mid-September at the latest. There's a sixty-day fuse on the buy-sell. So I'll have to give Kennedy notice not later than mid-July, or a little more than a month from now." He looked at Chester. "Where does that leave us?"

"Why don't we terminate Norcal's obligation if Kennedy hasn't tendered his shares for purchase by, say, September 30th, 1957?"

There was a general murmur of assent and the meeting broke up, with the two lawyers going off together to put the agreement in final form.

"I love you, Mark, but I'm not at all sure I'm ready for marriage. I'm thinking very seriously about taking a post-graduate degree in economics. I really dig that stuff."

"I think you should go ahead, if you feel that way. But there's no reason why you can't do that and be married at the same time. If things work out the way I think they will, I'll be practically living in San Francisco for the next couple of years."

"Your deal with Norcal must be really coming along?"

"It's so close, I can almost taste it."

"If Dad knew that, he'd have a fit."

Mark was tempted to tell her that her father had given up, but that was not something she should hear from him. He shrugged and said, "He's dead in the water and he knows it. He hasn't got enough gas to light the kitchen stove."

Jane frowned. "Don't ever make the mistake of underestimating my father, Mark."

"I'm not. But, realistically, there's nothing he can do."

With something close to terror, Norman Andrews looked down at Jane. The moon had retreated behind a wisp of cloud and her face, upraised to his as she said good night, was unbearably beautiful in its soft light. With a groan, knowing he was in danger of making a fool of himself but unable to stop, he bent down and kissed her. Her lips were cool and passive, but he was astonished to feel her fingers reaching for his crotch. Startled, he took an involuntary step backward, letting his hands drop to his sides. She blinked, gave a tiny shake of her head as if to clear it, whispered "I'm sorry, Norman. Good night," and ran into the residence.

The badly shaken professor stood rooted to the sidewalk, scarcely believing what had happened. The Jane Marsden he had worked with so closely and — he finally admitted it to himself — had fallen in love with, had suddenly, shockingly, stepped out of character. The face that looked up at him as he took her in his arms had somehow changed from the poised, supremely intelligent young student he thought he knew. What was that look? It came to him that it was the closed, almost blind, look of someone who is doing what is expected of her. Almost like an automaton. He shivered and began to walk. There would be no sleep for him tonight.

The next afternoon she came to his office with her research all neatly summarized and typed, and told him she would be driving back to Calgary in the morning.

23

Mark gingerly picked his way through the crowd of Indians, most of them on horse-back, milling around the entrance to the Palliser. Cameras clicked furiously as tourists, carefully stepping around the lumps of horse manure that littered the street and sidewalk, recorded the colourful scene. In keeping with Stampede Week, the lobby had gone Western — featuring a chuckwagon surrounded with straw bales and fake rail fences lining the walls. Next to the entrance of the Rimrock Room a Western band swung into a toe-tapping number.

An elevator door slid open to disgorge a pathetic trio. Two men, the older one with a weary, resigned look on his face, struggled to keep D.R. Cullen upright as they made their way across the lobby. Mark recognized the older man as Peerless's chief pilot whose job description should have included acting as a nursemaid to his boss. Dave Green, whom Mark was meeting for lunch, came up to stand beside him as the sad little group lurched past. Cullen seemed to recognize Mark for he raised his hand in what could have been a wave.

"That poor bastard," Dave Green muttered as they watched the two men strug-gling to get Cullen through the revolving door. Jack, the millionaire doorman, rushed over to unsnap the panels and fold them back so that they could maneuver Cullen through sideways.

Like everyone else in sight, including the doorman, both Mark and Dave were dressed in Western attire, although Dave's outfit was much more elaborate than Mark's jeans and Western shirt. Dave had decked himself out as a Mississippi river-boat gambler, complete with striped pants, black jacket and string tie.

"Old D.R. seemed to recognize you, which is pretty remarkable when you consider the state he was in," observed Dave after an overweight waitress, dressed in a shiny black cowgirl's costume, had shown them to a table. "He looked a little ashamed to be seen like that."

"He shouldn't be drinking, not with his heart condition."

"Maybe he can't stand the suspense. He went independent on that offshore California well, you know."

"I heard that. The big boys said no thanks, but he went ahead anyway. He's got balls, you have to give him that."

They hurried through their lunch and skipped coffee. Today was a half-holiday to let the citizens of Calgary take in the Stampede. That morning Dave had gone down to the Stampede grounds to line up for tickets that were put on sale daily for the infield bleachers.

The wild-cow milking was underway by the time Mark and Dave found their seats. This was an event that required more foolhardiness and brawn than skill, and was shunned by the regular cowboy contestants. The stars of the more glamorous bronc and bull-riding events tried to relax in the aisle behind the chutes as they waited their turn. A number of the cowboys were surrounded by their own court of rodeo groupies — lithe young girls clad in bottom-hugging jeans. The cowboys called them "buckle bunnies" since they all lusted after the silver and gold buckles that most of the major rodeos awarded to the champions of each event. The Stampede awarded the much coveted Charlie Beil sculptures instead of buckles, but any cowboy who wanted to make out in Calgary would have the foresight to pack a buckle or two along with his rodeo gear. With an unpleasant start, Mark realized that the girl with the whipcord body, whose finger was hooked under a cowboy's belt buckle while she gazed up at him with that look of naked hunger, was Sue. The cowboy laughed at something she said and cupped a hand around her tight little buttocks.

"Ol' Barry's having himself a bang-up Stampede." The voice, a lazy, Texas drawl, came from the row of seats immediately behind Mark. "Wins the saddle bronc go-round and gets fucked to death by the lil' ridin' instructor."

"Last year she took on Marty Quinn." The second voice was high-pitched with a built-in snicker. "Screwed him right into the ground. The poor sucker ain't won an event since."

"They say she really goes ape with a hot cock inside her. All a guy has to do is stay aboard."

Ears burning, Mark stole a quick glance over his shoulder. The two cowboys wore numbers pinned to their shirts, identifying them as rodeo contestants.

Dave had also been eavesdropping with awestruck intensity. "Sounds like the kind of girl we should add to our invitation list. She would sure as hell liven up a party. I wonder which one is her?"

Mark, who could have told him, merely shrugged. But Dave was not to be defeated. He studied the printed program, looking for a saddle bronc contestant named Barry. There was only one — Barry Newsome, contestant number 146. The cowboy standing beside Sue had 146 pinned to the back and front of his shirt. "There she is." He pointed her out to Mark. "The one that looks like a goddamn gymnast. I'm getting a hard-on just thinking about what it'd be like."

The loudspeaker blared an announcement about the upcoming saddle bronc event and Barry bent down to pick up his saddle. As he turned away, Sue let her finger tips trail across his crotch.

"Did you see that?" breathed Dave. "Why don't we mosey down and chat her up while her boyfriend does his thing with the broncs?"

Depressed, Mark shook his head. "Too risky. A girl who puts out like that could have every disease in the book."

"Yeah, I guess you're right," Dave reluctantly agreed. Then he brightened. "Hey, maybe we could let Roger Farris have first dibs and see if he comes down with anything. Sort of like a food taster to a king."

"Watch the goddamn rodeo for Christ's sake," growled Mark.

Dave stared at his friend in astonishment. "What's with you? Just because you're in love and pure as the driven snow doesn't mean the rest of us can't have some fun."

Cliff Marsden was out of town. He was in Toronto where, according to Jane, he spent a lot of time setting up a new business. As a result, she was almost carefree as she met Mark at their pre-arranged rendezvous on a country road just south of the city limits. For his part, Mark felt an undeniable sense of relief that the decision about what to do with Sue had been so rudely taken out of his hands. The relief was tempered with an equally undeniable sense of loss that never again would he experience the pure sexual excitement of her unleashed passion.

"It's been months since I've heard you laugh like that," Mark finally ventured. "Getting you away from the academic grind seems to have done wonders for you."

"I don't think that's it, really. I think it's more being back here with all that blue sky and open space. No matter where I go, this is the place I will always want to come back to."

"Amen to that," replied Mark fervently.

"Speaking of the academic grind, I have definitely decided to take a post-graduate course. But not at Stanford. I've applied to Columbia."

Mark digested this in silence. Her being in New York was a very different matter from being just down the road in California. He felt a familiar sense of frustration returning, but here was nothing he could do. "Are you going to instruct at Borden's this summer?" he asked, almost fearfully.

"No. The summer's half over already. Besides, I feel sort of played out. The best thing for me would be to rest up and maybe get in some tennis. Do you play tennis?"

"Never had a chance to learn. But how about we go riding together?"

"Horseback riding? I didn't know you rode."

"There are a lot of things you don't know about me," he said with mock mysteriousness. "But not at Borden's. Isn't there a place with better horses?"

"Their horses are pretty good, actually. For a riding academy. But we have much better ones at our place." She thought for a moment. "I can pony a horse out to meet you somewhere. Do you ride Western or English?"

"Whichever." Although Mark was much more secure with the deep Western saddle, he had ridden English style enough to be able to post to the trot and steer with both reins instead of neck-reining.

"Okay. I've got just the horse for you. Here's where we'll meet." She fished the last cigarette out of a package, tore it open, and sketched a crude map on it. "You can park alongside the fence at the south end of this field. I feel terrible about not being able to have you come directly to our stable, but you know how it is."

"I do indeed. Speaking of parking, why don't you pull in over there. I haven't kissed you properly yet."

Somewhat to his surprise, for he could never predict how she would react, she complied and turned into an overgrown track leading to an abandoned farm.

Harrison Dobbs was on the phone, wanting to know if Mark had reached a decision about activating the buy-sell clause. Mark told him he had just that morning received an evaluation report from a firm of independent geological consultants. They had valued a half-interest in Central Resources at $3-million on the low side and four on the high side with the most appropriate figure being in the middle of the range.

"We don't want to leave anything on the table by offering too much," Harrison said as if thinking out loud. "Have you taken Kennedy's pulse lately?"

"I get the impression that my offering him the shares is the last thing he wants. I think he tested the water to see if he could raise the necessary cash and came up short. Just like I did."

"Which suggests we should come in with a low bid?"

"I guess so," Mark replied uncertainly. "But the thought of losing the company scares the hell out of me. It should worry you too, Harrison, because California will never see a cubic foot of that gas if Kennedy has anything to do with it. He's still absolutely convinced that we'd be much better off just letting the gas stay in the ground for a few years. In a way you've got more to lose than I do."

"I realize that. I guess I'm so gung-ho because I'm confident he'll take his money and run." Harrison paused before adding, "Remember we don't have all the time in the world, Mark."

"I've still got a few days in hand. I just wish there wasn't so much at stake."

"You make it sound as though it were all or nothing for you. Don't forget that even at the worst you'll end up a very wealthy man."

"That's not what I want, Harrison. There'll only be one Claymore in my lifetime, and I want to be the one to develop it and build that pipeline."

When his conversation with Dobbs was finished, Mark's secretary told him that Mr. Crawford was holding on another line.

"I just wanted to tell you that you're changing the way we think about natural gas, Mark."

"How's that, Bill?"

"I just drilled a gas discovery a few miles east of Camrose. Up until now, I would have cursed my bad luck and moved on to another area. But this morning I ordered three delineation wells to be drilled to find out how much gas is there. And I know other companies are doing the same thing. It's all because of a market you're opening up."

"Thanks for telling me that, Bill. I appreciate it. I trust those new reserves will be dedicated to my pipeline."

"Count on it." Crawford seemed unwilling to let go of the subject. "You know, Mark," he went on in a thoughtful voice, "what you're doing is really important. Much more important than individual wildcatters like me who are just trying to find the stuff and build a successful oil company. Your pipeline project will influence the entire industry. I think I'm just a little bit envious."

It was enormously gratifying to hear someone like Bill Crawford confirm exactly what Mark had come to realize on his own. "Thank you for saying that, Bill. There are times when I feel almost like a traitor now that I've left the explorationist end of the business and become a pipeline promoter. Anyway," he added thoughtfully, "we're both essential — those who are out there finding the gas and those who are trying to develop a market."

"Yes. But your impact is industry wide." Bill paused briefly, then went on in a brisker tone. "That's enough philosophizing for one day. How about lunch on Thursday?"

"Done. I'll meet you at the Pete Club at twelve." Mark crossed over to the window and gazed out at the booming young city while he thought about what Bill had said. It was absolutely true. Accessing a vast and growing market by pipeline would have a profound effect on the way the industry would develop. He would succeed come hell or high water.

"Say, you're good! I'm really impressed." Jane cantered up beside Mark.

"Anybody would look good on this horse!" Mark laughed with sheer pleasure as his superbly trained mount maintained his smooth, collected gait. "He's the Cadillac of horseflesh!"

"He's had a fair bit of dressage training. But you look great on him."

With her dark hair pulled back under her velvet hunt cap, Jane looked like a photo in the society section of some glossy magazine. As usual, her eyes were hidden behind huge sunglasses, but her tanned skin glowed with a faint, healthy flush and her smile would have made an orthodontist weep with envy. She was breathtakingly lovely and Mark ached with longing.

Red-tailed hawks wheeled and screamed in the blue sky above them as they pulled up at the edge of a cliff that fell abruptly away to a meandering creek bed. Mark's horse stood rock-still as he dismounted and, following Jane's example, loosened the girth a few holes. A kingbird darted from the top branch of a poplar in pursuit of a giant dragonfly almost as big as itself.

"There's some fresh alfalfa and clover over here." Jane's horse threw his head and whinnied as she led him over to a patch of dark green grass. "I always let them have a few mouthfuls as a little treat."

While the horses cropped greedily at the succulent grass, Jane tilted her cap back on her head and looked around her with a smile that seemed to express pure, unalloyed joy.

"I can see why you feel so strongly about this place," Mark murmured, his eyes never leaving her face. He took a hesitant step forward and kissed her lightly on the lips. Her free hand rested on his forearm and the kiss lingered and grew.

"I want to spend a lifetime with you," he whispered as they finally drew apart.

"Maybe we should do something about that," she whispered back, making his heart leap with sudden, wild hope.

"Like marriage, maybe?" Mark struggled to keep the tremor out of his voice.

"Maybe. Not right now. But sometime. Maybe next summer, after I've finished my year at Columbia. Can you wait that long?"

"I can wait forever if it means being with you."

Mark finished the ride in a euphoric daze. Jane apologized once again for her family's treatment of him as he dismounted beside his parked car. "Time will take care of that," he told her airily as he handed her his horse's reins, giving the animal an affectionate pat on the neck. Feeling as if he could conquer the world, he watched her ride away, his horse trotting obediently at her side, until she disappeared from view down a coulee.

Cliff enjoyed giving instructions to Kennedy. It was like having an intelligent robot that you wound up and sent out to do battle. Kennedy, who had had an undistinguished career as a character actor before Cullen found him, was a quick study. He also insisted on knowing the purpose behind each move, explaining that it enabled him to give a more convincing performance and to react appropriately when necessary.

Now Cliff was telling him that they were at the most crucial and delicate stage of the operation. The object was to make Mark put his shares, and to do that Kennedy must convince him that his response to the put would be to sell his own shares. "Once he makes the put, we've got him by the short hairs," Cliff crowed. "Now, go do your stuff!"

Mark would have given anything to know what was going on inside Kennedy's head, but the full, red face blinking amiably back at him was unreadable. Unexpectedly Garth heaved a sigh and said, "This ain't any fun at all, old buddy. I know you think I'm a stubborn son of a bitch and a lousy partner for bucking you on this deal. I've been thinking that life's too short for this kind of hassle."

"What do you have in mind, Garth?"

"Maybe you should buy me out."

"You mean you'd sell me your shares?"

"At the right price, why not? I'm not cut out for this office routine."

"You got a price in mind?"

"That's where the buy-sell agreement comes in. Keeps both of us honest. You have to offer a price that you'd accept for your own shares."

"The only problem is that the shares aren't very bankable."

"Yeah. I found that out already. Well, think on it, boy." With some effort Garth pushed back his shirtsleeve so he could see the wristwatch on his thick wrist. "I'm late for lunch," he grunted and heaved himself out of his chair.

Mark sat unmoving behind his desk while he tried to work out the ramifications of what Kennedy had said. Then he reached for the phone and placed a call to San Francisco.

"I think it's time to make our move," he said when Harrison came on that line.

"That's good news, Mark. I was beginning to worry about the way you were dragging your heels."

"It hasn't been an easy decision to make, Harrison. Believe me. I still don't know which way my partner will jump even though he's making noises like he wants to sell out."

"We've analyzed all that pretty thoroughly, Mark," Harrison replied almost testily. "For one thing, we're almost positive he doesn't have the necessary financial resources. If he seems anxious to sell out, maybe we can come in on the low side."

"That's a risk I'm not prepared to run." Mark took a deep breath. "I've decided to offer my shares for five million."

There was a long silence on the other end of the phone before Dobbs said, "Do you really think it's necessary to go that high? Especially if the man wants to sell?"

"I want to make it as attractive as possible for him to sell and as unattractive as possible for him to buy."

"I can see that. But five million! I don't like to say this, Mark, but you're in a bit of a conflict here."

"How do you mean?"

"It's pretty obvious isn't it? Getting five million for your shares would be a real financial coup for you."

"The whole point of offering the five million is that I don't sell my shares," an exasperated Mark replied. "Anyway, I've got the right to go that high under our agreement."

"True enough. Okay, Mark, do what you think best. Just make sure you've got all the legal technicalities covered."

"I'm going to have Chester Martin draw up the put letter," Mark assured him.

"Five million!" Kennedy whistled as he read the two-paragraph letter. "You really must want to get rid of me! I didn't know you had this kind of dough, Mark. Is this for real?"

"It's for real, Garth. And the money's ready whenever you are. Do you want to accept it right now? All you have to do is sign the copy."

"There's no rush, ol' buddy. I got sixty days to think about it." As Garth refolded the letter and stuffed it into his inside breast pocket, Mark thought he caught a glimmer of triumph in those bloodshot eyes. It was probably because the price was so much higher than he expected, but, if so, why didn't the guy accept the offer right here and now?

24

"Mother," Jane put down her magazine and held her mother's unwilling gaze. "You know perfectly well that I've been seeing Mark, and yet I can't let him come to the house. That's dishonest and hypocritical and I hate it. Tonight we're going to a movie and he's coming to the front door to pick me up."

"Oh God, Jane, please don't force the issue like that." Eleanor Marsden sat bolt upright in the chaise longue. "Your father will find out about it as soon as he gets back from Toronto and you know how upset he'll be."

"He'll be more than upset. He'll make a disgraceful scene, but I can handle it. It's time we faced up to the issue. I may end up marrying Mark."

"Mar ...? Are you out of your mind? That will tear this family apart. Your father won't stand for it!"

"I didn't say for sure that I was going to marry him, Mother. But I might some-time down the road. And I certainly intend to go on seeing him and it's high time this family faced up to that fact."

Eleanor shuddered and drained the last dregs of her Bloody Mary.

"By the way, when is Dad coming home? He seems to be spending an awful lot of time in Toronto this summer. And he never seems to go to Montreal any more. What is this new business he's so involved in, anyway?"

"Something to do with oil well pumps, I believe," her mother replied vaguely.

"Mother apologizes for not being here to meet you, but she's not feeling well and is lying down."

"I understand," replied Mark, looking about him with some awe. The Marsden establishment, a sprawling ranch-style structure nestled in its own valley, was obviously designed for entertaining on a large scale. The entrance hall with its timbered two-storey ceiling and the sunken living room stretching interminably into the distance could easily accommodate three hundred guests.

"That's some spread," Mark murmured as the heavy, ironwood door clicked smoothly shut behind them. The Olds looked like a child's toy in the immensity of the paved front yard.

"Spread is right. It's got more than twelve thousand square feet. And there are times," Jane added a little grimly as she slid into the seat, "when we need every square inch of it. When my father finds out about tonight promises to be one of them."

"He might not find out. Your mother won't tell him, will she?"

"Not on your life. But the servants will. And I know exactly which one."

"You stay out of this Eleanor. This is between Jane and myself." Cliff and his wife were alone in his study. He made as if to push his wife bodily out of the way, but she stood her ground, blocking the doorway.

"No it isn't. She's my daughter too. I know I have failed her in the past, failed her terribly, but this is one time I'm going to stand up for her."

Cliff's thick lips curled with contempt. "All right, you've stood up for her. Now get out of my way."

"I know why you used to spend so much time in Montreal, Cliff."

His half-raised hand dropped to his side. "The reason I used to spend so much time in Montreal is that I had a business there. A valve manufacturing business, if you remember. Which has now been sold. At a good profit, I might add."

"You also have a second family there."

"What? Who's been feeding you that crap?" he blustered.

"Don't bother denying it, Cliff. I've known about Denise and your little love nest for years."

"It doesn't seem to bother you very much."

"Our marriage died a long time ago, Cliff. And you know why. All I cared about was that it didn't turn into a scandal. But I don't even care about that any more. What about you? Do you mind if the world finds out that you've been maintaining two households and that you've fathered a second family out of wedlock?"

"If you don't care, then maybe I shouldn't," replied Cliff, but the sweat breaking out on his forehead gave away his bluff.

Eleanor took a deep breath. "Do you want the world to find out about Jamie?"

"Damn you, Ellie!" Cliff raised his hand as if to strike her, then abruptly turned his back on her and strode over to the sliding glass doors that looked out on the pool, its calm unruffled surface glinting in the sunlight. "Okay, Ellie," he said through clenched teeth, "I will not read the riot act to Jane, and you will keep this Montreal business to yourself. Deal?"

"And you will allow her friend to call for her and she can entertain him in this house, which also happens to be her home. You don't have to see him," she added hastily when he spun around and she saw the look of fury on his face. "You can lock yourself away in your study whenever he's here."

"People will think I'm a goddamned wimp, giving the free run of my house to the bastard who nearly killed me."

Eleanor almost smiled. "No one will ever think you are a wimp, dear. Believe me."

Cliff made a snarling sound in his throat and dropped heavily into a leather armchair. He sat there brooding alone while the slowly descending sun sent lengthening shafts of light across the polished floor and Oriental rug. So Ellie had known about the Montreal set-up all along. How she must have gloated when Jamie turned out to be handicapped! She would know that begetting a son like that would almost destroy him. When, shortly after Jane was born, they found out that she couldn't have any more children, he had given her a hard time about how his superior genes were being wasted.

One good thing though. There was no need to worry about her keeping her part of the bargain. She was good at bottling things up. And it wouldn't make a particle of difference to a marriage that was nothing more than a convenient facade. Her being so matter-of-fact about everything kind of rankled, though. But it was the thought of that bastard, Hunter, driving boldly up to the front door and whisking Jane away, that was making his guts churn.

The only consolation was that he had Hunter completely in his power. Wait until he found out that it was none other than Cliff Marsden who would end up with one hundred per cent of Claymore, and the California project. Once the shares were safely his, he'd make sure that Hunter wouldn't be around to enjoy his fortune. At first Cliff was shaken and more than a little frightened as that murderous thought sprang unbidden into his mind, but gradually he began to accept it, and then to savour it. Antonelli's friends could make it look like an accident. The sudden appearance of Jane in an electric-blue bathing suit, bouncing up and down on the springboard before diving cleanly into the pool, brought him out of his evil reverie.

As if to reassure himself, Cliff crossed over to the fireplace wall, moved an oil painting aside, and dialed the combination of a small safe. Garth Kennedy's signature, duly witnessed, was on both copies of the letter agreeing to buy Hunter's shares for $5-million. Paper-clipped to the letter was another document, also signed by Kennedy, which transferred ownership of all the shares of Central Resources to Clifford Marsden.

It was a month today since he had activated the buy-sell clause and Kennedy still hadn't tipped his hand. In fact Kennedy had completely disappeared from the scene. Two weeks ago he had casually informed a dumbfounded Mark that he was going to treat himself to a little holiday. In vain Mark pleaded with him to tender his shares before he left. Mark tried to tell himself that the smirk on Kennedy's face was merely because he revelled in keeping his partner in suspense.

Mark tried to ease his anxiety by talking to the only two people he could confide in — Harrison Dobbs and Chester Martin. Dobbs was supremely confident that Kennedy simply couldn't refuse an offer that Dobbs still thought was outrageously inflated, while Martin, in his lawyer-like way, could only shrug and tell Mark to "abide the event." Seeing that this was cold comfort to a despondent Mark, he went on, "There's absolutely nothing you can do. The ball is in Kennedy's court, as we full well knew it would be when we offered to sell your shares."

"Christ, it's like a furnace out there!" Dave threw his coat jacket down on a chair and rushed into the kitchen for a cold beer. "I thought the hot weather only lasted while the Stampede was on." He took a long pull from the bottle and sighed. "Ah, that's better. Much better." Plopping into a chair across from Mark, he said, "Old D.R. blew it. That California well was dry and abandoned."

"Damn! I was hoping the old wildcatter could pull it off one more time."

"His wildcatting days are over, after this fiasco."

"I wouldn't count him out just yet. The Cullen name still has magic in the oil patch. It wouldn't surprise me if he came up with the financing for another exploration venture."

"That's not what the street is saying. The word is that the banks are set to move in."

"The poor bastard. This could kill him, you know."

"It probably will, especially if he keeps hitting the bottle. You like the old reprobate, don't you?"

"Yes, I really do. I always felt we have something in common. Probably because we both feel the same way about the oil game — that there's nothing else like it. And I'll never forget how he tried to help me when I was breaking into the oil industry."

"Well, the guy will always be a legend in the patch. They can't take that away from him." Dave chug-a-lugged the last of his beer. "You got a date with the toothsome Miss Marsden tonight?"

"Yep. I'm calling for her at eight."

"I gotta hand it to you for the way you managed to storm the Marsden fortress. Somehow I can't picture old Cliff welcoming you with open arms."

"He doesn't. I never lay eyes on him. He's out of town a lot, and when he's at home he makes himself scarce when he knows I'm coming. I wish I could meet him face to face. I'm sure we could put all this crap behind us if we could only talk."

"Dream on." Dave hefted the empty beer bottle and got to his feet.

"I dropped in at Borden's today. I thought I should pay them a little courtesy call."

"Oh?" Mark's heartbeat quickened as he waited for whatever was coming next.

"I told Sue you were a credit to her. That you were riding as if you had been doing it all your life."

"That must have pleased her," replied Mark carefully.

"Not so you'd notice. She just shrugged. And she didn't seem the least bit glad to see me." Jane's sideways glance at Mark was speculative. "The funny part is that we got on beautifully last summer when I was instructing at Pony Club."

"She's probably upset over losing a good customer since I don't go out there any more now that I'm riding with you."

"That could explain it," Jane agreed and dropped the subject, to Mark's intense relief. If she ever found out about his short-lived affair with Sue, he would lose her.

As it was, he still couldn't be sure of her, from one moment to the next. Her moods had a distressing habit of swinging from calm and loving to misgivings about whether she should be tying herself down so early in life. Her attitude, combined with his inability to get a decision from Kennedy, filled him with a restless sense of helplessness.

"Mark?" Dave sounded agitated on the phone. "I just had a call from Bea Cullen. D.R.'s had a massive heart attack. The doctors don't think he'll survive this one. He's conscious and insists on seeing you. The plastic duchess wants you to see him right away. He's in intensive care at the Holy. They're expecting you. Can do?"

"I'm on my way."

An oxygen tank stood beside Don Cullen's bed and a plastic tube dripped a clear fluid into his forearm. His eyelids flickered open as Mark came in and the nurse removed the oxygen mask from his face. His voice was a harsh rasp and Mark leaned close to catch the whispered words.

"I was the money behind Kennedy," the dying oilman said.

"Then I have a lot to thank you for. You made it possible for me to find the Claymore field."

"I sold you out, boy. I sold my interest to ... to Cliff Marsden, so I could drill that California wildcat."

"Cliff Marsden? He owns Kennedy's shares?"

Tears filled Don's eyes and flowed down his blotched cheeks. The nurse wiped them away with a tissue and shot Mark a severe look, but stepped back out of the way. Don's breath rattled in his throat, but from somewhere he found the strength to whisper, "Kennedy's share was held in trust for me. I sold the declaration of trust to Cliff. For $7-million. It was the worst thing I ever did in my life. But I just had to drill that well, Mark. I just had to."

"I understand. We're a pair of wildcatters, you and me. I don't hold it against you, Don. Honest."

Don's eyes rolled supplicatingly toward the nurse and she clapped the mask over his face. His hand felt for Mark's and he squeezed it. Mark returned the pressure.

In the corridor outside Cullen's room, Mark stood stock-still while he tried to come to grips with the blow he had just been dealt. Cliff Marsden controlled Kennedy. That bastard must have been hugging himself with sadistic glee these past few weeks! That explained why there had been no word from Kennedy. Marsden was deliberately stringing out the suspense to extract the last possible drop of malicious satisfaction from his revenge. Mark squared his shoulders and opened the swinging doors. Bea Cullen and Dave Green were sitting on a plastic bench in the small waiting area. They were holding hands. Was there something between these two? Dave saw the stricken look on his friend's face and blurted, "Is he ... is he gone?"

"No," Mark replied tonelessly.

"I better go to him." Bea disengaged herself from Dave and stood up.

"I'm afraid that what they have done is perfectly legal," said Chester Martin when Mark had finished. "They haven't interfered with your rights under the buy-sell agreement, except that now we know Kennedy will buy the shares, as he is entitled to. What he does with them after that is immaterial from a legal point of view."

"He will hand them over to Marsden, damn his soul."

"Yes. That's how it will work. Of course, you will have the consolation of ..."

Mark held up a hand to interrupt him. "Don't say it. It's not what I want. I want the California project."

Chester gazed sorrowfully at his client. "I greatly fear you have just lost it."

Sitting two pews behind the Marsden family, Mark saw with a certain grim amusement that Cliff had a conspicuous bald spot on the back of his head. There were some things in life that even the omnipotent magnate couldn't control. The oil company president who was giving the eulogy cleared his throat nervously, the amplified sound echoing around the packed church. Somewhat guiltily, Mark began to listen. The speaker was making a valiant but utterly unconvincing effort to endow the deceased with the conventional human virtues. It was only when he reached the point where he could talk about Cullen as an oilman that he hit his stride.

When the brief service was over, Cliff, along with the other honorary pallbearers, preceded the coffin out of the church to form an honour guard on the sidewalk, as Mark and the other active pallbearers carried it to the waiting hearse. Mark spotted Jane standing beside her mother in the crowd milling about in the bright sunlight and deliberately walked over and began to chat with them. That should raise Marsden's blood pressure a few notches. But he immediately regretted the gesture when he saw the look of fear in Eleanor's eyes. Jane's eyes, as usual, were hidden behind sunglasses, but she quickly turned aside and said something to Rhodes Taylor who was standing next to her. It was an awkward little scene, and Mark was grateful when the flunkey from the funeral home tapped him on the shoulder and said they were ready to move off.

"I'll see you tonight," he called, half-defiantly, over his shoulder to Jane before he climbed into the waiting limousine.

"Okay, so I pulled a bonehead play at the funeral. But you don't have to make a federal case out of it. You've hardly said a word all night."

"You don't seem to realize, Mark, that when Daddy gets upset, life gets pretty miserable around the Marsden household. Mother went to bed with a migraine, and Daddy tore off in the Lincoln. He must have been doing a hundred by the time he reached the end of the driveway."

"Since your driveway is at least two miles long, that could easily be." A vision of a lifeless Marsden pinned underneath his overturned car flitted pleasurably through Mark's head. But life was never that simple. "What's happening to us, Jane?" he asked plaintively. "It used to be fun and games — a laugh a minute with us. Now I hardly know what to do or say, for fear of how you will react. Is this how love is supposed to be?"

"I just don't know, Mark." Jane looked out the open window at the moon-drenched nightscape. They drove past a field where deer grazed among a herd of horses standing still as statues. "I have this vague feeling of being uneasy all the time. As if there's something just beneath the surface busting to come out." She gave a shaky little laugh. "Sometimes I wonder if I'm going crazy. Maybe we better stop seeing each other for a while, and see if that helps."

"Jesus, Jane, I wish you'd stop talking like that," an agonized Mark pleaded. In an attempt to change the subject and lighten the mood, he said, "Guess what? I got me an invite to the Oilmen's Golf Tournament."

"Really?" Jane was impressed. "That's a feather in your cap!"

Mark nodded agreement. The annual tournament, held in Banff during the last week of August, had rapidly become one of the most prestigious events in the international oil industry. Chief executives from the States and England schemed and clamoured for the precious invitations. The fact that he had been invited to attend, albeit as a social, non-playing member like all first-time guests, meant that he had been recognized by his peers as an industry leader. He had a lot to thank Claymore for. "You'll be there, of course?"

"Oh, yes. Daddy wouldn't miss it. It's a good thing he wasn't on the invitation committee or you'd never have made it."

25

Bill Crawford paid off the taxi and stood for a moment in the driveway of his house, drawing in deep lungfuls of the cool night air. It was intoxicatingly fresh and invigorating, especially after the sticky heat of Toronto. In that moment he decided that he would live out his life and his career in Calgary. It had everything he needed or wanted — a young oil industry with all the challenges and opportunities an ambitious man could wish for, an almost small-town atmosphere in which to raise a family, and the cleanest, purest air in the whole wide world. It was true the winters could be long and dreary, but there were always the faithful chinooks to dispel the winter chill, the beckoning ski slopes of Banff, and the subtropical and easily accessible charms of Hawaii.

He shivered as if the night had turned suddenly cooler. Marianne. She hated the place. She had been miserable ever since they left Texas, and had steadfastly refused to make any attempt to adjust. Except that recently Sharon Livingston seemed to have taken her up. That might make a difference in her attitude. As a friend of Sharon's she would be welcome everywhere and anywhere in Calgary. That could help this weird insecurity she had. On the other hand ... The living room drapes suddenly parted and he saw Anne Fleming looking out. Bill gave her a reassuring wave and picked up his suitcase.

"Hi, Anne," he said as she opened the door for him. "My meeting finished a day earlier than I expected. Where's Mrs. Crawford?"

Anne's youthful cheeks were flushed and she seemed oddly flustered. "She was meeting Mrs. Livingston and they were going somewhere. Maybe to a movie."

Bill looked at his watch. "In that case, she should be home pretty soon. Everything okay around here? The kids in bed?"

"Sound asleep."

"Great." Bill knew his heartiness sounded false, but he was trying to reassure the youngster who really did look upset. "Let me pay you and then I'll walk you home."

Walking the short distance to the Fleming house, Bill was tempted to ask Anne if she did much babysitting for Marianne while he was away, but refrained. He didn't want her to think he was spying on his wife, and it wouldn't be fair to put her on the spot.

Back in his own house, Bill carried his suitcase up the flight of stairs to the bedroom level and swiftly unpacked. Carrying an armload of dirty clothes, he walked down the hall to the laundry chute. Halfway through stuffing his laundry down the chute, he paused. In the morning, Marianne would have to pick up his dirty clothes and put them in the washer. Not exactly an exciting or challenging task. A boring, repetitive chore, really. Like most of the things she had to do. Not for her the excitement of drilling a wildcat well, negotiating a farm-in, or travelling to other cities to package a new finance deal. All these were part of his daily existence, while she had to look after the children, prepare meals — although she wasn't any great shakes at that — do the laundry, and generally try to keep the household running. Thoughtfully, Bill sent his shirts to follow his socks and underwear down the chute.

His frown faded as he gently opened the door of Debbie's bedroom and gazed down at her. She was sleeping on her side, bright blonde hair cushioning her head against the pillow, a soft smile on her tender lips. She was a happy, determined child and, with Billy, the most precious thing in Bill's life. He was tempted to kiss her forehead but knew it would waken her. He propped the doll he had brought her against her pillow and tiptoed out of the room.

Billy, as usual, lay sprawled across his bed, with his covers lying in a heap on the floor. He still clutched his favourite car in his hand. Bill placed the new racing-car he had bought Billy on the bedside table then bent down, picked the covers off the floor and covered his son. He looked at his child and swallowed hard as he saw the young man that could already be seen in Billy's sleep-softened face. Not for the first time, he realized that the business trips that were such an essential part of his life were robbing him of his family life. He closed his son's bedroom door and walked quietly downstairs.

For perhaps the tenth time, Bill checked his watch. Five minutes of twelve — he still hadn't come round to the Canadian way of saying "to" the hour. Even if she and Sharon had taken in the late show, Marianne should have been home by now. Maybe they had stopped for a cup of coffee somewhere.

It was almost an hour later that he saw their station wagon creeping down the streets, without lights. Marianne obviously did not want the neighbours to see her arriving home at this hour. She was drunk. Plastered. And she looked a mess. Her blonde hair was tousled, her lipstick smeared, and her dress was rumpled and creased as if she had slept in it. Dismayed, Bill realized he was confronting something more than a dipsomaniac wife. There was an almost palpable air of stale sex about her.

Grasping the banister for support, she squinted with drunken belligerence up at Bill, who was standing at the head of the short flight of stairs that led up from the garage.

"Wha' you doing home?" she demanded. With a visible effort she overcame the slur in her voice. "You're not supposed to be here till tomorrow night."

Bill's emotions were in turmoil. He was assailed with successive waves of rage at her betrayal, wounded male pride, and a desperate, almost helpless concern for Marianne herself. But there was no point in discussing anything while she was in this state. "Come to bed, Marianne. We'll talk in the morning."

"I need a drink." Clinging to the banister like the railing of a ship in heavy seas, she climbed up the stairs and headed for the kitchen, bumping against Bill on the way. He watched helplessly as she opened a kitchen cupboard and brought out a half-full bottle of Jack Daniels. "Want one?" she asked as she poured herself a stiff jolt.

Bill shook his head. He had never seen Marianne in a mood quite like this — despondent, guilty, tearful, yes, but never openly defiant like this.

She retched and nearly threw up as she swallowed the last of the drink. He reached out to help her, but she knocked his hand away. He walked around her, ready to catch her if she fell, as she climbed the stairs and staggered down the hall, knocking a colour photograph of a Venture oil well off the wall. The carpeted floor saved the glass from shattering. She collapsed on the bed and passed out. Bill started to undress her, but stopped after he had unbuttoned her skirt. He didn't want to see what he might find. Lifting her unresisting body, he pulled back the bedspread and covered her with a blanket.

Lying beside his unconscious and snoring wife, Bill tried to figure out how he really felt, and what he should do. He was surprised at how detached he was. For the first time he admitted to himself that he no longer loved his wife. He should have bitten the bullet and left her behind in Texas when he came to Canada. They both would have been happier. But there were the children. And that traumatic business with Rose. He hadn't heard a word from or about her since he had sent the money order.

He seemed to be making all the right moves on the business front, but when it came to the domestic scene he screwed up every time. Except for Billy and Debbie. Billy was a source of great pride for Bill, and no father could wish for a better relationship than he had with his precocious young daughter. If he were in love with another woman, what had happened tonight would have made him leave Marianne for her. He found himself almost wishing that there was such a person in his life. It would help him come to a decision. But there wasn't. Certainly no one serious. The oil business was his mistress. At least at this stage of his career. The bedroom furniture was beginning to take shape in the pre-dawn lightening of the sky before his unhappy thoughts let Bill fall into a troubled sleep.

The smell of frying — more accurately, burning — bacon woke Bill. Marianne would be trying to make amends — and punish herself — by cooking bacon and eggs for breakfast. It was strange, he thought as he hurriedly brushed his teeth, how much he knew about her without really knowing her.

"There's juice on the table," she said without looking at him. Thankfully, Bill retreated to the dining room where the smoke was less overpowering. Billy was playing with his new car and Debbie was having breakfast with her new doll.

Billy gave his father a big grin while Debbie squealed with delight at the sight of her father. "She's beautiful, Daddy! Thank you," she cried and flung her little arms around his neck and hugged him when he picked her up. Holding her, Bill knew that he could never abandon his children to be brought up by someone as unstable and unhappy as Marianne. And from what little he knew of the law, she would get custody. At least to start with. He might eventually succeed in proving her an unfit mother, but by that time the damage would have been done. And he had no stomach for the kind of mudslinging a custody battle would entail.

"Why don't you two kids run next door and show Joan your new toys?" Marianne said as she plunked down a plate in front of Bill. Billy stood up and Debbie obediently scrambled down from Bill's lap and headed for the front door. Marianne sat down in her own chair and took a sip of black coffee. Bill was alarmed to see her hand shake.

"I guess I really messed up last night, huh?" It was offered as an apology, but there was an underlying note of defiance in her voice. Bill wondered if she had taken a restorative drink. He couldn't smell anything; but the pall of acrid smoke would explain that. What was wrong with him? How could he be so dispassionate about what was going on?

"You certainly *were* a mess by the time you got home," he grunted, buttering a piece of blackened toast. "Care to tell me about it?"

"I went over to Sharon's — her husband's out of town too — and we had a few drinks. I guess I had a few too many and I got a little tight."

"I see." A piece of overcooked bacon splintered into tiny fragments when Bill tried to cut it with a knife. He gave up the struggle and picked up the next slice in his fingers. "Aren't you getting a little bit worried about the way you're drinking?"

"I can handle it," she said almost absently, waiting for the second shoe to drop. When several minutes passed without him saying anything more, she began to breathe easier. Maybe he had put her dishevelled state down to her being so drunk. If he only knew what had really happened last night! She had fought off Cliff Marsden for as long as she could. But she was confused and weakened by the alcohol she had consumed and when he threw her to the floor and held her down, she had given up and let him have his way. It hadn't amounted to very much, but his leer was triumphant as he climbed off her and zippered his pants. She'd give herself a douche as soon as Bill left for the office. It took her a moment to realize that he was speaking to her. Oh, oh, here it comes. But he was going on about the Oilmen's Golf Tournament, of all things!

"The Oilmen's is on next week," he was saying. "I don't have to tell you how important it is to me. I want your promise that you will behave yourself."

So, all you're worried about is your precious Oilmen's where you can suck up to the big boys. You don't give a good goddamn about your wife, or what happens to her. With these vicious thoughts swirling through her aching head, Marianne smiled reassuringly at her husband and said, "I'll do you proud, Bill. You can count on it."

26

Mark waited until the trail ride, some of the riders clutching the pommels of their saddles with white-knuckled apprehension, had crossed the road before he turned into the entrance of the hotel. The Banff Springs Hotel, built with stone carved from Mount Rundle and designed to resemble a baronial Scottish castle, looked totally out of place against the backdrop of rock-ribbed, pine-clad mountains, but it was so massive and imposing that it created an environment all of its own. The Scottish motif was repeated in the Highland attire of the bellboy who came forward to take Mark's suitcase. The registration desk for the tournament was inside the main lobby, against a panelled wall and directly underneath a lugubrious moose head. Some joke-ster had placed a cigarette between its pendulous lips and hung a golf cap on its antlers.

As a first-time, non-playing guest, Mark was low man on the totem pole and his accommodation was a tiny broom closet of a room tucked under the eaves. Peering out through the narrow casement window, Mark felt like the Hunchback of Notre Dame. But he was in no mood to complain. It was a signal honour for someone his age to have been invited to the tournament, and it was also an unequalled opportunity to rub shoulders with the "Who's Who" of the oil industry. More importantly, Jane would be there. And he would get to spend time with her. The Oilmen's was definitely oriented toward couples and families, but it was also an occasion to mingle and expand one's circle of acquaintances in the patch. Mark hefted a thick envelope stuffed with invitations to hospitality suites and tickets to lunches, dinner dances, and a costume ball. And during the day, he could count on Cliff's being totally preoccupied with golf. He was in the Pembina flight — all the flights were named after major oilfields, with Redwater being the championship flight — and he was determined to bring home the trophy. According to Jane, he had been taking lessons from one of the top pros in the country all the time he was in Toronto.

The kit that Mark had been given when he checked in included a printed guest list. Scanning it, he was mildly surprised to see Harrison and Estelle Dobbs listed under the Ds. When you thought about it, though, it made sense that Dobbs would be invited. Due primarily to Mark's pioneering efforts, northern California was coming to be recognized as an important potential market for shut-in Canadian gas and Norcal was literally the only way it could be accessed. Mark might have been first on the scene but he would not be the one to build the line. His smile was self-derisive as he thought of how neatly he had been dealt out of the game. Except that as far as Dobbs knew, he was still very much in the picture, although Kennedy's long delay in accepting the offer must be making him wonder. Mark dialed the hotel operator and asked to be connected with Dobbs's room.

Harrison sounded delighted to hear from him, but when Mark asked if he could join them for dinner, he was told that they had already arranged to sit with the Marsdens. But, since it was also Harrison's first time at the tournament, he assured Mark they would have plenty of time to talk while the others were out on the golf course. They agreed to have coffee together at eleven in the morning.

He saw Jane that night, but only from a distance. The Marsden party was seated at a table on the opposite side of the cavernous Alhambra Room. If Mark hadn't been so preoccupied with thoughts of Jane, he might have had a fairly entertaining evening. He was seated with Rhodes Taylor and Brenda Lester and a middle-aged couple from Dallas who were accompanied by their twenty-year-old daughter. At first, she could hardly believe her good fortune in finding a handsome, unattached male to rescue her from the boredom of watching her parents and their contemporaries partying it up, and making fools of themselves in the process. She began to sulk when Mark responded to her overtures with a polite lack of interest. She started to light a cigarette, but Rhodes hissed at her, "You can't smoke yet. We haven't had the Queen."

The girl, the unlit cigarette dangling from her lips, stared at him blankly.

"You're not supposed to smoke until they give the toast to the Queen," he explained more calmly.

"I don't believe this," she muttered as she put the cigarette back in an embossed gold case and snapped it shut. She made one more try as the dinner party broke up, asking Mark if he was interested in taking a stroll around the hotel grounds. Mark, his eyes intent on Jane's departing back, begged off, saying there were some people he had to get in touch with.

He left a note in Jane's box asking her to be in her room at noon on the following day to take his phone call.

Harrison came directly to the point. "What's taking this Kennedy character so long?" he asked as they waited for the waitress to bring the coffee. "We're beginning to run out of time."

"Maybe he figures the price is too low." Mark's grin was mischievous as he enjoyed the shocked look on Harrison's face.

"I'm surprised you can joke about it," the urbane Harrison said rather huffily. "I was under the impression that the project was rather important to you."

Mark was tempted to blurt out the whole story of how he had been out-manoeuvred by Marsden, but he held back. If Dobbs knew the truth, he would lose all interest in Mark and begin to court Marsden in earnest. Mark knew his situation was hopeless, but the final whistle hadn't blown yet.

As Harrison went on to urge Mark to track Kennedy down and persuade him to sell the shares, Mark realized that Norcal must be desperate for Alberta gas. That meant the pipeline would be given top priority status. If Norcal really turned the heat on, the pipeline would be completed and gas would be flowing within two years. Marsden would have the whole damn thing handed to him on a platter. He would have exactly what he had always craved — recognition and status as an international pipeline tycoon.

"What's the matter, Mark? You look upset."

Mark slipped a tip for the waitress under the saucer and stood up. "I am. For the same reason you are. I don't like the way Kennedy is acting. Not one damn bit."

Jane couldn't meet him for lunch; her father wanted her to caddy for him and he had a 12:15 tee-off time. She was, however, going to have a swim in the pool at five o'clock, come hell or high water, and Mark could join her then, if he liked.

"I like," he assured her fervently.

"How did the game go?"

"Don't ask," replied Jane with a shudder as she slipped out of her terrycloth robe.

"As bad as that?"

"Worse. It was downright embarrassing, in fact. Poor father, he's his own worst enemy in so many ways. He got off to a horrendous start by driving two balls into the Spray River from the first tee. For a minute I thought he was going to throw his clubs in after them. He managed to settle down enough to finish the eighteen, but it was pretty grim. The two Americans in the foursome were giving him some mighty strange looks, but he was so frustrated and fed up with himself I don't think he cared."

"What was his score?"

"Ninety-eight," she flung over her shoulder as she dove cleanly into the pool. She did twenty lengths, slicing through the water with a hard, driving crawl that Mark had no chance of keeping up with. When she emerged from the pool the tension seemed to have drained from her.

"There's something almost sinful about this place." She stretched out on a chaise longue and sighed contentedly as the warm sun caressed her tanned body. "It's so close to the city, yet it's so different. Everybody seems to relax and let their hair down."

Except for your father. Prudently, Mark left the thought unspoken. This was a different Jane, and once again he was excited, yet oddly disturbed. He stole a glance at her smooth, tanned thighs, barely restraining the urge to lean over and kiss them. As though sensing his thoughts, Jane opened her eyes, smiled, and closed them again. All too soon, the sun dropped behind Sulphur Mountain. Jane shivered and sat up. "I told Dad in no uncertain terms that after the way he behaved today he could get his pet thug, Antonelli, to caddy for him."

"Which means you have tomorrow afternoon free. Right?"

"Right. How does the idea of a horseback ride in the mountains grab you?"

"Right where I live." Mark was ecstatic. "I'll make the arrangements."

The fragrant aroma of Cliff's thick Havana cigar wafted through the still, cool night air as the two men walked down the elevated boardwalk that led to the clubhouse.

"I had coffee with young Hunter this morning," said Harrison. "He still seems to think he's going to get the shares."

"Of course he does." Cliff put one hand on the railing and looked down at the dense stand of lodgepole pine, the needles silvery green in the moonlight. "He has no way of knowing that I control Kennedy."

"I wish you'd stop playing cat and mouse with Hunter. I really want to sign up that gas and get on with the job."

Cliff smiled to himself in the darkness. Whether Dobbs knew it or not, the price of the gas had just gone up. But all he said was, "Don't deny me one of life's little pleasures, Harrison. I'm getting a large charge out of keeping that son of a bitch dangling in the dark until I decide to cut the rope."

"That's all very well, Cliff. But while you're getting your jollies, I'm losing precious time. Don't forget that I made all this possible for you. If Norcal hadn't agreed to come up with the five million, Hunter would never have put his shares."

"I realize that, Harrison. But you did all right for yourself. A million dollars cash is a pretty handsome supplement to anyone's retirement fund. I sometimes wonder what your board of directors would think if they knew about your numbered Swiss bank account."

"Are you threatening me, Cliff?" Harrison's voice was steely.

"Hell, no. We're partners. Just don't rush me, that's all." Cliff ground his cigar butt under his heel. "It's getting chilly. Let's go back to the suite and have a brandy."

"You know, Cliff," mused Harrison as they climbed back up the wooden steps, "you've spent an awful lot of money to defeat Hunter ..."

"It's a good investment," Cliff interrupted. "It's peanuts compared to what the pipeline project will generate."

"I agree with that," Harrison conceded. "Still, it's well-known that you hate Hunter's guts. And yet, everywhere I go, I hear he's a favourite candidate to become your son-in-law."

Cliff whirled and grabbed him by the upper arms as if to shake him. "Don't talk like that!" he almost screamed, drops of saliva raining down on Harrison's face. "That's not going to happen! You hear me? I'm not going to let it happen!"

"I hear you," replied a shaken Harrison. "Now let go of me and let's have that brandy."

While Dobbs and Marsden were warily eyeing each other over their brandy snifters, Marianne Crawford was angrily confronting her husband in their hotel room. "Damn it, Bill, you insisted that I come up here with you, which is the last thing I want to do, then you carry on as if I didn't exist."

"We've been through all this, Marianne," replied Bill with weary patience. "This is a golden opportunity for me to make contacts. Contacts that will lead to deals. All I'm asking of you is to stay sober and put in an appearance at some functions."

"The ladies' program," she said mockingly. "Kaffeeklatschs and fashion shows to entertain the little woman while her husband struts around playing golf and making deals. Or pretending to." She paused, then asked with a little giggle, "Want to know the only reason Astrid's here? She made Gerald promise to buy her a mink coat."

Bill frowned. "I don't think you should be seeing so much of Astrid Winslow. She has a reputation for being pretty wild."

"She's not wild. She's *bored*. We all are." Marianne stood up and tied the belt of her bathrobe. "I'm going to have a nightcap. Want one?"

He started to protest, but she cut him off. "Look, I've only had three drinks all night and I'm going to have one more whether you like it or not."

Turning away from the dresser with a dark brown drink in her hand, Marianne, as sometimes happened, was caught off guard with the sudden realization that her husband was a devastatingly attractive man. "Feel like making love?" she asked in a husky whisper.

Was that a look of distaste that flickered across his handsome face? He flashed a deprecating grin and said, "I better take a rain check, dear. I've got a breakfast meeting first thing in the morning."

"Suit yourself." Marianne shrugged indifferently, but inwardly she was seething at the rebuff. "I'll get you for that, buster," she muttered to herself, knocking back her drink.

"Sue!" Mark quickly recovered from his surprise. After all, it was perfectly logical for her to have switched jobs. Riding in the mountains would be a lot more exciting than the familiar trails around Borden's. Her faded jeans were so tight he could see the bulge of her pubic mound. He couldn't help wincing inwardly when he saw the ornate gold and silver belt buckle she was wearing.

"Hello, Mark," she said tonelessly, not meeting his eyes. "I didn't know it was going to be you. All they told me was to break out a couple of horses for experienced riders. I guess Jane is the other one, huh?"

"Yes. She'll be along in a minute. How've you been, Sue?"

"Okay, I guess. Things were real slow at Borden's so I hired on with this outfit." She handed him the reins of a bay quarter horse. "This is Chaparral. He's a good 'un." Still without looking at him, she asked in a breathless voice, "How come you dropped me so cold, Mark? Because Jane came home?"

"That's right." No point in bringing up that rodeo groupie stuff.

"You could still have seen me now and then. We were good together."

"Hello, Sue. I didn't expect to find you here." Mark froze at the sound of Jane's voice. Had she heard? It was impossible to tell from her expression as she took the reins of a chestnut mare from Sue and expertly adjusted the length of the stirrups.

"Look, you guys," Sue was apologetic, "I know you don't want me tagging along, but the rules say every ride that goes out has to be accompanied by a guide."

"That's fine, Sue." Jane touched the mare's flanks with her heels and led the way out of the corral. "You can show us the best trails. It's been a long time since I've ridden in the mountains."

Bringing up the rear, Mark convinced himself that Jane couldn't have overheard anything. It was true she was a little cool and distant to Sue, but that could be explained by the way Sue had behaved when Jane paid her courtesy call to Borden's. Jane was definitely not the type to take being snubbed lightly. When she felt like it, she could put on a lady-of-the-manor air with the best of them.

The two-hour ride was an almost unbearable erotic experience for Mark. Riding behind the two women, he was tormented with memories of Sue's rock-hard body writhing under him as her panting rose to its wild crescendo. Jane would never be able to let herself go like that, nor would he want her to. Even after all this time, and even though they were virtually engaged, at least as far as he was concerned, she would almost panic if he tried anything more intimate than French kissing. Except, of course, for that incredible night when she had gone down on him. And he knew with a sick heart it wasn't the first time she had done it, either. She had known exactly how to go about it. God, how he wished it had never happened, while at the same time aching for it to happen again.

"I enjoyed that!" exclaimed Jane as she dismounted at the end of the ride. "This little beauty didn't put a foot wrong!"

"Dulcie is a real mountain horse," Sue agreed enthusiastically. "I've never seen her so much as stumble. And you should see her pick her way through a deadfall!"

Walking back to the hotel, Mark tried to take Jane in his arms, but she held him off. "Not in broad daylight," she said in a fierce whisper. Smiling at his crestfallen expression, she relented and added, "Wait until tonight."

Mark kissed her lightly on the cheek and released her. Tonight was the big costume ball. It was the highlight of the social program, and, under pressure from his wife, Cliff had grudgingly agreed that Mark could escort Jane to it.

"I still can't get over Daddy letting you take me to the ball," said Jane in a wondering tone as they continued down the woodland path.

"Your mother's on our side."

"I know she is. But he's never paid any attention to what she says. At least, not until recently. It's very strange."

Mark touched her arm and pointed to a mule deer and her two young browsing among the trees only a few yards away. "Maybe your mother's got something on him," he said jokingly after they had duly admired the sleek, healthy-looking animals.

"Maybe she has," Jane said musingly. "It would explain a lot of things."

"Anyway, I get to take you, and that's all I care about. You know," he added thoughtfully, "everyone will think I must have his seal of approval. After all, he can't very well refuse your hand in marriage after I escort you to the costume ball!"

As always when he broached the subject of marriage, he was careful to speak in a lighthearted, teasing manner, but nonetheless her face took on that half-frightened look he had learned to hate. "Forget it. I was only joking," he said brusquely.

27

This year the theme of the costume ball was "Gunslingers and Molls." Mark checked his appearance in the bathroom mirror and decided that, with his silver-trimmed black shirt and string tie, he was the very model of a Wild West gunfighter.

The Marsden suite was on the sixth floor. Jane had instructed him to knock on the door of her adjoining room, 648, so that he wouldn't run into her father. Mark gulped audibly when she opened the door. Her form-fitting strapless black dress showed off her tanned shoulders and the smooth swell of her breasts. She wore a diamond choker around her neck and the slit in her skirt revealed tantalizing glimpses of an embroidered garter encircling a shapely thigh. She would never look like a gangster's moll but she would turn every man's head that night.

Two floors above, in their much less commodious accommodation, the Crawfords were also getting ready for the night's festivities. Marianne cleared her throat nervously. "I'm going to have to skip Rhodes's cocktail party."

Bill raised an inquiring eyebrow and waited for her to go on.

"The ladies have worked up a little skit for tonight."

"And you're in it?" Bill sounded both surprised and pleased. Having his wife act in a skit at the Oilmen's would show the world that the Crawfords were really 'in.'

"I've got one of the lead roles," Marianne said with a proud little smile. "Sharon wrote it. She's real clever that way."

"That's great!" Bill enthused. Getting up on a stage and acting a part, even if it was only an amateur skit, seemed totally out of character for his wife, but maybe she was finally coming out of her shell. Palling around with Sharon Livingston seemed to be doing wonderful things for Marianne's self-confidence. He wanted to tell her to watch her drinking, but knew that would send her spinning off into one of her defiant moods where anything could happen.

Bill finished adjusting his bolo tie and gave his wife a peck on the cheek. She wouldn't thank him for smearing her lipstick. "Okay, I'm off to Rhodes's little soiree. Knock 'em dead, sweetheart!"

"You'll have to go into dinner by yourself, too," Marianne told him. "Sharon's organized things so we go on early, before everybody gets too plastered."

The pre-dinner reception was sponsored by Apex Drilling, Rhodes Taylor's company. He and Brenda Lester stood just inside the entrance of the Alberta Room to welcome their colourfully garbed guests. Many of the Calgarians had simply dusted off their Stampede clothes, but the gun moll theme had given some of the younger women an excuse to wear dresses that were blatantly sexy. Jane, normally so collegiate in skirt and sweater, outshone them all. Men swarmed around her in a way that reminded Mark of how Betty MacDonald used to hold court. Except that with The Bod, it had mainly amused him, but now he was anything but amused. At one point he whispered in an aside to her, "You're sure showing your wares tonight!" He meant it to be jocular but it came out sounding petulant and puerile.

She blushed and her hand instinctively went to her throat, covering her cleavage. Then she deliberately dropped it and turned away from Mark to say something to the man standing next to her. Cursing himself for his stupidity, Mark pasted on a smile and joined in the party chatter. After all, she was his date — for all the world to see. He caught a glimpse of a scowling Cliff Marsden hovering at the edge of the crowd. Mark laughed at something that was said and came back with an amusing rejoinder, for which he was rewarded with a forgiving smile from Jane.

Rhodes tapped the live microphone and a few muffled groans went up at the prospect of a speech from the host. Brenda Lester, a radiant smile softening her mannish features, stood beside him at the mike.

"She's wearing a ring," Jane whispered to Mark. "She wasn't when we came in."

Rhodes waited while an army of waiters circulated through the crowd, serving each guest with a glass of champagne. There were audible gasps from some of the women who were close enough to get a good view of the spectacular diamond.

"Four carats at least," Estelle Dobbs pronounced, with the air of someone who knows.

"Only the best for Rhodes," Mark murmured without malice.

"I'm a very happy man tonight, folks." And the tense, high-strung oilman *did* look happy, and as relaxed as anyone had ever seen him. "Brenda has consented to be my wife."

Standing in the centre of the crowd, Bill Crawford raised his glass and called out, "To Brenda and Rhodes. May they find much happiness together!"

Which is more than you and Marianne have, thought Mark as he joined in Bill's toast to the engaged couple. He looked around for Marianne but couldn't spot her in the crowd.

Rhodes and his fiancée mingled with their guests for a few minutes, accepting congratulations and good wishes, then the room lights dimmed three times, signalling that it was time to move into the Alhambra Room for dinner and dancing. The loud voices of the men boomed out a hearty mixture of golf and business as the costumed procession wended its way along the wide, medieval-looking hallways. Mark and Jane were to sit with Rhodes and Brenda and two other couples whom they hadn't met. They exchanged glances when they located their table and saw the other two couples who were already seated. They were somewhere in their fifties, the men red-faced and paunchy and the women with bright yellow hair and recent face lifts. All four were obviously intoxicated, one of the men almost tripping over his feet as he stood up to introduce himself as Al Perkins from Dallas. "As are these other good folks," he added with a wave of his hand that nearly unbalanced him.

"This is God's country you folks got up heah," Al drawled as he carefully lowered himself back into his chair. "How come we ain't never heard of it until now?"

"We prefer to keep it a secret," said Jane sweetly as she unfolded her napkin. Mark picked up the toy six-shooter that had been placed beside each bread and butter plate as a party favour. "Looks like the real thing," he muttered as he put it down.

The big-name band imported from Philadelphia struck up a tune and Mark and Jane gratefully fled to the dance floor. It was so crowded it was impossible to do much more than stand and sway in the same place. "What do you think of our table companions?" she asked, wincing as a lurching body bumped into her.

Mark looked down at her, to be mesmerized by the valley between her breasts. "Diamonds in the rough. But harmless," he said finally.

Rhodes and Brenda had arrived by the time they made it back to the table. The two women from Dallas were oohing and aahing over Brenda's ring. The contrast between the Texans and the fastidious, almost effete, Taylor was striking, but Rhodes hadn't built up a prosperous drilling company without learning how to get along with types like this. He listened attentively while Al, who seemed to do most of the talking, told him how he had inherited a few "dinky little stripper wells" from his father and parlayed them into a company that produced a thousand barrels a day. "And it's all mine, every last barrel," he boasted.

Rhodes was impressed and showed it. The noise and sweat level steadily rose, but they got through the soup course without incident, except for a few buns being lobbed at the head table. Then a man in a Lone Ranger mask commandeered the microphone and announced with a flourish, "Ladies and gentlemen! The main course!"

He raised his arm and pointed with a dramatic flourish to a procession of masked men marching in under one of the archways. They carried on their shoulders two large sheets of plywood each bearing an enormous silver tureen.

"You folks sure know how to do things in style," marvelled Al as the little parade came to a halt next to the serving station in the centre of the floor. "What's under them silver dishes? Roast pig?"

Two of the masked men positioned themselves so they could lift the covers off the tureens. The masked figure at the microphone asked the bandleader for a drum roll. The drummer obliged, and as the roll ended with a tricky rim shot, the covers were snatched off and a gasp went through the crowd.

Lying curled on the trays were two blonde women, totally naked except for small red masks. After that one spontaneous and collective intake of breath, the dinner crowd was silent as the women slowly raised themselves until they were resting on their knees with their legs tucked underneath. They began to sway from side to side, their breasts moving in sensuous rhythm. They stood upright and an excited hum, underlaid with sexuality, ran through the cavernous ballroom as the trays were slowly rotated so that everyone could see.

"Who are they?" someone asked.

"They must be professional entertainers," a woman ventured.

"The hell they are!" A man's voice boomed out. "That's Astrid Winslow. I'd recognize them big brown nipples anywhere."

Mark who, like everyone else, was on his feet, suddenly exclaimed, "My God, it's Marianne Crawford! She must be bombed out of her mind!"

As he spoke, he saw Bill Crawford fighting his way through the crowd, stripping off his Western-cut jacket as he went. Marianne's mouth, fixed in a forced, defiant smile, turned tremulous when she saw her husband and she let herself fall forward into his arms. Gently, almost tenderly, he lifted her down and wrapped her in his jacket. With a set face, he steered his wife to the nearest exit. Gerald Winslow was too intoxicated to do anything more than sit in his chair, a glassy smile pasted on his sweating face. His naked wife held her arms over her head as she was borne triumphantly from the room.

"Jesus Christ!" muttered a shaken Mark. "Why did she have to pull a stunt like that? Maybe this will convince her that she needs help."

Jane didn't seem to hear him. She was staring straight ahead, her eyes unfocussed. Once she flinched and gasped as though someone had struck her. It was almost as if she were having some kind of attack.

"Jane, are you all right?" asked a worried Mark. Again, she didn't seem to hear him, her eyes fixed unblinkingly at the spot where Marianne and Astrid had put on their little show. Then the maitre d', frowning with disapproval at the unseemly goings-on, stationed himself in the middle of the floor and began to direct traffic. Waiters scurried to pour the wine and serve the main course. Mark touched Jane's arm and she sank into her seat, still without looking at him. He thought he heard her whispering "no, no," to herself, but couldn't be sure with all the background noise.

Al Perkins, still bug-eyed from the display of female flesh, was drinking the wine — vintage claret — as if it were coloured water. A waiter obligingly stood at his elbow and refilled his glass three times before leaving to attend to another table. Gazing morosely at the dregs in his glass, Perkins absently began to play with the toy gun. "Hey, this thing's a water pistol! Let's see if it works."

Dipping the end of the barrel into a glass of ice water, he pulled the plunger, sucking up all the water in the glass. Before anyone could stop him, he aimed a stream of water at the delinquent wine waiter hovering over a nearby table. The water found its target but it also sprayed a hot-tempered oilman who immediately snatched up his water pistol and squirted Perkins in the eye.

Chortling with glee, Perkins refilled his pistol, but this time with red wine from his wife's glass. His victim spluttered with fury as his shiny white satin shirt turned blood red. Bellowing with rage, he filled his pistol from a wineglass and squeezed the trigger, scoring a bull's-eye on Perkins and also soaking his wife. Looking down at her ruined costume, she swore and reached for her own gun.

The banquet was swept with a kind of mania as men from other tables gleefully joined in the fray, while their womenfolk screamed and wept over ruined dresses. Someone, probably envious of the moneyed and successful Taylor, took advantage of the confusion to hit him in the face with a full load of red wine. Rhodes wiped at his eyes, trying to clear them of the stinging liquid. "I think I better go upstairs and change," he said mildly, peering down at the stains on his jacket.

"I'm coming with you," Brenda announced and took his arm.

Mark got to his feet, pulling Jane up with him. Now she was finally looking directly at him, but there was still that strange, almost vacant, look in her eyes. "We're getting out of here," he muttered, tugging at her arm.

She nodded, almost indifferently, and followed him as they, along with some of the saner guests, retreated to a far corner of the ballroom. Mark stared in amazement at the incredible scene. With arcing jets of red wine filling the air, it looked like a miniature battlefield. The band continued to play until a woman on the dance floor took dead aim at the female vocalist and another sprayed the orchestra leader. Livid with rage, he motioned the band to stop and told the crowd they were going to take an intermission until "this craziness stops."

No one could hear him above the pandemonium. How in God's name could grown-up, educated people behave like that? Disgusted by the spectacle, Mark said, "The party's over." He pointed to an exit sign. "I think we can make it to there without getting in firing range."

Outside the hotel, the moon shone down on the majestic mountain peaks, glinting on little pockets of snow that still lingered in some high, sheltered crevices. Mark breathed deeply of the mountain air and shook his head. "It makes you wonder about the human race, doesn't it?"

Jane, lost in some world of her own, made no reply. The moon, high and silver in the sky, suddenly emerged from behind a cloud and Mark was astonished to see a look of unbearable anguish on her face. As if her whole body were screaming, a high-pitched wailing sound seemed to surround her. Then her lips began to form words. "Why did you do it, Daddy? How could you do it, Daddy?"

"What is it, Jane? What are you talking about?"

"It's true. It's all true. I remember everything. Oh, my God!" Jane bit the back of her hand to keep from screaming. "He used to take off my nightie and make me stand on the bed and move my hips in a dance — like ... like they were doing in there. He called me his little showgirl. And he would make me ... do terrible things."

"My God, Jane, do you know what you're saying?"

"It's all coming back to me." She seemed to be aware of Mark for the first time. "I'm not dreaming, am I?"

"It's no dream," he said grimly. "Let me try to get this straight, Jane. Are you saying your father abused you?"

"Yes." She swayed on her feet and Mark grabbed her arm to keep her from falling. She gave him a grateful little smile that tore at his heart. Still in that same wondering tone of voice she went on, "Daddy was always the one who put me to bed and tucked me in. It was his "special time" with me. He used to ... to touch me, even when I was very small. He made me touch him, too. Oh God, Mark, what am I going to do?"

"Keep talking. You have to share this with someone who loves you."

"Do you love me, Mark? After this?"

"I love you." He kissed her, but she didn't respond. Somewhere out in the darkness, a coyote gave its yip-yipping howl and was answered from further down the valley. "Did he ... you know?"

"Yes. I must have been ten or eleven when ... God, it hurt."

"Jesus Christ, Jane!"

"I know. It's horrible, isn't it? That's probably why I was able to block it out. I remember going to school and feeling I had this terrible secret that set me apart from everybody else. I always led the class and I was captain of the girls' volleyball and field hockey teams but that didn't help. I still felt soiled. Unclean. And I knew that if anyone found out I would be branded as something abnormal and perverted. Like an untouchable. Then I had to go home to ..." For the first time, her voice faltered.

Mark was overcome with horror and compassion. It explained so much about her, especially her strange sexual behaviour. "When did it stop?"

"When I was fifteen. I told him I would tell Mother if he didn't. He ... he wanted to have a child by me. I would go away to have it, and then he and mother would adopt it. That must have been the final straw that made me sublimate the whole horrible business."

"The man's insane! Why didn't you tell your mother what was going on?"

"I couldn't. I was so ashamed I couldn't bear the thought of anyone else knowing. And I guess I must have realized that mother is not what you would call a strong character. It would have destroyed her."

"Instead, you let it almost destroy you." Mark winced at the thought of her as a child bravely trying to protect her family from the terrible burden she was carrying. No wonder she had finally taken refuge by blocking it out.

"God, Mark, what am I going to do?"

"Marry me." He put his arms around her, holding her close to his chest.

"I can't, Mark," she whispered. "I can't marry anybody. Ever."

"Don't talk like that!" Alarmed, he almost shook her. "It wasn't your fault. It has nothing to do with you. Nothing. You must believe that."

"It happened, though. I did all those dirty things."

"We'll get help for you. There are psychiatrists who specialize in child abuse cases. They can help you put all this in the right perspective."

"I don't want anybody poking around in my psyche. I'll deal with this myself."

"I know how you feel. But professional help is there if we decide we need it."

She shivered suddenly. "I'm cold. But I don't want to be alone. Not yet."

"Let's change into something warmer and go for a walk."

Hand in hand, they walked, for the most part in silence, along the velvety fairways. At one point, Jane asked in a little-girl voice, "What am I going to do about Daddy?"

Mark thought for a few moments before replying, "I think you're going to have to act as though nothing has changed. At least until we have time to sort this out."

"I'm not sure I can do that. But I'll try."

The moonlight was bright enough for her to read her watch. "It's almost midnight. I better get back."

"Will you be all right by yourself?"

"I think so. I'm awfully glad you were there when it happened, Mark. Thank you for being so understanding."

"Jesus, Jane. There's no need to thank me. I love you. Can't you understand that?"

She pressed a finger against his lips and said with a forlorn little smile, "All I know is that you've been wonderful to me."

They paused for a moment beside the outdoor pool before entering the hotel. "You do believe me, don't you, Mark?"

Astonished, he stared down at her. "Believe you? What about?"

"That my father did those things to me."

"Of course I believe you. Nobody in their right mind would lie about something like that."

28

"Hunter!" The shout stopped Mark dead in his tracks. He spun around. Cliff Marsden, his face set in a belligerent scowl, strode across the lobby toward him. "What have you done with Jane, you son of a bitch?" he demanded.

Mark looked at him with loathing. There were no words to describe a man who would do what he had done to his own child. The bastard should be in prison. Then the import of what Cliff had said filtered through the haze of his fury. "What are you talking about?" he demanded, unclenching his fists as anxiety displaced his anger. "What's happened to her?"

"She's disappeared. I can't find her anywhere." He shook his fist in Mark's face. "If you've harmed so much as a hair on her head, I'll have your balls!" Cliff's face took on an unhealthy mottled hue and he was breathing heavily. "You were with her last night. What time did you leave her?" he asked in a voice that quavered as it struggled for control.

"I said good night to her just after midnight and haven't seen her since." Mark cursed himself for not staying with her and helping her make it through the night. He should have realized that after the trauma she had suffered, anything could happen. But at the time she had seemed to be in control of herself. Damn and triple damn. But there was no time for vain regrets. "Have you searched her room?"

"Her mother and I did. Most of her stuff is still there, but a few things are missing. According to her mother, she would be wearing jeans, jodhpur boots, and either a plain blue or white shirt."

"Sounds to me as though she just decided to go for an early morning ride. I'll go over to the stables and check it out."

"It's not that simple. I wish it was. She also took a couple of changes of underwear and her toilet things. Like she intended to be gone for a while. My wife and I were afraid maybe you two had eloped."

"That's what we should have done. I'm still going to check out the stables."

"Let me know what you find out. I'll keep looking around the hotel grounds."

Mark stared at Jane's father. He was scum. Beneath contempt. But for the moment they shared a common cause. Finding Jane. And with as little fuss as possible. "I'll be in touch," he said tersely.

"No, I haven't seen her. Not since yesterday." The faint lines of a frown appeared between Sue's pale, sun-bleached eyebrows. "Dulcie's gone."

"What? Oh, isn't that the horse she was riding yesterday afternoon?"

"That's the one. She really seemed to like that mare. Someone took her out of the corral during the night, and that same someone broke into the tack room and stole a bridle." Sue paused and added, as if determined to be fair. "I guess "stole" isn't exactly right, because whoever it was left an envelope with a couple of hundred dollars cash."

"What about a saddle?"

"Nope. They're all still on the racks. But an experienced rider wouldn't need a saddle. Not with a horse like Dulcie." She gave him a shrewd look. "Why are you lookin' for her? You two have a fight?"

"No. Nothing like that. I just thought she might have gone for a ride. She's probably somewhere around the hotel. I hope you get Dulcie back. Give me a call and let me know what happens."

"Sure. And you let me know when you find Jane. Or even if you don't find her."

Mark gave her a quizzical backward look over his shoulder but made no reply.

"No sign of her over at the stables." Mark had decided to postpone telling Marsden about the missing horse until they were sure Jane was nowhere about the hotel. "Let's do a square search for her before we hit the panic button."

Harrison Dobbs, strolling with his wife down by the tennis courts, stared in amazement at the sight of Mark and Cliff walking side-by-side. "Now that's something I never expected to see," he remarked thoughtfully. They seemed to be in a tearing hurry. The peace of his morning stroll was dispelled as his restless mind uneasily explored the consequences for him if those two blood enemies ever made peace.

A half-hour's intensive search turned up no sign of Jane. As those who knew about their well-publicized feud stared in disbelief, Mark and Cliff walked into the writing room and sat down together, Cliff popping into his chair with a weary sigh. Maybe the son of a bitch will have a heart attack and die before this is over, thought Mark, surprised at how appealing he found the idea to be. After last night's revelations Marsden was no longer fit to be treated as a member of the human race and Mark told himself that he could watch him die with equanimity. Meanwhile though, Jane was still out there somewhere.

He cleared his throat to get Cliff's attention and said, "Something strange happened over at the stables and it's just possible it may be somehow connected with Jane. A horse was stolen during the night — the same horse that she rode yesterday. And the tack room was broken into and a bridle is missing."

"A horse stolen and a tack room broken into?" Cliff asked incredulously. "And you think Jane might be involved? That's bullshit. She would never do anything like that. Not Jane."

"She was disturbed enough last night to do pretty well anything."

"Just what the hell did you do to her? Once this is over, boy, you and I are going to have a reckoning!"

"That we are," Mark replied grimly. "But it's not over." He got to his feet. "I'm going to get a horse and look for her in the mountains. Why don't you get in your car and drive around Banff to see if you can spot her? It would be a good idea to take Mrs. Marsden to help you look."

"Mrs. Marsden has probably passed out by now," muttered Cliff. "That's her way of dealing with emergencies." He got heavily to his feet. "I'll get Antonelli to help me look."

"Do you think that's wise?"

"Sure I do. He's got eyes and he'll keep his mouth shut."

The thought of the thug-like Antonelli looking for Jane gave Mark a queasy feeling but he had to admit that another pair of eyes would be useful. "Okay," he agreed reluctantly. "We'll meet back here in two hours. If Jane hasn't been found by then, we better think about organizing a search party."

"Over my dead body! Do you think I want everyone to know my daughter has run away? Besides, it's the last thing she'd want." Mark had to acknowledge the truth of that. If it ever got out that Jane had run away from her family at the Oilmen's, the story would dog her for the rest of her life. Just like the silver platter episode would forever haunt Marianne Crawford.

"I'll go with you and help you look," said Sue as she tightened Chaparral's girth before handing the reins to Mark.

"That's great, Sue. Otherwise I can see myself getting lost in the first fifteen minutes. You know, that could have happened to Jane. She could have lost her way up in the mountains."

"No way. All she has to do is give Dulcie her head and that mare would bring her right back to the stables." Sue backed a spotted Appaloosa away from the rail and vaulted into the saddle with a litheness that not even Jane could duplicate.

"I just don't see Jane pulling a stunt like this," said Sue as they scrambled up a steep rocky slope in a fast trot. "But you seem so positive that she did. That must have been some fight you two had."

"I told you, we didn't have a fight. But she was upset about something. Very upset. But I'm sure she'll come back when she feels like it. After all, she doesn't have any food or supplies."

"She has money, doesn't she? Easy enough for her to ride into Banff and buy whatever she needs and head back into the hills. I figure she can stay out as long as she wants. She wasn't upset enough to kill herself, was she?"

"Jesus, Sue. Don't say things like that."

They worked their way up the mountain, taking turns calling Jane's name. There was no reply, just the breeze whispering through the pines. They met up with a group of trail riders strung out along a narrow ridge, but they reported having seen no trace of any one else since starting out in the early morning.

Sue told Mark that if he had to meet someone back at the hotel by one o'clock, he should join up with the trail ride. "They go right past our stables."

"What about you?"

"I'm going to stay out here till I find her."

"I'll settle up with the stables later. For the horses and your time."

"You take your money and shove it, Mark Hunter!"

On the way back, Mark acknowledged to himself that it was foolish to think their puny efforts had any real hope of finding Jane. Sue had told him that a network of trails extended for miles in all directions. Furthermore, since Jane was on horseback, she wouldn't be confined to trails but could roam wherever she wished. People got lost in the mountains for days even with search parties looking for them. She could be lying out there badly injured, crying for help. It was time to stop fooling around and report it to the park wardens and get a full-scale search underway. He'd have to convince Marsden somehow. Unless, of course, Marsden had found her, or she had turned up on her own account.

No such luck. Marsden and Antonelli had drawn a complete blank in town. Marsden had called Calgary on the off chance she had returned home. "I didn't ask directly, of course, but when the housekeeper asked if Jane was having a good time ..." He shrugged.

"We've got to talk, Mr. Marsden." Even under these circumstances, Mark couldn't bring himself to call the child abuser by his first name. "Let's go out on the terrace."

"By the way, I've cancelled my game for the afternoon." Cliff made it sound as if he had made a major sacrifice. "I had no chance of winning my flight anyway," he added, making Mark wonder whether the game would have been cancelled if he had still been in the running.

"This is more serious than you seem to realize. Your daughter is in a frame of mind where she could do harm to herself. I say we can't delay any longer in organizing a search party."

"And I say we do no such thing. We went through this earlier. What the hell do you mean about her frame of mind? Just what did you do to her last night?"

"Not me, Marsden. You. Jane remembered her childhood last night. All of it."

"What's that supposed to mean, for Christ's sake?" Cliff blustered, but Mark saw the look of fear that suddenly leapt into his narrowed eyes.

"It's called child abuse. Jane had locked it away in her subconscious but it all came pouring out last night."

"What kind of crap is this? You know what I think? I think you killed her. You probably raped her when she wouldn't give in to you and then you killed her to shut her up. And now you're trying to frame me with this child abuse bullshit."

"I'm not trying to frame anybody. I'm trying to find the girl I love while she's still alive. And our best chance of doing that is to bring the experts in."

"Not yet." Cliff, still in a state of shock over Mark's devastating accusation, spoke mechanically. Then he shook his head as if to concentrate on first things first. "Listen to me. We've got to think of Jane's reputation. We've still got a few hours of daylight left. And this girl Sue is out looking for her on horseback. Right?"

"Yes. But that's one person trying to cover hundreds of square miles. You sound as if you know her?"

"Sue?" Cliff shrugged. "I saw her a couple of times when Jane used to instruct at Borden's." He suddenly wheeled on Mark, demanding, "Did you tell her about this child abuse nonsense?"

"No. She thinks Jane and I had a fight."

"Does anyone else know?"

"Hell, no. It's not exactly the sort of thing one spreads around. Unfortunately," Mark added bitterly, "the victim gets just as badly tainted as the criminal."

Mark's deliberate use of the word criminal made Cliff wince, but he continued to stonewall. "I'm telling you it's a crock of shit. And you know it. But we can go into that after we find Jane. If you haven't killed her already, that is. Let's make a deal. If she hasn't turned up by nightfall, we report her missing. Between now and then you and I and Antonelli will look for her on foot, while Sue searches the high country on horseback. Agreed?"

Mark, thinking of what Jane would want, nodded grudging assent. It was bizarre, the way he and Marsden were acting so matter-of-factly. It was only because everything else was subordinate to Jane's safety. And to give the bastard his due, Marsden seemed to feel the same way. He obviously had no intention of confessing to child abuse but, like he said, that could wait.

Marsden was talking again, suggesting that they get his car and drive across the other side of the river to start their search. "Jane used to like to ride over there when she was a youngster." The memory of those far-off days almost made him smile until the full force of Mark's accusations came back to fill him with terror. Scowling, he said, "I'll go collect Antonelli. Meet us in the parking lot in fifteen minutes."

Since they had talked about it more than once, Cliff was reasonably certain of his man. But when it got right down to the nut-cutting you never could tell.

"Here's your chance to earn yourself a bonus," he said as he and his bodyguard went through the revolving door of the hotel entrance.

"Hunter?"

"Yeah. He's getting on my nerves."

"How much did you have in mind, boss?"

"Ten thousand."

"Make it fifteen and you're on."

"Okay. But it has to be done right away. While we're all out on the trail together."

"That's not so smart, boss. These things need to be planned."

"No time. Besides I know exactly how we're going to do it. He's going to take a ride down the Bow Falls. Nobody can survive that. You've got your sap, haven't you?"

Joe Antonelli patted his jacket. "Never without it. You know that."

"Good. You knock him out in the woods just before we reach the path. I'll tell you when. Then we wait until the coast is clear and throw him over the cliff. The falls will do the rest. By the time they finish with him nobody will be able to tell he's been sapped."

"As simple as that? Yeah, it might work."

Cliff greeted Mark, who was waiting for them by the Lincoln, in a manner that was almost jovial, making Mark wonder if the unspeakable monster had flipped over the edge.

29

"Steady, boy," Sue murmured as the Appaloosa's steel-shod hooves slipped on the bare rock. When the horse had recovered his footing, she called again for Jane. Her throat was raw from shouting and she was growing more discouraged by the minute. It was hopeless trying to find one horse and rider in this vast wilderness area. She looked at her wristwatch — three-thirty. The day was fast closing in. She called again but the only response was the loud cry of a whisky-jack, peering curiously at her from the top of a stunted pine. "What's the matter, Appy?" Sue stroked his neck to soothe him. "You don't like being way up here, do you, boy?" She frowned as she felt a quiver run along the muscles of his neck.

Skirting a large limestone outcrop, they came upon a small alpine meadow. The wildflowers had ceased blooming but there was a large patch of wild raspberries. Sue decided to help herself to a few handfuls; she had had nothing to eat since her seven o'clock breakfast. A low, rumbling growl, that seemed to come from the bowels of the earth, raised the hairs on the back of her neck. Her horse snorted with fear and rolled a wild eye back at her. The bear, huge, brown, and menacing, stood up on its hindquarters in the middle of the berry patch. One look at its immense size and dished face told Sue she was dealing with a grizzly and not the less fearsome black bear. Two smaller brown shapes continued to stuff themselves with the luscious berries, oblivious of the mounted intruder. God in heaven, she had blundered into the worst possible bear scenario — a sow with cubs, fattening up on berries for the winter hibernation. Still there were numerous contacts between humans and grizzlies that turned out harmlessly. Sue managed to control her own fear, but there was nothing she could do with the panic-stricken horse. Sweating and trembling, it reared as the sow suddenly dropped to her haunches and charged. Realizing the horse had lost his balance and was going to topple over backward with her underneath, she frantically tried to bail out. Her left foot caught in the stirrup and she heard something snap. Then she was falling, to land with a jarring crump on the bare rock.

The horse's terrorized neighing rose to a near scream as it struggled to regain its feet and flee down the mountainside. But the bear, moving with awesome speed for so huge an animal, was upon it before it had taken two strides. In shock, but still conscious, Sue watched with horror as the giant bear mauled the doomed horse. Its blood-chilling ululations were abruptly choked off as the grizzly broke its neck with one swipe of a mighty paw. Throbbing with pain, Sue lay still, praying that the bear would make a meal of the dead horse and leave her alone. To her horror, she saw one of the cubs, its endearingly cute face alive with curiosity, padding in her direction. The sow let out a barking roar and charged. Knowing her young life was over, and too paralyzed with fright to close her eyes, Sue watched the brown behemoth hurtling toward her. She smelled the sweet smell of blood on its breath, then it suddenly veered away to intercept the venturesome cub. Giving it a cuff that made it squeal with outrage, the sow sent it running back to join its sibling. Then she drove them both, squalling in protest, out of the berry patch and into the trees.

Sue, who unconsciously had been holding her breath, released it in a long shuddering sigh. Would the sow come back to finish her off after escorting her cubs to safety? Suddenly she became aware of a familiar sound, the frenzied neighing of a horse. Propping herself up on her right elbow, ignoring the pain that shot through her left side, Sue shouted, "Is anybody there? Can you hear me? I'm hurt. I need help."

There was no answer, but the neighing and whickering snorts seemed to be closer. It was coming from somewhere beyond a large, smoothly-rounded hump of rock. Sue called out again and this time there was an answer. "Hang on, I'm coming." It was a woman's voice. Then horse and rider appeared against the skyline and Sue almost fainted with relief when she recognized Jane astride Dulcie.

"My God, Sue, what happened to you?" cried Jane as she slipped off Dulcie's back and knelt beside the fallen rider. The mare, terrified by the bear smell, danced and tossed her head, but Jane had a firm grip on the reins.

"Bear attack," replied Sue tersely, saying everything that needed to be said.

"What did he do to you?" Jane looked for the horrible signs of a bear mauling but found none.

"It was a she-bear. With cubs. She didn't touch me. She killed Appy and made what the fellows around the stable call a 'bluff' charge at me. It was being thrown that bent me out of shape." Trying to be nonchalant, Sue unconsciously slipped into the macho lingo of the rodeo cowboy. With Jane's help, she managed to sit all the way up. "We gotta get outa here. That old sow could come roaring back any minute."

"And we have to get you to a hospital. If I help you, can you get on Dulcie's back?"

"Easy. Just grab me under my left arm and hold me up. I think my left ankle's snapped and my wrist feels like it's broken."

With Jane supporting her, Sue draped herself across the mare's withers. Nervous quivers rippled underneath the horse's hide but, obediently, she stood still as Sue hooked her good right leg over her back and pulled herself on board. Jane jumped on behind and they got out of there at a brisk trot, Dulcie snorting with fear as they gave the carcass of the dead Appaloosa a wide berth.

"What were you doing way out here?" Jane asked, then answered her own question. "Dear God, you were looking for me."

"Yep. You got some people mighty worried about you. Especially Mark."

"I had to get away. To be by myself for a while to sort some things out. I guess I never thought what it would do to other people. I find it hard to deal with the fact that you were hurt on my account, Sue."

"It's a long way from my heart." Sue thought to herself that most likely what Jane had to think about was whether or not to marry Mark. If it had been her, she sure as hell wouldn't have had to go off by herself in the woods to find the answer. But it would never be her. Jane was the type of girl men like Mark ended up marrying.

Despite herself, Sue was unable to stifle a groan as Dulcie, carefully working her way down a steep boulder-strewn path, suddenly propped both forefeet on a rock ledge to keep from pitching forward.

"Are you okay?" The horse's sudden movement brought Jane hard against Sue's tight little rump. Jane put a supporting arm around Sue's waist as Dulcie recovered her balance and resumed her cautious progress. "Maybe you should stay here and let me bring back a stretcher party. I know exactly where we are."

"You kidding? I'm not staying on any damn mountain where the bears are having themselves a picnic. It's just that my wrist hurts something fierce when it gets jiggled."

"Some sort of splint would help." Jane brought the mare to a halt and slid off. "We should be out of that bear's territory by now."

She snapped some small branches from a dead larch and placed them around Sue's wrist. "I'm not going to try to set it, but I'll do my best to immobilize it," she said as she wrapped the sticks with spare undies from the bag tied around her waist.

"Looks like you were planning to spend some time out here," observed Sue, eyeing the lacy undergarments.

"I was so upset I don't think I was planning anything."

"Feel like talking about it?" asked Sue as Jane climbed up behind her and took the reins.

"Unfortunately, it's not something I can talk about. It's something I have to deal with myself. No offence."

"None taken. You know where we're going, by the way?"

"Yes. I figure the fastest way to get you some medical attention is to go down to the river and ride around the top of the cliff to the parking lot. Somebody will drive you to the hospital from there."

"You sure seem to know your way around these parts. How come?"

"My family spent a lot of time in Banff when I was a child." As she spoke she was assailed with a sudden vivid memory of her father coming into her bedroom at the cottage, pulling her nightgown over her head and running his hands over her naked little body. Then he would whisper what he wanted her to do. They had to speak in whispers because the walls in the cottage were so thin. *Oh God, Daddy, why did you do this to me? What made you do it?* Jane's head spun dizzily and she put a hand on Sue's shoulder to keep from falling. Sue smiled and reached up to squeeze it.

Now that the veil had been lifted, she would be tormented by these horrible memories at every turn. How she wished they had remained forever locked in her subconscious. Maybe a psychiatrist could block them out once again. No, she had to face up to the reality of what had happened and come to terms with it.

Cliff looked sideways at Antonelli and received a slight affirmative nod. It was going to happen. He realized now that he could never have gone through with it himself, he would have panicked at the last minute. But Antonelli seemed to treat it as being all in a day's work. Cliff's pulse was pounding in his ears and his breath was coming in uneven gasps at the enormity of what he had set in motion. But he had no choice. With Hunter alive to expose him — and the son of a bitch would like nothing better — he would be an outcast, despised and reviled on all sides. He might be able to tough that one out; he had long since grown accustomed to being thought of as an egotistical prick, but it wouldn't stop there. He could end up being prosecuted and sentenced to a stiff term in prison. That he could not and would not take.

Jane would never let her father go to prison. He was sure of that. The knowledge that he would end up in jail if she talked would guarantee her silence. Mark was the real danger. With him out of the way, everything would be controllable. They were almost at the spot.

Mark brushed away the pine needles that stuck to the sweat on his forehead and squinted up at the small patch of sky that was visible through the tops of the towering pines. The trees cast long shadows on the trail. "We don't have much time left." He had to raise his voice slightly to be heard above the muted roar of Bow Falls thundering through a rocky gorge somewhere up ahead.

Cliff gave Antonelli the go-ahead sign and stepped back to let the killer precede him. Antonelli hefted the lethal blackjack in his right hand, selecting the spot he would aim for. He had to be careful not to kill Mark, he would have to be still breathing when he went over the cliff so there would be water in his lungs.

Taking a quick look back up the trail to make sure the coast was clear, Cliff shouted, "Did you hear that? I think I heard somebody calling. It sounded like a girl."

Mark halted in his tracks. "Where?"

"It seemed to come from over there. To our right. Can you hear anything?"

"No." Mark strained to hear, cupping his hand to his ear.

The blackjack hissed through the air in a short, deadly arc, and Mark crumpled without uttering a sound. Blood oozed from a wound at the base of his skull as he lay sprawled on the trail. Antonelli examined his weapon for traces of blood. Finding none, he pocketed it with a self-satisfied smile. Then he and an agitated Marsden began to drag Mark down the trail.

Cliff had chosen his spot well. Sightseers mostly kept to the other side of the river, and the pine trees that stubbornly clung to the rocky face of the cliff would screen them from view so long as they stayed low to the ground. And he had a story prepared — a story about how their friend had taken a nasty fall — if someone did come along the trail. The real danger lay in those unavoidable few seconds when they had to push Mark over the cliff. But they would hug the ground and make their move only when there was no one else in sight.

"What the hell are those guys playing at?" Sue pointed with her uninjured right arm to the figures further down the trail. They were acting damn peculiar. All three were flat on the ground, one guy was wiggling along on his stomach while another lay on his back, pulling the third man after him, as if towing him to shore. Except it wasn't the shore they were heading for; it was the cliff. Only a few yards separated them from the edge.

"I don't think they're playing." Jane urged Dulcie into a trot. The sound of the hooves striking the hard-packed ground made Cliff look around. "It's your father," said Sue in an awed voice. "And Mark. What's the matter with him? My God, they're going to throw him over the cliff!"

Jane gave an anguished cry and vaulted off the moving horse. "Stop it, Daddy. Don't do it!"

She flung herself on the recumbent Antonelli, pummelling him with her clenched fists. Antonelli released his grip on the unconscious Mark and reached for her, pinioning her arms. While Antonelli's seasoned criminal mind was assessing the situation, Sue slid off Dulcie's back, landing on her good right foot. Hopping on one leg, she made her awkward way toward Mark, pleading with him not to be dead. With the reins trailing on the ground, Dulcie stood as if tethered. Sue reached Mark and half-fell, half-dropped, on top of him. Her searching fingers found a pulse in his wrist, and a tigerish grin spread over her fierce little face. No way was he going over the cliff.

Still lying on his back and still pinioning Jane's arms, Antonelli looked at the defiant Sue with cool indifference. He'd get to her after he had taken care of Jane. The toll of the mountain tragedy had just increased by two. He had no intention of taking the rap for attempted murder and spending the next ten years behind bars. Life on the outside was just too sweet. Twisting Jane's left arm behind her back until it almost snapped, he forced her to her feet and began to frog march her toward the cliff.

"Daddy! Help me! Help me, Daddy!" Jane screamed.

Galvanized by the terror in his daughter's voice, Cliff hurled himself at Antonelli, blindly reaching for his throat. Antonelli, knocked off balance by the fury of Cliff's attack, staggered forward a few steps, clawing at the suffocating grip with his free hand. But Cliff's hands remained firmly clamped around his throat, thumbs pressing against the base of his skull and fingers digging into Antonelli's larynx. The killer, his eyes beginning to pop, released his hold on Jane's arm and, using both hands, tried to pry Cliff's grip open. Marsden, knowing his own life was now also at stake, hung on grimly as they struggled. Antonelli, beginning to be seriously short of breath, suddenly changed tactics and began to bludgeon Cliff's midriff with his elbows. He heard Cliff grunt with pain and felt his grip begin to slacken. Confident that it was all over, Antonelli took a step backward to give himself leverage and reached up to tear Cliff's hands away. Cliff's scream exploded in his ear before Antonelli realized they were falling.

The two bodies remained locked together until they hit the face of the cliff where it jutted out some fifty feet below. Then they bounced and tumbled down the rest of the cliff, their screams only ceasing when the foaming cataract engulfed them. Jane watched in horror as the two men, only their heads visible above the swirling white water, were swept over the thundering waterfall. Sue hopped over to stand silently beside her. Sue looked across at the other side of the river; there was no one in sight. Two men had plunged to their death after a violent struggle and she and Jane were the only ones to have seen it happen. Without being aware of what she was doing, Jane was rubbing the arm that Antonelli had so cruelly twisted. Sue gently touched her arm and urged her back from the edge of the precipice.

Mark, struggling to sit up, stared at them groggily. "You missed all the excitement," Sue, a little giddy with shock and relief, said as she sat on the ground beside him and used her uninjured hand to help him to a sitting position. Gingerly Mark touched the lump on the back of his head and cried out with the pain. "What the hell happened?" he asked as the throbbing inside his head gradually subsided.

"Want me to tell him?" asked Sue. Jane, still in a state of shock, nodded indifferently. She seemed not to be aware of the hand Mark held out to her.

"When Jane and I rode around that bend back there we saw Mr. Marsden and another man dragging you toward the cliff. You were out cold. Jane tried to save you, the other guy grabbed her and was going to throw her over the cliff when her dad jumped him. They fought and then they both went over the edge."

Mark, his head much clearer now, stared at her in amazement. "Is this true?" he asked Jane who replied with a toneless, "Yes."

"And you saved me." He struggled unsteadily to his feet, ignoring the white stab of pain, and took an unresisting Jane in his arms.

"It was Daddy who saved us. All of us," she whispered against his shoulder. Mark's lips brushed her forehead. "Maybe now you'll be able to forgive him," he murmured.

"I don't know. I'll try."

Still sitting on the ground, Sue made a small clucking noise and Dulcie, stepping carefully to avoid the trailing reins, came over to her. Sue's injuries, now that adrenalin was no longer flooding into her arteries, sent waves of pain lancing through her body. Between them, Mark and Jane hoisted her onto the horse's back as gently as possible.

"What'll we tell the police?" asked Sue, as she picked up the reins Jane handed her. "There'll be an investigation. I remember the time somebody was killed by a horse at Borden's."

"We can't have a scandal," Jane blurted, her eyes wide with fright.

"We won't," Mark assured her. "We'll keep it simple," he said, picking up a good-sized rock and placing it just below the edge of the cliff. "Mr. Marsden and his companion were walking along the path, deep in conversation. Antonelli — we'll make your father the hero — stumbled over a rock and your father tried to grab hold of him and they both went over. Just another one of those unfortunate accidents that happen in the mountains."

Jane looked up at Sue. "Will you go along with that, Sue?"

"Me? Sure. Like Mark says: accidents happen all the time up here."

30

These funerals are making a regular churchgoer out of me, thought Mark as he slid into the pew next to Marianne Crawford. Bill, as a pallbearer, was seated in the front row. Marianne gave him a wan little smile, as if grateful for his company. She smelt strongly of mint and her fingers plucked nervously at a handkerchief in her lap.

Mark knew there was no point in looking around the packed church for a glimpse of Jane. She would be sitting in a screened alcove with her mother. In the six days that had elapsed since the bodies had been fished out of the pool below the falls, Mark had seen a great deal of Jane and her mother. He had been at Jane's side throughout the inquiry conducted by the RCMP, except for the half-hour when the sergeant in charge of the Banff detachment interrogated her in private. With three eye witnesses all telling the same story, the file was soon closed with a finding of accidental death. In order to avoid exciting suspicion, Mark had taken a chance that his head wound would heal by itself and, despite Jane's pleas, had refused to go to the hospital to have it treated. He knew that he had been severely concussed, but now, six days later, there were no lingering after-effects.

The congregation rose to sing one of the hymns Jane had selected. Sharing a hymn book with Marianne, Mark droned out the words with his thoughts still focused on Jane. Outwardly composed, she had made all the arrangements for the funeral with crisp efficiency, but every now and then her eyes would take on a desperate, haunted look as if seeing something too awful to bear. Mark cringed inwardly whenever he saw that look, but he quickly learned not to try to comfort her. The one time he had tried to do so by taking her in his arms, she had backed away with a look of wild alarm. He also had the good sense to know this was not the time to bring up their own situation, and wisely contented himself with helping her by running errands and acting as chauffeur.

When the service ended with a benediction from the Anglican priest, the congregation filed out, pew by pew, starting at the front. When their turn came, Mark took Marianne's arm and led her down the centre aisle. He saw the surreptitious looks and heard the whispers as they passed. Marianne's lips were beginning to tremble. He squeezed her hand and whispered something to her so she would look at him and not the curious crowd. Propped up on her crutches, Sue was standing near the back of the church. She winked at him and he motioned that he would talk to her outside.

The sunlight was just as bright as it had been for Cullen's funeral, but already there was a hint of autumn in the air. People pointed out a patch of yellowing leaves on a small poplar across the street and shook their heads. Calgary's too-brief summer was almost over.

Jane decided to have her father cremated — something that was still comparatively rare in Calgary — so her decision had created a mild sensation. Mark had never discussed it with her, but he was sure it was an attempt on her part to remove the last vestige of her father from the earth. Having the body that had so sordidly and callously abused her, consumed by flames might help to exorcise the devils within her. Because there would be no graveside service, Bill's duties as a pallbearer were over as soon as the coffin was loaded in the hearse. He immediately began to make his way over to where Marianne and Mark were standing. Mark heard a woman telling someone in an excited whisper about Marianne's escapade at the Oilmen's. Marianne heard it too, although she pretended not to. She intercepted her husband and led him down the hill to where their car was parked. Left to his own devices, Mark looked around for Sue. Leaning on her crutches, hampered by the casts on her left wrist and ankle, she was poised uncertainly at the top of the short flight of concrete steps.

"You look as if you could use some help," he said with a wide grin as he swept her up in his arms.

"I like this!" Sue pressed her cheek against his, then complained, "But it's over too soon," as he placed her gently on the ground. Jane and her mother had slipped out a side door to a waiting limousine and, with no family members present to receive condolences, the crowd was rapidly dispersing.

"Are you going to the reception?" Mark asked Sue.

"Naw. I don't belong with that crowd. Besides, I had a nice visit with Jane this morning. We met for coffee downtown." She paused as a dusty GMC pickup, Banff Trail Rides painted on the door, pulled up at the curb. "I'll just be a couple of minutes, Bob," she called out through the open window of the truck. The driver, his face obscured by a battered cowboy hat, nodded casual agreement and lit a cigarette.

"I need some advice, Mark. Jane offered to back me so I could set up my own riding stable. I told her that I couldn't take money from her, and then she said she'd make it a loan. What do you think?"

"The look on your face tells me that you really want to do it. Right?"

"It's what I've always wanted. More than anything."

"Well, there's your answer. Take her up on it. She can afford to lose it."

"She won't lose it." Sue bared her teeth in one of her fierce little grins. "Just watch me. I'm going to put Borden's out of business."

Using her crutches, she headed for the waiting truck. Halfway there, she looked back with a teasing smile. "Will you rent a horse from me, Mark?"

"I'll be a regular customer." He smiled as he said it, but looking at her taut little figure, he wondered if he really was joking.

"You've been a great help through all of this, Mark," said Eleanor Marsden after the last guests took their leave with murmured condolences. Jane's mother didn't look like a person in need of condolence — she looked more alive and with it than Mark had ever seen her. Living all those years with a domineering bastard like Cliff had exacted a terrible toll. With his oppressive presence removed, maybe she could still find some pleasure in life. Mark hoped so; he had come to like her as a person, although he could never forgive her for not stopping her husband's terrible abuse of their daughter. Jane had convinced herself that her mother couldn't have known what was going on, and outwardly Mark went along with that. But in his heart he knew she must have known. She had deliberately let Jane, doing her valiant childish best to protect her family, bear the full brunt of her father's incestuous acts.

Eleanor seemed to be aware of what he was thinking for she gave him a look that was almost pleading as she said, "I'm exhausted. I think I'll lie down for a while."

"Mother's right, you know. You've been wonderful. Especially to me. I don't think I would have survived without you."

"You would have survived all right. You're tougher than you think."

The catering staff bustled about, clearing up after the reception. Cliff had never been popular — in fact, he had been widely detested — but the Marsden name carried a lot of weight and nearly two hundred people had made the long trek out to the family home to pay their last respects.

"We're just in the way here," said Jane. "Let's go out on the patio. I'll get a sweater."

The cashmere sweater draped over her shoulders gave Jane that collegiate look Mark had come to dislike. It always made him feel she had retreated into a world where he couldn't go. It wasn't an educational gap — he had a university degree — it was just that that part of his life was in the past, while it was very much part of the present for her.

"Sue told me what you offered to do for her. I think it's great."

"What did she say? Is she going to accept? She left it kind of up in the air this morning."

"Definitely. She's really excited about the idea."

"I'm glad. She's a super little person. She really likes you, Mark."

"She's a good friend of both of us."

Jane raised a quizzical eyebrow but didn't pursue the matter. Instead she said, "It must have been a terrible strain for you, knowing that my father had you in his power like that."

"The worst part was knowing there was absolutely nothing I could do about it. Thank God he held off as long as he did." Mark paused and looked directly at Jane. "You don't have to sell me the shares, you know."

"I know I don't have to, but I'm going to. The certificates are in his name, by the way, not the company's. We'll do the paperwork when you get back from California."

"Wonderful. You know how much this means to me, Jane."

"I do know. And that makes me very happy. At least I can right one wrong my father did." A bitter grimace twisted Jane's lips and she quickly changed the subject. "Tell me about your California trip. Is it to let Norcal know that you're partners in the California project?"

"They already know. I talked to Dobbs on the phone and told him I expected to acquire Kennedy's shares in the next few days."

"What did he say? Was he pleased?"

"He didn't say much of anything. But he did agree that Norcal would make the funds available as per our agreement." Mark gave a grim little smile. "The real fun will come when I tell him I want control. This business with Kennedy and your father has taught me that a fifty-fifty split just won't work."

"Do you think there'll be a problem?"

"There'll be a problem all right. Chester Martin doesn't think much of my chances, I might add."

"Is he going with you?"

"Yes. I want to come away from that meeting with everything nailed down legally."

"Good luck," smiled Jane. For the first time since that terrible night at the Oilmen's she had taken a keen interest in something. It was a good sign and Mark knew he shouldn't undo it by telling her how much he loved her. But how he longed to!

31

"I have a feeling this is going to be a long, hard day," Chester Martin muttered when Mark joined him for breakfast in the Fairmont coffee shop.

"We're in for some mighty tough bargaining, that's for sure." Figuring he would need all the energy he could muster, Mark ordered a substantial breakfast of bacon and eggs. On the flight down he and the lawyer had discussed his desire to get control of the project without coming up with any sure-fire method of achieving it.

Chester took the last sip of his orange juice and asked, "You expect Dobbs to insist on a full fifty per cent equity position?"

"I'm sure of it. And the hell of it is that's what I told him Norcal could have. I should have had the brains to set a limit below fifty per cent."

"You're going to hear plenty about that in the next few hours. How do you propose to handle it? Did any bright ideas occur to you overnight?"

Mark swallowed a piece of bacon and cut into a fried egg. "You've told me it's not legally binding, right?"

"Strictly speaking, that's correct. You made an offer that has not yet been officially accepted. I mean, Norcal has never said, 'yes, we will participate and want fifty per cent of the equity.' Legally, you can withdraw the offer before it's accepted. But if you're going to do that, you'll have to do it right away before they have the chance to say they accept. But we both know that if you do that it will blow the meeting right out of the water."

"I'm not going to do it that way. I want to play it straight across the plate. I'm going to tell them that after my disastrous experience with Kennedy I have come to realize that a fifty-fifty split just doesn't work. Harrison knows what I went through with that character and I think he'll be sympathetic."

The lawyer looked sceptical. "He may be sympathetic as hell, but he's still got a responsibility to his shareholders. I think we can expect him to hang tough. What then?"

"I have no choice but to live up to my word and let them in for a full fifty per cent."

Harrison's normally pale complexion grew steadily pinker as he heard Mark out. "Are you comparing Norcal to this Kennedy person?" he spluttered when Mark was through.

"Certainly not. I recognize that Norcal will be an excellent partner and I want you in. But I've learned through bitter experience that an equal division of control is plain unworkable."

Harrison turned to his gas-supply manager. "George, were you not in this very room when Mark offered us up to fifty per cent participation in the pipeline?"

MacGregor nodded emphatically. "I most certainly was. And it's in my written notes of the meeting. I can get them if you want."

"That won't be necessary," said Mark. "I'm not denying that's what I said. But the point is that somebody has to have the final say on this project and that person is me. I was the one who initially conceived the idea of moving Alberta gas to California and I'm the one with the gas supply."

Harrison was almost beside himself. "Why you young pup! If you hadn't talked Marsden's daughter into ..."

"Talked her into what, Harrison?" Mark asked softly.

"Nothing. Forget it. It doesn't matter."

Mark's mind was racing. If what he was beginning to suspect turned out to be true then all bets were off, and he was no longer bound by his verbal undertaking to Norcal.

"I think it does matter, Harrison. And I think you and I need to talk. Alone."

Harrison looked as if he wanted to refuse. Then he gave a grudging nod and said, "Very well. If you think it will do any good."

When Martin, MacGregor, and the Norcal in-house attorney had filed silently out of the office, Mark said, "Let me finish the sentence for you, Harrison. You were about to say if I hadn't talked Marsden's daughter into selling me the shares."

"So what?" The urbane Harrison Dobbs was actually blustering.

"Only a very few people knew that it was Cliff Marsden who owned those shares. And you aren't one of them. Or you shouldn't be."

"He told me about it at the Oilmen's."

This was plausible enough to give Mark pause. But if that was the case, why was Harrison so palpably uneasy? There was even a sheen of sweat on his forehead, though the air-conditioned office was uncomfortably chilly.

"I think you knew about it long before that. In fact, Harrison, I think you knew all about Cliff's little scheme when Norcal made the funds available so I would put my shares and Cliff could get his hands on them."

Harrison expression told him he was on the right track and he pressed on. "You know what else I think, Harrison? I can't see you doing this just to oblige Cliff Marsden. I'll bet there's been a payoff to you somewhere along the line."

"You realize you can't prove any of this?"

"Not now, maybe. But it's amazing what a thorough corporate investigation can turn up."

Harrison cleared his throat. "Part of Norcal's business philosophy has always been not to have unhappy partners. What kind of an equity split would you feel comfortable with?"

"Sixty per cent to me and forty to Norcal."

"Sounds reasonable to me. Why don't we call the lawyers back in and tell them to draw up the agreements on that basis?"

"I realize my father paid seven million for Mr. Cullen's interest and that we're selling it for less than that," Jane said to the representative of the trust company that had been appointed her co-executor under Marsden's will. "But the price he paid had nothing to do with economics. He had other reasons for going that high."

"Probably because he wanted to help Mr. Cullen out of the financial bind he was in." The trust officer paused as if to pay tribute to Marsden's generosity, then went on, "And to give his life trying to save his chauffeur! You must be very proud of him."

"A friend of mine used to call him a prince among men," murmured Jane, unable to resist a small inward smile. She glanced at her watch. "We're due in Mr. Martin's office in thirty minutes."

"Very satisfactory." Chester Martin accepted the share certificate from the lawyer for the estate and glanced briefly at the executors' signatures before passing it on to Mark. "The Marsden estate receives $5-million, and Mark gets the California project."

Mark fingered the embossed lettering of the ornate certificate. Strange how much power resided in a single, harmless-looking piece of paper. He handed the certificate back to the lawyer for safekeeping and stood up. "Come on, Jane, I'll buy you a cup of coffee."

Jane let him take her hand as they walked the four blocks to the Crest Cafe. Gazing around the restaurant's unprepossessing interior, Mark thought of all that had happened since he had last been there. A small-time operator — what was his name? Bernie Andrews — bought him lunch and tried to swab him down for Permex's lease acquisition plans. How long ago was that? He had no trouble recalling the exact date — April 29th, 1956, the day he had formed Hunter Oil Limited. He made a mental note to talk to Chester about changing the name of Central Resources to Hunter Oil. It suddenly hit Mark that, as incredible as it seemed, he hadn't even met Jane by then. And now she was leaving. She was flying to New York in the morning. To make matters worse, she had decided they wouldn't see each other until she came back for the Christmas holidays. Mark had protested, but she was adamant, saying that she needed the time to sort things out for herself. That was a hard one to argue against, even though there was a good chance that when she did sort her life out there would be no room left in it for him.

Jane broke into his thoughts by asking how he could work with a man like Dobbs who had done his best to double-cross him.

Mark shrugged. "Realistically I have no choice. I need Norcal and they need me. It's that simple."

"I remember a quotation I used in a thesis at Stanford, 'Who sups with the Devil should have a long spoon.'"

Mark laughed. "I'll keep that in mind." His expression sobered as he added, "I'm going to be seeing a great deal of that particular devil in the next few months. There's one hell of a lot to be done before the construction crews take the field."

"Good. That will give you something to do while I'm gone."

"It won't keep me from missing you." He reached across the table for her hand. He was tempted to renew his plea to be allowed to visit her during the fall term but realized it wouldn't do any good. It would only increase the tension between them. However, if things started to come apart for her, that was another matter.

"Promise me that if things start to get ... difficult for you, you will let me know," he said.

She smiled and squeezed his hand.

"Of course I will. You're the only person I can talk to. I honestly feel I'm going to be okay, but if I have a relapse, and those old hobgoblins start prowling around, I'll be on the phone." She paused, then said quietly. "I'm going to date, Mark, and I want you to do the same."

Her words hit him like blows from a hammer. He was losing her and there was absolutely nothing he could do about it. More for something to say than anything else, he muttered, "My date's going to be the California project."

"You do what you think best, Mark. But I'm through with feeling guilty."

As Mark paid the bill, the middle-aged cashier beamed at them, obviously thinking what a handsome and happy couple they made. How appearances could deceive! Mark smiled grimly to himself as he held the door for Jane.

Outside on the sidewalk, he remembered something that had been bothering him. "By the way, what are you going to do with your father's ashes? I keep expecting an urn to show up at your house."

Jane lifted her sunglasses and looked at him. "I flushed them down the toilet."

The Devil's Lighter

I

The DC-8 dropped rapidly under reduced thrust. Rod Fraser stirred uneasily, floating upward to the shimmering surface of consciousness. Easing himself erect, he looked out the window. The cold moonlight coated the port wing with dull silver as it dipped and revealed a sprawling cluster of lights glittering and sparkling on the dark land. Their brilliance startled Rod; he had forgotten how clear the skies were in these high, northern latitudes. He remembered now. It was a combination of the altitude and the use of natural gas as fuel — free from the heavy residues that blackened the atmospheres of most cities. His spirits lifted as the plane swooped down to the beckoning lights.

As the jet taxied to its berth he saw a large illuminated sign on the terminal — WELCOME TO CALGARY. Walking through the tunnel of the unloading bridge, he wondered just what sort of welcome he would find. He stood for a moment outside the terminal while the other passengers hurried by, and took several deep breaths, drawing the thin air into his lungs. He felt the chill of the night finger its insidious way through his tropical suit and light trench coat. There was a long line of taxis, but Rod decided that, since he was unemployed, he had better start acting like it.

Suitcase in either hand, he clambered into a minibus which quickly filled with passengers and luggage and pulled away from the terminal. It was ten-thirty by the time he had checked into the Calgary Inn; long habit forced him to unpack completely and hang up his clothes, rumpled with travel, before he fell on the bed and dropped instantly into sleep.

The night's sleep erased the fatigue of the long hours of flying. He decided to walk to his first appointment. It was only a few blocks away and the bright sunlight was inviting, fitting his mood. The city had changed a lot since his brief visit four years ago. It had thrown up a new skyline of high-rise buildings. He had been on his way to Venezuela then, the first stop in a bright new career — one whose brightness had darkened considerably in the last few months. Now, four years later, he was walking through sun-washed streets to another new career, although one maybe not so bright this time. And yet, he reminded himself sternly, at thirty-one he was still young enough to do just that, walk away from what lies behind and start all over again.

He had chosen the first company very carefully: small enough not to have international connections, big enough to participate in the costly deep-reef play in the north. The personnel manager was tall and imposing, grey hair contrasting with smooth pink skin. He was the product of a nicely controlled martini intake, steam-baths, and massages. He spent half an hour with Rod and companionably sipped a cup of coffee with him. Only once did Rod manage to ask about a job. The manager looked pained, smiled uncomfortably, and muttered, "Afraid it's no go, old man. We're up to full complement, as it happens. But you won't have any trouble finding a berth — with your training and experience."

It was the same story at the other two oil companies Rod called on that morning. He wondered where he had ever gotten the idea it would be a cinch for a geologist to find a job in Calgary.

Discouraged, he slipped into an aluminum-and-glass telephone booth on a windy corner. Closing the door against the penetrating cold, he dialled the number of the Inter-Continental Oil Company. In a moment the familiar voice of Tim Murphy rattled in his ear. Rod fancied he detected a slight hesitation in Tim's welcome, then cursed himself for becoming an oversensitive fool.

If Tim had felt any hesitation, he soon recovered, and now he was booming a command for Rod to lunch with him. Rod felt a good deal more cheerful as he left the tiny booth. It was only a few blocks to the Petroleum Club where he was to join Tim; he had fifteen minutes, and once again he decided to walk. The downtown core of this city was so tightly knit, the places of business were so close together and park-ing so impossible, that everyone walked to each appointment unless pressed for time, or if the temperature had plummeted to below zero.

During the morning a Chinook had started to blow through the city — that warm west wind that came off the Pacific Ocean and climbed the Rockies, dumping its moisture on the western slopes but keeping much of its warmth as it swept over the eastern foothills. It had a strong effect on the climate of the prairie towns that lay in its path. It defrosted the northern winters and rolled up snowfields like so many carpets. The cloudy conditions that usually accompanied the chinook wind had by now blurred the brilliant sunshine of early morning.

Chinook or not, it was barely above freezing, and Rod, his blood thinned by four years in the tropics and his light trench coat scant protection against the seeking wind, soon found himself hurrying in a rapid dogtrot.

The club had a whole building to itself; low and two-storied, it crouched at the feet of its high-rise neighbours. Rod's cold-inspired rush had brought him there ahead of his host. He found the cloakroom, hung his light coat among the rows of heavier ones, and returned to the lobby where he sank into a deep leather chair. The Petroleum Club could have been located in Tulsa, Houston, Dallas, or Caracas — wherever oilmen gathered. It was richly appointed, with deep burgundy carpeting, dark walnut panelling on the walls, and black leather furniture. It was precisely the sort of club that the oil industry created wherever it went. When the Arctic Circle yields sufficient volumes of oil, thought Rod, a club just like this will spring into being on the nearest iceberg.

The men greeted each other, forming and re-forming into small groups as they moved into the main dining room; all seemed to be cast from the same mould. The soft accents of the American southwest floated through the air; their greetings were elaborately courteous. Each handshake was followed by a tap on the shoulder or a squeeze of the arm — oil people touch each other a lot. To an outsider they appeared forced and insincere, but Rod had gotten used to them during his stay in Venezuela and knew how deceptive their outward appearance could be. When any deal got down to the "nut-cracking," these same men would act with breathtaking speed and decisiveness. Business over, they would slide effortlessly back into their courtly pleasantries.

He rose as Tim sprinted up the short flight of stairs. With a length of woollen muffler wrapped carelessly around his neck, rough tweed coat flying open, bright red hair flowing about the ears, Tim was like a flamingo in a flock of crows. His manner of dress and his way of talking were half affectation, half his own flamboyant nature. He had been born in Canada and had never set foot in Ireland, but there was a distinct Celtic rhythm and swing to his speech. Rod had once accused him of speaking "Hollywood Irish" and Tim had happily agreed. "It's the blood of me ancestors. It cannot be denied. Besides, me mother was born and raised in the auld country and she spoke like the angels." It spoke well for the tolerance of the company for which he worked that not only had he continued in its employ but he had also prospered and risen in its ranks. A pure geologist, he had few interests beyond his beloved samples and maps.

Rod waved away the offer of a drink. "I need to be bright-eyed and bushy-tailed for any interviews I might be able to scrape up this afternoon. That is, if anyone will condescend to see me," he added gloomily. "I thought this place was such a hotbed of activity that all I had to do was present myself, mention my Venezuela experience, and I'd be on my way to an oilfield before I could blink."

"Well, me boy, you're rather a hot item just now. For instance" — Tim surveyed the huge room packed with an all-male noontime crowd — "I'll bet the news that I had lunch with Rod Fraser gets back to the office before I do."

Rod was struck with a sudden misgiving. "Well, I'm damned. I hope I haven't put you on the spot in any way."

Tim shrugged. "Don't fret yourself. I'm good at what I do; they don't dare raise so much as an eyebrow at me." He was complacent, the professional sure of his abilities. "What companies have you talked to so far?"

He nodded sagely as Rod listed them. "I can see why you never got past the personnel manager with those boys. They wouldn't touch you if you were the only wellsite geologist in western Canada and they had a well just reaching its target formation."

Exasperated, Rod put down his knife and fork and glared at his companion. "I'm damned if I can see why. Not one of them is an international company. I checked them out carefully and all their holdings and property are in Canada. Why should they care about Venezuela production? Hell, you'd think they'd be cheering me on, that they'd want access to the Montreal crude market. I don't get it!"

"There's something a lot more important to them than selling oil to Montreal." Murphy paused. "I don't suppose you know anything about the land situation here?"

Rod shook his head. "No, I haven't the foggiest."

Murphy glanced around the crowded room. The people at the nearby tables were all absorbed in their own conversations. "The major international oil companies have been in this province a long time, Rod. The majority of the mineral rights are under lease to them." He paused while a busboy filled their coffee cups.

Rod gloomily stirred a cube of sugar into his coffee. "I think I get the picture. The same boys that have all those reserves of oil down in Venezuela. Oil they are mighty anxious to sell."

Tim shrugged. "It's a fact of life. If you're a small independent trying to assemble some land so you can drill a well, the chances are you'll have to deal with the majors."

Rod sipped his coffee. It had grown cold but he waved away a waitress advancing with a silver jug. "Do you really think a major company would turn down a good offer for its leases just because you'd hired a lowly geologist who tramped on a few toes way down in Venezuela?"

Tom lit a cigarillo and leaned back in his chair. "Probably not, but it's a screwy business, you know that. Is it a chance you'd want to take, if you were a small independent like those companies you saw this morning?"

"Damn it, Tim, this business is all I know! Apart from that short stretch in mining, I haven't done anything else and I don't want to. There must be some outfit that will take me on."

"There's one thing in your favour. Every well needs a geologist. The problem is finding a company that has a desperate need for a geologist and maybe doesn't have too much concern about ruffling a few feathers. There's only one I can think of —" he hesitated. "It's sort of a ramshackle outfit, but they need a geologist in the worst way. They had one but he was killed last week, and if they don't find a replacement pretty damn soon they may have to shut down their drilling."

"Sounds like they might be desperate enough to hire even an outcast like me. Who are they? Is there anyone you can call?"

"That's easy, it's essentially a one-man proposition — Thistle Oils." Tim paused — he had grown accustomed to the security of big-oil operations — and continued somewhat uncertainly. "It's a pretty shaky outfit, by all accounts. Rumour has it that everything they've got is sunk in this one hole in the Zama area. Even if they take you on, I wouldn't plan on anything long-term." He looked at Rod anxiously.

"For God's sake, man, I'm in no position to worry about security and a long-term career. All I want is a toehold and maybe this Thistle Oils can give it to me. Why don't you get on the phone right now and see if you can fix me up with an appointment?"

Tim laid down his napkin and followed Rod's impatient progress to the lobby. When he emerged from the tiny telephone cubicle, he had a slip of paper in his hand. "Well, so far, so good. The president's in, and he'll see you. His name is Mac MacPherson and he's a good old bucko. Here's the address; it's just a few blocks south of here."

Rod seized the paper and hustled into his coat. Tim walked to the door with him and stood for a moment with a slight, embarrassed grin. "God and Mary and Patrick be with you. I'd like fine to invite you to the house for dinner, but, you see ..." His voice trailed off. Rod grinned to himself; he understood his friend's uncharacteristic embarrassment. Tim's matrimonial arrangements with his fiery Kathie were a legend.

He said, "I take it Kathie's gone back to Vancouver?"

Tim nodded miserably. "She claims I spend all my time at the office and neglect her."

"I'd think with the rate at which you two manufacture little Murphys, she'd be grateful for a spot of neglect. Anyway, I'm at the Calgary Inn. Join me there about five-thirty. We'll have a few drinks and a bang-up dinner. I'll tell you how I made out at Thistle and you can clue me in on the regional geology."

2

The address on the slip of paper was for one of the few remaining older buildings in that section of the city. It was big enough to still represent a fairly economic use of the expensive downtown land, especially since its construction cost had been written off, not only by the original builder, but also by a parade of subsequent purchasers and speculators. Some years before it had received a facelift and now narrow slabs of black marble and aluminum strips covered its old-fashioned front. There had also been a half-hearted attempt to modernize the interior, at least to the extent of a coat of light-green paint and a rearrangement of some of the partitions and interior walls. The renovations didn't include an elevator, however, and Rod, studying the small directory, saw that his quarry was located on the top floor, three flights up.

As he climbed the last few steps, he saw a door with a frosted-glass window bearing the legend Thistle Oils Limited and a crudely painted replica of the flower that lent its name to the enterprise. Rod stopped for a moment to catch his breath, then walked the last remaining steps across the plastic-tiled floor. Small letters on the lower right-hand corner of the window directed the world to WALK IN. The head office of Thistle Oils was far from elaborate; no shareholder could complain that the executives lavished luxuries on themselves. There were only three rooms — a combined reception area and secretary's office in which Rod stood, another small room partitioned with frosted glass, and, off to the left, a tiny cubbyhole completely filled with rolled-up maps and filing cabinets. The girl smiling up at Rod would have graced the most luxurious, carpeted, and softly lit reception area that any company could boast. Her hair was a deep auburn, and she wore it long so that it curled over her shoulders. It swirled gently around her young glowing face as she turned. Her voice was low-pitched and warm with a lilt of gaiety.

"Mr. Fraser? I'll tell Mr. MacPherson you're here." The office was so tiny that Mr. MacPherson could have been in no doubt that he had a visitor, or of his identity. But it gave Rod a chance to see the rest of her as she stood up behind the metal typing desk, edged her way carefully through the cramped space, and stood outlined in the doorway of the inner office. She was tall and slender with a long, swinging line of leg.

She turned back to Rod. "Mr. MacPherson will see you now."

He was sorry that MacPherson was so accommodating, and an impish gleam in those glorious brown eyes showed his disappointment was more transparent than he meant it to be.

In an industry and a city where the accent was on youth, MacPherson was out of place. He was sixty-six years old, but the fire of optimism still burned inside him. Like an old-time gold prospector, he sought only the big strike and spurned the cautious step-out drilling which stayed as close as possible to an already producing well. Cautious operators, adding one small discovery to another, had amassed fortunes in this manner, but it was not for MacPherson. He was a devotee of the wildcat — located miles from any previous discovery — the one that if it hit at all, came in big. The new fields in the north were irresistible to him with their thick pay zones and the tantalizing reefs. Up there, every well was a wildcat and the rewards of success were correspondingly great; while the cost of failure — because of the depth of the formations, the remoteness of the region, and the forbidding terrain — was ruinously high.

Pumping Rod's hand vigorously, MacPherson swept a bundle of contour maps from a chair and invited him to sit down. The desk and two chairs were of a hideous, bright-yellow oak. The walls were covered with maps of all sizes, tacked or taped to the plaster, some spotted with multicoloured pins and others covered with elongated circles. A green filing cabinet squatted in one corner, and papers, maps, and white Styrofoam coffee cups overflowed from the desk onto the adjoining window ledge.

"You have some very impressive credentials, Mr. Fraser." There was a slight, unmistakable burr to the voice, an almost imperceptible rolling of the rs. He was regarding Rod with an apologetic air. "I really wish I had your training. Geology has been the passion of my life, but I've had to pick it up as I go along. To no good effect, as you can plainly see." With a good-humoured chuckle, he waved his hand at his unprepossessing office.

He was remarkably easy to talk to and knew personally many of the men Rod had encountered in Venezuela. Calgary, South America, and the Middle East often served as way stations for junior executives on the way up. Some of Rod's co-workers had arrived at Maracaibo directly from Calgary and some had left the tropics to take up postings in western Canada. MacPherson seemed to know them all. He paused and gazed out the window as he said, "I understand you ... ah ... tore up the pea patch down there."

Rod answered with a quick burst of irritation. "You could say so, if you like. For my part, I looked at it differently then, and still do."

MacPherson was instantly contrite. "I didn't mean it that way. I'm sorry. What you did was admirable, quite admirable! I meant only ...," he left the sentence unfinished.

Rod grinned rather sheepishly. "Sorry. I guess I'm still a little raw on that point. No need to apologize, sir, I can easily understand your position." He started to rise.

"Sit down, man, sit down!" MacPherson fairly shouted at him. "What you did, or didn't do, thousands of miles from here is nothing to me. I daresay, I'm one of the few operators in the whole city who could truthfully make that statement. I don't have to look to the majors for any favours. Time has taken care of that very nicely.

The way things have worked out, everything has boiled down to this one well. If it strikes or turns out to be a dry hole — either way, the problem's solved as far as I'm concerned. It's too late for this old wildcatter to start over again."

He spoke lightheartedly, as one who had staked everything on the next turn of the cards and was content.

He continued, "As your friend Murphy undoubtedly told you, I need a wellsite geologist. I had a good one all lined up — Jack Walsh — but he got himself killed last week. He was a first-class professional. Only trouble was, he drank too much for his own good."

He sighed heavily. "That's why he was still doing wellsite work. He was better off in the bush, away from temptation."

He picked up a small, round core of light-grey rock, and smiled. "Mississippian limestone at a depth of five thousand feet. The best well I ever drilled; she could pull three hundred barrels a day. Jack was the geologist on that one ten years ago."

Rod blinked, he couldn't help himself. MacPherson chuckled. "Big wells seem out of place in a set-up like this, don't they? I only had a small piece of the action, and I sold that long ago to drill a few more dry holes."

There was no reply to this, so Rod answered, "How was he killed, sir?"

MacPherson gently replaced the rock on his desk. "Call me Mac; everybody does." He stood up, pushed aside some rolled-up maps, and leaned against the window ledge. "It was just another one of those accidents that happen all the time in the north. Jack was visiting another camp last Thursday night; he took a pickup and drove over to one of Empire's rigs about fifty miles away. I guess his friend had smuggled some booze into the camp because Jack had had a few before he started back home about eleven o'clock. He never made it."

"Who found him?"

"A seismic crew spotted him and his truck the next morning, upside down in a frozen creek bed. The pickup had gone over a bank, rolled over, and crashed through the ice. Jack drowned in about a foot of water inside the cab." He shook his head sadly. "The crash must have knocked him out and he ended up face-down in the water."

"I'm sorry." Rod continued. "It sounds like the sort of accident that can happen easily enough on an oilfield road, particularly in winter."

Mac nodded absently. "Yes." He looked down at the small piece of grey rock and sighed. "Jack knew those roads, though. He drove over to the camp by a shortcut, but when he started home he must have decided to use the main route. It's longer but the road was in better shape. Drunks develop quite a sense of self-preservation."

Rod smiled. "I'm sure they do."

"What Jack didn't know was that two days earlier a road crew had moved the temporary bridge a hundred yards downstream. He kept on driving to where the bridge had been and that's where he went over. Still can't figure out why he didn't see the barrier."

He shook his head, then went on in a brisker tone. "Well, all the fussing in the world won't help Jack now. The point is, Mr. Fraser, I need a wellsite geologist and I need one right now. Since you need work, it stands to reason we should be able to get together. In all fairness, I must tell you it will have to be pretty much a one-shot deal. There's just the test well. Thistle Oils, I'm afraid, is in no position to embark on a wholesale drilling program." He held up a hand as Rod was about to speak and continued, "One more thing, the pay isn't too hot," he looked troubled and embarrassed, "the best I can offer is a thousand a month, plus your keep and transportation, of course. I know it's not much for a man of your qualifications but it's all this operation can stand."

"You've just hired yourself a geologist! When do I start?"

"Why don't you report in here tomorrow, we'll sign you on. That shouldn't take long as we don't go in much for fringe benefits. You'll have to get outfitted and then we'll arrange transportation to the field. Sheila!" He raised his voice, although the girl couldn't have avoided hearing every word in the tiny office. "Come in here and meet the newest member of our staff. This is Mr. Fraser — Rod Fraser — meet Sheila Robinson." He beamed at her. "Sheila's my secretary, but also a great deal more. She's the whole head office of the company. Without her, things would get so fouled up we'd have to lock the door and walk away from it."

She smiled at Rod. "Mr. MacPherson exaggerates. I'm so glad you will be with us. We do need help, rather badly."

At precisely five-thirty the room telephone rang. It was Murphy in the hotel lobby. "Reporting for drink duty." Rod exuberantly told him to come up and enjoy the hospitality of a gainfully employed geologist.

"That's great, just great. I couldn't be more delighted!" Tim's voice rang with sincerity as he gripped his friend's hand. He looked quickly at the circular table and advanced toward it, rubbing his hands. "Ah, sure and we have all the ingredients to toast your entry into the western Canadian oil patch!"

The hotel room was luxurious, the Scotch was first-class, and once more he was a part of his beloved oil industry. Rod felt good. He began to question his friend about the geological features of the northern oilfields. "I must confess my ideas are pretty hazy. As you know, I'd kidded myself into thinking they were the same as the fault blocks of Venezuela."

"In some parts, particularly in what they call North Zama, it's not unlike the Venezuelan geology — there's a lot of violent faulting, with upthrust blocks trapping the oil. But mostly, it's straight reef formation — the type usually associated with salt domes. Only thing about them is they're real haystacks — so narrow that if you're even a few feet off-target you miss them completely. While they may be small laterally, they're thick. Man, are they thick! As much as eight hundred feet of pay zone, just oozing and dripping with all that lovely black oil!"

Rod whistled appreciatively. Murphy acknowledged his reaction with a grin as he continued. "Yeah, I know. It sounds more like Middle East stuff than North America, but it's there. God, is it there! Only trick is, how do you find it? One thing, with that type of structure they don't expect us simple-minded geologists to pick out the wildcat locations. The geophysical boys with all their seismic surveys and shot holes are on the hot seat this time. They've got to interpret their wiggly little lines and guess whether or not there's a reef six thousand feet below. All we can do is sit on the well and call the shots as we go down. That's what you'll be doing and here's what to look for ..."

The conversation became technical, speaker and listener both absorbed as Tim drew rough sketches and pointed out the typical formations and how each one could be recognized by an analysis of the tiny cuttings that came up from the well bore.

Rod concentrated intently on Murphy's lecture, grinning inwardly as Tim's Irish affectations disappeared. They always did when he became absorbed in professional talk.

Finally, Tim croaked, "Bejesus but I'm dry!" and splashed a generous shot of Black Label into his glass. He studied the depths of the dark brown drink and said, "Now it's your turn. What sort of jackpot did you land in down in South America? You must have shaken things up in pretty good style, judging from the accounts that got back here."

Fraser shrugged helplessly. "It's the damnedest thing. I still can't believe all that's happened since. It seemed so unimportant at the time." He drew a deep breath and took a thoughtful swallow of his drink.

"When I first arrived in Venezuela, Universal Oils sent me to Lake Maracaibo to work on the wells. My boss was a man called Fenwick — Hal Fenwick — a good guy, a company man through and through, and determined to get ahead. We hit it off right from the start. As you may remember, I've always liked economics, finances — that sort of thing."

Tim nodded.

"I got to be pretty good at working out the economic justification for a proposed well — you know, payout, risk evaluation, all that stuff."

Tim poured himself another drink. "Can't stand that economic bullshit meself, but I know you like it."

Rod walked over to the small table near the window and poured a careful inch of Scotch. He smiled as he dropped in the ice cubes. "Fenwick didn't care much for it either, but he was red-hot on operations, and with me making the snowballs, his presentations made him look good to the brass. After I'd been there about two years he was promoted to the Caracas office and made responsible for liaison with the government. He was good at that; he was likeable, straight from the shoulder, and people respected him."

"Everything sounds lovely in the garden so far. What went sour?"

Rod smiled bleakly. "Nothing, until I was asked to work up the case for the Venezuelan government against the construction of a pipeline from western Canada to serve the Montreal area."

Tim whistled softly but said nothing.

"You know how important the Montreal market is to Venezuela; it takes about half a million barrels a day of their production. They don't want to lose it."

"I think I can guess the rest."

Rod gave a short laugh. "Yeah, maybe I was being too naive and self-important, but I couldn't see myself helping a foreign country do something I believed was against the best interests of my own country."

"So you resigned."

"So I resigned. And here I am in Calgary, where I'm treated like someone with the plague by the very people I thought I was helping."

Tim was shaking his head in wonder. "Holy Mary, David with his sling shot, that's my boy. You really have a gift for it, don't you? Why, when I remember the swath you cut in the mining game ..." He swallowed his reminiscent chuckle as he saw the look on Rod's face.

Rod hastily gulped down his drink and stood up, his expression blank and impassive. His voice had a tone of forced cheerfulness as he said, "Let's go down to the dining room. I don't know about you, but I need to anchor this cargo of booze with some solid food."

Tim followed him meekly enough to the elevator, but he was not in the least intimidated by his old friend's abrupt reversal of mood. As the elevator dropped silently, he was still shaking his head in amused wonder. "To think that they accuse us bog-trotters of being unstable. I'll say this, old buddy, for a staid, conservative Scots-Canadian, you've been making mighty big tracks."

Tim was in good form throughout dinner and Rod's black mood soon lifted. With the coffee, a delicate little hostess appeared at their table offering steaming hand towels. Rod, patting his face with the hot, scented cloth, thought of the contrast with the harsh environment of his new job. Tomorrow was the start of a new oil career, and nothing would go wrong this time.

He shook his head to Tim's suggestion of a liqueur and rose from the table. "Tim, you won't mind if I hit the sack? I'm going to have enough on my hands tomorrow without fighting my way uphill through a hangover."

"You're right, of course. I'll betake myself to me own sober and lonely bed. Call me tomorrow and let me know how you're making out."

3

The resonant voice of the radio announcer assured Calgarians that their city was still wrapped in its warm Chinook blanket. Rod, as he knotted his tie, listened to the complacent litany of temperatures in other parts of the province. It soon became obvious that Calgary stood alone with its relatively balmy thirty-eight degrees above zero. The temperature dropped steadily as the announcer's voice rolled northwards: Red Deer — fifteen above; Edmonton — five below; Grand Prairie — twelve below; Fort Vermilion — twenty-eight below. Rod recognized the last place as being somewhere near the Thistle well. Standing in his warm hotel room, he shivered. He didn't know much about the north country, but he did know that the frigid temperatures were not entirely unwelcome. Deep winter froze and hardened the quaking muskeg and made it passable for wheeled traffic. Summer operations were kept to a minimum since they required the use of specially designed tracked crawlers and giant air-freighters. Freeze-up was the signal for a flurry of activity.

Rod snapped out of his reverie with a start as he saw it was already seven-thirty. The oil industry was noted for grabbing an early start on each day; even in the city its offices opened at eight o'clock. Rod grabbed the trench coat from the closet and ran toward the elevators. At the coffee-shop counter he gulped down scalding hot coffee and a piece of toast. The doorman, shiveringly resplendent in the quaint garb of a London Tower guard, whistled up a taxi.

Rod threw a dollar bill at the driver and sprinted up the three flights of stairs. It was just eight o'clock but, as he panted up the last few steps, he could see the light shining through the frosted-glass door. The day had already begun for Thistle Oils Limited.

Sheila smiled up at him as he hung his coat on the wooden rack. "Mr. MacPherson's in his office, waiting on a call from the field. You can go in."

Mac was hunched at his desk, scowling ferociously at the telephone. It was ominously silent. He waved Rod to a seat with a preoccupied motion. "This damn thing's the only connection we have with the field. It's tied into the northern radio network. At least, everybody calls it a network, but it's just a screeching party line trying to make itself heard through the northern lights. The toolpush is supposed to report in today, but the good Lord only knows if he'll get a chance, what with everybody calling his wife, drillers begging their sweethearts to be good, and all the other companies and rigs reporting in to their head offices. Even if he does manage to get through, chances are we won't be able to hear properly with all the static and interference."

Mac grinned suddenly. "You know, up north, listening to the mobile radio is a favourite entertainment. They never turn them off. It beats any old soap opera. They block out the field end of the conversation, all you hear is 'beep, beep.' But everybody can hear what's said on this end. You get so you can listen to one side of the conversation and guess what's being said on the other end.

"The things people will say over an open line. The last time I was in the north a roughneck's wife was telling him she would have to move, her landlord had lowered the boom. You couldn't hear what he said, but you could tell that he wanted to come out and see what he could do. She was having none of that; told him just to send money and not to worry about her; she would find a place somewhere. It was clear the last thing she wanted was to see him; she was only interested in the money he could earn freezing his butt in the boondocks. Poor devil's probably all busted up wondering if she's shacked up with somebody. Most likely get so upset about it, he'll forget to duck when the tongs and chains start flying. Well, it looks as though Larry isn't going to make it ..." He broke off as Sheila called, "The rig's phoning in."

Mac pressed a switch and said, "I'll turn on the speaker attachment so you can hear."

The speaker cut in with a sudden blast of static and the hollow sound of a voice saying, "This is Cheyenne Three calling Thistle. Do you read?"

Mac spoke into the microphone. "We read you, Larry. I've got you on the conference speaker. Our new geologist, Rod Fraser, is here with me. I want him to hear what you have to say. He'll be going up to the rig pretty soon. Go ahead, please."

The distant voice reported that they had just made a trip and were drilling ahead through crumbling shale at a depth of two thousand feet. Rod understood the phrases coming out of the set. "Making a trip" meant the laborious process of hauling up the strings of drill pipe, uncoupling and stacking them, removing the worn-out drilling bit from the last string of pipe, replacing it with a new one, then recoupling all the strings and lowering them back into the hole until they were once more on bottom and ready to drill again. At their present shallow depth it wasn't much of a chore, but it would get steadily worse as the bit chewed deeper into the earth's crust.

Mac snapped off the set with a satisfied grunt. "At least we're moving again! I don't know whether I told you or not, but we've got a deadline on this well. There's a land sale exactly four weeks from today, including a drilling reservation right next to this well. We've got to reach total depth before the sale."

"What's your estimated total depth?"

"It varies, but at least fifty-five hundred feet, maybe six thousand feet subsurface."

Rod whistled. "You *have* cut it a bit fine. I don't know your drilling conditions, of course, but it seems to me you still should make it all right."

"We should, I agree. But God knows anything can happen, especially up there in the back of beyond. Too damn much has happened already!"

He brooded for a moment, then collected himself with a faint shiver and looked at Rod. "Well, Fraser, I suppose we had better figure out what to do with you." He leaned forward, placing his elbows on the battered desk. "I'm afraid Thistle is a little short of hands just now. In fact, you, Sheila, and I represent the entire salaried staff of this great oil empire. Primarily, of course, you'll have to sit on the well, but if you don't mind, I'd like you to double in brass. Maybe you could lend a hand on the financial end of things, so to speak."

At first, Rod thought that the old veteran was putting the bite on him, gently leading up to an invitation to invest some funds in the well. He was inwardly cursing the loss of his job even before it started, but as he listened to Mac he soon realized that he wasn't looking for a direct financial contribution.

"I've managed, one way or another, to scrape together enough funds to see the bottom of this hole; made a deal with the drilling contractor and brought in some outside investors. But bidding at the Crown sale for that drilling reservation is another matter. There are some Montreal investors who are interested, but they don't know the first thing about the oil industry or its economics. I'm not too hot on all this financial talk — payouts, cash flow, market analysis, all that sort of stuff is out of my line. But I know it's meat and drink to you, so I may call on you as we get closer to the sale. Okay by you?"

Nothing could have suited Rod better; he agreed eagerly. Mac smiled. "Good enough. Meanwhile," he rummaged around in a file of papers, extricated two or three long sheets of paper clipped together, and threw them onto the centre of his desk, "here's the well prognosis. Now what you'll have to be watching for is dark shale from this formation ..."

Midway through the morning, Sheila interrupted their concentration with coffee. Both men thanked her absently and raised the steaming cups to their lips without lifting their eyes from the maps and diagrams.

Mac finally laid down his pencil and leaned back in his chair. "Well, that's the needle we're looking for. Remember, I'm always at the other end of the phone — providing you can get through, of course." He looked across at Rod. "You'd better get yourself outfitted for some mighty rough conditions. I don't suppose you have any cold-weather gear." It was more a statement than a question. "Ever been up in the north?"

"Not really. About five years ago, when I was in mining, I spent quite a bit of time several hundred miles up the coast from Vancouver. It was cold all right, but nothing like the far north, I'm sure."

"You'd better believe it. In winter up there we only have three kinds of weather:

cold, colder, and frigid. I looked at a weather map this morning and a big high-pressure ridge is sitting right on top of Fort Vermillion. That always means a long siege of the real deep-freeze. It's standard practice in the industry for a man to supply his own working clothes. Okay?"

Rod nodded stiffly. Accustomed to big company operations where money, once a project was underway, was never a problem, he was unsettled by this acute and ever-present concern with it.

Mac was busily writing out a long list of supplies. "Let's see, you'll need long winter underwear, heavy socks, safety boots — you better get at least one pair of felts with the steel toecap, rubber galoshes — Fort St. John slippers, we call 'em — to wear over them, a parka, several wool sweaters, and a hard hat. Whew, that's quite a list! Sheila!" He suddenly raised his voice. "Draw up a cheque for one hundred dollars for Mr. Fraser and charge it to supplies." Turning back to Rod, he said, "That won't cover it all by a long shot, but it'll help, and you may not have any more use for these things after the well is finished. Here's the address of a surplus store. You better get on with it. Check back this afternoon if you're finished in time."

It was late afternoon by the time Rod had tracked down everything on the list. He felt a little self-conscious as the taxi deposited him and his small mountain of rough clothing outside the luxurious hotel. He needn't have worried. Heavy boots, duffel bags, bedrolls, these were all an old story to the staff of the Calgary Inn, where so many oilmen stayed before jumping off to the northern fields.

Mac had left and Sheila was just slipping the cover over her typewriter by the time Rod got back to the office. She looked very appealing, the taut young lines of her body outlined as she leaned over the machine. Not giving himself time to hesitate, Rod asked her to have dinner with him. She looked at him for a long moment. "I'd like that, Rod."

Sheila lived midway up a high-rise apartment block shaped like a narrow diamond with both ends cut off and rising from the broad base of a four-storied parking structure. She was ready when Rod arrived. The apartment was bigger than he expected — the walls a warm, light shade of beige, the furniture plain and modern. A bottle of gin was chilling in the refrigerator. "Let's have a martini here before we go out. Would you like to build it?"

She talked in a relaxed and easy fashion while Rod measured out the ice-cold drinks into frosted glasses. She shared the apartment with another girl, already out on a dinner date, who worked as a secretary to one of the senior executives in a large oil company. "There are two bedrooms, we're very compatible, and by splitting the rent we can each afford a much better apartment than we ever could on our own."

Sipping his drink, Rod enquired casually where she would like to go for dinner. It took him an amused minute to realize that Sheila, skating all around the subject, was attempting tactfully to suggest a place that wouldn't be too great a strain on his pocketbook. Taking over the lead, he said, "Look, I'm going to be a long time in the bush, far removed from any sort of creature comforts — let alone the chance of having a wonderful dinner with a gorgeous redhead. I've got a whole bundle of tropic pay just burning a hole in my pocket, so you name the best place that this city can offer and that's where we go!"

Sheila's laugh was rueful. "Was I really that transparent? All right, if the best is what you want, we'll go to my favourite — *Hy's*. It's too far to walk and we'd have to wait too long for a taxi. Let's take my car."

Her car — a blue Rambler — was on the second floor of the open parkade. The wind tore at them as they left the elevator and rushed across the snow-flecked floor.

In front of the restaurant Rod handed the car over to a muffled parking lot attendant and he and Sheila ran down the long passageway to the entrance. Electrical heating coils in the cement walk melted the light snow cover into thin tendrils of steam.

The restaurant was dark, with red-shaded lamps making pools of light over small tables covered with gleaming white damask. The decor was determinedly Spanish, with iron grillwork, dark-grained panelling, and furnishings artfully antiqued. Like a good many things about Calgary, it seemed wildly incongruous with the cold wintry air.

Sheila was a delightful companion. She had a naturally shy temperament, which the years had balanced with poise. The combination made her a wonderful conversationalist — a non-aggressive, sympathetic listener with interesting gambits and contributions of her own. Their talk, spiced with physical attraction, bounced and skipped lightly over many subjects. Sheila's face sobered momentarily as she spoke of her employer. "He's quite a guy, you know. He's always followed his own line, always maintained his own independence, even when it would have been so easy and profitable for him to join forces with the big companies. I know that years ago he was very much sought after by the majors; they wanted his experience and know-how. They say he turned down countless offers of vice-presidencies with big salaries and big fat stock options. Not now, of course; things have sort of swept by him. He knows this is his last big play, his last chance to make a major oil discovery. I'm sure the discovery itself means far more to him than any financial rewards. Anyway, he's thrown all his resources into this well. He sold off all his overriding royalties and interests in other wells to raise the money. He's got all his eggs in one basket, that's for sure!" She gazed gravely into her empty cup.

"What about his family? I saw a picture of a woman in his office. I take it that's his wife."

Sheila nodded her head slowly. "She's dead. It was tragic. They didn't have any children. It happened before I met Mac, but I know the story. Mac was away all the time, out in the field nursing wells, or in the States trying to raise money. Mary was left alone, to rattle around in a big house he bought for her in Mount Royal. She started to drink, and it got steadily worse. I guess near the end it was pathetic. She would stumble around with glazed eyes, hair a mess, clutching a drink, and a cigarette always drooping from her mouth."

"God, it must have torn Mac apart."

"Yes, and the old dear wouldn't be able to cope with it. I can see him now, standing around looking distressed, trying not to believe what was happening, feeling too guilty himself to criticize her, hoping it would somehow get better. And fleeing back out to the field."

"What finally happened to her?"

"One of those accidents you see in the paper all the time. She was in bed, drunk and smoking a cigarette. Mac was away, of course. She fell asleep, the mattress started to smoulder, and she was asphyxiated. They found her the next morning when a neighbour spotted the smoke seeping out of the bedroom window."

Rod spoke softly. "The poor old boy."

"It just about killed him. But he didn't let it show, his pride wouldn't let him do anything else. Mr. Sanderson — you'll meet him, he's head of Cheyenne Drilling — told me Mac was magnificent, always courteous and self-contained. He sold the house and all the belongings and moved into an apartment just one block away from the office."

Sheila shook her head with a slight smile. "You should see that apartment. It's just like a field camp — he sleeps in a sleeping bag, cooks on a two-burner hot plate, and there's nothing else but a clutter of maps, files of geology books, and notes."

"Sounds like he's reduced life to its basics — nothing to interfere with the search of oil."

"That's just what he's done. It's been five years, but he's felt the guilt every day. He told me that once. I think that's partly why he has given up whatever security he had and thrown everything into this well. If he finally hits something big it might justify all the times he left her alone."

They were silent; her thoughts gave her face a pensive quality — the serene, contemplative look of a Madonna.

After a long moment, he spoke. "And what about Sheila Robinson? Somehow she seems out of place in Thistle Oils. I picture her as the elegant, efficient, very, very private and confidential secretary to the president of a major oil company — polishing her nails in her own hushed office while the boss reports to the board of directors in New York. How did someone like this end up at Thistle?"

Sheila laughed. "By a fairly roundabout route. I started on the road to becoming just that — a secretary in a big company — when I first came to Calgary. Winnipeg is my hometown, but I fled the winters as soon as I was independent. I worked for a major — Inter-Continental, as a matter-of-fact. Then I decided life must have more to offer, something full of glamour and excitement, so I became a stewardess with Air Canada. The glamour wore off after a few weeks. It took me only that long to realize

I was just an airborne waitress. I stuck it out for a year and on the whole I enjoyed it
— I visited a lot of places I had never expected to see. When I came back, I had
changed just enough so that I couldn't be comfortable with the smooth, insulated life
of a big company job. So, I landed at Thistle and I've honestly loved every minute.
Satisfied my female craving to be needed, I guess. Besides, old Mac's such a dear, he
has always treated me as though I were his daughter."

They huddled deep in their coats while the boy brought the car around. The
heater blasted a jet of frigid air until Rod, blindly searching the unfamiliar dash,
found the switch and turned off the fan. The Rambler creaked protestingly the short
distance to the apartment block, and the green light on the instrument panel
remained uncompromisingly at COLD.

She handed him her key and they walked into the foyer of the apartment building. At the elevator she turned and held out her hand. Rod was surprised at its firm
strength. "Tennis?"

She shook her head, smiling. "No. But I hike in the mountains and camp out
every chance I get."

4

By the next day, Rod was feeling decidedly superfluous around the cramped office. He had purchased all his gear, learned what he could about the local geology; there was nothing further he could do until he arrived at the well. Mac nodded sympathetically when Rod pointed this out. "You're absolutely right. As a matter of fact, we've booked you on Air Canada's two o'clock flight to Edmonton this afternoon. But before you go, I want you to meet the owner of the company that's drilling the well. I think he wants you to get some valves in Edmonton and take them to the well. He said he'd drop over this morning for sure."

They did not have long to wait. Rod, flipping idly through a back copy of *Oilweek*, heard the voice booming in the outer office. Joe Sanderson was tall, at least six feet four, Rod thought, with a body constructed along the general outlines of a pear. Below an oval, elongated head, narrow shoulders bulged out to the soft lines of a rounded belly and wide hips. Moist, pendulous lips made love to a green cigar. He was dressed in a western-cut suit of light brown; his shirt was of a slightly darker shade of the same colour, and his tie was a leather thong, tipped with silver and strung through a rough, gold-flecked, quartz-like stone. It was difficult to judge his age; the soft flesh of his face smoothed out any telltale wrinkles. His voice, when he spoke to Rod, was deep, with the soft, measured accents of the south.

Sanderson's greeting was more of an embrace than a handshake as his left hand massaged Rod's upper arm while he held his hand in a grip of surprising strength. Mild, blue eyes gazed placidly at Rod from the unlined face. "Happy to make your acquaintance, suh! I understand you all will be going up to the well? I expect you'll find things a mite different from Maracaibo. For one thing, the air might be a shade crisper!" He chuckled happily at his own mild joke.

Joe Sanderson had spent most of his adult life in the employ of the same drilling company, starting as a roughneck in the Texas Panhandle. He had come to Canada in the distant days of the first boom following the Leduc discovery. In a few years he was made a vice-president and put in charge of his company's Canadian operations. By this time, despite his drawling accent, he was more Canadian than American. His children went to school in Canada, and the youngest had been born in the country. Five years ago, he had made two decisive steps: he took out Canadian citizenship and resigned from his secure, highly paid position to set up his own drilling company. His company — Cheyenne Drilling Limited — now owned three heavily financed rigs, two small ones on shallow holes in Saskatchewan and the flagship — an old, fourth-hand Continental Emsco g.b. 500 — drilling the Thistle well.

Sanderson's demands for Rod's services in Edmonton proved to be light. If Rod could locate two valves to replace others that had split in the sub-zero temperatures, Sanderson would be "greatly obliged, suh, greatly obliged!"

The Air Canada dc-9 whistled gently over the flat, snow-dusted geography of the western plains. In less than an hour, Rod was walking through the subterranean passages of the Nisku International Airport, twenty miles south of Edmonton. The brightly lit passages with walls painted in blocks of glaring colours finally emptied into an echoing concourse the size of a football field. In recent years, the Department of Transport had flung starkly modern terminals across the breadth of Canada and stocked them with chunks of sculpture and gigantic paintings, all unrelentingly modern. Sometimes these terminals-cum-museums emerged as integrated functional wholes; other times not. The Nisku terminal was one of the latter.

He was signing the hotel registration form when he heard her voice. "Rod! It *is* Rod, isn't it?" The lobby seemed to shift and rock before springing back into focus. Rod blindly handed the form to the clerk, took a deep, shuddering breath, braced himself against the encounter, and turned slowly to meet his past. He was afraid he wouldn't be able to speak.

Melinda — how the name suited her — stood before him. She was tiny — not more than five foot three — but she carried herself with an imperious bearing that made mere height totally irrelevant. She was dressed for the outdoors in an ankle-length white coat whose white mink hood framed her dark hair. She pushed back the hood and tilted her small elegant head to look up at him with those extraordinary green eyes.

"You really are a beautiful man, Rod. Maturity seems to go with those stern good looks. How long has it been? Now let me think ..." She broke off. Rod, who could have told her to the precise minute, said nothing. "Why, it must be four years, or more! Too long, anyway —" she pouted. "You're staying here, aren't you?"

As she talked, Rod managed to slow the wild pounding of his heart and to ease the choking sensation in his throat. His voice was almost free of a telltale quaver as he said, "Only for tonight, I'm afraid. Tomorrow I take off for the north."

She frowned slightly. "What a bore! I find you only to lose you. After all, you are my favourite correspondent!" A mocking light glinted in her eyes. Rod said nothing. The old familiar pattern was there once more; Melinda flicking him with the pronged whip of her cool self-possession while he stood there, a great shaggy dog waiting in vain for a crumb of kindness.

She moved closer, her movement stirring little trails of a tantalizing scent. She spoke in an urgent whisper. "Be in your room at ten-thirty tonight. I'll come to you then. Don't try to call me. I'm here with my new husband." Not waiting for his answer, she turned away and walked across the lobby to the main entrance. The bell-hop had loaded Rod's gear onto a wheeled trolley and was waiting patiently. Rod followed him to the elevator.

Melinda! The dark queen of his thoughts. Here in Edmonton and remarried! She was oddly suited to the cold northern capital; with its mantle of sun-burnished snow, the rounded spires of the Ukrainian churches, the hurrying, and bundled figures, it had something of the air of old Russia. Wrapped in furs, she could have been the reincarnation of some fabled czarina.

Reining in his racing memory, Rod picked up the telephone. He had to call four supply houses before he found one with the right valves in stock. The insatiable demands of northern exploration were sucking equipment out of Edmonton like a giant vacuum cleaner. They agreed to set the valves aside until he called for them on his way to the airport. He replaced the receiver reluctantly. The routine chore had been a welcome distraction.

After his lonely dinner, over which he lingered with many cups of coffee, he walked the frozen streets until the penetrating chill drove him inside. Back in his room he walked over to the low bureau and splashed a generous slug of Black Label into a glass. By the time he added ice, there wasn't much room for water. He took a deep swallow and realized, with distaste, that his hand was trembling. He picked up a paperback novel. His eyes spelled out the individual words, but they were meaningless. He was on page thirty-seven and it could have been a cookbook for all he knew. With a sigh, he put it down and looked at his watch. Ten-twenty-five; five minutes to go. She would be on time, she always was. At ten-thirty precisely he heard the light, imperious knock. He put down his glass slowly and walked over to the door.

She was dressed in a long black dress with a white shawl. As Rod took the shawl he saw her bare back flowing to the delicious curve of her hips. She stood motionless, while he moved toward the bureau. "Would you like a drink?"

"No, thanks. I'll have *you* first." She lifted her arms to him and he bent to her parted lips.

He felt her fingers lightly caressing, squeezing, kneading. It was glorious, unbearable. He held back as long as he could, then climaxed with hard strokes deep into her. Rod buried his chin in her dark hair and whispered, "That's beautiful, the way you do that."

"The way I do what, darling?" She was running her fingers lightly across his back.

"The way you fondle and squeeze my balls just as I'm about to come. It really lights the afterburner! I've never forgotten it in all the time we've been apart. And you know just when to do it!"

"You're not exactly secretive about when you're coming. Now you can get me that drink."

Rod held a match to her cigarette. She said, "Know something, Rod? You've changed. Four years ago you would never have said that word 'balls' to me. Screw the ass off me, sure, but never use a dirty word. You were such a square, my pet, such a delightful, lovable square!"

"Compared to you, I'm still one. I don't want to know, but you'd better tell me about this new husband."

"His name is Mason, George Mason. I like the sound of Melinda Mason, don't you?" Rod groaned and she smiled. "No, I guess you wouldn't. Anyway, we've been married six months. He's old and I think very rich, although I'm not as sure of that now as when I married him."

"Sounds great, just great!" Rod said bitterly. "Suppose he starts pounding on that door?"

"Relax. He's out like a light. He takes his first drink at exactly four o'clock and keeps pouring them in until ten when he collapses into bed. Tonight his nightcap had just a little touch of Seconal for insurance. He's not going anywhere." She squinted thoughtfully through the smoke. I'm not sure what he'd do, anyway. He's really kinky. I think he knows a lot more about my activities than he lets on. I'd just as soon not find out, though."

Rod cringed inwardly at her icy recital. But this time he was determined to meet her on her own terms. If she wanted to play it cool — well, so would he.

He propped himself on one elbow and hooked his left hand under the sheet, flipping it back to uncover her. She didn't move as he looked down the length of her body. Her breasts were so firm the nipples curved upwards, begging to be sucked. He said, "Did anyone ever tell you that you talk too much?"

He had caught her off-balance, he could see that. Then she arched her head back on the pillow and laughed. "Beautiful!" she murmured as she leaned over him to stub her cigarette. She bent over him, nibbling at him, her dark hair falling in a cloud over his body, each cool strand caressing his skin. He started to roll on top of her, but she held him back. "Wait, Rod. I want you in my mouth first."

5

The taxi driver, assured of a long, uninterrupted trip, shut off the crackling static of his two-way radio and turned up the transistor set lying on the seat beside him. A western singer nasally lamented the faithlessness of his love. Rod smiled sourly. *That's what you suffer from, Rod, my boy,* he told himself, *the bad-girl fascination.*

The taxi stopped outside the supply store, its exhaust bubbling a stream of white vapour. The valves were packed and ready. When he lifted the small parcel from the counter he was jolted by its weight. The valves were made of a heavy brass alloy, inches thick, but they cracked like tinfoil under the brutal temperatures.

The northern flights still used the old municipal airport in the very heart of the city. Its approaches, between tall buildings and directly over a sprawling railroad yard, were narrow nightmares of downdrafts and obstructions.

The taxi deposited Rod outside an old-fashioned terminal building covered with white asbestos shingles. It took him several trips to lug all his stuff to the check-in counter. The crowded, green-painted lobby vibrated with a dry heat. Roughly dressed men, some with beards and most showing the after-effects of several nights on the town, endured the heat, not even bothering to unbutton their heavy clothing. An ancient DC 6-B stood patiently on the tarmac.

One by one the motors coughed, belched blue smoke, and settled into a steady roar. As Rod buckled himself in, he saw every seat was occupied. He plunged into a deep sleep as the plane milled its way northwest into the deepening cold.

Hours later, they let down into the town of Peace River, the one scheduled stop before leaping into the real northern bush. Rod came groggily awake and peered through the tiny square window at the hooded figures scurrying busily around the plane. He felt the cold air seeping through the overheated cabin. At a shouted order from outside, the door slammed shut and they took off in a swirl of ice crystals. Now wide-awake, Rod looked out at the forbidding country unrolling beneath them. He could see, far off to the right, the bold slash that was the Mackenzie Highway. Apart from that umbilical cord to civilization, the entire countryside was carpeted with a dense growth of tightly packed evergreens blanketed with snow. The woods were crisscrossed with irregular patterns of straight lines. These were trails hacked through the wilderness by seismic exploration parties as they mapped the under-lying formations with shallow explosions and recording devices. The larger animals quickly adopted the paths and used them as broad highways and protected browsing grounds. He saw the convoluted outline of a river, a frozen snake coiling across the land in tightly spaced loops.

It was a desolate scene; it seemed impossible that this barren environment could support any form of life. A good many of the native animals — the bears and rodents — had long ago learned to escape the rigours through hibernation; but others — moose, caribou, wolves, and lynx — driven by the relentless goad of hunger, were abroad at all seasons.

There were also signs of human activity. Billowing clouds of steam pinpointed the location of drilling rigs. The plane flew directly over seven, evenly-spaced columns of smoke rising above a pipeline route. Men below were burning straw bales to thaw the ground so the ditching machines could scoop out a trench.

They lost height rapidly; the small dial in the cockpit that registered the outside temperature spun crazily. At five hundred feet it was a relatively balmy eight below, while the ground-level reading stood at minus forty. The needle quivered as it raced to record the falling temperatures. A towering plume of smoke from a flare-pit showed the precise point at which the temperature inversion occurred. The smoke rose straight and dense for three hundred feet, then, as though cut by a gigantic cleaver, stopped abruptly and slid along the ceiling of air, trailing off to the eastern horizon in a thick black streamer.

The warning light flashed red. The plane pitched slightly as the flaps and wheels dropped; then they were rolling smoothly down the frozen runway. They pulled to a stop beside a group of small, white-painted buildings. Cars and pickup trucks, engines running, waited behind a snow fence. As soon as the propellers had swung to a standstill, two ground-crew members, awkward in their heavy clothing, fastened wooden shields over the open nacelles to conserve vital heat. Rod squinted into the glare of the yellow sun, which already hung low over the horizon although it was still early afternoon. Its rays struck the crusted snow at a shallow angle and threw long shadows. A twin-engined de Havilland Caribou, designed specifically for bush flying, lumbered down the runway they had just quitted. It looked awkward and cumbersome with its thick body and upswept tail but it sprang into the air after an impossibly short takeoff run. A helicopter, Plexiglas windows glinting in the pale light, whickered in over the low buildings and settled gently on the ground inside the snow fence.

Suddenly the cold hit Rod. He was wearing heavy insulated gloves but his fingertips burned, and his skin contracted in a tight band across his forehead. He looked around for the driver he had been told would be there. By now, most of the passengers had sorted themselves out and were busily stowing luggage in the vehicles; the temporary crowd was rapidly dissipating. Rod felt a light touch on his arm. "You the geologist for Cheyenne No. 3?" The speaker was young, with a narrow, ferret-like face. Rod could see that, underneath the loose-fitting hood of his parka, he wore long curling sideburns. He was about two days from his last shave. "Truck's over here."

He turned, seeming not to see Rod's outstretched hand, and led the way to a battered pickup painted a dark green. They slung Rod's gear into the open back, just behind the spare gas tank welded in place behind the cab. He looked at Rod. "You ate on the plane?" He pronounced it "et" and it was more a statement than a question. Rod, forcing himself to sound cheerful and trying to ignore the misgivings that the cold-blasted scene had stirred in him, replied heartily that the airline had stuffed him so full he couldn't even face the thought of food.

His companion received this false heartiness with a laconic, "We better get started, then," as he swung himself into the cab. The windshield, like that of every other vehicle in the north, was starred and crisscrossed with fractures from flung gravel. The wheels thumped and bumped as they turned, until the flat spots frozen into the tires while the truck was parked were pounded back into circular shape. They drove west along a narrow, curved road that skirted the metal buildings of the townsite. Great transport trucks trailing sour clouds of diesel exhaust and loaded with strings of pipe, storage tanks, or dismantled drilling rigs, ground heavily by.

Batteries of oil tanks stood in neat clusters near the road, flowlines rising out of the ground like bloated snakes to couple with their valves. The air was polluted with the most appalling stench. It was as if some obscene giant had broken wind. Rod recognized it immediately: hydrogen sulphide gas escaping from sour crude. Gagging, he asked, "How come the Energy Board hasn't made them do something about that God-awful smell?"

"Dunno, I guess everybody's been too busy to worry about it."

"Well, they better start. It must be near lethal limits right now."

For the first time his companion smiled briefly. "Sure makes you want to light a match, don't it?"

They clattered and banged steadily west into the low-lying sun until the tiny townsite of Rainbow Lake was far behind; then the road angled north.

Rod soon discovered that the driver, whose name — Jerry Fleming — he had extracted with much difficulty, was not as surly and vicious as he had seemed at first. His rudeness stemmed from shyness and insecurity, not animosity. Jerry was one of life's buck privates and the rigidly structured world of the drilling rig suited him to perfection. So long as a fellow did what he was told, pulled his own weight, and endured the cold and other physical hardships, he was accepted by his peers. Nothing more was expected or required of him. The occasional binge or infrequent excursion to the outside world was an accepted thing; he had earned it, and there was plenty of time to recover in the long, cold months to come.

The pattern was flawed to some extent in Jerry's case by a young wife whom he had acquired somehow in the alcoholic daze of a brief stay in Edmonton. She was a riddle he didn't try to understand. Most of the time he managed to keep her very existence bottled up in the back of his mind, but occasionally he was summoned to the toolpush's office to stand before the squawking mobile, mute and miserable, while Thelma's voice, querulous and plaintive, complained of his neglect. He had already half-decided that the next time he hired on with a new rig he would simply forget to list her as a dependant, and maybe even this unwelcome intrusion from the outside world would disappear.

The road grew steadily worse. Soon it was nothing more than a frozen, corrugated slash. Jerry rode the brakes constantly, but it was still a rough, bone-shattering ride as they swooped and pitched, shock absorbers wildly thrumming, fenders banging and slamming. Vehicles and machinery aged quickly in the north; the freezing cold sucked out the last ounce of elasticity from metal and the demands of the appalling terrain completed the job.

There appeared to be quite a few rigs operating in the area. Rod saw signs — crudely painted or pencilled — pointing down roads to Valley No. 4, Turner No. 10, Red Indian No. 14, and others. Sometimes he could see the drilling mast fingering the skyline; more often the branch road simply disappeared over the horizon.

It was warm in the small cab. The heater blasted hot air and the defroster blew fans of clear glass on the frosted windshield. But there were veins and eddies of cold seeping through the floorboards and the door edges. Rod slumped down in the seat, head resting on the collar of his jacket, and fell into a semi-doze. He came suddenly and violently awake as the blunt noise of an enormous truck, air horn blatting, air brakes hissing, barrelled around a blind corner. Jerry drove the pickup straight into a snowbank and there they waited in helpless tension as the metal sides of the behemoth pounded by, the iron angles of a rig substructure jutting far beyond the low-boy trailer. Rod braced himself for the impact, for the sound of metal tearing as those harsh outlines sliced into the cab. At the last possible moment the trailer slewed slightly to the right, just enough to permit its murderous cargo to slide by the motionless truck. Jerry had ducked down in the seat covering his head with his arms. He slowly raised his head and expelled his breath in a long whistling sigh. "I figured we'd had it that time, for sure," he grunted as he pushed open the door and stepped out into the snow.

The huge diesel had ground to a stop a quarter-mile down the road and was slowly reversing. The driver's helper jumped down from the cab and fastened a chain to the stranded pickup. Then the giant tractor unit rumbled forward in compound low gear and yanked the small, green truck free of the snowbank. The driver, grinning hugely, craned out of his window and waved, while his helper matter-of-factly unhooked the chain and clambered back into the cab. Jerry had recovered from his initial shock and now treated the whole affair very calmly. It was obviously routine. A trailer rig highballing with its heavy load couldn't stop; it was up to the smaller vehicle to take evasive action. It was standard practice to drive right off the road — snow is a lot softer than steel. Afterwards, the giant rig, if its crew were well-disposed, would return to either pull out the stranded victim or disentangle the crumpled mass of metal. The crew, secure in their mighty machines, often showed a lamentable tendency to treat the whole affair as a huge joke. It was one of the most unpleasant hazards of travel in the north.

The northern night dropped down over them like a velvet cloak. The headlights had been on all through the daylight hours in the faint hope of giving some advance warning to the onrushing trucks; now their beams strengthened, highlighting the waves of mounds and valleys over which they pounded their painful way. Jerry exhaled a long sigh of relief. "That's better. It's safer driving these roads at night, you can see the other guys' lights and maybe have time to do something — like get the hell and gone out of their way!"

He reached his right hand down to the floor, fumbled around, and turned a switch to cut in the spare gas tank. Peering at his watch in the dim glare from the dashboard, he said, "Five o'clock. Chow time. There's some sandwiches and coffee behind the seat. We'll stop up the road at the turnoff to Barrow No. 7. Can't eat while we're bouncing like this, that's for damn sure."

The cab vibrated and shook with the roughly idling motor as they chewed on thick meat sandwiches and drank coffee from plastic cups. Standing outside the truck to relieve himself, Rod gasped involuntarily as he looked at the magic landscape. A frozen lagoon of stars floated across the night sky. The starshine struck glittering diamonds on the wind-polished snow. The trees carried their burden of snow in a mosaic of black and white. There was no moon. The cold, no longer checked by the feeble resistance of the sun, held the whole scene in icy stillness.

They drove on through the night. Occasionally the erect tower of a drilling rig, festooned with lights, blazed brightly in the distance like an abstract Christmas tree. But mostly there was just the pounding clatter of tortured springs and shock absorbers, the hissing of heater and defroster, and the yellow cone of light thrusting into the hovering darkness. Rod moved away from the drafty door; the coffee and the heavy sandwiches made a warm glow in his stomach. Drowsily his thoughts drifted back to last night and the soft, scented warmth of Melinda. The vision of her shimmering before him; she seemed to be beckoning him, but she was running away ... always running ...

6

The party was at the home of Tom Vanning, vice-president of D'or Mines Limited, the company for which Rod Fraser, with his freshly minted Master's degree in geology, toiled. The long, low house, perched expensively on Marine Drive overlooking Vancouver's Burrard Inlet, suited Tom, with his blonde good looks, his big frame and air of easy confidence. Tom was thirty-eight and had come a long way in the large mining company with a parlay of a handsome face, commanding physical presence, and big chunks of drive and energy. In the last couple of years it had become painfully clear to his superiors, and a troubled few of his more perceptive friends, that he had also come as far as he could go. The impressive body had thickened perceptibly; the soft skin was beginning to pull away from the firm lines of the jaw; the clear blue eyes were becoming evasive. He had begun to meet life sideways, passing its problems over his shoulder with a slight shrug and another drink. With eyes permanently out of focus, it was reasonably easy to overlook the things he didn't want to see.

The reason for Tom's decline stood before the amused eyes of Rod Fraser. Tom mumbled a hasty introduction: "Melinda, this is our new geologist — Rod Fraser. Rod — my wife, Melinda."

She was beautiful, tempting, totally challenging, and completely off-limits. She made the other women, mostly wives of the mining company employees, look colourless and dowdy.

Her voice was low with just a touch of huskiness as she offered a slender hand. "Hello, Mr. Fraser, Tom has talked about how clever you are." She glanced up at her husband. "But he didn't tell me you were so good-looking."

Looking down at her cool perfection, Rod felt a fine line of sweat beading his forehead. He hoped she couldn't see it. He dropped her hand and muttered, "How do you do, Mrs. Vanning."

"So very formal, Mr. Fraser! Please call me Melinda —" she was interrupted by Tom, who reappeared with another guest to be introduced. Rod fled to the improvised bar at the far end of the garden. He recognized several fellow-employees and managed to lose himself for the next hour in a flow of introductions and polite small talk. Occasionally he would catch a flash of white and hear her voice as she circulated easily among the cluster of guests, cat-green eyes transfixing the men. She wore her hair long then.

At the end of an hour of correct conversation and a conservative two gin-and-tonics, the young geologist took his leave of his host and hostess. Tom was in a small group of men by the bar; he was carrying a pretty good load but he handled it well. He waved a casual hand at Rod. "Glad to have you, old man. We'll make a point of seeing you again before too long."

Melinda was being gracious to some ladies in the shade of a giant cedar. When she saw Rod leaving, she eased herself away to intercept him. "Leaving, Mr. Fraser? If you must go, I'll walk you to the door."

Her arm rested lightly on his as they walked through the sliding doors, across the carpeted width of a drawing room and over the polished slate of a square entrance-hall filled with golden light that streamed in through amber-tinted windows. Just before she removed her hand, Rod thought he felt a slight increase of pressure. He brushed away the thought as a hallucination of his own too-ready nervous system. She stood in the open doorway, smiling up at him. "Goodbye, Rod. Would you buy me lunch sometime this week? You can call me here at home anytime after nine in the morning. We're in the book."

Rod stared at the face smiling so serenely up at him. She might have been any dutiful company wife bidding a pleasant impersonal farewell to a junior employee. Had those delectable lips really framed that incredible invitation? Her smile deepened as she said, "Rod, you mustn't look so startled. It's not the least bit flattering. You will call me, won't you?"

Rod managed to nod, fumbled awkwardly with her hand, and stumbled across the asphalt parking lot to his shiny new Pontiac.

Tom had watched their departure from the garden with narrowed eyes. He stood looking for several long minutes at the door through which they had disappeared. When he turned back to his companions, he looked ten years older. There was an embarrassed, awkward pause until he signalled a waiter with a peremptory snap of his fingers.

There was nothing in Rod Fraser's background to prepare him for Melinda Vanning. His father had been the railway station agent in a small mountain community on the CPR right-of-way. Life in Stanton was remarkably uncomplicated; his father's pay was sufficient to keep the small family — Rod had one brother, Harry, ten years older — in reasonable comfort. There were girls, of course; girls with pigtails in grade school; girls grown suddenly tall and mysterious in high school with its occasional gymnasium dances, where they moved to the playing of assorted barbers, truck drivers, and railway hands, transformed into musicians by the setting sun. There were nights of necking and of furtive acts that went beyond necking, in the back seat of the family car. There was one girl in particular — every town, village, and hamlet has one — who, without any discernible passion, opened her legs to the fumbling and bursting eagerness of high-school cocks.

Rod had been able to attend university without any undue financial strain. His father helped; there were interest-free loans, and with the proceeds of summer jobs Rod was able to concentrate on his studies without the distraction of outside work. These financial resources also enabled him to join a fraternity, to buy the occasional bottle of rye whisky, and to date the more than occasional girl. Mostly he sought his dates within the confines of the university, presenting himself scrubbed and shining at the massive stone entrance to the girls' residence. Sometimes he sought other pleasures at the local dance halls, moving with practised ease through the shoals of young female flesh; trying an experimental dance with that one, discarding this one, sitting out a dance to share a rye-spiked coke with another, until finally by a process of elimination or sheer desperation he had winnowed out his partner for the night. Sometimes they made out, sometimes not. On two occasions, beguiled by clear glowing skin, the lift of breast and flash of thigh, he fell mildly in love, and just as mildly out.

He spent a year bumming around Europe after he got his Bachelor of Science degree from the University of British Columbia. There were lots of girls that year: American co-eds, a blonde Danish divorcee, and, in the last two months, a quiet little English mouse. She was majoring in literature, devoured books, and had a beautiful, questing intelligence. In the long summer nights of quiet lovemaking and deep conversation, Rod came to know that he was not yet finished with university life. He left her in Rome and went to Denver to study for his Master's. By the time he began to work for D'or Mines there had been many girls in Rod's life, but there had been no one remotely resembling Melinda Vanning.

Tom stood, swaying uncertainly in the doorway, dark-brown drink clutched in his left hand, a lighted cigarette in the right. He felt half sick and wholly desperate. He was licked before he started and he knew it. Melinda, her hair softened and fluffed by the pillows, looked up from her book with a cool, enquiring eyebrow. Lying there, soft in the lamplight, the frilled peignoir giving her a little-girl look, she was the picture of the demure wife, a *Ladies' Home Journal* bride. Tom shuddered and took a hasty pull at his Scotch. He tried to strike a light note. "Melinda, we really can't have you vamping young Fraser. Company policy, you know. Can't have promising young geologists put off their feed and their work by the vice-president's devastating young wife. Just won't do." His voice darkened and thickened. "Lay off, damn it! This one I won't stand still for. My position in the company is all I've got left, all you haven't managed to take from me. You fool around with Fraser and I'll be a laughingstock in my own office as well as everywhere else in this bloody town."

"Whatever are you talking about, Tom?" The low voice had an undertone of sheer pleasure. "I was merely being charming to Mr. Fraser to further your precious career. I thought I was the very model of a loyal wife. You mustn't let these fancies run away with you like that." The tip of a pointed tongue flashed pinkly against gleaming teeth.

"Darling, you really have been neglecting poor Melinda, you know." She threw back the silken coverlet and flowed out of the bed to stand before him, moving her body in a slow rhythmic undulation, her great eyes glowing.

With a cry of despair Tom dropped his glass, the brown stain darkening on the white rug, and fled blindly down the hall to his own bedroom pursued by peal after peal of laughter.

The dime bonged deep in the inner workings of the telephone. Rod's hand was steady as he spun the dial but there was a broad band of tension across his diaphragm, robbing him of breath. A voice, clear and modulated and with unmistakably brown African tones, announced, "This is the Vanning residence." Sucking in a deep breath, Rod asked for Mrs. Vanning.

She came on the line, her voice a polished blend of neutral accents until the maid was out of earshot. She accepted Rod's hesitant invitation with a brisk alacrity, told him when and where they would meet for lunch, and rang off.

And so it began for Rod Fraser. Late afternoons and occasional nights of single-minded, driving passion. She was the perfect vessel of sexuality, practised and devoted. Rod rapidly fell into a state of near-schizophrenia, distracted by her beauty, informed by her experienced passion. Tortured by his conventional assortment of boy-girl concepts and ideals, he loved and hated her.

During that summer, his work deteriorated badly. He could whip himself into brief spells of concentration but couldn't maintain the sustained energy and absorption that should be lavished on a first job. He had been with the company for less than a year, and he could sense he was about to be ignominiously fired. He could see it in the withdrawn, cool attitude of his immediate superior, the chief geologist, and in the concerned eyes of the president. The thought of a failure so crushing, so unnecessary, was bitter bile in his mouth, but he was deep in the sweet misery of Melinda and there was no escape.

Rod's failure to perform in the office, while performing so valiantly in bed, became purely academic with the passkey entrance of two polite, impersonal gentlemen, with Vanning's face sick and pale behind the popping glare of the flashbulbs.

Rod was named as co-respondent in the divorce, but he didn't stay around for it. Miles Coleman, D'or's president, gave him the chance to resign before he got the chop and Rod seized it gratefully. At their final interview, Coleman shook his neat grey head. "It's too bad, my young friend, but you were way out of your depth. It's like catching a disease, but it needn't be fatal. This town's too hot for you right now. I know they always say to stick it out and face them down, but in your case I advise against it. You're still very young. Get away from here, as far as you can, and make yourself a new career. There's a big demand for geologists — you won't have any trouble getting another job."

The real demand for geologists turned out to be not in mining but in the oil industry, and this gave Rod the first professional lift he had felt in months. In those infrequent intervals when his mind was not completely immersed in Melinda, he had begun to think about the fascination of tracking the elusive black gold lurking under thousands of feet of rock. It was the most exciting action on the geological scene. Coleman did him the final favour of arranging an interview with Universal Oils, and Rod was hired by the giant, international oil company as a very junior geologist for their Venezuelan operation.

It seemed to him like the answer to everything. He and Melinda could marry and start a new life together. The divorce and all the unpleasant rumpus would turn out to be a blessing in disguise. Like knocking up the girl that you loved anyway.

The acid scorn with which Melinda had greeted his suggestion etched a livid scar across his psyche. The memory of it even now made him groan; he stirred and gazed groggily around the swaying, dimly lit cab. The realization that he was pounding over a God-awful road en route to a frozen hell jarred him back to reality.

7

Rod leaned forward to hold his wristwatch under the feeble light of the dashboard. It was ten o'clock and they were still in the ass-end of nowhere. Jerry must be absolutely beat. Guiltily, he volunteered to spell Jerry at the wheel, but his offer was rejected with a firm shake of the head. His conscience relieved, and thankful he didn't have to manhandle the unfamiliar vehicle over the impossible road, Rod sank back against the seat. Like a finger picking at a scab, his memory wandered back to Melinda — now Melinda Mason, newly married to one George Mason, who sounded like a real creep. "Kinky," she had said. His imagination was just beginning to explore the revolting implications of this when the motor coughed, hesitated, then lurched forward, spat twice, and quit with an ominous air of finality. Rod sat bolt upright, the unfunny implications of a night in the bush at minus forty swarming through his head. He knew what extreme cold could do to a person, how quickly it sapped the will to survive, how quietly and painlessly it invaded the body to extinguish the very cell of life.

Jerry snapped off the lights to conserve the battery, then leaned across Rod and popped open the glove compartment. His teeth gleamed briefly in the cold starlight. "No sweat," he said as he fumbled around in the compartment, finally extracting two small, bronze-coloured tins. A quick twist and both cans opened with a faint hiss of escaping air.

"Carburetor and gas line froze up, that's all. Just needs some of this medicine."

He opened the door and stood on the running board, unscrewed the gas tank cover, and emptied both cans into it. The engine turned over and caught, running smoothly as the mixture of alcohol and glycol dissolved the ice deposits.

Rod said, "That's great stuff. I hope you've got lots more of it."

"Nope. Only had two cans, but that's enough to get us to the rig."

Rod stared at him. "Christ, I hope you're right."

It was almost midnight when they saw the faint glow in the sky. Jerry spoke. "That's our rig. We're almost there."

Rod had sweated out every mile, waiting for the dread sound of missing cylinders that would condemn them to a frozen night. He held his breath every time Jerry took his foot off the gas pedal to ease them over the rolling bumps. Seldom had he been as glad to see anything as that blur of light. Now, even if the motor did conk out, they could walk to the camp.

He peered through the frost-bordered windshield waiting for the sharp, precise outline of the drilling derrick to resolve itself out of the night. It didn't. All that happened was that the blur of indistinct light grew stronger and larger, swinging more and more to their right as they approached. Finally, Jerry slowed to a crawl and turned down a road branching off at a right angle. Rod stared hard at the shape standing squarely at the end of the short road, a mile distant. He realized now what he was looking at, but he still didn't believe it. The entire drilling derrick was encased in canvas; the lights glowed dimly through the heavy material and clouds of steam swirled around it, making it look like a giant rocket in the final stages of the countdown.

Jerry grinned at his reaction. "She's a tight hole."

"She sure as hell is!" Rod breathed in awe. He had heard of "tight holes" before, where every security precaution was taken to prevent competitors from learning anything about the well — they had lots of them in Venezuela. But to build a tent over the whole damn thing? His racing mind quickly appreciated the advantages of the cover. Competitors' spies — or scouts as they were euphemistically called in the industry — training binoculars on the well from the cover of a bush or low-flying aircraft wouldn't be able to see what was going on. For the first time, Rod began to fully appreciate the immensity of the stakes they were playing for.

They pulled up at the camp, a quarter-mile from the shrouded rig. Jerry drove the truck close against the sheltering side of one of the camp buildings and plugged in a long length of black electric cord. It was connected to a small heater under the hood, which would, hopefully, keep the engine block warm enough so it would start. Up here, vehicles were either plugged in, their engines were left running, or they were forgotten until the spring thaw.

Rod climbed stiffly down from the truck. There was something unusual about the sound of that rig. He could hear the powerful motors; they were running all right, but they didn't seem to be pulling any power. Because of the canvas, he couldn't see whether they were making hole or not, but it sure as hell didn't sound like it. Both he and Jerry saw the trucks at the same time: two of them, huge, orange and black, each with a large cylindrical tank, hydraulic pumps just aft of the cabs, and thick hoses feeding into the substructure of the rig. Men swarmed over them ripping open small sacks and emptying them into the open tank hatches. They were cement trucks, and both roughneck and geologist knew they meant only one thing — trouble in the hole!

"Come on, I'll show you where you bunk down." There was a rough edge in Jerry's voice. The trouble wasn't his responsibility, but he didn't like it, any more than a sailor liked it when something went wrong with his ship.

The camp was simple and, like the rig itself, highly mobile. It consisted of four units, each about forty feet long, two placed end to end and parallel to the other pair, leaving an alleyway about ten feet wide. This alleyway had been boarded to make a rough sort of mall joining the trailer units. While the wooden partitions kept out the wind, the passageway was unheated and so made for a mighty chilly walk from one room to the next. All doors opened onto it, facing each other across its frigid width. It was a natural deep-freeze and cartons of food and perishables were stacked along its length. The rough wooden door squeaked harshly open as Jerry toted Rod's luggage inside. Rod levered his duffel bag from the back of the pickup, dumped it heavily on the ground, and stood for a moment, looking down the road at the steaming rig. It was a far cry from the lush, populous, warm city of Caracas. Misgiving churned deep in his guts; maybe he'd been crazy to fight so hard to get into this white hell. There sure wasn't much he could do about it tonight, however. He hoisted the bag and followed after Jerry.

Inside the passageway, the trailers with their shining white metal sides, their metal doors with refrigerator-type handles, resembled a string of cold-storage lockers. Each door had a badly painted sign: DINER, TOOLPUSH, BATHROOM, etc. "The tool-push lives there." Jerry said unnecessarily, jerking a thumb at the well-labelled door. "His name is Larry Quigley. He'll be down at the rig, though. Let's go in here and get some coffee and see if we can get find a bed for you. Should be some free bunks unless we got some visitors. Anyway, you can always latch onto a 'hot bed.'"

He pushed open the door marked DINER. Rod puzzled over the reference to "hot bed." Surely they didn't have any home comforts like camp-followers in this remote corner of hell. Then it came to him — they worked the clock around in eight-hour tours (pronounced "towers" for some long-forgotten reason). That meant one-third of the crew was always on duty, leaving freshly quitted beds available until their owners came off tour. He fervently hoped there were no other visitors.

The diner was fitted out with four tables, each covered with a red plastic top; the forward part of the room was a large kitchen. Two men dressed in faded dungarees leaned against the sink, carefully peeling apples, dividing the white fruit into meticulous crescents, then popping them into their mouths and chewing with great deliberation. They nodded at Jerry, more distantly at Rod. "Coffee's on and there's pie over there."

"This here's the new geologist." Jerry's introduction was sketchy. They nodded gravely once more but offered no names.

Sipping gratefully at a thick cup of steaming coffee, Rod said in a carefully neutral voice, "They seem to be having a little trouble down at the rig."

Both men considered this for a moment, then nodded sober agreement. One had a broad band of dead white skin across his prominent nose and right cheek, souvenir of a severe frostbite.

Finally, one of them confided what the problem was — deviation. When the crew had pulled out the drill pipe to replace the old bit, they ran a survey and found the hole had kicked badly to the right. It was running a full eight degrees off the vertical; the permissible maximum was three degrees. It meant they had to plug the hole with cement back to the point where it had twisted off course, then drill again, praying that this time the bit would cut straight. It meant aggravating delays: for the cement trucks to be contacted, load up, and drive out to the wellsite; for the cement to be made up and pumped down the hole; and finally — the worst delay of all — for the thirty to forty-eight hours it took "waiting on cement" — waiting for it to harden and set.

Rod thought of going down to the rig to let the toolpush know he had arrived, but finally decided against it. There was nothing he could do; he knew Quigley would have his hands full and, if he were anything like all the pushes Rod had ever known, he would also be in a savage temper. Jerry had found him a vacant bunk in a room at the far end of the corridor. Opening his suitcase, which was so cold it burned his bare hands, he fished out his leather toilet case and ran down the frigid length of the corridor to the door so decorously marked BATHROOM.

He gazed in blank astonishment at the tube of toothpaste. Frozen solid, it steadfastly refused to flow, or ooze, or whatever it was toothpaste was supposed to do. "Christ, what a country!" Rod threw the stubborn tube back in the case and stumbled off to his bunk.

"Time to hit the deck, fella, get the hell out of that sack!" The voice was sharp with impatience and its command was emphasized by a rough shaking of Rod's shoulder.

Half-awake, Rod instinctively pushed at the stranger's hand. He awoke with a start. There were no fingers on the hand, only stumps, with white skin folded over the tips. He looked at his wristwatch — it was seven-thirty.

"I'm Quigley, Larry Quigley, the toolpush of this bloody rig. You better get a quick wash-up and meet me in the diner for some chow." His voice was rough with fatigue.

Rod made another hurried dash down the arctic length of the corridor, then entered the warm, brightly lit diner.

There were several men seated at the long tables. They looked up as the door opened, then quickly returned their gaze to their plates. Rod saw Jerry Fleming and nodded as he walked to the kitchen-end of the room. Two middle-aged women bustled around the cluttered stoves, their broad, fleshy faces flushed with heat and exertion. Ron ladled some scrambled eggs and bacon onto his plate, poured a mug of steaming coffee, and went back to join Quigley, who did not bother to look up.

"I guess you've had some trouble?" Might as well take the bull by the horns, Rod thought.

"Some." Larry cradled his coffee mug, pressing the stumps of his right hand against its scalding heat. Reluctantly, he continued. "The cement's in the hole, now we sit on our ass till it sets up. I'll take you down to the rig after breakfast, show you around, and then I'm going to sack out!"

The towering rig was eerily silent as they walked across the squeaking snow. There was the muted hum of idling motors, the resounding crash of a metal door, but the ground-shaking roar of a rig under full power was missing. The canvas cover, hanging in loose shrouds, gave it the appearance of a ship becalmed in some unknown frozen sea. They climbed the steep flight of metal steps to the rig floor. Rod noted with some surprise that both the substructure of the rig, poking out from its canvas skirt, and the doghouse were made of heavy metal, painted the same dark green as the pickup. Must have some connection with the fact that these rigs are constantly on the go — steel would stand up a lot better than plywood to the wear and tear of moving and being torn down and rigged up. The door of the tiny, cramped doghouse slammed noisily shut behind them. His exposed face was stinging from the cold and the tips of his fingers already tingled inside the thick gloves.

The doghouse was divided into two parts. The first section was lined on both sides with tall steel lockers, and at the far corner a triangular steel bench was welded into place. It was littered with small bottles, a hand-driven centrifugal machine, and piles of cloth bags. This tiny bench and the small trailer parked near the camp were Rod's working quarters, where he would collect, examine, and classify the samples of rock washed up with the drilling mud.

The second compartment housed two machines: one had inked graphs and dials that showed the depth, the drilling pressure, and other data. Its graph pens and indicators were stationary, mute evidence that the rig was down. Across from it stood a machine that looked much like an intricate weigh-scale with its thin levers and chains. This was the rig's autopilot; under normal drilling conditions it could be set to regulate the speed and horsepower of the motors and the drilling weight on the string of pipe. It, too, was ominously silent. There was another triangle of steel, larger than Rod's bench, in the opposite corner. It was covered with copies of logs that were filled in by the driller in charge of each tour.

Larry wrenched open the half top of the heavy steel door leading to the rig floor. Rod sucked in his breath. It was a scene of indescribable confusion. Great shards and piles of ice were everywhere; coating the valves, the wheels, every projecting corner; hanging down in great bayonets and spears. The drilling floor was covered with grey, frozen mud. The whole scene resembled nothing so much as a ship reaching port after surviving a winter Atlantic gale, its superstructure laden with tons of ice. The crew had rigged steam-hoses in an effort to control the avalanche of ice, and white clouds of steam swirled damply within the confines of the canvas cover.

Larry's dark-brown eyes, almost buried in the depths of round, vein-splotched cheeks, regarded Rod with sardonic amusement. "Not much like the lush operations in Venezuela, eh? But you'll learn that when you've got eighty degrees of frost, you're doing damn well to keep anything working, let alone in shipshape condition. If you think this is bad, come down below and take a look at the blow-out preventers!"

They clattered back down the metal steps to the substructure where the great valves were housed. The blowout preventers — BOPS — were the last line of defence against a wild well. Huge and bulbous, they were bolted to the surface casing — several hundred feet of steel pipe cemented into place at the top of the hole. The valves were powerful ramjets that could be triggered by any one of three levers spotted around the rig. One of these levers was placed hundreds of yards from the derrick, offering a last chance of regaining control when fire or poisonous gas drove everyone back from the rig.

Dim figures stumbled about in the yellow light of two bare bulbs. Hampered by their heavy clothing and the numbing cold, they reeled and slipped heavily, some trying with clumsy motions to chip away layers of ice encrusting a dial while others directed a jet of steam at a heavy bolt-and-nut assembly. One applied a giant wrench to the nut, heaved once, and swore as the long handle broke cleanly in two. He flung the broken piece on the ground and brushed by Rod and Larry on his way to the toolhouse for a replacement. Larry grabbed him by the arm and shouted tersely that next time he'd "better fucking-well make sure" the nut was completely thawed before he tried to loosen it. They didn't have any wrenches to waste. The roughneck, young, with a blank, sullen face, nodded indifferently and lurched off.

Back in the relative warmth and quiet of the doghouse, Rod, although he already knew the answer, asked how much deviation they had found.

"Eight God-damn degrees off the vertical!"

Rod raised an eyebrow slightly.

"I know, God damn it, I don't need you to tell me we should have caught it. We're supposed to take surveys every ten feet or so, but I decided to hell with it. I figured it was just a waste of time and time is something we don't have. We were in shale and none of the other rigs in the area have ever run into any serious deviation in shale, so I reckoned we'd be safe in forgetting about surveys until it was time to change bits. Did three hundred feet in the soft shale with one bit and went off eight degrees. It's my fault, but if they don't like it in Calgary, they can stuff it — get someone else to run this fucking rig. But they won't; nobody else knows how to keep the damn thing glued together. I'm going back to camp. You might as well stay here and get your stuff sorted out, if you want."

There wasn't much to do. Rod did his best to clean up the litter on the desk and stow some of it in a small cabinet. While he worked, the members of the crew retreated one at a time from the derrick floor to thaw out briefly in the doghouse. They glanced at him curiously, exchanged a word or two about the bloody weather, but made no attempt to introduce themselves. Rod looked up as he heard a voice enquiring, "Are you the new geologist?"

Rod nodded and held out his hand, which the other man shook dubiously.

"Bob Reiner, sir. I'm supposed to get your samples for you." He grinned. "Been a soft touch, so far. We've spent most of our time just standing still. Do you want to take a look at the shaker?"

Rod shrugged his way into his heavy parka and followed Bob outside. They walked by the sump pit with its viscous mass of waste and contaminated mud, climbed up to a catwalk and over the metal tanks where the drilling mud was recycled and cleaned. The mud was pumped down the hole and then brought back to the surface slivers of rock chewed up by the drilling bit; these pieces were shaken out as the mud flowed over a vibrating screen, much as in the old-time panning of gold. The rock splinters were collected at regular intervals and brought to the geologist for analysis.

Rod looked dispiritedly at the frozen mass of material that had spilled over the shaker. While they stood there silently contemplating the unlovely pile of rubble, a helicopter dragonflied in slow circles just above the shrouded derrick. Bob watched it make three leisurely swings and depart. As it dimmed in the distance, he spoke without rancour. "Now everybody and his uncle will know that Cheyenne Three is down again. But that's all they'll know."

Using the doghouse as a fortress of warmth, Rod made exploratory sorties about the rig. It was old and it showed its age. But the two diesel motors that supplied the power looked sound enough, and the running gear of multi-sheaved blocks, steel cables, and swivels were in good order. The housekeeping was appalling; spare parts, broken tools, odd remnants of obsolete equipment lay about everywhere, solidly embedded in the ice. The supporting facilities, boiler house, toolhouse, and fuel tanks were strung in a straight line out from the substructure. Poking around in the small toolhouse, Rod wondered why in the world anyone would bother to insulate it, since it was not connected to the heating system. His exploratory finger, touching the white layer of insulation, sank into it without resistance. It was frost, three inches of it! Some insulation!

Because meals were important in camps, serving to break the grinding monotony, supper was served sharply at five o'clock. Larry, looking more rested and considerably more cheerful, banged his plate down on the table and sat on the bench beside Rod. "Well, the cement boys tell us we can drill ahead by noon tomorrow."

"Good. I felt about as useful as tits on a boar, all day."

"Did you mosey around and make yourself acquainted? Hell of a mess, ain't it?" Larry spoke with cheerful lack of care, little eyes gleaming in their pouches of fat.

"Still won't be an awful lot for you to do at first. We've got to drill through the cement plug and I don't figure that will be of much geological interest. Then we've got some more shale to drill. Beats me why they sent you up here so early."

"Well, of course, they didn't know about the cement job when I left Calgary. I imagine they just don't want to take any chances with this hole. After all, they had Walsh up here from day one."

"Yeah. But that was different. Old Mac sent him up here to dry out before we hit anything interesting." Larry gazed gloomily at his plate. "He was a good hand, old Jack, but the bottle won every time. He always used to say it would finish him, and it did — it sure as hell did!"

"Ever think it might not have been an accident? MacPherson seemed puzzled by the way it happened."

"You kidding? There was old Walsh with a skinful, and he didn't know they had moved the bridge. No, it was an accident, all right."

Rod decided to change the subject. "Maybe you can tell me something. Are we flying completely blind up here or is there any sort of geological control or information?"

"What there is ain't none too encouraging. There's a dry hole about six miles to the south. Paramount Drilling dug it for some Vancouver outfit — Argent Oils, or some name like that. They abandoned it early in December. It's just on the other side of the drilling reservation that's coming up for sale, the one we're trying to beat with this hole."

8

Mac sighed heavily as he put down the receiver. He looked across the desk at Sheila. "They're trying to crowd the old man. That was Jim Carruthers from Vancouver. He's making noises as though he and his friends want out."

"But they can't do that!"

"I'm afraid they can. And if they pull out now, it means we have to close the well down. We've already pared everything to the bone, and if they shut off the funds, we can't last a day."

He thought for a moment and then said, "We could possibly hold their feet to the fire. What really bothers me is that I don't feel I can cope with it. Getting old and decrepit, I guess — can't hack it any more."

"You're no such thing. It's just that everything has come at you so suddenly. They've given their promise; they can't go back on it now, surely."

"Maybe. But I can see what's on their mind. That dry hole on the other side of the reservation cooled them off. A thing like that sort of dampens one's enthusiasm, makes you realize that a dry hole is still a likely, and damn unpleasant, prospect. Jim sounded sort of funny, almost strained, as though he had some pressure on him. Probably loud and long complaints from some unhappy partners, that's usually enough!"

"Did he say definitely they were pulling out?"

"No, he just sort of hinted, like he was preparing the way. I wish to God I could take a stronger line with him. But how can I, with that confounded well shutting down every other day? He mentioned that all right — how concerned they all were over the breakdowns, the delays, and over expenditure."

"It seems to me we need some way to create a little counterpressure." She hesitated, took a deep breath, and plunged ahead gamely. "Look, didn't you say Rod had a lot of experience in things of this sort? Doesn't he know about finances and contracts? He can't be doing anything very useful up at the well with it shut down. Why don't you call him and see if he can do something with the Vancouver investors? See if he can't think of some way of stiffening their spines! You just can't give up at this stage; you're too near the answer! I won't let you!"

She broke off as Mac stared at her. "That was quite a speech, young lady! We have a 'sked' on the radio tomorrow morning. I'll talk to your young man and see what he has to say."

"He's not 'my young man' — yet, or maybe ever. But I do think he can do some good."

The noise on the rig floor was deafening. The motors whined, then roared with a deeper note as the driller let out the clutch. Men slipped on the treacherous slickness of the mud-covered floor as they strained to control the heavy pipe. Their movements were clumsy but co-ordinated. They watched while the derrick man, teetering on his tiny platform far above their heads, fastened the huge clamps onto a string of pipe. A surge of power brought the pipe swaying over them. Grunting, three roughnecks heaved against it until it hung over the threaded joint of pipe protruding from the hole. The driller watched them carefully. As soon as the two ends were aligned, he jerked at a lever and the descending pipe clumped onto its fellow with a hollow splat. Now the two sections had to be screwed together. One of the roughnecks looped several coils of chain around the pipe; the driller's foot pressed a clutch and he pulled another lever. The unwinding chain turned the pipe and tightened it on the threads. As soon as the chain had spun off, the roughnecks picked up the huge tongs — gigantic wrenches — and fastened them to the pipe; again the motor strained, cables tightened, tugged, loosened and tugged, loosened and tugged again. A signal from one of the roughnecks and the pressure was eased, the tongs were swung to one side, and the new joint of pipe was dropped smoothly into the hole.

Luke Willard, the driller, stopped its swift descent while the last three feet still protruded above the floor. Two floormen slung metal slips around it to hold it in place while another length was swung into position. It was back-breaking work, repeated endlessly. The punishing temperature made it just that much worse.

Rod Fraser stood on the right-hand side of the driller beside the drawworks. He was watching Luke with admiration; the man was an artist with his delicate mastery of the controls.

Rod still had not managed to sort out the crew members; there were too many of them to be absorbed at once. But he remembered Luke. He was black, which alone would make him stand out — very few blacks could be found around a drilling rig. His face was arresting. Rod looked at it now, half-hidden beneath the shiny safety helmet with its neatly stencilled WILLARD. It was a young face with sharply etched, handsome features and dark-brown skin. Deep lines scimitared down from the nose, and the thickly carved lips curved downwards at the corners, touching the face with cruelty. His eyes were narrow, restless slits, dark brown and liquid.

He was superb at his job. As the driller he was in charge of his tour and Rod could see that he was getting a lot out of the frozen crew. He worked with a smoothly co-ordinated energy and drive that inspired the others.

In a moment of comparative quiet, while a roughneck wound the chain around the pipe. Luke turned to Rod and said, with a downward twist of his lips, "Last week, over at Border No. 5 rig, they killed a guy standing right where you are. The chain snapped off the pipe in a neat little loop and wrapped itself around his neck just as nice as you please. They peeled him off the drawworks in two pieces."

Involuntarily, Rod stepped back as the chain grew taut and began to unroll from the pipe. He looked through the half-open door of the doghouse and saw Larry motioning to him.

"There's a special message for you coming through on the mobile in five or ten minutes. I'll go back to the camp with you to make sure the damn thing works."

Yesterday's clear blue skies had given way to a dense, ice-crystal fog. The grey blanket hung everywhere. It didn't raise the temperature; it just made it more unendurable. Ice-crystal fogs and unremitting temperatures of minus fifty had been known to last for weeks on end, driving machinery to breakdowns and men to suicide.

The static burping out of the grey box was appalling and they could barely hear Mac's shouting voice. Rod finally grasped that he was to come back to Calgary as soon as he could and to shout his understanding of the order. Anything more — any explanation as to why he was being yanked out almost as soon as he arrived — was utterly beyond the screeching, howling mobile.

Rod was in no mood to question any order that took him away from this frozen isolation. Anyway, he felt completely useless on the wellsite. They were drilling ahead now, through the cement, but they weren't anywhere near the critical formations. He turned to the toolpush with a slight shrug that only half masked his pleasure. "How do I go about getting back to Calgary?"

"That's no problem. We'll get Fleming to drive you out to Rainbow in the pickup. There's a flight leaves Rainbow around two tomorrow afternoon; you can catch that one."

Rod apologized to Jerry as they ground their way back over the same bone-shattering road. "I'm afraid I've been a hell of a nuisance, making you drive so much."

Jerry dismissed this with a gesture of his hand and his quick, shy smile. "It's okay. I don't mind; I kind of like it."

It was true enough; he did like the long drive, insulated in the warm cab from the outside world. It was something he could do and do well; he didn't mind the constant braking, the unceasing shifting of gears. He was always a little sad and a little frightened when the journey was finished and he had to open the door and step out into the land of people.

They jolted along in silence for a few miles, then Rod said, "The push — Larry — he seems a little feisty. Have you worked with him before?"

"Sure, lots of times. Larry's okay; his hand hurts like hell, and I guess what with the trouble at the rig ..." Fleming's voice trailed off.

"What happened to his hand?"

"The tongs. It was about five years ago. He was working on the floor, making a trip. His gloves got wet and froze to the pipe. When the other floorman threw his tongs, Larry couldn't get his hand out of the way — hell, it happens all the time."

"I know. But you'd think after five years it wouldn't hurt any more."

"It's the fucking cold. If you've got something missing that's where the cold hits. I had a buddy who got the tip of his little finger cut off. Just one finger, for Christ's sake! But the cold got to him so bad he had to give up drilling. He didn't want to; he didn't know how to do nothing else, but he couldn't take the cold in that finger."

It was after one in the morning when they turned off the lease road onto the more travelled section that traversed the last few miles into Rainbow. Rod coughed as the sickening miasma of sour crude entered the cab. Jerry grinned in sympathy, but kept his eyes on the road, where a parade of heavy diesels straining in low gear roared past them, their headlights splintering on the frozen crystals that rimmed the windshield. They followed the gentle curve past a green-painted Quonset hut; past a fenced-in yard where tracked vehicles stood in silent ranks patiently waiting until the summer thawed the frozen land into a restless sea of muskeg where only they could venture; past a new curling rink whose unpainted wood was raw and unfinished in the cold starlight. Jerry swung the wheel sharply to the right, and their headlights picked out the gleaming pink metal sides of trailer units, stripped of their wheels and grouped together like a child's building blocks.

"The Rainbow Hilton." Jerry smiled self-consciously as he produced the well-used joke.

They were both cramped and stumbling with fatigue as Jerry lifted Rod's suitcase, limned with a thin film of frost, and climbed a short flight of wooden steps to the door marked ENTRANCE. A clerk, a growth of grey stubble silvering his many rolls of chin, sleepily took their money in advance and slapped down two keys on the counter. "138 and 139. You know how to find them, Jerry."

They set off down the creaking wooden corridors. The hotel was simply a rig camp writ large, with many trailers connected together and portable heaters that made at least a pretence of keeping the corridors warm. The sleeping accommodations were in a rough square, while the trailers in the centre contained the dining room and a large compartment identified by a roughly lettered sign as The Recreation Room. A card table, a bulletin board with a few tattered messages, a ping-pong table with a severe list to starboard, and imitation-leather furniture that once graced a sergeants' mess gave scant promise of recreation.

"There you are." Jerry handed Rod a key and a sleeping bag. "There's a bunk in there, but you'd better just sling your bedroll on top and climb into it. The can's halfway down the hall. Goodnight."

The mass of light brown blankets and grey sheets was vaguely repellent and Rod realized his advice was good. Wearily, he untied the rolled sleeping bag, spread it on the bed, stripped off the outer layers of his clothes, and climbed in, to fall instantly asleep.

"When are you heading back to camp?" Rod drained the last of his coffee. He felt good; he was rested, and he was leaving, however temporarily, this damnable cold.

"Mr. Quigley told me to pick up some stuff that's coming in on PWA, so I have to wait around for the flight. It's one of the last times we'll be allowed away from camp."

Rod slowly lowered his camp and stared at Jerry. "What the hell do you mean by that?"

"Pretty soon we'll be getting deep enough that the company won't let any of the drilling employees off the lease, or near the mobile or a phone or anything. Or if they do, they make sure there's a company man with them. So they can't give out information, call their broker, or anything, you know."

Rod pondered this in silence. He wondered just where Thistle would find the personnel to police this security. "Probably good old versatile Fraser!" he thought.

They spent part of the morning aimlessly wandering the few streets of the settlement until the relentless cold drove them back to the hotel, where they sat in the barren recreation room blankly staring into space. The tiny community had taken its name from the oil discovery and existed only to serve its insatiable demands. Totally cut off from the outside world, save by air, it was the marshalling ground for men and machines on their way to the oilfields pushing steadily northward in the wake of wildcat wells. Machinery and heavy equipment lay everywhere, sometimes in tangled heaps blanketed with snow, more often in orderly rows. Nearly all of the buildings were mobile: some still perched on wheels, others, like the hotel, dismounted and placed on pilings with wooden skirts hiding their migratory nature.

Young as the community was, it had already survived one fire and, in rebuilding, some of the mobile units had been replaced with more permanent structures. There was talk of an all-weather road, to be built through the muskeg, which would connect with the Mackenzie Highway and civilization. Except for a few matronly cooks, there were no women and no children; it was still a gigantic field-camp, but already the pipeline and the steady increase in producing wells had brought a new kind of worker — men who were used to a settled way of life and who were used to being surrounded by their families. Soon, they would be followed by their wives and children; soon there would be schools and churches; and the camp would become a town with its own permanent population, its own character.

For the hundredth time, Rod looked at his watch. "We'd better get going. Can you give me a hand with some of this stuff?"`

"Sure, sure." Jerry blinked and smiled as he came back from some blissful nirvana where everybody behaved as they were expected to, where wives were quiet and loving, not always bursting into tears or disappearing God knows where for days at a time.

"There's no rush, though. No sense in going over there much before the plane arrives. That hangar ain't heated."

"We can sit in the truck. I just want to get the hell and gone out of this hotel."

So they sat in the truck, motor running over to generate warm air that blew fit-fully through the heater. Soon, they were joined by other vehicles — mostly half-ton trucks. The new arrivals parked against the snow fence, motors throbbing, exhaust bubbling, faces indistinct behind frosted windows. There was a slam of doors as people climbed out of the vehicles and stood on the hard-packed snow watching the DC-6B touch down and roll to a stop.

Flying south, passenger seats replaced the freight and mailbags that had crammed the front compartment on the northern leg. Most of the seats were empty. The heavy traffic in people and cargo was northward — into the bush.

Rod dozed through most of the flight. One of the advantages of northern winter flying, possibly the only one, was the complete freedom from turbulence. Cold air was still air. Through half-open eyes he sleepily watched the two stewardesses bustling up and down the aisle in their skin-tight blue stretch slacks and parkas of white fur. The slacks suited the slender roundness of one to perfection, but were a disaster on the ample hips and bottom of the other. His thoughts veered away to Melinda.

A series of unrelated memories of Melinda, snapshot vignettes, tumbled through his mind. Melinda, patrician in a black dress; Melinda smiling her cool smile while her telltale eyes darkened; the white breasts with their thrusting, seeking nipples, the soft incurve of belly; Melinda snarling her need deep in her throat, demanding, surging, the cords of her neck taut and stretched, fists drumming a frantic tattoo.

Someone was shaking him, gently. It was the slim dark girl, the young stewardess with the obsidian eyes that had flickered at him when he first came aboard but whose glow had dimmed as he sank deeper into his reverie of Melinda.

"We'll soon be landing in Edmonton, sir. You are going on to Calgary, aren't you? There's an airbus leaving for there fifteen minutes after we land. You can just catch it, if you hurry."

Rod heard her with mingled relief and regret. The choice had been taken from him. Now there would be no time to call Melinda, to find out if she was still in Edmonton. On the credit side, it meant he could have a good rest tonight and be fresh for whatever it was that had prompted old MacPherson to yank him out of the north.

After a frantic scramble with luggage, he found a seat on the airbus flying its regular schedule between the two cities. There were no reservations, no tickets; it was first-come, first-served, and you paid for your passage en route, the steward collecting fares like an airborne bus conductor.

Returning to Calgary, he experienced, with a sense of pleasure, the impression of coming home. He relaxed as they rolled through the darkened streets. The Chinook had blown itself out and a cold wind chased gritty particles of old snow along the deserted sidewalks. Every lamppost had its own little mound of grey, dirty snow heaped around its base.

9

"Where do I reach you?" The voice was lazy, heavy with assurance.

"You don't." Melinda closed her handbag with a brisk click and turned from the mirror to look down at the young man sprawled on the bed, linen sheet draped carelessly over his naked body.

He scrambled to a half-sitting position, his voice high and squeaky with disbelief. "What do you mean, we don't see each other? You can't just break it off like that! We were good together, weren't we?"

"We were, I can, and I am. Look, we met and we made love and the love was good, for which I am truly grateful. Period."

He stared at her, he didn't know how to handle this one and that was a fact. The whole evening had had an air of unreality for the young salesman of drilling mud. He had been quietly nursing a beer at the bar downstairs when she appeared in the doorway. She hesitated there a moment while every eye turned on her. She seemed to be looking for someone; he remembered thinking that he must be a real VIP to rate a girl like that. To his amazement, she walked over to the bar and sat down beside him, fishing in her handbag for a cigarette and waiting patiently until he managed to strike a match. She carried the conversation and he soon realized that he had been effectively picked up. It was expertly done; that meant only one thing, she had to be a pro. He was convinced when she placed her drink on the bar and asked directly, "Are you staying in the hotel?"

"Yes, I am, but look here, I'm really not interested ... I mean, damn it ..." he blurted, "look, I don't pay for my parties."

The green eyes flared open in mock astonishment. "Who said anything about paying? Do you have your key?"

He followed her in a daze. She had had to ask him for his floor number and push the elevator button. Once inside the room, she hadn't waited for him to pour a token drink before she started to undo her clothes. It was all so bizarre, so incredible, that he wondered if he could perform adequately, but that had been all right, she had seen to that.

Now she was about to walk out of his life as unceremoniously as she had entered it. He felt used, like an orange that had been sucked dry and thrown away. He had enough sense to realize that nothing he could do or say would influence her; he was outclassed and he knew it. He consoled himself with the thought that, whatever

242 / JOHN BALLEM

happened, he — Tom Dorf — had made love to this fantastic creature; nothing could change that. Besides, some instinct of self-preservation warned him he would not survive any protracted exposure to this strange goddess. A comforting vision of his gentle wife and two small children in the suburban Calgary home swam into focus. He had no misgivings about his betrayal of them. It was, he told himself, something beyond his control — an act of God, and people couldn't able held responsible for those, could they? With a comfortable sense of a risk accepted and met, and an escape narrowly won, he was able to meet her cool dismissal with a veneer of sophistication.

"Sure. It's been fun. I hope we meet again." He was proud of his voice; it had, he thought, just the right tone of detachment. The door closed behind her slim figure.

She pressed the button that took her down to the hotel's underground parking. The doors slid open with a pneumatic hiss and she stepped out into the reverberating cement cave. Flipping a casual wave at the attendant in his lighted booth, she walked down the sloping ramp, high heels clicking on the bare floor. She walked by ranks of parked cars until she came to a pale pink Mustang GT 500 squatting on its outsize, competition tires. The left side of the hood bulged to accommodate the supercharger; ventilating louvres had been cut into the wheel wells to cool the disc brakes, and a broad rally stripe of dark orange asymmetrically bisected the hood from the steering wheel to the grille. Despite its colour, it looked menacing and muscular.

Melinda threaded her way expertly through the light city traffic, the engine snarling in the lower ranges of the syncromesh transmission. Soon she was driving through the outskirts where the broad highway to Calgary stretched, black and bare, snow banked high on both sides. Her tiny foot pressed down on the accelerator, the engine growled deep in its throat, and the speedometer needle swung clockwise. She sat upright in the bucket seat, hands lightly clasping the wheel; her face, reflected in the subdued light of the instrument panel, was serene, almost exultant. On and on she tore through the black night, the powerful car devouring the miles of asphalt. Finally the coiled tension of her body relaxed. The hectic pace slowed and she searched the roadside for a turnoff. She dawdled back to the city, the engine muttering under its hood.

She and her husband shared a large suite in a hotel, a living room opening on either side to separate bedrooms. She was astonished to find George still awake. He sat in an amber pool of mellow lamplight, fingers steepled and gazing absently into space. He looked up as Melinda entered and struggled to his feet.

"Hello, George. This is a surprise, I must say. Have you suddenly turned into an insomniac?"

"Purely temporary, I assure you. You look distraught, my dear. Is everything all right?"

"I'm okay. I just needed to breathe, so I took the Mustang for a spin."

He followed her across the living room and stood in the bedroom doorway as she slipped out of her coat. She looked at him in surprise.

"Do you want anything ...?"

"No, no, my dear. I'm just concerned about you. I do worry, you know." It seemed incongruous from such an extraordinary source, but there was no doubt that this strange and tortured man had thawed sufficiently to let a tiny crack of concern splinter his glacial composure. She knew that with him indifference was something more than a shell; it had become the man himself, a way of life — so much so that, in order to do anything, he first had to set himself arbitrary goals and objectives, like a person devising a new game. If it came to the test, she supposed he would once again retreat behind his wall, but she was in no position to turn away any element of human compassion, however unlikely the source might be. Her smile became an affectionate grin. God, what a magnificent old wreck he was. Standing there with those eyebrows slanting down over his eyes like window awnings; those blue eyes all watery like a bloodhound's, that purply nose. He was a caricature of a plantation owner gone badly to seed! She chuckled delightedly to herself.

"That's better! Much better. Would you like a drink?"

"A light Scotch, please. That reminds me, my old sot, where's your daily dose of poison?"

"I'm so intrigued with this current caper of ours that I've decided to give it the full benefit of my mind, unclouded by the fogs of alcohol. Suddenly, miraculously, I'm not bored. As I think you may have guessed, my dear, drink for me is a refuge from ennui. By late afternoon of the average day I find people and life so insupportable that I must seek my daily oblivion. But not now. Not while I have this engaging problem to entertain me. We go back to Vancouver tomorrow, a top-level conference is overdue. I think it might be better if Wally drove the Mustang and you flew with me. As you wish, of course. I regret that we shall have to fly commercial. But not for long; when we bring this one off we'll straddle the world in our very own jet!"

"Okay. But I'll talk to him first, I want her handled with kid gloves. The last time he drove her it took me a week to adjust the timing. Tell me something ... this business of not having your own aircraft and some of the other more obvious trappings of wealth really bugs you, doesn't it? Why? You've reasoned your way through life until now you're all alone on some remote plateau where no one can reach you. How is it that you still care about such things?"

He smiled. "Simply because they are the symbols of victory. That's all that matters. Life is a game; it becomes intolerable if you treat it otherwise. If you collect enough of these baubles, you've won, that's all. It has lately dawned on me that I haven't collected enough. That's why the matter at hand has become so important to me."

"George, I always thought you were big rich. We certainly live like you were."

"I'm not really, not big rich. According to some people's tests, I guess you could call me reasonably well off. But in the eyes of those who have true wealth, enough so that it gives them power, unbelievable power, I'm nothing. And quite suddenly it matters to me; it matters very much. What I have is not only truly insignificant, it's decidedly shaky, a house of cards built on credit. And credit is a very uncertain foundation. One little whisper of doubt and it dries up and blows away like sand in a windstorm. I'm in the same boat as MacPherson, this is my last opportunity. I must succeed!"

"God knows we've all risked enough! Tell me, doesn't the thought of ... well, violence ... doesn't that bother you? Not the violence itself, so much, but what would happen if you were discovered. We've come pretty far down the road, you know."

He smiled with genuine delight. "That only makes it more interesting. One false move and there's disgrace, imprisonment, maybe even death. On the other hand, there's the prospect of unbelievable riches. It's delicious. Goodnight, my dear."

10

Rod stood in the doorway and stared at Sheila. She was all the warm tones of daylight. She smiled at him. "Welcome back! How did you like your first taste of the north?"

"It's nice to be back. There's nothing that can begin to compare with what's right here."

Her smile widened. "Nice of you to notice!"

Mac came out of his little office, hand outstretched. "Sorry to haul you back on such short notice, my boy, but we need help. Come in. Sheila, you might sit in with us, I would value your views."

"Don't apologize. I was glad to get away," Rod said hastily.

Mac looked at him as he settled himself behind the desk. "What are your impressions of the situation at the rig?"

Rod shrugged. "I can't really tell. Of course, I spent very little time there, and they were shut down until just before I left. I still haven't got the feel of it; it's completely different from tropical operations and you have to make allowances for that impossible cold. In a way, mere survival is a triumph. I have an uneasy feeling about it, though. The atmosphere isn't good, but that could be just the weather. The toolpush — Quigley — impressed me as knowing what he's doing."

"Yes. Larry's a good hand. He goes on some pretty wild binges every now and then, and his reputation makes quite a few people steer clear of him, but when he's sober, which he normally is when he's working, he's one of the best. It'll all become highly academic if we can't do something about the latest development, though. I had a call from the stud duck for our financial backers in Vancouver — Jim Carruthers. He's making noises like they want out."

"Oh? That doesn't make much sense. We're just getting to the place where we start to find out some things — things that will let us look down everybody's throat at the sale. To pull out now is just plain crazy!"

"I agree. You're absolutely right. But that's what they seem to have in mind. That's why I asked you to come down. I can't really cope with something like this, but I kind of thought, and so did Sheila, that you might be able to do something."

"I don't know about that, but I'm willing to do whatever I can. You better fill me in on the background."

"It's pretty straightforward. You know the sort of patchwork financing I've got. Well, I had the quarter-section of land and Joe Sanderson had the rig. But we needed cash to operate and that's where Jim Carruthers came in. He put together a small syndicate — mostly friends of his, I guess — mining people who wanted to take a fling at oil. They agreed to put up the cash and they have, so far."

"Were these arrangements all verbal or was there anything in writing?"

"Oh, there are letters and agreements of a sort; it's all on the file."

"I'll get it for you." Sheila rose and returned with a brown file folder. The file wasn't very thick. Mac moved out from behind the desk.

"I've got to meet some people and then join them for lunch. You sit here and go through it and I'll see you this afternoon."

The file followed a chronological sequence, with the oldest items at the rear. The earliest documents were the petroleum and natural gas lease and letters from the Department of Minerals. Then the Vancouver syndicate entered the picture. Rod studied this correspondence very carefully, checking for signatures, analyzing the wording, and making notes from time to time. Finally he replaced all the materials in the file and handed it back to Sheila.

"Let's pick up a sandwich. Where's the nearest place?"

"They will all be crowded at lunchtime. The coffee shop at the Inn is probably as good a bet as any."

He gave her his impressions on the file as they ate their sandwiches.

"As far as I can tell, and I'm no lawyer by a long shot, I think Carruthers and his friends are committed. They undertook to provide certain funds and it looks to me like an absolute obligation. Maybe I'm missing something but I couldn't spot any escape routes open to them. I think we can hold their feet to the fire, all right."

"Good, I was sure we could. But old Mac, bless him, doesn't want to do it. First of all, I don't think he really believes he has the power, and it goes against his grain. It's not the way he operates."

"I can appreciate that, but there's so much at stake he can't just sit on his hands and do nothing."

"I hope so," Sheila sighed. "You may be able to persuade him. If you can convince him that his position is as strong as we think it is, and that these people could be pulling a fast one, he may go along. Particularly since you are here to do the dirty work and he can stay in the background. He hates unpleasantness."

"I'm not all that fond of it myself. But sometimes it's the only way; otherwise you end up with great muddy footprints all over you. Well, let's go back and see what he wants to do."

Mac proved to be surprisingly amenable. "Well, if you think that's the situation, then I agree we should talk to them. It won't do any good over the phone; you'll have to go out there and meet Carruthers face-to-face. I wouldn't threaten a law suit or anything like that — remember they haven't withdrawn yet — just sort of encourage them to stay hitched. You probably know what to do a damn sight better than I do. Sheila, see if you can get Mr. Carruthers on the phone."

There was a wait while Carruthers returned from his own lunch hour, but when he came on the line he readily agreed to see Rod at his office the following afternoon.

"The evening flights are all booked," Sheila told Rod, "so I've got you on the flight that leaves at eight in the morning. You'll be there in lots of time for your meeting. Do you want to be wait-listed on the evening flights?"

"Not if you'll have dinner with me."

"I'd like that very much, but this time I do the cooking. We'll have dinner at the apartment and you can contribute a bottle of wine, if you like. Let's make it at seven?"

"It's only three-thirty now. I think I'll amble over and see Tim and swab him down for some background. I have a feeling that tomorrow I'm going to need all the ammunition I can scrape up."

Tim's office was on the twenty-sixth floor; it was a large uncarpeted room with floor-to-ceiling windows overlooking frozen Bow River. Two of the walls were metal and covered with a forest of maps and contour outlines held in place by small magnets. The desk was purely functional, dark grey metal, and more maps were spread out on a long metal table, held down by little leather bags filled with shot.

He waved at Rod through the open door. "Come in, come in! You're as welcome as the flowers in May! The very man I wanted to see."

"Great, that makes it mutual. You shoot first."

"Good old Inter-Continental has put me in the devil of a spot. The vice-president told me yesterday they want me to take on the job of exploration manager."

"But that's great! Or is it?"

"That's what I've been asking meself. Hell, Rod, I'm a geologist, not an administrator. If I accept, I'll be saying goodbye to geology; it'll be all management meetings, employee relations, personnel problems, shuffling files. It's the old Peter Principle in operation — promote somebody to his level of incompetence. The blessed Saint Patrick preserve us all, but I don't know what to do."

"I see your problem. It would be an easy decision for me; I think I like the executive end more than pure geology. But you, my friend, are a true scientist. I can tell you one thing, though."

"And what might that be?"

"If you turn it down, your days with Inter-Continental are numbered. The big boys like to see their key employees move ever onward and upward with a clear eye and confident step. You break that pattern and sooner or later you'll find yourself at a dead end, with all the action bypassing you. Your Irish temperament won't let you stand still for that, so you'll end up on the street. Then you have two choices: either hire on with another large outfit as a geologist, which is only a sideways move, or operate independently. You've got very valuable talent and knowledge, Tim. Operating independently with the right combination of people might be the solution. Lots of other people have made it pay off."

Tim sighed. "You've isolated the problem, Rod. It's whether I stay on with Inter-Continental or not. I've thought of going on my own, who hasn't? But with Kathie and the brood —" he brightened. "She called yesterday; she's still breathing pretty hard, but it was a definite peace-feeler."

Rod grinned. "She'll be back. It's just the Irish in both of you. The next time I come down from the north I'll find you surrounded by all your redheads. Do you realize there must be at least three of your kids I've never met? When do you have to let the company know about the job?"

"Not for a month. They're pretty good about it — they know what a change it is for me, and about Kathie being away. It's been good to talk, Rod; it'll help me sort things out in my own mind. Now, you, me boy, how come you're back so soon? I hear you've got some deviation problems in the hole?"

Rod shook his head. "I won't even ask how you know about that. But I'm on something else. Our Vancouver backers are getting a little nervous. I'm meeting with them tomorrow and I need some background to convince them to hang in with us. I need some specifics about the potential of this play."

"If the well finds production, the figures are astronomical. You could have as much as ten million barrels of oil under those one hundred and sixty acres you're drilling on. The oil sells for $2.50 at the wellhead, you have to pay royalty to the government and your operating costs. That leaves you with an average net of let's say $1.75 per barrel — which gives you a total value of $17,750,000. A foine, handsome sum."

"Jesus, yes!" Rod breathed. "And then there's the drilling reservation."

"Ah, sure, it's the icing on the cake. If you get that well down in time, nobody can bid against you, unless there's a leak of information at your end. If even that part of the reservation nearest the well turns out to be productive, it's another bonanza." He looked at Rod. "How's old Mac going to scrape up the bid money? Has he got it flanged up?"

Rod sighed. "Not in the way you and I are used to. Apparently there's a group of Montreal high rollers who may come in, but it's all very indefinite."

"That's the way a lot of things are in the oil patch out here. I've known of drilling rigs being financed on a handshake and a three-martini lunch! Which reminds me, it's drinking time in these here mountains, let's go!"

"Not tonight, I'm having dinner with Sheila Robinson."

"Our boy wastes little time. That's a *real* girl, Sheila. With that gorgeous hair she could even be Irish!"

Rod goggled at the girl in the doorway. At first he thought it was the wrong apartment, but she smiled and said, "Hello. I'm Barbara Harris. Sheila's just applying the finishing touches. Come in, won't you?"

As soon as Rod saw the white-handled broom leaning against a chair in the living room, he understood Barbara's odd garb. Curling! That explained the thick tartan sweater, bespattered with badges and shields, and the hairy tam-o-shanter hat, bright red marbled with green. Despite the flamboyance of her attire, Barbara looked very mild and wholesome. She wore glasses with colourless plastic rims and she had a nice smile. She was smiling now as she said, "Sheila asked me to pour you a martini. May I help you with that?"

Gratefully Rod handed her the bottle of wine wrapped in brown paper. "What about you, aren't you having one?"

She looked slightly shocked. "Me, oh ... no, no thank you. We're in a bonspiel; our next match is in half an hour."

"I see. Well, we can't have your aim spoiled by strong drink, can we?"

Barbara smiled good-naturedly at the teasing note in his voice. "That's right, we can't. Serious things, these bonspiels. Here's Sheila." She stood up. "Well, I must be off. My lead is picking me up at seven-fifteen and we can't be late. Goodbye, Mr. Fraser; I'm sure I'll see you again."

"I hope so, Miss Harris. Good luck to you and your ... what's the word ... rink?"

"Right. You'll soon be an expert."

Rod turned to Sheila as the door closed. "She seems very nice, but my God, what a getup! I like yours much better — much better!" He eyed the green velvet pantsuit, which did great things with her long, tapered legs.

"I'm glad you're still noticing! Barbara is very nice, and all curlers dress like that. She's also loads of fun but right now she's all tied up over this bonspiel. It's the first time she's ever skipped a rink and she takes it seriously."

"She sure does. You don't curl, do you?"

Smiling, Sheila shook her head.

"Thank God for that. The sight of you decked out like that might blow my mind."

He brought her a martini.

"Can we take a moment for a council-of-war? Have you ever met this fellow — Carruthers?"

"No, I've never actually met him. I've placed a lot of calls to him for Mac, and there's been the correspondence, which you saw. Why?"

"I don't really know. Just looking for a handle, I guess. Some sort of clue as to why he wants out at this stage."

"Probably for the very reasons he gave Mac. His people know mining but they know nothing about oil. The rig has had one breakdown after another and that dry hole that Argent abandoned doesn't help much."

"Yeah, I guess it wouldn't at that. Quigley mentioned it. Still, it's six miles away and really doesn't affect our chances at all. With that kind of reef even a few hundred yards can make all the difference."

"You know that, and I know it, but our Vancouver friends don't. I bet this oil business, where you can't count on anything for sure, makes them as nervous as cats. One thing — Mac seems to think there might have been some sort of pressure on

Carruthers. He wasn't too definite; it was just a feeling he had. Since you ask, I think you had the right approach this afternoon: take it for granted they won't back out, with maybe just a subtle hint that they are bound by their written agreements. Meet pressure with pressure."

"There's really no other choice. Maybe all he needs is a little pep talk. I must say, Miss Robinson, you have a remarkably clear grasp of how these things work."

"Thank you for not adding 'for a girl,' even though you were probably thinking it. It fascinates me and it's not all that difficult once you discover the fundamentals. I'm in the wrong business, though. There's no room in oil for a woman, except as a secretary or receptionist. It's a man's world and it's going to stay that way. Anyway, things are exciting enough at good old Thistle Oils. It's been a wonderful experience. With nobody else around, Mac has had to rely on me."

Sheila put her glass down on the low coffee table. "Now this business girl will become very domestic. Dinner is pretty basic — stroganoff and Caesar salad. That's why I was late, I had to go to three stores before I found any crisp lettuce."

After dinner they sat comfortably relaxed with coffee. Sheila stood up. "Would you like some mood music?"

He kissed her as she turned from the stereo. Her lips were cool and exciting. For a long moment she responded, then she leaned back and pushed gently against his chest. She smiled and returned to the couch, sitting at her own end and very erect.

"Would you like some more coffee?"

Later, brown eyes regarding him gravely, Sheila said, "I ran into Tim Murphy at one of the stores, he was shopping for himself. Apparently Kathie's gone back to mother again. I knew him when I worked at Inter-Continental. He said he'd seen you and we talked about your Vancouver trip. He said ... he said something about someone you had once known out there ... a girl. He said you had gotten into a pretty bad scrape with her. He seemed awfully concerned."

Rod felt the familiar kick in the guts the memory of Melinda always brought. He said, "In his absent-minded, bumbling way, old Tim can be quite a busybody. Sure, I was in a scrape, a messy one, but it was four years ago. Her name is Melinda and she's still in Vancouver."

"Oh."

"Does it matter?"

"Does it matter? Maybe it does ... to me."

When he left he merely brushed her lips. She whispered, "Good luck. I'll be thinking of you all tomorrow."

II

The steady sound of rain drummed through the open door. As Rod edged along in the line of disembarking passengers he could see heavy drops gathering and splashing in the small crack where the covered ramp nestled against the curved side of the fuselage.

He was in good time to have lunch and keep his appointment with Carruthers. Lifting his suitcase from the revolving luggage carousel, he went outside and splashed his way over to the bus.

"I'm glad to see you, Mr. Fraser. Please sit down." The speaker was tall, with a pleasantly lined face. The eyes were shrewd but tolerant. Jim Carruthers looked every inch the experienced, successful investor.

"It's very good of you to take the time to see me, sir." There was just enough difference in their ages to justify the "sir."

"Not at all. On the contrary, I am indebted to you for making the trip."

"Well, Mac wanted me to bring you up to date. I haven't been in the picture very long myself, as you may know, but at least I have been up at the well."

"I don't even pretend to know anything about the oil industry, but it doesn't look very good, does it?"

"No. It's had its problems right from the start. However, we're drilling ahead now and maybe the worst is behind us. We still have plenty of time to find out what we need to know before the sale."

"I certainly hope so. After all, that's the whole point of the exercise." Carruthers shifted slightly on the long leather couch. "Look, Mr. Fraser, I regard the well as Mac's problem, and yours. I can't help there and I won't interfere. My problem, and Mac knows this, is that with all these accidents and breakdowns, you are running way over the budget. This syndicate of ours is a small group and not a particularly affluent one; the members can't just throw their money down on the ground and walk away. We agreed to put up $100,000 and for that amount of money we were to see the bottom of the hole. Mac already has spent almost all of it and you know how far we still have to go."

"I know." Rod looked at him in sober alarm. If what Carruthers said was right and they had already used up most of the commitment, they were in a spot, for sure. His clever ploy of subtly hinting about the syndicate's obligations had evaporated, blown away by the friendly, knowledgeable voice of Carruthers.

"You tell Mac I'm on his side. I'll do my part, but he's got to get that well straightened out. We'll be all right up to the hundred thousand and I may be able to persuade my partners to kick in a certain amount over and above that. But not much. They're restless and uneasy, and small wonder! We keep getting feedback of very unsettling rumours. Nothing you can pin down, but there's a feeling in the street, here in Vancouver anyway, that there's something radically wrong with the entire operation, almost as though it were doomed from the start." He held up his hand as Rod started to interrupt. "Sure, we knew it was risky. But my people are promoters. Luck is a magic word with them. A failure rubs off some of that magic."

"I can understand that, sir." Rod was subdued. "But we must remember that, if we win, the payoff is fantastic. We could have ten million barrels under that well. That could net $17-million over the life of the well."

"I agree the potential is there. The risk-gain ratio is impressively high. That's why we've strung along so far. And we'll continue, but there's a limit. Tell me, how is old Mac these days?"

The talk drifted into casual channels. Carruthers was easy to talk to; his comments on people and places were acute, but threaded with a tolerant vein of humour. Finally, he looked directly at Rod and remarked, "I understand you were in the mining game for a while yourself. D'or Mines, wasn't it?"

"I had a brief fling at it, yes. I was with them slightly over a year, just before I went to Venezuela."

Carruthers smiled briefly. "Yes, I seem to remember something about the circumstances that may have prompted you to go to Venezuela. Remarkable woman, Melinda. Delightful, thoroughly delightful. She's living here, did you know?"

"I had heard, yes."

"She married again, just recently. A real eccentric, a genius I guess, but a damned odd fellow — George Mason. Old enough to be her father. They say he's brilliant — drinks himself into a stupor every day. He's sort of on the fringes of mining; he's rumoured to have played shadowy roles in a number of deals. Never gets directly involved himself. Don't know how he manages it, inhaling booze the way he does, but he seems to live well enough. You know Vanning's dead, I suppose?"

It hit Rod hard. "No! I hadn't heard that. When did it happen?"

"I guess it would be about five or six months ago. He had moved to California after the D'or people tied a can to his tail. He went into public relations work, got taken on as an account executive with one of the firms. I didn't hear anything more of him, didn't even think of him really for years until I read in the paper that he was dead. Stuck a gun in his mouth and blew out the back of his head. Messy, but remarkably sure. Sorry if I've given you a jolt. No need to blame yourself. As I understand it, you were just the proverbial straw that broke the camel's back." He gave a short, strained laugh. "That's quite a girl, Melinda, quite a girl."

Rod knew with a sure, sick feeling that the older man had been Melinda's lover.

He sensed that Carruthers was still in thrall to her, however unwillingly. The light mocking tones of his voice didn't quite mask the underlying hurt. The air prickled with tension between the two men. This guy, sitting over there smiling at me, probably hates my guts, Rod thought; he's thinking right now of my lying with her, wondering whether I'll be with her tonight. But I don't hate him; we're practically blood brothers, members of Melinda's Legion of the Lost, with the most effective recruiting campaign in history!

The older man stood up and held out his hand. "I wish we could have dined together. Unfortunately, Mrs. Carruthers and I have a long-standing engagement we just can't break. We'll make a point of having you on your next trip. In the meantime, my best regards to Mac, and please tell him I will do my very best to keep everybody on side, and I expect him to hold up his end."

Rod stood in the recessed doorway, trying to spot an empty taxi. The drenching rain had placed its usual premium on their services and they streamed indifferently by, passengers dim and bulky behind fogged windows. Pedestrians splashed along the wet sidewalks, each cowering beneath an open umbrella. The packed ranks of umbrellas, mostly a somber black, undulated like the canvas of a midway ride. He saw what looked to be an empty taxi bearing down on him. He ran out and waved, braced for the disappointment of seeing a resident passenger looming through the opaque windows. His luck held and he settled back with a sigh of relief and gave the name of his hotel.

Sheila's cool clear voice came over the wire. "Thistle Oils, good afternoon!"

"Good afternoon yourself, and how are all things with Thistle, that colossus of the oil industry?"

"Rod! I'm so glad it's you; we've been waiting for your call. Hang on a second, I'll get Mac."

Mac's voice came booming through the receiver. Rod could hear him instructing Sheila to stay on the extension. "Now, my boy. How did you make out with Carruthers?"

"There's no immediate danger. He told me definitely they will not pull out just yet. It looks like he personally wants to string along, but is on the receiving end of a lot of static from his syndicate. Of course, this may just be the very impression he wants us to have. But I don't think so. I'm convinced he's genuine and there's no doubt he's under pressure from his group. I think he'd just as soon they had never heard of the deal. It's pretty clear that somebody's been at work, undermining our position, but whether it's a member of the syndicate or an outsider, I can't even guess."

"Well, at least they're not going to shut us down right now. That's something at any rate."

"Yeah. He said our budget is badly overspent."

"I guess it is. It could hardly be otherwise with all the problems."

"How bad is it, Mac?"

"Oh, I don't know exactly. There's always a time lag before the invoices come in, but we must have spent somewhere around $90,000."

"As much as that? We have got a problem!"

"Sure we have. Bu there are ways, son, there are ways. For one thing, a good many of our creditors are used to waiting ninety days for their money. By that time we'll know what we need to know. Just don't make waves!"

"Okay, if you say so. But I don't like it. How are things at the rig?"

"They called in this morning; they're through the plug and drilling ahead. Maybe you should get back up there."

"Right. Sheila, are there any connections from here?"

"There *is* a flight out of here, but I'm not sure it goes every day. Wait a moment while I look at the schedule ... It only leaves Vancouver on Thursdays and Saturdays, so that's no good. Your best bet would be to catch an early morning flight to Edmonton and connect with PWA there."

"Okay. That's what I'll do. But it means I don't see you."

"I know and I couldn't be sorrier. But there will be other times."

"That there will be! Lots of them."

Rod was smiling as he put down the receiver. Well, he was in Vancouver for the night anyway. First thing is to make sure of the airline space, unpack, and then what? Melinda? She was probably back by now.

He busied himself with Air Canada, booking an economy passage on the flight to Edmonton, continuing PWA to Rainbow. He unpacked completely, stacking his shirts neatly in the drawers, his suits and ties in the closet. He sat and looked at the phone. It rang suddenly, making him jump. His voice rasped as he croaked, "Hello?"

"Rod, is that you? It doesn't sound like you." The familiar voice purred throatily through the receiver. "Were you going to leave Vancouver without calling me?"

"I was just about to call," he replied truthfully.

"I'll buy that, I think. You are staying in Vancouver tonight." It was a statement rather than a question. "I can meet you by seven."

"Super. Where shall we go? There must be all sorts of new places since I left here."

"Your room at seven. We'll dine, as they say ... privately." Rod heard the click as she rang off.

"My, my, has our lover boy been reading *Kama Sutra*? Just how do you propose to untangle us, my virile lord?"

"We could always call room service."

Her eyes, glinting green beneath the dark lashes, smiled up at him and laughter bubbled in her throat. "I love you when you're like this! When you're funny — not so full of gloom and doom. That's what life is for — love and fun!"

"For a gal who talks so much about fun and the gay, mad world, you spend a lot of time down where the blues are deep and dark." He grunted as he rolled to one side. A caressing finger followed the outline of his nose, the curve of his lips.

"You are sinfully handsome, and you know it." She snuggled closer to him. "Maybe it's just that I have more reason than most to hit the blue notes. Maybe that's why I try harder. Did you know Tom killed himself?"

"I heard it today. From Jim Carruthers." Rod was careful not to look at her as he said Carruthers' name but he could feel the slender body stiffen against him. So I was right! he thought bitterly.

"When did he do it?" he asked.

"Six months ago. Right after it happened, I decided to marry George Mason. They were terrible to Tom. As soon as the divorce was final, Miles Coleman called him in and gave him one of those dreadful 'for your own good' speeches. They couldn't wait to get rid of him; he didn't have a prayer, poor lamb."

"An impartial observer might feel that you made your own little contribution," Rod said drily.

"There's no need to be cruel — you didn't have to say that! I've never denied it, have I? All I thought was that once I was out of the picture they might have given Tom another chance. But not them, they washed their sanctimonious hands of him as fast as they could. It knocked the last prop from under him. From that day on, he was just a suicide waiting to happen. I knew it but there was nothing I could do; he wouldn't even speak to me, poor darling. And that Miles Coleman would have had me between the sheets if I had so much as batted an eye!"

"I don't, God knows, pretend to understand what makes you tick. But what is the possible connection behind Tom's death and your marriage to an old creep like Mason?" Rod was trying very hard to maintain an air of detachment, for he knew that with the first hint of concern or condemnation she would close the shutters on herself.

"I wanted to get at them somehow. To prove I could live in their world — compete on their terms. Maybe they could toss Tom aside, but I could survive. Sounds screwy, doesn't it? Anyway, that's what I thought and still do. I married George mainly because I had an idea we would make a good team. He has the brains, but somewhere they left out that ingredient called incentive from his makeup. Maybe he's so damn intelligent he realizes life is a bloody sham — I don't know. But I thought I could stir him up, get him involved, throw that mind of his into gear. It wasn't so much a marriage as a partnership."

"Oh ..." Rod probed an old wound, "I would have thought it next to impossible to keep on a platonic plane with you."

"Oh, we make love from time to time, in a sort of way, that is!" She grinned maliciously.

"You have to do it, don't you? Get that old needle out and dig it in."

"If you had to go through life with what I've got tearing away at me, you'd feel like doing a little hurting yourself." She gazed at her own perfect body, at the glowing skin, the pink-tipped cones. "You wouldn't think there was a tiger prowling around inside that smooth skin, would you? But there is; he never gives me any peace and sometimes I know he will destroy me."

"The men ... the ones you ... do it with. Do you love them, do you feel anything for them?"

"Does an alcoholic love each bottle of rye he drinks, the glutton the meat he eats, the addict the clear drops of dope he shoves into his veins? He uses them, that's all — they fill a need. He doesn't love them; he probably hates them, hates himself. That answer your question? Present company always excepted, of course."

She was talking more openly than ever before to him. Her voice was pensive; she might have been alone, exploring something that had long troubled her. She was quiet now, not looking at him.

The pent-up words tumbled from him in a hoarse, urgent whisper. "Melinda, my darling, listen to me, please listen. It could work, it really could. It has with others. They say that love, the sense of being needed, can cure it. God knows I love you, and I need you. We could try it, Melinda, we could!"

She looked up at him, tears spilling down her face. "That's the most wonderful thing anyone has ever done or said to me, my darling!" She touched his face gently, wonderingly. "It won't work. I love you too much to ever let you take that risk, but thank you, my dear, thank you!"

She stood up. "Now, I'm going to get dressed and leave and I'm going to hug what you said to me, very, very closely. Don't you move or say another word, don't change a thing until we meet again."

12

A swirling cloud of steam blurred the yellow glow of two caged light bulbs. It condensed and froze instantly whenever it touched any surface, adding to the stalactites and stalagmites of ice that hung and grew everywhere. Luke Willard, made clumsy by muffling layers of heavy clothing, lurched through the steaming clouds to where the black casing protruded above the lumpy shapes of the blow-out valves. The open casing stopped a few feet short of the derrick floor, ready to swallow the strings of drill pipe now stacked above it in even ranks.

They had just finished a trip out of the hole to change a worn bit. Any minute now the new one would be fixed to the first section of drill pipe, heavy collars — thick short lengths of pipe — would be screwed on and the monotonous business of tripping back into the hole would begin.

The heavily clad figure slipped, cursing softly as he recovered, and pulled himself against the bulging outline of the blow-out preventers. Pressing his right knee against the bulge, he levered himself upward, his arm raised in a slow, careful arc. There was a dull gleam of metal as the heavy wrench dropped into the casing and began its long tumbling fall. He dropped back to the frozen ground, breathing heavily.

"Hey, what the hell are you doing?"

He went rigid as the voice sounded almost in his ear. The intruder was staring at him, hesitant, not completely sure of what he had seen in the dim light. Luke stooped and grabbed a discarded valve, not yet welded into place by the creeping ice, and struck savagely, aiming at the vulnerable spot just below the metal rim of the safety helmet. The dull crump was lost in the distant hum of the motors and the slamming of heavy metal as the crew prepared the new bit. The roughneck crumpled without a sound. Luke dropped the valve and pulled the inert figure to a corner of the substructure, deep in shadow. Grunting with exertion, he propped him half-sitting against the wall, then walked to the plywood door. It opened with a shriek, bumping roughly against the polished lumps of ice. Satisfied that the rest of the crew were fully occupied on the derrick floor, he walked to the toolhouse, taking care to hug the protecting wall of the substructure. He retraced his steps, now burdened with a murderous wrench. Carefully, almost tenderly, he removed the hard hat, stretched the unconscious figure on the ground — so it was White; well, too bad for him — turned him over on his back, and with one brutal blow stove in the back of his skull.

With the same macabre care, he adjusted the metal hat over the pulpy mess, cleaned the weapon by ramming it into the hard-packed snow, and returned it to the jumbled tangle of the toolhouse. A few kicks at the snow and all traces of blood were obliterated. He took stock, wanting a cigarette badly. Time enough for that later, when he had disposed of White. He was sure he was dead — nobody could survive that blow; it didn't matter anyway if he wasn't, the cold would finish him off.

He started violently as the motors throbbed into pulsing life and the serrated teeth of the rock-bit clattered through the drilling table. It hesitated a moment, seemed to be groping for the hole, then dropped smoothly into the open end of the casing.

I can't leave him here, he thought. That's for triple-damned sure! If I can just get him away from the camp, they won't find him until breakup. If he doesn't freeze solid first, the ravens and the lynx will work him over so even his own mother won't recognize him. But how? His mind raced. Now was the best time to move him. Pretty soon they'd start looking for White — the push had probably sent him down here to check the BOPs, and wouldn't expect him to be gone for long.

Once again he opened the squealing door and stood in the shadow looking up at the shrouded rig. Off to his right, a floodlight illuminated the evil-looking sump pit. Christ, it was a temptation just to dump old White in there and be done with it. He wouldn't sink, though; with all these clothes he'd just float on top of that muck like a fucking great scarecrow.

He had never realized before just how much light there was, even with the canvas shroud over the mast — it was like Times Square, for Christ's sake! Hugging the wall, he tugged his awkward burden to the rear of the rig, where the square outlines of the shale-shaker and the mud tanks provided some shadow. He paused for a moment, breathing heavily. He could feel the ice forming on the hairs of his nostrils, on his eyebrows, and around the rim of his parka hood. No sense in rushing it! A guy could burn holes in his lungs if he overdid things.

Next came the tricky part: he had to cross the lighted area alongside the sump pit. A hundred yards farther and he would be beyond the range of the lights, safe in the enveloping dark. No startled shout, no harsh command to halt interrupted Luke's progress. He backed into the shadow and let White's head and shoulders thump heavily to the ground.

The snow was deeper here; spruce trees, black against the reflected light of the snow, stood in tightly packed ranks a few hundred yards ahead. If he could get inside their dense growth, no one would find White in a million years. But they might just as well be miles away for all the good they would do Luke. He couldn't stagger with his load through the waist-deep snow and, anyway, if he had had the stamina, the broken trail would be an arrow pointing right to White's grave.

The snow was covered with a hard crust but underneath it was soft. He pounded with his mittened hands on the crust, breaking it, and scooped at the soft snow until he had a depression big enough for his purpose. He patted and smoothed the snow over the body and his own deep footsteps. It wasn't perfect, but nobody went tramping around at forty below, and the wind would soon glaze it with a sheen indistinguishable from its surroundings. The next snowfall would complete the job.

Luke walked back up the road to the camp, keeping in the shadow of the trees. He had picked a time when his mate was on tour and he had the room to himself. Cautiously he inched open the door. The bleak corridor was empty, and the frozen boards crunched under his feet as he stumbled to his room. The dry heat hit him like a blast furnace. He stripped out of his outer clothes, but not his pants and shirt. With shaking fingers he lit a cigarette and inhaled the smoke with a gusty sigh. Throwing a towel over his shoulder, he walked down the corridor to the washroom. He was in the clear now. If anyone spotted him, he could say he had just got up to take a leak. Meanwhile, he could examine himself under the brilliant fluorescent lights of the washroom for any betraying signs of blood.

Too bad about White; he wasn't such a bad sort in his own way. Tough luck he had to barge in just when he did. Luke's mind picked at the thought that it hadn't been all that unpleasant, sort of exciting in a way. Much more direct than the way he had taken care of Jack Walsh. He forced his thoughts away from that dark void.

The wrench had ricocheted its clattering way down the casing, bouncing off the smooth metal walls. The casing only went to a depth of six hundred feet. From there to the bottom the hole was bare, smoothed by the sealing action of the drilling mud but still soft enough that the heavy tool scored long furrows in the sides. Eight hundred feet from the bottom the wrench dug in and wedged itself firmly across the hole.

Labouring through the long night, the crew made up lengths of pipe reaching ever deeper into the hole. Just before dawn the rock bit ran into the tightly wedged wrench and stopped. The driller felt it through the long-handled gears of the draw-works. He glanced at the pipe and up at the immense travelling block. They hung motionless, fifty feet of pipe projecting above the derrick floor. He cursed softly to himself. Goddamn, more trouble! This fucking hole is jinxed! Maybe it was just a small cave-in; maybe a piece of rock had worked its way into the mud wall.

He tested the obstacle by slacking the tension of the travelling block, placing more weight on the drill string. The increased pressure down-hole might break through the barrier. The string inched down, then stopped once more. Holding his breath, the driller reversed the motors and raised the string two or three feet; then he slammed in the clutch and dropped the thousands of pounds of metal in a jarring crash. The wrench gave way, raking deep gouges in the walls until finally it broke free and fell to the bottom.

Russ Fogarty, the driller, was worried. They had jarred themselves free but God only knew what was waiting on the bottom for them. Maybe it was just a failure in the hole wall and wouldn't give them any more trouble; the only way to find out was to keep lowering away. He wondered how White was getting along. He had taken him on as an extra this hour to see if he couldn't make a dent in the ice buildup in the BOPS. Good man, that White; so far as Russ could tell he hadn't even taken a break to come into the doghouse and warm up. Probably figured that since the crew couldn't — they had to stay right with it when making a trip — he'd do the same thing. Poor bastard must be pretty miserable, hacking away at the steam line, though.

Russ carefully noted the time and depth at which they had encountered the obstruction. He would enter it in the log when he wrote up the tour. The man-killing process of making up the drilling string continued: elevators clamped on, pipe manhandled into position, dropped, chained, tonged. Men strained on the slippery floor, their bodies sweating and overheated with exertion, their breath coming in clouds of frozen vapour, their exposed cheeks on fire with the cold. Finally, in the grey, bleak lightening that passes for dawn in the northern latitudes, the last string was connected and lowered carefully into the hole. They were on the bottom. It had taken them almost the entire eight-hour tour.

"Everybody in the doghouse. Ten minutes for a smoke and a warm-up. I want to make sure we get her turning to the right before the next crew comes on!"

Wearily, the figures stumbled through the doorway, to stand huddled and silent. Every now and then one would catch another's eye and shake his head slowly, ruefully, as though to say, "What a Christless way to make a living!" Mixed in with the wry self-deprecation was a generous dose of pride; without it no man could endure the killing conditions. As feeling returned to their tortured bodies, they moved clumsily to the iron lockers and opened thermoses of steaming coffee and cellophane packets of sandwiches.

As soon as his fingers thawed enough, Russ wrote up his log, duly recording the fact they had to jar loose an unknown obstruction at 2,015 feet. He sipped his coffee from the plastic thermos top, looking down the narrow length of the dog-house trying to locate White. He wasn't there; that meant he, Russ, would have to climb down and tell the crazy bastard to knock it off. Maybe White had taken a break earlier and he just hadn't seen him.

Sighing, he put his mug down on the tiny table, drew on his heavy mitts, and clambered down the metal stairs. He peered in at the steaming nightmare of the substructure. No sign of White. He walked by the valves and saw that one of the steam lines, the one that White was supposed to clear, was still lying stiff and solid on the ground. He felt a faint twinge of alarm and crossed quickly to where the diesels hummed softly beside the great mud pumps with their thick tubes and hydraulic pistons. No sign of White anywhere.

Maybe he had felt sick and gone back to the camp. He should have reported first, though. Now thoroughly alarmed, the driller climbed back to the doghouse and told one of the crew to go back to the camp and wake Quigley.

Meanwhile, they might just as well start making hole, by God! They trooped back onto the drilling platform and Russ kicked in the gear to start the rotary table turning. This rotated the square section of pipe, the "kelly" which was connected to the top section of drill pipe. Slowly the whole string began to turn and the cutting surface of the bit dug into the tempered steel of the wrench. The pitch of the motors changed; the gear lever bucked and jumped in Russ's hand. He was prepared for it and he slammed in the clutch, neutralizing the strain.

The members of the crew looked at each other wordlessly. Once more Russ eased the motors into gear, gradually increasing the rpm. Nothing gave; the pipe remained obstinately still and the noise of the motors changed to an ominous scream. He didn't dare put on any more pressure or the whole string might twist off. Next he tried to smash whatever it was on bottom by alternately raising and dropping the string. That didn't work either. Whatever it was, it was a damn sight tougher than the bit.

He turned away from the drawworks with a snarl of rage and disappointment. Quigley, little eyes puffy with sleep, was looking at him sourly.

"What is it this time?"

"We're stuck on bottom. I can't jar it loose. Looks like we got ourselves a fishing job. And White's disappeared, unless he went back to camp. Did you see him up there?"

"Hell, no, I haven't seen him. Didn't he report to you?"

"No. I don't know what happened to him; all I know is that he's not anywhere on this damn rig. He's probably back at camp, but I just don't know."

"Well, you better send one of the boys up to look for him. Let me see if I can feel what's holding us up."

Larry and Russ played a tune on the gears of the drawworks. At the end of ten minutes and every trick they knew, they both realized that the bit was firmly stuck. It meant another trip out of the hole and then a tedious fishing job with a special grappling tool lowered into the hole to probe blindly for the obstruction. A fishing job could last for weeks, and if it wasn't successful, it meant the abandonment of the well.

The first thing, though, was to get hold of a fishing tool. These specialized instruments weren't part of a rig's normal equipment. They would have to locate one, with luck in Rainbow, maybe in Fort Nelson, or they might have to bring one all the way from Edmonton.

"I'll tell you one goddamned thing ..." Larry spoke heavily, "I'm sure as hell not looking forward to reporting this to head office. Well, I better get on the blower. You tell the next crew to start breaking out." He shook his head and stomped away.

13

The telephone rang in sharp demanding peals. It meant business. Rod swung his legs to the floor and crossed the room to scoop up the receiver.

It wasn't his wake-up call after all. The operator was saying, "Mr. Fraser? One moment, please, I have a long-distance call for you. I'll put you through."

Sheila's voice was low and urgent.

"Rod? Thank heaven I've caught you in time. I can't talk over the phone but there's trouble, bad trouble at the well. Mac's called a meeting with Mr. Sanderson and Pete Berry and he wants you to attend. You'll have to scrub your flight to Edmonton. There's an eight o'clock flight from Vancouver to Calgary that you should be able to catch. Unless I hear from you, I'll assume you're on it, and I, or somebody else, will meet you at the airport. Bye."

Rod hardly had time to mutter goodbye before she rang off, leaving him staring blankly at the receiver.

He recovered fast. He had an hour to make it. He flung his clothes into the suitcase, took a split-second shower, checked out, and jumped into a waiting cab. He would breakfast on the plane.

There were a lot of youngsters on the flight. Girls with long shaggy hair and boys with equally long shaggy hair. Both sexes wore bulky dun-coloured turtleneck sweaters and faded blue jeans. Ski enthusiasts undoubtedly, heading for Banff and the Rockies. As soon as the pilot throttled back at their cruising altitude, Rod heard the high-pitched sound. At first he thought it was a ukulele but the notes were too high and piercing. A zither, that was it! Probably the kids would have a singalong — but they seemed as puzzled by the music as he was; he saw two of them exchange amused smiles across the aisle. Intrigued, he sat up straighter and looked around for the source of the strange music. A middle-aged Ukrainian, old-fashioned grey felt fedora placed squarely on his round head, sat bolt upright, fingers restlessly plucking the strings. As Rod watched, he turned to his companion. "You like the music? I don't know what to do with my hands, I never fly before, and they shake, so I play."

Grinning to himself, Rod sat back. He had a window seat: far below, the snow-covered mountains were rumpled and folded like used linen sheets.

He wondered about the well. What in hell could have gone wrong this time? The sunlight streamed in through the window as he ate his breakfast, which had sat too long on some steam table. Melinda had been different last night, more vulnerable than he had ever seen her. Funny how she talked about the pursuit of fun — the poor little devil really didn't even know the meaning of the word. For the first time he thought of her with a trace of pity.

They were clear of the mountains by the time the stewardess had removed his tray and they lost height rapidly.

He could see Sheila in the crowd just inside the plate-glass windows. He kissed her soundly, murmuring against her ear, "Everybody does this at airports. We can't look conspicuous, you know."

"Really? I must come out here more often."

She had left the Rambler in the passenger loading zone, where a uniformed commissionaire was glaring balefully at it. Rod slung his single suitcase into the rear seat and asked, "Would you like me to drive?"

"Yes, please. That way I can concentrate on what I have to tell you."

He eased it into gear and pulled away to join the stream of traffic.

"Whenever you're ready, shoot."

She took a moment to compose her thoughts, then told him about the fishing job at the well and the mysterious disappearance of a roughneck. She finished on a doubtful note.

"I suppose all these things could have some perfectly normal explanation. But with one thing piled on top of another, it's just too much. They're all over at Cheyenne's office, waiting for us. It's on Sixth Avenue, between Fourth and Fifth Streets — there's a parkade just across the street."

Mac stood up as they came through the door.

"Glad you got here all right. You remember Joe Sanderson? I don't think you have met Pete Berry — Joe's drilling superintendent. We hauled him out of the wilds of Saskatchewan to see if he could help with our problems."

Rod shook hands with Sanderson and Pete Berry. The drilling superintendent was young — about his own age, with light-brown hair and clear blue eyes etched with sun wrinkles. His face was open and friendly and he smiled easily. Rod liked him on the spot.

"Sheila filled me in on the way from the airport. Locating a fishing tool?"

"Yes, and it's the first break we've had. One of the service companies had one in Rainbow, just released from another job. It's on the way out to the rig right now."

"That's good news. I just hope nobody hijacks it on the way!"

"I take it, Rod, you think this is something more than just a run of bad luck?" Berry smiled at Rod as he asked the question.

Rod shrugged. "I really don't know what to think. But it's straining coincidence pretty far, isn't it? After all, a geologist is killed in a truck accident, the rig gets into a deviation jackpot, they no sooner recover from that then they hit something on the bottom, and then a roughneck disappears. I think I could swallow all of it, except the missing crew member. Any sign of him yet?"

Pete Berry shook his head. "Not yet. I agree with you that we can't ignore the possibility of sabotage. Question is, what's to be done about it?"

Mac sighed wearily. "It all seems incredible to me. What do you think, Joe?"

"Whatever it is — bad luck, bad management, sabotage — it's damn sure got to stop! And we ain't going to stop it from down here. I'm sending Berry up as soon as he can get transportation and I'm flying up myself in a day or two to take a look-see. Are you going, Rod?"

Rod nodded. "Just as soon as a flight leaves. Which I guess is tomorrow morning. What about your personnel records? They might tell us something."

"Pete thought so too. I've got the files on every member of the crew right here."

"Good! We may just spot something."

Joe snapped open a brown leather briefcase and flipped a bundle of file folders on the desk. The files didn't prove to be very helpful. As Rod expected, they revealed the migratory nature of the oilfield workers; they drifted from rig to rig as work was available. The toolpush, Quigley, had the longest service — ten years.

They lunched on sandwiches and instant coffee. After completing the unrewarding scrutiny of the files, they talked, searching for anything that might give them a lead. It was pointless. Finally, Pete got to his feet.

"We've come to a dead end. If there is an answer, we won't find it here but at the rig. I've just got time to catch the airbus to Edmonton. That gives me tonight to clean up some things at the head office. I guess I'll see you at the Municipal Airport tomorrow?" He shook hands with Rod, blew Sheila a kiss, and left. Joe went with him.

"Pete's right, we can't do anything here" — Rod looked at Mac — "but maybe we should talk about what happens if we do happen to reach total depth before the sale. What about the mysterious Montreal bankers, how firm is your deal with them?"

Mac leaned forward. "I was going to speak to you about that. I've been so caught up in all these accidents, I haven't done much about it. We need some kind of presentation I can send to them, the usual stuff — payout, prices, reserves, present worth, and so on."

As he spoke, Sheila walked over to a filing cabinet, selected a thin file, and laid it in front of Rod.

Mac continued. "There are some rough notes and figures in that file, but it needs a lot more work."

Rod flipped rapidly through the file. "Sure, I can put a proposal together. But I'm worried as hell about security on the rig." He stuffed the file into his briefcase. "I'll just have to find a good hiding-place for it."

That night Sheila and Rod had dinner with Mac. They all tried hard to be gay and at times almost succeeded, but thoughts of the doomed well lurked around every corner. Rod shook his head at Sheila's half-hearted offer of a nightcap. She pressed herself against him for a moment as she murmured, "Promise me you'll be careful, Rod. So much is happening, I'm afraid for you."

Early next morning he caught the first flight to Edmonton.

14

The penthouse looked down on English Bay, twenty octagonal-shaped floors below. Tonight there wasn't much of English Bay to be seen as Vancouver's winter rains slanted down, blurring lights and driving pedestrians indoors. In the dining room the drapes had been drawn.

The penthouse was new; its furnishings had the simple uncluttered look of good design and lots of money. If it looked a bit like a decorator's set piece, at least the decorator had known what he was doing. It belonged to Frederick Lazarus: English financier, student of human nature, frustrated social climber. He had a striking appearance: iron-grey hair with matching sideburns, a deep tan, regular features, and date-brown eyes, watchful in their deep foxholes. He spoke with a precise, careful diction; when he smiled, his eyes didn't.

He regarded his feminine guest with the appreciative air of the born connoisseur. How Melinda's dark flaming beauty contrasted with and complemented the statuesque flamboyance of his own creation! He smiled down the length of the table at Anne, who wrinkled her nose companionably.

Never would he forget the first time he had seen her. It was a bright sunwashed morning on a Jamaican beach. He had come down from his cabin armed with suntan lotion, dark glasses, towels, and a paperback novel. He was at ease with himself and the world, the weather was superb, the sun strong, and he had earned the vacation with a modest but neatly executed coup on the market. He wrestled with a beach chair until he had it at the desired angle and was busily arranging everything within easy reach when he saw Anne.

She was sitting on the beach near the water, half turned away from him as she chatted idly with an older couple. He stared, electrified by the flowing lines of her long-waisted body. She was tall and narrowly built but all the curves were there; the skimpy blue bikini made no secret of that. Her hair fell straight to her shoulders in a gold and copper cloud. It gleamed in the sun.

As he watched, oblivious of everyone else on the crowded beach, she, still talking quietly to her companions, plaited the gleaming strands into two long braids, then stood up and waded into the quiet surf, rounded buttocks swivelling rhythmically on long legs. That slender, rounded back, those glorious legs right up to the armpits, that was his weakness! And red-gold hair! It was too much. Scarcely conscious of what he was doing, Frederick followed her into the water.

She waded in the warm shallow water until it closed over her rounded hips, and dove headfirst with a flick of long legs. She swam a few strokes, then stood in the water gazing out to sea where a white banana boat rode easily at anchor. Frederick stalked her, walking on the sandy bottom; he didn't want to dive and muss his distinguished grey hair. As he waded, he cudgelled his brain for some deft opening remark. He was not good at conversational gambits. Normally he had no need of them. His usual female companions were fully aware of his accomplishments and were of a type certain to be impressed. The prospect of exciting parties and expensive presents was always in the background. He admitted to himself that, consciously or not, he had drifted into the easy path, where conquest was sure and superiority taken for granted. Not this time, however; these were unchartered waters!

The goddess turned and his dream world shattered. That heaven-designed body, that glistening crown of hair, was matched to a face that stopped short at the mouth and receded with an appalling angularity to the slender throat. The lower lip hung loose and pendulous.

Frederick backed up furiously but it was too late. So impetuous had been his advance that he was practically on top of the unfortunate girl, the light of conquest rapidly dimming in his brown eyes. There was no escape. Not for nothing had the years schooled him to mask his emotions. He prized his reputation of keeping his cool, whether chance and the stock market smiled or frowned on him. God knew they had done both often enough! He was able to choke out some banality without averting his eyes. She replied pleasantly enough; her voice was undistinguished, but at least it didn't grate on the ears.

They were the only two people in the water, and they had begun a conversation. So they stayed together, alternately floating and swimming a few awkward strokes, filling in the blanks with desultory remarks.

They left the water together. Frederick fell back a few steps until the perfection of her body struck him anew. With practised movements she undid the plaits and let loose a cascade of copper hair. It would be churlish to ignore her on the beach. Frederick dragged over his beach chair. She seemed good-naturedly indifferent; if he wanted to talk — fine; if not — also fine.

The hotel was on the modified American plan, which meant breakfast and dinner were charged against the room whether eaten or not. As a result, guests were remarkably faithful to the cuisine of their own hotel. Frederick, rested and fit after a long afternoon nap, came down to the open-air bar where she sat alone at a table. They exchanged glances; not to sit together would be an intolerable snub. So they had a drink, dinner, and then a drive in his rented car up the winding narrow road to the bar of another hotel.

In the days that followed, they spent more and more time together. She was good company, singularly undemanding, independent and infinitely more intelligent than the pneumatic playgirls who were his normal bill of fare. Her name was Anne

Cameron and she was a model from New York. He smothered his astonishment when she told him this, but she explained casually, "A very specialized sort of modelling — only photos of legs. You know — hosiery, depilatories, suntan lotion: things like that. Sometimes also bathing suits from the rear." She spoke without bitterness.

He was enjoying himself. The sun was hot, the water warm, the vodka plentiful, and Anne's company increasingly pleasant. She asked nothing of him; there was no strain, no sweat. More important, and he was astute enough to realize this, she was a considerable notch above any woman he had ever felt comfortable with before. She had a quality he desired in women but had always avoided in the past, not caring to expose his sensitive ego to the risk of a snub. Her disfigurement took care of that problem. If anyone did any rejecting, it wouldn't be her!

He never kissed her, never attempted to make love to her. If only there had been some way of enjoying that magnificent body without first saluting the sucker-like mouth. But even his ingenious mind couldn't find the solution to that one.

Gradually he found himself watching her with an almost clinical eye. There was something grotesquely fascinating about the contrast between her body and her tragic face. The other guests felt it too. He watched their reaction. They liked her; the men because they could dream all sorts of dreams when they couldn't see her face, the women because her face was always there.

As they talked or simply lay in the sun, he studied her covertly. The upper teeth were of normal size and shape, slightly overlapping in front. No insurmountable problem there. The trouble started with the lower jaw; it was sickeningly underslung. He estimated that the lower teeth missed the uppers by a full inch. For the most part her lower teeth were hidden, but occasionally when she threw back her head to laugh he could see them. They were short and stubby, just barely poking through the gum line, and they didn't seem to have any enamel. They reminded him of a rodent gnawing at the bars of its cage.

An idea was slowly forming in his mind. Screwy, maybe, but he might as well take it down to the end of the road and see what happened. He placed a long-distance call to his Vancouver doctor, who passed him on to an orthodontist. Carefully, reading from notes, he detailed Anne's deformity. The orthodontist listened silently, so silently that Frederick stopped several times to inquire anxiously, "Are you still there, Doctor?"

"I'm listening. Continue, please."

Finally he came to the end of his recital. He took a deep breath, surprised to find his palm was wet against the receiver.

"What's the verdict, Doctor? Do you think anything can be done?"

A long silence hummed over the wire. The orthodontist cleared his throat noisily and said, "You realize that I have not examined this person. From what you have told me, however, I would say that there could be a considerable improvement if she wanted to do this very badly, if she had unlimited time, and if she had a great deal of money. The first ingredient is the most important. Surgery of this type is very painful and prolonged. It would have to be done in stages."

"How much time are we talking about, Doctor?"

"I would say at least two years. That's why the personal element is so important. It's like going to jail for two years, except that there's a lot of physical pain thrown in."

"I see. And how much money?"

"Well, that's hard to predict. First this person would have to be supported for two years; she certainly won't be able to earn her own living. Then there's the question of several complicated operations and protracted hospitalization. Apart from any question of living costs for two years, I would say the medical and hospital bills would approximate $12,000, maybe more."

"Thank you, Doctor. You have been most helpful."

He replaced the receiver thoughtfully. The money was all right. He could manage that. But the rest of it. Two years? Several operations? Physical pain? Who did he think he was, God?

Still, she must be damn sick and tired of lugging that face around, like a Halloween mask on that luscious body. As for him, hell, he was forty-five and he liked that girl; it was exciting in an offbeat way.

Next problem. How does one say to a girl, "Look, why don't we do something about that ugly mug of yours?" Perhaps, "Would you like to go to a hospital and let them do bone grafts and straighten your teeth and then cap them and a few other little details like that?"

When he finally did broach the subject, on the day before he was to leave, it turned out to be remarkably simple. She listened to him intently, her head tilted to one side, her rather nice eyes fixed steadily on his. He gained courage as he talked and wound up with a plea whose passion surprised him. "Look, I know this really is none of my business. But I want to make it mine. You are the one who would have to endure everything. The decision is entirely yours, of course, but if you accept, then I would be privileged to look after all the arrangements."

Her voice was very low, husky with emotion. "Why would you do this?"

"Because, my dear, I love you. I had hoped that maybe during the next few years, your feelings toward me might make it possible to think of marriage." He spoke stiffly.

"Then I will do it! I've often thought about it, but it all seemed so impossibly long and painful. Now I can face up to it. You see, my darling, I love you too!"

She was in his arms, her beautiful body moulding with his. Hungrily he kissed her, his lips blindly seeking hers. He whispered hoarsely, "Let's forget all that business about the operations. Marry me now, just as you are, my beautiful darling."

She pushed him away gently. "Thank you for saying that. But I want to be beautiful for you, and I want you to be proud of my beauty. We'll get this old face of mine fixed up, and then, and only then, we'll marry. You tell me where I'm to report and

I'll be there and they can do their worst. One thing I insist on, however. You must not try to see me until I let you know. Promise?"

Reluctantly he agreed.

The hospital was in Chicago and the remodelling took just under two years. Not once in that time did they meet. Lazarus cherished the long letters he received. She wrote freely of herself, hiding behind no barriers. When one's face is being ripped apart and restructured, when one can only drink and eat through a straw with a face swathed in bandages, there isn't much point in reticence. So her whole personality poured itself onto the pages which he read with compassion and a steadily growing love.

The reunion took place in New York. At the appointed hour he stood in the lobby of the Plaza Hotel, outwardly at ease in black tie, inwardly churning with a mixture of impatience and dread. Now that the moment was at hand, he would have given much to postpone it.

It had been so pleasant to think and dream while everything was at a safe remove. One could weave fantasies comfortably sniffing the aroma of fine cognac, preferably while sated with the young flesh of a complaisant partner. With a sense of panic he saw the fabric and pattern of his life shifting to take on new and unknown forms. They were strangers! Worse, he felt his old self-doubts rising like yellow bile in his throat.

The elevator doors slid back; he saw her standing tall and statuesque. She advanced serenely into the lobby, her eyes composedly searching; her step quickened as she saw him. His heart took a great bound. It was all right, everything was one hundred per cent!

They were married within the week. As an unexpected bonus she proved to be adept and demanding in bed. She was also, as he was at some pains to discover, faithful to him. For the rest, she was pleasant, discreetly uninterested in his business affairs, and a gracious and charming hostess.

He looked at her now, her beautifully formed breasts and rounded shoulders rising from her low-cut black gown. He leaned forward across the whiteness of the table. "My dear, we have some tiresome business matters to discuss. Possibly we could join you later?"

"Of course. Melinda, you are staying with the men? How I admire your grasp of everything. I will be with my coffee in the drawing-room when you are through. Will you excuse me?"

Her husband ceremoniously escorted her from the room and brushed her cheek lightly as she settled in a low chair before the fire. She smiled up at him.

"I shall be quite comfortable, my dear. Don't worry about me, just come out as soon as you have finished."

There was a decanter of port and a humidor of cigars on the table. He was a stickler for English traditions he had never known.

As the port went round, he looked askance at Melinda; he had forgotten that she would, of course, remain. He poured the ruby liquid into her glass, and she smiled at him. "Aren't you going to offer me a cigar, my dear Frederick?"

"But of course, if you would enjoy one?"

The thick greenish cigar looked obscene in her sensuous mouth. She inhaled luxuriously and blew pale blue smoke at her host. Frederick controlled himself with difficulty. What a trying woman she was! Years ago, when she was still married to poor old Tom Vanning, there had been a brief affair, or to be more accurate, he had been swept into the vortex of her sexuality. It hadn't lasted long; she was too rich for his blood by a long chalk!

"Well, I suppose we might just as well get started, if you are all quite comfortable? Possibly it would be helpful if I briefly reviewed the situation, or better still, if Kondar here would bring us up to date on the current status of the well."

He inclined his head with grave courtesy toward the fourth member of the group, a small, slender man in his mid-forties with a dark, brooding appearance. He had been silent during the meal, his eyes glazed like those of a deaf man who switches off his hearing aid and turns his thoughts inward. Now — the amenities of dinner safely past — he was all attention, nervous fingers drumming a soft tattoo on the tablecloth. He spoke slowly; he was easy to understand despite a heavy central-European accent.

"The rig is presently down, as a result of a wrench carelessly dropped in the hole. This means a fishing job, which will consume days or weeks, depending on their luck. I am sorry to report they have had one piece of good fortune; there was a fishing tool available at the Rainbow townsite, so they have gained a few days. Unfortunately, a roughneck blundered upon Willard at a critical moment and had to be eliminated. They will certainly be searching for this man and it would be highly embarrassing, if you will permit the understatement, if the body were to be discovered."

His voice trailed off. For a moment no one spoke, until Frederick, elaborately casual, said, "You know, my dear Kondar, these unfortunate deaths rather change the nature of the game. It escalates the affair from a harmless bit of industrial espionage to a murder charge. As I am sure you understand, under the law we are all equally guilty even if we had no actual part in the killing."

"I am fully aware of that. The legal principle you are thinking of, I believe, states that a conspirator in an unlawful act is automatically guilty of murder if a person is killed as a result of the commission of that act, regardless of whether or not the particular individual played any part in the actual killing. He may have violently opposed it, or even, like us, have known nothing about it until too late. Guilt by association." He spoke pedantically, letting a trace of arrogance show through. He gazed thoughtfully around the table and continued, "We can, however, take some comfort from the fact that we have been in this uncomfortable position ever since

Walsh overheard a certain conversation and had to be silenced before he realized its significance."

"That's true, but in the case of Walsh, the police appear to be satisfied that it was an accident — caused by his getting drunk and not seeing the barrier. We are in the clear on that one. But it'll be a different matter if they stumble across this fellow's body. How was he killed, by the way? Any chance they'll think he simply became lost and died of exposure?" Frederick looked hopefully at Kondar, who shook his head.

"I am very much afraid not. The information I have indicates that he had to be killed on the spot. His head was caved in with a heavy wrench, so there will not be much doubt about how he died. However, we must hope there will be no discovery, for without a body they can only speculate. So long as it remains hidden, the most logical explanation must be that the unfortunate fellow collapsed or became lost in some manner."

"Right, quite right. There is not much point in brooding about it. Let us assume that the incident will remain closed and concentrate on what steps we should take to ensure success. Let me recapitulate for a moment. It is now the night of" — Frederick shot back his cuff to glance at the calendar dial of his wrist watch — "January twenty-eighth. The sale takes place on the fifteenth of February. That gives them ..." He paused to calculate but Kondar broke in coldly.

"Precisely eighteen days."

"Thank you, eighteen days. They are now stuck on bottom at ...?" He looked questioningly at Kondar.

"Two thousand eight hundred twenty-two feet."

"Thank you. And their target formation is at what depth?"

"The muskeg formation should come in — if it's there at all — somewhere between fifty-four hundred and fifty-six hundred feet. Say fifty-five hundred and you won't be far wrong."

"Exactly. That means our friends must drill just under twenty-seven hundred feet in less than three weeks. Is this possible?"

"Easily, with a trouble-free operation. Everything now depends on how long they are delayed with this fishing job. I can't be too optimistic on that score, particularly since they have obtained a tool so quickly. If they get squared away in the next few days, they won't have any trouble. Unless some other unfortunate accident occurs, of course."

George Mason stirred. He had been slouched down in his chair staring morosely at his untouched glass of port, occasionally peering at his companions from under his tangled tent of eyebrows. Now he spoke.

"Possibly we can do something on the financial end, dry up their funds. Any luck with Carruthers, Fred?"

He knew how Lazarus hated to be called Fred.

Frederick looked down the table at George Mason. Damn odd to see him cold stone sober at this hour of the night. All of a sudden he's taking things very seriously. Well, it can't but help us.

He replied with careful courtesy. "Not too much as yet, I'm afraid. Jim's group committed themselves pretty firmly, I understand. It wouldn't do their reputation any good if they pulled out now, apart altogether from any legal consequences. We've got the rumour mill going full blast, of course — how the well is jinxed, the rig a dangerous wreck, the budget heavily overspent, and so forth. But that sort of thing is indirect at best; it takes time. Probably too much time, unless they run into real difficulties and heavy additional expenditures. Then I believe the syndicate would be happy to cut their losses and run. That dry hole we drilled isn't bolstering their enthusiasm either, I'm sure."

"That reminds me." George turned to the engineer. "What about the phony abandonment? Won't we have our necks in the wringer when the authorities find out we have a thick pay zone instead of a dry hole?"

"We've been through all this before." Kondar Podoroff spoke impatiently. "First and most important, there is no chance anyone will discover our harmless little deception until after the sale. By then it will be too late; the lands will be securely registered in the name of our new company, Golden Oils Limited — so aptly named by the charming Melinda." He bowed to her and she smiled faintly; she had chosen the name with considerable care and with many bitter thoughts of Tom's former employers — "which has no connection with the company that drilled the well and fraudulently abandoned it. There is always the chance, and it's a real one, that the little deception may never be discovered. It may prove possible to drain the oil from a well drilled close to the adjoining border of the reservation, or we may have the old Argent company sell the lease to Golden and have Golden drill a well at a new location and happily discover oil. In any case, the worst that can happen is that Argent Oils gets a stiff fine and forfeits a quarter-section lease. That would be unfortunate indeed, because it is underlain with a great deal of oil, but it's insignificant compared with the drilling reservation. Just remember, my friends, that reservation will cover twelve whole sections, which could mean nearly half a billion barrels of oil. Think of it! We are gambling for wealth that is virtually beyond comprehension and certainly beyond any individual's capacity to spend, no matter how talented he may be. A sum of that dimension would grow faster than you could get rid of it."

They listened to him avidly. This was the dream that fired their searching souls — proof positive for George that he could be staggeringly successful if he but tried; wealth that would automatically command respect and acceptance for Frederick, and a personal vindication for Melinda!

Mason was the first to speak. "We must make absolutely sure that the well never reaches the bottom! So far, we've just been nibbling at the problem, not solving it. Pinning out hopes on piddling little accidents. I say we must think of something that will put them out of the running once and for all! As our friend Kondar has so thoughtfully reminded us, we are in this thing up to our necks already, so we have nothing to lose — nothing! If we play our cards right, I can see us ending up with MacPherson's lease as well."

There was a murmur of assent. Frederick turned to Kondar. "It seems we are all in accord. Can we do it?"

A half-smile twisted the secretive mouth. "There is one possibility. It's virtually a certainty that the well will encounter gas in a formation somewhere around one thousand feet above the muskeg formation. There is no connection between the two zones and right now the gas has no value because there is no way of selling it. All it means is an extra hazard, an added danger. They'll have to be very careful when they run into the gas, they'll have to cement it off and generally treat it with kid gloves. It's under very high pressure and, of course, it's highly inflammable. The slightest miscalculation and they would blow that rig sky-high!"

"I suppose it would always be possible to arrange for a 'slight miscalculation'?" Frederick's expression was a nice blend of distaste and fascination as he asked the question.

"In theory, yes. If you invite the devil to escape, you can be certain he will accept. The real problem will be to persuade our man to unleash him. After all, he will be on the rig when it happens and that's rather like asking someone to picnic in a nuclear range. I expect he'll do it all right, but it may take some persuasion. I'm not sure our code system will prove to be eloquent enough."

"I'm sure you can arrange it, Kondar." Frederick's voice was smooth; he looked around the table for any sign of disagreement. Finding none, he said, "That appears to be settled. We'll leave it in your capable hands."

"Very well. I'll see what can be done. But shouldn't we at least consider the possibility of something less dangerous? How about infiltrating their people?"

"A good idea, but what are the possibilities? How about that toolpush, what's his name — Quigley? I understand he has fought some memorable battles with the bottle."

Kondar shook his head slowly. "It won't go. Quigley is a booze hound all right; he's been suspended by Sanderson several times for it. But he leaves it alone when he's on a well; it's only when he's between jobs that he gets into trouble. I don't think there's any hope in that direction." He paused and looked at Melinda. "What about that new geologist — Fraser? I understand he used to be an admirer or yours?"

George stirred, as though to intercede; he half raised his arm, then let it drop.

Without raising her gaze from the table, Melinda shook her head. "There's no way. Weaknesses Rod may have, but betraying an employer is completely out of character. He lives by his own code and I can tell you that working behind the backs of people who employ him, people who trust him, is not part of it. No, you better forget Rod Fraser."

"Okay, I was just asking."

"It would seem we are still very much on our own. So much the better, I say."
Frederick frowned as he continued. "I dislike mentioning this, but our own financial
support isn't as strong as one might wish. I had a long telephone conversation with
old Thompson this very afternoon. He's getting restless, decidedly restless."

George groaned. "Christ, what does he want now?"

"I think he merely wanted to flex his financial muscles, not being overly blessed
with muscles of any other description. We must remember, however, that he is
essential to our plans. Our bid must be substantial. The majors are quite capable of
putting in a 'stink bid' far beyond our present capacities, even with no information
to go on. Not only that, but the government will reject any bid they consider too low.
With so much at stake, we simply can't afford to come in low. Nothing to compare
with the value of the oil reserves, of course, but nonetheless a considerable piece of
change. And so, the good offices of the venerable Thompson are very important.
He complained, my dear Melinda, that he had called you several times but you seem
never to be at home and that you neglect to return his calls. I really do think you
should call him, don't you?"

Slowly, without raising her eyes, Melinda nodded assent. "I'll call him tomorrow,"
she whispered.

For a moment no one spoke. Her sexuality was a dark thread running through the
fabric of the group. Frederick broke the silence.

"Well, that seems to cover everything. Shall we adjourn for coffee?"

Later, as they were standing in the carpeted hallway waiting for the elevator,
George drew Kondar to one side. "I think it might be desirable if our young geologist friend were to meet with an accident — a fatal one!"

"You think so? As for myself, I don't think he is much of a hazard. If you wish,
I will try to arrange something with Willard. But I'll leave the decision strictly up to
him. If he thinks it will be too risky, I'm not going to argue. It may happen anyway,
if he's around the rig at the right time!"

With a soft, sighing swish the elevator deposited them on Parking Level 2. They
walked toward the pink Mustang, Melinda's heels echoing in the concrete cavern.
George climbed awkwardly into the passenger seat, fumbled with the safety belt,
then gave it up as a bad job. He was silent as she expertly tooled the car through the
wet black night. While they waited for a light to change, he remarked idly, "I haven't
seen you driving the Volvo recently. Where is it?"

"It's in the shop, getting tuned and fitted with stud tires for the winter rally on
Sunday."

"Of course, I had forgotten. Somehow a winter rally seems even more dangerous
than the usual kind."

"Not really, not with the studs. I want very badly to win it." She cut her eyes at
him as they pulled swiftly away from the intersection. "I'm afraid it's going to cost a
bit, I went a little ape on some new instruments."

He smiled briefly as he continued to stare at the mesmerizing sweep of the clacking wipers. "That shouldn't pose any undue problems. You are entered in the open division, I suppose?"

"You suppose right, I already know I can beat the pants off the spreading back-sides of anyone in the powder-puff set. There are some first-class drivers in the open but I think I have a chance."

"Is Tony navigating for you?"

"Yes, he is. And I hope he is getting lots of sleep; the weather reports aren't very encouraging!"

Braking smoothly, she turned into the driveway of their apartment block, switch-ing off the wipers as they passed through the automatic door.

Their apartment was older and a good deal less pretentious than the one they had just left, but it was still very luxurious. Heavy lamps anchored end tables at either end of a huge sofa; a low circular coffee table carried its burden of outsize ashtrays before a false fireplace filled with fresh flowers — pink roses, which also stood in tall vases throughout the large room. Heavy plum-coloured drapes had been pulled across the floor-length windows, shutting out the inclement night.

George took her wrap as they stood in the marble-floored foyer. He wanted a drink so badly he could feel it in his toenails, but he willed his mind to ignore the clamouring demands of his nerve-ends. He followed Melinda into the living room and stood behind her as she flicked a light to her cigarette. Timidly he pressed her shoulders, then ran his hands lightly down her bare arms.

She blew out a cloud of smoke and looked up at him over her bare shoulder. She spoke in a carefully expressionless voice. "George, do you want me to get the ... you know, the machine?"

With a sigh, he dropped his hands. "No, not tonight. The way I feel now, it would be too degrading."

"I'm sorry, George. I didn't mean to upset you."

He kissed her hair. "I know you didn't, you meant to help me and I thank you. But I'd like to talk."

"Fix me a very light drink while I change."

He could see the warm tones of her skin through the sheer lounging pyjamas as she curled herself into an armchair opposite him. George said, "This Rod Fraser means something to you, doesn't he? I mean, more than the others."

Her eyes widened; this was tricky ground.

"Rod? You know all about him. I knew him when I was married to Tom. He was the man Tom named as co-respondent when he divorced me. I had an affair with him. So what else is new?"

"Only that you have been with him at least twice since he got fired down in Venezuela. That young man has a gift for getting crossways with his superiors. But I meant more than just physical love. You feel for him, Melinda, don't you? He's not just another man to sleep with."

"Just how much do you know about me, George?"

"Quite a bit. Let's see, in the recent past there's been that bartender from the Red Door, there's been Rick Harvey, old Thompson, but that's in the line of duty, and a young drilling-mud salesman up in Edmonton. There are probably others, but they don't matter." He smiled bleakly. "I think of them as proxy pricks. But your feeling for Fraser goes much deeper."

Melinda was on her feet, tiny fists clenched, white and shaking with rage. "You want to possess me, don't you? You can't take my body, so you want to rape my soul. Men! You're all alike; with everything, it's 'I own it;' 'I want it;' 'You're mine.' Well, nobody owns Melinda, not Rod Fraser, not you, not anybody!"

She ran out of the room. George sat slumped in an armchair while the black surface of the window gradually turned grey with the reluctant dawn.

15

They were cramped in the narrow cab. Rod Fraser, sitting in the middle with no door or steering wheel for support, bounced helplessly as they rose and dipped over the endless humps. He was wretchedly uncomfortable. He couldn't stretch his legs without hitting the sharp metal edges of the asthmatic heater; the fan-shaped arcs of the defroster left a solid line of frost bisecting the windshield directly in front of his eyes.

They weren't talking much. Jerry, never loquacious, concentrated on his driving. Pete, trying to keep his right side from touching the frigid door, was sunk in the gloomy silence.

Rod flung a casual question at Jerry. "White was a friend of yours, wasn't he?"

Jerry's eyes widened as he considered the startling implications of the word friend. Pleased, he nodded, his lips forming a shy smile.

"Yeah, yeah — he was. We were buddies!"

"What do you suppose happened to him?"

Jerry wrestled with the difficulties of logical thought as he shifted down to ease them over another hillock.

"I dunno. He was a steady guy, Mike was. He wouldn't go wandering off in the bush just for the hell of it. Way I figure, he maybe got sick, an attack of something ..." He gestured vaguely. "Started out for the camp and got lost and the cold got him. You can get attacks that twist you all up so you don't know where you're at, can't you?"

"Yes, I think a stroke would do it. But it doesn't seem likely."

"It sure as hell don't. Mike was strong like a horse. But I can't figure out what else could have happened to him."

Pete chipped in. "They haven't found any trace of him yet?"

"Not up to the time I left camp. We all was out looking for him, or his tracks. But there wasn't a sign of anything. Funny. Maybe he just kept on walking down the road right past the camp. That way there wouldn't be no tracks and he could keep moving till he fell into a snowbank anywheres along the road. We ain't had no snow to cover his footprints, so he must of been walking where there was no deep snow."

Pete mused. "Damn odd he disappeared right as the bit got jammed in the hole."

"Old Mike didn't have nothing to do with that, Mr. Berry. He was as straight as they come, old Mike was. If there was any funny work going on, he wouldn't have no part of it."

Pete leaned forward to light a cigarette, the flame of the propane lighter throwing his face into sharp relief.

"How is the fishing job? They making any progress?"

"I dunno, Mr. Berry." Rod noted that the drilling superintendent always rated a "mister" from the niche-conscious Jerry; it was a rare attitude in the drilling business. "As soon as I unloaded the fishing tool at the site I pretty well had to turn around and come back for you."

"You've really been logging the miles, Jerry. A damn good effort!"

"Thanks, Mr. Berry. I do what I can." Rod could see that Jerry was pleased with the recognition. Berry knew how to handle men.

"I'll check in with Larry," Pete said as they climbed stiffly out of the truck. He looked briefly down the road to the rig, its lights shining through the canvas, and turned to the camp. "He's probably in his room."

Larry Quigley looked up from his bunk, an open copy of *Sports Illustrated*, two months old, face down beside him. He smiled and got up to shake Pete's hand. It was the first time Rod had seen him shake hands with anyone.

"Hi, Pete. Glad you got here."

"Larry, good to see you. How are things?"

"No great hell. We got a break by locating a fishing tool in Rainbow. We've made one trip out and brought up some stuff. There's still more down there, though, and we ran the tool back in."

"What sort of junk is it bringing up?"

Larry looked at him steadily. "The very best of tempered steel. It's chewed all to hell but it's easy enough to tell what it is — a twenty-four-inch wrench!"

Pete swore softly; he looked at Rod. "Beautiful!" His voice was bitter as he asked, "Any idea how it got there?"

Larry shrugged. "It could have been an accident; somebody could have dropped or kicked it in while we were between trips and been too frightened to report it. Might have figured it would be chewed up and nobody would ever know. Or it could have been sabotage."

"Any sign of White?"

"None. We've combed the whole area. Nothing. He most likely buggered off."

"Where in the hell would he go?"

Larry shrugged. "Shit, I don't know. Maybe he had some place picked out to hole up for the night and somebody to pick him up on the main road the next day. All I know for sure is that he ain't here!"

"There's not much we can do about it at the moment. I want a cup of coffee and then I want to see the rig."

The night was clear, but a sharp ground wind had sprung up and it clawed at them with its icy breath. It was just a few hundred yards to the rig but they took the still-warm pickup. Larry pulled it close to the protection of the substructure wall and left the motor running.

He turned to Rod. "I nearly forgot. There was a guy on the radio last night, Lee Crozier, I think he said his name was — he was asking for you, said he knew you in Venezuela. He's the geologist sitting on the new hole down the road a piece. Wants to see you."

"Crozier, is he up here? I'd like to see the old bastard! Where is this well?"

"About seventy-five miles of godawful road from here. They rigged up just a few days ago, so the geologist won't have too much to do and the hole won't go tight for a while. So, if you want to visit him, you better do it soon. We'll still be fucking around with this fish all tomorrow. If you want, you can take the pickup. Jerry can tell you how to get there."

"Thanks, I'll just do that."

Inside the doghouse Larry led them to the triangular bench where a few broken and badly chewed pieces of metal had been placed carefully on a sheet of white cardboard.

"That's what we got on our first trip." He pointed to the scraps. "One good-size section of a handle, the lower part of the jaws, and some slivers. I reckon it will take at least three more trips to get it all and even at that we'll have to be lucky."

Pete looked at the pieces. "Is that one of our wrenches?"

"Yeah. The first thing we did was make a count of the tools. A twenty-four wrench turned up missing, so I ordered a magnetic fishing tool."

Pete nodded approvingly.

Larry listened to the motors. He peered out the doghouse window and said, "They're coming out of the hole. Let's see what they've got."

The heavy metal door clanged shut behind them as they crowded onto the rig floor. The driller stood by the drawworks, one hand on the gear levers, never taking his eyes from the pipe slowly emerging from the hole. High above, the derrick man stood on his tiny platform, ready to wrestle the disengaged stand of pipe into the rack. The roughnecks stood poised by the tongs and slips, waiting to unscrew each section.

With a fish the trip was even more tedious and arduous than normal. The fishing tool was a powerful magnet set inside a steel sleeve threaded onto the last section of pipe. The magnet was dropped on bottom, rotated a few times to stir up the fish, and raised — slowly and carefully, so the pieces of metal would not be jarred loose from its embrace. More important, the turning action of the rotary table could not be used to unscrew the sections. Each one had to be laboriously disconnected, using only the power tongs and chains.

Larry spoke briefly to Luke Willard, who was the driller on duty, and then told Pete, "He figures it will take a half-hour to break out the last few strings."

Pete nodded. "Okay. Might as well poke around the rig."

Other than a quick nod from Luke Willard, the rest of the crew had ignored their presence. They realized who Pete was, but as members of a floating, nomadic workforce, none of them except the driller knew him personally. In the age-old tradition of keeping the head down, their eyes were riveted on the ascending pipe.

Pete said nothing as he viewed the eerie mixture of ice and steam in the substructure. He looked directly at Larry, who grinned wryly.

"A bitch, ain't it? In this weather, we just can't seem to get ahead of it. You set up a steam line and the damn thing freezes and splits wide open. Try and chip at the ice and the tool shatters in your hand."

Pete made no reply, just led the way to the mud-pump section. Later he would chew out Larry for the state of the BOPS and Larry knew it. No excuses could be accepted; the powerful rams had to be kept free so they could seal off the well in split-seconds.

The last section rose slowly out of the hole, gobs of grey drilling mud dripping and spurting from it. A roughneck slipped to one side and hastily dropped a steel cover over the square hole in the rotary table. Others pushed the pipe to one side. Three small pieces of metal hung from the magnet; it took a powerful jerk to free them.

Luke carried them inside and placed them with their fellows. He looked at the others crowding around him and said, "Not much, Larry."

Larry sighed heavily. "I'll say. Just the ends of the handle and a couple of pieces that look as though they were part of the handle, too. That leaves practically all of the head still down there. Well, we just have to keep hacking away at it. Start another trip."

Jerry opened the door for Rod. "She's all set, the engine has been running for an hour, gas tank's full. I poured in a can of de-icer and there's two more cans in the glove compartment. You know how to get there?"

"Yeah, thanks, Jerry. Forty miles down our road, then a turnoff to the left. There's a wooden arrow sign that says Barrow No. 8 — right?"

"Check. Pretty hard to miss; it's the only turnoff until you hit the main road to Rainbow." Jerry grinned. "Don't drink too much and do what Mr. Walsh did."

The wind was still blowing, rustling the ranks of spruce like robed monks at some pagan mass. The sun gleamed weakly in the blue sky. A hawk owl, perched on the top branches of a dead evergreen, surveyed his frozen domain for the telltale movements of an unwary rodent. The carcass of a lynx, skinned and left hanging from a wooden frame, swayed grotesquely in the wind.

It was brutal, fatiguing work. Shift down, brake, shift up, accelerate, and always the terrifying prospect of a heavy transport rig snorting around each blind corner. There was no traffic, however; he was alone in a frozen world. The wind whipped ice crystals from the crusted snow and drove them in swirling eddies across the road.

Idly he speculated about the chill factor. The thermometer at the camp registered minus forty, and with a wind like this, the combined result was probably somewhere between minus sixty and minus seventy. Christ!

He spotted the sign without any difficulty; it was an arrow pointing to the turnoff. For the last few miles he had been driving through a region completely free of trees. It must be all muskeg in summer, he thought. He could see the towering mast of Barrow No. 8 while it was still miles away. It turned out to be a much more modern rig than the battered Cheyenne outfit, but the general arrangement was identical. The latticework of the derrick was open, they were not using a canvas cover.

He waited in the diner of the camp while one of the crew brought Lee from the rig.

"Rod! It's damn good to see you! What in hell brings you into these frozen parts?"

"I might ask you the same question. Just a bit different from our last assignment."

They shook hands warmly. They were of the same age and had been good friends during Lee's tour of duty at Maracaibo. A Canadian working for an international company, he had been rotated to Venezuela on a two-year tour to gain experience. A year ago, his stint completed, he had been brought back to Calgary.

The off-duty crews filed into the diner to heap their plates with a midday meal of staggering proportions. Afterward, the two friends sat in the deserted room, swallowing cup after cup of coffee as they relived tropical nights in Caracas. Lee had made many friends there and was anxious for the latest news.

Finally, he pushed back the bench and said, "Come on. You might as well see the rig while you're here. We haven't put security regulations into effect yet, so it's okay."

They climbed into a Chevrolet sedan and drove the short distance to the rig.

"I'm just getting things organized, setting up my sample trays and so on."

Rod was curious. He knew that Lee was a comer. People liked him and he was a damn good geologist. Sitting on a well was not exactly a plum job for a major-company geologist; usually, it was handled by a junior. Casually he asked, "How come a VIP like you is sitting on a well? I thought you just sat behind an acre of desk and dispatched troops of minions to freeze their asses."

Lee grinned. "Strictly by choice. The reserves up here are so important that I wanted to get first-hand experience, so I assigned myself to sit this one."

"Makes sense. That reminds me, I better start getting back to my own."

"No rush. You're safer driving at night and, anyway, you can't leave without supper. Speaking of your well, I keep hearing the most intriguing rumours about it. Can you comment?"

"Afraid not. I need the job."

Rod unplugged the block heater, started the pickup, and left it idling while he stuffed himself with an enormous meal. The early northern night was firmly clamped in place when he started back. He felt bloated and uncomfortable.

The headlights gouged great slices in the night. The wind had grown steadily all day and now it was blowing directly from the Arctic Ocean, shaking the light vehicle and driving frozen pellets of snow that reflected with a white glitter in the glare of the lights. Rod hunched over the wheel, squinting through the windshield. Finally he saw the solitary signpost and turned north on the road to his own well. He lifted his foot from the gas pedal and shifted down. Horrified, he saw the lights flicker and dim. Frantically he gunned the motor with the clutch engaged, and the lights glowed back to life, but the engine gave an ominous cough as he eased it back into second gear.

"Gas line freezing, that's all," Rod assured himself. "All it needs is a can of de-icer dumped into the gas tank."

He pulled the truck to a complete stop. The motor spluttered, roared back into life as he pumped the pedal, then went cold with a convulsive shudder. The lights faded to an orange glow, barely lighting the snow in front of them. He cut off the light switch; they would drain his battery in a minute, and if the battery couldn't turn the motor over, all the de-icer in the world wouldn't help him. Time to worry about the battery when he had dealt with the gas line freezing. He fought to control the panic that was beginning to nibble at the edges of his mind.

He leaned over and punched the lock on the glove compartment. The door fell open; his mittened hand fumbled inside for the small cans. He felt a flashlight, switched it on, and focused it on the small compartment. Apart from a few dusty credit cards and a plastic ice-scraper, it was empty. There was no trace of the precious bronze cans. Christ! They had to be there. Fleming had said they were, hadn't he? He distinctly remembered Jerry saying he had put two of them in the glove compartment. Maybe they were on the floor, rolled under the seat or something.

With increasing desperation and fading hope, he played the light under the seat. Standing in the open door he lifted the seat cushions — no cans there, nor in the cargo compartment, nor on the shelf behind the seat.

His mind raced. Well, might as well see if it'll start now, because if it doesn't it sure won't in a few minutes!

He turned the ignition key; the warmth of the engine, no longer dispersed by the forward motion, had caused a partial melting of the ice, and the engine caught. With a surge of hope he eased into low gear.

He drove on, hands sweating inside the leather mittens as they clutched the wheel. He reviewed his situation; it wasn't very promising. Damn near forty miles to go, no de-icer, this clunker could give up the ghost any moment, there wouldn't be any traffic on the road, and he didn't even have a sleeping bag!

He pounded the wheel in impotent fury as he thought of the bedroll. He had been incredibly stupid not to make sure there was one in the truck. A sleeping bag was the life belt in the north and he hadn't even given it a thought as he drove blithely away from the camp. You'd think he was just going to the corner drugstore. Well, it looked as though he was about to pay for his folly!

The lights began their ominous dimming. He tried everything he could think of to keep the motor turning over: gunning it with the clutch in every time he had to shift down; dropping into low gear; alternately praying and cursing; but slowly, inexorably, the misses grew more frequent, the return of power slower and weaker, until finally the motor quivered and was still.

He counted the seconds, trying to judge the moment when the heat from the motor would have thawed the gas line and before the battery had lost its charge. Prayerfully, he turned the key. The battery groaned sluggishly but there was still enough juice to spin the flywheel. The motor caught, but its note was faltering, uneven. A few hundred yards down the road it quit, this time for good. When Rod turned the key, the only response was a series of clicks, empty and final.

He made one last, frantic search for the de-icer. It was futile, as he had known it would be, and the light from his flashlight was dimming fast as the cold sucked at the battery. The truck cooled with the cracks and clicks of contracting metal. Soon it would be as cold inside the cab as in the white world outside. From somewhere he had a dim idea that the first step when marooned like this was to start a fire. But he, bloody fool, had no matches and there was no wood in sight. He could see in the distance a dark blue line of spruce, but the woods were at least a mile away, a mile of deep packed snow. He could never make it.

He should keep moving, that was it. But he remembered another cardinal rule of survival — "Stay with your vehicle!" Besides, there was no place to aim for, he would be dead long before he could hope to reach the rig. But he could walk up and down the road and keep his blood circulating.

The wind tore at him, sticking its icy bayonets into his face, picking its way under his parka, buffeting him with its force. He felt the burning start in his fingers; the ache in his feet climbed to his ankles. In the cab, he would be out of this hellish wind, at least. Awkwardly, he pried open the door and clambered in. It was peaceful and quiet, sheltered from the stunning blast.

He watched the ice crystals form on the fur rim of his parka hood; by looking up he could see the frost on his eyebrows. His fingers were really sore now and his face felt as though it were on fire, but the pain in his feet was lessening. Funny, you'd think that, sitting in the cab like this, you would be warm. But there was no heat, the truck was just a frozen mass of metal. He couldn't feel his feet now at all. He supposed that was a bad sign but the relief from the pain was welcome. His mind turned over heavily; maybe the cold had worked its way inside his skull and was slowing down the revolutions. It was difficult to think straight, difficult to think at all. He fell back on the seat, sprawling clumsily. Struggling, he sat up. Goddamn it, this wouldn't do. He wasn't going to sit there and just quietly freeze to death! He stamped his feet on the floor, but he couldn't feel them. Pounding his hands together, he was rewarded with a sensation of pinpricks, but deep down he knew there was no escape from the creeping, unrelenting cold. It lay over everything, muffling every spark of life. What a damn silly, pointless way to die!

He blinked and raised his head, staring at the frost-crazed windshield. For a

284 / JOHN BALLEM

moment he thought he had seen a glint, a sparkle of reflected light. There it was again; it couldn't be starlight, it was too bright for that. It came again, brighter this time, now the whole windshield was shining in its light. Somebody was coming! It couldn't be anything else! He struggled to sit up, fumbling with the door latch.

He pitched forward on his face as his legs buckled under him, but he clambered back to his feet, hanging onto the door. Straining his eyes he could see the lights moving along the road, sometimes disappearing as they dipped to follow its undulations but always moving nearer. What if they turned down the road to the Barrow rig? He prayed silently. They kept coming, growing steadily brighter. Surely by now they were beyond the turnoff, they must be coming his way!

The red truck pulled to a stop, the bearded driver staring in open-mouthed disbelief at the haggard figure clinging to the side of the stranded pickup. Rod almost fell as he released his hold on the door handle and turned to his rescuer.

"Take it easy, old buddy. Let me have a look at you." He led Rod into the glare of the headlights.

His passenger, also bearded, leaned across the seat and looked at Rod keenly. "How long have you been stranded?"

A wild sense of relief, of escape, coursed through Rod. He replied, "I don't know. A couple of hours, I guess. But I'll be all right now, thanks to you fellows."

The driver grunted. "His cheeks have a touch of frostbite, which means his feet will have it too. Okay, my friend, we'll just walk a while, until we get the blood moving."

Rod was too weak to protest as the burly driver half-supported, half-dragged him up the road. "Rub your face with your hands, and keep walking."

"Christ, I'm frozen. Let me get in your truck and get warm," Rod mumbled.

"You can in a few minutes, once we've got some circulation going. If you were exposed to that heat right now, you'd lose a few bits and pieces of yourself, and you wouldn't want that. What's the trouble with your truck?"

"Gas line froze and I had no de-icer."

The other simply looked at him. "You mean to tell me you've been driving around up here with no de-icer in your truck? Christ, what a bloody hero!"

"And no sleeping bag either." Rod managed a sheepish grin.

"Did you hear that, Charlie?" The driver shouted against the driving wind. "Our little tenderfoot here has been wandering around with no de-icer and no bedroll!"

"Mother of Jesus! But if it's only a frozen gas line we should be able to get the pickup moving. I'll pour in some fluid and see if it thaws out the line."

The heat of the cab made Rod gasp. His cheeks were a million pinpricks, his eyes watered and stung, and his feet and hands burned with an excruciating agony.

"How do you feel?"

"Like Joan of Arc when they lit the bonfire. I never knew that sub-zero cold could be so damn hot!"

The other peered at him in the light of the dash. "You'll be all right. You'll lose part of the end of your nose but it'll grow back, and you'll have some black bruises on your face but they'll fade after a while. What rig are you from?"

"Cheyenne Three."

"That's Quigley's. What's an old hand like him mean by letting people drive around without proper equipment?"

"It's not his fault. It was my own damn stupidity. I thought I had plenty of fluid when I started out and I never even thought of a sleeping bag."

"You better start thinking of it. A few more hours without one in that truck and you would have been just so much frozen meat."

"Yeah, I know. How come you fellows happened along?"

"We're on a seismic survey. We're heading north of your rig. Feel warm enough to get your vehicle started?"

Rod nodded. "Yes, but the battery is dead."

"That's no problem, we'll push you until you can turn her over in gear."

It was a rough start; with no battery the pickup had no lights, so the only illumination was the diffused glare from the seismic truck as it butted from the rear. The heavy metal grille grated and jarred as the two vehicles rose and fell with each dip in the road. It was impossible to gain any speed so Rod finally let out the clutch, relying on the brute power of his rescuers' motor. The pickup's engine caught, reluctantly, then steadied. Rod snapped on the lights and watched them grow in intensity. Now under his own power, he was able to pull away from the jarring impact of the heavier vehicle.

The lights stayed behind him, twin beacons of security. The clogging sludge of ice was dissolved by the fluid, the engine ran without a miss, and even managed to generate some warm air through the heater. All the way to the rig Rod was filled with an overwhelming sense of relief. Never had the world looked so good to him.

Even the bleak, cheerless camp was a haven of shelter and blessed warmth. He stood in the diner gulping a steaming mug of coffee. The only other occupants were two water-haulers, truckers who transported water under contract from a nearby river where they kept open holes in the ice. They looked at Rod with guarded curiosity. One of them ventured, "Have any trouble?"

"A bit." Rod had decided to play it cool, minimize the narrowness of his escape. "Gas line froze up and I thought I was in for a long, cold night but some seismic boys showed up and got me going."

"That ain't no fun!"

The other nodded sagely and soon they were deep in reminiscing over similar experiences. Every year mechanical breakdowns and the deadly cold claimed their share of victims.

Rod felt the reaction hitting him. He excused himself and fell heavily onto his bunk, staying awake only for a long appreciative look around the tiny, warm room as he pulled the covers up to his neck.

16

"I thought you said there was de-icer in the pickup?"

Jerry looked up from the wash basin, water streaming from his face. "I did, I know there was. I checked it before you left, just like I told you."

Rod shrugged, looking into the mirror as he wiped his razor. "All I know is that when she conked out on me there was no de-icer."

Jerry started. "She conked out on you? How in hell did you get out of it?"

"Luck, sheer blazing luck. A seismic truck came along after I'd been stalled for a couple of hours. Even at that, I've picked up some battle scars. Look at that." He turned toward Fleming.

"Jumping Christ! Your nose is as red as a nanny goat's arse. You got bit, all right, but real good." Jerry breathed in awe. "But there was fluid in that truck, I saw it."

"Okay. I believe you. But sometime between your checking it and ten o'clock last night, it disappeared. Maybe somebody just glommed onto it."

Jerry shook his head doubtfully. "Maybe, but I don't think so. Anybody took it they would let me know. That stuff is too important up here. It looks like somebody meant to get you ..." He paused as a new thought struck him. "Maybe they were after me."

"I don't think they were after either of us. Most likely somebody needed the cans and took them without thinking. Anyway, that's what I keep telling myself. Are you going on tour?"

"No. Just came off. I'm going to get me a couple of hours shut-eye and then go back looking for Mike."

"Looking for him? How?"

"I got me a metal rod and I walk along poking it in the snow. If I feel anything, I dig. That's what they do when they look for a skier buried in an avalanche. I know damn well old Mike didn't just up and leave. He wouldn't act that way. I walked up on both sides of the road yesterday, didn't find anything but an old dead wolf. Man, was he frozen solid!"

Rod swallowed. "Well, good luck. Except I don't mean good luck, I hope your friend is safely shacked up with some blonde in Edmonton."

"I hope so too, but I know he ain't."

"Let's get some breakfast. Then I'll go down to the rig. Are they getting anywhere?"

"Yeah. This should be the last fish; they got a big hunk of the wrench the last trip."

Pete turned as Rod walked into the doghouse. He smiled cheerfully. "Welcome back. With a little luck, we might have some work for you before too long."

"Things looking up, eh?"

"Not bad. We'll be out of the hole in six or seven strings, and if we have a few pieces of metal sticking to that old magnet, we'll be back in business. I don't think we'll ever get all the pieces, but if we get enough we'll take a chance and drill ahead. Matter of fact, I thought we could have lowered the bit after the last fish, but Quigley didn't agree. How was your trip?"

"Reasonably exciting toward the end. The gas line froze and I spent a couple of hours wondering how many toes I was going to lose."

"Well, I'm damned! How come you broke down?"

"I'm afraid my tenderfeet were showing. I didn't check for de-icer. However —" he shrugged slightly, dismissing the subject, "it all worked out and I learned a lesson, one I won't forget."

"It happens to the best of us. Just about everybody up here has a brush with death at one time or another. One little slip, one moment of forgetfulness, and you pay a hell of a price." Pete leaned to one side to gaze through the grimy window. "Looks like the last string. Let's see what goodies they've fished out for us."

Larry raised a hand in casual salute and returned his gaze to the magnet now rising slowly above the floor. As the hole cover dropped into place, he sighed with satisfaction. "Two good hunks, that should just about complete our jigsaw puzzle, men."

And it did. When he had fitted the new pieces into the design, the only gaps were thin cracks and broken corners.

"We can go through what's left without any trouble. All right men, now we drill!"

Luke Willard caught the drive in Larry's voice. He turned to the crew who had crowded into the tiny room to absorb a moment's warmth. "Come on, let's get cracking on a new bit and get this goddamn show on the road!"

They trooped out behind him.

"That's a good 'un." Larry watched Luke as he stood by the drawworks. "He's just about ready to start pushing, Pete."

"I agree. He gets the next rig, provided we ever get off this blasted hole. He's a credit to you, Larry, you brought him along just right."

"I didn't have much to do with it. The black bastard's just got it, that's all."

Luke felt good as he handled the levers with cool confidence. He enjoyed the smooth response of his body as he swung the drill pipe into position in one easy flow. Lately he had begun to accept the idea that men would follow him — treat him as boss. It took a while; he had grown up in Africville, the black ghetto of Halifax; its squalor and open sewers didn't lead to much self-confidence. But he had the qualities that worked in the drilling business, energy and physical ability. It was beginning to pose a problem for Luke. Sometimes he felt so spaced-out just leading his crew that he was tempted to give up his other dreams, the dark ones, and make it the straight way. Become a name in the drilling industry on his own. But it was too slow; he wanted to live, man, and he wanted it right now!

Jerry burst through the far door, his parka hood thrown back. He was breathing heavily, his face ashen. "Larry — Mr. Berry — I found him! I found Mike; he's out there under the snow, frozen so hard I can't move him."

Pete took command. "You lead the way, Jerry. Show us where you found him."

White's eyes stared up at them through the hole Jerry had pawed and scraped in the snow. They glittered brilliantly in the sunlight, the fluid of the eye frozen into a hard, shiny surface. His heavy eyebrows were caked with ice and the hair stood out in frozen spikes.

"My God!" Pete breathed, bending over the corpse. "I can't close his eyes, they're frozen open. What's this?" He dug at the snow, uncovering a mittened hand reaching up from the body. "If I try and force his arm down, I'll break it off. We'll have to dig him out, but be careful, for God's sake!"

The body, when finally uncovered, was completely encased in its shroud of ice. One leg stuck straight down while the other was doubled up close to the torso and frozen in place.

Larry whispered, "How do we carry him? He's sticking out at all angles."

"We'll just have to take him the way he is. We can't do anything with him until he ... thaws out." Pete spoke through clenched teeth.

With a strangled sob, Jerry lurched a few paces and was violently sick in the snow. Wiping his mouth with a mittened hand, he mumbled, "I'm sorry, he was my friend."

"He was a friend of all of us ..." Larry spoke softly. "I wonder how he ended up out here." He kneeled and half lifted, half turned the rigid carcass, the frozen neck supporting the head as it moved free of the snow. He drew in his breath sharply as the battered skull came into view. "There was some fucker who, by Jesus, was no friend of his. Look at that! Some bastard sure worked him over!" He looked up at Pete. "This is out of my line, Pete, but it looks to me like we better call the Mounties and leave poor old Mike right here. He sure ain't going to deteriorate any and ain't there some law about not moving the corpse?"

Before Pete could reply, Jerry burst out, "You're not going to leave Mike out here! We've got to take him inside where it's warm."

Pete touched his shoulder. "It doesn't matter to him now, Jerry. But I think we should move him in. There's nothing for the police out here. If there ever were any clues, we've trampled and dug them out of existence. We can't just leave him out in the open where everybody can look at him. It isn't decent. We'll carry him in, and if we get any static from the horsemen, I'll take the blame."

Afterward, Rod was never able to remember much of that nightmare journey. He had a kaleidoscopic impression of fighting down waves of nausea, of clutching a rigid arm pointing straight up to the blue sky, of a head and neck remaining stiffly and horribly horizontal as they stumbled over the hard-packed snow. He remembered Pete muttering hysterically, as he grappled with the bent leg, "Mike was one hell of a good hand, but right now he's just a big problem in logistics."

No one spotted their lurching, straining progress. The crew on the rig were screened by the plywood walls, except for the derrick man, who was too busy maneuvring a heavy string of pipe to pay attention to anything else. The off-duty crews were indoors.

"We'll put him in the office," Pete grunted as they reached the camp. There was a horrible moment while they struggled to get him through the door. Finally they had to tilt him at an angle.

"Christ, I need a drink, need one real bad," Larry muttered as the frozen eyes glittered up at him.

They placed him gently on a bed. "Man, I never seen anything like that and if I never do again it'll be too soon!" Larry gazed in horror at the grotesque figure. "We better get on the blower. The nearest detachment is at Rainbow. What do I tell them?"

Pete was breathing heavily. "Just report that there has been an accident — a fatal one. You don't have to say anything else, the Mounties will come out. No sense broadcasting that it's murder. For all we know, it might even have been an accident. He could have been hit by something and wandered out in the snow and collapsed."

Larry went over to the radio set. "You know better than that. He was hit, all right, but by somebody, not something, and more than once. You take a look at the back of his head; it's like a hunk of frozen hamburger. What's the priority sign? Hell, I'll just tell everybody to stop transmitting because we've got an emergency." He began to speak into the microphone.

"I apologize for dragging you out of the sack, but I thought you all should know ..." Pete Berry looked at the men crowding the small diner, most of them heavy-eyed with sleep. "We found Mike White — he's dead. I don't know whether it was an accident or what. The police have been called and are on their way. That's all, fellows."

He left the men buzzing with excited conversation and crossed over to the toolpush's room, where Rod stood an uneasy vigil over the body.

"That's a good idea." He nodded approvingly at the blanket Rod had draped over the top bunk to conceal the appalling occupant of the lower.

"It was a matter of preserving my own sanity. That arm was getting to me."

"Larry went back to the rig?"

"Yes. He planned to bring the tour crew into the doghouse and tell them about ... our discovery, and then order them back to work."

"Of course. You know, that Jerry has shown an amazing amount of initiative. I never thought he had it in him, frankly. Sometimes the damnedest people surprise you and really come on strong. We will have to do some shuffling because of White's death. I was thinking I should suggest to Larry that we promote Jerry to derrick man on Jim Hunter's crew. What do you think?"

"I don't know whether Jerry would like the idea. He doesn't strike me as the type who wants any more responsibility than he has as an ordinary roughneck. Still, as you say, you never know. Maybe you should give him a shot at it. Jesus! What was that?"

A long, shuddering groan came softly from behind the grey blanket.

"Just old Mike starting to thaw a bit. I doubt if it's anything as dramatic as a resurrection. We better take a look."

"Be my guest."

Pete gingerly tugged at the blanket. "Yeah, that's what it is. His arm has dropped a bit and I guess it forced some air out of his lungs. I'll see if I can lower his arm." He bent over as he applied pressure. "Nope. We'll have to wait until he thaws a bit more. Hand me a towel — there's some hanging in the can — the ice has melted and he looks like he's sweating. I'll wipe him off." He straightened up with a grunt of satisfaction. "I managed to get his eyes closed. He looks a damn sight more presentable now."

"Jesus, but you're a callous bastard!"

Pete looked at him, then said quietly. "Not really, I was just doing what I could for him. It's not much, but at least he has a little more dignity now."

"You're right. I'm sorry. This whole thing has got me a bit unravelled. When do the Mounties get here?"

"Hard to tell. The detachment HQ at Rainbow told Quigley they have a cruiser in the general area. They said they could reach them by radio."

Three hours later, the black-and-white cruiser drove up to the camp. There were two Mounties, both young with broad, unlined faces. They looked like identical twins in their rakish fur hats, blue parkas, and broad yellow stripe running down the side of their dark-blue pant legs. The car doors slammed with the thin rattle of frozen metal. They strode across the hard-packed yard, pushed open the door to the corridor, and walked over to the toolpush's office.

"I'm Constable Harper and this is Constable Mirkowski. Are either of you gentlemen in charge here?"

Pete stood up and shook hands. "I am. Pete Berry — drilling superintendent for Cheyenne Drilling. This is Rod Fraser, the geologist on the well. Larry Quigley is the toolpush — he's down at the rig at the moment."

"Fine. We'll see Mr. Quigley later. Maybe you could just give us the particulars."

"As far as I know them." Pete launched into a summary of White's disappearance and grisly materialization. Harper listened intently, seldom interrupting, while the other Mountie unobtrusively took notes.

"Well, sir, that's an admirable account. Very helpful. Now if we could just see the … ah … body?"

"That's easy. It's on the bunk, right beside you."

"Really ..." The Mountie gulped audibly. "That's very convenient. Behind the blanket, I take it? Well, let's have a look at him."

They examined the corpse minutely, finally rolling it over to view the crushed skull. The body had thawed rapidly in the dry heat of the room and was now quite pliable. There was a large pinkish stain on the pillow where the head had rested. Harper looked at his companion and whistled softly. "Several blows. We can rule out accident, wouldn't you say? And he certainly didn't commit suicide!" He straightened up and faced Pete.

"Could you show us where you found him, sir?" He added in a tone of mild reproof, "You really shouldn't have moved him, you know. Still, I suppose it was the natural thing to do under the circumstances."

"We weren't about to leave him in the snow like a frozen side of beef, that's for sure!" Pete retorted angrily, but when he saw the Mountie was sympathetic, he calmed down. "Sorry, it's just that I knew White well and liked him. I didn't find him, one of our hands did — Jerry Fleming. He's standing by in the diner. If you like, we can get him and have him show you where and how he found the body."

"First-rate. Shall we go?"

It was dark by the time the two Mounties had finished with the snowbank where White had been found.

"Can you put us up for the night?" Harper asked Larry.

He shrugged. "We always seem to be able to find room somewhere. If we could do something with old Mike, Pete and I could find some other bunks and you could use my room."

"That's damn good of you and it would be mighty handy. It'll give us a place to question your men in private. As for the body, we'll have to find some way of moving it to Rainbow tomorrow. It will have to be flown to Edmonton for an autopsy. In the meantime ..." He hesitated, cleared his throat uneasily, and asked Larry, "Ah ... ah ... do you have a building where there is no heat?"

Larry stared at him incredulously. "You mean you want to put old Mike back in the deep-freeze? Like hell you are!"

Harper spoke soothingly. "It really doesn't matter to your friend; he's beyond that now. And, I don't like to mention this, but he has a long journey ahead of him and the process of decomposition isn't too dignified, you know. I'm sure, if he had a choice, he would rather make the trip safely frozen rather than be remembered by everyone up here for ... ah ... some of the unpleasant by-products of decomposition." He added gently, "We really have nothing in the way of facilities up here. It's the best way."

"Yeah. I guess so. There's a shed out back. For God's sake, we can't let anybody see us. The boys wouldn't understand."

That night they questioned everyone in the camp. They concentrated on the members of the crew that was on tour when White was killed.

Pete Berry and Rod Fraser sat in the diner, drinking cup after cup of coffee. Rod said, "I don't know when I wanted a drink so badly."

"I know what you mean. I've never cursed that old rule about no liquor on rigs more than I have today. Have some more coffee?"

"Thanks. They're really bearing down on the duty crew."

"Yeah, and I think they're making a mistake. That crew was making a trip, everybody would have his work cut out; if anybody left his station he'd be noticed right away. Well, they know what they're doing, I guess. Anyway, there's not a hell of a lot we can do about it." He dismissed it with a shrug. "You seem to be running into lots of excitement. How do you like the north?"

"How does anyone like the north? You let down your guard for a minute and it nails you to the cross. Machinery can't function, metal splinters like glass, and I get the feeling the whole damn place is just lying there in wait like a great patient beast. It's a cold-punished land and it wants revenge. And yet, in a crazy way, I'm beginning to like it. Maybe that means I'm getting bushed."

Pete nodded sympathetically. "I know how you feel. It's like being at war all the time. One thing about it, though, if you can hack it, there are some pretty good rewards to be picked up. The individual still has a chance up here, a chance to make a stake and" — he grinned — "get the hell and gone back to where it's warm!"

He looked thoughtfully at Rod. "You know something, Rod? You and I are in a unique position. We're both young, both in small companies — one-man operations, really — and the owners are about ready to step down. A couple of the right sort of breaks and we'd be locked in. I'm prepared to do any amount of work and tolerate any kind of conditions for a parlay like we have. Maybe we should form a partnership."

"Maybe we should at that." The suggestion had been thrown out casually, but as Rod thought about it he could see its advantages. "Deserves some thought at least, although I think I would be getting the best of it. You know the area, I don't, and you are a take-charge guy, I can see that. You really handled things today!"

Pete dismissed the compliment. "It's part of my job. This rig and the crew are my responsibility. If I couldn't handle them, I wouldn't be much of a drilling superintendent."

"How did you end up in the drilling business?"

"Simple. For the same reason I work for a small, one-man company. I don't have a college education; I quit school right after high-school graduation. It didn't take me long to find out that there is precious little room at the top for an eager young buck with no university degree. The drilling industry was one place where a guy with his eye on the ball could really make it, provided he didn't mind man-killing work, twenty-four-hour days, godawful working conditions, and could handle some of the damnedest misfits that ever trod this earth in human form.

That's why I chose drilling; it was the best route to where I want to go."

He leaned forward, eyes shining. "I don't plan on sticking to the drilling business. The real payoff's in your end — exploration. And the big plays — the elephants — the Arctic and the North Sea, hell, the whole world! If a guy could put together a big enough stake, he could operate anywhere. Start with a Canadian company and put it right in the international big time! That's where I'm going —" he broke off as the door opened and the Mounties walked in. "You two have been making quite a night of it. How about some coffee? Make yourself a lunch."

"Sounds great. My throat is raw as sandpaper from all that talking."

"I thought the police were supposed to do the listening, not the talking?"

Constable Harper nodded as he piled slices of beef on his plate. "That's the theory all right, but with this bunch it doesn't seem to work out that way. They're not what you'd call talkative, so we had to do a fair amount of digging."

"Did your spade work turn up anything interesting?"

"No comment, I'm afraid. Now, how do we move the body to Rainbow? As I explained to you, Mr. Berry, it's really better if it stays frozen. Sounds heartless, I know, but there it is."

"Wait just a moment and I'll get Fleming. He does practically all our driving and he was a pretty good friend of Mike's. He'd want to do whatever he could."

Jerry looked apprehensively around the diner. Pete talked to him quietly. "As Constable Harper says, it's better all around if Mike's body remains frozen. You understand that, don't you?" Jerry nodded miserably. It seemed all wrong somehow, but he knew that Mike wouldn't want to stink or anything like that on his last ride. He never wanted to bother anybody, old Mike didn't.

Pete continued, "We thought the best way might be to wrap the body, cover it all up, and place it in the open back of the pickup. That way, he ... would stay ... frozen. Jerry, I know it's a lot to ask, but could you drive him down?"

"Sure ... sure, I'll do it. I'll leave right now, might be better to do it while it's still dark."

"Good man!" Harper stood up. "When you get to Rainbow drive right to our office. They'll be ready for you and they'll take care of everything." He looked at Jerry and laid a comforting hand on his shoulder. "It really is the best way. You're doing one final service for your friend."

17

Sheila was worried about Mac; he looked so haggard and worn. He kept himself under control, and only the constant telephone calls to Joe Sanderson betrayed his tension; but she could see the strain was getting to him. There was nothing to distract him, no other business, no other exploratory plays, no deals — nothing. There was just that damn well. Thistle Oils existed only in Cheyenne Number Three, slashing through the unreceptive rock in a frozen hell. In Calgary they had just the daily drilling reports spluttering over the radio-telephone hookup. They were on full security now and their questions and answers were very guarded. Every mobile in the north would be listening, hoping to learn something about the well. In the past few days the reports were a lot more encouraging.

Sheila smiled at Mac. "Don't be so glum. They've been going great ever since they finished the fish."

Mac muttered, "I'm afraid to even think about it. Whoever dropped that wrench down the hole won't give up that easily. Our only hope is that he won't get a chance now that everybody knows what's going on."

Sheila shivered. "It's frightening to know there's somebody on the rig ready to kill, to do anything. Sometimes I wonder how Rod can stand it."

"Now there's an interesting young man. You like him a lot, don't you?"

She nodded. "Yes, very much."

"He looks to me like someone who finally is discovering what he wants to do. I think this oil game is for him, all of it. He sees the whole picture now, and he's learning how to do it." He looked anxiously at Sheila. "He'll become a driven man. I don't want you to get hurt."

"Mac, it's all right, honestly. I've got my eyes wide open. I'm not looking for the orange blossom bit; if it happens, and we both want it, wonderful! But I don't even know if I want to give that kind of a commitment. At this stage, all I know is that I like him." She laughed. "Anyway, if he heard this conversation, he'd catch the next plane back to Venezuela. It's okay, Mac, but I love you for worrying about me."

Rod called in that afternoon. For once, the connection was reasonably clear. He had been working on his notes for the proposal to the Montreal group. It was ready to be dictated and typed in final form. Mac bellowed into the speaker attachment, "Sheila's the only one who can do that, Rod. We can't trust anyone else with those figures."

Rod's voice sounded tired. "I know that. But she'll have to come up to Edmonton,

I don't like being even that far away from the well right now. I'll come on the morning flight. Ask her to meet me in the lobby of the MacDonald not later than two in the afternoon."

"Okay." Mac pressed the off button and spoke to Sheila without looking at her. "You better check the airbus schedule. I think there's one that leaves at eleven; it'll get you there in lots of time."

"Pretty, isn't it?" Rod grinned at her through cracked lips.

Sheila wanted to touch him, but she was afraid to. His face looked so sore! "It's going to be all right, isn't it, Rod? Mac talked to his doctor and he said you shouldn't have any permanent damage."

"That's what they tell me. In fact, as frostbite goes, I guess this is fairly mild. I'm healing, don't worry, my lips have stopped bleeding and my nose doesn't hurt anymore. Looks like hell, though, doesn't it?"

She shook her head. "It doesn't matter. All that's important is that you will get over it."

"I'll check in." He walked across the lobby, carrying a slim black attaché case that looked out of place with his heavy northern clothing.

Upstairs in the room he dictated steadily for two hours. He had his thoughts well organized and the figures carefully worked out. Finally, he stuffed his notes back into the briefcase and said, "That's it. There's nothing more I can tell those James Street boys."

"I'll type it tomorrow, back in Calgary. Is there any way you can check it?"

Rod shook his head. "I'm going back to Rainbow in the morning. Just let Mac read it over; he'll spot anything that may be out of line."

"It sounds awfully persuasive. Is it really that good?"

"If our well finds oil, it's the best deal in Canada. If the well is dry — forget it. The trick is to get the well tested before the sale. Then we know which way to jump. The Montreal boys are really getting in on the inside track, but there'll be so little time. They need to know all the factors. The only thing missing is one essential fact — whether there's oil or not."

Sheila moved toward the closet to get her coat. "I'll go out to the airport. There's a Calgary flight in an hour."

Rod turned her gently towards him. She came into his arms with a low moan. He could feel her body trembling against his; her lips were cool and exciting.

"Sheila." His voice was husky as he whispered into her hair. "Don't go back tonight; stay with me and go down in the morning. Please."

She drew back and looked at him, brown eyes steady. "Is that what you want, Rod?"

He kissed her. "More than anything."

She nibbled gently at his lips as their tongues flickered. She stopped suddenly and whispered, "Oh darling, your poor lips! I'm sorry."

"They're healed, I tell you. Even if they weren't, I love it."

"Let's not wait, Rod. I'm so ready for you, I'm almost ashamed."

She moved under him with rhythmic pulses of hips and rounded belly. Eyes closed, she breathed, "It feels so good; God, it feels good!"

Rod stroked deeper and faster until he exploded in exquisite release. Sheila gave a small, sharp cry. They lay together quietly; he could feel himself throbbing in her warm wetness. She opened her eyes and gently touched his discoloured nose. "Aren't bodies wonderful? And everybody has one!"

Rod said, "You climaxed, didn't you?"

She smiled contentedly. "With you."

He smiled. "And here I thought you were shy and inexperienced! Seems I underestimated you."

"No, you haven't. I'm really not that experienced, and I am shy. But not with you, it all just seems so natural."

"Let me look at you." Rod sat back on the bed and gazed down at her. She was beautiful in the warm lamplight, auburn hair spilling over the pillow, white skin glowing, the triangle of soft pubic hair, a lighter red, curling down the valley between her legs.

She opened her arms. "Don't stay out there. Come back where it's warm."

They lay in each other's arms all night making love with a deep sureness. Long before the winter dawn, Rod eased himself out of bed, flicked on the bathroom light, and began to shave. When he came out, freshly showered, Sheila could see he was preoccupied and tense. She had the sheet pulled up to her neck as she watched him start to dress.

"You're back at the well, aren't you darling?"

He grinned ruefully. "Yeah, I guess I am." His grin changed to a smile, so warm and tender it made her heart turn over. "I didn't think about it once all last night. It was beautiful."

"Yes, beautiful — in every way."

"You've really turned me around. I've got some thinking to do."

"Rod." She sat up, the sheet slipping to her waist, exposing her breasts. "Don't think about anything now. Give all your attention to the well, concentrate on it, please. It's so dangerous. I'd never forgive myself if something happened to you because you were thinking about me. There'll be lots of time afterwards. Rod, I couldn't bear to see you hurt anymore."

"Message received. I'll check out and catch my flight to Rainbow." He kissed her. "What will your roommate think about this — not coming home all night?"

She chuckled. "I don't know what she'll think, but she won't say anything. We don't invade each other's privacy, or exchange girlish confidences, that's why we get along so well." She pressed herself against him. "Be careful, my love, so careful! I want you to come back to me."

18

Frederick Lazarus glanced around at the echoing emptiness of the cavernous bar. He was well satisfied — apart from his own group, there were only two dark-suited businessmen slumped in their chairs in a far corner and a young couple self-consciously sipping nauseous-looking drinks. He turned back to his own table.

"I asked all of you to meet with me here since I anticipated that the bar would be virtually empty, and we also present to the outside world an innocuous picture of friends joining for a casual drink." His smooth voice held a note of complacency. It irritated George Mason, who stirred restlessly on the imitation-leather banquette.

"Very clever, I'm sure. Now, shall we get on with it?"

Frederick stared at him in mild surprise. Here was a change! Why, George was actually sitting upright and fidgeting with impatience. And there was something else — eyebrows, that was it! The old bastard had clipped that jungly growth. He looked almost human; this might create some unexpected problems. He smiled kindly at George. "I know, my old friend, how upsetting it must be for you to sit in a bar and toy with ginger ale. We shall, as you ask, get on with it and reduce your discomfort to a minimum."

"I'm all right," George growled, "or I would be if we could get down to business."

"Very well." Frederick looked quickly at Melinda and Kondar, cleared his throat, and began. "The fact of the matter is that they are making good progress at the well. Much too good for our purposes. The fishing job didn't hold them up for as long as we had planned. They had a good break in finding a fishing tool still at Rainbow and it certainly didn't take them long to clear the hole. What was down there anyway, Kondar?"

"Just an ordinary wrench from the toolhouse."

"I see — ingenious. Well, in any event, they fished it out and are going full steam ahead. What's more, the body of that unfortunate man has been discovered."

Melinda's glass made a sharp click as it struck the shiny tabletop. "That means the police, doesn't it? I don't like it, not one little bit."

"None of us do, my dear. It was unfortunate in the extreme. And the police have been called in; they were at the rig all day yesterday. But we must remember there is nothing to connect us with the rig in any way, absolutely nothing. But it does mean that we must stop playing around. We have to shut the rig down, once and for all. These fringe harassments are simply not enough."

"Amen to that. I have been of that opinion ever since we started." George leaned forward. "Kondar, what do you suggest?"

"The same thing as at our last meeting. They should be almost into that gas zone, if it's there. Once they hit gas much can go wrong."

"You mean, much will go wrong!" George grinned mirthlessly as he spoke. "I vote we have a shot at it."

Frederick said, "I agree. Kondar, you can get the message through?"

"I've been thinking about that and I've made some arrangements. There will simply be a message over the mobile that so-and-so's daughter was taken to the hospital with an attack of appendicitis and will be operated on as soon as possible. That will be the signal to put the plan into effect."

"It will be awfully risky, won't it?" Melinda tapped her cigarette nervously in the ashtray.

"Risky?" Kondar stared at her. "Certainly it's risky. For those at the rig, but that's a long way from here."

"I take it, then, we are agreed." Frederick signalled for the check.

"George, I don't feel like it. I just don't feel like it! Please!"

George smiled thinly as he cruelly tightened his grip on the firm flesh. She gasped, blinking back the tears.

"George, what have I done to deserve that? From you, of all people! Just tell me, what have I done?"

"I'm sorry, my dear." But his eyes and voice weren't sorry. "It's just that I have difficulty visualizing you ever not feeling like it. Except, of course, with me."

"Oh, stop it. Stop it, George. What's gotten into you? I just don't feel like the vibrator and the whole bit at this particular minute, that's all. It's that simple."

"It's Fraser, isn't it?" he persisted. "You're in love with him, aren't you? Aren't you?"

Melinda moved her shoulders helplessly. "I told you before, I'm not in love with anybody, not you, not Rod, not anybody. Can't you understand? I don't — repeat, don't — love anybody."

"You always were a superb actress. But you forget how well I know you. You fancy yourself in love with Fraser. But he won't be around long enough for you to love, you may be sure of that!" He paused. "Dammit, Melinda, I'm sorry, I didn't mean that." He looked at her beseechingly. "Couldn't you ever love me? Just a little bit, to start with?"

"George, please. Let's drop the subject." She stared at him in growing dismay. Damn men, anyhow. Why couldn't he have stayed the way he was — kind, quizzical, undemanding. If only he knew how ludicrous he was. With his clipped eyebrows; those stupid exercises he performed so sheepishly but so religiously, his pitiful attempts at lovemaking.

Her original pity for George had turned to actual revulsion whenever he touched her. How she hated it! His groping fingers, his sobbing breath, his frantic foreplay with the vibrator, his lonely little ejaculations that left her unmoved. And she knew he sensed her withdrawal. He was sliding into cruelty. That bite the other night, like the squeeze a few minutes ago: that wasn't passion; that was sadism. And it would get worse.

She buttoned her blouse. "George, I'm going out for a while, for a drive. I need to be alone. And I may go away for a few days. I don't know, it's all too much for me."

He looked at her with hooded eyes. "Very well, my dear. As you wish. I'll be waiting for you when you come back."

"No, please, George, not tonight. I have to pull myself together."

The pink Mustang blasted through the tunnel of the night. As always, the blinding speed of her passage calmed her and soon she was able to think rationally. George meant to have Rod killed. She was in a trap and she wanted out. But merely running away wasn't the solution. There was still no reason why even now she couldn't salvage everything. But it would have to be done in stages. Once the oil reservation was safely in their hands, she would sell her shares in the Golden Company and quietly disengage herself from George. Frederick would be eager to buy them; he'd love to have a lever over George. And Rod, what about Rod?

She thought of their last meeting. Her guard had been down, way down; she had told him so much about herself and yet he still wanted to marry her. That must mean something, that a man like Rod could want her as his wife even after he knew all those awful things about her. God, how she wished he were here beside her, right now. She would turn the car up the very next side road and they would make love — how they would make love!

Thinking of Rod had aroused her. She felt the hot metal taste of sex in her mouth. She wanted a man, now, tonight!

She glanced at the dashboard clock — twelve-thirty. The bar at the Red Door closed at one. She spun the wheel and gunned the Mustang back toward the city.

19

A Javelin — turbo-prop engines mounted on an old Convair airframe — replaced the slower DC-6B. There was no cargo on the flight but it had a full load of passengers. Melinda stared unseeing at the white landscape unfolding beneath the wing. Last night had convinced her; George was determined that Rod must be killed. Somehow in the last few weeks his reason had tipped over the edge. She knew he would soon succeed in tracing her, but she wasn't worried about her own safety. For the moment at least, she was a love-object for George, the touchstone of his strange resurrection. He wanted to own her. Goddamn men! How she hated that stupid look of male arrogance. Like Jerry the other night — he thought he had satisfied her! The fool!

She stood uncertainly in the narrow passageway as motors whined to a halt. She was the only woman passenger on the plane. She had dressed in the heaviest clothing she could find — a quilted ski jacket, ski pants, and fur-lined boots; they effectively blocked out the rounded charms of her body, but nothing short of the grave could blur her essential femaleness. She was the focus of hot male stares as she walked down the ramp into the blinding sunlight of the snow-draped Rainbow airport. One of the stewardesses had told her that she would have to charter a plane to reach the well. She walked into the wooden hangar and across the echoing cement floor to the door marked Northern Flying Services Ltd.

The canvas cover fitted snugly over the engine nacelle, and covered the propellor like an outsize gun case. Two figures worked on the plane, a small Cessna, painted light blue; one of the men switched off the portable heater while the other, who seemed to be in charge, unzipped the canvas, folded it neatly, and stowed it behind the rear seat. He turned to where she stood freezing in the still air. A broad smile split his round face, showing teeth so large and so astonishingly white that Melinda jumped back as though she were being attacked.

"Okay, miss. You can climb in now."

She swung aboard, nimble as a cat, while he shoved the seat forward and handed her both ends of the safety belt. He walked around the rear of the small craft and climbed through the other door. The engine sprang to life, the propellor a silver arc in the thin sunlight. He pushed the throttle forward and the metal skis squeaked across the hard snow. Several times he throttled back and jumped out to tug and heave at the tail section; it was the only way that the plane could be steered on the ground. It was hard work and Melinda wished she could help; she felt so useless just sitting there. Finally he had the plane turned into the wind at the end of the runway. He was breathing heavily as he settled back in his seat, spoke briefly into a hand mike, and gunned the motor.

When they reached cruising altitude and he had throttled back, they began a shouted conversation. He smiled at her as he pushed the fur-lined hood back from his head. His hair was black and coarse and stood straight up from his scalp in a short crewcut.

Melinda leaned forward. "I'm sorry, I didn't quite catch your name."

"Nick, Nick Kikooak, ma'am."

She struggled with the unfamiliar sounds, finally getting the name right. He grinned happily at her. "Good! That's it. No Eskimo could do it any better."

She looked at him in surprise. "Are you an Eskimo? I mean, you're so big and flying a plane ..." She raised a hand to her mouth. "Oh, I'm sorry, I didn't mean that the way it sounded."

"That's okay." He soothed her. "Nobody expects to find Eskimos piloting planes; most of my people stay close to the old way of life. But I am pure Eskimo. As for my size" — he grinned — "well, maybe there was a big Scottish trapper who took advantage of the old-fashioned Eskimo hospitality."

"May I smoke?"

"Sure. There's an ashtray right in front of you."

She smoked in silence, gazing at the forbidding country. So this was where Rod worked. God, it was awful. She glanced uneasily at the single propellor. "Have you ever made a forced landing? In winter like this?"

"Twice. It's never any fun but people can survive if they don't get too badly racked up in the crash. We carry everything we need — bedrolls, emergency rations, and radio."

She shivered inside her jacket. "Are we anywhere near the well?"

"We're getting close. They don't have a landing strip, but there's one at an abandoned well about ten miles away. We'll buzz the rig and somebody will drive over to get us. The Cheyenne rig is the farthest one from Rainbow." He grinned his huge grin. "That's how we navigate up here now — by the rigs. You can't miss them, night or day."

Looking ahead, Melinda saw what he meant. The rigs marched below them like giant signposts, each with its plume of billowing steam.

"There it is, sticking up right on the horizon." The giant Eskimo pointed a thick finger. As they flew on, Melinda picked out the triangular shape. It swam rapidly into focus until it was directly below them. Nick cut the power and put them into a tight diving turn. Melinda felt her stomach sink to her crotch and try to divide itself and slide down her legs. She grabbed the top of the instrument panel and hung on — hard. He raised the wing until they were once more on an even keel. She released her grip and sat back in her seat. This was fun! She liked this! She laughed aloud with sheer delight as he dipped the other wing and swung them into another gut-tightening turn.

They were very low, the drilling mast was just below their wing tip. Several figures stood in front of the camp, looking up at them; she could see they had their hands over their eyes to shield them from the sun's glare.

"They probably think we're scouts from some other oil company. I'll make a pass right over the camp." He swung wide, away from the rig, then turned and flew directly over the huts, rocking his wings form side to side.

"There's somebody heading for a car. They've got the message," he shouted as he pulled up in a steep climb.

"That was wonderful! I hate to stop. I'm going to learn to fly just as soon as I get back to Vancouver!" She exulted, cheeks flushed, green eyes glowing.

"It's the best thing in the world, that's all. There's nothing else that even comes close. I'll give you your first lesson on the way back."

They could see the car, a dark green toy, below them.

"This strip ain't used very often. I'll make a pass to see if it's safe to land."

Their shadow chased them across the bright ground. The Eskimo's deep-set eyes searched for any bumps or ruts hidden under the snow. "Looks okay," he laughed happily as he pulled back on the stick. "You really like it, don't you, ma'am?"

"Oh! I love it, and don't call me ma'am. My name is Melinda."

"Okay, Melinda. Hang tight, we're touching down and it might be a shade rough."

He pulled back hard on the wheel, deliberately stalling them a little high; he wanted to hit and stick. They landed hard, bounced once, and the skis rooster-tailed through the cover of loose snow. Nick increased the throttle before they came to a complete stop and taxied to a gap in the snowbank midway up the strip.

"This is where they'll come. We'll wait here."

Motor idling, propellor making lazy circles, they watched the car bounding toward them.

"You might as well stay in the plane. I'll tell them you want to talk to Mr. Fraser — Rod Fraser. They'll have to go back for him. You're sure you don't want to drive back and see him at the rig?"

"Quite sure. So long as the plane stays warm, I would much rather have him come here."

"Okay, I'll talk to them." He walked over to the car. "Do you have a geologist named Fraser at the rig?"

"Yeah, he's over at the rig now." Jerry rolled down the frosted window and looked up at the burly Eskimo.

"Good. There's a young lady in the plane who wants to see him. Could you ask him to come out? Tell him a Mrs. Mason wants to see him — she flew in from Vancouver, so it must be urgent."

"Okay." Jerry was impressed. "I'll tell him. You people be all right here?"

"Sure. We'll leave the motor turning over, it keeps the cabin warm enough."

Melinda stared at Rod's battered face.

"What in the world have they done to you, my poor darling?"

Rod laughed self-consciously. "It looks worse than it is. Just a touch of frostbite, I got a little careless. It'll pass. What in God's green world are you doing here? When Jerry told me a Mrs. Mason wanted to see me, I never would have believed him, except he's not smart enough to think up a lie."

Melinda leaned forward to touch her cigarette to the glowing end of the lighter. She exhaled, blowing smoke against the car's windshield. "I'm here to warn you."

"Warn me ... Against what?"

"Against my husband. He plans to have you killed."

"You've got to be kidding!"

"I'm deadly serious. And so is he. You must believe me. You remember I told you how indifferent he was, that he didn't care?"

"Yes."

"Well, I was wrong. He wants to possess me, not physically so much, but to control me, my emotions, my thoughts. I'm his new hobby, or something. He knows about you and me — it never was exactly a secret — and he's convinced I'm emotionally involved with you. You are the big stumbling block and you've got to go! It's that simple to him. He scares me."

"He scares me, too." Rod felt a quick stab of jealousy. "Is he making love to you?"

She shrugged. "Yes, in a sick sort of way. But what has that got to do with anything? I'm trying to make you see that your life is in danger, serious danger. I know him and right now that man is capable of anything. He is going to kill you, can't you understand?"

"With everything that's happened at the rig, I'm prepared to believe anything." He stared at her narrowly. "Is he behind all the trouble at the well?"

"I haven't the foggiest idea what you're talking about. George doesn't know anything about the oil business. The only business he understands is the buying and selling of stocks. No, it's purely personal. He has this idea that you and I are in love; it's an obsession with him. He threatened to kill you last night and he means it. Then he and I will live happily ever after. Oh, God, it's too much!" She stubbed her cigarette viciously. "What do you mean, trouble at the rig? What sort of trouble?"

"Oh, murder, fatal accidents, trifles of that sort. I appreciate your warning, but I don't know what in hell I can do about it. If somebody is really after me, sooner or later he is bound to get me. It's true of kings and presidents and it's true of just plain people. Anybody wants to kill you bad enough, he can do it."

"At least you can be on your guard. Please take me seriously, Rod."

"I do. If you tell me your husband is insane and determined to kill me, I believe you. I just don't know what to do about it, that's all. But I'll keep my eyes open, okay?"

"I guess so. But Rod, darling, do be careful?"

"Sure, and ... thank you! When Jerry told me you were here, I thought you must have come to give me an answer to that question, you know, that simple little question I asked you in Vancouver — How did it go? Yes, now I remember — will you marry me?"

She looked at him steadily, then held another cigarette while he pushed the lighter.

"You know something, Rod? You've changed. I don't think you really care anymore about my answer. You meant it when you asked me in Vancouver, and I'm grateful for that, but now you don't. You're only asking to be polite — gallant, or something."

"Do I get an answer?"

"You get an answer, but in my own way." She paused, staring blankly ahead, luminous eyes widening until they devoured her face. "After I'm through you will be cured, completely. Because of the way we talked the last time in Vancouver, you already know me better than anyone else. What you said then is very precious to me, to know that I could be ... what I am, and still a person like you could want to share his life with me. That means a lot to me, Rod, more than you could possibly know."

She was speaking slowly, her words dropping into the silence between them. "You know nothing of my childhood; I never thought I could tell anyone, but you must know ... so you will have no doubts ... and be free of Melinda. Rod ... I wasn't even toilet trained until I was seven —"

"Well, for Christ's sake, that's hardly enough to blight the rest of your days!"

She ignored his interruption and continued. "What's important is why I wasn't toilet trained until then. Over the years I've managed to fit together most of the pieces of my childhood. They don't make a pretty picture. When I was one year old, my mother deserted me and my older brother. She left a note saying that since my father was so cosy with his new woman she was leaving them a ready-made family.

"I never saw my mother again. Until I was ten I thought the other woman was my mother. I was so happy when I found out she wasn't. She had two kids of her own from some other arrangement, a boy and a girl, both older than my brother and me. She and dad drank all the time. When they weren't fighting with each other, they knocked us kids around. It was all right, I guess; I didn't know anything different. But it got worse, a lot worse, when my father decided he'd had a bellyful and pulled out. Just like that, he was gone. I'd be a little over three, I guess. Jean — that was her name — Jean was left on her own with the bottle and us kids. There was only one thing she wanted to do — drink — and only one way she could get the drink — men. They were at our place all the time: great, filthy brutes with big bellies, long underwear all yellow under the arms, hair sticking out all over them — like great smelly bears, they were.

"At first Jean would be all ladylike and genteel, hair combed, maybe a clean dress, a few petunias stuck in a jar, things like that. Then they'd get into the booze and the man would start grabbing at her and us kids would get shoved into a room and locked in. She left us in there while they roared and bellowed and screwed and fought and drank. Sometimes they kept it up for three or four days. Occasionally the door would open and they'd throw in some slices of bread and a pail of water, enough to keep us alive, but she wouldn't let us out, not until they had drunk themselves out and the man had left. Then we had to clean our mess. Sometimes the man she was with wouldn't let her open the door even to throw us some food; the smell got so bad. Then she'd wait until he was asleep and throw something in to us. I remember that; she didn't let us starve.

"I was ten the time one of them said, 'Don't put this little gal away just yet, Jean. Let her stay out and talk to us for a while.'

"My mother — Jean — screamed at him, 'You keep your hands off her, you ape!' But he grabbed me by the arm, holding me, and hit her until she was still. And he raped me there on the kitchen floor, it was linoleum — green with a brown pattern. His whole body was covered with great mats of black hair; he smelled of sweat and his breath stank. He hurt me, oh God, did he hurt me! My brother heard me screaming but he was locked in the room. After that I couldn't go into a trance any more. Before, I could always sort of dissociate myself, you know, from what was going on around me — sort of escape from everything — but not after that. I bled for three days but Mom was afraid to take me to a doctor."

Rod expelled his breath in a long sigh. She looked at him quickly. "Don't say anything! I don't want you to say anything. There's nothing that anybody can do or say that will do any good.

"The only reason I told you this about me is so you will realize why I can't love you or anyone. All the love was burned and scalded out of me before it ever had a chance to get started. I'm like a machine with the wires and fuses all blown and burnt. There's nothing there — maybe a bit of compassion — but love, no, not ever."

She touched his arm lightly. "Rod, my dear, there is simply no way. You need a woman who can return your love, not just a shell. The Melinda you once thought you loved didn't exist — she couldn't — and she never will."

"Just slow down a minute and let me get this straight. You're telling me that you don't love me — which I knew anyway — but also that you never can love me?"

"If you want it that bluntly, well, then — yes. But I am also telling you why. It isn't you, Rod; it's me — I can't."

"I can understand that, I guess. It's all right, Melinda, don't tear yourself apart, I'll be okay."

"Dear God, I hope so. I want you to be free. Maybe that's a sign of love, I don't know. For sure it's the first time I ever wanted a man to be free of me. Always I've wanted to keep them mounted on pins like an insect collection. But when Tom killed himself ... Oh, Rod, sometimes I'm so scared of what's happened to me!"

"Melinda, look, is there anything I can do ... anything?"

She shook her head. "Nothing. Except live your own life and fill it with good things. I'm an emotional cripple, I know that. But you're not. Every time I see you, you seem like a better, stronger person. I'd like to think that I was not a curse to every man who loved me. So stay away from me, Rod." She leaned across and brushed his blackened cheek with her lips. "Now, come and meet my Eskimo pilot."

Nick climbed out of the plane as they approached. He beamed widely at Rod. "I wonder, mister, if you could give me a hand. She's damn hard to swing in this loose snow." He looked at Rod ruefully. "I'm afraid I'll need some help at the other end of the strip, too. Have to turn her into the wind."

"Sure, sure, I'll give you a hand." He kissed Melinda lightly on the mouth. "I will miss you ... always. And I do understand."

When they were in the air, Nick pointed at the instruments. "This is the altimeter; it tells you how high we are. In a minute I want you to keep it right on the five thousand mark. This is your turn-and-bank indicator; just keep that little black ball centred between those two lines. This one is your artificial horizon — the straight line is the horizon and the little bar that moves, see" — he banked the plane slightly — "shows the position of the wings. Okay, take hold of the wheel. I have her trimmed for level flight, so you don't have to work at it."

Gingerly Melinda held the wheel, her eyes glued to the altimeter. The needle started to climb.

"You're hauling back on it; ease it forward."

She pushed forward and the needle dropped with alarming suddenness. She could feel the wind rushing by the wing. Desperately she pulled back.

"You're over-controlling, don't fight it. If you leave it alone, it will just about fly itself." His voice was calm and reassuring.

"Oh, damn. I'll never get it."

"Sure you will. See, it's settling down now. Take it easy, that's the most important thing."

Concentrating on the dial, moving the wheel in small, cautious jerks, she finally got the needle to remain reasonably steady. Slowly her confidence increased as they flew through the still air. He showed her how to turn the plane in slow, gentle banks. "Watch the horizon, keep the nose glued right on it. I'll handle the throttle. Good! That's it, you're getting it now."

Her shoulder and back muscles ached from the strain, her hands were moist on the wheel, but she had never enjoyed herself more.

He pointed down to the left. "Moose! Three of them, can you see them?"

"Where? I don't see anything."

"Down there, on that seismic trail. Let's go take a look. I've got it."

Gratefully she released the controls and leaned back in her seat. He cut the power and they swooped out of the sky on silent wings. Now she could see the moose:

brown dots rapidly growing and taking shape against the snow. They looked up as the motor cut in with a roar, flattening out from the dive a few feet above the trees. The animals floundered through the heavy snow, fleeing the thunder that pursued them down the narrow clearing. In a moment the Cessna had flashed over them as they galloped clumsily but with astonishing speed through the heavy drifts. Nick pulled up sharply, turned, and dived at them once again, this time from the front.

"They'll head into the woods now," he shouted. "There they go!"

She grabbed his arm. "Let's fly like this all the way back to Rainbow. Right over the trees and full throttle!"

He grinned at her, shaking his head. "You are a live one, aren't you? Afraid no can do, this Eskimo boy would get his licence lifted if anyone spotted us, and this old bucket of bolts would come unstuck if we kept pulling this much power. Hang on, we're going up!"

He hauled back on the wheel, smiling at her as she reacted to the sudden upward thrust.

"There she goes." They watched as the red disc of the sun briefly lit the western sky and dropped quickly from sight behind a range of low-lying hills. "We better turn on a few of our own lights." He reached forward and flipped three switches, lighting the instrument panel in a subdued green glow and the red and green riding lights on the wing tips.

She was momentarily frightened by the darkness that dropped on them so suddenly, blotting out the white world below. "Does this mean anything? I mean, are we equipped to fly at night?"

"Sure. And they've got runway lights at Rainbow. You can see them for miles. No problem."

She was sorry when they saw the long double row of lights. She turned to Nick; his heavy-featured face was intent in the cold light of the instrument panel. "Thanks to you, I know what I'm going to do with the next few years of my life."

He smiled broadly, not taking his eyes from the runway. "You mean flying? Yeah, that's for you, baby. You belong."

The hangar was empty and dark. Nick switched on some overhead lights and led the way to the office. "I'll log in the hours and get your suitcase and we'll get you settled at the hotel."

"I'll pay you now for the flight. How much is it?"

He looked embarrassed, almost shy. "Well, it's just over four hours at fifty an hour. Make it two hundred. Okay?"

"Very much okay. Not only did you find Rod for me, you opened up a whole new world." She counted out the notes and laid them on the desk. He stuffed them into a drawer as though anxious to be rid of them.

"I don't know if they have ever had a lady stay here before, but I'm sure we can get you a room."

The desk clerk, stubbled cheeks sagging around a cold cigar, a dirty woollen shirt bulging over his belt like untrimmed pie crust, looked at her dubiously.

"Come off it, Ned. The lady has got to stay somewhere. It's only for one night. Just give her a room, she won't bother anybody." Nick picked up her bag as he spoke, holding out his hand for the room key.

The desk clerk gave in grudgingly. "All right. Put her in 57. Turn left, then right and down at the end of the corridor."

Melinda surveyed the tiny room, which was almost entirely taken up with the double tier of bunks. She said cheerfully, "Not quite the Ritz, is it? But it will do, it will do beautifully. There's a bottle of very good Scotch in my suitcase. Can I buy you a drink?"

"You sure can." The Eskimo smiled easily, pulling off his parka.

She said, "That's beautiful, what's the fur?"

"The body part is plain old wolf. But the lining of the hood is wolverine. It's the only fur that doesn't frost up with your breath. *Prosit.*"

"That sounds funny." She giggled.

"What does?"

"That toast, coming from an Eskimo."

"Oh, we are a very adaptable lot, easygoing."

"So I see. How about another?"

"Great! But we'd better do something about feeding you. I'm not sure the management would take kindly to your presence in the dining hall. Why don't I nip down and bring us back a tray."

"Wonderful. While you're gone, maybe I can slip across the hall and use the facilities. I didn't see any marked LADIES."

He laughed. "You won't. Just be quick and lock the door. I'll be right back."

It must be the clear northern air, she thought, a little shocked at the quantity of food she had wolfed down. Long after she had finished, however, Nick continued to methodically chew his way through prodigious mounds of overdone beef and rubbery chicken. She watched him, fascinated.

"You like to eat."

He nodded amiably. "There's a lot of Eskimo to feed."

"Is there? Show me." She reached for him.

He held her hand and looked at her. Their eyes were level although he was sitting and she was on her feet, colour flaming in her cheeks, eyes bright with desire.

He carefully placed his tray on the floor and smiled. "You want to make love? That's good."

She pinched his flesh in wonder. "But you're not fat, at all. Your body is so hard and lean!"

"Everybody thinks my people are fat. I guess it's our round faces smiling out from fur-lined parkas. But our bodies aren't fat — they couldn't be, we're hunters and live on meat. But it's changing; the Eskimo is hanging around the white man's bars and eating his food and getting sloppy fat."

As he spoke, she ran her hands lightly over his wide brown body. His erection was huge; she had never seen anything like it. He tried to enter her gently; when he was less than halfway in he stopped and looked down at her anxiously. "Is it all right? Sometimes I hurt people."

She murmured through clenched teeth, "Give it to me, I want it!" She wrapped her legs around him and drew him all the way into her with one convulsive jerk. For a moment she couldn't move; she felt impaled, as though he had gone right up her throat. He waited, then began a gentle, deep stroking. Suddenly he withdrew and covered her with great sucking kisses. He raised his head and leaned back on his knees between her legs. She slowly raised her body until her body was level with the pulsing tip of his cock. He could see moisture glistening on the fine, black hair; the pale lips, twitching, beckoning. It was the single most erotic moment of his life. With a deep moan, he mounted her, hammering her into the mattress.

Afterwards, she looked up at him. "I feel all stretched and smashed in. I like it."

"You're beautiful! When you lift yourself like that — man, it's out of sight!"

"How would you like me to move up here and live with you for a while? You could teach me to fly and we could make love every night."

He shook his head gently. "It wouldn't work and you know it. Not that I wouldn't enjoy it, but," he added with a quick grin, "I don't think my wife and four little Eskimos at Tuk would be too happy about it."

"There is always that, isn't there? Where did you say this family was?"

He grinned. "Tuk — really Tuktoyaktuk." He pronounced each syllable. "It's a tiny Eskimo settlement on the edge of the Arctic sea. My home base, although I seem to spend less and less time there."

He began kissing her. "The first one was for me," he murmured against her skin, "but this one's for you, too." Her eyes were expressionless.

This time he took her standing up, one huge hand under her buttocks, her legs wrapped around him. As his breathing quickened, she rode his erection with deep, panting thrusts of her pelvis. Her head was thrown back, she was crying, mouthing half-heard obscenities, tiny fists beating against his chest. He spurted deep within her.

Slowly he opened his eyes and looked down at the perfect doll-like body that seemed to be growing out of his own. Tears glistened under her closed eyelids.

"You didn't make it, did you?" His voice was gentle.

Slowly she shook her head, her eyes still closed.

"You never do come, do you?" The opaque brown eyes were dark with sympathy.

"No. I can't fool you, can I? Funny, I can fool all the others. I'm all right until the man starts to reach his climax, then I'm turned off, just like there was a switch. I thought maybe with you, everything about you is so great, and I like you so much. But that switch is still there. Put me down, please."

She placed her lighter back on the rickety bedside table and touched his face tenderly. "Don't feel bad, Nick. I'm all right. I've learned how to live with it. I only miss the last part, I like everything that goes before. It feels like you're still in me; it'll feel that way for days." She grinned. "You didn't know you were coming back to Vancouver with me, did you? Even if it's only the feeling of you inside me."

He looked up at her from the bed. "And if I do come to Vancouver sometime, will you see me?"

"Of course. Any time. It's been wild — the best ever, for me. Honestly."

He rolled easily to his feet and started to dress. "I've got a charter to Norman Wells first thing in the morning."

He paused for a moment, his hand on the doorknob. "That guy up at the rig — Fraser. He mean anything to you?"

Drowsily, she shook her head. "He's a closed chapter. That's the story of my life, a book full of closed chapters. But I opened up a new one today, on our flight. I'll sleep now and dream of all the new and shiny airplanes I'm going to fly. Goodnight, my Eskimo lover."

They were waiting for her. Frederick, always the gentleman, rose to his feet as she stood in the entry of the apartment. "My dear, we were so concerned over you." He spoke with a note of mild reproach. "You really shouldn't have gone off like that, without letting us know."

Kondar leaned forward, black eyes smouldering. "Damn it, Lazarus, why do you always insist on behaving as though we were at some goddamn pink tea. All right, Melinda, how much did you tell him? We might as well know the worst."

She gave him a long level stare. Her heart was in her throat, choking her, but when she spoke she was relieved that her voice sounded calm. She turned and looked directly at George. "I went up there to tell Rod Fraser I had no intention of leaving you to marry him. The last time I met him he was so insistent I really didn't know what he might do next." She forced herself to smile at George. "I wanted him out of my life, completely. So I flew up and told him, it's that simple."

She watched George's face and knew he wanted to believe her. He said mildly, "I must say you are very impetuous, my dear. But in a good cause, a very good cause. You are quite sure he doesn't connect you with what's going on at the rig?"

"Absolutely. As far as he's concerned, you're my husband, nothing more. He's jealous, not suspicious."

Frederick let out his breath in a long sigh. "Well, that's very satisfactory, I must say. I feel I should congratulate you, my dear George. You never cease to surprise me. Kondar, I have the distinct impression we are rather superfluous here. Shall we leave and allow our two good friends to enjoy their reunion?"

Kondar muttered unhappily as they waited for the elevator. "I still don't like it. She wouldn't go to all that trouble just to tell a guy she wasn't going to marry him."

"My dear Podoroff, you just have no understanding of these affairs of the heart. Obviously she is anxious to start a new life with Mason with a clean slate."

"That slate will take some cleaning!"

As soon as the door closed behind them George held her close. She felt him trembling. "I was so worried! I was afraid you had fled to Fraser and that you would tell him everything. You know something? The thought of losing you was much more painful than the prospect of being discovered — of jail, even!"

She stood within his embrace and smiled up at him. How she would have loved to tell him that last night she had been with an Eskimo, a real man, and that she still throbbed with the pain of it. But not yet; now she must smile at him, fondle him. "I'm a bit travel-stained, I'm afraid. Wait till I change into something more comfortable."

20

"Man, that's what I call making hole." Quigley grunted with satisfaction as he studied the dials. "Four hundred feet a day for the last three days and it looks like we'll do it again today. That's living, ain't it?"

The others grinned back at him. There was a new atmosphere around the rig. Even the shock of White's murder was blurred by the exhilaration of a smooth-running job. The two Mounties still showed up occasionally and asked a few questions, but they didn't seem to be getting anywhere. Meanwhile, they were knocking off four hundred feet a day and life was good.

"There's nothing like that good old Simpson shale! It's just like drilling through smooth cream," Luke said, teeth gleaming whitely against his brown face. "You got any idea how long we'll be in the shale, Rod?"

"Thank you, my friend, for asking the one question I can answer with some hope of being right. Tim Murphy — you know him?"

Larry interjected briefly, "Heard of him — he's a wheel over at Inter-Continental, ain't he?"

"Yeah, he's their top geologist. Anyway, back in Calgary he told me the Simpson shale is sixteen hundred feet thick around here. He also told me when you spot the Jean Marie marker you know you're right on top of the shale. We picked up the Jean Marie right at 2,650 — just before we had the fishing job. So this is our fourth day in the Simpson and we've been averaging four hundred feet a day. We should come out of it before your tour is over, Luke."

Luke nodded. "The way she's cutting we should make it, easy."

"Then things start to get interesting." Larry looked at Rod. "We tap into some gas, don't we?"

"Probably. God, I wish we knew more. Everybody is so damned secretive around here; they won't even tell you if the sun is shining. Flying blind, that's what it amounts to."

"Yeah, a little bit of straight dope would sure help. We should get ready for high-pressure gas, though. How about the mud, do we weight up?"

Pete Berry spoke for the first time. "I don't see why, Larry. We must be carrying ten pounds per gallon right now. Remember our mud got clobbered pretty good in that fishing job and it will have picked up weight going through the shale. Ten-pound mud should hold anything, and every time we make it heavier we slow down our drilling. Remember, we've got a deadline. But it's up to you."

Larry considered. "You're probably right, but I hate to take chances with that stuff. I think we should dump in some barites. How about you, Luke?"

"Near as I can figure, the mud is running around nine and three-quarter pounds right now. Let's take it up to ten point five. That should hold anything and it won't slow us down enough to notice."

"Sounds good to me. Get somebody onto it, will you, Luke?" Larry turned to Rod. "Is that gas likely to be sour?"

Rod shrugged. "Search me. Slave Point gas normally is sweet, but it can be sour. We'll just have to wait and see."

"That's just great, just great!" Larry grunted as he thought of the powder keg they were playing with. It was bad enough to bore into a formation where the volatile, inflammable gas was trapped under unbelievably high pressure, but if it was sour to boot — if it contained hydrogen sulphide, the smallest trace of which could kill a man in seconds — sweet mother of God! There was the devil's own brew waiting for them down there!

Luke was thinking furiously as he walked onto the rig floor. This was it! Soon the beast would show its claws, and those Vancouver bastards expected him to tie a can to its tail! If he was ever going to blow this operation out of the tub, the time to do it was when they hit the Slave Point. He shivered. Did they realize what they were asking him to do? They were nice and safe, a thousand miles and a mountain range away, but he was right on top of the fucking horror. He didn't have to do anything; he could leave the beast in its cage. He'd be safe; they would never hang White's murder on him. But he would also be broke. If he could keep them from reaching the muskeg zone before the blasted sale, he'd be rich, richer than he had ever dreamed possible. Rich enough to leave this godforsaken place, get free of the smell of diesel, and surround himself with pale, soft-breasted blondes and barrels of rye whisky.

The first thing he'd do was get a room in some classy hotel where it was warm, and buy himself four blondes. He'd make them lie in a circle, bare-assed naked, and he'd stand in the centre of that circle and jack off. He'd turn slow, real slow, and lay his hot seed on all four white bellies. Then he'd get on with the fucking!

He felt himself swelling. Son of a bitch, if that wasn't something! Standing on the floor of a godforsaken rig at forty-five below zero with a hard on. He shook his head. He'd better forget those ideas and start figuring out some way of lighting the torch without burning himself to a crisp.

Timing, that was it! There was a way! If they hit the Slave Point before his tour was over, he could set the stage for the next crew, so they would blow the well like pulling a cork out of a bottle. And he would be snug and safe in his own bunk. He grinned as the pieces fell into place. What crew took over from him? Jim Hunter's crew; yeah, that's right. Too bad, Jim; I'm really sorry, fellows, but better you than me, much better! Everything depended on reaching the Slave Point by not later than eleven tonight. What time was it now? Seven-thirty; okay, we've got three-and-a-half hours, no more.

He walked over to the controls. "Okay, men, let's lean into it!"

Forty-five hundred feet below, the whirling bit sliced through the black shale. They were using a jet bit with three openings through which the mud was propelled at high velocity, driving against the smooth shale to soften it for the cutting edges. Fifty feet below the turning bit, natural gas pressed against the impervious caprock at a pressure of thirty-five hundred pounds on every square inch of unyielding stone. As Larry had feared, it was sour; poisonous hydrogen sulphide made up a lethal five per cent of its volume. Steadily the bit churned its way toward this hellish force while Luke on the derrick floor pondered his plan. It took courage to even think of twisting the tail of this tiger, but he had passed the stage of initial shock and was now busily fitting the details into place.

The idea was simple, but the slightest miscalculation and it would be his crew, not Hunter's, that would go into orbit. The thick mud filled the hole behind the bit in a column forty-five hundred feet high; this made a hydrostatic head powerful enough to hold the gas — unless something were done to disturb the balance. And disturb the balance was precisely what Luke intended to do. As soon as they hit the gas he would call for a change of bits and haul the drill pipe out of the hole as fast as his crew could break out the string. The ascending pipe would swab the hole like a giant pump, sucking the gas behind it. Every time they removed a string of pipe the driller was supposed to pump in mud to replace it and to maintain the hydrostatic head. By forgetting to do this a few times he could lighten the combined weight of the drill pipe and mud. At some point the balance would shift and the gas would blow free.

The hours crept on; every fifteen minutes he left the floor to check the mud tanks. At nine o'clock Rod walked onto the rig floor. He shouted at Luke over the roar of the motors.

"We must be damn close to Slave Point. Did you weight up? That could be the grandfather of all volcanoes down there."

Luke nodded. "I know it. We're at ten point five. I've been checking the mud but so far no bubbles. Have you looked at the samples?"

"Yeah, still black shale. The Slave is white limestone, easy to pick out. If you're checking for bubbles, you'll spot it before I do."

At ten forty-five Luke saw the telltale bubbles breaking the sluggish surface of the heavy mud. Right on schedule! He took a deep breath; he could feel the sweat prickling the hairs of his armpits, and running down the palms of his hands.

Rod watched a roughneck dump a sample from the shale-shaker. He looked up at Luke. "That's limestone, all right. We're in the Slave Point, did you see any gas bubbles?"

Luke nodded. "Yeah. Everything's right on target so far. The bit's worn out, I've got to change it."

He shouted at the crew. "Time to change the bit. Let's show some hustle. Old Jim gets pissed off when we leave him with too much of a trip to finish! We start out in ten minutes, as soon as I check out the BOPs."

Down at ground level he walked to the master switch that controlled the entire blow-out system. It was on a plywood panel mounted between the light-plant hut and the mud tank. He pulled it to the off position and opened a valve to bleed out any back pressure. Now there would be a big fat nothing when the panic-stricken driller hit the switch on the rig floor. Just so long as that panic-stricken driller wasn't Luke Willard!

He used the brake pedal sparingly and let the steel cables run swiftly over the crown block, grinning encouragingly at his crew toiling with the tongs and chains, while his blood ran cold. He was walking a tightrope and he knew it. As well as almost a mile of drill pipe, there were eighteen drill collars placed directly over the bit. They provided the weight to force the bit into the resisting ground — each collar was twenty-five hundred pounds of solid metal, thirty feet long. Luke figured if all the collars were still in the hole there would be too much weight to be blown out by the deadly gas bubble he was so carefully building. But once old Hunter broke out the top few collars, good-bye world! He would leave two stands of drill pipe plus all the collars in the hole; that should give him plenty of time to be long gone before it went up.

He counted the stands carefully as they were racked against the derrick. He looked at his watch; eleven-forty — perfect! They could break out one more stand.

"All right, boys, leave it on the slips. Time to sign out."

He hurried into the doghouse, where the new crew was changing into their heavy work clothes. Quickly he stepped out of his stained work parka and insulated outer pants and bent over the steel table to write up the log of his tour.

"She's all yours, Jim. We're just about out of the hole, two strings and then the collars. Nothing unusual."

"Good. At least we won't have to freeze our butts off making both legs on the trip. I know some guys who would have kept on turning a drill bit until their tour was over. I appreciate that, Luke."

"Forget it. We ran into some gas, but with that ten point five mud she's not kicking back." He left the doghouse and walked quickly up the road to the camp.

Rod turned to Jim. "Look, your crew will have their hands full this tour with that gas. I know what formation we're in, so there's no panic about the samples. I'll collect my own."

"Thanks, Rod. Let's hit it, gang."

The new crew took their places on the derrick floor. All except Jerry Fleming, who had to climb ninety feet up the ladder to his tiny platform. He hated it; the ladder was outside the canvas cover, which swayed and ballooned against him as he climbed. He didn't dare look down and it wasn't any better on the narrow platform. He wished fervently that he had been left at peace in the anonymous security of a floorman. Tomorrow he would speak to Larry. This was his third tour as a derrick-man, they couldn't say he hadn't given it a fair try.

Below, Jim Hunter eased off the brake handle, the cables took up the strain of the pipe, the floormen removed the slips, and the interrupted trip continued. They had broken out six collars when he saw the heavy string move, heard the first telltale hiss of escaping gas, and saw the first gobbets of mud spurting from the hole. The collars rose slowly at first, riding their column of gas like a spaceship in the first reluctant stage of its flight. Eyes dilating with terror, Jim Hunter reached behind and to his left, grabbing at the lever by the doghouse door. He jerked it down; it came easily — too easily. The valves weren't closing; she was going up!

His hoarse shout was lost in the increasing hiss of gas; he bolted for the doghouse. Now the gas pressed upward with growing force. It had slammed shut the floating valve in the jet bit, making a solid wall against which it lifted slowly, remorselessly. The string of drill collars picked up speed, surging out of the hole. The mounting pressure forced the gas to escape around the string, pumping out of the hole with great pulsing gouts of mud and a shifting, dancing veil of vapour.

The floormen, ears blasted with the dreadful hissing roar, deserted their tongs and chains and ran to the crude doors cut into the plywood sides. Scrambling, all four of them arrived at the same door; a frantic wrench and it came half off its hinges. Impelled by the awful sounds behind them, they crowded through and dropped twenty feet to the frozen ground. They landed running, oblivious to the injuries caused by the fall. One of them sprained both ankles, another broke two ribs, but all of them fled across the hard-packed snow with terror snapping at their heels.

Ninety feet above the drill floor, Jerry Fleming heard the surging hiss; the last string of the heavy collars had been difficult to handle; he was sweating with the strain of guiding it into its slot. He stared down with wide unbelieving eyes at the deserted drawworks, the pipe swaying out of the hole like a monstrous snake, the slack cables and the waterfall of mud, pumping and pulsing — a severed artery in the earth, bleeding grey blood.

He fought his way through the canvas opening to the escape line. He had always viewed this contraption with profound distrust: a steel cable that looped its way to the ground a hundred yards from the rig, two sets of wheels dangling an iron T between them, and a bar that was supposed to act as a brake. The thought of sitting down on the T-bar and casting off had haunted Jerry's dreams. Now he was faced with it, except that the cable was so coated and encrusted with ice that the wheels were rigidly locked in place. He couldn't budge them. He felt an odd sense of relief that he couldn't use the escape mechanism; the decision was out of his hands. He began to clamber down the ladder, clawing at the canvas as it flapped against him.

Rod Fraser was standing by the shale-shaker digging his trowel into the mound of rock fragments when he heard the motors begin their wild pounding race to destruction. Then came the shrill scream of escaping gas. She was going up! He dropped his trowel and sample bags and floundered through the soft snow, sinking to his knees at every second step. Hampered by his heavy clothing, he struggled clumsily to his feet, only to fall once again. The explosion would come at any moment now.

Time stood still. The same thought kept spinning around in his head, like a revolving neon sign. "If I had kept my mouth shut in Venezuela, I wouldn't be in this fix ..."

The choking, deadly gas was trapped by the shroud. Soon it filled the entire working area; it drifted over the motor compartment and was sucked into the diesel engines. To them it was a fuel, an intoxicating fuel that sent them wildly out of control. The drill collars arched upward — a string of iron sausages — and crashed through the heavy crown block at the top of the derrick, smashing and splintering solid metal, dropping the enormous pulley one hundred and twenty feet to the floor below. As metal struck metal, sparks crackled and ignited the hellish fog. The "devil's lighter" flamed against the northern sky.

The explosion came before the first flicker of fire; an appalling concussion of force which split the air, ripped the canvas shroud like tissue paper, shifted and bent the derrick on its base, and pulverized windows in the distant camp. It came as Jerry was on the sixth rung from the top. It picked him up and threw him, arms and legs outflung, spreadeagled in a pathetic attempt to find support in the riven air, to land in a broken, crumpled heap three hundred feet away.

It caught Jim Hunter near the exit door of the doghouse and flung him against the steel lockers, splitting his head with a soggy thump. It threw Rod off his feet and flattened him in the snow. He lay there for a moment while the shock wave washed over him, then he stumbled upright and continued his shambling run.

A gust of wind, stepchild of the explosion, tore at the long plume of gas cascading from the rig and blew it groundwards in a capricious sweep. It settled over one of the fleeing roughnecks, the slowest one, and his straining lungs sucked in the deadly vapour. Veins bursting, he fell to the ground, writhed once, and lay still, staring up at the night sky with sightless red eyes.

Luke had locked the door and crawled under the bunk, stretched out flat on the cold floor. He felt the building shake, felt it strain upwards, and settle back; he heard the tinkle of glass as it shattered and fell into the room. Next came an onrushing torrent of sound, smashing at his eardrums, pounding him into the floorboards. Then it passed and all was still, except for a strange trembling and a distant, roaring hiss. He crawled out from under the bed and got the door open before he vomited with convulsive retches onto the wooden floor of the hallway.

Larry was pouring a cup of coffee in the diner. The pot was torn from his grasp and smashed against the wall, coffee running down the white surface in slow brown streams. The cup flew to the ceiling and stuck there, embedded in the plywood. He felt himself sliding helplessly on his back over the polished formica tabletop to land with a crash on the floor. Dazed, he sat still for a moment until the sickening realization washed over him. Blowout! He ran for the door.

The corridor was filling with startled, frightened men. As the initial shock wore off, they found their voices with an increasing babel of sound. They streamed toward the door to stand dumbfounded in the eerie, flickering light.

It illuminated two forms stumbling up the road, two more lying crumpled and dark against the snow, and the black curve of the drill collars. The flame — dark orange edged with an oily, dark band and a crown of white vapour — jetted three hundred feet into the air. Already the metal framework of the derrick had an incandescent glow. Soon the A-frame supporting the base would melt and the entire structure would crumple into the frame. The heat blasted at their faces as they watched.

With an oath, Larry ran to the first figure, calling to the crowd, "Lend a hand, grab that other one!" Supporting the tottering roughneck, he said, "Easy, take it easy, you're all right, you're safe now. You're not burnt." Leaning back, he searched the other's face. "It's you, Timmins. Well, you made it. How about the others?"

Sobbing, his voice raw and harsh in his throat, Timmins said, "Don't know. I just ran as fast as I could. There wasn't any time; she just went. My chest hurts ... hurts like hell."

Signalling two men to lead Timmins into the shattered camp, Larry turned to the second survivor. He was another roughneck, Pete Visic, and he could barely stand. Larry took one quick, searching look at his face; the man was in shock, there was nothing to be learned from him.

Pete spoke at his elbow. "She's going straight up. Thank God it's not shooting out in all directions. We should be able to get fairly close. Pick two more men and let's see if there is anything we can do for those other poor bastards."

Quigley nodded briskly. "Right. First, let's find out who's missing." He glanced rapidly over the shifting crowd. "Fraser. He must be down there!"

"That figures. He would want to be there when they hit the Slave Point."

"They sure as hell hit it!" Larry's voice was bitter.

"Who else is missing?"

"All the rest of the crew. Jim Hunter — the driller, Jerry Fleming, and Osbrowski. Two of them are out there, the poor bastards." He pointed to the inert forms. "Okay, boys, first we find out how bad we're hurt. Luke," he jerked his head at Willard, "I want you and O'Leary to come with Pete and me. Don't try and be bloody heroes, there's nobody still alive in there. Keep out of the path of that derrick in case she falls."

The fierce heat fanned out at them, keeping them back. They managed to retrieve Osbrowski's body, but Jerry Fleming was just beyond their reach. The snow was starting to melt and wisps of steam curled upward from his motionless form. Pete peered at him, shielding his face and eyes from the orange glare. "There's not much we can do for him, anyway, the poor little bugger."

Rod had worked his way in a wide circle, walking the circumference of bearable heat. Cushioned by the loose snow, he had escaped injury, but he was in the early stages of shock. He forced one leg to follow the other, and fought down an insane impulse to rush back to the flaming rig.

Pete was the first to spot him. "There's somebody! Over there — by the trees! Christ, he's going to fall." Shouting encouragement, Pete floundered through the snow.

"Rod! Thank God it's you. For a moment I thought I had lost a partner. Come on, fella, we'll get you out of this."

21

Joe Sanderson slumped heavily on the side of the bed. He replaced the telephone receiver and looked with unseeing eyes at the sleeping form of his wife, an indistinct rounded shape in the darkened room. He shook his head, trying to absorb the news and gear himself to the things that must be done.

Number Three in flames, three of his men killed! Jim Hunter — one of his oldest and best employees — they hadn't found his body yet but, as Pete said, he had to be dead. He remembered Fleming, a funny little guy, always seemed to be looking for a corner to hide in. He didn't know the third one — Osbrowski — he had just joined the crew at Number Three. Joe thought of the painful phone calls it was his duty to make. God! There was Mac; he had forgotten about him. Poor devil! His dreams of one final coup had gone up in flames along with the rig. Well, he'd better get with it. Sighing gustily, he padded downstairs.

He poured himself a stiff drink of Scotch at the bar in his panelled study and picked up the telephone.

With the advancing years, Mac had become a very light sleeper. He scooped up the receiver on the second ring, automatically looking at the luminous dial of his alarm clock. Two forty-five in the morning — it was the well — it had to be — what the devil had gone wrong now? He cleared his throat and rasped a foggy hello.

"I'm afraid I have bad news, Mac. Very bad news. The rig is on fire, the well has blown out, and three men are dead. Your fellow Fraser had a close call but he's okay. It's a bad one."

A strange calm descended on Mac as he listened. Well, that was that; it was out of his hands now. There was nothing more he could do, except to co-operate with Joe and help bring the situation under control. They would never complete the well now. He said quietly, "It's a blow, all right. But I feel a lot worse about those men. Have you called anyone else?"

"No. As soon as we hang up, I'll call the insurance company and the Energy Conservation Board. After that I have to try to locate the families of the dead men. I'm not looking forward to that. Then I'm going up to the rig."

"I'm going with you. Look, I'll call Sheila, then wake up my Vancouver partners and give them the bad news. Let's meet at your office as soon as possible; we'll operate from there."

"Okay. I should be there in about an hour. The press boys will be onto the story any minute now so we'll be hearing from them."

Mac dialled as soon as Joe had hung up. "Sheila, I'm sorry to have to call you at this hour, but something has happened."

"That's all right, Mac, don't apologize. Just tell me what it is, quickly."

"It's the well, there's bad trouble, it's out of control. Your Rod is all right. He had a close call, apparently, but he escaped."

Sheila felt the relief wash over her. Rod was safe! So long as she knew that, she could face anything. Briskly, she agreed to meet them at the office.

Five hours later, a winter sun bathing Calgary's skyline in pale golden light, Joe Sanderson hung up the phone and turned to his companions. "That wraps up all we can do at this end. Everybody that should be notified has been. I've arranged for a Cessna 310 — wheels up at ten o'clock. Sheila, there won't be much to do down here, anything that comes up can be handled out of our Edmonton office. But you could be mighty useful at the well, there will be so many things to arrange for, to expedite and coordinate. It will be rough, but it sure won't be dull. Do you think you could come?"

"Yes, of course. I'll go pack. Where do we meet?"

"It would be quicker if we all made our way independently to the airport. Let's be at the executive aircraft terminal at nine forty-five. Your taxi driver will know how to find it."

Late in the afternoon of the same day, George Mason gave a triumphant shout and slammed a copy of the *Vancouver Sun* down on the coffee table. He looked at Melinda.

"They really blew her out of the water this time! Well, that should write finis to their chances of reaching the muskeg. All we have to do now is sit back and wait for a whole river of oil to fall in our lap. We're rich, my dear!"

"I'll believe that when Golden Oils owns the reservation, not before."

"It will, my dear, it will. There's no one who can bid against us." He reread the paper hungrily.

"Damn! Your friend Fraser appears to have survived. That's unfortunate, most unfortunate."

"Don't say that. You know perfectly well I went up there and told him it was all over between us. You can forget him; he means nothing to me, nothing!"

"Maybe. But he has made love to you. If I had my way, every man who has ever touched you would be struck dead — obliterated!"

"Oh George. You can't undo the past." She smiled wickedly. "Besides, if you set out to kill every man who has made love to me, you'd have to hire yourself a battalion of killers!" She paused as she saw the stricken look on his face. "I'm sorry, George, truly sorry. I didn't mean to hurt you. It's just that it's all so hopeless when you get in this mood. There's nothing we can do about my past, or yours either, for that matter. We simply must learn to forget what is gone and look to the future."

That night she, outwardly all feminine willingness and desire, contracted herself so that George, groan and strain and sweat as he might, could not enter her. Afterwards, she giggled helplessly into her pillow as she listened to his restless pacing across the living-room floor.

22

The twin-engined Cessna bucked and shuddered in the troubled air. The pilot fought the wheel and rode the rudder pedals in a vain attempt to keep the plane steady.

Clinging desperately to their seats, first thrown against their safety belts and then slammed deep into the cushions, his three passengers squinted at the brilliant light. Joe was the first to find his voice. "That's a pretty fair bonfire. They're burning up enough gas to heat a whole damn city!"

Mac shouted, "I'd say it's making about ten million cubic feet a day, but look at the steam coming off the top. There's a lot of water vapour mixed in with it."

"I hate to see gas wasted like that. In a few years they'll be begging for it down south."

Mac nodded. "You're right, of course. But I can't see anybody building a gas pipeline into this area for at least another five years, and until they do, it's just a dangerous nuisance. It won't do us any good, anyway, we can't last out the five years," he concluded gloomily.

Below them, the searing heat of the fire had melted the snow in an even, brown circle seven hundred feet across. They could see frenzied activity; the area around the camp was jammed with trucks, pickups, and a few muddy sedans. A low-boy trailer laboured up the road burdened with a D-8 Caterpillar tractor. Farther back, another tractor-trailer rig carried mobile housing units. Already three of the portable buildings had been hastily assembled to house the extra personnel.

The heat boomed in waves of sound against the cabin. The pilot turned to Joe, who was beside him. "There's a car pulling out from the camp. It'll be our ride back from the strip. Have you seen enough?"

"More than enough. Put her down."

Two other planes — a sturdy Beaver and its big brother, the Otter — were parked on the strip as the Cessna touched down. The pilot identified them immediately. "The Beaver is owned by the Mounties, and the Otter is a charter job out of Edmonton."

Sheila gasped with the numbing shock of the cold as she stepped on the wing. She peered anxiously at the heavily clad, hooded figure advancing from the car. She climbed down the two steps projecting from the side of the plane and walked uncertainly toward him. Yes, it was Rod! She started to run. He opened his arms and held her, tight.

The plane took off on its return trip to Calgary as they piled into the car. Sheila sat beside Rod in front, with Mac and Joe in the rear.

Mac said quietly, "Maybe you could bring us up to date, Rod."

"Yes, sir. I don't know how much Pete told you. She blew just after the graveyard tour came on, about twenty minutes after midnight. So far we have recovered two bodies, Osbrowski and Jerry Fleming —." He hesitated as he mentioned Jerry's name, then continued, "Jerry landed too close to the fire so it took us a while, but we rigged up a protective shield and finally managed to hook onto his clothing with a long pole and pull him out. Jim Hunter is still missing but one of the roughnecks who escaped said he saw him running into the doghouse just before the explosion. He would still have been inside when the blast came. Anyway, I'm afraid all that's left of him now will be ashes. The doghouse is red-hot all over. The derrick is about ready to let go, the fire has melted the A-frame.

"The insurance boys are here; they flew in on that Otter. We had a council of war and, for the moment at least, have decided to bring it under control ourselves. With your approval, of course." He looked in the rear-view mirror at Joe, who nodded. "There was some thought at first that maybe we should get Red Adair's outfit, but I knew he and all his top hands have been over in Libya for the past two months with a real bad one. Anyway, the insurance boys okayed our decision and they're the ones who are picking up the tab right now."

"Thank God for that!" Joe interjected.

"Amen. We've been on the radio all day. The Mounties brought in another set, and that helps. I passed a truck bringing in a big cat on the way to the strip."

Joe nodded. "We saw it from the air. What are you going to do, make a cherry picker?"

"Yeah. We've got some welders working on the boom right now." He grinned at Sheila. "A cherry picker isn't what you might think. We have to get all that hot metal away from the flame before we blow it out, otherwise it would just re-ignite, and we'd be right back where we started. So we take a tractor, build a shiny aluminum shield to reflect the heat and protect the operator. Then we attach a long boom, complete with cables and pulleys and hooks, to grapple onto the derrick and other chunks of debris and haul it away from the fire."

Sheila smiled sweetly. "Thank you for the explanation. And I really didn't have any theories as to what a cherry picker was, lewd or otherwise."

Rod winked at her amiably. "Of course not." He sobered quickly. "The real problem is water. We need tons of it to cool things down so the cat can work in close. We managed to corral another five water trucks. The plan is to bolt together a storage tank, heat it with steam lines so the water won't freeze, and build up a reserve that way."

"Good. Looks like you boys are doing what has to be done." They pulled to a stop in the bustle of the parking area as Joe spoke.

Everything seethed with controlled, purposeful activity. Powerful motors groaned in low gear; men strained and shouted as they unloaded the heavy trucks. Blue acetylene sparks flashed and bounced off the masks of welders readying the long boom for the gigantic cat, now backing slowly down the ramp.

Pete Berry and Larry Quigley were waiting for them. Larry shook his head remorsefully as he greeted Joe.

"I sure feel bad, Mr. Sanderson. I hate to let you down like this."

Joe gripped him by the arm. "You didn't let anybody down, Larry. It happened, that's all. A well can get away from a crew anytime, especially up here where nobody knows which end is up. Don't blame yourself, I don't."

Larry was visibly cheered. When he spoke, his voice was closer to its usual laconic note. "Well, she's sure one bearcat, no mistake. We're going to have some sport when the time comes to bell this baby."

Pete said, "Let's get you fixed up with some bunks and then we can take a closer look." He smiled at Sheila. "We've arranged for you to stay with our two cooks, both of them very respectable and matronly ladies."

Rod picked up her suitcase. "Their trailer is over here, I'll show you." As they ducked and squeezed their way between the parked vehicles and hurrying men, he said, "I was really floored when I heard you were coming. Bringing you was a real inspiration of Mac's. You can be a tremendous help, not to mention your effect on morale."

"I'm glad you approve. I was a little worried about how you would take it. The idea was Joe's, not Mac's, and I accepted before either of them could have any second thoughts. I wanted to be with you. But I must say you look remarkably self-sufficient. You're enjoying yourself, aren't you?"

"In a way I guess I am. It's a challenge, to put it mildly. I did some work around a real heller down in Venezuela, so I have an idea of what we are up against."

"Rod ..." she paused outside the trailer door. "You won't be too directly involved, will you? I mean, it's more Pete's and Mr. Quigley's line, isn't it?"

He laughed easily. "It's everybody's line. Everybody has to do whatever he can at a time like this. We're all involved. Pete has the final word, I guess, but we're all thinking alike as to how to handle it. We make a pretty good team, as a matter of fact."

She looked at him, at his face so alive and alert. All her adult life she had wondered about the type of man she would fall in love with when the time came. It had never occurred to her that it would be someone with Rod's type of conventional, neat-featured good looks. In her imagination, her lifetime lover had always been comfortably rugged with appropriately craggy features. There was nothing even remotely craggy about Rod's smooth face, framed in the fur-lined parka. Disturbingly handsome and wilful were the apt words of description. So much for intuition.

He was introducing her to a beaming woman, spotless and cheery in a starched white uniform. "Mrs. Spangel, our young tenderfoot looks charming in that ski outfit, but she won't stay warm very long. Do you think you can find something suitable for her?"

"Sure, sure. Come in, my child. My clothes will fit you like a tent, but you'll be warm, at least."

They stood in a group at the edge of the melted circle. The ground trembled under their feet and made their flesh jiggle and vibrate. It was an eerie feeling. Heat waves from the appalling flame shimmered and danced in the air, making a vacuum that tugged at their eardrums. The heat fanning against their faces was almost unbearable, while their backs froze.

As they watched in silent wonder, the yellow sun completed its shallow swing over the horizon. The early darkness made the blaze seem even brighter; it illuminated the open area between the wrecked rig and the camp and sent long flickering shadows into the yard where men toiled under artificial lights. Great gobs of liquid metal dripped and splashed from the derrick. Pete said, "She'll cave in anytime now."

As if waiting for its cue, the towering mast swayed — a giant metronome — momentarily righted itself, then slowly telescoped to earth. One of its supporting struts had not been completely melted and this tipped it outwards so that it landed in a diagonal away from the hole. The hot metal plunging into small pools of water threw up a barrage of white clouds.

Pete expelled a deep breath. "Now we can really get to work. Thank God, it didn't foul up that nice clean jet. When do you figure the cherry picker will be ready, Larry?"

"Should be sometime late tonight or early tomorrow morning." Larry added casually, "It'll seem kind of funny to be back at the controls of one of them cats."

Pete stared at him. "You! What the hell do you know about handling a cat?"

"Plenty. I spent the best years of my life as a cat skinner before I started pushing rigs." He held up his mutilated right hand. "If you're thinking about this, don't worry. I can still handle the controls. Besides, there's no other choice. The jockey who came in the tractor don't want no part of that little firecracker out here. Just keep the water going and keep old Quigley nice and cool, that's all I ask."

A roughneck pounded Larry's shoulder and shouted in his ear, "Rainbow is calling. There's a Mr. Carruthers from Vancouver who wants to know if he can fly up here."

Larry looked inquiringly at his companions.

Mac nodded. "Let him come ahead. After all, there's a good chunk of his money going up in that flame."

Jim Carruthers arrived with the morning's first light. Dressed in rough, heavy clothes, he seemed a different person from the urbane, self-assured financier Rod had met in Vancouver. He was stunned by the naked power erupting from the very bowels of the earth. He stood by Mac and stared at the towering flame.

Mac shouted above the roar. "In the oil patch we call it the devil's lighter. I've always thought it was a good name: when a well blows wild, it's like opening the gates of hell."

Jim touched his arm. "For the first time I think I understand you, Mac. To deal with forces like this — win, lose, or draw — it's the only game in town. My God, even the ground is shaking! Mac, I wouldn't miss this for anything. I feel like I'm being reborn!"

They watched Larry trundle the unwieldy cherry picker into position at the edge of the melted circle. Larry climbed down from the huge machine and walked over to where they stood.

"Reckon we're about ready. It'll take him a few minutes to finish rigging the water hoses. I'm for a cup of java; any takers?"

They sat over their steaming mugs in a final conference before going into action. Mac was apologizing to his backer. "You have no idea, Jim, how sorry I am it had to end this way. I'm afraid we haven't given you a very good run for your money."

Jim shrugged off his apology. "Don't worry about that. All of us are over twenty-one; we knew the risks. Although I must admit I had no idea of the appalling forces you people play with. That show out there makes the lumber industry seem pretty tame. We'll just have to write off the hundred thou —" he shot a quick grin at Mac — "closer to a hundred and twenty-five, really. It isn't pleasant, but we've done it before."

"You may not have to." Rod dropped his bombshell in as casual a voice as he could muster.

They all stared at him, but Mac was the first to speak. "What do you mean, Rod? Surely there's no way we can meet the deadline now?"

"It's close, I admit it, but with a good helping of luck we might just bring it off. Look, here's the way I figure it." He turned to Quigley. "How many days to clear the junk out of there?"

"With luck, one and a half, not more than two."

"Make it two. Then one more full day to douse the fire and bolt down a new BOP. That's if we can do it at all, of course. That leaves us eight days to get a new rig and punch her down to the muskeg formation. It's cutting it awfully fine, but it can be done."

Mac said, "It just might be possible. Wouldn't that be something?" Then the fire died in his eyes. "Ah, well, it's out of the question anyway. We've no rig and no money either. We can't ask Jim's group for anything more."

Jim nodded absently, eyes intent on Rod. "There's no way we could raise the money in time. If there were, I'd back you all the way."

Rod took a deep breath. "I still think we can do it. There's a rig lying on its side at the Royal dry hole not more than fifty miles from here. They haven't found any work for it since they abandoned that hole, so it's mothballed but all ready to go. I bet you could make a deal with the owners — it's a Blackstock Company rig — for them to move in and finish the hole for a percentage of the action. We might even make a deal with Royal if they've got it under contract."

Jim chuckled. "You've got a real wheeler-dealer on your hands, Mac. I'm prepared to reduce our share if they'll come in; what about you other fellows?"

Joe nodded. "I'll go along."

Mac said, "She's all yours, Rod. See what sort of a deal you can make. At least it's better than sitting on our hands doing nothing."

Larry stood up from the bench, dark eyes alight. He slapped Rod on the back. "By God, boy, we're not dead yet! Let's go get that flaming bitch!"

Larry felt the fingers of heat flicking at him as he manoeuvred the giant tractor, teetering and top-heavy with the weight of the boom. He wore dark goggles but still the glare stung his eyeballs. The hoses played over him and the advancing tractor. The thick steams pummelled him unmercifully but without the cooling water he couldn't work near the flame.

The water turned to steam as it struck the sizzling metal. Larry squinted through a dense white veil as he edged closer to the derrick.

Finally the boom was poised over the base of the derrick. He dropped the hook so that it caught in the angle of two intersecting beams. Keeping a steady strain on the cable, he threw the tractor into reverse. The burnt-out metal snapped and fragmented. Sweating, cursing the heat and the punishing water, he moved in to engage the derrick higher up. The hook refused to bite; it kept sliding and bouncing off the closely knit girders. Finally it caught, and this time the metal held under the strain. Belching black diesel smoke from its stack, the D-8 tugged until the derrick grudgingly began to slide across the swampy ground. As the tractor worked further back from the scorching heat, Larry's clothes became coated with ice. They were as stiff as a suit of armour, impeding his movements. However, after a full two hours the twisted derrick was safely out of range of the fire.

The melting ice made a pool on the floor where Larry stood sipping a mug of steaming coffee. He thought longingly of how much a great slug of rye would improve the flavour. When they got the fiery bitch under wraps, was he going to drink up a storm! He wouldn't draw a sober breath for two weeks!

Joe was watching him closely. "Mighty rough duty out there, Larry. You're doing one hell of a job."

Larry put down the heavy mug and turned to the door. "Thanks, Joe. The worst is yet to come. This is the easy part!"

Things improved for him as the day wore on. The main derrick tower had been the hardest; the smaller pieces came away readily once he managed to set the hook. Better still, when Larry took a breather after his second spell near the fire, the cat's regular skinner climbed into the seat without a word. Grinning through his fatigue and discomfort, Larry punched him on the shoulder. "Go get him, tiger!" Man, that was a break! Now they could work nonstop.

It was the cat skinner who later came up with the idea of securing a heavy timber to the cable, allowing them to drag and scrape the smaller bits and pieces out of range. The tractor, bright yellow at the start, gradually turned black as the paint blistered and cracked.

Rod had a very delicate task. Somehow he had to sell what was at best a very dubious and risky proposition to the president of Blackstock Drilling. From Mac he had learned that the president's name was Lawrence Davison, but his name and reputation for tough, shrewd bargaining were all Mac knew of him. Rod sought help from the experienced Carruthers. They spent their time in the Mounties' radio shack.

During a lull while they waited for another call from Davison, Jim said, "You remember I mentioned those rumours about the well that were floating around Vancouver?"

"Yes. They turned out to be pretty accurate."

"Almost suspiciously so. I found out who started them."

"Who?"

"A fellow by the name of Lazarus. He's a pretentious bastard, carries on like he's a belted earl. Can't stand him, myself. He has a remarkably nice wife, though. Anyway, he's the one that started it all. Two members of our syndicate know him slightly and he told the same story to both of them. He's mighty thick with the Masons, by the way."

Rod didn't like the turn his thoughts were taking; but they took it anyway — all tires screaming.

Sheila fitted smoothly into the furious activity. She quickly became indispensable to Berry, making lists of what supplies were needed and where they could be found. Pete was superbly organized. He knew exactly where to locate each item and who could best expedite delivery. Topping the list were twelve packs of high explosives with electric cables and a detonator; these were to be flown in from Edmonton, nestled in a bed of Styrofoam.

Sheila's unspoken fear that she would be uncomfortably conspicuous, even resented, in this ultra-masculine setting proved to be groundless. She was doing a job that urgently needed doing and so she was accepted. It was as simple as that. The motherly presence of the two cooks also comforted her.

She didn't see much of Rod; he seemed to spend all his time deep in consultation with Jim Carruthers, seldom venturing away from the radio. But for a brief, precious moment they were alone together in the diner. Rod said, "Well, at least I've got them interested enough so that the president and the toolpush are flying up for a look-see. No commitments, mind you, but we get a chance to talk to them."

Sheila smiled. "You know something? The Rod Fraser of today is quite a different person from the one who walked through our office door in Calgary."

"You may be right. One way or another, I've discovered a few things about myself."

"Such as?"

"Such as, this is what I want to do with my life. Build something right here in this country, even in the godforsaken north, if need be. Such as, I can never work for a large company again. I want something that exists only because I exist. In a big company, things might go better, more smoothly, and more economically because of your efforts, but they would still take place whether you were there or not. At some point in my life I want to be able to look back on something. Maybe an oilfield, maybe a gas plant or a pipeline, maybe just an oil company, like Thistle, teetering on the edge of bankruptcy. But good or bad, it'll be me. I guess you could call it monument-building, I don't know. I only know I've never felt like this before about anything. Corny, isn't it?"

"It doesn't sound corny to me. Not the least bit."

"I've kicked it around with Pete. We think a lot alike. Once this is all over we may team up."

"From what I've seen of him in action, you couldn't find a better partner. He's so efficient it's almost frightening and he has a real talent with people. The men worship him."

Rod gave a low whistle. "Say, what gives? Sounds like my partner has been making time behind my back. I think maybe I'm jealous."

Sheila made a face at him. "I'd love it if you were, but somehow you don't make it sound very convincing."

He laughed, then held her close. "I can feel your body even through all these damn clothes."

She giggled. "I bet not as much as I can feel you!"

They drew apart guiltily when the door was flung open. Jim Carruthers came in and said, "If I'm interrupting something, I apologize. Davison's plane has just taken off from Rainbow. He should be here in a couple of hours." His eyes sparkled, he was eating this up. They'd never get him out of the oil patch after this!

"If that ain't a ring-tailed, brass-bound hellcat, then I swear I never did see one!" The slow Texas drawl emphasized and underlined the words. The speaker turned to Mac, holding out his mittened hand. "Lawrence Davison, at your service, suh. Mr. Fraser, here, did mention that you all had yourselves a right cheerful little barbecue, but I never did reckon it would be this impressive."

Mac shook the proffered mitten and peered at the speaker's face behind the fur-lined hood. He saw what the slow, courtly drawl had led him to expect: a shrewd, lean face, bright with interest and glowing with the prospect of a deal to be negotiated. There are men who place the parry and thrust of negotiation above a good woman, a good meal, or a good wine. Lawrence Davison was clearly one of them.

"Happy to know you, sir," he assured Davison. "Let's go inside where we can get some coffee and escape this hellish din."

"Gentlemen, it's been a pure pleasure to come up here and feel the ground tremble and see that thundering great blaze light up the sky. If nothing else comes of this trip but that glorious sight, I'll count it well taken, indeed I will. But my young friend here" — faded blue eyes glanced at Rod from a face not much more than ten years his senior — "tells me you still have hopes of beating this here Crown sale. How can I help you, gentlemen?"

The others glanced at Rod. He said, "Just to review the bidding, Mr. Davison ..."

"Lawrence, please, suh," the other corrected smoothly.

"Thank you. Well ... Lawrence ... Thistle Oils bought this Crown lease — it's only a quarter-section — but then they had to find some financial backing so they could drill the test-well. Cheyenne had a rig that wasn't working and Joe Sanderson here agreed that we could use it without charge. That left the drilling and operating costs and that's where Mr. Carruthers' group entered the picture. They underwrote the costs up to a specified limit — which has already been exceeded, I'm afraid. Cheyenne and the Vancouver group were each to acquire a quarter-interest in the lease and the right to participate in any joint bid on the drilling reservation." He broke off apologetically. "I'm afraid I may have confused you."

"I understand the deal perfectly so far — you talk like a lawyer."

"Well, we sort of poor-boyed the well along. We had our share of trouble, that's for damn sure, but it still looked like we'd make it okay, when she blew on us." He paused to emphasize his next words. "We still think we can make it."

Davison blinked. "Really? Let me see, the sale is on the fifteenth. That gives you ..." he counted on his fingers, "seven days including what's left of today. I admire your determination, I surely do."

"What if we could give you the hole — under control — sometime tomorrow?"

Davison whistled softly. "That's a pretty big if. The blue eyes went blank as he calculated. "If we started the move right now, we could be rigged up the day after tomorrow. That would give us four days to drill and test."

He looked at Ken Howard, the toolpush he had brought with him. "What about it, Ken?"

Howard nodded slowly. "It's possible — barely. Provided the hole is in good enough shape to use." His voice was flat and unemotional but inwardly he exulted. This race against time would become a legend in the drilling industry and he, Ken Howard, would be a part of it. And that big National 55 was the baby that just might bring it off!

Rod spoke with considerably more assurance than he felt. "The hole should be okay. There's only one jet, but it hasn't cratered or leaked around the well bore. If we can get a clean snuff job, it should be workable."

"Interesting, very interesting. Well, gentlemen, I am always anxious to find work for my rigs. What rate did you have in mind?"

"Before we come to that, could you tell us if you are under contract or tied in any way to Royal? Your rig is stacked on one of their locations."

"No. No problem there. We left it there after the abandonment because we figured they would have more work for us in the area, and we still expect that they will. But there are no strings; we are not committed to them in any way, I'm happy to say."

"Good, I was hoping that was the case." Rod felt the tension easing. "As for rates, like I said earlier, we are really not in any position to pay cash. We had in mind more of a share position — a partnership if you like."

The Texan unwrapped a cigar, inspected it with a critical eye, and finally held a match to it. His drawl was even more exaggerated as he said, "Well, now, that's a risky undertaking, mighty risky. That's a pile of cash you're asking me to gamble. Let's see, now, it'll cost me fifteen thousand to move and rig up."

"Nine thousand," Joe corrected automatically.

"Well, then, nine thousand, if we are lucky, very lucky. Fortunately the rig hasn't been down long and she's ready to be moved. Then" — with a quick look at Joe — "it will cost at least fifteen hundred a day to keep the rig on the hole. That's a lot of money, gentlemen."

Joe cut in. "It's a damn cheap price to pay for a stake in this game and you know it!"

Lawrence Davison was unperturbed. "All right, gentlemen. Assume I'm interested; what sort of a split did you have in mind?"

Rod was embarrassed to detect a slight quiver in his voice as he replied, "We think, Lawrence, something in the order of ten per cent would be fair."

Davison snorted politely. "Ten per cent don't sound like a very generous offer from folks between a rock and a hard place like you all appear to be."

Finally, it was agreed he would come in for twenty per cent.

As soon as they had agreed on the deal, Davison underwent a complete metamorphosis from disinterested dilettante to man of direct action. He issued clear and precise directions to Ken Howard. The radio sets sparked into renewed activity. Davison turned to the group with a wide, boyish grin.

"Would you be surprised to learn the rig is already on the road? I gave the order for them to start loading before we left the ground at Calgary."

Joe gave a shout of laughter. "That's the way to hack it, Davison! Damn it, if I don't watch myself, I'll end up liking you!"

The Blackstock toolpush went into a quick huddle with Pete Berry. Since Blackstock's regular crew had moved on to new jobs, the survivors of the burned-out rig would man the new rig. Howard knew that pushing a strange crew on a crash program in a damaged hole would test his skills to their outer limits. He listened intently as Pete began to talk.

Later, Pete paused for a moment beside Constable Harper, who was staring in silent wonder at the acres of fire. "Hi, Jim. How goes the sleuthing?"

Jim Harper shook his head. "Not good. So far as White's murder is concerned, we have a nice round number of potential suspects — twenty to be exact. Everybody who was in camp that night. We've pretty much ruled out the possibility of an outsider wandering in from the blue and killing him. It's not like going to the corner drugstore for a milkshake. I suppose twenty suspects is better than the whole world, but not much." He jerked his head at the soaring flame and the labouring cherry picker. "Ever occur to you this could be more of the same?"

"No, I never even thought of it. I don't see how it could be. Fooling around with a well is a very different thing from banging a guy on the head. The wrong person can get killed."

"I guess you're right." The Mountie shook his head gloomily. "Still, you can only stretch coincidence so far before the old lady's garter snaps. When do you figure they'll be ready for the big show?"

"From the way they're scraping that junk out of there, I'd guess sometime tonight. We'll wait until morning regardless of when they finish. We need lots of light to do what has to be done."

"Will you be going in yourself, sir?" The speaker wore gold sergeant's stripes on his blue sleeve. "I'm Sergeant Streeter, in charge of the Rainbow detachment."

"Nice to know you, Sergeant." Pete shook hands. "Yes, I'm part of the team."

"You're a brave man." The senior Mountie spoke simply. "How large an area should we cordon off?"

"When that flame goes out there'll be poisonous gas blowing over the countryside. You should clear out all the people and keep them at least five miles away. At that distance the gas will be high enough so there shouldn't be any danger. It depends a lot on the wind, of course."

Streeter nodded and shouted back, "I agree. We'll set up our roadblocks five miles to the west."

"What about any strangers in the area? Trappers, seismic crews, people like that?"

"There'll be a chopper patrolling downwind. If they spot anybody they'll get them out somehow."

The explosives expert had appropriated Rod's trailer for his delicate chore. The welders had cut the top from a steel drum and he stuffed it with the twelve packets of TNT, each trailing a thick electric cord. He was careful to surround each blue package with a cushion of white Styrofoam. Whistling, he stood up. "There, nice and cosy. Now to connect it to the detonator and we're all set. Let me see, I think two hundred and fifty feet should be ample for Mr. Quigley — as long as he's behind sandbags, of course."

Late that night the welders went back to work on the cherry picker. This time they attached the reel that would spin out the cables connecting the detonator to the deadly cargo in the steel drum. All the smouldering debris had been cleared away and the Mounties began to evacuate the camp.

Reluctantly Sheila climbed into the car beside Mac, her lips still warm with Rod's parting kiss, her mind filled with foreboding. She had, she thought, managed to keep her fear from showing and her voice under control. She had tried so hard to be casual when she asked, "Darling, I know you don't want to be bothered with my stupid questions, but please just tell me what part you'll play in all this?"

She saw he was nervous, and it sent a stab of fear through her. He spoke hurriedly, not meeting her eyes.

"When Larry puts out the flame, somebody has to go in and bolt the new blow-out preventer in place, so we can shut off the gas. That's where Pete and I come in."

Her eyes widened. "But that's the most dangerous part, isn't it? I mean, when the fire is out and there's all that gas just waiting for something to set it off?"

He was trying to be offhand. "It's not as bad as it sounds. We'll make sure there are no sparks and both Pete and I will be wearing air-paks so the hydrogen sulphide won't get us. Besides, there are two of us, so if ... anything ... does happen, we can help each other."

She stared at him helplessly. It was awful, worse than she had dreamed it would be. He was going to walk right up to the mouth of the appalling monster, where the slightest mischance meant a horrible death! He didn't like the prospect either: she could see that. But there was nothing either of them could do; the pattern was set. From somewhere she had found the strength to say nothing more as they clung together for a brief moment.

Mac looked at her anxiously as they bounced and bumped their way to the checkpoint. He patted her knee clumsily and said, "The boys know what they're doing, Sheila. They'll be all right ..." His voice trailed off uncertainly.

They would go in with the grey half-light of the day's beginning.

23

There were four of them left behind when the last vehicle had rumbled down the road: Larry who would handle the tractor; Pete and Rod to secure the new blowout preventer; and Luke, whom Larry had asked to remain as a back-up in case of trouble.

It was strange to be alone, after all the frenzied hustle and bustle. They stood for a moment outside the suddenly deserted camp buildings. The wind was just right, blowing light and steady from the west, with no gusts, bending the flame in a gentle arc away from them. The dawn grew slowly; the day would be clear. Over the past few days a warming trend had set in, and the thermometer showed a relatively balmy twenty-four degrees below zero. It made a difference; one's face didn't freeze quite so fast; it took a little longer for the cold to penetrate to fingers and toes; metal was a little more responsive.

Larry slapped his hands together and moved purposefully toward the idling tractor, saying, "Let's get the fucking show on the road!" He climbed up to the operator's perch and sat for a long moment gazing at the inferno with a smile that was almost affectionate. He whispered softly, "Okay, old girl, we're coming in after you!" He wrenched the machine into gear.

The first job was his alone. Gingerly he pulled back on the lever and watched the boom slowly rise. He saw the cable tighten and the deadly barrel sway above the ground. He studied the flame carefully; he had to place the barrel right at the interface between gas and fire. The gas jetted about eight feet into the air before it burst into flame and he had to allow another seven feet for the BOPs; fifteen feet should do it. He wanted to have everything just right before he got in where it was hot!

Slowly the tractor lumbered across the ground, water squirting and splashing under its wide tracks. Larry kept an anxious eye on the reel playing out the electric cable. This time there was no water playing on the tractor since it was supposed to be a fast in-and-out proposition.

Mother of God, but the heat was something! It singed his eyebrows, he could almost smell them burning. His eyeballs felt like they were frying in their sockets, but he couldn't afford to even blink as he manoeuvred closer to the blaze. The dry, hot air shrivelled the very lining of his nostrils, and sweat ran down his body in streaming rivulets. Even the stumps of his missing fingers felt warm. It seemed impossible that the explosive hadn't gone off. He could see tendrils of white smoke curling above the barrel. Christ! Was that smoke or steam? How he would love to throw the bloody great machine into reverse and get out of there! There, the barrel was right in the flame, swaying and swinging like a goddamned pendulum! That was better; now the flame was flowing around it. Time to bail out!

He half jumped, half fell from the tractor and ran to the detonator. He flung himself down beside the red box, threw a hasty look at the blackened barrel smoking in the flame, and pressed down on the plunger.

The explosion shook the ground, dislodging two sandbags from the wall in front of Larry. Suddenly it was darker. The fire was out! Cautiously he raised his head above the sandbags. In place of the towering flame, there was an arc of deadly gas sweeping downwind.

The cherry picker had taken a beating. The heat shield was crushed and draped over the driver's seat. There was something else wrong, though. He peered more closely — it sat still and motionless in its tracks. It was stalled! What a jam they'd be in if he couldn't restart it. And if he didn't get it going damn smartly it would freeze up solid.

He bolted for the cat, tearing and pulling at the broken shield. The shattered pieces came away easily, clearing the controls. Not daring to think, he pressed the starter. The powerful diesel rumbled into life. Weak with reaction, Larry slammed it into reverse. He was grinning broadly as he drove it over to his three companions.

Five miles away at the checkpoint, they saw the flame suddenly roll up into itself and wink out. A ragged cheer went up, only to die uncertainly as they gazed at the towering column of gas sweeping downwind in a giant fan. The water vapour in the gas turned into billowing clouds of steam. Vehicles were strung out along the narrow road in a mile-long column from the barrier. Fifteen enormous diesel units, puffing clouds of black smoke from upright stacks, loomed over the others. They were loaded with all the components of the dismantled Blackstock rig. Ken Howard had been there to watch them grind up to the barrier and had checked every piece of equipment.

He beamed when he saw that two of the rig's regular drillers were with the caravan. He told them, "Boys, we've got the job to end all jobs! We're going to rig up on top of that wild well and drive her down to the muskeg in four fucking days. How do you like them apples?"

"I'm freezing to death in my own sweat!" Larry shouted as they crowded around him, pummelling him with congratulations.

"Do you want to change your clothes?" Pete asked.

Larry shook his head. "No time. We've got to shut off that gas before we knock off everybody from here to Edmonton. You fellows ready?" They nodded. "Okay, let's hook up."

With a preventer swinging on the cherry picker's boom, Rod and Pete adjusted their air-paks. The apparatus resembled a scuba diver's outfit, with two tanks strapped on the back and a clear Plexiglas face-piece. Since it was essential that they be able to communicate, each wore a throat mike and earphones. Pete's voice rattled metallically in Rod's ear. "Have you got the bolts? Okay, I'll carry the wrench. Let's move in."

The giant valve, much heavier than the barrel of explosives, dropped easily through the gas stream. From his seat in the cat, Larry couldn't judge whether it was exactly over the hole. He would have to rely on hand signals from Pete for that, and also for the more delicate task of lining up the ten bolt holes with their mates.

They walked to the far side of the jet, Rod carrying the bolts, each wrapped in soft cloth, and Pete cradling a long-handled wrench. Rod saw that the new BOP was sitting squarely on top of the old one; old Larry was quite an artist with that cherry picker! Gently he placed the bolts on the ground. Pete walked forward to check the alignment of the bolt holes. Rod saw him step from behind the new valve assembly and signal Larry.

Obediently the boom swung to the left, shifting its heavy load. They had gone too far! A thin jet of gas shot out; blown downwind, it swirled about them in a deadly fog. Well, that's why they were wearing the air-paks; no harm done, but he wished Pete would connect it and get rid of this damn gas. What was delaying him?

He heard a sharp intake of breath vibrate in his earphones. Startled, he looked back and saw the wrench descending in a murderous arc. He jumped to one side, enough to make it miss his head, but not enough to escape altogether. It struck him on the shoulder, the numbing blow almost buckling his knees.

Thrown off balance, Berry felt the heavy wrench sliding from his grasp to fall on the wet, now-freezing ground and slide toward the steel side of the wellhead, stopping an inch away. One scant inch separated it from a spark that would have wrapped them in a curtain of fire. He reached for it, but Rod, now fully awake to his danger, dove at him, pushing him back. They grappled clumsily, hampered by their heavy clothing. It wasn't a very scientific fight, just two amateurs swinging at each other and tumbling on the slippery ground. Their breath whistled and roared through their throat mikes.

For a long straining moment they stood up and grappled face to face. Rod hooked a foot behind Pete's legs and gave him a sudden shove. It was enough to throw Pete off balance and he fell heavily to the ground. Rod jumped on him before he could move.

Sitting astride Pete, knees pinning his shoulders to the ground, Rod reached behind and squeezed the air tubes. He could see Berry's eyes, dilated and frantic, peering up at him through the face-piece, now beginning to fog.

Larry stared at the struggling figures in astonishment. He hadn't seen Pete's murderous attack behind the wellhead. This had been the essence of Pete's plan. If the

338 / JOHN BALLEM

first blow had succeeded, he would have rigged up another "accident," one that would have left Rod a charred corpse with all signs of the killing blow obliterated by the fire.

Larry was helpless and he knew it. Without an air-pak no one could venture near the swirling gas. From this distance, he couldn't even risk lifting the preventer. Without directions he might move it out of line so that the whole damn stream would come blasting out the side, or, worse still, he might strike a spark and blow them all to the other side of hell.

The other spectator wasn't helpless, but he cursed softly, viciously, as he watched the struggle. That damn Pete had torn it for fair, the stupid bastard. Now the question was, how much could he salvage? Maybe there'd be three victims instead of just one, and only one survivor — himself. Smiling, Luke raised the rifle. It no longer mattered which one he hit. They all had to go.

At first he couldn't believe it, but the iron-hard pressure under his jaw increased and the long barrel of the service revolver dug deeper into his side. The voice repeated, "I said, 'Drop it, Luke.' I'm taking you out of play."

Unable to move his head, Luke squinted sideways and up; he stared into the grim young face of Harper. The Mountie spoke again. "Lay it down nice and easy. It's all over."

Ever a realist, Luke considered his position. There was no way he could regain the advantage. Disdainfully he dropped the rifle in the snow.

Rod hooked his fingers under the face-piece and said, "You can hear me, Pete. Look, I'm releasing the tubes, you can breathe." He paused, listening to the harsh, laboured sobs as Pete sucked in precious air. His own breathing wasn't all that steady, but he managed to keep his voice even as he continued. "Feels good, doesn't it? One jerk and the mask comes off. They say it takes ten seconds for the stuff to kill you, but those will be the longest ten seconds of your life. It ruptures your blood vessels, did you know that?"

He let Pete squirm for a moment before he went on. "Say something, my friend. If you don't — goodbye mask. Melinda is in this with you, isn't she?" He stared intently at the ashen face behind the Plexiglas.

An inexpressible sadness spread through him as Pete croaked eagerly, "Yes, yes! She and that creep Mason — we were going to make the big stake."

"And who else?" He had to tread softly here, pretend knowledge he didn't have.

But Pete, eyes staring at the gas hissing around the preventer, was beyond thinking. He babbled, "Lazarus, Frederick Lazarus, he's some kind of big-shot in Vancouver. And Kondar Podoroff — he's an engineer Royal fired years ago. They're all in it — it was a one-shot deal. For God's sake, Rod, let me up."

Rod wasn't sure how much oxygen was left in the tanks. He couldn't take any chances of running short since he had to return at least once more into the lethal fog.

He shifted position, interrupting Pete's tale. "Who's your accomplice on the rig? You weren't anywhere near here when White was killed, or that geologist, either. Who is it, Pete? Tell me."

But Pete, belatedly aware that he had said far too much and sensing Rod's uncertainty, clamped his lips and defiantly shook his head. Rod took a firm grip on the air tubes and grunted, "Okay, Pete. On your feet and quick march!"

"They were coming at you both ways," Harper greeted him. "Our friend here had you nicely sighted in the cross hairs."

Luke spat venomously at Pete. "It would have been you first, you stupid bastard what can't even take a man out from behind." He turned to the Mountie. "And that's the last fucking word you get from me!"

"I think maybe Mr. Fraser here has learned everything we need to know. Right?" He looked enquiringly at Rod.

Rod nodded. "I sure as hell have! But it will have to keep. Right now, I've got to do something about that well. That gas it's spewing out is a killer!"

A very puzzled Larry locked the controls of the cat and walked over to join them. Rod eyed him carefully; God alone knew who was involved in this little caper. Still, old Larry had knocked himself out fighting the well, risking his life every minute. Quickly he told Larry what had happened.

"Mr. Fraser, would you cover me while I search them?" Harper politely handed his revolver to Rod and efficiently frisked both Willard and Berry. "Clean," he grunted as he straightened up. "Now, what about the well?"

"The same as before, except this time I go in alone. I'll be one hell of a lot safer without my 'buddy.' Larry, you'll have to drag the preventer back in place. You had it bang on the first time."

Larry scratched his head. "That's what I thought. I couldn't figure what in hell Pete was playing at. I figured the bolt holes must have been lined up wrong. You just signal me where you want it, and I'll lay it right in there, light as a feather and no sparks."

Constable Harper said, "Maybe I better go in with you. In case of trouble I could always drag you out."

Rod shook his head. "No, thanks. Somebody has to watch this pair. I can do it alone."

"I'll take the extra air-pak with me on the cat and if anything comes unstuck I'll come in after you. I'll get you out."

"I know you will, Larry." Rod punched him lightly.

The preventer slid gently over its base. When Rod saw the holes line up, he chopped his hand. The rest was easy; the bolts dropped smoothly into place. He had to make sure the metal touched metal with only the gentlest of kisses, but the bolting-down was routine.

He and Larry stood for a moment by the control switch. With a slight bow, Rod said, "It's your well."

Grinning, Larry pulled the lever and the ramjets slammed shut and suddenly, unbelievably, all was still, the hellish racket was no more.

The crowd at the checkpoint watched the arching plume of gas shred and disappear against the sky. "Thank God," Mac muttered, "I was beginning to think they were in trouble."

Jim Carruthers stared at the cracked windshield of the pickup. "Taming that inferno is something Rod will never forget as long as he lives. I envy him."

The radio in the black-and-white cruiser crackled into life. Sergeant Streeter slid into the driver's seat and listened intently. He beckoned to Mirkowski. "Jim has himself a real jackpot in there. We were right — there was a connection between White's murder and the wild well. Keep everybody here until I pass the word." He put the car in gear and drive to the camp, red lights flashing.

Rod heard the wail of the approaching siren. He said to Larry, "Tell the Mountie I'll be there in a moment. I have to go to the can."

Larry nodded. "I don't blame you."

Inside the corridor, Rod raced to the toolpush's office and picked up the microphone. In a moment he was connected with the outside telephone network. A brief wait and he was put through to Vancouver.

24

The pink Mustang GT grumbled impatiently while the overhead door rolled upwards. With a squeal of tires it surged onto the glistening wet pavement. Melinda drove savagely, gunning the car in snarling acceleration from stop signs, weaving through traffic, shooting the yellow lights. The obedient power soothed her; gradually the numbing shock was replaced by an icy detachment. If only she could will herself into one of her childhood trances!

The car boomed through a long cement tunnel and burst out the other end. Before her stretched the open four-lane highway, but, with its heavy traffic and ever-present police, it wasn't what she wanted. She knew her destination — a little-travelled sideroad that branched off five miles down the highway. It was one of her favourite routes on the long, lonely night drives. The teeming rain had slackened to a light drizzle, and the air had a steely quality as the sun struggled feebly through a grey overcast.

Rod's voice kept drifting and tumbling across her mind. He had sounded tender and compassionate, but the words he spoke had been so definite, so devastating: "Confessed everything" ... "They caught Willard too" ... "Murder." The dreadful litany went on and on, eating into her soul.

It was the last thing he could do for her — the warning before the police arrived. He had given her a choice.

Braking hard, shifting down, she tooled through the interchange and blasted down the secondary road. It was an exciting piece of road, blacktopped with sweeping turns, a few real hairpins, and some good long straights. The Mustang lifted on its high-test tires.

The voice was right in her ear, the hurtling car swerved violently. She fought down the waves of revulsion and fear that crawled under her skin, and mechanically corrected the spin. Coolly she looked in the rear-view mirror. "You make a very effective spook, my dear George. That depraved face of yours is enough to give any innocent girl the screaming meemies, let alone this new twist of suddenly popping up behind car seats. Has it ever occurred to you that you missed your true calling — that you could have made it big on the late-night horror shows?"

George brushed aside her feeble attempt at mockery. He levered himself onto the cramped back seat and leaned forward. "I heard you talking to Fraser. The whole operation has been blown, hasn't it?"

She nodded sombrely. "Right. They know everything; names, plans — everything."

He considered this. "Of course, there's always the problem of proving it. There's quite a difference between knowing something and being able to prove it before a jury."

She said flatly, "Forget it. Pete has been babbling like a drain. He will probably turn — what do they call it — Crown witness."

"That's close enough. Well, where do we go from here?"

"*We* go nowhere. I stop the car and you get out."

"I don't think so," he said quietly. "This gun is small but it's remarkably effective at short range, and we are at very short range indeed."

Melinda shrugged indifferently. "All right, if that's what you want, lover-boy. I don't want you messing up my farewell scene, but so be it. You leave me no choice."

His eyes sought the rear-view mirror as he tried to read her expression. It had that damnable remote, withdrawn look — a beautiful, cold mask. Her attitude puzzled him. He said, "Very clever of you, to take this sideroad and avoid the main border post. They won't have had time to seal off the small border crossings. I'm afraid our escape will be very temporary, without funds. Did you bring any money?"

"We won't need any money where we're going."

He stared at her. "What do you mean?"

"Figure it out for yourself. This is when little Melinda escapes from everything — men, money, gossip — the whole shitty world. And you invited yourself, remember that."

He screamed at her. "Stop! Stop this instant; let me out. I'll shoot. I mean it."

She shook her head. "Shoot if you like. That will only speed matters up. It'll soon be over."

She could see it now, the place where the road swept around a gentle curve, so gradual that there was no guardrail, only a green shoulder sloping into the adjoining meadow. An ancient cedar stood in lonely dignity thirty feet from the road. It was a local landmark and an old friend to Melinda. It pleased her that the final act of her life would require all her driving skill. Aiming the car like a bullet, she barrelled into the curve and held the wheel steady as they tore across the narrow strip of grass. Then they were in the air.

Jim Carruthers left the toolpush's room and went looking for Rod. He found him a hundred yards down the road, staring blankly at the swarming activity around the new rig.

He touched his arm; it was strange not to have to shout. "She's dead, Rod. They found her in a field on a roadside. She wasn't marked at all, just lying there like a doll someone had thrown aside. The car burned and Mason burned with it. The Mounties figure he must have been in the rear seat and there was a gun. Beyond that, they're simply guessing, but it doesn't take much imagination to figure out what happened."

"Jesus! She was beautiful, so damn beautiful!"

"I know, Rod. I feel like somebody kicked a big hole in my guts. But we both know she could never have lasted through the trial and jail. It's for the best, really it is."

"I hope you're right. I sure hope so. What about the others?"

"They're to appear in court tomorrow to be formally charged. Harper said it will probably be two months before the actual trial. Apparently, Pete really clammed up once they got him down in Vancouver. He just shakes his head and flatly refuses to answer. So God only knows how much they'll be able to prove at the trial. They think they have Willard nailed to the cross, but they're not so sure about the other two."

Rod shook his head. "You know, the one I still can't understand is Pete. Hell, I know he was ambitious; he made no secret of that. But, murder! He must have wanted something awful bad."

"I know what he wanted — power. Naked power! I've met a few like that in my time. They think of nothing else, and they don't let anything stand in the way. I liked Pete, but when he started to talk about his plans for vast international operations, I was getting some peculiar vibrations. I bet he'll crack up in the next few months."

Sheila stood uncertainly in the doorway of Rod's small trailer. He was slumped against the littered bench. She asked quietly, "May I come in?"

He struggled to his feet, smiling wanly. "Sure, just let me clear some junk off this stool. I know it's an appalling mess. That's why geologists get their own trailer-laboratory — they can't stand us around the rig."

She stared at the floor, uncertain how to start. "Constable Harper told me that ... she ... Melinda ... is dead." Now she looked straight at him, brown eyes warm with concern. "I'm sorry, Rod — desperately sorry. She meant a great deal to you, didn't she?"

He nodded slowly. "For five years she dominated my life. Dominated it, and twisted it. But it wasn't her fault, she was herself and she could never change."

"I know," Sheila said softly. "I know how it is."

He looked at Sheila. Her beauty had all the warm golden tones of autumn and made him think of trees and clear water, sparkling and glinting in a mountain stream. He shook his head with a weary smile. "You can't possibly know."

25

The new rig, bright with paint, metal parts gleaming, looked strange to eyes accustomed to the dinginess of battered old Cheyenne Number Three. But it could make hole, God couldn't it make hole!

Larry prowled happily around the rig, patting the powerful motors, admiring the gleaming orderliness of the doghouse, the latest equipment on the drawworks. Man, wouldn't it be something to push a rig like this! At first he had felt awkward, afraid that Ken Howard would resent his presence. But Ken had made him feel easy; they were both charter members in a tough brotherhood.

He often thought of Luke Willard. That bastard had ice in his veins for sure. That was something, by God — to stand on the derrick floor and coolly whistle the devil up the hole. No matter what they did to Luke, he would always have that. And Larry knew that he, too, had gained something. He was agreeably aware that he had new stature because of his part in taming the well. Maybe he should stay sober and enjoy it. He'd give it some thought.

"How is it going?" Mac looked up from his coffee at the young-looking president of Blackstock Drilling.

"Never had it so good," Lawrence Davison said in his yawningly, drawly voice. "We're making four hundred fifty feet a day and Rod reckons we're getting close, mighty close. That's why he's sticking so tight to the rig. He asked me to apologize to you, ma'am." He smiled down at Sheila.

By now their establishment had given up all pretence of being a conventional drilling camp. Mac had readily agreed when Sheila timidly asked if she could remain to see it through. "But of course, my dear. There is absolutely nothing for you to do in Calgary. Everything that Thistle Oils possesses is right here and, what's more, you're out of range of people who would try to swab you down for information. Besides" — this with a gentle smile — "you belong here."

Jim Carruthers seemed to belong, too. He was everywhere, deep in long conversations with Rod and Larry, standing by the hour on the freezing drill floor — he was getting a cram course in oil.

Joe Sanderson had left the site to begin negotiations with the insurance company, leaving Larry to represent Cheyenne. The hordes of workers and officials had disappeared, and security was once more in force, although each day several planes flew low around the rig. Now there was no canvas shroud. There hadn't been time and

Lawrence hated them. "We'll confuse our friends by stacking drill pipe all over the place. Anyway, there's so much crap left over from that fire, they'll never be able to figure it out."

Lawrence muttered, "You know, the sale is the day after tomorrow. Suppose we got ourselves a big ol' river of oil down there. That's nice, but it won't mean much without the adjoining reservation. And we're not going to get it without the scratch — bundles of it; much more than I can lay my hands on. I don't know about you ..." he paused delicately.

Mac shook his head with a rueful smile. "Me? I'm not even sure I can finance my return air ticket to Calgary! But Rod seems to have that pretty much under control. He's been in touch with Inter-Continental. Tim Murphy — he's one of their hotshot geologists — is an old friend. They've arranged if we hit anything we'll let them know, and if they agree with our analysis, they'll put up the money for a joint bid. Murphy is standing by at Rainbow with a plane. When we give the word they'll fly up to the strip and take a look at what we have. They're prepared to bid whatever figure Murphy recommends. It means we all water down our interests, of course."

Lawrence whistled softly. "Well, I'll be triple damned!" He flashed his sudden, charming smile at Sheila. "That young man of yours is one goin' Jessie!"

Rod studied the jumping figures on the narrow dial — 5450-5451-5452 — they must be very close to the interface. He wished fervently he knew more of the regional geology; with all this secrecy, it was like trying to package fog. He turned to Ken Howard. "We just can't afford to take a chance. You'll have to shut her down until I can look at some samples. For all I know, we could be in the muskeg right now."

Ken nodded and ordered the crew to stop drilling and to circulate mud. The motors hummed quietly, powering the pumps, and Rod waited while the mud flowed down the pipe and back up the hole. He thought it would take about thirty minutes to bring the most recent cuttings to the surface. Ten minutes before that, he left the doghouse and walked to the rear of the rig, where the mud spilled over the metal screen of the shale-shaker. He scooped at it with his trowel and dumped each scoopful into a separate cloth bag. Finally, when he had filled each bag, he dogtrotted over to his trailer.

At this stage the geologist was in complete command, like a pilot guiding a giant ocean liner through the treacherous waters of his own harbour. The rig waited, circulating quietly.

He washed each sample to remove the coating of mud. The rinsing left the rock splinters dark and wet. These he dried on saucepans over the hot plate. All his samples remained obstinately black — they were still in the shale. He returned to the rig and ordered Ken to drill ahead another forty feet. The rotary table began to turn, picking up speed; the numbers on the dial resumed their march — 5453-5454. At 5482 — thirty feet after they had resumed drilling — the figures suddenly accelerated, the black numbers dropping into place at twice their former rate. An excited murmur rippled through the crowded doghouse. They had a "drilling break," the strongest indication that they were in a new formation. Rod waited until the numbers climbed to 5492 before he ordered drilling to stop.

Back in his trailer with the new samples, he repeated the same procedures, but this time the cuttings from the deepest zone turned white as they dried. It was limestone — Devonian limestone deposited three hundred and fifty million years ago when the sea covered the land. Now to check the porosity. Solid limestone wasn't any good; it had to be honeycombed with minute spaces where the oil could be stored. He placed a particle under the microscope, anxiously fumbling with the knobs until it sprang into focus. There they were — tiny pores and fissures breaking the smooth white surface of the rock. Rod's hands were shaking as he sat back on the stool.

Now he had the answer to two of the questions. The limestone formation was there, and it was porous. Only one question remained, the all-important one — was there any oil? There was only one way to find the answer: tap into the formation and bring to the surface whatever substance lurked within it.

He entered the expectant doghouse, shouting jubilantly, "All signals are go! We're in limestone and it's got porosity! I'm calling for a drill-stem test."

The test utilized another of the ingenious instruments that oilmen have developed to enable them to probe thousands of feet below the surface. They would substitute a special tool for the drilling bit. It was a slotted section of pipe with a rubber ring that could be inflated against the wall of the hole to isolate the test formation.

There was a long wait while the drill string was lifted out of the hole so the substitution could be made. Nearly everybody went back to the camp to ease the wait with coffee and cigarettes. The conversation was disjointed and scattered, as each speaker broke off to concentrate on his own inner excitement. Rod couldn't sit still, the rig kept tugging at him. Gulping his coffee, he stood up to leave. A wide, exultant grin lit his face as he said to Sheila, "This is what I live for, the moment when you win or lose — when the last card is turned face-up on the table."

She pressed his arm. "Go back to your well. I'll come down later with Mac."

Hours later they were ready. The testing tool had been attached and laboriously lowered into the hole; the driller had tapped bottom with the string and then raised it one precise foot.

A flare line, made from sections of pipe screwed together, led from the blowout preventer to a pit ninety feet away. Whatever came out of the hole could be dumped in the pit and, if necessary, burned. A small bleed-off tube was inserted into the first section of the line. Below the tube, in the dead centre of the derrick floor, there was an ordinary, galvanized bucket. This plain household pail was the repository of all their hopes and dreams. It was the ballot box in which the verdict of success or failure would be rendered.

Five thousand four hundred eighty feet below them the rubber ring pressed against the hole and sealed off the hydrostatic head. Immediately the formation flowed through the narrow slots and mounted to the surface, pushing the column of mud before it in its furious climb. A gout of mud splattered in the pail. "She's coming at us!" Larry breathed reverently. "Come on, baby, let's have you!" They watched breathlessly as the mud continued to splat and drip against the sides and bottom of the bucket. More to break the silence than anything else, Ken Howard said, "She's got pressure, that's for sure. That mud is coming out like an express train."

Mud splashed into the bucket for a full five minutes. Then, without warning, the grey goblets were replaced by a steady stream of white chalky fluid, the exact colour of skim milk. A stricken silence settled over them. Even Sheila, coached by Rod, knew what the milky fluid was — salt water! They had tapped an ancient underground ocean — the reservoir was filled with sea water, not oil!

Larry was the first to find his voice. Shaking his head, he muttered, "Dry as a popcorn fart! Christ!"

They were still cocooned in shock as they sat in the diner. Lawrence Davison, ever the gambler, was the first to recover. With a shrug, he said, "Well, I guess there's nothing left but to pee on the fire and move on," and left for the strip to wait for his aircraft. Sheila's heart ached for Mac; she longed to comfort him but couldn't find the words.

Rod was beginning to shake off the effects of the stunning upset. They had been so sure, so very sure! Still, it wasn't the end of the world, although old Mac looked as though it might just as well be. Mustering a shaky grin he asked him, "Where does Thistle Oils go from here?"

Blinking, Mac slowly focused on him. "Nowhere. This is the end of the line. For Thistle and for me."

Rod leaned forward. He held Sheila's hand and spoke with growing intensity. "It doesn't have to be. We can take Thistle back where she belongs for a while — in the fairway of Alberta and over in Saskatchewan. Hell, the wells over in Saskatchewan are so shallow they're just deep fence-post holes!" He looked at Jim Carruthers. "What do you think, Jim? Can we scrape together enough funds to drill some shallow, low-risk wells?"

"Hell, yes! Like I say, it's the only game in town. I'm not about to leave now."

Rod was starting to grin. "Good. We'll build up our production and when we've got some steady revenue we can bring Thistle back up here for another crack at the big stuff."

Mac's eyes were glowing. "It just might work!"

Sheila reached across and squeezed his hand. "Of course it will. We'll make it work!"

Larry watched them with growing wonder. He looked at Ken Howard, shrugged helplessly, and said, "Jesus H. Christ! Here we go again!"

Oilpatch Empire

I

"The lady really did a number on you, Bill." The lawyer's lips were compressed in a grimace of distaste as he unsnapped his briefcase and took out a copy of *Tomorrow*, holding the magazine with his fingertips as though it might suddenly explode in his face.

Bill Crawford's heart thudded uncomfortably as the import of Chester Martin's words struck home. Wordlessly, he reached for the magazine. There was a picture of him on the cover, posing in the doorway of the Lear, trench coat draped carelessly over his left arm. He looked like a playboy setting off on a journey to some exotic destination. He and Margo's photographer had spent the better part of a morning at the Calgary airport, the motor-driven Nikon clicking its way through roll after roll of film. The cover caption, in large white letters, read: "The Sumptuous Lifestyle of a Canadian Oil Baron."

Bill felt his cheeks grow warm as he opened the magazine and scanned the list of contents. The article under the by-line of Margo Jones began on page eight.

The whine of the twin engines subsided as the Lear completed its long climb-out from the refuelling stop at Frobisher Bay and levelled off at 45,000 feet, well above the commercial jet traffic. The Lear's power-to-weight ratio made this the most economical cruising altitude, and the pilot liked to joke that at this height there were only themselves, God, and "the occasional B-52." Chester, unable to stand upright in the aircraft's small cabin, bent over the bar to pour two stiff Scotches from a cut-glass decanter. He handed one to Bill and tactfully went back to the rear while the oilman read the damning article.

Margo had done a masterly hatchet job. Without ever coming right out and saying it, she depicted Bill Crawford — at fifty-three, the chairman of the board and chief executive officer of Venture Oils Limited — as a pleasure-seeking parasite, living a life of opulent luxury totally removed from the realities of everyday existence.

There were photos of the ranch, his mansion in Mount Royal, Debbie in formal riding clothes accepting a prize at the Stampede horse show, and the new head office of Venture Oils, now nearing completion in downtown Calgary. Somehow Margo had got hold of the three-dimensional model of his office suite, and there was a picture of it in full colour, along with the comment that the chairman's office alone was expected to cost a quarter of a million dollars. She had included a couple of quotes from some unnamed employees of Venture Oils saying they didn't see much of Mr. Crawford around the office: the clear implication being that he was too busy leading the life of a globe-trotting jet-setter to bother about mundane business affairs. Titillating little items about the well-stocked bar on the Lear and spur-of-the-moment trips to Caribbean luxury resorts were sprinkled throughout. The final and most damning paragraph posed the question of whether there should not be some limit on the extent to which a private individual could leverage natural resources that belonged to the public. "Granted," Margo had written, "Bill Crawford, born in Texas and a 'Canadian by choice,' has spent his lifetime exploring for oil in Alberta and has been marvellously successful at it; does that mean he is entitled to go on forever adding to a fortune that has already attained indecent proportions?"

Bill took a swallow of whisky without tasting it. Strangely, there was no anger, just an empty feeling of loss. He had been callously used to further the ambitions of a very determined female journalist. He winced at the memory of that sleek head, with its close-cropped dark curls, cocked to one side in alert attention to every word he uttered, the dark brown eyes bright with interest and, finally, the spare, exciting body next to his. All so she could get the inside goods on the oil industry.

On one trip to Toronto, he had picked up the intercom and told the pilots he didn't want to be disturbed for the next half-hour, and he and Margo had made love, rather awkwardly, on the short, bench-like couch where Chester Martin was now perched with his Scotch. It had been her suggestion; Bill remembered being more than a little put off by the idea. With the benefit of hindsight, he realized she had done it so she could throw in a reference to "sex at 45,000 feet" with impunity. She had done a beautiful job of setting him up.

And, dear God, he had been thinking seriously of proposing marriage! In the few weeks they had spent together while she was researching her "story," her stylish good looks, restlessly inquiring mind, and scintillating conversation had completely captivated him. He could find abundant sex and female beauty wherever he travelled, but Margo was quite simply the most entertaining companion he had ever known.

There was more than twenty years' difference in their ages, but that was nothing unusual in some of the circles he travelled in. Many of the men were in their second or third marriages, and May-December combinations were almost the rule. Besides, she seemed every bit as infatuated as he was. He had even worked out a little speech about how marriage wouldn't affect the career she was so determined on. It was only her abrupt and unexpected departure on an assignment to El Salvador that had prevented him from making a prize fool of himself. Now, of course, it was obvious that she had wanted to be well out of range when the article appeared.

Shaking his head over his own naivety, Bill flipped back to the front page of the magazine. There was a brief note about the cover photo, along with a statement that the article was the first of two and that the second instalment would feature a mosaic of the colourful inhabitants of the oil patch by freelance investigative reporter, Margo Jones. Sweet Christ! She had used him to get next to the movers and shakers of the oil industry, and now she was going to turn her venomous pen on the friends he had so trustingly introduced her to. She had made him into a traitor to his own kind.

Chester Martin came forward and dropped into the seat facing him across the narrow aisle. Chester pointed at Bill's empty glass, but the oilman silently shook his head.

"I had a call just before we took off from Heathrow that the magazine was on the stands in Canada and that the article really savaged you," Chester said. "I picked up a copy at the newsstand while we were on the ground in Frobisher and you were in the VIP lounge making your call to New York. I figured it would be best for you to find out about it while we were in the air where nobody could reach you. I'm sorry as hell to have to be the one to throw it in your face."

"You did the right thing, Ches. Tell me," Bill went on after a short pause, "is that how I come across to people? Some kind of super-rich jerk who freeloads off the country and never does a tap of work?"

"Hell, no, Bill. The people who know you realize how hard you've worked for what you've got and how much it's cost you in personal terms. There may be some jealousy because you've been so incredibly successful, but no one tries to downplay what you've accomplished. Of course," the lawyer gave a helpless shrug, "it's a different matter with the guy in the street who reads this piece of shit and turns pea-green with envy. He'd trade places with you in a shot, but that won't stop him from figuring you're a Yankee son of a bitch who's come up here and made his fortune by out-smarting the good grey Canadians. The one thing she was very careful not to attack was your business ability and integrity. It's your wealth and high-flying lifestyle she zeroed in on." Frowning thoughtfully, Chester Martin rolled the empty whisky tumbler between his palms. "I'm no expert on the law of defamation, but it strikes me that a number of the statements about your personal conduct could be actionable. Unless she can establish they're true, of course." He raised an enquiring eyebrow at Bill.

"Let's just say the lady has covered her ass very effectively." Bill leaned back against the headrest with a weary sigh. "The quotes she used are wildly out of context, but I'm sure she has them all documented. As for the other things ... well, she could probably prove some of them at least, if she were forced to the wall. Anyway, I've got no appetite for that kind of lawsuit."

"It's usually a mug's game all right," the lawyer agreed, knowing that if even a few of the more serious allegations could be proved in court, a defamation action would be suicidal for Bill.

The silver-and-blue jet sped westward, its fuselage hammered from time to time by clear-air turbulence as it bucked the prevailing headwind. Finally, Bill Crawford roused himself from his painful reverie and switched on the overhead reading light. "We might as well go over the final draft of that farm-in agreement."

"Right." Chester reached for his briefcase. "I'm still not happy with the wording of the earning clause," he muttered as he laid a stack of printed and stapled pages on the fold-out desk. "I don't care how Jenkins interprets it, it says that unless the well reaches a total depth of not less than 10,000 feet we don't earn a damn thing."

"Redraft it so that our interest is earned if either a total depth of 10,000 feet is reached or the mid-Jurassic formation is encountered."

"That's exactly what I'd like to do, but do you think Trans Ocean will buy it?" asked the lawyer dubiously. "They really hung tough on that point."

"They'll buy it," Bill replied confidently. "I finally got through on that call, and my New York source claims that Trans Ocean needs this deal desperately. They lost their ass on that well in the northern block."

"Can we treat it on a deal or no-deal basis?"

Bill hesitated only briefly before saying, "Go for it."

"Okay." The lawyer pencilled some notes in the margin. "I'll cable a new clause over first thing in the morning. There are a couple of other small points," he went on, and both men pored over the agreement whereby Venture Oils's UK subsidiary would earn, or "farm in," an interest in a block of oil lands under the North Sea by picking up a share of the cost of drilling a wildcat well. The well was authorized for expenditure (AFEd) to cost $4-million, and Venture's share would be considerably higher than the percentage interest it would earn. It was the amount of this "premium" that had involved Bill in the toughest bargaining sessions. It was finally agreed that Venture would pay forty per cent of the cost to earn a twenty-five per cent interest in the exciting and costly North Sea oil play, and Bill managed temporarily to blank out the pain of Margo's treachery while he and the lawyer concentrated on the documents. Then the voice of Tim Connors, Venture's chief pilot, announced that they were beginning the descent into Calgary.

Debbie's white Mustang convertible was parked beside the Avitat hangar, and Bill spotted her standing inside the lighted reception area, waiting for the shrieking jets to be turned off before she opened the door and stepped out onto the tarmac. Whenever he saw his daughter after an absence, no matter how brief, Bill was struck anew by how much she resembled her dead mother. Slightly under medium height, she had the same bright blonde hair that stopped just this side of brassiness and a spectacularly voluptuous figure that had made Marianne a fantasy object for every male employee of Consolidated Petroleum back in the days when she'd been a legal secretary in the Houston head office and Bill Crawford was a rookie geologist just a few months out of the Rice Institute. Debbie's eyes were her father's, though — cool blue-grey under arcing dark eyebrows.

Bill stood at the foot of the ramp, breathing in the crisp night air and moving his shoulders to shake off the fatigue of the long overseas flight. Smiling with affectionate pleasure, he opened his arms as Debbie ran up. She buried her face against his shoulder for a moment, then leaned back to peer up at him. "You've read it already, haven't you?"

The smile faded from his face. "I have. Ches picked up a copy in Frobisher. Not exactly flattering, is it?"

"When I think of how that two-faced bitch used you!" she stormed.

"She made me look pretty foolish all right," Bill agreed ruefully. Dismayed by his air of resigned acceptance, Debbie glared at him, but he forestalled her angry retort by excusing himself to go to the washroom. The toilet facilities on the Lear were for emergency use only.

"We're going to sue her for everything she's got, right Ches?" Debbie said as she swung the Mustang onto the main exit road.

Chester Martin, crammed with his suitcase and bulging briefcase into the cramped back seat, leaned forward. "We discussed that on the plane, Debbie. Your father is very reluctant to involve himself in that kind of mud-slinging contest, and I tend to agree with him."

Debbie gave an exasperated sideways glance at her father. He was staring straight ahead, his handsome, clean-cut profile illuminated by the glow of the dashboard light. His mouth, which normally curved in an amused half-smile that saved his expression from being too remote and aloof, was set in a grim straight line. Debbie knew what that meant, but still she expostulated, "Well I think it would be an absolute crime to let that awful woman get away with what she's done!"

"Drop it, Debbie," her father said quietly.

Her lips pouted mutinously, but she reached over and squeezed his hand. "Okay, if that's what you want."

They dropped Chester Martin off at his Mount Royal home and drove in silence the few blocks to the Crawford residence, an imposing pile of sandstone and brick on Prospect Avenue. Oddly enough, the immense old mansion had been Marianne's choice. It had seemed totally at variance with her alcoholic retreat from the world, but Bill had finally come to understand that it was her world, and that wandering through its many rooms was her substitute for going outside and actually participating in life. After her hideous death, he had fully intended to sell the place, but two years later he still hadn't got around to putting it on the market.

When he suggested that Debbie come in for a nightcap, the tone of his voice made it clear he didn't want to be left alone just yet.

"Love to," she agreed. "But I don't want to keep you up. You must be exhausted. How long did the flight take this time?"

"The usual eleven hours, give or take a few minutes, including refuelling stops at Reykjavik and Frobisher. You get used to it after a while."

The front door opened and Chong, the Chinese manservant, hurried down the path to take the luggage. Bill had hired him when the Crawford's long-time housekeeper, Mrs. MacLeod, distraught at Marianne's death and blaming herself for it, had gone back to her native Scotland. It had taken some pretty forceful persuasion by Bill before the proud old lady finally agreed to accept the monthly pension that allowed her to live comfortably in her Highland home.

"Margo was sort of special to you, wasn't she, Dad?" Debbie asked when they were settled with their drinks.

"Not any more," Bill answered bleakly. "What about your brother?" he asked after a long pause. "Does he know about this garbage?"

"Not from me. The magazine isn't published in the States, so there's no danger of Frank spotting it on the newsstands down there. He's due in on Saturday, and I thought it could wait until then."

Bill frowned. "I don't think it can. Some of his classmates at the School of Mines are from Calgary, and you can bet their families will send along copies of the article. I'll call him tomorrow." He glanced at Debbie. "You coming out to the airport with me to meet him?"

"Of course. He's really excited about coming home. He's full of great plans for the ranch. You better brace yourself for some pretty radical changes around the Circle C, Dad."

Bill smiled indulgently. "He really loves that place. I can still remember the look on his face when I put him on the back of his first pony. He comes by that feeling for the land honestly enough. My paternal grandfather was a homesteader in Oklahoma." The strained look was easing from Bill's face as he talked about family matters. "And at the same time, Frank has done all right in that petroleum engineering course."

"He's really worked at it. Did he ever tell you that he audited some agricultural courses on the side?"

"The hell he did! That's why he sounds like some kind of scientist when he talks about breeding cattle. The boy's a double threat."

Relieved to see her father's good humour restored, Debbie finished her drink and stood up to leave.

Debbie's thoughts were still on Frank as she drove downtown. Ever since her older brother, Billy, had been killed in that crazy, heartbreaking accident, Frank seemed to feel an obligation to equip himself to follow his father into Venture Oils. She was almost sure that his heart had been set on attending agricultural college; yet, without telling anyone, he had enrolled in the petroleum engineering course at the Colorado School of Mines. Damn you, Billy, why did you have to die such a stupid, pointless death? She'd make a point of going for some long rides with Frank out at the ranch, and maybe he'd open up about his plans.

Her father sure wasn't opening up about that awful article. If it had been up to her, she would have sued the ass off that Jones bitch. Unless, of course, there was no chance of winning. That had to be the reason. Dad must know inside himself that Margo could make some of the filth stick. He hadn't got to where he was without being pretty pragmatic about things, and he had obviously decided to take his lumps and ride this one out.

By the time she had parked the Mustang in its underground stall and taken the elevator to her high-rise apartment, Debbie had acknowledged to herself that there would be no lawsuit. That only meant, however, that vengeance would have to take a different form — a more deadly form.

Debbie's apartment was a showplace, with a sunken living room, a marble fire-place, deep carpeting, and a panoramic view of the rapidly growing city skyline. It was the pad of a rich man's daughter, but that didn't faze Debbie. There were some things that simply were not worth bothering about. If her father happened to be wealthy enough to give her a fabulous living allowance, so be it. She had no doubts about being able to survive very nicely on her own if the circumstances had been different.

She moved restlessly about the apartment, picking up the black argillite Haida carvings, that she collected on a sporadic basis, and putting them down again with-out really seeing them, while her analytical mind searched for an avenue of attack against the poised and sophisticated Margo Jones. Debbie wasn't forcing the pace; she was just letting her thoughts wander over the various possibilities, confident that in time inspiration would strike.

She nearly dropped a tiny, intricately carved totem pole when the harsh ring of the phone shattered the air-conditioned silence. It was Pete, slightly tipsy, wanting to come over. She turned him down, not bothering to be polite about it. He was a good-looking hunk and not bad in bed, but his narcissistic preoccupation with his own body was beginning to drive her right up the wall. Maintaining an even suntan was the height of his ambition.

Ambition! This was where Margo Jones lived! Whatever one might think of her methods, she was fiercely determined to establish herself in the front rank of the new breed of female journalists. Destroying her credibility as a professional journalist would be the most devastating punishment that could be inflicted on someone like her.

2

There was no copy of the offending issue of *Tomorrow* in the neat array of current magazines spread out on the coffee table in Venture Oils's reception area. Normally it would have been on display along with *Time, Oilweek,* and *Fortune,* but someone, either the receptionist or more likely Lisa Pollock, Bill's private secretary, had banished it.

The immaculately groomed Lisa made no mention of the article as she welcomed Bill back to the office and enquired politely about his trip. Tactful discretion was a prerequisite for being an executive secretary, along with the ability to sit for endless hours at a desk without appearing bored while the boss was away on protracted business trips. The higher her boss's position, the less actual work there was for his secretary to do, but she was expected to slip smoothly into high gear whenever he returned. With an open dictation book in her hand, Lisa stood in front of Bill's walnut desk, which was bare of any papers or ornament except a core of reservoir rock from Bent River No. 2, the oil discovery that was the key to Venture's success.

"I wasn't sure how heavy a schedule you wanted on your first day back, so I haven't confirmed any appointments except one with Mr. Wilson at ten." Bill nodded agreement. Dave Wilson was Venture's exploration manager, and would bring Bill up to speed on the exploratory wells that were drilling and any new land plays that might be in the works.

Lisa made a little tick beside Wilson's name and continued smoothly: "Here are the people who would like to see you as soon as possible ..." She read out a list of ten names, mostly senior company personnel along with some top executives from other oil companies. Bill told her the ones he would see that day and which ones to put off until the following week.

Dave Wilson was short, tubby, and bald and looked more like a successful used-car salesman than the scientist he was. Like most geologists, he was optimistic by nature, although a lifetime of dealing with the mysteries and disappointments of the "black art" of finding oil had given a wry, laconic slant to his personality. His report didn't take very long; road bans were in effect and drilling operations were shut down on all but one of Venture's wells. The one that was still drilling ahead was within a couple of miles of a main highway, and it was economically practical to stockpile enough fuel and supplies to last through the spring breakup.

The door had barely closed behind the exploration manager when Lisa came through on the intercom to announce that Clint Boyle was calling. Bill told her to put him through; he was the Canadian manager of Paragon Petroleums, a large multinational company with headquarters in Houston. It had impressive landholdings in Alberta, but its head office was beginning to doubt the wisdom of continuing to spend huge sums of money in Canada, which made it a prime source for farm-outs. Within the past six months, Venture Oils had completed two successful farm-out wells on Paragon lands. Bill didn't particularly care for Boyle's bluff, boisterous manner, but his voice was warm and cordial when he spoke into the phone.

His greeting, however, was swept aside by the torrent of sound issuing from the earpiece. "If you want to make a fucking spectacle of yourself, that's okay by me," Boyle was thundering. "Be my guest. But, by Jesus, I'm not about to stand still while that cunt dumps all over me!"

"What the hell are you talking about, Clint?" Bill instinctively stalled for time, although he already knew the answer. He had arranged for Margo to have lunch with Clint, and the florid-faced oilman with his General Bullmoose style would be an irresistible target for her.

"You know fucking well what I'm talking about," Clint raged. "There's another article coming out in the next issue of that rag, and I'm in it. Front and centre."

"What can I say, Clint? Except that I'm sorry as hell. Some of these things can't be controlled, you know."

"Well, by Christ, I'm going to control this one! My attorney's already been on the telephone to the editors telling them we'll have their ass if they don't kill that story."

"Great stuff!" Bill was elated. If Boyle managed to block the second instalment, it would preserve a number of reputations and keep Bill Crawford off the permanent shit list of some very influential people.

"Except that it ain't goin' to work," Boyle growled. "They as good as told my lawyer to stuff it; claimed there was nothing libellous in the article, that Miss Jones was a first-class journalist who always documented her sources and all that crap. Henry Stevens," Bill recognized the name of one of Calgary's leading trial lawyers, "figures it might cool 'em down when you sue them. He thinks you should get your action started right away, while there's still time to yank the next article."

"I'm not planning to sue, Clint," Bill said slowly.

"Tell me you didn't say what I thought you said," pleaded a dumbfounded Boyle.

"My lawyer advises against it." Bill mentally apologized to Chester Martin for putting words in his mouth. "It's the kind of situation where a plaintiff loses even if he wins."

"I used to have a lot of respect for you, Crawford," Boyle said in a voice that was no longer a rant and was all the more deadly for it. "But if you just lie down and take this like a whipped cur dog, I'll ... I'll ..." Sputtering with rage, he slammed down the receiver.

It was Bill's custom, on those days when he had no specific appointment for lunch, to walk over to the Petroleum Club and sit at the community table. The service was fast and efficient, and the matronly waitresses usually placed a bowl of consommé in front of him before he'd had time to fill out the luncheon chit. The menu even included a "Crawford special," a turkey salad served with cottage cheese and sliced pears. Bill had ordered it so often that the club had named the dish after him. Lunching at the long table was also a very effective way of keeping up with current happenings in the oil patch, with much useful information to be gleaned from the banter and gossip. But it would be open season on him if he showed up there today. The wisecracks he could take; but he didn't want to face the anxiety and animosity of those who might be crucified in Margo's second article. Using the backlog of paperwork as an excuse, he decided to remain at his desk and have Lisa bring him a sandwich.

Finished his modest lunch, Bill wiped his hands on the paper serviette and dropped it on the plate. He still felt sticky so he went into the private washroom adjoining his office. It was little more than a glorified closet, nothing like the elaborate layout in the new building. Staring into the mirror over the sink, he was assailed with an unfamiliar sense of weary defeat. He was fifty-three years old, for Christ's sake! What had possessed him to think he was capable of attracting the love of a talented and beautiful girl still in her early thirties? Being sucked up to for his wealth and power, yes, he could expect that, but love for love's own sake was behind him. Shaking his head impatiently at his own mawkishness, he turned on the tap. As he reached for a towel, however, he had a sudden image of Margo's elegant little face, delectable lips curving back to reveal perfect white teeth, dark eyes dancing. He was in for some rough sessions before he got that lady out of his system.

In the intervals between his afternoon appointments, he fielded two more calls from close friends who were alarmed at what Margo might write about them. The first one at least had the good grace to commiserate with Bill over the way the article had cut Bill up before launching into his own woes, but Ted Riley had been too overwrought to bother with such niceties. "Damn it, Bill," he had wailed, "you're single, and that stuff about making out in the Lear won't do you any harm at all. But if that bitch prints any of that sort of crap about me, Jean will be on the next flight south!"

Since it was common knowledge that Jean Riley, née Filberg, had all the money in the Riley household, Ted's panic was understandable. Bill told him to contact the magazine's management, either directly or through his lawyers, and demand to see an advance copy of Margo's article. If enough pressure were brought to bear, they might get the wind up sufficiently to tone it down if not withdraw it altogether.

When his last visitors had departed, Lisa came in with an engraved invitation. "You haven't forgotten the bank reception, have you?"

Bill sighed and reached for the card. "I sure haven't. I'll have to go." The National Bank was holding a meeting of its board of directors in Calgary and, to mark the occasion, was hosting a large reception at the Westin Hotel. To oilmen like Bill, dependent on bank loans to finance their search for oil and gas, the invitation was tantamount to a royal command.

His route took him past the partially completed Venture Tower. Work was finished for the day, and the site was deserted except for a uniformed commissionaire standing outside the security shack. The topping-off ceremony had been held a couple of weeks before he had left for England, and since then they had made good progress installing the outside curtain wall. The tower dominated the city landscape and had far more space than would be required to house Venture's employees, who were presently scattered in eight different locations throughout the downtown area. Bill's travels in the Middle East had convinced him that the world oil scene was in for some radical changes and that one of the side effects would be a sharp upswing in industry activity in the province of Alberta. He saw it as a golden opportunity to build a head office that would serve the needs of Venture Oils far into the future and would also be a profit centre in its own right if the excess space were leased out until required by his growing company. His view prevailed, even though Lee Travis, one of his directors, grumbled that Venture was an oil company, not a goddamn real-estate developer.

Events seemed to be proving Lee right. So far, only two of the floors other than the ones reserved for Venture had been leased. Al Medford, the representative of the leasing agency, who was one of his afternoon appointments, made no attempt to minimize the gravity of the situation. "It looks like we could be two or three years ahead of the times. However," he added cautiously, "I have had some indication of interest from a possible tenant who might take ten floors."

"That's the best news I've had all day," Bill enthused. "Sign 'em up!"

"It's still a long way from the signing stage." Al started to reach in his pocket for a pack of cigarettes, then remembered Bill didn't smoke, changed pockets, and produced a crumpled Kleenex tissue. "There's just one thing," he muttered, blowing his nose unnecessarily. "The people I'm dealing with are another oil company, and since they would be the major tenant, they feel they should have the right to name the building."

"Never!"

Al Medford shrugged. "That's your privilege, of course. Don't forget, though, that ten-floor tenants aren't exactly easy to come by."

Margo had written about the possibility that the new building would turn into a "disastrous white elephant." And that's exactly what could happen, Bill reflected as he stood on the sidewalk and squinted up at his creation. If the rental income failed to materialize, Venture's revenues would be eaten up servicing the mortgage instead of being reinvested in finding new reserves of oil and gas.

"Admiring your erection?" A hearty voice intruded on Bill's depressing chain of thought.

"Just as long as it's not my last one." Bill responded amiably to the well-worn joke and shook hands with Ernie Foster, an extroverted promoter who had been hanging around the periphery of the patch for years, surviving quite nicely on low-risk edgewell farm-outs, and by flipping small land plays.

They walked together the few remaining blocks to the Westin. "I just got back from the UK last night, and I've been chained to my desk all day," Bill said casually, "so I haven't picked up on any of the scuttlebutt. I imagine that *Tomorrow* article provided a lot of laughs?"

"It was the talk of the town all right. To be honest, I don't think it did you a whole lot of good."

"I know," Bill replied sombrely as the doorman opened the glass door and tipped his brown Stetson respectfully to the chief of Venture Oils.

Ernie Foster, happy to be seen in this exalted company, stayed beside Bill as they went down the reception line of bank directors, identified by the white carnations in their buttonholes. A trio of scantily clad models handed a name tag to each guest as soon as he had shaken the hand of the most junior vice-president on the far end of the line. Apart from the waitresses, these were the only females in a crowd of some five hundred people. The oil patch was very much a male preserve.

The model took her time affixing Bill's name tag, holding his lapel while she smoothed the adhesive tag with her fingertips. She gave it a final lingering pat and smiled up at him. "There you go, Mr. Crawford." Bill thanked her and turned away, to be met with a row of outstretched hands. Venture Oils was among the top five of the independent oil companies, and Bill ranked high in the petroleum hierarchy. The press, impressed with his still-boyish good looks and easy way with words, sometimes referred to him as the "Crown Prince of the Canadian oil industry."

A number of the men looked a little uneasy, as if wondering whether to mention the article or not — with no one willing to be the first to bring it up, until a tall, beefy man with a mane of white hair dipped a shrimp in the cocktail sauce, swallowed it with a noisy smacking of lips, and chortled, "You was snakebit the day you met that reporter gal, Billy boy."

"I can't deny that, Jess," Bill replied in an even tone that did not encourage further discussion. The others chuckled appreciatively, relieved that the troublesome item had been duly brought up and disposed of, and they could get back to the things that really mattered, like whether ol' J.C. had honest-to-God found Devonian oil in his Nisku wildcat or was simply priming the market so he could unload a few shares of his stock.

"Can we talk, Bill?" The question was accompanied by a light touch of his elbow, and Bill looked down to see Jim Goulder, one of the senior partners of Confederation Securities, standing beside him. Jim's brokerage firm had done the underwriting of the two public issues of Venture stock. As always, Goulder looked rumpled and bone-weary, as if ready to topple over from sheer fatigue, but Bill knew he was quite capable of sitting through the marathon all-night sessions that for some mysterious reason seemed to be an essential part of every stock underwriting.

"I just came in on the afternoon flight from Toronto," the broker said as they worked their way through the press of people, many detaining Bill for a brief handshake, while others eyed him speculatively. Eventually, he and Goulder found a quiet backwater at the rear of the long reception line, and Jim muttered, "The TSE was buzzing with rumours about Venture."

"The stock's been strong," Bill replied, with the automatic defensiveness of a chief executive of a publicly listed company.

"Very. While every other oil stock was dropping, it gained one and a half points this week." Jim paused as if to pay tribute to this admirable performance, then blinked up at Bill with watery brown eyes that seemed perpetually out of focus but could pounce with unerring accuracy upon a misplaced comma in a hundred-page prospectus. "I expect it will be even stronger when the market opens on Monday. The rumour is that someone may be trying to take it over."

"What?" Stunned, Bill took a step backward. It had been the possibility that a corporate raider might take a run at the company, his company, which had made him so reluctant to go public, even though the company desperately needed the funds to finance its expanding exploration programs. The experts from Confederation Securities had assured him that the large block he owned personally, together with the holdings of his US backers, made the company virtually immune to outside attacks.

"You told me it couldn't happen." Bill let his anger show.

"What we said was," Jim corrected him, "that it couldn't happen without the co-operation of yourself or the consortium."

"Well, I'm sure as hell not co-operating with anybody who's trying to steal my company. And it doesn't make sense that the investor groups would either. They're not interested in hands-on management, and Venture's been one hell of an investment for them."

"The rumour could easily be wrong. Some broker could have started it to kill time on a dull day. Or a buyer could be accumulating a position for straight investment purposes. Still, the activity really picked up when that appalling article appeared, almost as if somebody is trying to capitalize on it and knock you out of the box."

The panic that had struck Bill at the thought of losing his company was giving way to a steely determination to keep it at all costs. "So what do we do now?" he asked through gritted teeth.

"See if we can get some reading from the market action on Monday. In the meantime, I'm going to check all my traplines and see if I can find out who's doing the buying. If it turns out to be an institutional investor, like a pension fund, then there's no cause for alarm." Jim lifted his shoulders in an apologetic shrug. "I'm sorry to lay this on you, Bill. It's just that I feel we have to stay on top of things like this."

"You're damn right we do." Bill placed his empty glass on a tray carried by a passing waiter. He was still shaken by the possibility that someone out there who was completely unknown to him might be taking dead aim at Venture Oils. "I'll be out at the ranch for the weekend. You can reach me there any time."

3

Frank wanted to go directly to the ranch. That didn't surprise Debbie; she knew that the Mount Royal mansion held even unhappier memories for him than it did for her. As a teenager, she had gradually learned to dissociate herself from her mother's alcoholism — after a few humiliating experiences she had simply stopped bringing friends home after school and found her fun elsewhere. But Frank, four years younger and with a father who seemed to be always away on business trips, had been trapped. He had also displayed a compassion and understanding beyond his years and had done what he could to comfort and help his mother as she retreated further and further into the bottle.

They were in the big, silver Mercedes. Bill asked his son if he wanted to drive, but Frank declined — he didn't want to miss a single glimpse of his beloved foothill country en route to the ranch. The Circle C had formerly been two separate ranches, which had faced each other across a river that was little more than a creek for most of the year. In late April, however, the spring runoff from the mountains was in full spate, and brown water coiled along the foot of the sandstone banks as the heavy sedan rumbled over the private bridge. There had been times when Bill had despaired of ever getting permission to build that bridge. The Calling Bird River was officially listed as a navigable waterway, despite the fact that even a rowboat had difficulty negotiating its rocky shallows, and it had taken two years and all his influence, together with Chester Martin's legal arguments, before the go-ahead had been given.

The main house was on the south side of the river. It was a low, modern structure of Montana stone and cedar siding built in the shape of a square *U*, with a dramatic view of the Rocky Mountains, smoky blue in the distance. Debbie had phoned ahead, and the horses were ready for them in the corral — quarter horses with Western saddles for the two men and a thoroughbred hunter for her.

"The Calgary horse show's coming up pretty soon, isn't it?" asked Frank as they trotted out of the yard, the spirited thoroughbred dancing and snorting with excitement.

"The week after next," Debbie told him. She stroked her horse's neck. "But this old boy won't be in it this year. I've retired him."

"You've still got Star Song, though?" Frank shot his sister a questioning glance.

"Oh, yes. She's entered in the show. I've got her stabled at Blue Meadows where I can school her every day. That's where I've got my new horse, Imperial Way. He's still green, but he's got conformation to burn and loves to jump. Give him a year and watch out!"

Debbie put her horse at a wooden panel set into the barbed-wire fence, and he soared over it. Bill reined in to admire her smooth jumping style. Some of his friends joked that their daughters lost interest in horses as soon as they discovered boys. But Debbie had discovered boys years ago, with a vengeance, without it perceptibly diminishing her enthusiasm for horses. Frank had ridden over to the barbed-wire gate and was holding it open while his horse stood quietly. The quarter horse might not be built for jumping fences, but he sure was handy around gates and cattle.

They stayed out most of the afternoon, confined to the south side of the river by the swirling waters of the runoff that made the usual fording places impassable. Several times they stopped to check the herds of cattle with the *C* brand on their flanks. The herds were of above-average quality, but Bill knew they should be better, considering the money that was lavished on the ranching operation. "It looks to me like we could use some new bulls," he remarked as they inspected some white-faced Herefords grazing on a sunlit hillside.

"We need more than that, Dad," Frank replied. "We should cull the herd and build up a new one from scratch. And we should be thinking seriously about some of the exotic breeds, too."

"Hold on," Bill laughed. "It's just a hobby operation. A place for the family to relax."

"It could be much more than that. It could be a ..." Frank broke off as his father spurred his horse into a canter and led the way back to the river and home.

The telephone started ringing for Debbie well before dinner and kept up until nine o'clock. Bill and Frank exchanged wry smiles as they listened to the practised ease with which she refused the invitations, leaving the door open for another occasion. Except for Pete. Whoever he was, the unfortunate young man had clearly played out his string with Debbie.

"Don't stay in on our account," Bill said after she had hung up on the fifth call. "I don't know about Frank, but I'm beat after all that riding this afternoon, and I'm going to turn in early." A sudden yawn proved his point.

"I'm perfectly happy right here with my two favourite men." She smiled and tucked her shapely legs underneath her on the couch.

If Bill and Debbie had been alone, Bill might have mentioned Goulder's suspicions about a possible takeover attempt on Venture. While Debbie was still in her early teens, Bill had discovered that his daughter possessed a very cool and analytical brain behind that pretty face, and he had begun to discuss his business affairs with her. At first it was a means of educating her and stimulating her interest, but gradually he had come to realize how much it was helping his own decision-making; not only because it forced him to talk his way through a problem, but also because of Debbie's increasingly astute questions and suggestions.

He had never been able to establish that kind of rapport with the boys. His glance strayed to the silver-framed photo of Billy on the mantel. It was just a few weeks short of five years since Billy had missed a turn on a mountain road and plunged over a cliff. The car had landed right side up, but the four young people inside it had died, their necks snapped by the sheer hundred-foot drop. Billy and his sidekick, Ben Snyder, had picked up a couple of girls who were barely out of high school and gone for a joyride. All four were bare-ass naked and stoned out of their skulls on hashish. Because of the evidence of drugs the insurance company had refused to pay, and it had cost Bill half a million dollars and change to settle the claims out of court. Bill had always tried to convince himself that if Billy had lived he would have outgrown his wild ways and done something worthwhile with his life. That was what well-meaning friends also kept assuring him when he was trying to cope with the trauma of losing his son. But Billy's wild, self-indulgent streak ran deep. It seemed to be a way of life by itself, without the counterbalance of the need to achieve that Bill realized was what kept his own life on the rails.

As for Frank — Bill smiled fondly at his youngest child sitting beside Debbie on the long leather couch — he was the straight arrow of the family. It was too bad in a way that Frank didn't have Debbie's keen interest in the world of business. His eyes had a tendency to glaze over when the discussion turned to the niceties of how a deal was put together. But he tried. Frank would always try, and maybe it would come with time — Bill had seen other young men suddenly turn on and start to do big things.

"What about wheels, Frank? If you're going to live out here, you'll need transportation. How about a convertible like Debbie's? It'll be your graduation present."

"If it's all the same to you, Dad, I'd like a pickup truck. Maybe one of those new Dodges with four-wheel drive."

Debbie burst out laughing at the look on her father's face. "Just be grateful he didn't ask for a tractor!"

Bill held up his hands in surrender. "A pickup it is. And you're also entitled to a trip. Where would you like to go?"

"Don't you think I should start work pretty soon?"

"No, I don't. You've just finished four gruelling years of college, and I think you need a break."

"Well, in that case, I'd really like to see Europe, particularly France and Italy."

France and Italy — the home of the exotic cattle-breeding industry. Bill knew how his son would spend his time — visiting every Charolais and Marchigiana breeder in Europe. He caught Debbie's eye, and she winked at him.

"Okay, Frank. Lisa will make the arrangements." Bill got to his feet. "I'm for bed. I expect I'll spend the morning on the phone, so I'll see you two at lunchtime."

When they were alone, Frank turned to Debbie with a troubled look and said that their father seemed to be losing interest in the ranch.

"I really don't think that's right. He just looks at it a little differently than you do.

To him, it's a retreat — a place to relax in, like he said this afternoon. On the other hand, you'd like it to become a real working ranch. Right?"

"It would be so easy to turn it around, it almost makes you weep. But," Frank sighed, "I'm going to have enough on my plate just trying to survive in the oil patch."

Bill and Debbie drove back to town late the following afternoon. True to his word, Bill had spent the morning on the phone, mostly on a conference call with Jim Goulder and Chester Martin. Nothing conclusive had emerged from the discussions, except that if a raid was in fact on, some kind of deal must have been struck with the principal American shareholders. Without their co-operation, it would be impossible for an outsider to gain control. Chester reminded Bill of the shareholders' agreement, which required the four major investors, including Bill, to give the others first refusal of any shares they wished to sell. It offered some protection, provided, of course, that one could raise the millions of dollars that would be necessary to buy up the shares. It was all very indefinite and unsatisfactory, and Bill felt a sense of foreboding over what signals the market would send out in the morning. He kept these grim thoughts to himself, however, and he and Debbie fell into a companionable silence as they joined the flow of Sunday drivers heading back to the city.

"The ranch is a great recharger," he said as he let Debbie off in front of her apartment block. "I'm ready to take on the world again."

She lifted her overnight bag from the rear seat and stood on the sidewalk to wave at him as he drove off in the direction of Mount Royal.

Chong had turned on the heater in the outside pool, and Bill decided on a quick dip before dinner despite the chill of the early evening. The spot where the firepit had been cemented in was still faintly visible on the concrete apron surrounding the pool, and Bill gave it a wide berth. He had been in New York the night Marianne had decided to have an impromptu poolside party for some of her drinking buddies. She would have spells where she would manage to cut down on her drinking and, in the typical manner of social alcoholics, be eager to display her comparative sobriety. There had been eight of them, including herself — three divorced women, confirmed lushes all, and two couples whose marriages were held together only by a mutual addiction to alcohol.

A tape of some old Tommy Dorsey favourites was playing through the patio speakers, and Marianne was dancing by herself, jitterbugging the way she had when she was the most popular girl in Midland Central High. Her guests applauded with drunken enthusiasm, unconsciously responding to the spirit of a vibrant young girl shining through the missed beats and ludicrously clumsy footwork. The tempo of the music increased, and Marianne's feet flew faster. Head thrown back, she was smiling exultantly when her ankles crossed, pitching her backwards into the blazing, kerosene-soaked logs.

Bill would never accept any explanation other than that she had struck her head on the concrete rim and been knocked unconscious immediately. She had lain motionless on the fatal pyre while the flames ignited her flimsy dress and blackened her flesh. It took her befuddled companions several precious seconds to grasp the full horror of what was happening. Their screams as they struggled to haul Marianne out of the pit brought the horrified housekeeper flying out of the house to extinguish the human torch with a mink coat grabbed from the front hall closet. By then Marianne had suffered second- and third-degree burns to seventy per cent of her body. It had taken her a week to die in the hospital, although the doctors had warned Bill from the start that she had no hope of survival.

Bill did ten laps at a punishing pace and was breathing hard when he hoisted himself out of the shallow end. Towelling himself vigorously, he resolved to call Al Medford in the morning and put the house on the market. Filling in the firepit and completely redecorating the interior had failed utterly to exorcise the ghost of the unhappy Marianne.

4

The market opened at 10:00 a.m. Toronto time, which meant that the Canadian brokers had to rise early and be at their phones by 8:00 a.m. Bill called Jim Goulder at 8:15 to be told that 5,000 shares had traded already at almost a point higher than Friday's close.

"Why don't we do a little buying ourselves?" asked Bill. "Anything wrong with that?"

"No," Jim replied after a pause. "In fact, a few outside orders might signal that speculators are anticipating a takeover and are starting to move in for the kill. It just might force the mysterious buyer to fill his basket before the price of the stock is driven out of sight. I'll jitney the orders out through a couple of the other houses so they won't be traced back to you. Five thousand at market seem about right?"

"Go ahead. I'm just leaving for the office. If you need me in the next ten minutes, call me on the car phone."

As it turned out, however, the broker didn't call back until eleven o'clock. Monday mornings were always busy at the Venture head office as the week's activities geared up, and with Gavin Anderson, the president and chief operating officer, not due back from San Francisco until early that afternoon, Bill's time was fully occupied. He dealt expeditiously with the operating decisions that had to be made, while a corner of his mind fretted over how the stock was acting.

"All the indicators are there." As usual Jim's wispy voice sounded as if it might trail off into nothing before he completed the sentence. "You got your five thousand — three at fifteen and the balance at fifteen and one-eighth. That trade seemed to trigger a real feeding frenzy. The volume is already in excess of fifty thousand for the day, and the price is sixteen and climbing." He paused as if struck by a sudden thought. "My God, do you ever think about your own personal worth at these levels?"

Bill brushed the thought aside. "Are you telling me there's definitely a raid underway?"

"I just can't come up with any other explanation for the way the stock is performing. It's the one bright spot on the board; the oil index is down nine points. If there were anything about the company itself, something like a spectacular new discovery, you would be the first to know about it. So ..." Bill could almost see the broker's shrug over the telephone.

When the telephone light blinked off on her call director, Lisa came through the intercom to tell Bill his next appointment was waiting. Instructing her to delay a few minutes before showing him in, he leaned back in his swivel chair and stared out the window. In the little park across the railway tracks that bisected the downtown area, leaves were beginning to sprout on the bare branches of the trees, and patches of green were crowding out winter's brown grass. None of this registered on Bill. Goulder's unexpected remark had forcefully reminded him of something he had come to take for granted — he was a fabulously wealthy individual. His holding of Venture stock alone — he reached into a drawer for a pocket calculator and quickly punched in the numbers — were worth nearly $20-million, at this morning's market price.

Maybe the smart thing would be not to fight the takeover but simply to pick up his winnings and walk away. Somebody else could worry about running the company; he'd be cruising the Greek isles on a yacht, with champagne cooling in a silver bucket and bikinied starlets sunbathing on the forward deck. Many of his contemporaries had done just that: sold off the companies they had built up and retired. And what were they doing now? Forced by the tax laws to take a five-year leave of absence from the oil industry, they drank tall Caesars and played high-stakes gin rummy in the card room at the Pete Club, or teed off on their sixth golf game of the week. Not for him. Besides, Venture Oils was in large measure the sum of his life; its daily production of 2,500 barrels of crude oil and seventy-five million cubic feet of gas represented the arithmetic of his achievement. He leaned forward and stabbed the intercom button to carry on with the day's business.

The fact that he hadn't even attempted to contact Gavin Anderson over the weekend to tell him of the possible raid was revealing in itself. The thought depressed Bill as he shook hands with the president of his company and waved him into an armchair. Gavin had obviously lunched well on the flight from San Francisco — his flushed face and mint-scented breath attested to that. Bill didn't mind; it went with the territory in an industry that required its executives to be constantly on the move. What did bother him about his old friend and associate was that Gavin had been promoted to his own personal level of incompetence. It happened all too frequently in the oil industry, particularly in the case of geologists whose brilliance or luck in finding oil often led to their being appointed exploration managers, where they proved to be hopelessly inept at dealing with administrative problems.

Gavin had been one of the best lease-hounds in the patch; no one could sweet-talk a farmer out of a wellsite lease or a freehold mineral owner out of an oil lease better than the extroverted, easygoing Gavin. He had been adequate, barely, as land manager, where he had to negotiate deals with other oil companies. As president, he just couldn't hack it, and the knowledge was buried deep in those eyes that once had faced the world with good-humoured confidence.

"How did the convention go?" Bill asked conversationally. Gavin had been attending the American Natural Gas Association's annual convention in San Francisco.

Gavin shrugged, embarrassed by the fact that attending industry conventions and conferences was becoming an increasingly large part of his workload. "The usual. They went and elected me third vice-president when my back was turned."

"Great stuff!" Bill managed to sound enthusiastic, but it didn't fool either one of them. "Anyway, I'm very glad you're back. I may have to go to Houston later this afternoon."

"Oh?" Gavin's expression indicated that if Bill wanted to tell him the reason for the sudden trip, that was fine. If not, that was okay, too. When it became clear that nothing more was forthcoming, he asked, "Any idea when you'll be back?"

"Before the end of the week."

"Fair enough. Well, if there's nothing more, I'll meander back to my office and start picking up the threads."

Lee Travis. He was the key. He held twenty per cent of the voting stock, the same as Bill himself. Travis, second-generation Texas oil money, had been a classmate of Bill's at Rice, and he had been the one Bill had turned to for financing when he decided to leave Consolidated Pete and strike out on his own. How that move had upset Marianne! With no paycheque coming in regularly every two weeks, she was convinced they would be evicted from their home and end up on welfare.

Lee could be as elusive as the Scarlet Pimpernel, but this afternoon he was in his Houston office and took Bill's call. "Say, ol' buddy," he drawled, "you're a famous man. I've just been reading all about you."

Trust Lee to take the high ground right from the start. He had an uncanny ability to exploit every advantage, whether in negotiating a deal or in ordinary conversation. "Don't believe everything you read," replied Bill, with an unconvincing laugh. "Anyway, it doesn't seem to have hurt the stock."

"Ain't that the truth? You boys must be doin' somethin' right up there."

"That's what puzzles me. As far as our operations are concerned, there's just no reason for the stock to be performing like this."

"You got any other explanation?" Was there a sudden note of wariness in Lee's voice?

"None. But I'd like to talk it over with you. I'm going to be in Houston tomorrow."

"Golly, Bill, my days are real crowded just now. Could you postpone it a couple of weeks?"

"I have to be in Houston on other business," Bill lied, "and since I'm going to be there anyway, I think we should get together. It needn't take long."

"I could ask Ted to see you. Would that be any help?" It was perilously close to an insult. Ted Reid was Lee's executive assistant and the second Travis nominee on the Venture board. Both Lee and Bill knew he was nothing more than a messenger boy. "I don't think there's much point in my seeing Ted," replied Bill. "But I think it would be very useful for you and me to have a visit."

"Tell you what. We're having a little get-together at our place tomorrow night.

Why don't you come to that? Carol would love to see you."

It wasn't at all what Bill wanted. Lee's "little get-togethers" never involved less than a hundred guests, and there would be scant opportunity to talk. Was Lee banking on that? Now he was asking Bill where he was staying and saying that the Rolls would pick him up at his hotel at seven o'clock. Bill cancelled his plans to fly down that afternoon and ordered an early morning takeoff for the next day.

It was odd how even the most intractable problem seemed to solve itself as soon as a bigger one came along. Bill had been agonizing for more than two years over whether Gavin could assume responsibilities of a CEO. It was partly to answer this question that he had begun to distance himself from the everyday affairs of the company and to spend more time away from Calgary. As the Lear began its takeoff roll at eight o'clock the following morning, he knew with absolute certainty that the man he had made president of the company would never be its chief executive officer.

Bill was disconcerted to find himself suddenly thinking about Frank. Was his son really suited for the oil business? He certainly seemed hell-bent on entering it. Bill examined his own conscience and found no reason to reproach himself. It had never been his idea for Frank to follow in his footsteps. His personal motto was "Live and let live," and he had always done his best to apply that to his children. Maybe too much so, but there it was. If Frank was labouring under a misguided sense of duty, it was something he had dreamed up himself. Now, there was a line of thought that might be worth pursuing. In the meantime, Frank's forthcoming trip would give them a breathing spell. Mildly ashamed of himself for linking Gavin's limitations with Frank's aptitude for business, Bill turned his attention to the matter of what in hell was going on in his company.

Was Lee involved in some fashion? He had been anything but his usual outgoing self on the phone. As the custodian of old wealth, loftily removed from the struggle for economic survival, Lee liked to pose as a man of the highest rectitude and principles. Certainly he had been completely straightforward in every dealing that Bill had had with him. To date, that is, Bill reminded himself.

He hadn't thought about it for months, but now he recalled an airline flight from Riyadh to London almost a year ago. He was seated in first-class next to a Saudi Arabian sheikh who, with the restrictions of his Islamic homeland safely behind him, kept the stewardess busy serving him double Scotches. The sheikh was attached to the oil industry in some capacity and had an inexhaustible fund of stories, mostly scandalous, about the leading figures of the international oil patch. All the people he mentioned were known to Bill, either personally or by reputation, and Bill found himself being entertained almost against his will. Then his seatmate snickered and started to talk about "the righteous Mr. Lee Travis from Houston."

According to the garrulous sheikh, Lee, working behind a screen of corporations and phantom transactions, was rumoured to have purchased "old" oil at the government-regulated price and laundered it into "new" oil, which he sold at several times the original price. Bill hadn't been particularly shocked; the staggering difference between the price for the two categories of oil was a challenge many of the wheelers and dealers of the industry couldn't resist, and an incredible amount of ingenuity had been expended in converting one into the other. All it proved was that Lee could be as greedy as the next man. Which, now that Bill thought of it, was not exactly reassuring in the present circumstances.

The co-pilot came back and served Bill a coffee and a Danish. He told Bill they would be landing in Houston in another two hours. Bill thanked him absently and went on thinking about his principal shareholders. The Dwight family of Boston held five per cent of Venture's shares. Lee had brought them in when the company was in desperate need of money to drill up the Blindman River prospect. In return for lending the company $1-million, they had been permitted to purchase voting shares. They acquired additional shares a couple of years later when the Abrams brothers got into a bind in the commodities market and needed to sell some of their Venture stock. It was a fairly small block, and Bill and Travis had agreed to let the Dwights buy it all.

The Dwights were hard to get a handle on. As far as Bill could make out, their wealth was held in a number of interlocking family trusts administered by professional advisers. Certainly, Richard P. Dwight, III, the titular head of the family, took little or no part in the management of their affairs. His entire life was dedicated to ocean racing, in which he had acquired an international reputation as a gracious loser. His son-in-law, Adrian Strickland, was the Dwight nominee on Venture's board. Strickland was a pain in the ass. The young Princeton graduate was bright enough — and altogether too articulate for his own good; he just couldn't resist showing off the debating skills he had acquired at business school. Recently, he had begun to needle Gavin Anderson at the quarterly board meetings. What made it worse was his phony way of treating Gavin with mock deference while he asked questions he knew the president couldn't answer. Bill usually managed to intervene before it got completely out of hand, but Strickland's sadistic glee was not pleasant to watch.

Lee Travis had little use for the ineffable Strickland and didn't trouble to hide it. Still, it was Lee who had brought the Dwights into the Venture picture in the first place. And the Abrams boys, who had fought their way up from New York's garment district, were in awe of the patrician Dwight name. Christ, the permutations and combinations were endless with that bunch of high rollers! There was no point in trying to plan too far ahead until he had some hard information. Bill spent the rest of the flight trying to think of a replacement for Gavin Anderson. By the time they landed, he had pretty well decided that he himself would have to act as both chairman and president on a pro tem basis.

5

The white Rolls-Royce purred up to the hotel entrance at precisely seven o'clock. The black chauffeur told Bill they would arrive half an hour before the other guests because Mr. Travis wanted to have a private visit with him. This was welcome news to Bill. At least he would have a chance to be eyeball to eyeball with his long-time friend and backer. Although Bill knew that he was considered a mover and shaker in the Canadian oil patch, he was uncomfortably aware of the difference between himself and the super-rich like Travis. They marched to the beat of a different drummer, and there were times when they succeeded in making him feel hopelessly provincial with his never-ending pursuit of oil and bottom-line profits. But his were the real values, he told himself as the Rolls conveyed him regally through the luxurious estates of River Oaks. And, by God, neither they nor anyone else were going to take his company away from him!

Lee Travis, with his narrow, bony face and eyes that seemed perpetually narrowed against the sun's glare, looked like he belonged on the range, herding cattle. In fact, the only horses Lee ever rode were polo ponies. He greeted Bill warmly, his Texas accent and mannerisms at about half-throttle, and led him into the library, which, with its deep leather chairs and dark woodwork, was the one room that had been off-limits to the second Mrs. Travis's interior decorator. The encounter began with some polite sparring: both men congratulating each other on the performance of the stock, and Lee slipping in some jocular asides about Bill's macho lifestyle as depicted in Margo's article. His comments had a barbed edge to them. Was Lee getting pompous in middle age?

Whatever it was, it made Bill uneasy, and he decided to make his move. If nothing else, it might bring things out into the open. "I want you to know, Lee, that I intend to take up my full share of any stock you sell," he said.

The Texan gaped at him. "What in God's green world are you talking about, partner?"

"The shareholders' agreement. It gives each one of us the right to buy a pro rata share of any stock one of the other parties may wish to sell."

"I have absolutely no intention of selling any shares," Lee declared flatly, in a voice that had lost all trace of Texas twang.

"I'm relieved to hear that," replied Bill. In fact, he was anything but. The strategy he and Chester Martin had worked out relied heavily on the shareholders' agreement.

As long as the banks were prepared to lend him the necessary funds, it would permit him to stay at least within range in the share-purchase battle. But it wasn't worth the paper it was written on if Lee, instead of selling his shares, simply voted them against him. But why would he want to do that?

A conversation with the young heir to a banking fortune during the cocktail hour furnished the necessary clue. The young man and his pale-blonde wife stood momentarily isolated with Bill in one of those little pockets that constantly form and dissolve in the rushing swirl of a large social gathering.

"I think our host will make an excellent ambassador, don't you agree?" the young man asked, by way of making conversation.

"The Australians will love him," his pale wife gushed with unexpected vivacity. "He's horsey, just like them, and he entertains so beautifully."

Now, there was a motive for you. Bill excused himself from the informative young couple and went off in search of his host. He found him listening with rapt attention to a white-haired dowager whose crépey neck and powdered bosom were ablaze with diamonds.

"I understand congratulations are in order, Lee." Bill touched his host's sleeve and held out his hand.

Lee ignored the outstretched hand and shot him a sharp look. "You're jumping the gun, ol' buddy. As I was just telling Mrs. Pennington here, it's nothing more than a rumour."

The dowager archly tapped his wrist with a jewelled purse. "I just know it's going to happen. It's so right. And you've got support in the places that count. Close to the President." She turned away to meet a languid young man who bent to kiss her hand.

"I must see you tomorrow, Lee. You name the time," Bill said in the brief moment he was alone with his host.

Lee looked as if he were going to refuse, then shrugged. "Okay. I guess I owe you that much. Ten-thirty. My office."

Bill had been careful not to overdrink at Lee's party, but, even so, he had consumed enough alcohol to make him fall asleep as soon as he climbed into bed. He was wide awake at four-thirty, his restless mind anxiously seeking a way out of the Venture maze. Lee wanted that ambassadorship so badly he could taste it. After dinner, while coffee and liqueurs were being served, Bill had heard him say that the Travises had always been creators and accumulators of wealth, and now it seemed appropriate to have one of them serve in a public capacity. Maybe all the uncertainty was making him paranoid, but Bill felt that Lee was uneasy in his presence. Once, when Bill had mentioned some concern over his own position, Lee had stared at him as if astonished that it should be mentioned in the same breath as an ambassadorship.

Although it was clear that nothing was official, there was an air of quiet confidence in the Travis camp, which was a little unexpected when you considered that Lee had never been a strong supporter of the present incumbent of the Oval Office. Maybe he had just made a handsome contribution to the Republican war chest.

No, it was the Dwights. It had to be! They were really wired-in to the White House. Adrian was always boasting about how his father-in-law was one of the few men in America who could count on having his calls returned by the President the same day. Jesus. If those two outfits were ganged up against Bill, his position was pretty precarious. Knowing that sleep was impossible, he phoned room service and ordered breakfast.

The offices of Fidelity Holdings, which seemed to be at the apex of the Travis financial pyramid, were in the Alliance Bank building. The bank itself just happened to be owned by a Travis subsidiary. Bill was known to the staff at Fidelity — to his mingled amusement and chagrin, they treated him like the manager of some important foreign branch operation. The receptionist brought him coffee, and Ted Reid came out to keep him company while he waited to see the boss man.

Lee had a reputation for enjoying his own parties; his voice was raspy, and the narrow, squinty eyes were bloodshot. Sometimes old Lee wasn't any too swift when he was in the grip of a hangover like this.

"This ambassadorship is connected with the takeover, isn't it?" asked Bill as he and Lee went through the ritualistic shaking of hands.

"What takeover?" Lee replied testily. "There's no damn takeover that I know of."

"It may not be a takeover in the technical sense," Bill retorted, "but it smells like a scheme to vote me out of control, and that's a takeover as far as I'm concerned."

"You're guessing."

"The hell I am. The only thing I haven't figured out is what's in it for the Dwights." As Bill spoke, the last piece of the puzzle fell into place. "Christ, it's a make-over project for dear Adrian. They want to make him the head of Venture."

The look in Lee's eyes confirmed it. The Texan obviously figured his position was unassailable, for he suddenly gave a nasty little grin and said, "You got it. I kinda think the idea of having Adrian up in Calgary, thousands of miles away from Boston, has a lot of appeal for ol' Richard P!"

The bile rose in Bill's throat at the thought of the enterprise he had so laboriously created being subject to the whims of the inexperienced and insufferable Adrian. "Good God, man!" he burst out. "Do you have any idea of what you're doing?"

Lee merely shrugged. It was obvious he regarded the risk of his investment in Venture going down the tubes as a reasonable trade-off for obtaining the diplomatic post he craved.

"I don't suppose the State Department would be exactly thrilled if they found out one of their ambassadors was involved in a hot oil scam." Bill played the only card he had left.

"What are you talking about?" The telltale flush started under Lee's chin and slowly rose to his forehead.

"You know damn well what I'm talking about." Bill studied his fingernails and observed mildly, "The feds put people in jail for that, you know, and the IRS come sniffing around like a pack of coon hounds looking for undeclared income. Remember a couple of months ago when they fined Permian $5-million and put Pete Demers in the slammer for two years?"

"That's blackmail, you son of a bitch!" Lee's fists were clenched.

"That's almost funny, coming from a guy who double-crosses his friends." Bill stared the Texan down. "You back off, and I back off. Deal?"

Lee swallowed and nodded grim assent.

As Bill walked the few blocks back to his hotel, he was aware that he had probably made a mortal enemy of Lee. On the other hand, he was still in control of Venture Oils. Or was he? What kind of control was it when he was at the mercy of a few powerful shareholders to whom the oil industry was no more meaningful than soybean futures or pork bellies?

As soon as he was back in his suite, Bill placed a call to Chester Martin. The lawyer was elated when Bill told him the situation was under control. "By God, I'll have two martinis before dinner tonight!"

"It may turn out to be just a temporary reprieve, Ches. I want you to crank up that legal mind of yours and figure out some way of making sure my control can't be challenged."

"Circle the wagons, eh? With or without the co-operation of the investor groups?"

"Without."

Chester whistled, rattling the receiver in Bill's ear. "That's like trying to make two and two add up to five, Bill."

"I'm aware of that. Nevertheless, I want you to start to work on it."

"Consider it done. Once again, Bill, congratulations. I'll think of you when I'm building those martinis."

Bill was grinning when he replaced the receiver. He was in the mood for a little celebration himself ... Nancy Holman. Good Lord, he had almost completely forgotten her since meeting Margo. Without giving himself time for second thoughts, he thumbed through his address book for Nancy's Houston number. Her answering service took the call. That was standard procedure; she never accepted calls directly and was highly selective about the ones she returned. She returned his within half an hour, her voice warm and inviting, with no hint of reproach that she hadn't heard from him in more than three months. Nor was she coy about the short notice of his dinner invitation. She accepted briskly, and the conversation was over.

The stock would fall right out of bed when the market realized that the rumoured takeover wasn't going to happen. The buying pressure would evaporate, and the speculators who had jumped in with the expectation of a quick profit would bail out in a mad panic. He could make a small fortune by selling short, but that was a definite no-no for an insider possessing confidential information. Besides, Bill would never sell Venture short, insider rules or not. In fact, he might step in with some buy orders to support the stock if the decline threatened to get out of control. He reached for the phone to call Jim Goulder, then slowly withdrew his hand. This kind of advance knowledge would be too much of a temptation for any broker. He was sure Goulder would never use it to line his pockets, but there were always special accounts and influential people an ambitious underwriter would like to impress. Better to let the market take its own course.

"Nightcap, Bill?" There was the tiniest catch in Nancy's voice.

"Best offer I've had all day." Bill helped her out of the hired limousine and told the driver he would have no further use for the car that night.

Nancy's apartment was on the fifth floor of a spacious old brick building with tight security. Bill didn't know how much the rent was, but it had to be at least three thousand a month. Nancy's mother was a much-divorced Dallas socialite who preferred to keep her daughter at a safe distance. Nancy played a lot of tennis, dabbled with the manuscript of a book that never seemed to get finished, and fucked like a mink.

The elevator opened directly into the foyer of her apartment. She went over to the bar that angled across a corner of the living room and poured cognac into two engraved glass snifters. Her dress was slit to the waist, and the golden skin between her small firm breasts glowed like smooth ivory.

He took both glasses from her and placed them on the bar. She went rigid when he kissed her, then her lips opened with a soft moan and her legs parted slightly to rub against his thigh. Her moans quickened into a ragged panting as he undid her belt, slid the narrow straps of her dress off her shoulders, and bent down to kiss her erect nipples. The sherry-brown eyes, glazed with desire, looked at him through half-closed lids, and she reached for his crotch.

Hours later, drained by their lovemaking, they fell asleep in her bed. The dawn was beginning to lighten the crack between the drapes when he felt her tongue lightly probing his navel. "Bill, are you awake?" she murmured as the tip of her tongue traced a course down his belly.

"I am now," he grunted as she took him in her mouth.

"I love to feel a cock grow hard," she whispered, tonguing him until he could stand it no longer and rolled her over on her back. She crossed her ankles and pressed her thighs together, laughing up at him. Her whipcord body twisted and writhed under him as she teasingly resisted his attempts to enter her.

"You forget, I've got the key," grinned Bill, rubbing his thumb along her clitoris. She gave a sharp little cry and drew him inside her, locking her legs over his hips, her pelvis straining upwards to ride his deep strokes.

6

The corporate offices of Sterling Investments Ltd. were on the twenty-third floor of the Traders Building, overlooking Vancouver's Burrard Inlet. A minor celebration was taking place in the panelled boardroom.

"Masterly, Ken!" The president raised his glass in tribute to a young man who had more the appearance of a university graduate than a financial buccaneer. "Your timing was flawless."

Ken Kwasny gave a diffident smile. "Sometimes it's more profitable to lose than to win."

"By a cool $2-million in this case," chimed in the third man, Sterling's treasurer and chief accountant.

Sterling Investments was a highly specialized company. It bought and sold the shares of other corporations, sometimes holding them for their growth potential, more frequently flipping them for a quick profit. Its success depended on the ability of its top executives to sniff out situations where a basically sound company was seriously undervalued by the market, or, better still, was ripe for a takeover bid.

The operation they were currently toasting with Dom Perignon was fairly typical of their modus operandi. Reliance Financial Services was a lacklustre organization burdened with a moribund management that was content to declare quarterly dividends and resolutely ignore any opportunities for expansion. The company had one major asset — a number of savings-and-loan branches in choice locations with a loyal clientele of widows and retired farmers. When Ken read an interview in the *Financial Post* in which the president of Global Finance said that his company planned to expand its operations in British Columbia, Sterling quietly began to pick up Reliance shares on the open market. As soon as they had acquired enough shares to make it worthwhile, they let it be known that they were after control of Reliance.

It was a gamble, but a calculated one. Ken's research had shown that the Reliance branches were located in areas where Global had little or no representation, and taking over a going concern, even with a substantial premium over the current market price, was bound to be more attractive to Global than starting from scratch. Sterling's announcement was enough to galvanize Global into action, and the price of Reliance shares quickly doubled. When the timing was right, Stan Winters, Sterling's president, placed a call to the Global head office, made a feeble joke about not being in a position to take on one of the big boys like Global, and offered to sell the Sterling block, which would guarantee control. The offer was accepted within twenty-four hours.

It had been only eight months since he had invited Ken to leave the brokerage house where he was employed as an analyst and join the high-flying Sterling firm, but already Stan Winters was a little in awe of his protégé. The young man had an instinctive understanding of figures; one swift glance at a balance sheet told Ken all he needed to know about a company's financial condition.

Stan's secretary entered the conference room and handed him a note. "I don't like to disturb you, but I thought you'd want to know about this."

Crumpling the note, he stuffed it in his pocket and said, "I'll take it in my office."

When Stan Winters came back, the accountant immediately sensed that the president wanted to be alone with Ken. He put down his empty glass, murmured, "Congratulations once again, Ken," and left.

"That was Davies calling from Toronto," Stan said. "The Venture deal collapsed." Alarmed by the stricken look on Ken's face, he added, "Hey, it's not the end of the world. We'll take a bath on the shares, but we can afford the loss."

"What happened?" demanded Ken.

"Travis backed out at the last minute. Apparently he got an attack of conscience or something."

"Shit." It was the first time Stan had ever heard Ken use the word.

"I know. The old human element backfires again. That's the one thing that bothered me about this deal right from the start. We were tinkering with people's motives and personal ambitions. A little bit too much like playing God for my taste."

Ken looked as if he were going to protest, then shrugged. "You're probably right. But I don't think we should sell those shares just yet."

The older man looked at him keenly. "This thing with Venture and Bill Crawford has really gotten under your skin, hasn't it? Just remember that in this business it's fatal to get emotionally involved in a project." He held up the bottle of Dom Perignon. "Have some more?"

"No. You finish it. All of a sudden I don't feel like champagne." Ken went back to his own office, coldly furious that Crawford had managed to escape the trap he had so carefully built for him. The smooth son of a bitch was turning out to be every bit as formidable an opponent as he was reputed to be. But the game had barely begun. Victory would be all the sweeter when it finally came.

The object of Ken's brooding was en route to Calgary, talking to Lee Travis on the newly installed flight phone. Lee had placed the call, and Bill had experienced a touch of panic when Connors told him who was on the line. Was Lee going to renege?

"I guess I won't have to buy those striped trousers after all, Bill. The appointment's not coming through."

382 / JOHN BALLEM

"Lee, I'm sorry. Sorry as hell." Which way would Travis jump now? "The Dwights withdrew their support, I take it?"

"No, that wasn't it. It seems like a cousin of the President's wife had the inside track all along."

"I can't tell you how relieved I am that it had nothing to do with our ... discussion."

"That's right, it didn't. Ol' Lee jes' ran afoul of some good old-fashioned political patronage."

"What about us, Lee? Where do we stand?"

"I reckon we stand about even, partner. What about you?"

"Suits me just fine." Bill was elated. Having a deadly enemy as a principal shareholder was definitely not the ideal way to run a company.

7

"Them good ol' boys sure know how to put the heat on." Lou Reznik's simian face was smiling, but he tugged nervously at the woolly grey hairs of a sideburn as he looked at Margo Jones. "I hope you got the goods, doll."

"Try me." Margo swung the briefcase onto her lap and unsnapped the clasps.

"You heard the lady. Give her your best shot." Encouraged by her air of quiet confidence, Reznik waved a hand at Howard Blescup, a lawyer specializing in libel cases who had been called in to advise the publisher of *Tomorrow* concerning the legal risks of running the second of Margo's articles.

The lawyer unsteepled his fingers and said, "Mr. Simpson of Brentwood Petroleums claims he will sue if we so much as mention his name. He's retained a lawyer who enjoys a certain reputation out west." The tone of Blescup's voice made it sound as if the lawyer was from the boonies and wouldn't last a minute in the big leagues in Toronto. "You say here," he continued, flipping through a couple of page proofs, "that the esteemed Mr. Simpson got his start by drilling crooked holes in Louisiana. You go on to explain that this means he drilled wells at an angle to siphon off the oil from adjoining leases." Blescup laid the pages in his lap and peered at Margo over his half-moon glasses. "I understand the oil industry regards that as a crime several degrees more serious than murder."

Margo placed a small Sony tape machine on the desk, selected a cassette from her briefcase, and ran it forward to the midway point. Then she pressed the play button and said, "The next voice you hear will be that of Mr. James Simpson, president of Brentwood Petroleums."

"Hell, honey." The booming voice filled the publisher's office. "It was the way things were done in them days. It was jes' like a kid takin' a straw to suck from his buddy's ice-cream soda. You'd drill straight down for a few hundred feet, and then you'd kinda encourage deviation, know what I mean? Of course, you'd have to square it with the drilling crew, but that didn't take much back then." The speaker broke into a wheezy laugh, and Margo pressed the stop button.

"That takes care of Mr. Simpson," the lawyer acknowledged with a slight smile. He turned a page. "Then there's this item about Paragon and an abandoned well."

"I'll have to change tapes." Margo consulted a typewritten list. "This is Bob Rumsey, who at one time was the toolpush on Paragon Rig Number 4."

"We wuz drilling up in the Peace River country back in the winter of seventy. We hit the Devonian around seven thousand feet, and that oil was practically leaping out of the hole at you." There was the sound of someone swallowing, followed by an unmistakable belch.

Margo pressed the pause button and said, "This conversation took place in a bar. Rumsey is bitter because Paragon ran him off last year, but he was sober enough to know exactly what he was saying."

The lawyer nodded and motioned for her to continue.

"I got orders direct from old man Boyle hisself not to run any tests on the well, just plug it with cement and move the rig off."

"Why on earth would he want you to do that?" Margo's taped voice asked.

"There was a Crown sale coming up that covered a whole bunch of land in the area. Half the friggin' oil companies in Alberta was scouting that well; you could almost feel them telescopes burning holes in your back."

"I still don't completely understand. Remember, it's a brand-new world to me." Margo's air of puzzlement was disarmingly feminine.

"It's simple." Rumsey was enjoying himself. "All them scouts report in to their head offices that the Paragon well is a duster, so nobody bids on the land. Paragon puts in a stink bid and picks up all the chips."

"It was beautiful the way you got him to put it all on the record," approved Blescup when Margo switched off the recorder.

Lou Reznik was squirming with delight. "You really nailed him to the cross, babe." He turned to the lawyer. "We run it, Howie? Okay?"

The lawyer, wincing inwardly at the detested "Howie," looked judicious. "On the whole ... I think so, yes. Still, what we have isn't the same as an admission from Boyle himself."

"The funny part is that it wasn't Paragon Pete who got the lands," Margo said softly. "I checked the records, and the successful bidder was an unknown company called Norquay Resources Limited. According to the Companies Branch in Edmonton, it was a shell company. You know, a lawyer and his secretary as the only shareholders. That kind of set-up."

"And you suspect the real owner might turn out to be none other than Clint Boyle?" The lawyer's eyes were bright with interest.

"Now that's what I call chutzpah," breathed Reznik. "Steal the fucking store right from underneath the boss's nose!"

"It's a pretty good guess." Margo frowned slightly. "But an educated guess is all it is. I couldn't prove it without the co-operation of the lawyer who incorporated the company."

"Who would immediately claim privilege on behalf of his client," Blescup said matter-of-factly.

"Right. And the mineral rights have been transferred half a dozen times since they were acquired by Norquay."

"Suggestive, but not conclusive," the lawyer muttered. "But," he turned to the publisher, "it at least makes me feel more comfortable about running the Paragon material."

"Terrific!" Reznik beamed. "Simpson and Paragon were the two hot spots you were worried about. Right, Howie?"

"Principally, yes. But there are several innuendoes about the sexual exploits of these people." Blescup pronounced "people" as though he were discussing alien creatures from another planet.

"The sex stays, Howie. That's the sizzle that sells the goddamn magazine." A pained expression crossed Reznik's face. "We coulda' sold a million copies of that last issue except we only printed three hundred thou. This time we're running a million. We need the sex, Howie."

"No one is mentioned specifically by name in any of the sex stuff," Margo pointed out.

"That's right, doll. No names, no pack drill. Right, Howie?"

"As a general rule, yes. But if there's enough description so an individual can be identified, you can still be sued."

"The closest I've come to that is with Ted Riley. He's married to a rich bitch who is as wide as she is tall, which may explain why Mr. Riley is always on the make."

"Riley isn't one of those who have threatened to sue, is he?" asked the lawyer.

"Haven't had a single peep outa the guy," replied Reznik eagerly. He was patting beads of perspiration from his tanned bald dome despite the air-conditioned chill of his office.

The lawyer didn't hear his answer. He was too busy watching Margo as she ejected the old cassette and inserted a new one. "Good Lord, you're not going to tell us you have him on tape?"

"Oh, yes I am," she replied with a gay laugh. "Naturally the amorous Mr. Riley had no idea he was being recorded," she added as she depressed the play button.

"Mr. Riley ..." On the tape, a man's voice interrupted her impatiently. "I've told you at least three times now to call me Ted."

"Beautiful. Just beautiful." Blescup looked at Margo and shook his head in wonder. "Name, rank, and serial number. You are a true artist, Ms. Jones." He whispered the aside without breaking his concentration on the running tape.

Ted Riley was blatantly propositioning Margo, asking her to fly out to Vancouver with him and spend a weekend on board his yacht. Margo skilfully led him on until his intentions were crystal clear, then begged off with the plausible excuse that she had to be back in Toronto that particular weekend to cover a story. At the end of the conversation, Riley had reason to believe he would eventually succeed in bedding the delectable Margo Jones.

"A remarkable performance!" Blescup got to his feet and held out his hand to Margo. "You are a professional journalist in every sense of the word." He placed the article on the desk in front of Reznik. "There's no need to change so much as a comma in my professional opinion."

Signalling Margo to remain, the jubilant publisher escorted his legal advisor to the elevators. While she waited, Margo wondered if she was in for another session of pawing from the odious little man. She remembered with crawling distaste the feel of his sweaty palm on her arm. Dear God, now that he had purchased two major articles from her he might expect a great deal more than a little playful clutch and grab. However, Reznik was all business when he returned. Going directly to his desk he congratulated her effusively and began to talk about the possibility of her doing a series for the magazine. He was, she suddenly realized, treating her with what he would call "respect." It seemed she had finally arrived.

However, his shrewd brown eyes soon began to glaze over as Margo described some of the projects she had in mind. Finally he held up his hand. "Listen to me, doll. You're talking about think pieces. Any half-assed professor picking his nose up in his ivory tower can write them things, and we got no use for that kind of shit anyways. You're an investigative reporter; you heard what that old fart Blescup said. You've got a God-given talent for digging up the dirt on people and making your facts stick. That's the kind of stuff we want from you. We'll pay you the top dollar, and we'll promote you until you're the best-known lady journalist in the whole damn country."

Closing her briefcase, Margo promised to come up with a short list of potential subjects.

"Hit list is what you mean," Reznik interjected with an explosive laugh as he walked her to the door.

The only trouble was that she hadn't the foggiest notion where to find another subject as sensational as her oil industry pieces. More sensational, in fact. That would be expected of her now. Despite the triumph she had just scored, Margo's thoughts were bleak as she pushed the plate-glass door open and stepped out into the mid-afternoon bustle of Bloor Street.

8

The drilling rig was in the middle of a stubble field about two hundred yards in from the road. Debbie peered out the driver's window as the rented Ford drove slowly past.

Murlex et al Provost 11-13-40-17-w4 — the numbers indicated the precise geographic location of the well by legal subdivision, section, township, range, and meridian — was her first well, the very first time her fledgling company, Pinnacle Petroleums, had participated in a drilling operation. Pinnacle had previously purchased a tiny interest in a gas unit with a modest down payment and a larger bank loan, and that gave it a small revenue stream. But drilling a well was a much riskier business than buying already proven reserves. If the well came in dry, you lost the whole bundle. Except, Debbie comforted herself, the drilling costs could be written off for tax purposes against the income from the gas unit.

The Murlex well was supposed to be a comparatively low-risk proposition, which was the reason Tom Burdon, a consulting petroleum engineer, had recommended it. With gas in the Viking Sand as its objective and an estimated total depth of 3,300 feet, it was AFEd at $75,000 for a dry hole and $120,000 completed as a potential producer. The Viking was widespread throughout the Provost area, but it was a "fingered" formation, and if you missed one of the fingers, you were out of luck. Debbie realized now that participating in a one-shot deal on this kind of play was not the best possible approach. Spreading the risk by taking smaller interests in a number of wells would shorten the odds considerably when dealing with an elusive formation like the Viking. Lesson learned, although she was aware that deals could seldom be tailored to suit the interests of the individual parties. In the present case, it was participate in the one well or not at all.

Debbie drove five miles west before she turned around to go by the well once more. It was the third time in the past week that she had motored along the road for a glimpse of the well. She used a different rental car each time so the crew wouldn't get suspicious about the same car driving by the wellsite.

When Debbie had finally surrendered to her overwhelming desire to become directly involved in the oil industry, she had made up her mind that she would keep her activities secret. Bill Crawford was such a prominent member of the oil community that everyone would automatically assume any success she might achieve would be because she was her father's daughter. The shares of Pinnacle Petroleums were registered in the name of an Edmonton lawyer, and his signed declaration that he held the shares in trust for her was locked away in her safety deposit box. Using an Edmonton rather than a Calgary law firm had been an added precaution against cocktail-party gossip about Bill Crawford's daughter amusing herself by dabbling in the oil business. As the provincial capital, Edmonton was a government town and not a part of the oil scene, with its endless intrigues and rumours.

Tom Burdon acted as the front man and represented Pinnacle whenever it was necessary to negotiate deals. The one place she could not avoid appearing on the record was the bank, where it was necessary for her personally to sign promissory notes and pledge some of her Venture shares as collateral for Pinnacle's loans. She had deliberately selected a bank her father had no dealings with, and she had made it clear to the manager that she would hold him personally responsible for any breach in security.

As she drove slowly by, Debbie saw the crew starting to lift the drill pipe out of the hole. They were making a "trip" to change the bit dulled by cutting through hundreds of feet of rock. Tom had told her they expected to reach the Viking some time over the weekend and that a drill-stem test might be run as early as Sunday. For some reason, everything in the oil patch seemed to happen on the weekend.

Exhilarated by her fling, however modest, at exploratory drilling, and enjoying the feel of the wind rushing in through the open window, Debbie was in high spirits as she turned onto the paved highway and headed back to Calgary. She thought of the many times her father must have experienced the same sensation during his long career as he waited for the verdict of success or failure to come in. He had been working like a fiend ever since his return from his last trip to Houston, spending long hours at the office every day. From what she heard, he was checking into everything and taking the reins of management back into his own hands. She wondered what that meant for that dear man, Gavin Anderson. Obviously, a decision had been made that he wasn't up to the top job. It didn't bother Gavin, though; he was looking more relaxed and cheerful than he had in years when Debbie ran into him at a cocktail party over the weekend.

She hadn't talked to her father since the current issue of *Tomorrow*, featuring Margo's second article, had appeared. The magazine had gone all out to give Margo the star treatment. There was a publisher's note, complete with a picture of the little creep himself, referring to all the pressure that had been brought to bear in an effort to suppress the article. There was some phony crap about the freedom of the press, plus words of praise for the writer's professional integrity and journalistic ability, followed by the statement that the article was being printed exactly as Margo Jones had written it. The two features had created so much interest in the States, the note concluded, that arrangements had been made to syndicate them, and they would shortly appear in major regional publications throughout the USA. That meant Bill Crawford would be crucified all over again and on a vastly larger scale. A muscle worked in Debbie's cheek as she unconsciously ground her teeth.

Her father wasn't even mentioned in the second article and, under other circumstances, Debbie would have been enormously entertained by its contents. There was a delicious bit about Ted Riley — he wasn't identified by name, but it had to be him — using his wife's money to buy jewellery for the chicks who spent weekends on his yacht. Ted had propositioned Debbie once; she might have taken him on except she couldn't stand his self-satisfied little smirk and the way he was always fingering his moustache. And that business of Paragon and the abandoned well up near Grimshaw — absolutely riveting! Who would have thought that blustering old windbag Clint Boyle would have the smarts to pull off something like that?

Great fun and games, except that by concentrating on a few dubious individuals, Margo had deliberately given a false and distorted view of the oil industry. What made it worse was that it was Debbie's father, a man who had devoted his entire life to the industry, who would be getting all the flak for the bad press. She would soon have a chance to find out how he was bearing up; they were due to drive out to the ranch to have dinner with Frank that evening. Tomorrow, Frank was to leave on his European jaunt.

"Clint Boyle's been recalled to Houston." Bill Crawford fiddled with the air-conditioning controls on the Mercedes' dash.

"To get his wrist slapped for embarrassing the company with that abandoned-well stunt?"

"He'll have some explaining to do over that, all right," her father agreed. "That may be only the tip of the iceberg, however. Rumour has it that what's really bugging the Paragon head office is that the company didn't get any of the lands in that Crown sale."

"You mean Boyle grabbed them for himself?"

"That's the story that's floating around the Pete Club."

"I'll be damned!" Debbie crowed delightedly. "That pompous old fraud. I love it!" Still chuckling, she asked, "What will happen to him?"

"Nothing much more serious than early retirement, I expect. Paragon won't be anxious to publicize the fact that they've been defrauded by one of their top executives."

"So Margo Jones claims another victim," Debbie said and shot a sidelong glance at her father. "Are the good ol' boys giving you a hard time?"

"There's a fair amount of resentment, yes," he admitted. "Nothing that I can't live with, however." He swung to the outside lane as they came up on the exit to the secondary highway that led to the ranch. "The oil business is kind of a closed circuit, honey. You keep dealing with the same people time after time, so it doesn't pay to deliberately go out of your way to make enemies. The guy you're sore at now could turn out to be your partner tomorrow. Anyway, the good ol' boys, as you call them, haven't been too hard on your old man."

"Venture being one of the big players doesn't hurt either," added Debbie, pleased that his morale was so obviously intact. She gave her father's knee an affectionate squeeze and changed the subject to Frank's forthcoming trip.

It was a good evening. Frank glowed with enthusiasm over his trip and what he was going to see. There was a long list of the exotic cattle breeders he had arranged to visit. As Frank reeled off the names, Bill finally interjected: "Don't forget to have some fun, for God's sake!"

His son stared at him. "But this is fun."

"Okay. Okay. Have it your way. But don't forget to visit the odd nightclub."

Bill and Debbie left for town not long after, with Debbie promising to run Frank out to the airport in the morning. Bill had downed a fair bit of Scotch in the course of the evening, and Debbie was a little concerned about the drive home. However, he didn't suggest that she take the wheel, so she slid into the passenger seat. He opened the electric roof panel and Debbie leaned back in her seat to gaze up at the star-filled sky.

Her father glanced at the dashboard clock and switched on the radio. "It was so peaceful out there I really don't want to hear the news. Still ..." He stopped talking as the newscaster's voice filled the interior of the car.

"The lead story tonight is the government's refusal to order a public inquiry into the alleged involvement of the minister of consumer affairs in the scandal surrounding the construction of the new federal building in Windsor, the minister's home riding. The prime minister informed the House of Commons this afternoon that a departmental investigation had found no evidence that would justify a further inquiry into a possible connection between Walter Ferguson and the contractor who has already been convicted of bribery in the affair. Mr. Ferguson, who has been hospitalized for the past week for exhaustion and strain brought on by the allegations, was not in the House at the time the announcement was made."

Turning down the volume, Bill muttered, "That Ferguson's got more lives than a cat. He's been accused of everything under the sun — using government aircraft for his own personal business, accepting huge campaign contributions from the unions — at the same time as he was minister of labour, for Christ's sake! — trying to influence judges, and now accepting kickbacks from contractors on government projects. And the PM just says 'naughty, naughty' and keeps him in the cabinet."

"Do you think people will really believe that he was innocent of the kickback business?" asked Debbie.

"Hell, no! They've got more sense. But what can you do when the government just sits there and stonewalls?"

"Talking about politics always gets you uptight." Debbie half turned in the leather seat to stare at her father. "You ever think of going into it yourself?"

He looked almost shocked. "Whatever put that idea in your head? My job in life is to find oil. It's just that it burns me up to see how cynical and self-serving some of these clods get after a few years in office."

"I know what you mean," agreed Debbie, letting the subject drop.

"I sold the house today," Bill suddenly announced as the lights of the city came into view.

"Did you, now? Debbie recovered quickly from her surprise; she had long since grown accustomed to her father's little habit of dropping bombshells of information in the most offhand manner. "Did you get a good price?" Painful memories of her mother drunk in the afternoon and of her school friends snickering behind their hands came flooding back.

"Not bad, all things considered. Three hundred and fifty thousand, to be precise. At least the buyer should be a good credit risk."

"Who bought it?"

"The US government, no less. It's to be the official residence of the consul general."

"Frank will be pleased. I think that old place kind of haunts him." Debbie rooted around in her bag for her apartment key as the Mercedes turned onto her street.

Debbie's weekend of suspense began early the next morning with a telephone call from Tom Burdon. He was leaving to "sit" the well in its final stages. He told her the cores they had pulled had been moderately encouraging; they showed fair porosity, which meant the gas, if there was any, could move freely into the well bore. However, they wouldn't know the answer to the all-important question of whether gas was actually present until they ran the tests.

She was poor company for her date that night, and that was kind of a shame because he was new in town and looked like he could be fun. He took her to dinner at the Owl's Nest, and Debbie knew he was splurging, which made her feel even guiltier when her thoughts kept straying to the drilling rig chewing its way through the last few feet of rock some two hundred miles northeast of the posh restaurant. Or had the rig got stuck in the hole? More than once she had seen the worried look on her father's face when a bit got twisted off and had to be fished out of the hole with special tools in an operation that could last for days, or even weeks.

Debbie's companion, who was accustomed to the full — and frequently adoring — attention of the women he dated, was put off by her air of distraction. When she did make an effort to concentrate on what he was saying, it was all too clear that she was only trying to be polite. Goddamn rich bitch! Just because she's got an old man who's loaded, she thinks she can get away with anything. She was a looker, though, with that yellow-blonde hair and a figure that made you suck your teeth. According to the form chart, she wasn't at all shy about making out if the guy happened to appeal to her. Which I obviously do not, he told himself with something close to disbelief as they stood awkwardly in the tiled lobby of her apartment building.

"Look," she blurted out suddenly, "I've been a real drag tonight, and I'm sorry. It has nothing to do with you. It's just that I've got something on my mind that

I can't turn off. I should have known better than to inflict myself on anybody tonight. Why don't you give me a call some time next week when I have my headspace straightened out?"

"Do you want me to, really?" he asked eagerly.

"I'm counting on it." She reached up and kissed him lightly on the lips, letting the soft firmness of her breasts brush against him. That should keep him on ice until she was ready.

Alone in her apartment all the next day, Debbie had moments when she regretted having given up cigarettes in her last year of college. It wasn't that the phone didn't ring. It rang too damn often, but it was never Tom Burdon calling her with news of the well. She cut all the calls short, wanting to keep the line clear.

Tom Burdon's call came shortly after ten that night. He was calling from a pay phone in Stettler, the closest town of any size to the wellsite. Her initial excitement faded when he told her they were just assembling the test tools for the first test; there had been a small delay because they had to condition the hole before hey could run the electric logs that would show the thickness of the formation.

"When will we have some results?" she asked.

"Possibly before morning, if everything goes just right and we don't have misruns."

"I want you to call me the instant you know anything. Good or bad."

"That could be four o'clock in the morning."

"I'll be waiting for your call."

She undressed and prepared herself for bed, although it was really just a way of killing time. She had no real hope of sleeping; what happened up in that farmer's pasture in the next few hours would be much too important for her future to permit that. Sitting up in bed, she studied a sheet of paper covered with columns of her neat handwritten figures. It was her estimate of the payout of her investment at various production rates. In order to earn her fifteen per cent interest, she had to put up thirty per cent of the drilling cost — or $25,000 net to her. If the well came in dry, the calculation was painfully simple — she could kiss the twenty-five thousand goodbye.

She suddenly realized that, even if the well came in dry as a bone, she would keep on trying to build Pinnacle into a viable oil company. She still had some Venture stock to use as collateral, and there were always plays that could be bought into. This piece of self-knowledge seemed to put the Murlex well into perspective, and Debbie unexpectedly dozed off. Her subconscious was still locked onto the well, however, and when the phone rang she snapped into instant wakefulness and picked up the receiver before it could ring a second time.

Tom was laconic. "I figure it's a keeper. The third drill-stem test indicated a daily volume of just over one million cubic feet. We tested an interval of twenty-two feet, and the logs indicate there may be nine feet of pay, which ain't bad for the Viking. It's sure as hell no barn burner, but it's worth completing."

"If it tested at a million cubic feet a day, what rate can we produce it at?" Debbie ran her index finger down the columns of figures on her payout sheet.

"Around three hundred thousand, if the pressure holds up. The drilling went smooth as cream, and there weren't any cost overruns, so you shouldn't have to wait too long for the payout."

"Just over three years," Debbie informed him crisply. "Sooner, if the prices go up, as I'm sure they will." Debbie felt the excitement building up inside her, but she still craved reassurance from the expert. "The well looks okay, huh, Tom?"

"It's better than a kick in the ass with a frozen boot, that's for sure," the petroleum engineer replied as he rang off.

Too excited to stay in her apartment, Debbie decided to drive to Banff for breakfast. With the top down and the wind blowing in her face, she was riding a natural high as the white convertible raced toward the Rockies.

9

Margo's article and Clint Boyle's recall in disgrace to the Paragon head office in Houston provided ample titillation for the cocktail-party circuit throughout the following week. Then on Friday afternoon, as soon as the stock market had closed, came an announcement that completely overshadowed even those juicy items: CNIC had made an offer to acquire all the outstanding shares of Berkley Petroleums!

There was nothing wrong with the offer from a monetary point of view. In fact, at a premium of forty per cent over Friday's close, it was a bonanza for the Berkley shareholders. But CNIC stood for Canadian National Investment Corporation, a Crown company designed to bring a government presence into the private sector. Up until now, it had limited its acquisitions to some petrochemical plants in Ontario, an ailing steel plant in Nova Scotia, and a couple of mines in British Columbia. That was bad enough, and an outrageous waste of public money to boot, but now it looked as if the government assholes were set to move in on the flourishing oil industry and fuck it up in their own inimitable style.

If Berkley had been a US-owned corporation, the government's move would have been more understandable, if not any less ominous. American companies owned or controlled an astonishing ninety per cent of the Canadian oil industry, and even the most fervent supporter of free enterprise had to concede that this might not be entirely consistent with the best interests of Canada. But Berkley's control resided in London, England, and its acquisition would do nothing to reduce the overwhelming American presence.

In the House of Commons, the minister of energy stoutly defended the takeover, pointing out that, although it might not affect the US hegemony, it did increase Canadian ownership. It would also, he said, give the government a window on the industry. Besides, he added almost petulantly, Berkley was the only company of the appropriate size that was for sale. It appeared that the US giants were in no hurry to liquidate their investment in an area as profitable and stable as Canada. The minister's revealing reference to a "window on the industry" sent shock waves rippling through the oil patch that were felt as far away as Houston and The Hague. Now there would be a goddamn government spy in their midst, and one with access to a great deal of information, since Berkley's holdings were widespread throughout the oil provinces and the company was a joint participant in a multitude of projects. The prospect of being in bed with the government made veteran oilmen choke on their steak sandwiches at the Pete Club.

No one was more concerned than Debbie. She could see the industry in which she intended to make her future disappearing just as she was getting started. She took no part in the acrimonious discussions that became a staple of every social gathering, but inwardly she alternated between anger and a hollow feeling of despair. If the feds, after getting a taste of the oil game, decided they wanted more, there seemed to be no way of stopping them from grabbing it all.

The general public ignored the larger implications of the government's action. What hit home to the man in the street were the overnight fortunes that resulted from the takeover. Berkley shares, which had edged steadily upward in the previous two weeks, had been trading at sixty dollars immediately prior to the CNIC offer of eighty-four dollars per share.

Ironically, it was the company's president who focused public attention on just how well the insiders had done for themselves. Paul Thorsby had been kept in the dark about the impending sale of the company of which he was the titular head until twenty-four hours before it was announced, for the very good reason that the owners knew he would oppose it vigorously. The thought of selling out to the government would have been anathema to Thorsby, and he had the kind of combative personality that was not averse to public confrontation. Fortunately for the owners, Thorsby was a professional manager not a proprietor, in the sense that his shareholdings were comparatively modest, so the owners had been able to deal around him.

Instead of pocketing his loot and accepting the sale as a fait accompli, as any "right-thinking" executive would have done, Thorsby went public. His former UK bosses were unruffled; their money was safely out of the country. But Thorsby was a great embarrassment to the government. Before launching his attack, Thorsby freely disclosed that he had made a profit of a quarter of a million dollars from the sale, which was a mere trifle, he casually added, compared to what some of the other insiders had made. To his considerable chagrin, it was this aspect and not the state's intervention in the private sector that the press pounced on.

The opposition parties immediately joined the hue and cry, and question period in the House was devoted almost exclusively to demands for information on insider trading in Berkley stock during the weeks preceding the sale. The New Democrats had a field day. The government purchase was in line with their socialistic beliefs, so they could support the principle of the transaction while roundly condemning the government for unnecessarily enriching a pack of undeserving investors. Each day in the week following Thorsby's disclosure, the leader of the NDP waded in with a series of loaded questions designed to show how the government had been duped by greedy foreign capitalists.

Debbie, appalled by the spectacle of grown men acting like unruly schoolboys, followed the debate on television. Tumult broke out in the government ranks when the NDP leader asked a loaded question about whether the cabinet had been aware of the intended purchase. There was an unspoken accusation that some of the "honourable members" on the government side might have shared in the windfall. Cries of "Shame!" "Withdraw!" "Expel him!" were hurled across the strip of green carpet that separated the government from the opposition. The television cameras panned along the front row of government benches where cabinet ministers flanked the prime minister on both sides. The PM sat stony-faced and silent amid the uproar, but some of his cabinet colleagues were not so restrained. The camera lingered on the controversial minister of consumer affairs who was on his feet, shaking his fist at the NDP leader. Thinking that the man looked more like a member of the Mafia than a cabinet minister, Debbie tightened her mouth in an expression of distaste as the camera zoomed in on Walter Ferguson's pasty face with its loose-lipped mouth that always seemed on the verge of drooling.

The camera switched to the prime minister as he rose to reply to the question. "Of course," he said in his disdainful way, "the cabinet was aware of the sale. We would not think of taking a step as important as this without full cabinet approval."

My God! Debbie uncurled her legs and sat bolt upright on the couch. The ideas were clicking into place like the pictures on the reels in a slot machine, but she forced herself to listen while the prime minister answered a supplemental question about when the cabinet was first informed of the proposed purchase.

"Three weeks ago," he replied tersely and sat down.

Suppose. Debbie's pulse quickened. Just suppose that Margo Jones published a story accusing a cabinet minister of secretly buying a large block of Berkley shares prior to the sale. The story would be a sensation right across the nation and would spell the end of the unfortunate minister's career. Except that it would be Margo Jones who would be finished when it turned out the story was completely false.

Walter Ferguson was the obvious choice as the victim. People were prepared to believe the worst of him, and he always had the press sniffing around his heels, convinced there was a scandal to end all scandals just waiting to be uncovered.

Could it be done? Debbie pushed the button to turn off the television and began to organize her thoughts. The scheme had a lot going for it. There was Ferguson's unsavoury reputation, Margo's unbridled ambition, and the sense of urgency and haste that always accompanies a fast-breaking story. Margo was a disciplined reporter and would need some kind of corroborating evidence, but it wouldn't have to be too elaborate — just enough to persuade her to go ahead with a scoop she would be aching to publish. Whether Margo sold it to *Tomorrow* or to a newspaper chain, there would be a frantic rush to get into print before the competition got wind of it.

Debbie was fully aware of the appalling risk she would be running. If her role was ever discovered ... she shivered with a mixture of fear and excitement that was strangely pleasurable. She could always call it off, right up to the moment when the bait was placed in the trap. In the meantime, there were a number of initial steps that could be taken without any risk whatsoever. Smiling slightly, she flipped through the Yellow Pages for the number of the law firm where Don Kilgour toiled in the corporate law section.

"It's pretty straightforward, actually." The young lawyer glanced covertly around the dimly lighted bar to see if there was anyone who might snitch to his wife that he was having a drink with Debbie Crawford. Reassured to see no one he knew, he drank some of his beer and continued, "The law says that the share register of a public company must be open for inspection during normal business hours."

"Where is this share register?" asked Debbie.

"At the company's transfer agent," he replied, adding, when Debbie looked blank, "that's a trust company that handles assignments of a company's shares and issues new certificates. It's a purely administrative function."

Debbie nodded her understanding. It should be a simple matter to find out what trust company acted for Berkley. "Do you have to be a shareholder to see the register?"

"No. Any member of the public is entitled to examine the register. If you're a shareholder, you can have copies made. That's the only difference."

"Can a person who doesn't happen to be a shareholder at least make notes?"

"Oh, sure." He made a big production out of lighting a cigarette. "This has to do with one of your father's companies, I assume?" Jesus, wouldn't it be something if he could bring some of the Crawford business in the door? Not Venture Oils, of course — Chester Martin had that one tied up; although you never knew these days — but just a slice of their family corporate business. It would mean a junior partnership for sure.

"You know I can't say anything about that," Debbie replied with a bat of her eyelids that told him his guess wasn't far off the mark.

"Ta, Don. You've been a great help. Let's keep in touch." She kissed the air beside his cheek and left.

An anonymous phone call to a brokerage firm produced the information that Atlantic Trust was the transfer agent for Berkley shares. The trust company had offices across the country, including a branch in Calgary; but one of the newspaper stories had included the fact that Berkley had been incorporated in Ontario, which meant that the share register would likely be located in Toronto. That suited Debbie's purposes even better because there would be less risk of her being noticed there. Before she left for Toronto, she visited her safety deposit box and made a photocopy of the declaration of trust that the Edmonton lawyer had drawn up for her own Pinnacle shares.

Once Margo became aware that she had been the victim of a hoax, she would use all her formidable investigative skills to find out who had zapped her. The knowledge wouldn't salvage her reputation, but it would enable her to drag her enemy down with her. Debbie booked her flight under a false name, paying cash for the ticket. She used yet another name when she checked into a second-rate motel, forestalling a request for a credit card by paying cash in advance. Transportation was more of a problem — car rental agencies would be one of the obvious places for Margo to check, and you couldn't rent a car without producing a driver's licence. Debbie's solution was to purchase a used Toyota from a dealer in one of Toronto's satellite communities. With the acquisition of a brunette wig, pancake makeup, and a frumpy brown suit, she was ready to make her first move.

The share transfer department was on the third floor of the Atlantic Trust building, an aluminum and glass tower two blocks east of Bay Street.

"I would like to examine the share register of Berkley Petroleums, please," Debbie said to the girl who slouched over the counter.

"You a shareholder?" she asked indifferently.

"No, I'm not. I just want to look at the register, that's all."

"Wait here." The girl sauntered off and returned with a brisk-looking woman in her mid-forties who introduced herself as Mrs. Turner, the account officer in charge of the Berkley register. "Ms. Freeman. Janice Freeman."

Mrs. Turner asked for some identification, and Debbie shook her head. "I understand any member of the public is entitled to look at a company's share registry during normal business hours," she said firmly, hoping that the Ontario rules were the same as those in Alberta.

It seemed they were. Mrs. Turner gave a slight shrug of resignation and led her to a cubicle with a metal desk. "If you will just wait in here, I'll have it brought to you."

The register was a thick packet of computer printouts, with every page neatly divided into little squares, each containing the name and address of a shareholder and the number of shares held. It was dated less than a month ago. No doubt it had been updated for the purposes of the takeover offer. Debbie was disappointed that there was no way of telling exactly when a shareholder had acquired his shares; she would have preferred to use someone who had bought shares within the last three weeks. Still, it wasn't a fatal flaw; it would just make it even more essential to compress the time available to Margo to check out the story.

The vast majority of the shares were held by English interests. Shaking her head over the hemorrhage of cash from Canada, Debbie took out her notebook and began to copy down some names. She chose individuals rather than corporations and looked for those whose share holdings were in the three to five thousand range. It would have been a nice touch if there had been a suitable candidate from Ferguson's hometown, but the Berkley roster of shareholders did not boast any Windsor residents. When she had written down ten names that fitted her requirements, she smiled her thanks and handed the register back to the sullen girl who, on Mrs. Turner's instructions, had stationed herself just inside the door.

Back in her motel room, Debbie studied her list. She had equipped herself with a massive city directory that, to some degree at least, fleshed out the sparse information contained in the share register. When she had finished cross-checking, she knew the occupation, place of business, and home address of eight of the ten names. Two were lawyers. There were also a dentist and an accountant. However, her eye kept coming back to Allen Cormack who was listed as the president of a pre-mix cement company. A connection between Walter Ferguson and a member of the construction industry had a plausible ring to it. Allen Cormack definitely warranted further investigation.

At four o'clock that afternoon Debbie was sitting in the Toyota across the street from the premises of Peerless Pre-Mix Concrete Company Limited. The cement company was one of a number of small businesses occupying a two-storey cinder-block building in a sprawling industrial park. Its single door and narrow sash-window were squeezed in between an appliance distributor and a plumbing company. It seemed to be little more than an office for taking orders and sending out bills. Notwithstanding its unimpressive quarters, Peerless Pre-Mix must have been a profitable enterprise, because its proprietor was the registered owner of forty-five hundred shares of Berkley Petroleums, now worth a cool $378,000, thanks to the generosity of the federal government.

At precisely four-thirty the door opened and a middle-aged woman stepped out, turned right, and walked briskly along the sidewalk. Debbie could see a fluorescent light fixture glowing whitely in the ceiling, suggesting there was still someone in the office. She waited, grateful that she had found room to park in the shade of the warehouse. An hour later the door was opened from the inside by a thickset man in a bright red sports shirt. Debbie had a good look at him as he locked the door and pocketed the key. She judged him to be somewhere in his mid-fifties. When he turned down a lane that led to the parking lot at the rear of the building, she reached for the ignition key. Chances were that the man was Allen Cormack, but she could put the matter beyond all doubt by simply following him home.

When the man's station wagon turned onto Middleton Road, Debbie had her answer; Allen Cormack's home address was listed in the city directory as 171 Middleton Road. Now, if tomorrow Mr. Cormack would be obliging enough to stay on in the office after his secretary had left for the day ...

On the long drive back to the motel Debbie began to refine her tentative timetable. *Tomorrow* was published every second Saturday and went to press on the preceding Friday afternoon. Wednesday was the magazine's deadline, but Debbie knew from a casual conversation with a Calgary reporter that new material, provided it was sensational enough to justify special treatment, could be inserted in either a magazine or a newspaper right up to the moment the presses started to roll. She figured that *Tomorrow* would likely be Margo's first choice if the story broke in time for the magazine to get it out as quickly as a daily newspaper. Even if Margo did go to a newspaper, Friday was still the best day to bait the trap. There might be time to check a couple of the basic facts, like whether Cormack actually was a shareholder of Berkley Petroleums, but that was all.

It was almost six when Debbie arrived back at the motel, which meant there was nothing more that could be done until morning. Still it was only Tuesday. That left her two full working days to assemble the pieces and fit them together.

Debbie entered the bank shortly after it opened at ten o'clock the next morning. She went first to the circular stand where the customers filled out their deposit slips and helped herself to a handful. Then she went over to the new-accounts section where she asked for some blank forms to open an account and an envelope to put them in, explaining that she was in a rush and wanted to fill them out back at the office. As she had hoped, the envelope had the bank's name and address printed on the top left-hand corner.

The typewriters were on the third floor of Eaton's, next to the camera counter. Debbie looked at them until a salesman materialized at her elbow wondering if he could be of assistance. She asked if it would be possible for her to try out a couple of the machines, pointing to a Smith-Corona and an Olivetti. He lifted them both onto the counter and plugged them in, inviting her to use them with a wave of his hand.

She placed the declaration of trust on the counter beside the Smith-Corona, inserted a sheet of high-quality bond, and began to type, picking out the words with extreme care. Then she switched to the Olivetti to type Allen Cormack's name and address on the bank envelope, adding "By Courier" in the top right corner. When the salesman saw she had finally finished, he strolled back down the aisle to point out some of the features of the two machines. She said something about wanting to think about it for a while, and he handed her his card with the request that she contact him if she decided to buy. Her next stop was a courier service, where she picked up a packet of delivery slips by simply asking for them.

The blank deposit slips inside the bank envelope made a businesslike package. Cormack would be puzzled when he opened it, but banks were always screwing up these days, so he'd probably just shrug and pitch the useless forms in the waste-basket. Even if he did try to follow it up, there was nothing either the bank or the courier service could tell him.

As she had done the day before, Cormack's secretary left at precisely four-thirty, turned right and strode in her no-nonsense fashion along the sidewalk. By now Debbie was sufficiently familiar with the area to know that she was almost certainly heading for the bus stop one block over and two blocks north. Five minutes later, Debbie, wearing blue jeans rolled up to her ankles, white sneakers, and with her hair stuffed under a nylon-mesh peaked cap, opened the door of Peerless Pre-Mix Concrete and called out, "Anybody home? Messenger service."

Today, Cormack's shirt was a pale, baby blue with short sleeves. He accepted the envelope, laboriously wrote his name on the delivery slip with a ballpoint, and went back into the inner office.

His signature was highly legible, each letter formed with almost childlike care. Using a ballpoint with the same colour of blue ink, Debbie practised until her version of his careful signature would deceive the average eye, even if it would never withstand the scrutiny of a handwriting expert. She put down the pen and rubbed her wrist, deciding to wait until morning before signing Cormack's name to the declaration of trust.

IO

The steady rhythm of the electric typewriter faltered, then died away. Swearing under her breath, Margo Jones ripped the page out of the machine, crumpled it into a ball and threw it into the wastebasket, which was already overflowing with discarded sheets of paper. The story she was working on had no sex appeal, and Margo knew it. Last week Lou Reznik had called, asking her to do something for the upcoming issue of *Tomorrow*, and she had put him off. What was happening to her? The publisher of a national magazine begs her for an article, and she can't come up with anything! Automatically she reached for another sheet of paper, but let her hand fall into her lap instead. She stared down at the empty IBM, oblivious of the sudden shaft of light pouring in through her apartment window from the mid-morning sun that had finally cleared the high-rise across the street. The silent typewriter mocked her.

Would she ever be able to match the sensationalism of the oil-patch articles? The thought of them still gave her a warm glow of achievement. Rumour had it that Bill Crawford felt betrayed. He was a pretty decent guy, but it was just his bad luck to get between her and a good story. As for those other yahoos — they deserved everything they got.

At the sudden harsh buzz of the apartment intercom, she jumped convulsively, striking one foot against the metal leg of the typewriter table. Recovering her composure, she crossed over to the wall unit and pressed the talk button. "Who is it?"

"Messenger service. I have an envelope for Margo Jones."

Margo hesitated. Then, assured by a glance at the chain lock on her door, told him to come up and pressed the switch that unlocked the main entrance at ground level. She kept the chain fastened while she accepted the envelope and signed the receipt. The envelope was plain white and letter size. She frowned uneasily at the sight of her name pasted on it with letters from a newspaper. *The Globe and Mail* from the look of the type.

She slit it open gingerly, expecting either a crank letter or some obscene threat. Instead there was a Xerox of a legal document headed "Declaration of Trust" and a brief message pasted together with newsprint in the same manner as her name on the envelope. She read the message first. Most of the words were lifted entirely from the newspaper, while others were composed of individual letters, including some random capitals. The meaning was clear enough, however: "exposé of oil industry Brilliant you are the one to destroy criminal cabinet minister if Not used by Monday, will give to Another source."

Margo quickly scanned the legal-looking document. One Allen Cormack, Executive, of the City of Toronto, Province of Ontario, declared that he held three thousand common shares of Berkley Petroleums Ltd. in trust for the sole use and benefit of one Walter H. Ferguson of the City of Windsor, Province of Ontario. The paper trembled slightly in Margo's hand as she read it a second time. Dynamite! Pure dynamite!

It happened all the time. Someone with a grudge against a prominent figure came into possession of an incriminating document and leaked it to the media. Her oil stories had given her a high profile as an investigative reporter, so it was logical that she should be chosen as the instrument for revenge, or whatever it was that motivated the informer. Heart pounding wildly in her chest, she checked her watch. Eleven-thirty. Two and a half hours before *Tomorrow* went to press. She reached for the phone and began to dial.

"Lou?" Margo sucked in a deep breath in an effort to keep her voice steady. "I may have uncovered the biggest story of the decade."

"I'm listening, doll."

"Can you have someone check and see if Allen Cormack is a shareholder of Berkley Petroleums?"

"Berkley Petroleums? I like it already."

"A search at the trust company that keeps the share register is all it takes."

"I know that, doll. While we're talking, it's happening. You got this big story down on paper yet?"

"No, but it won't take long. It's a stop-press item. My byline, though."

"I wouldn't have it any other way. We're gonna' make you a star, remember. Do I get another hint?"

"It may involve a well-known member of the cabinet."

"Ferguson." Reznik breathed the name almost reverently. "Please tell me it's Ferguson and that we're going to nail that low-life to the cross."

"I'll leave you in suspense until you read my piece," Margo replied with a gay, teasing laugh. It was so good to have her teeth into another blockbuster scandal. "I'll be there at one. We'll need confirmation on Cormack's share ownership by then, if at all possible."

"My secretary's standing right here with a note that Atlantic Trust is the transfer agent for Berkley. She's on her way there, and she'll phone in the results as soon as she has a peep at the records."

"Keep your fingers crossed."

"Baby, if I could cross my cock, I would. I'm praying for this one." Lou was almost shouting with excitement as the conversation ended.

The story wrote itself — it was all there in the Declaration of Trust. The biggest problem was to estimate the windfall profit Ferguson had made. It had to be at least $72,000, which was the amount of the premium over market price multiplied by three thousand shares. It would be substantially more than that if the shares had been obtained at a lower price some weeks before the takeover announcement. She would be perfectly safe in describing the cabinet minister's illegal profit as being "at least $72,000."

She began to type as soon as she had finished the arithmetic, her faith in the story unconsciously bolstered by working out the figures.

Lou Reznik sank into his chair without a word and feverishly read what Margo had written. Then he leaned back with a look of unholy glee on his ape-like face. "It sings. It dances. It flies!"

The grin faded as he was assailed with the perennial journalistic fear of being scooped. "This is an exclusive?" he asked pleadingly.

"Yes. But my source," Margo's voice lingered lovingly on the word, "has attached a very short time fuse to it. If I don't use the info right away, he'll go somewhere else." Why was she so certain her source was a man? She decided it was the wording of the note; that was the way a man — a well-educated man — would express himself. She could almost picture some disgruntled civil servant smiling viciously to himself while he cut out the words that would ruin the detested Ferguson.

"Now that you know what it's about, are you going to bring Mr. Blescup into it?" she asked.

"Naw. This is too hot for that old fart." He jabbed a thumb at his chest. "The buck stops here on this one, ba —" Reznick broke off as the phone gave its cricket chirp. "That's my secretary," he said in a voice that was suddenly dry and croaky. "I told them to hold all other calls."

"Okay. Gimme that again." With the earpiece propped up against his shoulder, Reznik scribbled a few notes on a desk pad, then said, "Good work, honey. Now get your ass back here. We got things to do."

With an expression that was unwontedly serious, he looked up at Margo and said quietly. "Allen Cormack is the registered owner of forty-five hundred common shares of Berkley."

"It fits, doesn't it? Two-thirds to Ferguson for supplying the insider information and one-third to Cormack for acting as front man." Margo placed her finger on the line in the Declaration of Trust that contained the reference to three thousand shares.

"That's the way it would work, all right." Reznick glanced sideways at the phone. "By rights, we should try and contact Ferguson and ask for his reaction. But we both know he'd only deny it, and the tipoff would give him time to throw up a smoke screen. Besides, we'd lose the scoop of a lifetime." He picked up the instrument. "You know, this is exactly the kind of deal a sleaze like Ferguson would pull."

"Is there any way we could verify Cormack's signature?" asked Margo.

"Between now and press time?" Reznick shook his head. "No way. We'd have to track the guy down and come up with some excuse to get him to sign something." He glanced at his gold wristwatch and shuddered. "We're running out of time. Look, doll, you're a pro. The best. You got faith in this source of yours?"

"Yes. Yes, I do," Margo found herself saying. "He's in a position to know the facts, and he has a good reason to hate Ferguson's guts." Why in God's name had she blurted that out? Well, it was done and she couldn't retract it. Not without making Lou think she had lost her marbles. Besides, she didn't want to retract it; her professional instinct told her the story was solid. Her inner debate was cut short by Reznik, who bussed her on both cheeks and squeezed her upper arms painfully as he cried, "That's good enough for me. We're going to print!"

II

The huge, vaulted chamber of the House of Commons crackled with almost intolerable tension as its members took their places for question period. The only absentees were three elderly MPs who were hospitalized and two cabinet ministers abroad on government business. The public and press galleries were jammed and seething with suppressed excitement. The acrimonious debate over the Berkley acquisition had already prolonged the session into the third week of July, well past the normal summer adjournment date of June 30, and now there was this sensational development. A low murmur, quickly hushed, ran through the crowd as the green baize curtain parted and the prime minister appeared with Walter Ferguson following directly behind. Then the rest of the cabinet trooped in, surrounding Ferguson in a show of support.

The Speaker recognized the leader of the NDP, who rose, holding a copy of Margo's damning article in his hand. Her piece had come out under the heading "Berkley Big Payday for Cabinet Minister" in bold black letters and featured a two-column photo of Ferguson that made him look even more villainous than usual. The NDPer's voice quavered slightly as he began to speak, whether from indignation or nerves it was impossible to tell. "This government," he intoned sonorously, "never wearies of boasting to this House about the strict conflict-of-interest rules it has imposed on its cabinet ministers. Would the prime minister be good enough to reconcile that with the report," he paused to brandish the magazine, "that the 'honourable'" — his voice dripped with sarcasm as he emphasized the word — "minister of consumer affairs has made a secret profit through illegal trading in the shares of Berkley Petroleums?"

The prime minister got to his feet and gave a little bow in the direction of the Speaker's chair on its raised dais. "The question was addressed to me, Mister Speaker, but I would prefer to have it answered by the honourable member from Windsor East."

Walter Ferguson's face was even paler than usual, and there were great dark bruises of fatigue under his eyes, but his voice was firm as he declared, "The report to which the Honourable Member refers is a complete fabrication and absolutely without foundation in fact. I do not know anyone by the name of Allen Cormack, and I have never owned, directly or indirectly, any shares of Berkley Petroleums. In due course, I shall be instructing my lawyer to file suit against the magazine and the individuals who were responsible for publishing that despicable pack of lies!"

He sat down amid an eruption of desk thumping from the government benches. The members of the opposition looked at each other, uncertain of their next move. Ferguson's categorical denial had deprived them of the bloodletting they had been anticipating. For the moment at least. Few of his colleagues in the House were prepared to accept his protestation of innocence at face value — the Berkley scandal was just the sort of disreputable conduct one would expect from old Walter. Still, he must be aware that automatic expulsion was the penalty for lying to the House, so one would think he'd be damn sure of his ground before making that statement. The question period fizzled out. The next chapter would have to wait until it was determined whether the magazine or Ferguson was telling the truth. In the beginning, most people were betting on the magazine.

Outside the House, Ferguson repeated his denial to a forest of microphones and television cameras. One enterprising reporter dashed to a pay phone and got through to Lou Reznik in the *Tomorrow* office.

"Hell, no, I'm not going to retract!" Lou roared. "Didn't you look at the byline? Margo Jones, the best investigative reporter in the country."

He still insisted they were sticking by the story when a second reporter called with the news that Cormack had also issued a denial. That was to be expected. He sure wished he could locate Margo, though. What a hell of a time for her to go missing! He looked up hopefully when his secretary appeared in the doorway, but she shook her head and said, "I keep calling her apartment, but all I get is her answering service, and they have no idea where she is. Mr. Blescup has arrived, though."

"A bad business, Lou." Blescup permitted himself a reproachful look. "You really should have consulted me, you know."

"There wasn't time," snapped Reznik. "Look, Howie, that story's okay. Margo has a Declaration of Trust signed by Cormack, for Chrissake!"

"Well, that's a help. I assume you have verified the signature?"

"Not exactly." Reznik avoided the lawyer's incredulous stare. He was saved from further embarrassment by his secretary's announcement that Margo was calling in on line one.

"Where the hell have you been?" Reznik screamed into the mouthpiece. "The shit hits the fan and you pull a disappearing act!"

He calmed down when Margo told him she had been busy tracking down Allen Cormack in the hope of getting a sample of his signature. It was impossible, though, she reported. Cormack's office was besieged by reporters, and she didn't dare show herself. She refrained from adding that the cement contractor appeared to be enjoying himself thoroughly, basking in the media attention as he steadfastly denied any connection between himself and Walter Ferguson. "I'm coming in," Margo said as she rang off. "There's nothing I can do out here."

The Declaration of Trust became Reznik's chief defence as the pressure either to confirm or retract steadily mounted. "The story stands," he bellowed into the

408 / JOHN BALLEM

constantly ringing telephone in a voice that was rapidly becoming hoarse. "When we get a copy of Cormack's signature, we'll have all the proof we need."

Tomorrow's reliance on the signature was broadcast across the nation that evening, and it produced an unexpected result. Early the next morning, Allen Cormack appeared on "Canada AM" and volunteered to provide the magazine with a copy of his signature.

"I don't like the sound of that," Blescup muttered darkly. He, Reznik, Margo, and the managing editor of the magazine were assembled for a breakfast meeting in the publisher's office. They all showed the effects of a sleepless night, except for the lawyer, whose slumber had been untroubled. "He has to be supremely confident to make an offer like that."

When the specimen signature finally arrived, Reznik was elated. "Look at that!" he crowed as he lined it up with the Declaration of Trust. "Didn't I tell ya? They're the fucking same!"

The handwriting expert's report, however, soon turned their elation into despair. "The two signatures are quite similar, but they are definitely not the same hand," he announced. Using a magnifying glass, he started to expound on the telltale differences, but the publisher waved him to silence.

"Christ Jesus." Reznik looked ill. He turned to Margo with a look that begged her to make everything right again. "The source, baby. We need your fucking source."

"I can't ask him to reveal himself. We reporters have a duty to protect our sources. You know that." Margo could feel the walls closing in on her.

Reznik seemed to be having trouble breathing; he looked to be on the verge of some kind of attack. Finally he spluttered in a strangled voice, "Listen, you little bitch, I'm the one who's out there twisting in the wind. The only reason we printed that story was because you had a reliable source. Now you fucking well produce him."

"Your desire to protect your source is commendable," Blescup interrupted smoothly. "It's in the highest tradition of journalism. But this is a desperate situation. You owe it to the magazine, to Lou, and to yourself to make him come forward." The lawyer was looking at her keenly.

Margo sensed that he suspected the truth. She knew she couldn't hope to maintain the charade much longer. At first she thought of asking to speak to Lou in private, but his emotional state was such that she was probably better off with a third party present. Gazing down at the carpet, she said dully. "There is no source."

"What?" Reznik screeched. "Are you saying you made the whole thing up?"

"No. But it looks like I've been set up. The ... that thing," Margo pointed to the Declaration of Trust on Reznik's desk, "was delivered to me by messenger on Friday morning."

"I believe we would be well advised to start drafting a retraction and an apology." Blescup opened his briefcase. "As abject as possible, and the retraction must be at least as conspicuous as the original article. That's very important."

"Out! Out!" Reznik was advancing towards Margo, one small fist raised as if to strike her. "Get out of my sight. Call yourself a reporter! You're ruined. Ruined! Do you understand that, you stupid cunt?" He picked up a marble pen stand and hurled it so hard it shattered against the door as it closed behind her.

12

"Margo seems to have gotten herself into a bit of a jam." Bill Crawford's face was expressionless as he raised the vodka martini to his lips.

So they were finally going to talk about it. Debbie and her father had been together for almost two hours, inspecting the new house he had purchased, without any mention of the sensational developments following the collapse of the allegations against Walter Ferguson. "It couldn't happen to a nicer person." Debbie grinned wickedly. The grin faded when she saw the telltale set of her father's mouth. "You aren't happy about it?" she said in a wondering tone. "After what she did to you?"

"She's a very ambitious lady. That's a quality I can understand."

"Who doesn't give one small damn about anyone else," rejoined Debbie hotly. "You've still got a thing —" She broke off as the waiter rolled a trolley up to their table and began the elaborate ritual of mixing a Caesar salad.

He served the salad and withdrew with a murmured "Enjoy," thereby setting Bill's teeth on edge. Debbie smiled at his little grimace of annoyance. "You're so transparent sometimes."

"An open book," her father agreed cheerfully as he picked up his fork. He held it suspended halfway to his mouth and said with a puzzled frown, "What I can't understand is how she came to let herself get caught like that."

"The same ambition you were just going on about," replied Debbie. "There was a suggestion in that statement the magazine released that she may have manufactured the evidence herself."

"The *Tomorrow* people sure dumped on her. All that sanctimonious bullshit about her professional reputation lulling them into publishing the story without checking it out first."

"What do you suppose will happen to her now?"

"She's finished as a journalist. Completely. Ferguson will win his lawsuit, but the magazine's insurers will pay the damages, so at least she won't be faced with a thundering great money judgment."

"I can't get over how concerned you are about her!"

"What do you want me to do — gloat?" Bill spoke lightly, but the look he gave his daughter was suddenly speculative.

Alarmed by the look and knowing how perceptive he could be when his curiosity was aroused, Debbie shrugged and began to enthuse about the new house. That wasn't hard — situated on five acres of land west of the city limits, it was a brand-new and luxurious ranch-style bungalow with an indoor pool. It was absolutely ideal for her father. When that pleasant subject had been satisfactorily disposed of, she gently touched the faint lines around his eyes. "You've been working awfully hard all summer. Ever since you came back from Houston, in fact. All day at the office and then closeted for hours with Chester. What are you two cooking up?"

"So far, we haven't even found the recipe," sighed Bill. And that was the unfortunate truth. All their ideas about how to place his control over Venture beyond the reach of outsiders foundered on the simple fact that he could be outvoted any time the investor groups decided to gang up on him.

"If only," Chester had said as their last session drew to a close, "they would assign their voting rights to you ..." His voice trailed off, and he let a wistful smile complete the fantasy.

"Don't hold your breath," advised Bill with a wry grin, briefly amused by the idea of the Dwights handing over voting control of their shares after the way he had thwarted their cosy little plan to install Strickland in his place. The Dwight block of shares was a loose cannon on the Venture corporate deck. The family showed no inclination to sell their shares, and their precious son-in-law, as irritatingly superior as ever, was still on the Venture board. It was as if there had never been a conspiracy to replace Bill with Adrian Strickland. Despite the surface appearance of normalcy, Bill knew they would eagerly join forces with anyone who could wrest control from him. Provided, of course, that the transaction netted them a tidy profit as well. Vengeance without profit was definitely not part of the Dwight family credo.

"The Travis block would be enough by itself," Chester had pointed out. "Somehow I don't think control matters all that much to Lee."

"It doesn't. If only we could come up with a way to make it worthwhile, I have a feeling he might go along. But it would have to be very much worth his while."

The waiter presenting the cheque snapped Bill back to the present. Debbie had brought her own car, so they said goodnight in the restaurant's parking lot. Her new lover was waiting for her at the apartment. He had a technique that was kind of a turn on: he would withdraw from her, rub the tip of his rock-hard penis against her clit, and then slide further away, making her squirm and wriggle after him across the bed. Being forced to chase after him like that was sort of humiliating, but that only seemed to increase her desire.

Speaking of chasing, she herself was most likely the object of another kind of chase right now. The Crawford family was bound to be high on Margo's list of suspects. However, suspicion was one thing and proof another. She'd been careful about fingerprints, and the only time she had appeared in person in the direct chain of events was when she arranged for the envelope to be delivered. No risk there; she'd been dressed as a man when she walked into the messenger service. Anyway, they'd been so swamped with the Friday morning rush that no one had given her a second look.

She let her lover slide away from her once; but the next time he entered her she locked her legs behind his buttocks and laughed mockingly up at him while she pumped him to a quick climax.

It was time to go back. Margo gazed around the tacky motel room as though seeing it for the first time. It had been her refuge during the soul-numbing days after the Ferguson fiasco, but now she wanted out. She packed quickly, stepping around the coffee table where the remains of a half-eaten club sandwich lay unappetizingly on a bed of soggy potato chips.

The comforting cocoon of anonymity surrounded her during the two-hour bus ride back to Toronto, but her nerve ends were prickling as she climbed the stairs of the subway station and walked the remaining block to her apartment building. There were no signs of any reporters or photographers waiting to waylay her. Common sense told her they would have given up the vigil long since. Even so, her pulse was racing as she hurried up the short cement walkway and stepped into the foyer. Her mailbox was crammed full, and there was a note from the building superintendent that he was holding more mail for her in his office.

"Yes, Ms. Jones, you do have some messages." The answering service operator sounded as though she didn't know whether to laugh or cry. "It's not so bad now, but it was pretty hot and heavy there for a coupla days."

Margo made apologetic noises and asked for a quick rundown.

"Well ..." The operator hesitated as if she were going to refuse, then gave in. "Okay. But it'll take some time. Hang on till I get someone to take over the board for me."

Nearly all the calls were from the media, but a Mr. Blescup wanted her to call on "a matter of extreme urgency," and a Bill Crawford had phoned several times. "He's got the sexiest voice." He had left a number, which, the operator informed her, was the Four Seasons Hotel on Avenue Road.

Why in the world was Bill Crawford calling her? Margo put that minor mystery to one side and dialled Blescup's number.

The lawyer came directly to the point. "We've been served with a writ by Ferguson's solicitors. You're named as a defendant along with the magazine, Lou Reznik, and the managing editor."

"Oh." Margo knew a lawsuit was inevitable, but that didn't help the sudden queasiness in her stomach. "How much is it for?"

"Two million. They won't get anything remotely like that, although the damages will be substantial. However," Blescup cleared his throat, "I wanted to point out to you that our positions may be adverse at the trial. The magazine and its management will argue that they were misled by relying on your professional integrity and expertise. It won't affect the liability, but it might mitigate the damages."

"So?"

"Under the circumstances, my dear, it will be impossible for this firm to represent you. I'm sure you can appreciate why. I would be happy to recommend other counsel for you."

"I can't afford to pay any goddamn legal fees. I don't need a lawyer anyway. I've already lost my reputation. What more can they take from me? My typewriter? They can have it."

Blescup was scandalized. "It would be folly for you not to be represented by counsel. Utter folly. As for the fees, I'll see if I can convince Lou to make some arrangement to cover them."

"Whatever you like," Margo said indifferently.

"Your reaction is perfectly understandable, my dear." Blescup was playing the role of the avuncular family solicitor. "But I insist on your having adequate representation. More than adequate; the very best. I will let you know when the arrangements have been completed. Meanwhile, I must advise you not to talk to the media. That's the one good thing about this libel action. You are to tell them that since the matter is the subject of litigation you are not free to discuss it."

"Suits me," Margo said as she rang off.

The operator was right. He did have a sexy voice. He sounded thrilled to hear from her, almost as if he had been sitting in his hotel room waiting for her call. Except that with Bill Crawford it would be a suite.

Margo was unresponsive. "What can I do for you, Bill?"

"You can have dinner with me. Tonight, if at all possible."

"I wouldn't be very good company," she demurred. What was with this guy, coming on like a friendly puppy after she had sliced him up and hung him out to dry?

"That's a risk I'd run any time," he was saying cheerfully. "You don't have to say one word all evening. I'd just like to be with you."

They arranged that she would take a taxi and pick him up at the hotel. They would dine at some out-of-the-way restaurant where they would be in little danger of being recognized.

Incredibly, the evening turned out to be a smashing success. Bill was lighthearted and entertaining; Margo had almost forgotten how charming he could be. She herself was in a strange, disoriented mood that made its own contribution to the spell. With her career and life in a free fall to disaster, she was almost beyond caring; and Bill's world, in which money seemed to make everything possible, was suddenly very appealing. He was saying something, but the words were lost in the popping of a cork as the waiter opened another bottle of champagne.

She leaned across the table. "Sorry, I didn't catch that. Did I hear something about the Riviera?"

"I was saying that we should go there. Tomorrow."

"Don't say that word." She frowned, then reached out and touched his hand when she saw his contrite expression. "I understand it's horribly crowded with vulgar tourists this time of the year," she said with mock haughtiness.

"It's never crowded at the place I have in mind. A villa at Cap d'Antibes with its own private beach."

"You're serious, aren't you?"

"Perfectly. The Lear is sitting out at the airport with its fuel tanks topped up, ready to take us wherever we want to go." He paused, then added quietly. "You'll be out of range. The European press has never heard of Walter Ferguson."

Margo would always look back on the next ten days as a magical, dreamlike interlude. Sun-drenched mornings on a beach with real sand instead of the gravelly shingle found on most Riviera beaches; long, lazy lunches and languorous nights. Their lovemaking, sure and unhurried, was the final grace note in a pampered, hedonistic existence. She got the curse at the end of the first week, but that didn't seem to matter. Satiated, they were content with loving caresses as they strolled through the villa's grounds.

High over the Atlantic on the return trip, Bill placed his briefcase in his lap and clicked it open.

"Going to catch up on some work?" Margo asked comfortably. She had grown accustomed to his frequent long-distance calls and occasional bouts of paper work.

He shook his head and smilingly handed her an exquisitely wrapped package. Underneath the gold foil was a Cartier box. Margo pressed the catch and blinked at the diamond and sapphire necklace nestled on a blue-velvet cushion. She gazed down at its sparkling perfection for a long moment, then closed the lid with a firm snap and handed the case back.

"I can't possibly accept this," she whispered. "It's too much. It makes me feel like some kind of love chick."

He pressed the case into her hand and closed her fingers around it. "I want you to keep it. As a favour to me. We both know you're not a love chick. It will be a reminder of a wonderful time, and" — he paused and looked directly into her eyes — "a safety net for you. It comes with no strings attached. You may use it as you wish."

He so obviously wanted her to have the necklace that it would be churlish and ungrateful to refuse. And God knew she might need a safety net; her prospects were not what one would call promising. A few days later she found out just how much of a safety net it was when Birks appraised it at $75,000.

The sound of the engines being throttled back signalled the start of their descent into Toronto. Margo's fingers flew to the necklace. "My God, what are you going to do about customs?"

"Declare it and pay duty like any good citizen," Bill replied calmly. Did a flicker of disappointment cross that lovely face? A story about a filthy rich oil baron smuggling jewellery into the country on his private jet would be almost irresistible to her. More so than the necklace. One couldn't afford to take chances around this lady.

A Cadillac limousine, trunk lid open, rolled onto the tarmac as the Lear whined to a halt in front of the executive aircraft terminal. An impressed customs officer led Bill inside the terminal to pay the duty on the necklace.

Bill kissed Margo lightly on the mouth as he fastened the necklace around her slender neck. She clung to him, whispering, "Oh, Bill. What can I say? For the necklace. For everything."

"It's been wonderful, Margo. Unforgettable."

She leaned out of the window and waved back at him as the limousine pulled away.

Alone in the cabin while the Lear arrowed west, Bill nursed a vodka tonic and let his thoughts travel back over the past then days. Unreal. It was given to few men to share an idyll with a companion as captivating as Margo. And now, of course, when she did begin the search for the person who had set her up for the Ferguson debacle, as she was sure to do, the trail would be cold. If that person happened to be Debbie — which was nothing more than a remote possibility, he sternly reminded himself — then the linkage would be that much harder for Margo to trace. As for the secondary purpose — that prolonged exposure might get Margo Jones out of his system — well, he couldn't be too sure about that. Not sure at all.

13

Standing by the luggage carousel at the Calgary airport, Ken Kwasny felt like a spy in the enemy camp. Coming to Calgary had been a sudden decision on his part, inspired by the announcement that Bill Crawford would be one of the featured speakers at the economic analysts' convention. Ken had never seen Crawford in person, and the conference would give him a chance to watch from the anonymity of the audience while his enemy stood up there on the platform. He would have to be careful, though — he was getting to be a bit of a celebrity himself in financial circles. After the Reliance deal, the press had taken to calling him the newest whiz kid on the block. He would be careful to keep very much in the background whenever Crawford was on the scene.

Economic analysts are not exactly thick on the ground, and the Calgary convention was a small affair as conventions go. The exhilarating sensation of being in enemy territory was still with Ken as he checked in at the registration desk on the mezzanine floor of the Westin. He was signing his name in the register when a hand descended on his shoulder, making him drop the pen.

"Kinda jumpy there, guy." It was Allen Hunt, a hearty bond salesman from one of the Vancouver brokerage houses. He had spotted Kwasny as a rising star and went out of his way to cultivate him. Ken retrieved the pen and made some offhand joke about being overworked.

"I got the cure for that, buddy boy. We have ourselves a hospitality suite on the sixteenth floor, and after that some of the local studs are going to show us the town."

The door to the hospitality suite was open, and Ken did a quick scan of the crowd. He would have no trouble recognizing Crawford — the newspapers had made a national icon out of his smiling, handsome face. Satisfied that the oil tycoon was not among those present, Ken ordered a glass of Perrier. Apart from the occasional champagne toast with Stan Winters, he almost never drank alcohol, preferring to keep his mental circuits free of static.

After an hour of inhaling other people's smoke and shouting to make himself heard, Ken prepared to leave, but Allen Hunt collared him. Everything was arranged — they were meeting some local lovelies and were going to have themselves a ball. Ordinarily, Ken would have declined; the kind of evening that was shaping up didn't sound like his style. But he had been only seventeen years old when he was last in Calgary, and he was eager to see the brash and exciting city through adult eyes. It was where the oil action was, and, while oil stocks weren't really his bag, they were an important segment of the stock market. Besides, Calgary was Crawford's turf, and there was a strange kind of excitement in exploring it.

I knew it. They're a bunch of overfed nerds. Watching the stockbrokers troop into the bar, Debbie made up her mind to leave. The other women could do as they liked, but she wasn't going to hang around and be pawed by this pack of red-faced jerks. When Dick Meyers asked her to join some of his out-of-town friends for a drink at Hy's, she had agreed to come against her better judgment. She was in between horse shows and bored out of her tree, and there was always an outside chance of meeting an attractive male. She had warned Dick that she would probably take off after one drink. Then she saw, bringing up the rear, the tall, scholarly looking guy with the lock of dark hair falling over his forehead. He didn't look as though he belonged with the others, but now Dick was introducing him. Ken Kwasny. From Vancouver. Debbie decided the evening showed promise after all.

His first night in Calgary and he runs into Bill Crawford's daughter! It was a jolt, but Ken quickly reminded himself that she wouldn't know him from Adam. Then he became aware of something else — the lady was definitely coming on to him. She was showing a lot of delectable cleavage as she smiled up at him and moved over to make room on the banquette seat. Easing himself down on the leather bench beside her, Ken was immediately conscious of an unsettling contradiction between the blatantly sexy curves of her body and the alert intelligence that shone from those remarkable eyes.

It was obvious that what Debbie wanted, Debbie got. While Ken was still adjusting to this unexpected encounter, she was smoothly leading the conversation, leaning forward to isolate the pair of them from the rest of the party. She didn't seem disturbed by his initial lack of response; she was probably used to men being struck dumb on their first exposure to her. Cursing the luck that had led her to select him as her target for the night, Ken confined himself to noncommittal replies while he tried to think of some way of extricating himself. She looked slightly startled when he ordered Perrier and more than a little miffed when he deliberately looked past her to address a remark to Allen Hunt, trying to include him in the conversation. My God, she was a tempting morsel; under any other circumstances, Ken would willingly have surrendered to her appeal. But Bill Crawford's daughter was strictly off-limits.

The only trouble was that, by appearing indifferent to her, he was also liable to arouse her curiosity. She looked the type that would regard him as a challenge. The last thing in this world he needed was to have a member of Crawford's family taking an interest in Ken Kwasny. If his campaign against the man was ever to succeed, he must be able to operate completely in the background, unknown and unseen. The rest of the group were making noises about moving into the dining room, and

Ken hurriedly excused himself, muttering something unconvincing about having a big day tomorrow.

She had sure blown that one, Debbie told herself as she said a cool goodnight to him. The first man she had been really attracted to in ages, and she had turned him off by coming on too strong. Could he be gay? Somehow she didn't think so — there just weren't those kind of vibes. Some men couldn't handle it when the woman made the first move.

"Don't let Ken get to you, Debbie," Hunt was saying. "He's not much of a mixer. Why don't I buy you dinner?"

Debbie shook her head and picked up her purse. "I told Dick I could only stay for one drink." She said goodnight to the others and swept out of the bar, holding her head with that slightly imperious tilt that was so reminiscent of her father. Waiting for the parking valet to bring the Mustang around, she found herself wondering if she would ever see the aloof Mr. Kwasny again. She was slightly shaken to find herself wanting to, despite the fact that the man had been barely civil to her.

Back in his hotel room, Ken was tempted to check out and catch a late flight back to Vancouver. Coming to Calgary had been a crazy — worse, an unnecessary — risk. Look at what had happened tonight. He told himself no real damage had been done. Debbie would simply dismiss him as an uninteresting boor, and that would be the end of that. Still, the enemy had had him in view, even if they didn't realize it. Unexpectedly, Ken shivered with excitement. Working this close to the bone could get addictive.

Crawford's talk was scheduled for the morning. As soon as it was over, Ken would grab the next flight to Vancouver and go to ground.

Sitting well back in the audience, Ken got his first look at the man who had tried to kill him. Crawford lived up to his advance billing. Handsome, assured, he looked every inch the crown prince of the oil industry. He started off by talking about his own company, Venture Oils. Nothing the man said was new to Ken, but he listened intently, alert for any scrap of information that he could add to what was already stored in the computer. Crawford made no mention of the aborted conspiracy of the Dwights and Lee Travis, passing off the wild swings in the stock price as the result of unfounded rumours. Ken wondered how Crawford would feel if he knew that the man behind the attempt to unseat him was in his audience, paying respectful attention to every word he said.

Bill had moved on to an overview of the Canadian oil industry as a whole. His voice quickened with enthusiasm when he began to talk about the potential of the Arctic basin, describing the huge geological structures that lurked beneath the Beaufort Sea. "It's real elephant country," he declared. "One of the few areas remaining in the free world where there is a possibility of finding truly astronomical oil reserves."

It was obvious the man was obsessed with the Arctic quest, and Ken, who was aware from his encyclopedic knowledge of Venture that the company had no stake up there, wondered why that was so. As if realizing that many members of the audience would be asking themselves the same question, Bill said, "As I'm sure a good many of you know, Venture has not participated in the Arctic." He paused and added with dramatic effect, "As yet." When the excited murmurs died down, he continued. "The reason is simple. Exploration in the Arctic is an incredibly expensive business. It could easily turn into a financial vacuum that could literally drain away all the resources of a company the size of Venture. Accordingly, I have always taken the position that in the best interest of our shareholders we should stick to the conventional areas where we can have some control over the costs."

A number of heads, including Ken's, nodded approvingly at this. Venture was a highly successful company; it would be folly to put it at risk in the Arctic. Leave that to the multinationals who could afford to absorb losses in the hundreds of millions of dollars.

"But, I'm here to tell you," Bill was saying with an infectious grin, "that if the right opportunity comes along, we'll take a hard look at it. I like to think that we've reached a stage where we can play with the big boys."

He sat down to warm applause and fielded questions with the candid expertise for which he was famous, until the chairman finally called a halt. Ken didn't hang around for the coffee break; he had run enough risks as it was. As he checked out of the hotel, his ever-active mind was turning over the implications of Crawford's obvious infatuation with the Arctic.

14

It was at the official opening of the Venture Tower that Bill stumbled onto a possible method of protecting his control position. The opening, despite the fact that it coincided with the first real snowfall of the season, was a gala affair, well attended by members of the business community and representatives of all levels of government. Bill had stood firm on the name despite constant pressure to let the prospective major tenant call it Columbia Plaza. "There's no other building in town where Columbia can rent the space it needs," he had repeatedly assured a nervous Al Medford. The real estate agent, panicked by the prospect of losing the biggest commission of his life, protested that the multinational company could put up its own building.

"No time," Bill had replied, with more conviction than he really felt. "Tell them we're about to lease three of the floors to somebody else, so if they want all ten floors, they'd better get with it."

The bluff had worked, and the top brass from the Columbia Resources head office in San Francisco were there to attend the opening. Their president made a gracious little speech, praising the new office building and saying how delighted his company was to have all the employees of its Canadian organization under one roof.

After the speeches were over, the invited guests assembled in the new Venture boardroom on the top floor for drinks and hors d'oeuvres. The most prominent political guest was Gilles Vachon, the federal minister of energy, and it was he who provided Bill with the germ of an idea. Speaking indistinctly through a mouthful of goose-liver pâté, Vachon waved an expansive hand around the boardroom and declaimed in a strong French-Canadian accent, "It is magnificent! Magnifique." He paused to wash down the pâté with a gulp of red wine before adding, "Too bad it is not Canadian."

"What do you mean?" Bill was affronted. "I'm a Canadian. Have been for years."

"That I know well, *mon cher ami.* But the company is not. Under FIRA, Venture Oils is what they call a 'non-eligible person.' If it wanted to acquire another Canadian business, it could not. The agency would not permit it."

The passage of the Foreign Investment Review Act had created a storm of controversy, particularly in Alberta, where it was regarded as yet another attack by the feds on the oil-fuelled economy of the province. Designed to restrict the acquisition of Canadian firms by foreign interests, the act established a government agency to vet all such proposed acquisitions and to reject any it did not feel were in the national interest. Apart from a feeling of distaste and uneasiness over yet another example of government intervention, Bill had not paid any particular attention to the legislation. Venture was not in the market to acquire any companies, Canadian or otherwise, so there had been no need to become familiar with the details. Still, it came as an unpleasant shock to be told so bluntly that you were "a non-eligible person" — it made you feel like a second-class citizen.

The mayor of Calgary came up and buttonholed Vachon, freeing Bill to seek out Chester Martin. "Are you up to speed on this foreign investment law?" he asked, drawing the lawyer to one side.

"FIRA? Depends on how much of the nitty-gritty you want. The basic philosophy is simple: if a corporation doesn't have the required degree of Canadian control, it has to get approval before it can acquire a Canadian company or set up a new business in Canada. If you like, I'll work up a written opinion on the nuts and bolts of the scheme."

"Vachon tells me Venture is caught by the act."

"What else would you expect with those big blocks of shares held by three American investors? In fact, Venture is probably the classic example of what the Act is all about."

"Can a company's status be changed?"

"The answer is yes. Everything depends on where the control of the corporation resides. Get the votes in Canadian hands and you join the ranks of the anointed."

"I want you to become an expert on that Act, Ches. How long will it take?"

"Two days. I'll have the office hold my calls and bury myself in the library."

"Let me know when you're ready to talk," instructed Bill as he moved away to mingle with his guests.

"I feel like I'm back in law school cramming for the final exams." Chester Martin gestured at the stack of books and loose-leaf case reports on his desk. He removed his glasses and massaged the bridge of his nose. "I've got to admit you surprise me, Bill. Taking over other companies has never been your style — you've always been able to make Venture grow by going out and finding oil and gas."

"A good deal is still a good deal, no matter how it's packaged," Bill replied.

"I can't argue with that. Well," the lawyer picked up a thick sheaf of typewritten notes, "I've boned up on FIRA to the point where I can quote the important sections word for word, and I'm telling you there's no way Venture can —." He broke off as the real reason behind Bill's sudden interest in FIRA finally dawned on him. "Sorry to be so slow on the uptake. You're out to get voting control."

"That's the bottom line. And this FIRA thing provides us with the perfect excuse to do it. Before we get carried away though, check me on one point. It's legal for a company to have both voting and non-voting shares, right?"

"No problem there."

Bill exhaled a small sigh of relief. "Thank the good Lord. Everything hinges on that. Now tell me exactly what it will take to turn Venture into a true-blue Canadian."

"To be absolutely sure, all three of the American blocks would have to surrender their votes. The Act catches you in two ways — the maximum total foreign owner-ship is twenty-five per cent, and no one foreign individual or corporation can hold more than five per cent. You could make some kind of an argument that the New York group is okay because it's composed of a number of individuals each holding less than five per cent of the company's shares, but I expect the agency would insist on treating them as one entity. In a nutshell, then, you would have to turn the Travis and Dwight shares into non-voting; and, in my opinion, you would have to do the same thing with the New York syndicates as well."

"That shouldn't be any problem," replied Bill. "In fact, I'm counting on the New York boys to help persuade the others to go along. They've got the incentive."

"Liquidity, I assume."

"Exactly. It's a constantly recurring problem with the Abrams brothers. This time I understand it's grain futures."

"Sounds like them. This has been a bumper crop year, so if they took a long posi-tion they could be in big trouble about now." The lawyer rescued a textbook that was about to slide off his desk. "Your plans seem to be pretty far advanced."

"Let's say I've got the basic ingredients. A corporate acquisition that would be highly beneficial to the company. Beneficial enough to fully justify the Canadianiza-tion of Venture. The sweetener will be an underwriting that will allow a foreign shareholder to tender his shares for cash if he wishes. Throw in some tax breaks, and I think we've got a package we can sell."

Formulating the plan turned out to be the easy part. Implementing it was some-thing else again. The biggest problem was to find a suitable takeover candidate. A believer in growth from within, Bill had never cast covetous glances at his corporate neighbours, so he was forced to start at baseline zero in his analysis. The acquisition had to be sizeable enough to justify the reorganization of Venture, and the opera-tions of the target company should be compatible with those of Venture. Most important, the takeover should be friendly, carried out with the approval and co-operation of the board of directors on the other side. Bill had no intention of embroiling Venture in a bitterly contested proxy battle.

It turned out to be a case of "the girl next door." Hampton Resources Inc. was a partner in a number of joint operations with Venture and had a land-spread that was uncannily complementary to the Venture holdings. It was run as a branch plant of the US corporation, which was registered in Edmonton as an extra-provincial company. The Hampton company was headquartered in Houston and operated on a large scale throughout the world. Bill had always got along extremely well with Steve Miller, the dynamic manager of Hampton's Canadian operations. Six months ago, however, Steve had been hastily recalled to Houston to supervise Hampton's exploration program off the coast of California. The company had paid the big dollar for some choice drilling permits when the US federal government put them up for bid, and then had proceeded to drill a succession of costly dry holes.

Recently, Hampton had begun to turn down proposals for new wells on lands it held jointly with Venture in Alberta. Under the terms of the typical joint operating agreement, a party had the right to propose the drilling of a new well on jointly owned lands. If all the parties agreed, the well was drilled for the joint account; but a party had the right to decline participation and incur a penalty instead. The penalty consisted of allowing the drilling party to recover from the proceeds of production three times the non-participating party's share of the cost. If the well came in dry, there would be no proceeds, and the cost would have to be absorbed entirely by the drilling party. It was a useful mechanism to prevent one joint-owner from stymieing the plans of its associates, while at the same time allocating the risk to only those parties who desired to go ahead with the drilling.

In the past, Hampton had always been an active participant, routinely joining in any drilling projects proposed by Venture and frequently proposing new wells in those fields where it was the operator.

"I don't know what's come over them bastards." Dave Wilson scowled at the terse letter. "Hampton's elected to go penalty on the Edson well."

"Maybe they know something we don't," Bill replied, half jokingly.

"Naw." The exploration manager shook his head. "It's the kind of project they would have been bugging us to drill a few months ago. This is the third time in a row they've turned us down. I don't get it."

"We're going on our own, I assume?" asked Bill.

"That's my recommendation. But this," Wilson brandished the Hampton letter, "has got me runnin' kinda scared. I wouldn't mind a second opinion on the well, if you got a minute."

"Sure thing," Bill replied with alacrity. He stood up for a better view of the isopach map Dave was unrolling on the desk. They spoke of "closure," "well control," "updip," and "net pay thickness" while their fingers traced the gently curving lines of the map.

"Hell, it's a picture play," Bill said finally. He seldom had a chance to practise pure geology any more, and he had thoroughly enjoyed the brief session. "What about the other times Hampton went the penalty route? How did the wells pan out?"

"We completed both as producers. It just don't make sense, Bill. Maybe Hampton shot its wad drilling them dry holes off Santa Barbara," Wilson added with a faint tinge of professional malice.

"Could be."

Bill's expression was thoughtful after his exploration manager left. He didn't believe for a moment that a shortage of funds was the reason behind Hampton's non-participation. The offshore program would be one hell of a drain on their treasury, no doubt about that, but their share of the well Wilson had been talking about was chicken feed — less than a hundred and fifty thousand to casing point. A more likely possibility was that the political climate in Canada had turned the Hampton management off so completely that they had decided not to make any further investments and to expatriate their profits out of the country while they could. For whatever reason, and unthinkable as it would have been only a few short months ago, the Canadian assets of Hampton Resources Inc. just might be up for grabs. My God, what a coup that would be!

After a restless night, Bill decided to set up an intracompany task force to evaluate the Hampton properties. The Venture staff would be uniquely qualified to carry out the analysis, since so many of the parcels of land were either jointly owned or in close proximity to each other. This fact only served to increase Bill's excitement. The two companies were a glass-slipper fit.

Dave Wilson's enthusiasm soon equalled his own. The thought of having the Hampton lands to work with jerked the exploration manager out of his chair and set him striding back and forth on Bill's brand-new broadloom. He nodded eager acceptance when Bill asked him to head up a team to examine Hampton's holdings. "All I need is a ballpark figure, Dave. Enough to tell me whether there's any point in chasing after the deal."

It was quickly agreed that the team should consist of Dave, another geologist to help him with the all-important reserve evaluation, a reservoir engineer, and a landman.

"Here are the guys I want. They're good at their work, and they know how to keep their traps shut." Dave scribbled three names down on a sheet of paper and shoved it across the desk.

"I would have picked the very same ones," approved Bill. "Tell them to drop whatever they're doing and concentrate full-time on this assignment. And, of course, that it's all very hush-hush."

Somewhat self-consciously, they agreed that the project required a code name. They finally chose "Operation Blowdown" because, as Dave suggested, anyone who happened to come across the file would conclude it was a confidential study on how best to produce the gas cap in one of Venture's mature oilfields that had been depleted to the final "blowdown" stage.

The report was on Bill's desk three weeks later. Familiar with Dave's method of presentation, Bill immediately turned to the second page where the results were summarized. Using the standard fifteen per cent discount rate, the present value of Hampton's proven and provable reserves, plus unexplored landholdings, totalled $105-million. Comfortably within Venture's financing capacity.

"A conservative estimate, I take it?" Bill glanced up from the report to look at Dave sitting across the desk from him. The exploration manager had the confident look of a man sure of his facts.

"Yes. And ballpark. There's a real plus factor because their land spread turned out to be a lot more extensive than we first thought. That Steve Miller knew what he was about."

"Excellent." Bill nodded appreciatively. An oil company's inventory of land was the foundation for its future growth and expansion.

"You'll find another surprise in that report," said Dave with a hint of mischief in his voice.

"Are you going to let me in on it? Or are you going to keep me in suspense until I read the whole report?"

"It's your old passion — the Arctic. Hampton's got a net two hundred thousand acres up there."

Serendipity. Like finding oil when you were drilling for gas. When a deal started to give off vibrations like that, it was one of life's sweetest moments. Bill felt a buzz of excitement as he said, "The Arctic's a big place. Just where are their lands?"

"It's kinda strange in a way." Wilson unfolded a map at the back of the report. "Almost like the Hampton people were reading your mind — or bugging your office." The afterthought was meant as a joke, but the paranoia latent in every exploration-ist was not far below the surface. Dave's gaze travelled around the panelled walls of Bill's office before he continued. "Their exploration permits are the hell and gone west of where Globe is drilling and finding nothing but a few pockets of gas. In deeper water, too, although most of it is within the capability of drill ships." He leaned back in his chair and watched Bill's expression as he examined the map of the Beaufort Sea. "See what I mean? That's the same area you used to be so high on."

Bill nodded without looking up from the map. He needed a few seconds to collect his thoughts. When he did speak, he found he had to clear his throat. Annoyed with himself, he said, "It's a coincidence all right. What value did you assign to these permits?"

"They're just whale pasture until somebody does some work on them. So I put them in at cost, which is purely nominal."

"They could turn out to be a real stumbling block to any negotiations if somebody in Hampton happens to be in love with them," mused Bill. "If we ever get to the negotiation stage, that is."

"Find out anything from Stauback?"

"Not really." The previous week, Bill had taken Tom Stauback, Steve Miller's successor as Hampton's Canadian manager, out to lunch and needled him politely about not participating in the recent joint operations. Stauback had shrugged apolo-getically and muttered something about his budget having been cut to shreds. The impact of the California drilling disaster was left unspoken, but it was implicit in the air between them.

Wilson's report was first class. It revealed as much about Hampton Resources as anyone would ever learn without having direct access to the company's files. When he had digested its contents, Bill knew he was positioned for the next stage — an

426 / JOHN BALLEM

overture to the owners of Hampton. It was also time to bring Jim Goulder into the act; a share underwriting would obviously have to be an essential part of any deal. Bill had no intention of contacting the Hampton people until he had at least the framework of a plan in place. He instructed Lisa to arrange a meeting with Goulder and Chester Martin as soon as possible.

After that, it would be back to Houston to find out whether he was correct in suspecting that Canada had lost its charm for Hampton's top management.

15

It was the Hampton in-house lawyer's intimate knowledge of FIRA that gave the game away. Up until then, the broad face of Peter Ketchin, Hampton's president, impassive behind a screen of cigar smoke, had expressed nothing more than polite interest in what Bill was saying. But when the lawyer, thinking he was reinforcing his superior's position and preening himself on his mastery of the subject, butted in to express his scepticism that the deal would ever clear FIRA, it immediately became obvious that the Hampton head office had conducted a detailed study of the political changes in the Canadian scene.

Ketchin acknowledged the crack in his defence with a resigned lift of an unkempt eyebrow, and Bill responded with a sympathetic grin that showed he too was familiar with the experience of being undermined by an overeager subordinate. "Now that the subject has been raised," Ketchin toyed with a silver cigar cutter, "just how do you propose to get over the FIRA hurdle?"

"By turning Venture into an eligible person under the act."

"Umm. Well, that's an alternative that's not open to us." Ketchin tucked the cigar clipper back into his vest pocket. "Tell me, do you agree with those people who say this FIRA thing is just the first step and that the Canadian government intends to move in on the industry in a big way?"

"It's really the second step. The first was CNIC's takeover of Berkley Pete. And, yes, I fear we haven't seen anything yet."

"Goddamn governments to hell. They're never satisfied until they've got every-thing screwed up beyond repair."

"The trouble is that sticking it to big oil is a no-lose situation for the politicians."

Smoothing his tangled eyebrows with patting motions of his hands, Ketchin squinted at Bill. "And yet you want to increase your stake up there. How come?"

"That's where my working life has been spent. I've been a Canadian citizen for the past ten years. Besides, the majority of Venture's assets are located there, so we're committed to Canada, whether we like it or not."

"Seems like you boys up there are going to spend more of your time playin' politics than lookin' for oil," grunted Ketchin. "I'm glad it's you and not me."

He invited Bill to join him for lunch in the executive dining room. Bill demurred, worried that his presence might start the rumour mill working. Ketchin overrrode his objection, saying that everyone knew Venture was closely associated with Hampton's

428 / JOHN BALLEM

Canadian operations. "You people are regarded as one hell of a good operator, too," he boomed, flinging an arm around Bill's shoulder and walking him out the door. "Anyway," he added with a laugh and a squeeze of his meaty hand, "there ain't nothin' to start a rumour about, is there?" Bill was to learn that Peter Ketchin was a physical negotiator; he was perpetually clapping people on the back, nudging them in the ribs, squeezing their biceps, and blowing cigar smoke in their faces. Fortunately, Bill had developed a high degree of tolerance for this type, which was by no means uncommon in the upper echelons of the oil industry.

Clarence Harris, chairman of the board and chief executive officer of Hampton Resources, presided at the head of the long rosewood table. Silver-haired, slim, and patrician, and within a year of mandatory retirement, he was the antithesis of his bluff second-in-command. Bill was not the only outside visitor; there was also the executive vice-president of a Texas pipeline company, a cabinet minister from Venezuela, and a burnoosed gentleman from the Emirates. Bill was seated on the chairman's right while Ketchin entertained the sheikh and the South American politician at the other end of the table. The atmosphere was comfortably privileged, and the conversation flowed easily around the universal topic of oil. Bill was pleasantly gratified to discover that Ketchin had been right about Venture's reputation. In his dry, whispery voice that carried clearly in the respectful silence, the chairman informed the table that Bill headed one of the most efficient companies that Hampton had the pleasure of being associated with throughout their worldwide operations. It was gracious and sincere, and it also explained Bill's presence very neatly.

After lunch, Bill and Ketchin were invited back to the chairman's office for a "chat." Bill started to sit down in the small leather chair directly in front of the desk, but Harris waved him into another one off to the side, insisting that he would find it much more comfortable. Somewhat mystified, since the chairs appeared to be identical, Bill did as he was told.

"I understand you have a proposal you wish to make." Harris sat stiffly erect in his swivel chair, looking as if he had undergone a spinal fusion at some stage in his life. He had obviously been briefed by Ketchin while drinks were being served before lunch.

"I wouldn't go so far as to call it a proposal," Bill protested mildly. "More of an exploratory meeting to see if something can be worked out to our mutual advantage. I should explain that I'm here on my own initiative; I haven't mentioned anything about this to my board as yet."

"I see." Harris gazed at him keenly through rimless spectacles. "From what little I understand of your plan, it would appear you will have quite a selling job to do on your major shareholders."

"I'm confident they will go along."

Harris's slender shoulders gave a barely perceptible shrug, and he gestured for Bill to continue.

"If you agree," Bill said carefully, "I suggest we have our staff people get together and see if they can come up with a valuation figure. It shouldn't be too difficult, since so many of the properties are common to both."

"And then?"

"And then we would make you an offer."

"In what form?"

"Venture shares."

"Forget it!" Ketchin interjected with an explosive snort. "Cash or nothing."

Bill was prepared for this reaction. "I think possibly you should check with your tax people first. Cash in your hands will be taxable, while a straight share exchange attracts no taxes whatever. Always assuming, of course, that Hampton is taxable." Bill already knew from the company's annual report that it was fully taxable, its revenues having long ago exceeded its write-offs.

"The manner of payment is a very complicated matter, Peter. One that will require much study before we can arrive at any final conclusions." The reproof in the chairman's voice made Bill wonder about the likelihood that Peter Ketchin would inherit the CEO mantle when Harris retired.

With the effortless ease of those accustomed to power, Harris switched the conversation to generalities, speaking fondly of the many visits he had made to Calgary over the years, his fascination with the limitless potential of the Athabasca oil sands, and the deteriorating political situation in the oil-producing African states. "We are in headlong retreat everywhere," he concluded sadly. "Soon we will be driven back within our own borders. I must admit I never thought it would happen with Canada, but ..." He rose to offer Bill a brief handshake. "All I can say to you is that we will take the matter under advisement. We will be in touch, I would hope ..." he glanced at Ketchin, who nodded agreement when he finished, "within two weeks."

Outside in the corridor, Ketchin lit a cigar and exhaled a cloud of smoke with a pent-up sigh of enjoyment. "You made a big hit with the old man," he said.

"How do you figure that?"

"Simple. You passed the chair test."

"What chair test?"

"The chair you were going to sit in until he waved you off — he's had the front legs shortened a couple of inches, so people find themselves sliding forward all the time and they don't know why. It's uncomfortable as hell, particularly with that shiny leather seat, so it doesn't encourage people to linger and waste his time. When he made you take the other one, I knew you were in."

Back in his own office, Ketchin returned to the question of payment, grumbling that a share exchange would just be giving away solid assets for bits of paper. A green phone on his desk rang suddenly, and he snatched it up. The conversation was short, and he did all the listening, saying only at the end, "He's still with me, sir. I'll ask him."

"That was the chairman," he informed Bill unnecessarily. "He wants to know how you expect to comply with FIRA if you give us Venture shares."

So the second shoe had finally dropped. "That's easy," replied Bill. "Your shares will be non-voting."

With his cigar suspended in mid-air, Ketchin stared speechlessly at Bill for a full thirty seconds before sputtering, "I don't believe it! What good is a fucking share if you can't vote it?"

"As good as any other share as far as the stock market is concerned. Most investors don't give a damn whether a share is voting or not; all they care about is whether the company is making profits and whether the price of the stock is going up."

"Well, I'll tell you right up front, Crawford, I don't like it one goddamn bit."

"Why don't we let the lawyers and accountants worry about that end of it, and you and I stay with what we do best — the horse-trading part."

Ketchin was still muttering to himself and shaking his massive head in disbelief when Bill took his leave. "I purely admire your balls," he said as they shook hands, "coming in here with a Mickey Mouse deal like that."

Bill laughed and told him he expected an affirmative answer in two weeks.

As it turned out, the answer was a qualified affirmative. Ketchin agreed to take the next step and form a committee of staff experts from the two companies and one independent geological consultant to review the data. The manner of payment would be left open until after the joint evaluation was completed. Bill was jubilant; it was all he could have hoped for at that stage.

It was decided that the joint study team should meet in Kansas City, a location sufficiently removed from the normal flyways of oilmen that there would be little chance of their presence becoming known. Both companies worked up cover stories for the sudden absence of certain key employees. In the case of Hampton, it was an intensive think-tank session on the disastrous Santa Barbara exploration program; and in the case of Venture, a rumour was leaked that the company was thinking about buying some producing oil wells in Oklahoma.

Now that his corporate target seemed to be co-operating, Bill was faced with the job of persuading his three big American shareholders to go along. In theory it shouldn't be too difficult — the Hampton acquisition was a once-in-a-lifetime opportunity, and making Venture eligible under FIRA would open up a dazzling potential for growth by further acquisitions. But he was dealing with powerful personalities accustomed all their lives to having things their own way. As always, Lee Travis was the key; if he balked, the whole scheme would never get off the ground.

As the head of his family's vast fortune, Lee's responsibility was to find places where significant amounts of money could be invested safely and profitably. The key was to find people like Bill and join forces with them. It would be completely self-defeating for Lee to get involved in the actual day-to-day operation of any of his far-flung investments.

Although he had spoken to him several times on the phone, Bill hadn't seen Travis since their toe-to-toe confrontation in Houston. Travis had been his usual cordial self on the phone, but that didn't necessarily mean anything — he could lay on that Texas smarm with the best of them.

Travis listened intently while Bill sketched in the details of the Hampton deal. They were having breakfast together in Bill's suite at the Houston Four Seasons. "What it amounts to," he muttered when Bill finished, "is that you want me to give up control. That's asking a lot, ol' buddy."

"Well, you don't have control now, if you get down to it. You and I have the same number of voting shares. But I grant you that I am asking quite a bit. However, you will also be getting quite a bit in return." Lee's lifted eyebrow invited him to continue. "Growth. What we are looking at is a unique chance to grow exponentially. Hampton isn't the only large American company that is jittery about its future in Canada. If we succeed in qualifying Venture under FIRA, we'll be ideally positioned to take advantage of these situations as they arise."

"Bird's nest on the ground, huh?"

"Exactly."

"What happens if I don't go along? Rumours about hot oil will start circulating around Washington, I suppose?"

Bill looked him in the eye. "Not from me they won't. There's no question of that, now or in the future, regardless of what happens."

"You just said the right thing, Bill. Tell me some more about the business side of this thing."

"Be glad to." Bill was almost dizzy with relief that the air between them had been cleared. "For starters, the growth I'm talking about will require no further investment on your part. We can bank it all."

"Yeah," replied Lee, then he added the cautious rider, "except for dilution in the value of the shares."

"If I do my job properly, there won't be any dilution."

"True enough. Which brings me to my real concern. I have a lot of confidence in your judgment, Bill, and the thought of handing over complete control to you doesn't bother me all that much. For all practical purposes, you've run the company since day one. But what happens when my good buddy Bill Crawford is no longer at the helm? I'd be crazy to put myself in a position where I'd be at the whim of some jerk I know nothing about."

This set Bill up to apply the clincher. "There's absolutely no danger of that. There will be a condition attached to the shares that they automatically will become

432 / JOHN BALLEM

entitled to vote if a 'Crawford event' occurs. A 'Crawford event' happens when I am no longer the chief executive officer of Venture, for whatever cause — death, incapacity, retirement, termination — any reason at all."

"Well, now, that does give me comfort. A lot of comfort. Okay, I'll buy it. The lawyers and bean-counters will have to check the fine print, of course, but basically I'll go along."

"You'll never regret it," Bill promised as he reached across the table to grip Lee's hand.

"What about the Abrams brothers and the Dwights? Have you talked to them yet?"

"No. I wanted to find out how you felt about the idea first. I'm not anticipating much of a problem with the Abrams."

"They'll jump at it," Lee agreed. "They need a transfusion of cash real bad. Those boys can't seem to leave that commodities market alone."

"The Dwights won't be so simple. In fact," Bill looked at the Texan, "I haven't figured out how I'm going to approach them."

"Leave them to me."

"There's something going on in that favourite company of yours, Ken." Stan Winters made the comment lightly, but his eyes were watchful as he waited for his young partner's reaction.

"Venture? What? Tell me."

"I just had a call from Alec Davies, who's been talking to Richard P. himself."

Ken nodded and braced himself for what was to come. Right from the start of his campaign against Bill Crawford he had realized he would have to stay completely in the background. Stan Winters had come up with the name of Alec Davies, the CEO of Frontenac Mines Ltd., which was sitting on a wagonload of cash as a result of having one of its big South American mines expropriated by the government. Finding the right home for that kind of money was the biggest problem facing Frontenac, and Alec had been receptive when Winters first began to talk about Venture. In the way that these things often arrange themselves, it turned out that Davies and Richard P. Dwight, III, were members of the same prestigious yacht club in Bermuda and were well-known to each other. It was Davies who, acting on Ken's instructions relayed through Winters, had set in motion the scheme to replace Crawford with Adrian Strickland.

"Alec wasn't very specific," Winters was saying. "Probably because Dwight didn't really understand it himself; but it's got something to do with FIRA and non-voting shares."

"That clever son of a bitch!" breathed Ken, with reluctant admiration. "He's going to make Venture eligible under FIRA by converting the US shares to non-voting. If he succeeds in doing that, his position is impregnable. We've got to stop him!"

"I don't know how."

"Simple. Have Davies persuade the Dwights to hold out. Their holdings are big enough to prevent Venture from becoming eligible."

"It's not on, Ken. Alec's still steaming over the last time. He figures he lost a lot of face. Besides, he definitely got the impression from old Richard P. that the deal was done already."

"If we don't do something now, that company will be forever out of our reach."

"I can live with that, Ken. There are lots of other outfits just waiting for us to take a run at them. Outfits that don't have a guy like Bill Crawford to repel boarders."

"You're probably right, Stan," conceded Ken. There was no point in alarming Winters by letting him know that he was still as determined as ever to wrest control of Venture away from Bill Crawford.

16

The joint evaluation committee, after three weeks of seclusion in Kansas City, finally came up with its report. It wasn't as clear-cut as Bill had hoped for — it came in with a range of $100-million to $125-million. As expected, the Arctic permits accounted for a good deal of the discrepancy; the Venture experts assigned the permits only their actual cost — a nominal two hundred thousand — while the Hampton representatives valued them at fifteen million. The independent geologist tended to side with the conservative approach taken by Venture, although he pointed out that the terms of some recent farm-outs in the Beaufort could justify a substantial mark-up over book cost. The wide range of values meant there would be some hard bargaining ahead, but with Travis onside and the Dwights temporarily docile, Bill knew he had enough flexibility to conclude a deal. He himself needed no convincing that the Arctic lands were worth a premium — just thinking about these enormous seismic anomalies set his wildcatting instincts on fire.

Now it was up to him to negotiate the final terms with Peter Ketchin. It was decided that it would be safe to carry out these negotiations in Houston. There was nothing unusual about Bill's presence in that city; he travelled there many times a year in the normal course of business. Whenever he needed to meet with Ketchin, he would simply flag a cab and pick up the Hampton executive at a pre-arranged corner, and they would cruise aimlessly through the suburbs while they talked. To Bill's chagrin, Ketchin persisted in playing it coy, blandly evading any attempt to get down to hard numbers. They're out beating the bushes for other suitors, Bill realized with gloomy certainty.

It had been decided that, even though the deal was not finalized, the FIRA people should be put in the picture. Bureaucrats do not react favourably to being confronted with a fait accompli. Chester Martin had gone down to Ottawa to brief the FIRA staff, and Bill, in between his frustrating sessions with Ketchin, talked to Martin frequently on long distance.

"They don't really like it," Chester reported. "But they can't seem to find anything actually wrong with it technically."

"For Christ's sake, it's exactly what the damn act was intended to achieve," Bill expostulated.

"That's what I keep telling them. And I think the message may finally be getting through. At least to the head honcho, and he's the only one that matters."

"Who's he?"

"A career bureaucrat by the name of Harold Trotter. A mandarin's mandarin. The guy looks like a grown-up Boy Scout, but he's got all the moves of a street fighter. He's the one you'll have to deal with when we get down to the nut-cutting."

Bill saw Nancy Holman once during his sojourn in Houston. When he called, she said she wasn't free to have dinner with him, but invited him to come round to her apartment at ten the following night. When he arrived, she was waiting for him, topless above a pair of filmy black harem pants. Taking his hand, she purred, "Come in, lover, I have a special treat for you."

"If it's some of your nose candy, I'll pass."

"It's much more exciting than that. I want you to meet Casey."

The girl couldn't have been any more than nineteen. Shoulder-length blonde hair framed a petulantly pretty face with lips parted in a pose of self-conscious sensuality. Full young breasts swelled under a diaphanous white gown that allowed tantalizing glimpses of her pink nipples.

"Lovely, isn't she?" Nancy was slowly turning a bottle of Mumm's Cordon Rouge in a silver bucket. Satisfied with its temperature, she lifted it out and expertly popped the cork. The muted, heady beat of a tango came from unseen speakers. Casey toasted Bill with her champagne glass and held up moist lips to be kissed.

"You have a gorgeous ass. You know that?" Nancy was squeezing his buttocks while Casey opened her mouth for his tongue. Then someone's fingers, he couldn't tell whose, were at his crotch, and the three of them began a slow lingering progress to the bedroom, shedding clothes and pausing for long sips of champagne as they went.

The night became a fantasy of naked bodies glowing and intertwining together, drawing apart only to come together again with renewed passion. The two women caressed and fondled each other as freely and naturally as they did Bill. He was adrift on a sea of warm, female flesh — burying his head in Casey's voluptuous breasts, groaning as Nancy took him in her mouth. She guided his erection into Casey's warm moistness only to pull him off as he neared climax and take his orgasm inside herself. Both women were snorting coke, inhaling the lines from small gold spoons.

He was deep inside Nancy when he felt a tongue gently probing his anus. Startled, Bill instinctively squirmed and tried to shift to one side, but Nancy's legs were locked around his ankles, pinning him to her straining body. Her eyes glittered up at him in the near darkness as she whispered, "Like it, Bill? Do you like it?" while Casey's tongue probed and licked and the rapturous sensation raced along his nerve ends to explode in a climax that seemed to go on forever.

Spent, and obscurely grateful that he was desensitized by alcohol, he propped himself against the headboard and drank deeply from the bottle of champagne. Casey, crooning endearments, tenderly washed him with a hot towel.

She stopped abruptly as Nancy stretched out her hand to cup Casey's breast. Giving Bill's quiescent organ an affectionate pat, she turned to kiss the other woman on the mouth. To Bill, watching them with half-closed eyes through a mist of alcohol, they wove an entrancing mosaic of golden flesh and alluring shadows as they made love in the semi-darkness.

"Did you enjoy my little treat?" Nancy's smile was wan, and the drawn expression on her face foreshadowed how she would look at forty. The pale light of approaching dawn made grey ghosts of the furniture as Bill pressed the button to summon the private elevator.

"It was a blast. In every sense of the word." Bill bent down to kiss her. "They threw away the mould after they made you, my love."

Just before the elevator doors swished shut he had a fleeting glimpse of Casey standing naked in the bedroom doorway. She was smiling at him as she rubbed the palms of her hands down her flat tummy.

He never saw Nancy Holman again. Shaken by that wild night, he let days go by without phoning her. When he finally got around to it, it was to learn that she had closed the apartment and gone to Europe. It would have been a simple matter to trace her, but Bill decided it was best to treat it as a closed chapter.

He had placed the call from the office that had been allocated to him in the Hampton building. By now, there was little point in trying to maintain a pretence of secrecy, since rumours of the impending deal were circulating freely on the street. Bill shrugged off the impulse that had led him to phone Nancy and headed for the conference room where Ketchin and the two negotiating teams awaited him.

"You've got competition!" Ketchin crowed as soon as Bill had taken his place at the leather-covered table.

Ketchin's triumphant announcement jarred Bill like an unexpected kick in the groin, but the only change in his expression was a politely raised eyebrow as he asked, "How can that be, Pete? We have a deal."

"The hell we have!" snarled Ketchin. "Show me one goddamn piece of paper with my signature on it. Just one."

"I think we'd better talk this over privately," Bill replied. Dave Wilson gave an eye signal, and the Venture team got to their feet as one man. The only sound was that of briefcases snapping shut as the meeting broke up.

"What's all this shit about us having a deal?" Ketchin, his face mottled with red blotches, kicked his office door shut with his heel and rounded on Bill.

"We've got one so far as I'm concerned," Bill countered. "Maybe not the kind that would stand up in court, but at least an agreement in principle."

"Principle be damned," Ketchin replied, but with considerably less heat. Bill's up-front admission that there was no legally binding commitment had effectively defused much of the tension between the two men.

"Who's my competition?"

Ketchin took his time lighting a cigar, to prolong his enjoyment of the irony. "Your own fucking government!" he finally roared, spluttering with laughter until he choked on cigar smoke. Still coughing and hacking, he wiped his streaming eyes with a Kleenex. "How about that? I told you they were nothing but a pack of raggedy-ass commies up there."

"Knowing how strongly you feel about government intervention in the private sector, I'm sure you'd never sell out to them," Bill replied smoothly, giving no sign of the dismay he felt.

"Not so fast, buddy." Ketchin's shrewd eyes were cold. "Money has no politics."

"What kind of deal are they offering?" Bill asked, adding when Ketchin hesitated, "You owe me that much at least."

"Competitive. Very competitive."

"It has to be a cash offer. That's the only way the government can deal."

"Damn right. Like I've been saying all along — cash is the only way to go."

"Not when it's treated as income in your hands and you pay taxes on it."

"The money we're pumping into our offshore California drilling program will take care of that."

"Come off it, Pete. We both know better. You're just beginning a new taxation year, and your North Sea production came on stream last March. California dry holes or not, you won't be able to spend money fast enough to offset that revenue."

"I like your style, Crawford. Any time you feel like moving up to the big time, we've got a place for you."

Bill let that one pass. Ketchin obviously believed that a professional manager running a huge worldwide operation like Hampton packed more clout than some-body with a significant ownership position in a much smaller outfit. In terms of absolute power, you couldn't disagree with him. At least for as long as the hired man-ager held the job.

"Where do we go from here?" Bill finally broke the pregnant silence.

"It's up to you," shrugged Ketchin. "You want to sweeten your offer, we'll be here." He couldn't resist a final taunt. "Those government boys have mighty deep pockets when it comes to spending the taxpayers' money."

Ketchin was right on that point. Bill had no illusions about the outcome of a bidding war with the government. On the short taxi ride back to his hotel, he acknowledged to himself that his only hope lay in finding a political solution. For that he needed to return to his home base in Calgary and go into a huddle with Chester Martin.

17

"Senator Fulton is very sympathetic." Chester Martin sounded pleased with himself as Lisa ushered him into Bill's office. Senator Fulton was the bagman in Alberta for the Liberals. Collecting money for a political party that was the object of deep suspicion on the part of both the oil companies and the ordinary citizen was a thankless task, but the senator performed it with good cheer and a surprising degree of success. Despite their distrust for the party and all its works, the oil companies were fully attuned to the political reality that the Liberals were mighty effective when it came to winning elections. As a result, the industry gave generously, if not joyously — rather like making peace offerings to a malevolent god. Venture had always been one of the leading contributors.

"He saw the point immediately when I described how your proposal would Canadianize both the Hampton operation and Venture, while the CNIC offer would only affect Hampton. It seems the senator has no love for those empire builders at CNIC anyway."

"I like it so far." Bill grinned across his desk at the lawyer. "The next question is whether he has enough influence in Ottawa to be of any real help."

"I'm not worried about that. Fulton's got the PM's ear, if only because he's one of the few surviving Liberals west of Ontario."

"There will be a price tag, I assume?"

"Well, he did mention how generous Venture had been in the past, and I assured him that if the Hampton acquisition went through he could expect a very substantial donation to the campaign war chest. I believe the sum of two hundred thousand crept into the conversation."

"Seems completely reasonable to me."

"There's more," Chester said quietly, an enigmatic expression on his face. Bill gestured with his hand for him to continue.

"It appears the PM feels a need to relax occasionally from his pressing duties. The idea is that if he could have some sort of country retreat close to Ottawa, he would be able to escape on weekends. A group of friends and concerned citizens are banding together to purchase a lakefront cottage in the Gatineau Hills for him. It must be some cottage, since the asking price is more than $400,000. The senator thought you might like to contribute personally."

"Good God! Is that legal?"

"Well, let's say it's not illegal. It's also not tax deductible, since it would be in the nature of a personal gift." The lawyer chuckled at the incredulous look on Bill's face. "I agree it may not be too smart from a political point of view, but we all know our revered leader doesn't worry himself about trifles like that. Believe it or not, there's ample precedent for this kind of thing in Canada: Mackenzie King's wealthy friends chipped in to fix up Laurier House for him, and Stornoway was restored for the Leader of the Opposition through private contributions."

"It makes me feel like I'm dealing with a banana republic. Still ... if that's the way they want to play it ..." Bill shrugged with a show of indifference he didn't really feel. "By the way, am I supposed to pick up the entire tab?"

"Good Lord, no. They're hoping to form a group of ten, so your share will be one tenth."

"I'll get the cash tomorrow," Bill muttered. "Hypocritical bastards!"

Chester chuckled sympathetically, then said, "You know, there's one person who's going to be really upset by this. Harold Trotter."

"The mandarin we're meeting with on Wednesday in Ottawa?"

"Yeah. And unless I completely misjudge the man, he's a bit of an idealist. It'll be interesting to see how he copes with this development. Anyway, I think we should find some excuse to postpone the meeting until next week, to give Fulton's intervention time to work its way through the system."

"I think that would be a mistake, Ches. Let's play it as if we didn't know any better."

"You're right, of course. I guess I'm just not thinking straight after being exposed to the senator and his politician's way of looking at things." Chester paused as if to collect himself, then brightened. "I'm looking forward to you finally meeting up with Trotter. You're in for quite an experience."

But it wasn't Harold Trotter who captured Bill's attention when the meeting got underway in FIRA's office. Seated beside the preppie-looking bureaucrat was a youngish woman of striking good looks. She had a mane of light-brown hair and straight dark eyebrows above grey eyes luminous with intelligence. She smiled briefly at a whispered aside from Trotter, and it was as if another light switch had been turned on in the already brightly lit room. Her shoulders were just a shade too wide, but that only served to enhance the impact of the spare, athletic body underneath the tailored suit. She had a presence that made her something more than just another beautiful woman.

"You never told me about her," Bill whispered to Chester Martin under cover of the rustle of papers being sorted out around the table.

"She's new," hissed Martin under his breath. "I've never laid eyes on her before this minute."

Trotter, as head of the agency, acted as chair of the meeting and started off the proceedings by quickly running through the names and titles of those present.

The vibrant beauty beside him turned out to be Hilary Marshall, a director of planning for the Department of Energy. Ches had prepared Bill for the grandiose titles used in the civil service — everybody seemed to be the director of this or that — but even so the formidable roll call sent a chill of apprehension through him. He half expected to hear a commissar joining the roster of directors and administrators.

It soon became clear that word of the fix engineered by Fulton had not yet filtered down to the bureaucratic level. If anything, the vibes seemed to indicate that an entirely different deal was in place — one between the agency and the energy department to smooth the way for a takeover by CNIC. Trotter's attitude was almost patronizing as he debated the issue of benefit to Canada. He suggested that the test should not be applied in isolation; rather it should be compared to the benefit that might accrue from other alternatives. There was little doubt that the alternative benefit Trotter had in mind was the increase of the government presence through the acquisition of Hampton by CNIC.

The first time he mentioned CNIC he paused, glanced at his watch, and gave a little smile that was close to a smirk. "I must correct myself. By now, the minister will have informed the House that a new Crown corporation has been formed to take over all the oil and gas operations of CNIC."

The stunned silence that greeted this announcement was broken only by the whirr of a battery-operated pencil sharpener. Trotter had the curious habit of emphasizing every telling point he made by sharpening one of the pencils that were ranged in orderly rows in his briefcase.

Jesus! Bill's heart sank. If the government was going to have its own oil company, instead of a hodgepodge of investments like CNIC, what better way to give it a head start than with the Hampton properties? More to break the tension-filled silence than from any real curiosity, he asked, "Does this new entity have a name?"

"CanOil." Trotter tried to sound enthusiastic, but didn't quite succeed.

Bill carefully avoided Chester's eyes, but he knew that Chester, too, was wondering if Fulton's deal could possibly survive this latest development.

Satisfied with the minor sensation he had created, Trotter turned the meeting over to Hilary Marshall. She methodically worked her way through a series of probing questions directed at the degree of duplication between the Hampton and Venture properties. The thrust of her interrogation was that the duplication was a negative factor, not positive as Venture claimed, because the properties would end up under precisely the same management as before. There would be no new geological interpretation or initiatives brought to bear, as would be the case if the Hampton properties were acquired by an outside party.

It was a new line of attack, one that not even Ches Martin's meticulous briefing had anticipated, and Bill was chagrined by the halting weakness of his initial response. His attempt to finesse the issue by pointing out that his proposal would result in the Canadianization of two large oil companies met with a cool, "Yes. You've been through that with Mr. Trotter. However, my department is more interested in the operation and proper development of the properties themselves. Now, if you would just look at this map of the Egmont field ..."

As the polite, relentless probing went on, it became apparent that the lady director from the energy department possessed an astonishing grasp of both the Venture and Hampton holdings. It filled Bill with a kind of anger — it was his company she was dissecting so calmly. The dismaying depth of her knowledge slowed Bill's normal reaction time, and it took a few minutes before he began to fight back with the argument that the increased revenues from the combined properties would enable Venture to expand its exploration efforts. He was able to make the point that Venture's record of reinvesting its earnings was outstanding. "In fact, we could be accused of shortchanging our shareholders by not paying out dividends and plowing all the money back into the business instead."

"Perhaps," she acknowledged with a faint frown. "But what they have not received in dividends, they have more than made up for by an increase in the value of the properties."

"They are always at risk," he reminded her. "They run the risk of losing both their dividends and capital."

The expression on her face indicated that she wasn't too impressed with the risk factor, but she let it pass.

He went on to develop the thesis that Venture was in the best position to optimize the development of the properties because of the body of data and the expertise it had acquired over the years. It was good stuff, and Bill could see Chester Martin and Dave Wilson perk up as he talked. The government people heard him out in silence. It was impossible to tell what effect, if any, his words were having. At least it was better than the disorganized retreat Hilary Marshall had almost managed to bring about with her superbly prepared cross-examination.

"Well, I must say this has been a very worthwhile exchange of ideas." Trotter beamed at Bill. "And it's been particularly helpful to have you here, Mr. Crawford." He smiled around the table as if bestowing a benediction. "I think that does it for today. Except," he corrected himself smoothly when Hilary touched his sleeve, "I understand there are some technical matters Ms. Marshall and her assistants wish to take up with your people, Mr. Crawford. Perhaps you and she could arrange a convenient time between you."

"We're entirely at your disposal," said Bill. "That's why we're here."

She came over after Trotter had shaken hands all round and departed, trailing his staff behind him. If anything, she was even more sensational-looking at close quarters. Her skin was flawless under the barest trace of makeup, and the grey eyes had a hint of green. Bill was acutely aware of her as a threat to his plans. Although the afternoon was well advanced, she was anxious to start the technical meeting immediately. Bill told her they had taken a suite at the Westin to use as a temporary office, and they agreed to meet there within the half-hour.

The Venture contingent consisted of himself, Chester Martin, Dave Wilson, and one senior geologist. They were using a rented Cadillac limousine for ease of transportation around the capital. It was practical and not much more expensive than taking taxis; none the less, Bill had given the chauffeur instructions to wait for them on a side street, well away from the main entrance of the government building. The sight of four oilmen piling into the luxurious limousine would have confirmed the darkest suspicions of the civil servants. Especially, he thought grimly, Hilary Marshall.

Dave Wilson and Ed Jensen, the geologist, went directly to the suite to set up the maps, leaving Bill and Chester alone on the ascending elevator.

"If your boy Fulton doesn't come through, we can kiss this deal goodbye, Ches. That CanOil thing couldn't have come at a worse time for us."

The lawyer nodded unhappily. "They did everything but spell out what they intend to do — use FIRA to take us out and give their new baby a clear run at Hampton."

The elevator stopped at Chester's floor, and Bill said, "There's no need for you to be in at the start of this meeting, Ches. It's purely technical. Why don't you collect some background material on this Marshall woman?"

Hilary was accompanied by two assistants from the energy department, and they seemed to know exactly what they wanted. They were principally interested in learning Venture's plans for the jointly held areas where little or no exploratory drilling had been done. As Hilary's questions grew more and more specific, Dave Wilson's face grew more and more choleric. Finally he balked. "Look, lady, this stuff is confidential. We don't give out that kind of information to anybody."

Hilary glanced enquiringly at Bill who asked, "Could you tell me why you feel you need this information?"

"Certainly. Our responsibility is to assess your proposal in terms of benefit to Canada. In order to do that properly, we need to know something about your exploration programs."

Grim-faced, Bill nodded at Dave to answer her questions. The wide-ranging examination continued for another hour, with the apoplectic exploration manager swearing under his breath as he reluctantly disclosed the company's most secret information."

Bill finally called a halt when she started in on Hampton's Arctic permits. "You can't expect us to come up with any plans for an area we've never operated in," he protested. "Give us some time, and we'll develop a rational program."

"Exploring the Arctic is one of our most important national objectives," she replied with a touch of severity. "The fact that your company has no experience in that area is not particularly reassuring."

"My exploration manager will tell you that I've been in love with the potential of the Arctic for years," he answered jokingly, trying not to get hung up on an issue that was so premature it was pointless.

"The fact remains, however, that you have never operated there," she persisted. "It is also a fact that many private companies are not prepared to spend money in the Arctic, since any returns on the investment cannot be realized until years down the road." Left unsaid was the implication that the government would not be deterred by such crass economic considerations.

Chester Martin entered the room at that point, giving Bill a look that told him he had the form chart on Hilary.

"It's late in the day," Bill said. "And it's obvious that we still have a lot of ground to cover. Why don't we hang it on the wrenches until tomorrow?"

Hilary looked baffled for a fraction of a second, then said coolly, "I assume that's an oilman's way of calling it a day. Shall we say nine-thirty in the morning?"

"Ten-thirty would be better. We need a fair amount of data from our Calgary office, and they're two hours behind us."

"Ten-thirty it is," she said briskly.

"Okay, Ches. What do we know about Dragon Lady?" asked Bill as soon as he and his legal adviser were alone in Bill's hotel suite.

"Quite a bit. All of it impressive." Ches accepted the Scotch and soda Bill handed him. "Nutshelling: she's thirty-three, divorced two years ago, has a four-year-old son who lives with her. BA with Honours in economics from U of T and a Master's from Queen's. Scholarships galore. After graduation she worked in "— he paused to take a swallow of his drink and to spin out the suspense — "would you believe Calgary? ... for almost a year. She was a junior economist in the evaluation section of Devonian Pete. Then she quit, or was fired — there seems to be some doubt on that score — and came to work for the government. Her rise in the civil service could best be described as meteoric."

"Christ. That's all we need! A female who couldn't cut it in the patch and has a hard-on for the private sector."

"Your metaphor is a trifle mixed, but I take your point," murmured Ches. "I should have the full story on her departure from Devonian some time tomorrow. For whatever reason, the lovely lady holds no brief for private enterprise, and one has to conclude that she'd like nothing more than to freeze us out of the picture."

"Here's to Fulton." Bill's smile was dubious as he raised his glass in a mock salute. Abruptly changing the subject, he asked, "What's the latest on Margo's trial?"

"They're throwing her to the wolves. Apparently Lou Reznik was on the stand most of the day, apologizing and fawning over the lot, and going on about how they were misled by Margo's outstanding reputation as an investigative journalist."

"They've done nothing but apologize ever since the story came out. You have to wonder why the damn thing ever got to trial."

"Simply because Ferguson wants his name cleared on the official record. I understand he's rejected all offers for an out-of-court settlement."

"Will they put Margo on the stand?"

"I would, if I were acting for *Tomorrow*. There's no issue about the libel itself, just the quantum of damages. If the magazine can persuade the court they were not motivated by malice but were misled by a fraudulent story that was planted on Margo, things will go much better for them. On the other hand, if Ferguson's lawyers could ever establish that Margo fabricated the whole thing herself" — the lawyer threw up his hands — "the sky's the limit, so far as damages are concerned."

"They'll tear her to shreds!" Bill glared at Chester as if holding him responsible for what his professional brethren were about to do.

"I'm afraid you're right."

"Goddamn it to hell!" Bill's knuckles whitened as he gripped his empty glass in frustration.

"There's absolutely nothing you can do about it. I trust you realize that?"

"I know. I know." Bill's lips were compressed in a thin line. "We'd better give Dave and Ed a call and have some dinner."

18

"There's another quaint little expression we have in the oil patch, Ms. Marshall." The tone of Bill's voice was mild but the telltale set of his mouth showed that he was at the end of his patience. "It's called 'swabbing down,' and that's precisely what you have been doing to us for the past two hours — swabbing us down for confidential information that cost millions of dollars to obtain."

Hilary's two assistants had the grace to look guilty and kept their gaze fixed on the seismic maps and electric logs spread out on the table. Hilary, however, was unruffled. "I had assumed that getting the approval was important to you, Mr. Crawford," she said icily.

"It is," he assured her. "Vitally important. Still, I have the feeling that what has been taking place here this morning goes far beyond anything that is required for a review of our application."

"Does that mean you are refusing to co-operate?" asked the younger of her two assistants with a flash of bureaucratic arrogance that was quickly extinguished by a stern look from Hilary.

"This might be a good time to adjourn for lunch," she said with an unexpected smile that made the breath catch in Bill's throat.

"I was wondering when you were going to lower the boom on that broad," muttered Dave Wilson when the Venture team was alone in the hotel suite. "Talk about giving away the crown jewels ..." Both he and the geologist looked reproachful as they rolled up the maps.

"Why don't you and Ed take a break for half an hour and meet back here for sandwiches and a strategy session?" suggested Bill, indicating that Chester Martin was to remain.

"I found out why the lady commissar left Devonian," the lawyer announced. "Seems like her immediate supervisor was hot to get into her pants, and she wasn't buying. He made life tough for her. She had the guts to complain to the top management and got laughed at for her pains. After that, it was a simple matter for her supervisor to force her to quit."

"Not exactly the kind of background that would make her a big fan of the industry, is it?" asked Bill glumly. "Any word from your tame senator?"

The lawyer started to reprove Bill for his cynicism, but held back, knowing how deeply offended the oilman was by the shabby little deal with Fulton.

"He's in town. Came in last night. As you can imagine, I questioned him pretty closely about this CanOil development."

"And?" asked Bill impatiently, when the lawyer paused.

"He doesn't seem to think it's too much of a problem. Says there'll be lots of other companies CanOil can take over down the road." Chester broke off to chuckle. "According to Fulton, they're calling it OilCan up on the Hill. Anyway, he's scheduled to have lunch with the PM's principal secretary tomorrow. Things should start falling into place after that."

"Tomorrow's Friday, so nothing much is likely to happen until next week. Right?"

"Considering that the weekend is sacred in government circles, I'd say that's a safe assumption. Of course, we still have to play out this charade with Trotter and the Marshall woman."

"I wish I could believe that's all it is — a charade," said Bill fretfully. "The bureaucrats strike me as being firmly in the saddle in this town."

The phone call from Hilary came as they were devouring a tray of room-service sandwiches. Dave Wilson, being the only one between bites, answered it, then handed the receiver to Bill with a muttered, "Miss Iron Pants wants to speak to you."

Fortunately, he had the good sense to place his hand over the mouthpiece, and Bill grinned at him sympathetically as he reached for the phone. He knew how badly his exploration manager had been upset by Hilary's insatiable demands for sensitive information.

"I have been thinking over your objection, and I agree that we perhaps overstepped the line," she said crisply.

"I'm happy to hear that. Where do we go from here?"

"We may be able to come up with a revised list of questions. We're working on that right now. Will your people still be available in Ottawa tomorrow?"

"Of course. Whatever it takes."

"In that case, I suggest we 'put it on the wrenches' until the morning."

"Fair enough." He acknowledged her mild sally with a polite chuckle.

"The ball is in their court for the moment," he told his associates after he hung up. "There's nothing more for us to do until we hear from them."

"What about the CPA reception tonight?" asked Dave Wilson. "Are you going?"

Bill was on the board of governors of the Canadian Petroleum Association, and their Ottawa office was throwing a large reception for government officials, journalists, and anyone else who might be able to advance the cause of the oil industry. A number of governors had flown in from Calgary for the occasion, and Bill had been under heavy pressure to attend.

"Thanks for reminding me, Dave. I was so sure we'd be working tonight I put it right out of my mind. I'd better go."

"I think it would be best if the rest of us had dinner in our rooms," Chester

Martin said. "This place will be awash with oil types tonight, and there's no point in advertising the fact that we're down here in force."

They stuck a rose in Bill's lapel and put him in the receiving line. His arrival seemed to generate an air of subdued excitement among his fellow governors. Being so engrossed with the delicate negotiations with the federal government, he at first put it down to the Hampton takeover. Then the president of Scope Resources muttered something about the goddamn *Tomorrow* rag finally getting what it deserved, and Bill realized that the publicity surrounding Ferguson's libel action had revived interest in Margo's infamous articles.

The other members of the receiving line chimed in, crowing with delight that Margo had been so completely discredited. Somehow that seemed to nullify the effect of her attack on the industry and to cast Bill in the role of an innocent victim of her duplicity, deserving of sympathy rather than censure. The room was crawling with reporters, and Bill was soon grateful for the diversion provided by the trial. The last thing the Hampton deal needed at this ultra-sensitive stage was the bright glare of publicity.

The procession of guests working their way down the line slowed to a halt, and Bill found himself with no one to shake hands with. He glanced to his left to see what the holdup was. Hilary Marshall had arrived and was being greeted effusively by Brian MacAvity, the chairman of the board of governors. He held both her hands while he exuded avuncular charm. Knowing from past experience that Brian, when excited, had an unfortunate tendency to spray those within range with a fine mist of saliva, Bill admired Hilary's poise as she smiled back at the chairman without flinching. He hadn't expected to see her at the reception, but now he realized her position would automatically entitle her to an invitation. MacAvity finally released her, and the steady flow of incoming guests resumed.

She was still glowing with the warmth of her welcome when she reached Bill. Smiling and devastatingly feminine, she was a different creature from the cool and dedicated civil servant he had come to know in the past two days. Could it possibly be only two days? The pileup of guests thirsting for the bar brooked no further delay so there was no chance for more than a fleeting smile and a hurried greeting as she went by. Bill promised he would seek her out the moment the reception line disbanded.

The arrival of Gilles Vachon, the minister of energy, caused another small commotion. Vachon obviously had been well briefed, for he had no need to peer at the name tags as he affably pumped hands and clapped shoulders. He had two diminutive Japanese businessmen in tow who, he explained, had come to Canada to investigate the possibility of securing a supply of Canadian energy to meet Japan's ever-growing requirements.

"So I thought, what better place for them to start than right here where all the big wheels are," he boomed down the reception line, while the two Japanese bowed politely.

Bill took pains to make sure he had their names right; the older one was Mr. Hashimoto, and the other, his dark suit daringly accented with a burgundy tie, was Mr. Kakisaki. The Canadian government obviously considered their mission to be important — they were getting the full red-carpet treatment from Gilles Vachon. The energy minister glowed with self-satisfaction; the CPA reception was a heaven-sent opportunity for him to impress his Japanese visitors with his industry contacts.

"Okay, boys. That should just about do it," Brian MacAvity announced after the minister had passed through the line. "Let's get out there and circulate."

Bill had been watching Hilary moving conscientiously from group to group, introducing herself as she went, taking full advantage of the opportunity to broaden her acquaintanceship in the industry. She held a glass of white wine, but it never seemed to reach her lips. He intercepted her as she was smilingly disengaging herself from a cluster of public relations types."

"I'm having the best time!" she enthused. "After this, I'll be able to put a face to so many people I deal with."

"That's the general idea," he agreed.

Bill was the ranking member of the oil hierarchy and as such was the nucleus of a constant flow of people anxious to pay their respects. He had long since become accustomed to this kind of attention, but tonight, with an obviously impressed Hilary at his side, he revelled in it.

As the number of guests began to dwindle, Gilles Vachon steered his two charges over to Bill's group. He saluted Hilary with Gallic verve, bending over to kiss her hand and informing the Japanese industrialists that she was one of his most valued assistants.

The gregarious cabinet minister was organizing a small dinner party for the two Japanese. He had already conscripted MacAvity, plus another executive whose company was heavily involved in the oil sands, and Director-General Ellen Holt, a dowdy, fortyish official from his own department. With airy assurance, he informed Hilary that she was included, and then made it flatteringly clear that the whole evening would be made if only Bill would join them. Bill accepted immediately, warmed by the amused glance he and Hilary exchanged over her minister's high-handed attitude.

The reception was in the Chateau Laurier, only a few blocks from Bill's hotel, and he had walked over, enjoying the crisp winter air. Vachon had reserved a table at one of the celebrated French restaurants in Hull and, to Bill's regret, he insisted that Bill accompany him and the Japanese in his ministerial Oldsmobile, leaving Hilary to bring the rest in her Toyota station wagon.

MacAvity drank too much wine and made an ass of himself, clumsily flirting with Hilary in his elephantine way. For the second time in his life, Bill became acutely and depressingly aware of his own age. She probably lumps us all together, he thought glumly — slobbering old lechers who should know better. Obscurely annoyed with himself and the world in general, he turned his attention to the Japanese, answering their queries with a concise competence that brought murmurs of admiration from them.

He got to ride back to the hotel with Hilary. The Japanese were anxious to learn more about the oil sands, so Vachon asked the executive from the oil sands company to join them in the Oldsmobile. MacAvity had reached the stage of intoxication where merely staying on his feet required all his concentration, and he was grateful when Bill unobtrusively helped him into the rear seat of the Toyota, beside a stiffly disapproving Ms. Holt. They dropped Ellen Holt off first at her downtown apartment building, then delivered MacAvity to the Chateau Laurier. Bill walked him as far as the elevator and made sure he had his room key and knew what floor button to press.

"You were brilliant tonight," Hilary said as she pulled up in front of the Westin.

"Hmmm?" Bill's attention was elsewhere. The light from the streetlamps was doing ravishing things to the lines of her profile. A perfectionist might say her nose was a shade too snub, but it was exactly and excitingly right for the cool, crisp quality of her beauty.

"The way you explained things to the Japanese. It was masterly." The grey eyes were dark in the night as she turned to face him. "You truly love the oil industry, don't you?"

"It's my life," he replied simply. It gradually dawned on him that her attitude was warm and admiring, definitely not that of a woman making polite noises to a member of the older generation.

"It looks like I'm stuck here for the weekend," he said. That was a bare-faced lie, since the Lear was parked at the airport, ready to take him to any destination he chose. "Do you suppose we could have dinner tomorrow night?"

"I think I'd like that." She smiled a goodnight at him, keeping both hands on the steering wheel. The courtesy light came on as he opened the passenger door, and he surprised an expression on her face that, strangely, seemed to hint at compassion. Maybe she was thinking about how badly he would feel when he lost the Hampton deal. Well, he'd remember not to gloat when it came through. If it came through.

"Take it easy on us tomorrow, will you?" he called out teasingly as he stood on the sidewalk.

"Why not?" she laughed through the open window. "We already have everything we need."

19

By the end of the weekend, Bill knew he was in love. He and Hilary had carried on like carefree tourists. They visited the National Gallery and took Jason, her young son, through the Museum of Man. On Sunday afternoon, Bill stood chilled on the sidelines while Hilary and the child skated on the Rideau Canal. Jason was still at the stage where he did more falling than skating, and he soon tired of the sport. Hilary brought him over to stand with Bill and then went for a spin on her own. She was an expert, her long legs flashing as she leaped and pirouetted through the crowd.

"Where in the world did you learn to skate like that?" asked Bill when she slid to a stop in front of him in a shower of ice crystals.

"My mother had ambitions for me," she said lightly. "Until I was old enough to realize I wanted no part of that life."

"Because you discovered you wanted to follow an academic career?"

"Something like that." She took her son's hand. "Jason and I know a place where they make scrummy hot chocolate."

To make up for the fact that she was a working mother, Hilary devoted much of her weekends to the child, and she felt guilty at having left him with a baby sitter for the last three nights. Sunday she insisted on cooking supper for the three of them at home in her apartment. In the manner of four-year-olds who are left much on their own, Jason was reserved and somewhat solemn. Understandably, he resented Bill's intrusion, but he was polite about it. Bill knew better than to try and force the pace; he played it cool and was rewarded by an unexpected handshake when Jason was on his way to bed.

Through the partly closed door of the bedroom, Bill could hear Hilary murmuring endearments to her son, drowsy from his day in the fresh air. Her apartment had two bedrooms and was furnished sparingly with understated good taste. Bill absently reached down and picked up Jason's toy dump truck, which lay on its side on the carpet.

The evening — the whole weekend — had been a bittersweet experience for Bill. On the one hand, he was thrilled that Hilary had spent so much time with him; but the torment of restraining himself from kissing that inviting mouth was almost more than he could bear. Damn that old goat MacAvity for making him feel so insecure about his age. He was still dithering like an awkward schoolboy when they said goodnight. Hilary made it easy by holding out her hand with a friendly grin. "It's been super, Bill. Thank you."

It had been arranged that on Monday the Venture team would wait in their hotel for a call from Trotter's staff to set up another meeting. When no call had come through by ten-thirty, Bill got to his feet, saying that he was going back to his own suite to make some long-distance calls.

It was mid-afternoon before they heard from Trotter. His secretary insisted that Bill come on the line first and waited while Bill was fetched from his suite.

"I am instructed to advise you," Trotter's voice sounded as constrained as his syntax, "that your application has been approved by the agency. It still must go before the cabinet, you understand?"

"Of course. That is very good news, Mr. Trotter. I want to thank you and your staff for the expeditious and fair way in which our case has been handled."

"Does that mean what I think it means?" Dave Wilson demanded as soon as Bill hung up.

"It does. Congratulations to all of you on a damn fine job. It still has to be approved by cabinet, but Ches and I" — Bill's glance sought out the lawyer who nodded agreement — "believe that should be a mere formality."

"By God, Eddie boy." The exploration manager punched his senior geologist in the shoulder. "We got us some drillin' to do."

"We're not home and dry just yet," cautioned Bill. "There's nothing to stop CanOil from upping their offer to Hampton."

"That's true," Chester Martin conceded. "However, I can't really see them doing that in the face of an official approval of your proposal. Still" — he shrugged — "when you're dealing with the government, any goddamned thing can happen.

That fear was put to rest within the hour when Senator Fulton called from Calgary. Bill and Ches were alone in the hotel suite when the call came through. Fulton accepted Chester's compliments on the way the FIRA situation had been handled, then smugly informed the lawyer that "OilCan" had been instructed to withdraw its offer.

Chester was holding the receiver so that Bill could hear what was being said. The oilman clasped his hands in a victory signal at the senator's words.

"Signed, sealed, and delivered." Chester looked slightly awed as he hung up. "Your girlfriend's not going to like that part. She strikes me as a true believer in government ownership."

"A couple of dinner dates doesn't make her my girlfriend, for Christ's sake."

The lawyer dismissed Bill's disclaimer with an airy wave of his hand. "I like that girl. I disagree with everything she stands for, but I like her. She's a real person."

"If you can bring yourself to stop talking about Hilary Marshall," said Bill with mild exasperation, "I want you to know that I intend to recommend to the directors that you be granted a substantial stock option. And this time you will damn well accept it. You deserve it, and it's high time you did something to look after Betty and the children." He paused and looked solemnly at his associate. "Neither of us is getting any younger, you know."

"That's the first time I've ever heard you mention age," said Chester wonderingly. "But I take your point, and I'll accept the option. Gratefully."

"I'll take care of it as soon as we get back to Calgary. That way we can put it in the prospectus for the new share issue." Bill paused to glance at his watch. "Why don't you round up Dave and Ed for a celebratory drink? I'll meet you in the bar in ten minutes."

As soon as he was alone, Bill dialed Hilary's office."

"I've just been talking to Harold," she said when he identified himself. "You must be over the moon. Congratulations." Her cool, professional tone gave nothing away.

"I'm pretty excited, all right. I've got great plans for Venture!"

"And now there's nothing to stop you," she replied, removing all doubt that she was fully aware of his real motive.

"Oh, I wouldn't say that, exactly. I have several thousand shareholders to answer to."

"Whom you can outvote any time you want."

"Hmmm. Look, I'm going back to Calgary in the morning, and I'd love to see you tonight. Drinks, dinner, cup of coffee — you name it."

"I'm sorry, Bill. I'm tied up this evening."

Bill was prepared for the disappointment, but he was not prepared for the sharp wrenching stab of jealousy. Who was she tied up with? "That's too bad," he said. "For me, I mean," he added hastily. "Look, I expect this takeover deal will bring me back here within a few weeks, and I'd like to feel I could call you."

"Please do! And Bill, I really do congratulate you and wish you all kinds of success with Hampton."

As he left the suite to join the others in the bar, Bill felt strangely out of sorts, not at all like someone who had just scored a major victory.

An artist's sketch of Margo's tense face stared up from the front page of the *Star* lying on the seat next to Chester. There was also a sketch of Howard Blescup looking grave while he listened to Ferguson's lawyer address the bench where the judge, hunched over and ominous in his black robes, presided.

"It looks like they'll finish tomorrow," remarked Chester as Bill picked up the paper. Dave and his geologist, seated on the other side of the booth, tactfully kept up a low-voiced conversation. Like everyone else in the company, they were aware that their boss had been involved in some fashion with the female reporter, and they didn't want to get caught in the crossfire.

"That's kind of interesting." Chester pointed to a paragraph halfway down an inside column. It said that Margo was supporting herself by working as a freelance investigator and researcher. The paragraph went on to state that her clients were rumoured to include several political figures in Ottawa.

"I wouldn't care to have her on my tail," shuddered Chester. "What she couldn't find out, she'd make up."

"Did they ever discover who framed her?" asked Bill.

"No. In fact," Chester tapped the sketch of Ferguson's lawyer, "he's claiming that she wasn't framed. His theory is that she engineered the whole thing from start to finish."

"I don't buy that. Underneath all that ambition she's still a professional journalist."

"That's the way I size her up, too." Chester leaned across the table to include the two geologists in the conversation. "You'd better start thinking about all the goodies we're going to put in the prospectus."

The next two months were strenuous and exhilarating for Bill. As winter reluctantly gave way to spring, he flew back and forth across the land, bringing his dog-and-pony show to underwriters and institutional investors. Armed with maps and charts, he outlined the expanded company's potential. He was a very effective salesman, primarily because he believed in what he was saying about Venture's prospects and was genuinely optimistic about the future of the oil industry in general.

The timing of the new issue was fortunate; the stock market was enjoying one of its periodic upturns and, on the whole, investors were receptive to Bill's sales pitch. Jim Goulder and Confederation Securities headed up the underwriting group and took what Jim liked to call a "cafeteria" approach to the shares that were offered to the foreign owners. At Peter Ketchin's insistence, half of the shares paid to Hampton Resources were retractable, non-voting preferred shares, which Hampton could require Venture to buy back for cash at specified intervals. The remaining fifty per cent of the preferred shares that Hampton received were redeemable at Venture's option. The other foreign investors were offered a choice of preferred shares or a new class of non-voting common stock. They were also given the right to sell fifty per cent of their holdings. As expected, the Abrams brothers took advantage of this opportunity, but they turned out to be the only ones to do so. The Dwights unexpectedly chose the new non-voting common shares and made no attempt to sell them. As agreed, the Travis interests took up their full allotment of non-voting stock.

As the representative of the lead underwriter, it was Jim Goulder who decided where Bill should do his show-and-tell routine and what investment groups he should speak to. The campaign concentrated on the principal financial centres — Toronto, Montreal, Vancouver, and Calgary, with one brief stopover in Winnipeg. So Jim was dumbfounded when Bill suggested that Ottawa be included in the itinerary. "That's civil-service territory, and those gutless bureaucrats won't invest in anything riskier than a Canada Savings Bond," he snorted. "It would be a complete waste of time."

"You may be right, but I still believe we should go there," Bill insisted. "For political reasons, if nothing else."

"I agree," put in Chester Martin with a glint of amusement in his eyes. "After the way the government supported us, they'll be expecting us to show the flag."

"Just so long as you don't expect to sell any shares." Goulder picked up the draft timetable and began to work out the necessary changes.

"I'd almost forgotten how rewarding this can be," Bill whispered to Hilary as they watched Jason eagerly open the package. The boy's eyes widened in wonder at the realistic detail of the miniature tow truck.

Hilary bent her head to sniff the yellow roses that filled her arms. "They're lovely," she murmured. "I really should scold you for spoiling us, but I'm not going to. I'll just thank you instead. Let me find a vase for these."

Leaving Jason contentedly playing with his new toy under the benign eye of a grandmotherly baby-sitter, Bill and Hilary took a taxi to a French restaurant in Hull. One thing about having a dedicated career woman for a date was that there was no problem finding things to talk about. Hilary wanted to hear every detail of the underwriting and the promotional campaign that was part of it. She was probably operating on the theory that the more you knew about your enemy, the better, thought Bill with a certain sense of irony. But it certainly made for easy conversation. It was almost like talking to Debbie.

Midway through dinner, she touched upon a point that had surfaced more than once during his dog-and-pony shows — Venture's lack of bench strength at the top executive level. "Your president is several years older than you," she said, making him wince inwardly, "and his duties seem to be strictly peripheral, totally removed from the chain of command."

"You're right. There is a gap. But I'm about to plug it." And he would, as soon as the underwriting was finished. He'd had some preliminary talks with Steve Miller, and it looked as though they wouldn't have much trouble coming to terms. Under Steve's direction, Hampton finally had its offshore operations under control, even if the company still couldn't seem to drill anything but dry holes. After years of working as a salaried employee of a major corporation, Steve was attracted by the idea of having a piece of the action. Chester Martin seemed to feel Steve would have no particular problem in obtaining a work permit: his unique familiarity with the newly acquired Hampton properties should satisfy the immigration authorities.

However, the lawyer had cautioned against finalizing any arrangements until after the underwriting. Replacing Gavin Anderson as president would be a "material fact" that could complicate matters with the prospectus and the security commissions. "Not that the financial community wouldn't welcome it," the lawyer had said. "We know they would, and it would actually make the stock easier to sell. But it would mean delays and additional filings that we sure as hell don't need."

"Will it work?" Hilary was asking. "Hiring a new president, I mean," she added when she saw his thoughts had been elsewhere. "There's this old adage about acorns not being able to grow in the shade of a giant oak."

"I assume I'm the giant oak?" Bill laughed. "I know what you mean, but it's been my intention for some time now to divorce myself from day-to-day operations. Once I have the right man in place, I may do just that."

"And what will Bill Crawford do then?"

"Oh, I don't know. Roam the world. Enjoy myself. Care to sign up for the cruise?" As soon as he uttered it, Bill wanted to retract the flippant question.

She dismissed it lightly. "Not at the moment, thank you. I still have some bridges to cross and hills to climb. And, unless I'm very much mistaken," she added unexpectedly, "so do you."

He kissed her at the door of her apartment — a light, noncommittal kiss, but still a kiss.

Bill was at the top of his form the next morning. After the session was over, Jim Goulder wandered around with a dazed expression. "I just don't believe it," he kept repeating. "Guardian Investments want to sign up for twenty-five thousand shares!"

"Are you going to give it to them?" asked Chester Martin. "The issue is almost oversubscribed as it is."

"God, yes." A gleeful look replaced Goulder's normal air of terminal fatigue. "I'll cut back on the allotment to Citadel. Wait till the street hears I placed shares with an Ottawa house! I mean, you placed them," he corrected himself with an apologetic nod in Bill's direction. "You were sensational."

"It's your campaign," Bill laughed, "so you get the credit. But now aren't you glad we came?"

"I know somebody else who's glad we came," Chester Martin said, smiling quizzically at Bill. "but not for the same reason."

"What's on the agenda for this afternoon?" Bill hastily changed the subject.

"Another show-and-tell for some of the local brokerage firms," Goulder replied.

"I think I'll pass," Chester said. "You don't need me, and I can spend my time more profitably making some courtesy calls over at Justice."

"Care to guess who I saw coming out of the West Block?" Chester asked Bill when they met for a debriefing drink at the end of the afternoon.

"Margo Jones."

"You've seen her then?"

"No. I remembered that item in the paper about her freelancing in Ottawa and connected it with the look on your face. She scares the shit out of you. Did you talk to her?"

Chester shook his head. "There was no chance. She ran out of the entrance and scuttled into a waiting taxi."

"I wonder who she's working for."

"Most likely digging up dirt for a member of the opposition. Some of the more prominent opposition MPs have offices in that block. Want me to find out?"

"Negative." Bill took a swallow of his drink. "You're pretty confident about the insurance company leaving her alone?"

"All I know for sure is that old Blescup warned them against it. That should be enough to make them think twice."

The court had awarded Walter $125,000 in damages plus legal costs, and there had been rumours that *Tomorrow*'s insurer was considering going after Margo for half. Chester had learned through his network of legal contacts that Howard Blescup had been infuriated by the suggestion.

"Apparently Blescup buys her story that she was the victim of a hoax and is guilty of nothing more than negligence — no intent to deceive, as it were. The old boy's become fiercely protective of her, I understand." The lawyer freshened his drink. "You got a heavy date with Hilary tonight?"

Bill threw his head back and laughed. "Jesus Christ, Ches, you sound like some kid in high school. Yes, I am taking Hilary to dinner. What time do we leave in the morning?"

"Goulder has a meeting set up for ten in Toronto."

"Okay. Get hold of Connors and tell him it's wheels up at eight."

The Venture issue was an unqualified success. The original offering had been over-subscribed, and the secondary market was up two points. Bill had never forgotten a remark that Lee Travis had once made about a famous tycoon. "Poor Larry," he had said. "He's never learned how to enjoy his successes. He should take the time to savour a victory before plunging into the next deal, but he just can't seem to."

Bill's way of both savouring his success and winding down after the strenuous campaign was to spend a restorative weekend at the Circle C. It also gave him a welcome chance to visit with Frank. He had been so tied up with Venture affairs that he hadn't seen enough of his son in the months since Frank had returned from his European trip and gone to work for TriPet Resources as a petroleum engineer. They had both agreed it would be better for him at least to start his career with a company other than Venture. Debbie had just gone east with her hunter, Imperial Way, for the opening show of the Ontario circuit, so the two men were alone in the sprawling ranch house.

By unspoken agreement, they spent most of the daylight hours on horseback. Although a spring Chinook had swept away most of the snow, patches of unmelted ice made the footing treacherous, and the range-wise horses picked their way with extreme care. Here and there Bill could see subtle signs of Frank's influence on the ranch. Nothing dramatic: just that the strands of barbed-wire fences seemed tighter, the gates were easier to open, and in the north pasture there was a new Hereford bull with the square, chunky conformation of top bloodlines. And Frank, tactful as always, had managed to implement these little improvements without ruffling the foreman's feathers. Harvey had been his usual taciturn self that morning in the corral, but there hadn't been the slightest hint of strain between him and Frank. Instead, there had been an air of easygoing camaraderie as the foreman helped saddle the two horses. Frank had a way with people, no question about that.

"The place has never looked better," Bill commented, as they turned around and headed home. "I can see you've been busy."

"Only on weekends. It hasn't interfered with my work at TriPet."

Disturbed by the defensive note in his son's voice, Bill said, "Hell, I know that. In fact, Charlie Boyd was telling me only last week that you're doing a good job for them."

"I'm sure giving it my best shot."

Frowning slightly, Bill touched his heel to Big Country's flank, and the two quarter horses broke into an easy lope. They carried their heads low, on the lookout for the gopher holes that pockmarked the ground as the little rodents emerged from their winter hibernation.

"You know," Bill stared into the fire and said musingly, as if thinking out loud, "I'm very happy with what I do. Looking for oil is really all I ever wanted to do with my life."

"You're lucky." Frank gave the already blazing log an unnecessary prod with the poker.

"Yeah." Bill straightened up in his chair and took a swallow of coffee. "I figure that if a person knows — really knows — what he wants to do, he shouldn't let anything get in the way. Take you, for instance. Somehow I always thought you were more interested in breeding cattle than analyzing oil reservoirs."

"Well, I guess that's true. But, I dunno, maybe because Billy died ... I kinda got the idea it was up to me."

"So you went off and put in four years at university slugging away at a subject that didn't really turn you on. Did well at it, too. You're quite a person, Frank. But I'm not out to build a dynasty. For what it's worth, I doubt very much if Billy would have gone into the oil industry, anyway. He just wasn't cut out for it."

"What are you saying, Dad?"

"That you should give ranching an all-out try. If you find you don't like it, or can't make it work, you can always fall back on your engineering qualifications. But I don't think you'd ever forgive yourself if you didn't take a shot at it."

"You'll never know how glad I am that we've had this talk."

"So am I. Now let's have a brandy to toast your new future!"

20

The man had turned the company into a fortress. Ken Kwasny stared at the green numbers on the screen; the computer couldn't come up with the answer either. Realizing he would have to find the way into the fortress by himself, he logged off. With the screen suddenly dark, the only illumination in the living room of Ken's spacious condominium came from a shaded reading light on the opposite wall.

Sitting in the semi-darkness, he called up the numbers on his own mental screen. The figures ran into the thousands, but the bottom line was always the same — Crawford controlled sixty-two per cent of the voting shares. In the guise of Canadianizing the company, he had dug himself in so firmly that there seemed to be no way of ever winkling him out. Frustrated with his fruitless attempts to solve the puzzle, Ken let his overworked mind slide back to that day when his secretary brought him the message that had so radically changed his life.

He had been with Sterling Investments for two months then, and the world had looked pretty good to Ken Kwasny. He had finally arrived at the point where his uncanny gift for figures was appreciated. And profitable. Growing up in a working-class area of Edmonton hadn't been the happiest experience for the slightly built boy with a near-photographic memory and a genius for mathematics. The adult world was much more congenial — the skills that had been scorned by his childhood peers turned out to be very much in demand. Ken knew that he was establishing a reputation as a comer in the brokerage house, but even so he was taken completely by surprise when the famous Stan Winters asked him to join Sterling Investments.

He had been in the Sterling conference room discussing his first major assignment with Winters when Karen came in with a stricken look on her face and said, "You're wanted on the phone, Ken. It's your father. He says it's urgent."

There was a hollow tightness in Ken's stomach as he hurried back to his office to take the call. His mother was desperately ill. She had undergone a mastectomy four years ago, then a second one, and still the cancer spread through her body.

"Mother's back in the hospital, Ken." His father's voice had the alcoholic slur that had become almost chronic after they had found the spot in Rose Kwasny's lung three months after her second operation.

"How bad is it this time, Dad?"

"The doc says it could ... could happen any time. It could be hours, days at the most. You better get up here."

Ken grabbed the edge of the credenza for support. He had been dreading this news for months, but that didn't make it any easier to bear.

Karen stood in the doorway, an airline schedule in each hand. "Your best way is to fly to Calgary and take the airbus to Edmonton. You can be there at eight o'clock tonight."

Ken told his father not to meet the plane but to stay at the hospital, and he would see him there around eight-thirty.

His father mashed out his cigarette in a standing ashtray, almost knocking it over, and got somewhat unsteadily to his feet when Ken hurried across the tiled floor to the hospital's information desk. Physically the two men were totally dissimilar — Ken, senior, had a thick, powerful torso, which, in recent years, had developed a round, hard belly that forced him to stand so stiffly upright he was almost leaning backward. His hands were calloused and scarred with a quarter-century of welding pipeline joints in the sub-zero cold of winter and the blazing heat of a desert sun. His son was a good three inches taller and had a spare physique that was a tailor's dream. The younger man's face, under a lock of dark hair that always needed to be brushed back from his forehead, was slightly aquiline with a reserved, almost scholarly look that many women found appealing, especially when he gave one of his rare smiles.

The two men were assailed with a scent of overpowering sweetness as they neared the end of the long hospital corridor. "I hate that goddamn perfume," Ken's father whispered fiercely. "They use it to cover up the smell of death."

Appalled, Ken realized that the sickening stench was coming from his mother's room. She was propped up against the pillows, with an intravenous tube feeding into her arm. Her face, frightening in its ashen pallor, but still bearing unmistakable vestiges of beauty, lit up with a translucent glow when she saw Ken. She tried to hold up her arms, but the effort was beyond her.

Tenderly, terrified he might crush the brittle bones, Ken held both her hands and bent over to brush his lips against her forehead. She was whispering his name, over and over, with a loving smile that tore at his heart. There was another smell underlying the cloying sweetness of the deodourizer, and he suddenly realized what it was — the smell of dead and decaying human cells — his mother's cells. He felt a terrible, helpless rage that life could do this to the lovely and loving woman his mother had been before the unspeakable disease had invaded her body. All through his lonely childhood he had felt a warm pride in her beauty; her glowing, brown-eyed good looks had put the mothers of all his schoolmates in the shade. He felt the pitifully frail hands go slack and saw that her eyes were closed. The nurse came over to the other side of the bed and gently smoothed the pillow. "She wants to rest now." Her fingers searched for the feebly fluttering pulse, and she looked at the dying woman's husband. "If you want to wait outside in the solarium, Mr. Kwasny, I'll let you know if there's any change."

Knowing that the only change would be for the worse, Ken followed his father into the small waiting room with its plastic and chrome furniture and a selection of outdated, tattered magazines. The elder Kwasny lit a cigarette. "She's going faster than they thought she would. I figure she wants to." A thin stream of smoke jetted out of his mouth as he went on. "I wanted to call you earlier, but she wouldn't hear of it. She knew you was working on some big deal. It's meant an awful lot to her — the way you've been doin' so good."

"I'm glad." Ken managed the pale imitation of a smile.

His father excused himself to go to the bathroom, and Ken could smell the whisky on his breath when he returned. He didn't blame him — this ordinary, working-class man had adored his beautiful wife with a single-minded devotion that had done much to bridge the gap between father and son. And there was a gap — partly because the older man's world was one of physical skills, and he couldn't relate to a youngster with Ken's formidable intellect. But there was more to it than that. The senior Kwasny seemed actually to want to keep a distance between himself and his precocious offspring. Inevitably, the growing boy had sensed this and come to resent it.

But there was no question that his father, whose trade as a pipeline welder was a highly paid one, had provided a secure and comfortable home. Whenever pipeline construction dried up in North America Kwasny had been perfectly willing to take his skills to the burning sands of the Middle East. He would cheerfully have supported Ken as far as he wanted to go in university, too, except that Ken, after two years of undergraduate study at UBC, realized that university training was holding him back from where he wanted to go, rather than helping him get there. Despite a standing that was in the top five per cent and the horrified protests of his professors, Ken had quit university to go and work for a brokerage house in Vancouver.

The elder Kwasny's face was flushed from his third visit to the bathroom, and he was beginning to take on the slightly belligerent air that sometimes accompanied his drinking. Ken was wondering if he dared tell him to take it easy, when the nurse came to summon them.

Rose Kwasny's eyes were half-open and seemed to be in focus. She smiled and murmured, "My two Kens." They stood on either side of the bed. Tears streamed down her husband's face as Rose whispered, "Goodbye, dearest Ken. You've been wonderful to me. Always."

Her head moved slightly on the pillow so she could gaze adoringly up at her son. He smiled down at her and whispered, "I love you, Mom."

Suddenly, she grew agitated. Her fingers flicked at the sheet, and her eyes, now feverishly bright, anxiously sought her husband's. "I think he should know. He ... he ..." Her voice failed her, but she drew a breath that bubbled horribly with phlegm and gasped out, "... has the right."

"You don't know what you're saying, Rose."

Her husband's reply seemed to make her even more agitated, and she said in a whisper that was almost fierce, "Yes, I do. I've been thinking —" She choked and couldn't finish. Her lips moved soundlessly, then her head lolled sideways, her eyes rolled up until only the whites showed, and she was gone.

The nurse bent over her, gently pressing her eyelids shut and straightening her head on the pillow. "I'm truly sorry, gentlemen. She was a lovely lady. But at least her suffering is over." Tucking Rose's skeletal hands under the sheet, she added, "I must find a doctor. Would you be good enough to wait in the solarium?"

"What is it that she wanted me to know, Dad?" Ken asked when they were alone in the small, cheerless lounge.

"Nothing. She was raving. People do that when they're dying."

"Her mind was perfectly clear, and you know it. She wanted me to know, Dad. She said I had the right."

"I gotta go to the can," his father mumbled. "Be back in a minute."

He stayed in the washroom so long Ken was about to go after him, and when he came out it was obvious that he had downed a great deal of whisky. Probably had a bottle stashed in there. Ken blamed himself for not having thought of that. His father's face was beet-red, and he scowled when he saw Ken waiting for him. It distressed Ken to see him like this, but he fully intended to take advantage of the opportunity it presented.

"C'mon, Dad, tell me what it's all about."

His father didn't seem to hear him. He was muttering to himself, "All those years and she can't forget it." His eyes filled with tears of self-pity.

"Forget what, Dad?"

Kwasny turned on him in a sudden rage and snarled, "That you're a fucking bastard. That's what!"

Kwasny looked stricken by the enormity of what he had blurted out. "Just forget it ... I didn't mean ..."

"You're not my real father. That's it, isn't it?"

"Yes, goddamn it. Your mother was pregnant when I married her."

An unexpected feeling of euphoria swept through Ken, making him feel slightly ashamed. The knowledge that he did not share this man's genes made him almost lightheaded with relief. And it explained so much. Still, this was the man who had brought him up; he was his father in everything but the biological sense.

"I didn't mean that about you being a bastard, Ken. I've always thought of you as my son."

"I know that, Dad." Ken put his arm around his father's shoulders. It was the first time in years he had done anything more than shake his hand. "Who is my natural father?" he asked casually.

"No need for you to know that, boy."

"I think I'm entitled."

"No. Maybe later. I just don't know ... I got to think ..."

"Let's go home, Dad."

When Ken awoke the next morning after a restless night in his old bed, he knew that he had to find out the identity of his true father. It had all taken place some twenty-seven years ago — plenty of time for people to die, move away, or forget. Still, he had some valuable pieces of information: he knew that both his mother and the man she married were of Ukrainian descent and that both had grown up in the small farming community of Mundell in northeastern Alberta. It was a lot more than most illegitimate or adopted children had to go on when they started the search for their biological parents. That afternoon, when he was going through his mother's few papers, he found another clue, although it was more corroboration of a known fact than a new lead. She hadn't left a will, but there was a copy of her marriage certificate. Ken Kwasny and Rose Andrichuk had been married in a civil ceremony in Edmonton five and a half months before his own birth. It was completely consistent with what his father had said in his anguished outburst.

Two days after the funeral, Ken told his father he had to get back to Vancouver. The elder Kwasny seemed to be in good enough shape to be left alone; he was drinking, but not out of control, and a couple of his construction buddies had taken to coming around to the house and spending time with him. He dropped Ken off at the Edmonton airport where, instead of catching his flight, Ken hired a car and set off for Mundell.

He had never been there before. To the best of his recollection, the only occasions on which his parents had gone back to their hometown had been to attend the funerals of their own parents, and each time they had left their young son with friends in Edmonton.

With its freshly painted, false-fronted wooden buildings and plank sidewalks, the main street of the little town looked like a movie set. Later, Ken was to learn that this was the result of a campaign by a charitable foundation to refurbish the main streets of small rural communities in an attempt to instill pride in farming as a way of life and stem the exodus of people to the cities. Several mud-caked pickups were parked in front of the general store, which was painted an unappetizing rust-orange. The two people running the store didn't look very promising — both the woman at the cash register and the man behind the counter were young, no older than Ken himself. Still, he had to start somewhere.

"I'm anxious to meet anyone who might have known Rose Andrichuk. She lived here until about twenty-seven years ago."

The young husband and wife looked at each other blankly. The woman, trying to be helpful, said, "There are some Andrichuks who farm over in the next township. They don't come in here very often, though."

"Who's asking?" The speaker, a beefy man with a sunburned face, came up to stand beside Ken.

"She was my mother."

"You say was. We heard she was sick with the cancer. Did she ...?"

"Last week."

The farmer looked jolted, as if the news reminded him of his own mortality. Then he peered at Ken. "You didn't take after her much."

"No, I don't, I'm sorry to say. Did you know her?"

"Had a crush on her all through high school. She was the best-lookin' girl ever to come out of this neck of the woods." He folded his arms and looked around the store for confirmation. One of the other men, who looked to be in his late forties, nodded enthusiastic agreement. Apart from the cashier, there were no women in the place, which probably went a long way to explain why his informant was being so outgoing.

"She was beautiful all her life." Ken's voice broke, and the weather-punished faces of the men softened. This young man, grieving for his mother, was Rose Andrichuk's boy — he was one of their own.

"How's your dad?" asked one of the men, with considerably less warmth. "We heard he made big money working on the pipelines."

"Dad's fine. He's pretty broken up about my mother, of course."

"He was crazy mad about her. I remember how it took everybody by surprise — the way they ran off together to Edmonton and got married. Eloped, they called it."

"They used to joke about that," lied Ken. "They thought it was romantic." He was on thin ice here; it wouldn't take much to start these sharp-eyed country folk adding two and two together. The beefy man's wife had joined her husband in the store and was listening avidly.

"I thought I'd like to drive around and look at the places where she went to school and where she worked before she left."

"You won't find the place where she worked," the farmer's wife sniffed. "She had a job as a cook's helper on a drilling rig, and as soon as they's finished, them rigs just pack up and leave like thieves in the night."

A tawdry little fling with some young roughneck on a drilling rig. Is that what it was? Ken experienced a faint sense of disillusionment, then was annoyed with himself for his disloyalty. His mother would have been scarcely twenty at the time and with no experience of the outside world.

"They was in the area for quite a while. Not that it did them much good," the beefy farmer added with the air of a man who had fought nature all his life and isn't averse to seeing someone else defeated by it. His audience nodded sagely; it was obvious that the era of the drilling rigs had passed into local folklore.

"Something did come out of it all, though," the farmer went on, completing what was clearly an oft-told tale. "This is the place where the famous Bill Crawford got his start in Canada. His company sent him up here from Texas as a geologist on them wells.

"Some geologist!" cackled another. "All they drilled was dry holes!"

"He must've seen something, though," asserted the first farmer. "Cause he came back up here to Canada to stay a couple of years after." He paused, lost in memory of those far-off days, then said with a reminiscent smile and a mischievous glance at his wife, "The story around town was that he and Rose kinda fancied each other. I remember being jealous as hell."

"He was a married man," said his wife with a disapproving frown. "No good could have come of it."

So there it was. So simple once you had the vital piece of information that made it all fit. Ken forced himself to remain and have a Coke with them and dutifully drove over to look at the high school his mother had attended. It was only when he was on the highway heading back to Edmonton that he allowed himself to absorb the full impact of what he had learned.

Bill Crawford, *the* Bill Crawford, was his true father! You could see how it happened — the handsome young geologist, Christ, the guy still looked like a movie star, and the beautiful young girl out here in the boondocks. You couldn't blame his mother; she would have been swept off her feet. It was sort of romantic, when you thought about it. And it explained a lot of things to Ken about himself — his special aptitudes and his predilection for financial and business matters. Bill Crawford was a genius along those lines — look at what he had achieved with Venture Oils. It was right up there with the majors.

It was late when he reached Edmonton and checked into a hotel. It would be better to confront his father — and Ken Kwasny would always be his father — in the morning when he would be sober and less inclined to belligerence. He was the only one who could supply the information Ken needed to be absolutely sure.

Ken Kwasny, senior, was helping himself to a beer from the fridge when his son walked in. "That was a quick trip," he muttered. "Want one?" He held out the bottle.

"Not just yet, thanks."

"Suit yourself." His father raised the bottle to his lips. "What brings you back?"

"It's Bill Crawford, isn't it?"

The beer bottle flew past Ken's head and bounced off a wall cabinet. "Don't you mention that prick's name in this house!"

Case closed. Bill Crawford was his natural father.

"Take it easy, Dad. I just had to know. It doesn't change anything!"

The older man was mopping up the spilled beer. He cherished the home he and Rose had built together. "If you get any ideas about having a big reunion with that son of a bitch, forget it. He knows from nothing about you."

"I wondered about that. Mother didn't tell him, I guess?"

"She told him all right. Wrote him a big long letter after he went back to Texas.

And you know what the cocksucker did?" His bloodshot eyes glittered with malice. "Seems he already had a wife and family back home, so he sent your mother a money order for $300 to have an abortion. He was going to kill you, boy!"

That had been months ago, but the emotional impact of the appalling revelation was still strong enough to jar Ken back to the present. He sat shivering in the dim light of his own living room, feeling an icy cold at the core of his being. His own father had tried to kill him — to extinguish his life while he was helpless inside his mother's womb. Ken realized he was being irrational — abortion was an everyday solution to one of life's commonest problems — but he couldn't help it. To be alive and to learn that someone had actually intended to do that to you was almost unbearable. Sometimes the intensity of his feelings frightened him; he recognized the danger that his hatred for Bill Crawford would become an obsession that could ruin his own life. No. It was still okay. Once he had achieved his revenge against Crawford, his own equilibrium would be restored.

Rubbing his eyes, he switched on a light and went back to his desk where the Venture documents of incorporation were arranged in neat little piles. Picking up the prospectus for the recently concluded underwriting he read, for possibly the hundredth time, the paragraph that dealt with the limitation of the voting rights of the class B common shares. They were not entitled to vote unless and until a "Crawford event" occurred. A Crawford event occurred if Bill died, was declared insane, let his own shareholdings fall below a certain minimum, or was no longer a director or chief executive officer of the company. If entry to the fortress was to be found anywhere, it was in that last provision. It was the shareholders who elected the directors, but it was the directors who elected the officers, including the chief executive officer. As the controlling shareholder, however, Crawford could make the board of directors do whatever he wanted. It was a circle that kept turning back on itself. Ken sighed and switched off the light.

21

Hilary's grey eyes, inches away, were laughing at him. He kissed her cool and inviting lips again.

"We're right for each other," he whispered against her cheek.

"It's too early to tell." She straightened up and patted his shoulder. "Want some more brandy?"

"I'll pass, thanks. I have to be sharp for those rapacious colleagues of yours in the morning."

"Funnee, funnee." She placed a playful finger on the tip of his nose. "You could chew them up and spit them out before breakfast and you know it. Incidentally," she rose from the sofa with graceful ease, "the department is wildly excited about your plans for the Arctic."

"It was an undertaking I had to give in return for the Hampton approval," he reminded her, although he knew it was unnecessary. "It's much more than mere plans, too. I've already committed to lease a drill ship for the upcoming drilling season."

"Expensive."

"Try $200,000 a day. My directors think I'm much too bullish."

"But they'll go along?"

"Oh, sure. They're used to my little ways."

"Good. The country needs that oil."

"So do I. If it's there. It's the damnedest thing." His grin was rueful. "Here I am, bursting to whisper sweet nothings in your shell-like ear and we always end up talking business like a pair of tycoons."

"You're the tycoon, not me. I'm just an underpaid servant of the public. Anyway it does give us something in common, doesn't it?"

"Amen to that!" he agreed eagerly.

"I'll call you a cab." She kissed his cheek and picked up the phone.

Bill was astute enough to realize that he was engaged in a true, old-fashioned courtship with a very uncertain outcome. He was running the risk of finding the one thing he wanted more than anything else in life only to learn it would forever remain beyond his reach.

The pursuit of Hilary meant that he was spending an inordinate amount of time in Ottawa. Once, while they waited for takeoff clearance at the Calgary airport, Tim

Connors came on the blower to joke that the Lear could fly to Ottawa on its own. Bill picked up the phone and made some offhand response about the time-wasting frustration of having to deal with the government. He knew Tim's little joke was innocent; the pilot would never knowingly make any reference to the chairman's love life. But Bill was under no illusions about the gossip that must be buzzing around Calgary concerning the real reason he was spending so much time in Ottawa.

On his next visit, he found the real reason looking particularly breathtaking: her shoulders tanned and bare above a low-cut, strapless dress. She stepped outside the apartment door to kiss him with an eagerness that seemed to carry its own message. Bill's pulse was pounding as they went inside to spend a few minutes with Jason. That was one area where he had made progress — the boy no longer viewed him with suspicion and resentment. Instead, the visits of Mr. Crawford had become a welcome addition to his life; the boy thought of Bill as someone he could talk to on a man-to-man basis about things that really mattered, like airplanes and cars. His conversion was complete when Bill, somewhat hesitantly because of Hilary's views about the profligate ways of the oil industry, had taken them up in the Lear, and Tim Connors had put the youngster in the co-pilot's seat and let him touch the controls.

They dined that night in the Canadian Grill at the Chateau Laurier where the band played the kind of music that Bill could keep up with. For the first time they danced like lovers, their bodies fitting together as if cast from reverse sides of the same mould. Bill could feel the delicious curve of her belly where it tucked in to join her pelvis. He could also feel his own arousal and discreetly bent away from her. She breathed something in his ear and moved closer, renewing the contact.

"I told the babysitter I might be late tonight." Hilary's face was slightly flushed, but the grey eyes held Bill's steadily.

"I hope that means what I think it means," Bill said as he hastily scrawled his signature on the credit-card slip.

They held each other all the way up in the elevator to Bill's hotel suite. Mixed in with his excitement was a haunting dread of failure. My God, what if he had this glorious woman naked and eager in his arms and couldn't perform. It had happened once when he had had a great deal to drink and no taste for the female he was with. Ever since, the fear of a recurrence had lurked uneasily in the back of his mind.

The first touch of her seeking hand dispelled any fear of impotence. If anything, his response was too eager. He desperately wanted their first lovemaking to be sure and satisfying, but the gathering tension in his groin warned him not to prolong the foreplay. To his dismay, he found himself coming almost as soon as he had achieved full penetration. He didn't lose his erection, however, and continued his stroking while she moved under him with soft little cries of pleasure.

The second time was better. Much better. He explored her body with slow, lingering delight until she reached out to pull him between her thighs.

"That was beautiful," she murmured as they lay side by side on the bed, basking in the afterglow of love.

"I feel as if you have given me a great and precious gift," said Bill almost reverently.

"If it was a gift, it was for both of us."

"Would this be an appropriate time to talk about love and mushy things like that?"

She propped herself on her side and kissed him, golden-brown hair lightly brushing his cheeks. "Why talk about it when we have it?"

Bill was being warned off, and he accepted it. He could scarcely expect more than she had already given that night.

Bill's life that summer was ruled by two passions — Hilary and the Arctic. Both gave — or promised — much, yet withheld the ultimate prize. His love for Hilary seemed to feed on itself. The more he was with her, the more he possessed her, the more he wanted her. Their lovemaking never became routine. For one thing, he could never be sure when it would happen — she never let it become an automatic, taken-for-granted part of the times they spent together.

The closest he came to revealing how he really felt was a contented, "I could spend the rest of my life like this," as he lay collapsed on top of her after a soaring orgasm. If she was aware he had given her a cue, she made no attempt to pick it up. Fearful of losing what he already had, he kissed her gently and rolled over on his side.

Hilary gave; she didn't take. The Arctic was a much more demanding mistress, exacting an appalling financial toll from those who would woo her. Bill had been both excited and more than a little apprehensive when it was discovered that Hampton had actually done a great deal more work on its Arctic properties than had first been thought. Their plans had been well advanced before the actions taken by the Canadian government turned them off. During the previous two summers they had shot hundreds of miles of seismic and identified no less than fifteen geological structures. Three of the structures were gigantic, true elephants, capable of containing billions of barrels of oil or trillions of cubic feet of gas — or nothing but salt water from some ancient sea. A discovery of that magnitude would vault Venture overnight into the ranks of world-scale corporations. It would also be a priceless asset for the country.

Like many oilmen, Bill had travelled extensively in the Middle East and had met with the powerful princes and energy ministers of the oil-producing states. The OPEC price squeezes and embargoes had come as no surprise to him; only their severity and rapidity were unexpected. Canada had the potential to produce enough oil and gas within its own borders to meet all its needs. To Bill, developing this potential and becoming self-sufficient in energy was the only national policy that made sense, although there was no doubt the cost would be staggering. Not crippling, however. Not if a proper development strategy was followed.

In the late sixties, watching OPEC gradually becoming aware of the enormous leverage it possessed and realizing that the western world's energy joyride was about to come to an abrupt and painful end, Bill had given much thought to the enormous oil reserves locked in Alberta's famous Athabasca tar sands. The oil was there all right, hundreds of billions of barrels. And the technology to recover it was available as well. One commercial-scale plant was already in operation and had proven that oil could be extracted from the tarry bitumen, although at ruinous cost. But if OPEC was able to get its act together and increase the price of world oil to the levels he had heard mentioned in Riyadh, tar sands production could become commercially viable. That line of reasoning, together with the dazzling promise of billions of barrels of oil, had led Bill into a brief flirtation with the oil sands. Venture had contributed some seed money to a pilot project located twenty miles north of Fort McMurray and earned the option to participate in the commercial development of the property.

It took him a while to understand why the tar sands held so little fascination for him. It was a mining operation. The risks were high, but they were technological and financial risks, not the wildcat risk of whether the drilling bit would tap into a valuable reservoir or come up dry. He was an explorationist, not a goddamn miner. Shortly after acquiring this piece of self-knowledge, Bill traded off Venture's position in the tar sands and concentrated on conventional drilling.

That was why the Arctic was so appealing to him; it was strictly an explorationist's play. Either the oil was there, or it wasn't. Everything had come to a head when the president of Globe Petroleum had taken him to lunch and told him that Globe had reshot the seismic over one of its proposed locations and concluded the structure was so heavily faulted it was not worth drilling. This meant that one of Globe's three drill ships was available for the summer drilling season if Bill was interested. It would be available only for the one season, the Globe executive added, but with reasonable luck it should be able to drill and test one well. To Bill it was an irresistible opportunity to get his Arctic program up and running, and he grabbed it.

Right from the start he had planned to spread the risk by farming out a share of Venture's interests to other oil companies. That hadn't worked out so far, however. New federal taxes had cut into the oil industry's cash flow, and the big players were reluctant to commit funds to a project that, even if it were successful in finding oil, was still years away from payout because of the long lead time required to bring the oil to market.

All the outside directors showed up for the August board meeting in Calgary, which might have been an indication of how seriously they viewed Venture's increasing commitment in the Arctic. Steve Miller, who had been on staff for the past six weeks, led off the agenda with a well-organized review of the company's Canadian operations. His presentation was greeted with low murmurs of approval; it was clear the new president was off to a good start. Gavin Anderson caught Bill's eye and gestured a quick thumbs up. Gavin had co-operated in every possible way to smooth the installation of Steve Miller as the new president, asking only that it be made clear that he was resigning the office at his own request. In fact, he had been quite prepared to leave the company's employ entirely; in his years of association with Bill he had become independently wealthy. However, when Bill made it clear that he wanted him to stay on in some capacity, he readily accepted the office of senior vice-president and remained a director of the company.

As Steve was winding up his presentation, Bill was surprised to hear him say, "I know you are all anxious to hear about the Arctic, so I'll turn the meeting back to the chairman, since that operation is really his baby." Steve was a product of corporate politics. Was he already starting to protect his own ass?

"There's not a great deal to report," Bill said uneasily. "It's a case of drilling ahead with no unusual operating problems. No luck in farming-out to date, unfortunately. We still have a couple of prospects we're pursuing, though."

"The market doesn't seem to think very much of that play. The stock's fallen right out of bed," said Lee Travis.

"Everyone thinks out exposure is too great," Bill conceded. "And I agree with them. It'll bounce back as soon as we announce a farm-out. And, of course, if we come up with a discovery, it'll go through the roof."

"You still expect to know the answer by the end of this drilling season?" Adrian Strickland asked sceptically.

Bill held up his hand with two fingers crossed. "Yes, if everything continues to stay on track."

"Correct me if I'm wrong, but we only have the drill ship for this season." With a nod from Travis, Ted Reid inserted himself into the debate.

"That's right," Bill replied patiently. "That point and the risk attached to it were fully discussed before we entered into the deal. You will recall that Globe refused to lease the drill ship on any other basis. They have work requirements they must meet next year in order to maintain their permits."

"You have a contingency plan, I assume?" Adrian Strickland looked as if he assumed no such thing."

"There are a limited number of options that may be open to us. But we'd better all pray that we don't run into any problems with that well," replied Bill, and the meeting adjourned on an uncharacteristically troubled note.

22

Phone calls in the middle of the night are part of an oilman's life, and Bill snapped instantly awake at the first ring of his bedside phone. Dave Wilson didn't waste any time on the niceties. "We got ourselves a problem up at the Inukshuk location."

How many times over the years had Dave wakened him with a similar report — that they had lost circulation in a well, or that the drill pipe had broken off in the hole, or, on one heart-stopping occasion, that a sour-gas well had blown wild? This could be the biggest of them all. Never before — except in the earliest stages, when the company's very existence might depend on a single well — had there been so much riding on one hole.

"How bad is it?"

"Can't tell yet. They've got gas bubbling to the surface all around the ship."

"Christ. Are we talking about a blowout?"

"Not yet. It's not coming up through the hole itself. It's all around, like the ship is floating inside a bottle of soda pop."

"Hydrates. The heat from the well has melted some permafrost that's been hold-ing gas in suspension, and now the gas is working its way up to the surface." Bill paused. "That's shooting from the hip, of course, so I'm probably off base."

"I've got an idea your aim is pretty good. That's what Johannsen thinks it is too. They're trying to get a sample of the stuff, and then they'll have a better idea."

"We didn't need this, Dave. Not now, not with this hole."

"Don't I know. But we got it, old buddy."

"Yeah. Okay, I'll meet you down at the office in half an hour. Gather up whoever you'll need, and we better have that new public relations type there as well. The media will be snapping at our heels on this one."

"Cocksuckers," Dave snarled as he hung up. The exploration manager had bitter memories of the time, five years ago, when the press had climbed all over him because they thought he was taking too long to control a wild well that was spewing toxic sour gas into the atmosphere. In reality, he had been doing a superb job of coping with an incredibly dangerous situation, but one newspaper, desperate to boost its declining circulation, had taken the line that he was dragging his feet and was afraid to move in and tame the monster. The paper apologized profusely after the well had been successfully capped with no loss of life, but Dave still seethed over the injustice that had been done him.

By eight o'clock in the morning, Bill's snap diagnosis had been pretty much confirmed. It was natural gas that was bubbling to the surface around the Inukshuk well. Bill had named the well after the humanoid stone figures that dot the flat Arctic landscape. Inukshuk in the language of the Inuit means "in place of man," and the stone structures were used to supplement the nomadic Eskimo's chronic shortage of manpower. They deceived the caribou herds into believing they were surrounded by hunters and frightened them into going where the real hunters waited in ambush. Over the centuries, the sites of these mysterious monuments have taken on a sacred connotation for the Inuit.

Fortunately, the gas was sweet with no poisonous hydrogen sulphide, and the pressure was extremely low, which meant that the formation from which it was escaping was high up in the hole, maybe only a few hundred feet beneath the surface.

At nine, Bill attended a hastily assembled press conference. Dave flatly refused to accompany him. The boardroom was packed with representatives of the media, laden with tape recorders and other paraphernalia of their craft. The red lights of the television cameras blinked on as Bill began to speak.

"As you all know by now, we are experiencing some operational difficulties at the Inukshuk location. We feel confident that we know the cause, and let me say right up front that it does not pose any danger to human life."

This brought some sceptical looks, but on the whole Bill's audience was sympathetic. The oil industry was the prime newsmaker for the Calgary media, and they were accustomed to its atmosphere of high risk and the élan with which it overcame seemingly impossible logistic and technical problems. They listened attentively and knowledgeably while Bill explained the hydrate theory — how the heat caused by the circulation of warm drilling mud could melt the permafrost in which the gas was trapped and allow it to escape.

"You say there's no danger." The representative of *Oilweek* asked the first question. "But I understand that with gas bubbling to the surface, a ship can lose buoyancy and sink like a stone."

"In theory that may be correct, Fred. But you're talking about an extreme case, where the gas actually replaces most of the water. We're not facing anything like that. Our exploration manager likens the Inukshuk situation to bubbles fizzing in a bottle of soda."

"Will Mr. Wilson be in charge of bringing the well under control?" It was a reporter from the *Clarion*, the paper that had pilloried Dave over the sour-gas well.

"As exploration manager, Mr. Wilson will be in overall charge, naturally. It's not a matter of bringing the well under control, though. It's an operating problem that Mr. Johannsen, Globe's drilling superintendent in charge of the *Arctic Explorer*, is perfectly capable of dealing with."

"Isn't the presence of gas an encouraging sign?" asked a voice. "From the exploration point of view, I mean?"

"I wish I could say it was," Bill replied. "However, it's too close to the surface and too small in volume to be of any significance. Of course, it does establish the presence of hydrocarbons in the general area, but Globe's earlier wells have already done that, although not in commercial volumes."

Some of the veteran reporters exchanged knowing looks. You could count on Bill Crawford not to try to pull a snow job on you.

"At the very least this will cause a delay, won't it?" It was *Oilweek* again. "And this is the third week of August, so you don't have much time to spare before the drilling season ends."

"You're right on both counts. Everything depends on how quickly we can get back to making hole. But it's a setback. No question about that. As soon as this conference is over, Mr. Wilson and I are flying up to check out the situation personally."

The moon pool — an unnervingly large opening in the ship's hull through which the well was drilled — was strangely quiet. There was just the faint hum of pumps circulating drilling mud to condition the hole and the slap of waves against the steel sides of the opening. The pounding roar of the powerful engines that drove the rotating drill bit was absent. Bill gazed down at the bubbles percolating up from the well bore. They surrounded the ship, extending outward for a radius of several hundred yards.

Swede Johannsen looked at Bill and grimaced. "It's a bitch, ain't it?"

"Not good. What's your plan of attack?"

"We've got a workboat over at Tuk waiting for the Hercules to land with the glycol. As soon as we get it aboard, we'll start pumping it down the hole and see if we can't freeze that mother off. I already told Ray" — the burly superintendent jerked his head at the government inspector assigned to monitor the drilling operations — "that there's just no way we can shut off all them bubbles. Some of that gas will still be coming to the surface ten years from now."

"It will have to be one hell of a lot better than it is right now before I can let you resume drilling," the inspector said grimly.

"That's understood," Bill assured him. He looked at the drill pipe riding up and down on the riser as the ship moved to the motion of the waves. "Damn, there's no more depressing sight than a rig that's not making hole!"

Bill decided there was little to be gained by his remaining on board; the drilling superintendent was perfectly capable of doing whatever could be done. Before leaving, they grabbed a quick cafeteria-style lunch in the mess hall, and Bill made a point of going around to all the tables and shaking hands with the men. They had the subdued air of a crew with a rig in trouble.

Bill laughingly turned down a second piece of apple pie and cheese and asked Johannsen, "How long do you figure it will take us to get back to drilling?"

"Two weeks. Minimum. More likely three. I don't have to tell you what that means."

Bill and his exploration manager nodded sombre agreement. Now there was no hope of completing the well by the end of the drilling season.

"We'll get out of your hair, Swede." Bill stood up and held out his hand. Johannsen was openly pleased at being left in charge, but Dave Wilson looked somewhat disgruntled.

As the helipad dropped away beneath them, they could see the ice only a few miles to the north, a solid mass of white stretching all the way to the horizon. When it began its relentless march southward with the onslaught of the Arctic winter, all drilling would come to a halt.

The pilot had adjusted the intercom so that the two passengers could talk over the clattering roar of the machine. They were both buckled into the orange flotation suits that were worn on all flights over the frigid ocean. Bill spoke into his microphone. "I know you feel that you should have stayed on board, but I have a much more important assignment for you."

Dave grinned at the man who had been his boss for all his working life. "Point me."

The pilot's voice broke in over the earphones to tell them they were coming up on one of the Globe locations. The drill ship, a sister ship to the one they had just left, attended by two powerful icebreaker workboats, floated on the dark blue water like a child's toy. Off in the distance, another sturdy workboat rode herd on a rogue iceberg.

"I want you," Bill went on as the drill site fell behind, "to locate the leading offshore drilling expert in the world."

"Globe's probably hired them all by now."

"Not the kind of person I have in mind. He'll be an independent consultant — an authority on the design and construction of drill ships for use in northern waters."

"And what do I do with this guy once I find him? Hire him?"

"Retain him as a consultant, preferably. Hire him if necessary. Just make sure he's the best available. You've got two weeks."

Dave's eyebrows jerked upward, but just then the chopper banked steeply to the right. He turned in his seat to squint out the window. They were approaching Tuktoyaktuk, the tiny Inuit village that had been transformed into a bustling harbour by Globe's drilling operations. They could see a Hercules transport parked on the airstrip and a workboat backing away from the dock. "That must be the glycol. The boys sure hit the deck running," muttered Dave with grudging approval.

Bill smiled to himself. His exploration manager was telling him that he accepted Bill's decision to let the Globe people handle the problem on their own.

They were directly over the harbour now. It was crowded with craft of all shapes and sizes, buzzing back and forth to the anchored cargo ship that had been converted into a giant floating base.

"You sure you want all this?" Dave asked as the chopper settled down within a hundred yards of the Lear.

"It's where the future is. I'm convinced of it."

Dave was grinning as he pulled off the headset.

"What's so funny?" asked Bill.

"Oh, I was just thinking — I've been a dry-land driller all my life, but now I guess I better sign up for some swimming lessons."

23

Ken Kwasny followed the newspaper accounts of the hydrate problem at the Inukshuk well with increasing excitement. Each day that passed made it less likely that the well would be tested before the advancing ice pack shut down drilling for the year. He had been tempted to recommend to his partners that Sterling take a substantial short position in Venture shares, but held back because he couldn't afford to make the slightest move that would attract Crawford's attention. Besides, there was always the "Crawford magic" that could turn the situation around and leave the shorts bleeding all over the stock exchange floor.

Ken didn't allow his obsession with the Crawford empire to interfere with his efforts on behalf of Sterling Investments. He had just engineered a deal whereby Sterling had acquired control of a corporation using the captured company's own liquid assets to finance the entire purchase. This feat of financial legerdemain resulted in another spate of publicity in the financial press. Initially, Ken had been apprehensive about the amount of press coverage he was receiving, until he realized it could be used to create a public persona that might limit any investigation of his family background to "the son of a pipeline welder." It was a natural in terms of public appeal, and he was careful to say nothing about his mother, except that she was no longer living.

He would have to be on his guard tomorrow. The notorious Margo Jones, publisher of a new financial newsletter, was in Vancouver on a combined fact-finding and promotional tour and had arranged to interview him over lunch.

"Let me say right up front, Mr. Kwasny ... very well, Ken then, thank you," she corrected herself when he protested, "that I am somewhat awed by you and that I was absolutely thrilled when Sterling Investments became one of my earliest subscribers."

"Information is a priceless commodity, Margo, and I believe you have a remarkable talent for ferreting it out. May I also say that I admire the way in which you have managed to recover from your recent ... ah, problems. Publishing the newsletter was a brilliant stroke."

"It was a great moment for me when I suddenly realized that there was nothing to prevent me from putting out a private publication, even though I had lost my credibility as a professional journalist." There was no point in telling him that this realization had occurred when Chester Martin had tracked her down in Toronto and taken her to lunch. By the time he had finished explaining that there was no legal impediment to her circulating a financial newsletter, she knew that she had found her salvation. "Bill sent you, didn't he?" she had asked.

"Let's just say I wouldn't be here if he didn't approve," he replied. "By the way, if you need some initial financing, I'm sure it can be arranged."

Margo's fingertips touched her slender neck as she thought of the necklace Bill had given her, now reposing on its bed of velvet in a bank vault. "That won't be necessary."

Six weeks later, the first issue of *The Jones Financial Update* had appeared. Complimentary copies together with subscription forms were mailed out to some five hundred prospective clients. As Margo had expected, the reaction had been decidedly mixed; many recipients were outraged that someone with her reputation would dare to take such a step. But, as Ken had just mentioned, accurate and timely information was beyond price, regardless of its source, and enough subscriptions had been taken out to meet operating expenses. She knew she could deliver the goods, so success was just a matter of time.

"I've recommended your service to a number of people," Ken was saying, echoing her thoughts about word-of-mouth advertising. "I feel there's a real need for it out here in lotus land. On this side of the Rockies, we tend to get out of touch with what's going on in the rest of the country."

He took a sip of Perrier. "Now, how can I help you? I hope you're not going in for personality profiles and things like that. Factual information and informed opinions are what your subscribers want."

"And that's what they'll get. What I'd like from you is an overview — your general impression of what we can expect in the next six months."

"Well," Ken swallowed a forkful of chef's salad. "I'm anything but bullish. The oils are in the doldrums, and it will take something dramatic like a discovery in the Arctic to revive them."

"Speaking of the Arctic, did you know that Venture has committed itself to building a new drill ship this winter?" She looked pleased at his incredulous expression. "It's true," she assured him. "It will be the lead item in the next issue of *Update*. They're converting an old Liberty cargo vessel in Galveston and building two ice-breaking workboats in the Victoria shipyards. The total cost is rumoured to be somewhere around one hundred and thirty million."

Ken's thoughts raced as he strove to assess the implications of this new development. Crawford was carrying on like a Mississippi riverboat gambler over the Arctic. Maybe, just maybe, he was finally exposing his Achilles heel.

"That's interesting," Ken said after a long pause. "I hope it means they're onto something up there."

"The story I hear is that the Globe ships are fully committed for the next two seasons at least, so Crawford decided to go for broke and build his own navy. I gather some of his directors aren't exactly carried away with the idea."

"You know him, don't you?"

She didn't come right out and say it was a dumb question, but there was a faint note of impatience in her voice as she replied wearily, "Everybody in the whole wide world knows we were lovers. But that was ages ago."

"You ever think he could be the one who set you up?"

"Do you know him?"

"Never met the man in my life."

"If you knew him, you'd also know it's just not his style. Some of the other so-called oil barons I worked over — absolutely. Bill Crawford — never."

Ken was surprised and more than a little disconcerted to find her so firmly in the Crawford camp. It didn't affect his intention to try and see more of Margo Jones, however. He would just have to be extra careful. Sleekly elegant and informed, she was one lady who had her act together. There was also an indefinable and exciting air about her, of one who had been through the fire and had been tempered by the ordeal. She was older than Ken by a good few years, but the women he dated were invariably in her age bracket.

It was her lunch, so she paid for it. Ken waited until she had signed for it before saying, "I realize you will have a very crowded agenda while you're here in Vancouver, but I would like to see you again."

The clever brown eyes looked directly into his. "I do have a crowded schedule, but I'll uncrowd it if it means seeing more of you, Ken. I truly believe you have one of the most original and exciting minds in the world of finance today."

"That's very flattering," grinned Ken. "But I was sort of hoping that the attraction was, shall we say ... on a little more physical plane."

"I thought that was so obvious it went without saying. But I do have this workaholic conscience that must be placated." She was smiling up at him as they left the restaurant.

At the end of the second evening she invited him up to her room for a drink. "I have a bottle of vintage Perrier on ice," she teased.

She was an ardent and expert lover. Ken, who had heard the stories of how she obtained her inside information by selectively sleeping around Ottawa, knew that her expertise came from long and varied experience. That didn't trouble him; he was prepared to accept whatever had gone into making her the woman she was, and he found the fact that she and Crawford had once been lovers strangely stimulating. Their lovemaking was fuelled by the physical attraction that flowed between them with an almost palpable force and spiced with an unspoken competitive edge. When Ken whispered good night at three o'clock they grinned companionably at each other, like two weary gladiators who have fought to an honourable draw.

"Have you seen the paper?" It was Margo, phoning in-between her morning appointments.

"I've got it right here in front of me." Ken glanced down at the business section of the *Province*. "Too bad about your scoop."

"When you only publish once a month, you can hardly expect to be first with the hard-core news." Margo was philosophical. "But I had it right, didn't I?"

"Bang on." The news story, which was based on a press release from Venture, confirmed that contracts had been let for the conversion of a freighter to an ice-strengthened drill ship and for the construction of two workboats. The total cost was estimated to be one hundred and thirty million, and Bill Crawford was quoted as being optimistic that the new drill ship, which was to be named *Polarex*, would be on station at the Inukshuk site by the commencement of the next drilling season.

"I've got to rush or else I'll keep Mr. Stone of BC Power waiting. And we wouldn't want that, would we?"

"We're still on for tonight?"

"No need to ask. I'm counting the minutes," she replied gaily and rang off.

Ken sat at his desk, thinking about Margo. He was pretty sure that the feeling he had for her wasn't love, but it gave a mighty pleasant buzz all the same. She was the perfect companion socially, sexually, and intellectually. It was a joy to be with an attractive woman whose mind was on the same wavelength as his. He suspected that her feelings about him probably would be much the same.

Satisfied, for the time being at least, that he had correctly categorized their relationship, he picked up the newspaper once again. One hundred and thirty million dollars was a fair chunk of change in any man's language. Venture could raise it easily enough, but it would put one hell of a crimp in their other activities. Unless Crawford had been able to arrange some ingenious off-balance sheet financing ...? No, this project was too risky to stand on its own — it could only be financed on the credit of Venture itself. Ken folded the newspaper and started to doodle on a pad of yellow writing paper.

"That's what I like to see. Our wonder boy lost in thought." Stan Winters stuck his head around the door of Ken's office. "I trust this means you're incubating another coup."

Ken looked up and brushed back the lock of hair that had fallen over his forehead. "A lot of things have to fall into place before this one hatches. If and when it does, you'll be the first to know." Ken casually slipped the yellow pad face down over the newspaper story. He didn't want Winters to know he was still on his Venture kick. Time enough for that when he had a foolproof plan worked out. Stan would probably dig in his heels at first, but the prize was so glittering that Ken was sure he could convince him to take another run at Venture — if he managed to come up with a plan that looked like a sure winner, that is.

"You're not going to tell me any more, are you?" asked Winters finally.

"Not another word," Ken told him cheerfully. "I've got to convince myself first. And that may never happen."

When he was alone once more, Ken went back to planning his campaign. The large blocks of shares held by the foreign investors were the key. At the moment they were Crawford's shield. The trick was somehow to turn them into a sword that would destroy him. The Travises and Dwights had lined up against Crawford once before, which meant they would do it again if the circumstances were right. Maybe the thing to do was just shake the tree and see what fell down.

Ken began to write: "Cause delay in construction program," frowned at it dubiously, then added a question mark. "Shareholder revolt" — that would likely turn out to be an essential element. It would require a leader. Alton Grant — the name leaped into his mind without conscious thought. Grant was a publicity hound, perpetually making speeches and writing articles about oil policy. Ken regarded him as a phony who didn't give a damn how much harm he caused so long as he got the nationwide publicity he craved. But the media loved him; he was always good for a quote on anything that happened in the patch, and to the general public he was the recognized guru of the oil industry. It should be a relatively simple matter to have Grant become a registered shareholder of Venture, and then start indirectly feeding him information that would show how Crawford's Arctic adventure was threatening the very existence of the company.

Next he wrote down, "Go Signal," and thought for a moment before adding: "When the market value of the shares falls below fifty per cent of the non-Arctic assets of the company, or when the company's next budget shows that the expenditures on conventional exploration have been sharply reduced, or ..."

As he wrote, a line from a nursery rhyme popped into his head. It was one his mother used to recite as his father, his "real" father, playfully tossed him into the air and caught him in those strong, calloused hands: "Humpty Dumpty took a great fall." Ken smiled grimly to himself and wrote on.

24

A wave of applause rolled down from the grandstand as Imperial Way cleared the last obstacle — a hedge and stone wall. The bay hunter had put in a smooth, clear round, and Debbie knew she had first place locked up as she led him, now stripped of his saddle, back into the outdoor ring for the conformation judging. The only other horse that could match him in conformation had ticked the picket fence and would be marked down on performance.

She was right. The judge walked along the lineup of the twelve finalists, scribbling some notes on his card, and waved Imperial Way to the head of the line. Debbie fastened the rosette to his bridle and led him out of the ring, to another round of applause. As expected, Myron Sheldon and his teenage daughter were waiting in the paddock. Myron had made a fortune building and selling condominiums and now was hell-bent to make his daughter, Anita, a star in the horse-show firmament. He had been following Debbie from show to show, trying to persuade her to sell Imperial Way.

"Terrific win, Debbie. Congratulations!" He gave Imperial Way a nervous pat, then quickly stepped back as the gelding tossed its head. Smiling his oily, ingratiating smile, he fished in his breast pocket and pulled out a cheque. "It's signed and made out to you, Debbie. All you have to do is fill in the amount."

Debbie examined the cheque. He wasn't bluffing — it was complete except for the dollar figure. She handed it back. "You're something else, Myron. But he's not for sale."

She smiled at Anita, feeling more than a little sorry for the kid who had become the instrument through which her father was determined to fulfill his own private dreams. "Stay cool, Myron," she said to the disappointed condo king and strolled away, following after her groom who was leading the horse back to the stables. In her formal riding habit with skin-tight white breeches, she drew every male eye as she sauntered along, lightly tapping her boot with the leather crop.

By the time Debbie was finally ready to leave the grounds, after making sure the horse was properly cooled out and overseeing the bandaging of his legs, the groom was setting up his cot outside Imperial Way's stall. He had been doing this ever since the hunter's string of victories began.

"People in this business can be pretty flaky," he had muttered darkly. "Some of them don't give a shit how they win, just so long as they win."

On her way to the parking lot, Debbie stopped to chat with several of her fellow competitors, seemingly oblivious to the stares and whispers of fans touring the stable area. She had received a great deal of publicity since bringing Imperial Way to Toronto: "Western rider triumphs on eastern circuit;" "Oilman's daughter conquers the east" — that sort of thing. To the public, she had become the personification of the glamorous horse-show world. Little did they know that to Debbie it had become nothing more than a cover for her real career. The Black Diamond well, her first drilling venture since last summer's Murlex gas well, was due to reach total depth any moment, and Tom Burdon should be calling in with the results sometime that night.

"The sand's tighter than a bull's ass in fly time," Tom said without any preamble.

"It's a bust, then?" Debbie's mouth was suddenly dry.

"As far as the target formation is concerned, yes. But the Atlas people still think they're on to something and want to drill deeper — a lot deeper." He paused, then went on when Debbie said nothing. "What they thought was the Rundle turned out to be the Basal Quartz. That means the Rundle could still be there but as much as two thousand feet deeper than we figured on. You remember all the trouble they had with deviations?"

"And the expense," Debbie interjected grimly. There had been days on end when they seemed to be making no progress at all, stopping every few hours to measure the deviation and frequently having to go back up the hole and resume drilling at an angle. The resulting cost overruns had stretched Pinnacle's slender financial resources to the limit.

"Atlas intends to keep on going until they either hit the Rundle or convince themselves it's not there. We have the right to participate, of course."

"How much will it cost?"

"Our share — you're paying a quarter of the cost to earn an eighth — will come to an additional one hundred and forty thousand, dry and abandoned." Oilmen have the unnerving practice of quoting drilling costs on a dry and abandoned basis since that is the amount of money at absolute risk. The additional cost of completing a successful well normally can be recovered from production revenues.

"What do you think, Tom?"

"It's a crapshoot. Like everything else in this game. The real risk is that the Rundle will be there all right but stretched out flat like on the plains with no trapping mechanism. If it's been thrust up into a reef, and if it happens to be filled with oil, it'll pay off like a demented slot machine. From a purely explorationist point of view, I like it, but the risk factor is high."

"We could always go the penalty route —" Debbie broke off and added, "It's four hundred per cent, isn't it? That's no good."

"It's a rank wildcat, and carries the maximum penalty for nonparticipation. There probably won't be much oil left after Atlas has recovered four times the cost. Some of these operations can be pretty creative when it comes to cost accounting."

"How much time do we have?"

"The rig is on the hole, so we've got just forty-eight hours. Starting at five o'clock this afternoon, Mountain Daylight Time."

"Right." Debbie picked up a pencil. "Now give me some figures to work with, will you?"

"We just can't afford to put a foot wrong today," Debbie whispered to Imperial Way, stroking the graceful arch of his neck. Then the PA system was blaring: "The next entry is number fourteen, Imperial Way, owned and ridden by Debbie Crawford of Calgary."

The outdoor ring, approximately the size of a football field, was crowded with obstacles meant to simulate those found in the hunting field — walls, ditches, and fences, all decorated with flowering plants, shrubs, or flags. It was the Open Hunter Championship — the big one, in which both working and conformation hunters competed. As a general rule, the working hunters, which were required only to be "hunting sound," were better over the fences than their counterparts, who had to be judged on their overall appearance and soundness as well as performance. However, Imperial Way was capable of putting in a round every bit as good as the best of the working hunters.

Trotting into the ring, Debbie realized she was too tense. A little bit of nerves was a good thing — it quickened one's reflexes. Too much, however, interfered with the rider's timing and judgment and, worse, could communicate itself to the horse and throw him off. Approaching the first fence, she willed herself to relax and to concentrate only on presenting the horse correctly at each obstacle. The water jump had been the nemesis of most of the entries who had gone before her. A shallow pool of water, twelve feet wide, with a low hedge marking the takeoff point, it was a formidable test in its own right. The course designer had made it worse by placing it off by itself, with a long approach that gave horse and rider altogether too much time to think about what could go wrong. Rounding the turn for the water jump, Debbie felt a faint touch of panic. The horse would need plenty of impulsion to clear the big spread, but if he had too much, he would flatten out and splash down in the middle of all that water. Besides, it wasn't enough just to clear the jump — he had to look picture perfect while doing it.

She checked Imperial Way, asking him to gather himself, and he responded smoothly, ears pricked forward. A few strides closer to the jump and she sensed him beginning to waver; another stride and he would start to prop or duck sideways. At precisely the right moment she exerted strong leg pressure, guiding him like a projectile, and he took off faultlessly. The crowd, which had been holding its breath, let out a long "Oooh" of appreciation.

There was another tricky bit right after the water jump. A straight-up-and-down picket fence that forced the horse to collect himself immediately on landing.

Debbie was ready for it, checking Imperial Way and making him look at the fence.

"That was fabulous, Debbie. Fantastic." Myron's gaze was riveted on the championship ribbon fluttering from Imperial Way's bridle. He would build special display cases when Anita started to win ribbons like that. Hell, he'd build a special trophy room.

"Do you still have that cheque, Myron?"

He gaped at her for a moment, then muttered, "Sure. You bet," and fumbled in his pocket.

Wordlessly she held out her hand for a pen and used his plump back as a desk, making him squirm with pleasure at being seen to be on such familiar terms with Debbie Crawford.

She handed back the cheque with the amount filled in. "Well?" she asked. "Do we have a deal?"

He blanched slightly when he saw the figure$140,000. It was an exorbitant price for a show horse, especially since the prize money was almost nominal and the real return on the investment had to be in prestige rather than cash."

"We have a deal." He swallowed, and handed over the cheque. "You're something else yourself, Debbie."

"Good luck with him, Anita. Make sure your father gets you a trainer who knows what he's doing." Debbie folded the cheque and stuffed it in the pocket of her breeches.

Within the hour she was on the phone to Tom Burdon, telling him to inform Atlas that Pinnacle would participate in deepening the well.

Once again Debbie was faced with the occupational hazard of the oil industry — the interminable waiting for results. In this case the period of waiting was deliberately prolonged in order to coincide with a Crown mineral sale. Normally, it would have taken no more than fifteen days to reach the deeper horizon, but Atlas had requested the government to post some adjoining Crown lands for sale, and the bid date was three weeks away. The idea was to have the information available just in time to evaluate the bid without giving the competitors a chance to find out the results for themselves.

It was a delicate balancing act, because the projected depth had to be tested before the sale or the Atlas group would be bidding as blindly as anyone else. Complete security was clamped around the location, although everyone knew that scouts from rival companies would be monitoring it around the clock, and there wasn't much that could be done about the low-flying helicopters that whickered overhead several times a day.

Debbie spent the first week in Toronto, amusing herself with two new conquests. One, a rising young stockbroker, took her seriously and fell into an emotional tailspin that caused him to break off his existing engagement and permanently skewed his attitude toward women.

She kept trying to reassure herself that Pinnacle Petroleums could survive even if the well came in dry. In a strictly literal sense, this was true; by selling the horse she had raised enough capital to finance the cost of deepening the well, and the company's existing revenues could service its present debt and, given enough time, eventually retire it. But that would be all it could do — it wouldn't have the financial capacity to enter into new plays and grow. She was out on a limb — something she had sworn she would never let happen. Still, she knew that there had been no real choice, that when an oil company was in its infancy there were times when its future must depend on a single turn of the cards. Fortified by this inescapable fact, she flew back to Calgary to resume the outward lifestyle of a carefree playgirl and wait for news from the wellsite.

One thing about Tom — he never kept her in suspense. "It looks good," were his opening words when he called the day before the sale. "The logs show seventy-five feet of pay in the Rundle. Atlas couldn't run the kind of tests they'd like because all that tankage on the lease would be a dead giveaway, but it flowed at the rate of twelve barrels an hour. Initial production could be well over two hundred barrels per day of sweet, high-quality crude."

Oil! That lovely black stuff that OPEC had made more valuable than gold. So much more exciting than natural gas. Now Pinnacle was truly an oil company.

"That's wonderful, Tom! Oh, God, give me a moment to catch my breath."

"Don't take too long," he joked in high glee. "There's a meeting at eight o'clock in the morning to finalize the bid figure, and I need your instructions."

"I want to go along, Tom. How much do you think it's going to cost?"

"They'll be prepared to pay the big dollar now. But we're looking down everybody else's throat because we have the data and they don't. I'm expecting a top of eleven hundred an acre — there's three sections of land or nineteen hundred and twenty acres, so your twelve and a half per cent is ..."

"Two hundred and sixty-four thousand dollars." Debbie had been punching the numbers into her calculator.

"Right. And," Tom added helpfully, "you might be able to bank just about all of it, what with the well being a real barn-burner an' all."

"Go along with whatever price they recommend, Tom."

The new Black Diamond oilfield took its place as the latest minor sensation of the oil patch. When the third producing well was brought in, on land bought at the Crown sale, executives of the company that had farmed out the lease to Atlas came in for a fair bit of ribbing about giving away the crown jewels. Pinnacle, as a participant in the successful consortium, was in the public eye for the first time. Debbie now owned a bona fide, honest-to-God oil company."

"I've decided to come out of the closet, Dad."

"I beg your pardon!"

"Not in that sense," laughed Debbie.

"I wouldn't think so, from the little I know of your activities."

"People in glass houses ..." Debbie said teasingly. Then she asked, "Have you ever heard of a company called Pinnacle Petroleums?"

"Not until recently. It's in on that Black Diamond play. Run by Tom Burdon. Funny, he's a first-class consultant, but I never thought he had enough of the royal jelly to ... Hey, don't tell me you're Pinnacle Pete?"

Debbie, unable to speak, nodded, and Bill rushed around his desk to hug her. "I'm so proud of you. Nothing — absolutely nothing — that you could have done could please me more than this."

Debbie blew her nose into a tissue. "I was hoping you'd feel that way about it. I hated the thought of doing anything behind your back."

"This way is much, much better. Doing it all on your own. This is a red-letter day for your father, believe me. So Burdon was just a front, eh?"

"Oh, no. A lot more than that. He gave me a tremendous amount of advice and guidance. I've persuaded him to stay on as president. I'll be chairman of the board."

"And CEO?"

"And CEO."

"A good decision. You need someone like that behind you. Someone you can trust not to stab you in the back." He tucked her hand in the crook of his arm. "Come on. I can hardly wait till Dave hears about this!"

No one was more stunned by Debbie's emergence as the head of her own oil company than Ken Kwasny. Her double life had escaped even the intensive surveillance he maintained on the Crawfords. He was convinced that she had really done it on her own, despite what the financial community might think. Of course, she had a tidy little block of Venture shares to use as collateral. But all the same, how many women in a similar position — and the wealthy widows of men who had worked themselves into an early grave owned by far the largest number of shares in North American corporations — ever did anything with them except collect dividends?

He could have gone to bed with her that night in Calgary. His own half-sister. Christ, if she only knew! Would she ever know? Supposing he did succeed in unseating Bill Crawford, would he disclose their true relationship? Or would he just gloat in secret? Shit, there were times when the whole thing made him feel like some kind of pervert. Like a voyeur always peering in from the outside.

25

Bill's decision to commit the company to the construction of a drill ship and support vessels was the first time there had ever been an open split in the Venture board. Lee Travis was in Argentina, desperately trying to salvage a foundering cattle business, and couldn't make the meeting, but Ted Reid, the second Travis director, pointedly abstained from the vote. Adrian Strickland voted against it, leaving the affirmative votes to be cast by the in-house directors, Bill, Dave Wilson, Gavin Anderson, and a very reluctant Steve Miller. It was obvious that if Miller had had any real choice in the matter he would have voted against the project. But as a salaried and very recent employee of the company, he was not in a position to go against Bill's wishes.

The outflow of significant dollars began almost immediately. Dr. Axelson, the Swedish marine engineer, whom Wilson had signed up in October after a worldwide search that took considerably longer than the allotted two weeks, knew of an ancient World War II Liberty ship. About the only thing that could be said in its favour was that it was the right size for the conversion.

In the course of his career, Bill had signed a number of multi-million dollar cheques. But none had ever given him as much pause as the one for $5-million that purchased the vessel from a consortium of overjoyed Greeks. He was taking Venture into uncharted waters in every sense of the word.

"God damn it, Lee, I didn't fly all the way down here to be called on the carpet like a schoolboy!" Bill's face was tight with barely controlled fury.

This time, however, Lee refused to be his usual conciliatory self. "You've been acting like a schoolboy, Bill. Ordering the construction of a drill ship and support-vessels without the full backing of your board."

"The board passed a resolution approving the project."

"True. But Ted abstained, and Adrian voted against it."

Bill waved a dismissive hand at the mention of Strickland's name.

"I know what you think of Adrian," said Lee. "But that doesn't change the fact that he's a member of your board. Ted's abstention meant that I also was opposed. You must have known that."

"You didn't bother to attend the meeting," Bill countered.

The thrust hit home. "Things were critical in Argentina right about then, and it was impossible for me to leave," Lee replied somewhat lamely. "But why all this sudden mad scramble? You've been signing contracts all over the goddamned world and taking out bank loans that could bring the company to its knees."

"Time." Bill was back on firmer ground. "We can't afford to lose a single day if we want to be on location next summer. We couldn't have done it at all if our consultant hadn't found that old Liberty cargo ship in Brooklyn."

"You've really got it bad for the Arctic, Bill. How come?"

"Because it's our best chance of finding something really big — big on a world scale. And we'd be the first. Globe hasn't found anything yet on its permits — just little pockets of gas that don't amount to a damn."

"I see." Lee was studying him thoughtfully. "And in order to be first, you're willing to risk everything we've built up?"

The oblique reference to his own personal ambitions didn't escape Bill, but he chose to ignore it. "The company's not at risk. We can make money, good money, by charging our partners for the use of the drill ship. Globe shows a handsome operating profit every year by doing that."

"Maybe. But Globe has partners and we don't."

"We're working on that."

"Without success so far," Lee pointed out, but in a milder tone. The prospect of eventually turning a profit had a calming effect.

"Maybe the government would like to become our partner," he joked as he walked Bill back to the reception area.

"We don't want them," Bill replied tersely. "Even crime wouldn't pay if those clods ran it!"

The two associates parted amicably, but each was aware that this time the rift between them had only been papered over.

One place where the drill ship project was greeted with unqualified enthusiasm was Ottawa. Harold Trotter's pencil sharpener whirred as he congratulated Bill both on the decision and the progress that had been made to date.

"I wish some of my shareholders felt the same way," Bill said. In the latest round of bureaucratic musical chairs, Trotter had been shifted from FIRA, promoted to the rank of assistant deputy minister, and placed in charge of the oil and gas division of the energy department. At first Bill had been uneasy over the new appointment, but Trotter treated Bill like an old and valued friend and gave no sign of bearing any grudge over the way Bill had gone over his head to nail down the Hampton deal.

"You mean Alton Grant, I assume?" Trotter inspected the point of a pencil, decided it couldn't justify another sharpening, and laid it on the table. "He does seem a trifle upset."

"He just wants to get his name in the papers," Bill snarled. The sudden emergence of Alton Grant as a dissident shareholder had been an unexpected and potentially dangerous development. When the first interview with Grant, in which he deplored the diversion of Venture's revenues into the expensive Arctic quest, had appeared in the *Clarion*, Bill had called the self-styled "industry spokesman" on the phone and tried to kid him out of it.

"I'm sorry it has to be you, Bill, because I have the highest regard for your ability." Grant was unctuous. "However, I cannot stand idly by and watch that splendid company go down the drain."

"Hell, Alton, you've only got a thousand shares. It doesn't mean one damn thing to you personally."

"I have a duty to all the small shareholders and, yes, to the entire country, to do what I can to prevent you from destroying Venture. It's a national asset."

With that, Bill knew there was no reasoning with the pompous old fart. He was hot on the publicity trail, and there would be no stopping him.

"This might be an appropriate time to issue a joint press release," Trotter was saying. "We could announce that construction is proceeding on schedule. That's an accurate statement, isn't it?" He smiled when Bill nodded confirmation and continued, "And there could be a statement by the department that the new addition to the drill ship fleet will speed the development of our frontier resources. We can both use some good press about now."

"Good idea," Bill approved, delighted to be able to accommodate the government so easily. The significance of Trotter's request was not lost on him; it seemed Ottawa needed a success in the Arctic as badly as he did.

Hilary confirmed his impression when he saw her that night. "Venture is the toast of the department," she told him. "The government's been getting so much flak over the energy program that they desperately need something positive, and they're banking on you. The Globe operation has lost a lot of its glamour because they just can't seem to find anything."

"I'm not sure I care for being under the gun like that. I warned Trotter this afternoon that the chances of making a major discovery this early in the game are slim to the point of non-existence." Bill swallowed some red wine and let his gaze roam around the small, intimate restaurant. It was in the eastern outskirts of Hull, and the conversation at the other tables was in rapid-fire French. "How are things going with your career, Hilary? With Trotter in charge it should take off like a rocket."

"It's done just the opposite, as a matter of fact." She put down her fork and looked at him with a troubled expression. "There was an opening I was in line for — director general of the gas division — and I didn't get it. I know I did well in the competition, and I have all the right qualifications, but it went to someone else."

"A man?"

"As it happens, yes. But that's not the answer. The civil service bends over backward not to discriminate against women. It's something else ..."

Her troubled and preoccupied mood lasted throughout the meal, and Bill knew it would be a mistake to suggest they go to his hotel. As he was helping her into her coat, someone called her name. Two of her co-workers from the department, out for a night on the town with some lobbyists from the coal industry, were heading for the upstairs bar. Hilary introduced them to Bill, and he winced as they called him "sir."

"You look awfully glum. What's the matter?" asked Hilary as they settled themselves in the rear seat of the cab.

"Your friends must think you were having dinner with your father. Did you hear what they called me? 'Sir,' for Chrissake!"

She looked at him in astonishment. "They called you that because of who you are. They're in awe of the famous Bill Crawford — I don't think you realize how well known you really are." She put a hand on his sleeve. "This age business really bugs you, doesn't it? It shouldn't. I'm thirty-four and I look it. I hope I'll look the same ten years from now, but I do look every minute of my age. You don't. You look about forty. Honestly, you do."

"I'm glad you said that. It helps." Bill held her close and whispered. "Look, if your career is bogged down, why don't you pack it in and marry me?"

"You're serious, aren't you?"

"I have never been more serious about anything in my life."

"We have each other, Bill. We don't need marriage. But I do need my career."

Hilary gave herself a week's cooling-off period before seeking an interview with Trotter.

"What can I do for you, Hilary?" He was at his preppie best — button-down shirt, striped tie, scrubbed face glowing with goodwill.

"You can tell me why Jacques got the promotion instead of me. We both know I rated higher than he did in the competition, and I've got just as much seniority. And," she added warningly when he opened his mouth to speak, "don't give me the francophone routine. The department is notorious for being top-heavy with francophones in senior positions, so there was no need to appoint another one."

He leaned back in his chair and stared at her without speaking. When she could no longer endure the silence, Hilary leaned forward and gripped the edge of his desk. "It's my career, Harold. If there's no future for me here, I'm entitled to know why."

"It's called fraternizing with the enemy. Your relationship with Bill Crawford has caused everyone a great deal of concern."

"Enemy?" she expostulated. "Bill Crawford's not the enemy!"

"In some ways he is. Think about it for a minute. There is always a suspicion — and suspicion is all it takes — that you might, accidentally or otherwise, pass on some confidential information, or that your relationship might influence a department decision affecting his company. A director general is in a position to make such decisions."

"Dear God, does that mean I'm finished here?"

"If you persist in maintaining your, ah ... friendship with Crawford, I'm afraid that's just what it means."

"And if I ... terminate this relationship? What then?"

"I am sure you could look forward to a rewarding career in government service," he replied blandly.

"Level with me, Harold. No black marks?"

"No black marks."

"Can I have a few days to think this through?"

"Of course. Need I say that I hope you will decide in favour of your career?"

Walking down the corridor, Hilary heard the buzz of the sharpener biting into a new pencil.

The bow of the dry-docked freighter, bristling with metal supports for the new outer shell it would be fitted with, loomed over the fleet of shrimp boats tied up at the jetty. The air was redolent with the smell of fish, and the leaden sky was just beginning to spit rain as Bill got out of the car. He walked around the hood to shake hands with Dr. Axelson, who immediately led the way through a maze of crates and machinery covered with tarpaulins. They climbed a metal staircase, its corrugated steps slick with grease, until they reached the top of the dock. The ship was spread out below them like a patient on the operating table: gaping holes had been cut into its deck; cables and hoses snaked everywhere. Axelson ducked into a small shed and returned with two hard hats. "The problem's at the stern," he said tersely and led the way down a steel gangway to the dock.

Hard-hatted workers swarmed over the ship, which resounded with the chatter of jackhammers and, up in the bow, the racketing roar of riveting machines. An overhead crane reached down to pluck a pile of scabrous-looking plates from the aft deck. Axelson looked up at them with a jaundiced eye. "There's your trouble. When we opened her up, we found she was just about rusted through."

"Couldn't this have been discovered during the pre-sale inspection?"

"Aye. It could have been. If we had put her in dry dock and taken her apart seam by seam. You will recall there was no time for that?" The bright blue eyes glared defiantly at Bill.

"I realize that. Don't think I'm blaming you in any way. The question is, can it be fixed; and if so, how long will it take?"

"The answer to the first is yes. We can replace the old plates so that she'll be better than the day she was launched. As for how long it will take ..." He shrugged. "Who the hell knows? We're working three shifts already, so there's not much to be done in that direction. It all depends on how fast the new plates get here. A month — maybe less."

Bill grimaced. Delays and set-backs were a normal part of any new project, but the Arctic program was having more than its share. First the hydrate problem that had made it impossible to complete the Inukshuk well in one season, and now this. Still, there was nothing for it but to soldier on.

"I wouldn't like to have word of this get around," he said.

"Are you daft, mon?" After years of working around shifts and dockyards, the Swede spoke English like a phony ersatz Scottish engineer. "You're not dealing with one of your oil wells out in the ass end of nowhere. This is Galveston, and these men live ashore and hit the bars every night. Everybody on the waterfront already knows that her stern section is rotten."

Bill stayed around the dockyard long enough to have an early supper with Axelson and *Polarex*'s newly hired drilling superintendent, then drove himself back to his motel. The road hugged the coastline of the Gulf, and his headlights picked out small wavelets lapping over the rocks as he followed its curves. The lights of jack-up rigs and production platforms sparkled like fallen stars out on the water. He pulled into a gravelled lookout point and got out to breathe the pungent odour of crude oil, to him the most enticing perfume in the world.

It was January, and even this far south there was a damp chill in the air that discouraged standing around for very long. He got back into the car and drove to the motel where the usual handful of messages awaited him. He flipped through them quickly, resigned to spending the next hour on the phone. The message from Hilary was on the bottom — she wanted him to call her in Ottawa ASAP.

"When are you leaving there, Bill?" Hilary asked almost as soon as she came on the line.

"In the morning. Early. Why?" Bill asked half-jokingly. "Do you want me to stop by on my way?"

"Would you do that?" she asked eagerly. "I must talk with you."

Bill was momentarily nonplussed. Ottawa was not exactly en route between Galveston and Calgary. In fact, it would involve a detour of some twenty-five hundred miles. Still, she clearly wanted to see him. God, was she in some kind of trouble? Or could it possibly be that she was going to say yes to the proposal he had made in the taxi coming back from Hull?

"Of course," he found himself saying. "I'll see you tomorrow night. Your place, around seven. Okay?"

"Perfect. See you then." She hung up before he could say anything more.

"Where's Jason?" Bill was holding a Dinky Toy he had picked up at the airport gift shop. He had always brought them to Frank and ... Billy ... when he returned from his constant business trips. Along with Barbie Doll clothes for Debbie.

"He's with his father this week. They've gone to Disney World."

"You know, that's the first time you've mentioned your ex-husband. What's he like?"

"Richard? Charming. Everybody loves Richard. The only trouble is, he doesn't want the party to stop."

"What's he do?"

"He's an account executive at Pearce Levitt advertising agency in Toronto." She paused, then added, "Knowing the way you operate, I find it difficult to believe you didn't know that already."

"Just making conversation." Bill grinned, though his uneasiness grew. Hilary was really on edge about something.

She cleared her throat, something he had never heard her do before. "I feel badly, dragging you out of your way like this. But I couldn't say what I have to say over the phone." She paused to look directly into his eyes. "I'm not going to see you any more, Bill."

"What?" Bill almost gasped out loud with the hurtful shock of what she was saying.

"I said I can't see you again. I mean it."

Looking at her, Bill realized that she did mean it. Her tone, her whole attitude, told him there was nothing to be gained by arguing or protesting. "Are you going to tell me why?" he asked finally.

"I think you know."

"Your career?"

She nodded silently, and he went on, "You don't need it. You could marry me."

"Yes. I could. Or you could give up Venture Oils, give up your dream of Arctic oil, move to Ottawa and be my faithful helpmate while I carve out my career in the civil service."

"Bitterness doesn't become you, Hilary." He reached for her hand. "If I were prepared to do exactly as you say, would you marry me?"

Tears glistened on her long eyelashes. "It wouldn't work. I'd just be Mrs. Bill Crawford, no matter what. You, of all people, should understand."

"Oh, I understand, all right," he replied bleakly. "It's just that I look at life without you and I don't like what I see."

26

The item was on the third page of the financial section. Frontenac Mines and the Minalta Lumber Corporation announced that, by mutual consent, negotiations that would have led to Frontenac's acquiring all the outstanding stock of the lumber company had been terminated. Ken felt like someone who had just survived a near miss by lightning. If the deal, about which he had known nothing, had gone through, he would have lost his prime vehicle for the raid on Venture. Frontenac would have been too busy digesting the giant lumber firm to even think of taking on Bill Crawford. And for all he knew they could be zeroing in on another takeover target this very minute.

All Ken's research had failed to turn up another Canadian company as uniquely suited for the task as Frontenac, with its vast surplus of cash. The pressure on Alec Davies and his board to find a home for all those dollars must be mounting almost daily. It had to be nearly two years since the two hundred million had been repatriated from South America, and that kind of cash just sitting on the books tends to make shareholders wonder whether they're getting the biggest bang for their buck. With any imagination a person should be able to figure out a way to take over Frontenac itself by using its own hoard of cash as a lever. A smile of pure enjoyment played over Ken's face as he toyed with the idea for a few minutes before putting it aside. He had other plans for the mining company. Plans that meant he had to crank up Stan Winters once again, and that would take a little doing the second time around.

It was Thursday, one of the days when Stan went to his health club for a workout and massage after the market closed. He was doing his best to convert a sceptical Ken to the rewards of keeping fit. Ken had gone so far as to rent a locker and buy some gym clothes, but his attendance record was lamentably spotty. Today, however, he would be the very model of a fitness freak.

The market didn't close until two o'clock Vancouver time, and by then the noon-hour hordes had departed, so they had the facilities virtually to themselves. A T-shirted instructor took Stan through his regular routine, while Ken did the exercises that appealed to him. Since he was, if anything, slightly underweight, the sit-ups and push-ups were child's play to him, a matter of chagrin to his more portly partner. After that, he slowly pedalled a stationary bicycle to nowhere, while Stan pounded out his mandatory two miles on the track. Then they showered and repaired to the steam room, which, as Ken had banked on, was deserted at this time of the day.

Stan was perspiring profusely before the first bead of sweat appeared on Ken's brow. He patted it with a towel and said, "I think the egg is ready to hatch, Stan."

"Good, let's hear it. I'm overdue for a little excitement."

"It'll be exciting, all right. It's Venture."

"What is it with that company, Ken? You can't seem to leave it alone."

"It's the richest prize in Canada, that's all."

By the time they stretched out on the massage tables, Ken had almost convinced his partner that his new scheme could work. The masseurs had the robot-like aloofness of their kind, but Ken and Stan were careful not to mention names as they continued their discussion.

As usual, Ken found himself wanting to get off the table almost as soon as he got on. Why people willingly subjected themselves to this torture was beyond him. "This time" — he grunted as steely fingers squeezed a muscle in his thigh — "our friend will be up front and out in the open. As soon as he has accumulated a respectable block of shares, he will make contact with the target and request a seat on the board. He will disavow — ouch, take it easy — any ambitions to take over control and will want a seat on the board merely to keep an eye on his investment. Since the target believes his position is impregnable, he will probably buy that. I have a strong hunch that they will give him a seat — he would bring the kind of prestige they badly need right now. And if he also dangles the promise of funding some joint exploration deals, they'll welcome him with open arms. Jesus Christ!" The masseur was doing his best to separate Ken's head from the rest of his body.

"So far, so good." Stan purred with pleasure while his masseur tugged at his fingers, making the knuckles pop. "But how do we persuade our friend to make a second attempt? He didn't enjoy what happened the last time."

"Yeah. But now we can guarantee him no loss of face and a good shot at the ultimate prize." The masseur was pummelling Ken's back, which meant his ordeal was almost over.

"How?"

"I'll tell you on the way back to the office." Ken waited until his semi-erection subsided, then climbed thankfully off the table.

"I hired on to run an oil company, Bill." Steve Miller had followed Bill to his office after the weekly management meeting adjourned. "And right now, Venture is not an oil company. It's just a cash cow that's being milked to finance the Arctic project."

"I know it's not easy, Steve." Next year's budget had been the subject of the meeting. The unforeseen repairs to the ship and a new wage settlement at the Victoria shipyard meant there would be an overrun of some $10-million in the drill ship program. The banks, disturbed by the delays and overruns, had refused to commit themselves any

496 / JOHN BALLEM

further, so the money had to come from Steve's budget for conventional exploration. Since it had already been slashed to the bone, the latest reduction meant that Venture would only carry out work that was absolutely necessary to maintain its inventory of land. It was strictly a caretaker operation, and Bill wasn't surprised that his dynamic new president chafed under it.

"It'll straighten itself out once we get some partners." Bill was painfully aware that his words lacked conviction.

"Come off it, Bill. Maybe you can sell that line to the outside directors, but I know what's going on out there. Money's tight everywhere, what with both the federal and provincial governments siphoning off revenues like there's no tomorrow. And the companies who still have funds will spend them right here in Alberta where they can start earning a return almost as soon as they make a discovery. Nobody's going to put up great chunks of cash for a project that won't generate a dime's worth of revenue for ten or fifteen years."

Steve paused to light a cigarette; he had taken up smoking again after having kicked the habit for almost two years. "Do you ever stop to think what a fantastic company Venture would be if it didn't have that damn Arctic millstone around its neck? That's the kind of company I thought I was signing on with."

It would be a sweet company all right, but it would have lost its chance of great-ness. Bill kept the thought to himself; if he started talking about greatness in their present predicament, Steve would call for the little men with the straitjacket. So he merely shrugged and said, "What can I tell you, Steve? We're just going to have to ride it out."

"It's worse than it ever was at Hampton. And I figured that all that crap about not participating in joint operations was behind me. Hell, I haven't dared to set foot in the Pete Club for weeks!"

In the middle of Steve's little outburst, Bill's knee pressed the button on the side of his desk that told Lisa he wanted to be interrupted. She immediately buzzed through on the intercom to inform him that Mr. Martin and Mr. Goulder were waiting to discuss the annual meeting with him.

"The president looks a trifle upset," Chester said as the door closed behind Steve Miller.

Bill sighed. "He has a right to be. I had to cut the last ounce of flesh from his exploration budget."

"That we did not need," Jim Goulder grunted as he bent over to unlock his brief-case. "Not with the annual meeting of the shareholders coming up in two weeks."

"How is Dave Wilson taking it?" asked Martin. "It's his department, after all."

"He doesn't like it. But he'll go along. He knows that the Arctic has to have a priority at this point in time."

"He's a different breed of cat from Miller," observed Chester. "Steve is a professional manager, and he believes in decision making the way they teach it at the charm schools — critical-path analysis, cost-benefit studies, the whole schmear."

"He was bitching to one of my people the other day about his stock option," Jim said. "How it had gone to rat-shit with the drop in the price of the shares."

"He hasn't said anything to me." Bill frowned. "He's right, though. His option price is a fair bit above the current market. Maybe I can persuade the board to adjust his price if the market doesn't improve."

"For God's sake, don't do anything until after the annual meeting," implored Chester.

"I won't," Bill promised. He turned to Goulder. "Speaking of the meeting, do we give Frontenac a seat on the board?"

"I recommend that we do. They own two hundred thousand voting shares." The broker gave an admiring shake of his head. "Lovely how they did that — buying on the market without driving the price up. Nominee accounts all over the place and never too big a slice — staying on the bid side and waiting for the orders to fill. And all within the last three weeks. Masterly." Jim paused once more, in tribute to this feat of market generalship, before continuing. "A block that size normally entitles the holder to representation on the board if he wants it; and it's my personal view that having an outfit like Frontenac Mines lined up with us would do a lot for our image. Which," he added ironically, "could stand a little touching up right about now."

Three days earlier, Bill had received a phone call from Alec Davies, the chairman of Frontenac Mines Ltd. Bill had never met Davies but knew him by reputation as an urbane and successful scion of a mining dynasty. Davies courteously explained that Frontenac had accumulated a block of shares, "purely for investment purposes," and would like one seat on the board just to keep an eye on its investment. There was nothing unusual in Frontenac's purchase; companies finding themselves with surplus cash frequently went onto the stock market in hopes of making a capital gain.

Davies had also mentioned that Frontenac might well be interested in participating in some exploration programs with Venture. Could it be that Bill had found his first partner in the Arctic?

"What about you, Ches? What do you think?" asked Bill after a thoughtful silence.

"I'm inclined to agree with Jim," the lawyer replied slowly. "Alec Davies is a bona fide pillar of the eastern establishment, and having him on board would give us credibility in those quarters — if that's what we want. I like the idea of having Davies on the board for another reason — we can keep an eye on what, if anything, he's up to. It's a lot easier to deal with a guy who's sitting across the table from you than someone on the outside plotting God knows what."

"I've been thinking along the same lines," said Bill. "That aspect has a lot of appeal to me."

"The problem is," the lawyer went on, "the company's bylaws provide for a maximum of seven directors, and we already have a full slate."

"Can't that be changed?" asked Bill.

"It can. But not at the upcoming annual meeting. We'd have to give notice of the proposed change, and there's not enough time for that. We can always call a special shareholders' meeting for a later date and pass the necessary resolution then."

"If there's one thing we don't need, it's another shareholders' meeting," Bill muttered. "Look, here's how we can do it — I know Gavin would really like to get off the board. He wants to travel and generally do his own thing. Suppose he doesn't stand for re-election, and we nominate Davies in his place. Anything wrong with that?"

"No problem there," the lawyer assured him. "The proxy statement clearly states that if any of the nominees are unable or unwilling to run, the proxy holders are free to vote for other candidates."

"Good." Bill got to his feet to end the conference. "I'll arrange to meet Davies personally and see if I think he'll fit in."

With the end of the long business day, images of Hilary came flooding back unchecked. It was far worse than anything he had gone through with Margo. That had been infatuation coupled with a sharp sense of betrayal. This was the sure knowledge that he had found the woman he wanted to share the rest of his life with, and she had rejected him. Forever. There was a woman who worked in the building who, from the back, looked a bit like Hilary. The first time he had seen that mane of light-brown hair and that erect walk he had rushed to catch the same elevator. The woman was attractive, she even had a touch of Hilary's look of distinction, but she wasn't Hilary. Was he doomed to feel this wrenching sense of loss every time he saw something in a woman that reminded him of Hilary?

Work was the only thing that kept the ever-present dull ache within bounds. He found himself almost embracing the controversy that was building up over his Arctic program. Coping with its problems and fending off its growing army of detractors provided at least a temporary escape from the bleak desolation of his thoughts.

Corporate annual meetings are usually sedate, well-ordered affairs with the players following a script that sees resolutions proposed, seconded, and approved with well-greased efficiency. The chairman then delivers a "state-of-the-union" report and answers a few soft questions carefully planted in the audience. Afterward, the docile shareholders are served light refreshments and afforded an opportunity to rub elbows with the top brass.

The television cameras were the first indication that this annual meeting was not going to follow the usual pattern. Newspapers routinely cover important annual meetings, but the electronic medium totally ignores them unless there's a chance that something dramatic and newsworthy will happen. Venture had booked the same conference hall in the Convention Centre that it always used for its annual meetings, but it couldn't begin to handle the overflow crowd. The centre's maintenance staff was hastily pushing back folded partitions to double its size. Alton Grant must have arrived early; he was ensconced in the middle of the first row of seats.

"We sure drew flies this morning," Dave Wilson whistled under his breath as he filed in with the other directors. His laconic attitude steadied Bill as he mounted the raised platform and called the meeting to order. There was an air of suppressed tension while the formalities were dealt with — the minutes of the last meeting were approved; the reports of the auditors and scrutineers were received. Bill listened with grim satisfaction as the scrutineer, a female clerk from Warranty Trust, reported that there were 1,976,076 voting shares present in person or by proxy. He had the right to vote no less than three-quarters of those shares.

The first ripple of excitement came with the election of the directors. A senior employee read off a list of six names in alphabetical order: William Crawford, Stephen Miller, Theodore Reid, Adrian Strickland, Lee Travis, and David Wilson. Those who checked their copies of the annual report saw that it was identical to the previous board, with the exception of Gavin Anderson. That was understandable; the former president was easing himself into retirement. Bill called for nominations from the floor, and another employee shareholder stood up and nominated Alexander Davies. Now that was interesting, and it also explained the presence of the mining magnate at the meeting. His nomination was seconded, and Bill asked if there were any more.

There was a stir in the back of the room and a shareholder stood up and nominated Alton Grant. It was immediately seconded. Bill ruled that there would be a secret vote since they now had more candidates than vacancies. The result was a foregone conclusion; the six existing directors and Alec Davies were declared elected. Alton Grant smiled enigmatically from his seat in the front row.

When the business part of the meeting was finished, Bill called on Steve Miller for a report on the company's operations. It was superbly done and illustrated with the appropriate graphs and charts. When it was over, Alton Grant was on his feet with a question. "Can you tell me, Mr. President, what is the latest projection of the company's cash flow for the next fiscal year?"

"I think I'll defer to the chairman for that one," Steve replied.

Folding his arms across his chest, Grant said, "I don't care who handles it, so long as I get a straight answer."

Bill walked over to the microphone. "It's a moving target, Mr. Grant. At this precise moment, it's negative. But you must remember that's only a snapshot of the situation at this particular moment in time. We fully expect the situation to correct itself when we start generating revenues from our drilling operations."

Grant pounced. "Exactly how much is this negative cash flow?"

A gasp went up when Bill reluctantly admitted, "Well, it's in the order of $70-million." His plea to bear in mind that it was only a temporary situation did little to cushion the shock.

Before the ripples caused by Bill's sensational disclosure had fully subsided, a shareholder rose to ask the annual cost to the company of operating a private jet. The TV cameras started to roll as he spoke. Bill, who had prepared himself to answer every conceivable question about the company's exploration and production programs, had to admit he didn't know. "But," he added as he saw a member of the accounting department hurrying up to the platform, "It looks as if I'll have the answer in just a minute.

"I'm told it's just under $1-million. And full value for the money, I might add. It allows your executives to make the best use of their time, instead of cooling their heels sitting around airport terminals."

A new questioner, a self-assured young man with a mop of permed hair, was at one of the floor microphones. "Is it not true, sir, that you use the aircraft to visit a lady friend in Ottawa?"

"That is not —" Bill began hotly, then broke off as someone handed him a hastily scrawled note from Martin. "Ask him if he's a shareholder," it read.

"Are you a shareholder, sir?"

"Yes, I am. My name is Herbert Sollis, and I am the registered owner of five shares of voting stock. Would you like me to repeat the question, sir?"

"No, I would not. It's no one's business who I visit, or where!"

The young man looked as if he intended to pursue the matter further, then shrugged as if to say no further comment was necessary and sat down.

Somebody took Bill off the hook by asking a straightforward question about the Arctic, which he fielded neatly, and the meeting was over.

"Damage control. Damage control. Report to the bridge," Dave Wilson whispered to Chester Martin as they rose from their seats.

27

The fiasco that the Venture annual meeting had turned into exceeded Ken's fondest hopes. As the architect of the debacle, he allowed himself a small smile of satisfaction while he counted up the gains: Crawford's reputation had suffered two telling blows from both the large projected loss in net revenues and the scandal over the corporate jet. Even better, Ken now had his own Trojan horse on Venture's board in the person of Stan's lifelong friend, Alec Davies.

"Just had a long chat with Davies," Stan Winters announced from the doorway of Ken's office. "He was calling from his home," he continued as he walked in and took a seat. The usual roles of chairman and junior associate had been reversed for the "Venture caper," which Stan couldn't resist calling it. It was Ken's play — Stan was nothing more than his intermediary. That was okay with Stan; he hadn't had this much fun since the Gold Creek Mines proxy fight when he had outsmarted the Montreal "Jewish Mafia." He snapped out of his musings when he realized Ken was waiting for him to say something more.

"Alec and his wife are attending some mining conference in Houston and, get this, Lee Travis has invited them to spend a weekend with him at his shooting preserve in north Texas. The chemistry between those two is good. Very good."

"They're from the same class," Ken said.

"I daresay you're right. Anyway, they hit it off from the start. When the annual meeting was over, Alec says he made some crack that being elected a director was like being put in command of the *Titanic* after it hit the iceberg, and Lee said, 'I know what you mean.' How about that?"

"All part of the game plan. If he manages to convert Lee to our side, we're halfway home."

Stan glanced at his watch. "It's late. I'm going to pop in at the club for a quick one. Join me?"

"I'll pass this time, Stan. I've got a date for dinner."

"Margo Jones?" Ken nodded, and Stan went on, "I heard she was back out here. The boys were talking about it at lunch. She's making a real go of that newsletter of hers." Not for the first time, Stan wondered if there was any connection between Ken's affair with Margo and the raid on Bill Crawford's company. Good God, was it possible that she was the brains behind the caper?

After the chairman had gone, Ken continued to sit behind the desk, brooding over his next move. He was alone; all the others on the floor had gone home. He suddenly found himself wondering if his natural father — that unfeeling son of a bitch — was sitting late at his desk across the mountains in Calgary, trying to come up with some way to carry on with the Arctic project without tearing his company apart. Ken's nightline rang. It was Margo; she had finished her last interview and was back at her hotel.

"I know who set you up," said Ken.

"What?" Margo sat upright in bed, the sheet sliding off her slim upper torso.

"I said I know who set you up," Ken repeated. "On the fake Ferguson story."

"Who was it?"

"Debbie Crawford."

"Oh, Jesus. Are you sure?"

"I'm sure."

"How did you find out?"

"Elementary, my dear Watson." His fingertip traced the indentation of her backbone. She was still sitting rigidly upright. "I figured the critical time period had to be the week immediately before the story came out. Everything had to be rush, rush, so there'd be no time for you to run the usual checks. Right?"

"Makes sense. I should have done them anyway, of course."

"Hindsight. While I can't trace exactly how and when she left Calgary, I'm satisfied she was not there during the crucial week. Unexpectedly not there."

"How do you know?"

"An annual social rite takes place on the Tuesday of that week in Calgary. A thundering great barbecue brunch at some oilman's ranch. One of those affairs that everybody who's anybody attends — you know the scene. Anyway, Debbie had accepted an invitation to last summer's festivities but didn't show up. Her hostess is still annoyed with her, I'm told."

"She could have been sick."

"She could have been. However, it seems that at the very same hour when she should have been putting on a Western costume to attend the high-society cookout, she was in the Toronto head office of Atlantic Trust asking to see the share register of Berkley Petroleums. Not conclusive in a court of law, perhaps, but highly suggestive, don't you agree?"

"You mean she just marched in and asked to see it?"

"Not quite. It seems the lady wore a disguise. The account officer, a very efficient woman by the name of Mrs. Turner, remembers her very well. Mrs. Turner didn't care for her high-handed attitude, and she remembers thinking that the girl could have made herself much more attractive if she had taken the least trouble with her grooming. When she was shown a newspaper photo of Debbie with a dark wig dubbed in, she said she was ninety per cent certain it was one and the same."

"You didn't carry out this investigation personally, did you? It doesn't sound like you did."

"It was all done through contacts and agents. Are you convinced?"

"I think so. Yes ... yes, I am. It's funny, I didn't even think of the Crawfords beyond Bill, and since I was positive he would never pull a stunt like that, I just put them out of my mind. As suspects, I mean."

"What do you intend to do about it?"

"Oh, God, I don't know. Probably nothing."

"Nothing?"

"I just don't know. I'm not sure I needed this right now; I feel pretty good about my life." She put her feet on the carpeted floor and stood up. "I'm going to take a hot bath. Help yourself to a Perrier."

Ken was astonished by her reaction. He had been counting on Margo to turn into an avenging fury, bent on revenge at any cost. If she had come on like he had expected, it had been his plan to drop a few hints about the campaign to bring the Crawford empire tumbling down. From there, it should have been an easy step to convert her to the cause. What an ally she would have been!

Margo opened the door and stepped out of the bathroom, wrapped in a silk peignoir and enveloped in a mist of steam.

"You've decided not to do anything. I can tell from the look on your face," said Ken.

"Right. I would raise a hell of a stink if I thought it would help reinstate me as a journalist. That, next to the success of *Update*, is what I want most in this world. But exposing her wouldn't make me look any less of a fool."

On the way back to his condo, Ken analysed how this new development would affect his relationship with Margo. She had said once that they were a bonus to each other, an unexpected dividend from life. That's how he'd play it; no reason why they shouldn't go on enjoying each other. And even if she wasn't his ally, she was an invaluable source of information.

That disposed of, his thoughts swung eagerly back to Venture Oils. The second series of retractable preferreds held by Hampton Resources were due to be put next week. Street gossip had it that Crawford had failed in his attempt to persuade Hampton to defer tendering the $10-million worth of shares for repurchase by Venture. Bill Crawford was a certified miracle worker, and it would be fascinating to see how he would wriggle out of this straitjacket. Ken was pretty sure he would find a way to bring it off, but it really didn't matter, the net was inexorably closing around the oilman, shutting down his options one by one.

A phone call on the following day from Alec Davies to Stan Winters brought advance news of how Bill was going to raise the ten million. Over Steve Miller's furious objections, he had arranged for Venture to sell one of its best oil-producing properties to raise the necessary cash. Davies, in keeping with the overall strategy of securing Crawford's confidence, had supported the sale in a telephone poll of the directors. "But," he told Stan, "it's come down to open warfare between Miller and Crawford."

Alton Grant took up the hue and cry as soon as the sale became public knowledge. Trumpeting that Crawford was "selling off the company piece by piece to keep his Arctic folly afloat," he immediately convened a full-scale press conference. By now, the long-standing romance between Bill and the press had definitely soured. Convinced that their erstwhile golden boy had finally lost his touch, they turned on him savagely, accusing him of everything from faulty business judgment to indulging a macho ego trip.

While the pressure on Bill steadily intensified, Ken spent long hours alone in the semi-dark of his living room, endlessly reviewing and reassembling the pieces of the Venture puzzle. He realized that the moment of decision was rapidly approaching — faster than he had ever thought possible. In a way, events were forcing his hand just as surely as they were closing in on Crawford. As he analyzed and tested every move, the decision gradually took shape: if Alec Davies returned with a favourable report from his visit with Lee Travis, it would be time to press the "fire" button.

28

"Debbie? This is Margo Jones."

"What do you want?" Debbie's voice bristled with hostility while her heart thumped suffocatingly in her chest. Had Margo finally discovered who was responsible for her downfall?

"I would like to do an interview with you for *Update*. There's a great deal of interest in what you've accomplished with Pinnacle."

Debbie gave a derisive snort of laughter. "I know you've got more nerve than the law allows, Margo, but this is the limit. How can you possibly think I'd grant you an interview after what you did to my father?" Debbie's grip on the telephone receiver relaxed as she realized her secret was still safe.

"I understand why you feel that way. But you have no cause to worry. As you must know, all the items in *Update* are brief and factual. I just want to get your views, in the form of direct personal quotes, on a number of the more pressing issues facing the industry. You're obviously going to be a force in the industry, and I think you owe it to the public — and yourself — to make your views known."

Debbie's relief over not having been found out was making her deliciously reckless. "And if I don't give you the interview, I suppose you'll feel free to print whatever you damn well please?"

"That's not the way *Update* operates." Margo sounded miffed by the suggestion. "I think it really would be in your best interest to see me."

"Call me back in half an hour and I'll let you know."

Debbie replaced the receiver, stared at it for a moment, then touched number one on her memory phone. Lisa told her that her father was in a meeting, but she'd be happy to get him out if Debbie thought it was important enough.

"Would you mind? I hate to disturb him, but I really must speak with him."

"As far as I'm concerned, there's no reason why you shouldn't see her," Bill said after Debbie told him about Margo's request. "In fact, if she asked me for an interview, I'd do it."

"That's super, Debbie," Margo enthused when Debbie said she would see her. "I'll be there at nine-thirty sharp."

"Very nice." Margo glanced approvingly around Debbie's corner office. "You realize, I'm sure, that you are the first woman to make it — really make it — in the oil industry? Oh, I know there are female vice-presidents of some big public companies, but they're nothing more than tokens. You're the only one who has her own company."

"I had some advantages," demurred Debbie. Margo was looking well, an air of assurance had replaced that journalist-on-the-make attitude.

"Granted. But at least you did something with them." Margo fished a notebook from her bag and flipped it open. "I'll make notes just to make sure I have everything down correctly, so there won't be any danger of your being misquoted."

That brought a lifted eyebrow from Debbie, but Margo appeared not to notice. She began asking questions, incisive, demanding questions that permitted no easy, pat answers. Debbie found herself enjoying the challenge, sensing that her own understanding of the crucial issues was being sharpened. Margo was a perceptive outsider, on the whole sympathetic to the industry, but fully aware of the deep distrust with which the general public viewed it. Debbie was almost sorry when Margo signalled the interview was over by closing her notebook.

"Terrific. I could devote an entire issue to this one interview." Margo smiled, and Debbie was astonished to find herself smiling back.

"How you must have enjoyed it, Debbie," Margo went on as if she were discussing the weather. "I can just see you hugging yourself while my world crashed in pieces around my feet. You must have laughed yourself sick."

"What in the world are you talking about? Have you lost your flipping mind?" Debbie's bluster was betrayed by the crack in her voice. She was on her feet, her fair skin flushing furiously as she glared down at her visitor. "I suppose you've got a tape recorder somewhere, trying to trap me. Well, it's not going to work."

"There's no tape recorder. I just wanted you to know that I know. Somehow, it seems to make us a little bit more even."

"Just what is it I'm supposed to know?"

"Let's not play games, Debbie. You were the one who framed me with that bogus Ferguson story. I can place you at the head office of Atlantic Trust, asking to see the share register of Berkley Petroleums. In disguise, yet."

"What is it you want from me?" asked Debbie, adding for the benefit of any tape that might be running. "Not that I accept a word of this crap."

"Very little, actually. In fact, I'm almost grateful to you, in a perverse sort of way. If it weren't for my being turfed out of journalism, I never would have gotten involved with *Update*, and that paper means more to me than anything in my whole life." She suddenly glanced up at Debbie. "Your father knows nothing about this cute little prank of yours, I take it?"

Debbie started to shake her head, then said hastily. "There's nothing for him to know."

"I want to tell him. Everything. That's my price for letting the whole thing drop."

"What could you do, anyway?"

"Sue the ass off you, Debbie. You wouldn't want the whole world to know that

Debbie Crawford, the darling of the horse-show circuit and now the toast of the oil patch, is a sneaky, scheming little bitch, would you?"

"You have no way of knowing whether I tell him or not."

"Oh yes, I do. Tell him to expect a phone call from me in the next week. And you can also tell him from me that he should watch himself around Steve Miller. He's putting your father down every chance he gets."

"You continue to astonish me," said Bill as he neatly aligned his knife and fork on the empty plate. "That was a superb meal. One of the best I've had in months, in fact. Whenever did you learn to cook like that?"

"It's catered," Debbie informed him, and father and daughter looked at each other and shook with helpless laughter.

"It's wonderful to hear you laugh like that." Debbie lightly kissed the air above his head as she went to the kitchen to get the coffee. The strain of the past few months was beginning to exact its toll on even her father's resilient constitution. The faint lines around his eyes were etched a little deeper, and he seemed to have lost some of the smooth, coordinated vitality that had always been his personal trademark. She poured him a Remy-Martin and, when he protested, told him he was going to need it.

The cool, blue-grey eyes gazed at her appraisingly over the rim of the snifter as he waited for her to continue.

"I don't think you're going to like this very much." Debbie settled herself on the sofa, drawing her legs up beside her in a characteristic motion. "I'm responsible for that article that got Margo into trouble."

"Does she know?" Bill carefully lowered his untasted drink onto a coffee table already crowded with Debbie's collection of Haida carvings. Then he answered his own question. "Of course she does. That's why she wanted the interview."

"Exactly."

"Jesus!"

"It's not as bad as it seems. At least I don't think it is. She claims she won't do anything about it, so long as I 'fess up to you."

"Thank the good Lord for that." Bill cupped the balloon glass in his hands and took an appreciative sniff.

"You don't seem particularly surprised," she said when he said nothing more.

"I think I suspected something like this from the first. But I carefully avoided doing anything that might confirm those suspicions. I am a little surprised that Margo seems to be letting you off the hook, though. That's the last thing I would have expected from her."

"The way I read it, she's so turned on with this financial newsletter of hers' that she's not at all keen on digging up the past."

"That could explain it. Getting what you want out of life can mellow a person."

"Plus the fact that she's got a real soft spot for you." Debbie was almost giddy with relief over the way he was taking the whole thing. She really shouldn't have expected anything else — they had always had an affectionate tolerance for each other's foibles. God, what she wouldn't give to see her father relaxed and happy again. Damn that Hilary Marshall!

"Margo also told me to warn you about Steve Miller. But you already know he's got a knife buried up to the hilt in your back, don't you?"

Bill nodded grimly. "I'm going to have to do something about that fellow. It's not exactly the best time for the company to jettison a top executive, but ..." He let the sentence trail off in a shrug. "It started out as a perfectly honest difference of opinion; he thinks I'm sending Venture down the tube with the Arctic program ..."

"I've wondered about that myself," Debbie interjected quietly.

"You too, eh? Surely you understand that it's been my intention all along to return to the conventional oil scene as soon as we've had a good look at the Arctic. Once we do that, it won't take long to restore Venture's revenues back to where they should be."

"I thought that had to be your strategy. Still," Debbie hesitated, then added, "there's always the nagging doubt that by then there may not be much of Venture left to revive."

"That's what my detractors claim." Debbie was distressed to hear her father give a small sigh before he continued. "Recently I've begun to fear they may have a point." He lightly pounded the arm of his chair with his closed fist. "I've just got to find some outside investors. It all comes down to that."

Suddenly the phone began to ring, jarring them both out of their gloomy thoughts. "Late date?" asked Bill with a strained smile.

"Whoever it is, I'll get rid of him pronto." Debbie picked up the receiver. Her impatient scowl disappeared as she listened. "Yes. He's here. Just a second, Dave," she said and handed the instrument to Bill.

"I've just had a call from Galveston," Wilson began, and Bill braced himself for the worst. "The welders walked off the job tonight. With the ship almost finished, they figure it's a good time to try the old squeeze play."

Bill swore under his breath. Welders were the prima donnas of the construction trades. Over the years, he'd had some frustrating experiences with them in pipeline construction, but it hadn't occurred to him that they could play the same critical role in a shipyard. "What do they want?" he asked wearily.

"Bonuses for every weld over a specified minimum. Hot lunches to be supplied free on the job site. Triple time after the first two hours of overtime. Little goodies like that."

"The shipbuilder is just going to have to come to terms with them. Another delay will kill us."

"I don't think it's going to be quite that simple. The welders are trying to set a pattern for future contracts. The builder knows if he caves in this time, it'll be game over. I got the impression the other shipbuilding companies are leaning on our guy to hang tough."

"I'll fly down in the morning, Dave. I think you'd better come with me. Mind giving Tim a call?"

Hilary cleared away the breakfast dishes and poured herself a second cup of coffee before opening the morning paper. As always, she began by scanning the column on the front page that summarized the leading news stories. Her eyes widened when she came to the second-last item: "Wildcat Strike Hits Drill ship." The main story was carried on page three and was datelined Galveston. Everything seemed to be going so horribly wrong for Bill's Arctic dream. He would be in an impossible fix if *Polarex* wasn't ready for the upcoming drilling season. A sudden desperate longing to be with him swept through her, leaving her physically shaken.

Twice last week she had picked up the phone and started to dial his Calgary number, getting as far as the area code before hanging up. God, how she missed that man! And it was getting worse, not better. She had tried going out with other men but it hadn't worked — they came across as callow imitations of the real thing. She still winced every time she thought of how she had imperiously summoned him to Ottawa and informed him that it was all over between them. By now that hurt had probably turned into a relief that he hadn't become involved with a self-centred bitch who could think of nothing but her career.

And that career was rapidly going nowhere. Her work, which she had always thought would sustain her through anything, had become flat and boring. Helping to formulate the departmental decisions, a process that used to fill her with a rush of adrenalin, now seemed almost irrelevant. She began to live in fear that her inattention might lead her into making some glaring mistake that could ruin her career as effectively as continuing her relationship with Bill. Wouldn't that be an exquisite piece of irony?

Fortunately, her responsibilities did not include Venture Oils. Harold Trotter had assigned that sensitive situation to himself. Hilary knew her boss was in touch with either Bill or Dave Wilson almost daily, but he never discussed it with her. She sometimes wondered if Bill fully understood just how important his project was to the government. The hope of a gigantic discovery in the Arctic was about the only thing that was keeping their battered energy policy together. On the other hand, a spectacular screw-up, like Venture going broke, or the drill ship failing to get on location, might be enough to bring the government down. One thing was sure: Trotter's career would never survive it.

"Ready for 'spection, mommy." Jason stood in the doorway of his bedroom.

Hilary followed him into the room. The bed was made, untidily to be sure, but the sheets had been pulled up, and some attention had been made to smooth the spread over the pillows.

She threw Jason a mock salute. "A-OK, trooper."

He grinned up at her, and she gave him a quick hug and a pat on the bum. "We'd better hurry."

He nodded matter-of-factly and went to the closet to get his jacket. With more than a little trepidation and a vague feeling of guilt, Hilary had enrolled him in a government-subsidized daycare centre. Somewhat to her surprise and very much to her relief, he seemed to have no trouble fitting in. An extrovert he was not, but his quiet good humour attracted his own circle of friends. Each child was allowed to bring one favourite toy; as he did nearly every day, Jason chose the tow truck Bill had given him.

Damn you, Bill Crawford. Why did you have to come into my life and mess it up like this? Hilary cast a lingering look at the silent telephone as she followed her son out of the apartment.

29

"You look like you've been rode hard and put away wet." Dave gazed at Bill, who was slumped down in his seat, and shook his head. Leaning a hip against the liquor cabinet to steady himself as the Lear ran into a patch of rough air, Dave managed to pour without spilling a drop, and handed it to Bill. "Try some of Dr. Wilson's celebrated nerve tonic." He poured himself a stiff whisky and said, "Well, you got action. I'll grant you that."

"But it cost. That's what you're thinking, isn't it?" Bill sipped his vodka and tonic carefully. It tasted almost too good after what they had been through in the past seventy-two hours. "We had no choice, Dave."

"Not if we want to finish drilling the Inukshuk well this year," Dave agreed. "It's the middle of May now, and that ship's got to be off Point Barrow when the ice starts to go out in July. But it burns my ass to give in to those bastards."

"Amen to that. However, we did manage to get that one vital concession. Toward the end, I was more worried about the shipyard's attitude than the welders'. If the union hadn't agreed not to treat the deal as a precedent for future negotiations, I'm convinced the shipyard's representatives wouldn't have budged."

"Ol' Ches came through like gangbusters," said Dave admiringly. "His idea of suing the union for damages kinda attracted the strikers' attention."

"It sure as hell impressed those Galveston lawyers. It never seemed to have occurred to them that it was actually possible to take a union to court." Bill raised his glass in a toast to his legal advisor whose suggestion, made during a long-distance conference call from Calgary, had broken the deadlock between the wildcat strikers and management.

"The bastards should be sued," growled Dave. "They broke their goddamn contract, blackmailed us for an extra five hundred thou in hourly rates, and caused a delay that will take a million dollars' worth of overtime to make up."

Bill winced. "I have a feeling I'm going to hear about that million and a half when we arrive back in Calgary."

"You better believe it. It won't matter that the men are back on the job and the ship will be finished more or less on schedule. All the board will think about is that another million or so has been tacked on to the cost of the Arctic program. Steve Miller will be foaming at the mouth."

"Dave," Bill paused to look his exploration manager in the eye. "I'm going to ask for Steve's resignation tomorrow."

"I wondered when you were going to get around to that little chore. He's been asking for it, almost since the day he arrived."

"In many ways I can't really blame him. It must be totally frustrating to want to run an aggressive oil company and have all your exploration and development funds taken away from you. But he's become so negative that he's really hurting the company." Bill glanced across the aisle at Wilson. "I'd welcome a second opinion."

"You're doing the right thing," Dave assured him. Seeing that Bill didn't want to discuss it any further, he pulled out a folding table and began to deal himself a hand of solitaire.

"Me? Resign? You've got to be kidding!" Steve's expression was torn between incredulity and anger.

"I'm prepared to offer you very generous terms. Severance pay equal to two years' full salary and a downward adjustment of the price of your stock option to account for the drop in the shares since you joined the company."

"Do you think that can even begin to compensate me for what I gave up when I left Hampton? I had a future there; but nobody in his right mind would hire me now, after the way this company has gone to hell in a handbasket. Besides, I don't want a golden handshake. I want to see this company back on the rails."

"That sounds fine, Steve. Unfortunately, it doesn't square with the way you've been acting." Bill paused. "Are there any other terms that might make it easier for you to resign?"

"I told you, I'm not resigning." Steve was on his feet, knuckles resting on the top of Bill's desk as he glared down at him.

"You leave me no choice," said Bill quietly.

"It may not be as easy to get rid of me as you seem to think," Steve fired the parting shot as he strode across Bill's carpet and angrily yanked the door open.

"The backfield's in motion!" Stan Winters announced excitedly.

Ken did not share the chairman's enthusiasm for team sports, but he smiled tolerantly. "What's happening?"

"Crawford demanded Miller's resignation and didn't get it. He's called a meeting of the board to fire Miller. The meeting's set for next Tuesday, right after the long weekend. It's to be held in Calgary, and all the directors will be there."

Ken was silent for a long moment as he digested the information. Watching him, Stan had a sudden mental image of that computer of a brain inside Ken's skull whizzing through logic sequences, analyzing the options, discarding some, retaining others. "That opens up some interesting possibilities," Ken finally murmured.

That was too much for Stan. "Interesting is hardly the word!" he snorted. "We just can't afford to lose Miller's vote on the board."

"That's not quite accurate, Stan. If we could capture the two Travis votes, we could still control the board. The real danger is that the directors might refuse to go along with Crawford and vote against firing Miller."

"I'm afraid you'll have to unpack that one for me."

"If Crawford senses that he's lost control of the board and that he can no longer count on its automatic support, he'll use his voting power to replace it with one he can depend on. If he doesn't recognize the danger, you can be sure that lawyer of his will."

"Are you saying we should have our people vote to fire Miller?"

"Isn't that something?" A look of triumph flickered briefly across Ken's face. "The two of us sitting here and making decisions for one of the country's largest oil companies!"

"That's not enough for you, though, is it, Ken? You want Crawford destroyed. That's your real goal. I sometimes wonder why. What's he ever done to you?"

"My *real* goal," said Ken with careful emphasis as he stickhandled his way around the question, "is, as always, to make a potful of money for Sterling Investments. If Crawford gets the chop, the bottom will drop out of Venture shares. Temporarily. We load up and wait for the price to recover as a new and responsible management puts the company back in the black."

"Ummm." Stan did not sound altogether convinced. "It still strikes me that we're involved in some pretty complicated manipulations just to make a profit on the stock market."

Ken looked at him in pretended astonishment. "Are you putting the knock on profits, Stan? I thought that was how people like you and me kept score — with dollars."

Stan conceded the point with a sheepish grin, and Ken went on, "Besides, the moment all those foreign shares become voting, Venture loses its eligibility under FIRA."

"That's good?" asked Stan dubiously.

"Damn right. For us. It makes Venture a prime target for any number of Canadian-controlled pools of capital. It's takeover time — and you know what that means!"

Stan nodded happily, much to Ken's relief. His questions had been getting uncomfortably close to the truth. Moreover, he had a valid point. What they were trying to do was to destabilize Venture, as though it were some Central American banana republic. To say the least, it was an unusual and highly risky way to make a killing on the stock market. No wonder Stan was suspicious of his motives. Not for the first time, Ken was struck with the similarity between his obsessive drive to topple his father and his father's obsessive drive to conquer the Arctic. Impatiently, he dismissed the thought and reached for a pad of paper. "Let's run through the numbers one more time. Davies is our point man. Strickland is with us." He paused to look across the desk at Winters. "This could be the moment the Dwights have been waiting for."

Stan nodded assent, and Ken continued. "Miller for sure. The other side can count on Crawford himself and Dave Wilson and, of course, they rely on Travis and that lackey of his, Ted Reid, to support them. Which just may turn out to be a fatal mistake on their part."

A beatific smile was spreading across Ken's face as he worked his way through the problem. "I'm beginning to like this. We should be able to turn it into a no-lose situation. If Davies can bring Travis on side between now and Monday, we go for broke. If not, we have Davies cast his vote in support of Crawford like a loyal little director and bide our time while Alec continues to cultivate Travis." Ken glanced across the desk at his partner. "Those two really seem to hit it off. The wives as well."

"They're extremely compatible, no question about that. People in the social stratosphere where those two couples live don't often encounter equals they feel completely at ease with. When they do, they tend to seek out each other's company."

Stan's greatest strength was his astute judgment of people, and Ken listened intently. Then he said, "Whatever the reason for it, we have to capitalize on the empathy between Travis and Alec. Have Alec convene a meeting of the outside directors. It's entirely logical that they would want to consult with each other before deciding what to do about Miller. Why doesn't Alec take that Gulfstream of his, pick up Strickland in Boston, and fly to Houston? He can work on Strickland on the way down."

"Strickland won't need any persuading," said Stan. "He hates Crawford's guts. What Davies really should do is to get Strickland to cool it at the meetings in Houston. Travis regards Adrian as a real lightweight, and if he came on strong in support of Alec's position it could turn Lee off completely."

"Agreed. And tell Davies that step number one in dealing with Travis is to find out how he feels about firing Miller. That will give us some idea of where we stand."

"I'll tell him to try, Ken. But remember, men like Travis know how to keep their own counsel."

As it happened, however, Travis was completely open about his intentions. Right off the top, he told both Alec and Adrian that he was going to vote against the motion and asked for their support in defeating it. He felt it would be both a salutary rebuke to Bill and a clear signal that the directors were fed up with "this Arctic bullshit."

Alec's biggest problem was to persuade Lee not to call Bill to warn him ahead of time that all four outside directors were opposed to firing Miller. That would be playing right into Bill's hands; he would be able to withdraw the motion and so prevent it from being voted down, and he would also be alerted to the fact that his board could no longer be trusted. Fortunately for Alec, this led directly into the most powerful argument Winters had provided him with. Adrian and Lee were stunned when he pointed out to them that Bill was almost certain to use his voting power to elect a new slate of directors.

"It would be unrealistic to expect him to sit idly by once he finds out that he can't fire his own president," Alec told his astounded listeners. Ted Reid wasn't present, but that was of no consequence since he would vote the way Lee told him to.

"He could really do that?" asked Adrian in alarm.

Alec nodded solemnly. "All he has to do is to call a special meeting of the share-holders and use his voting power to replace us."

"I can't see Bill doing that." Adrian was unconvinced.

"He can be totally ruthless when it suits his purpose," Lee said with the air of one who knows. The note of bitterness in his voice did not escape Alec. Was there an underlying enmity there that could be exploited?"

"What in God's name are we going to do?" Adrian wailed. "Maybe we should let him go ahead and turf Steve out. I kinda like being on that board."

Alec concealed a smile. Being a director of Venture was the only thing Adrian did that his wealthy in-laws approved of. "It strikes me," Alec said slowly, "that if the chairman's motion to fire the president is defeated, then the chairman himself should resign."

"You thinking of a Crawford event?" Lee's eyes were slitted as he squinted at Davies through a thin screen of blue cigarette smoke.

"Go to the head of the class, Lee." Alec reached into his briefcase for a thin sheaf of Xeroxed pages. "This is an extract from Venture's incorporation documents," he said, handing each of them a single sheet of paper. Two brief passages had been marked with a yellow highlighter. The paragraph was headed: "Limitation of Voting Rights Attached to Class B Common Shares" and began: "The holders of Class B Common Shares shall not be entitled to vote at meetings of the shareholders of the Corporation until such time as: ... (e) William Crawford is not a director and Chief Executive Officer of the Corporation."

"You will observe the presence of the word 'and'." Alec sounded like a lawyer, blissfully unaware that he was merely parroting Ken's words. "That means that the Travis and Dwight shares would become voting if Crawford ceases to be *either* a director *or* chief executive officer, but" — he paused to give his listeners a look that was freighted with meaning — "the officers of the company are elected by the board of directors."

"And being elected by the board, they can also be terminated by the board?" Lee suddenly jumped as the unheeded cigarette burnt his fingers.

"Exactly. It's our window of opportunity, gentlemen, and it will remain open for but a few minutes after the motion to terminate Steve is defeated."

"Why would we want to kick out ol' Bill?" Lee had slipped back into his familiar drawl. The dialogue was strictly between Lee and Alec now; Adrian was nothing more than an interested bystander.

"I don't know how you feel about it, but I don't enjoy watching a company with which I am identified in the public mind go down the drain. Nor do I care for the prospect of being kicked off the board like some junior clerk."

A faint nod of Lee's head acknowledged these points, and then he asked, "What about the FIRA business? Won't a bunch of Americans having control of the company screw it up?"

"Yes. But that doesn't matter. Hell, with the financial bind Venture is in, it couldn't buy out the corner grocery store."

"You sure as hell have given us something to think about, Alec." Lee was on his feet. "We can talk about it some more on the flight to Calgary tomorrow in that airplane of yours. Meanwhile, you all will be my guests for dinner tonight."

Much to Ken's consternation, things remained in limbo over the entire Victoria Day weekend. He and Stan were in constant touch by phone as Stan relayed the latest intelligence from Davies. An increasingly anxious Ken finally asked if Stan was positive Travis fully grasped that this could be their one and only chance to gain control of the company.

Stan assured him that Davies had laid it all out for them, then asked whether Ken had changed his mind about what to do if the American directors weren't prepared to run against Bill.

"No. The same strategy as before. Throw Miller to the wolves and keep our powder dry."

"Anyway, we won't have long to wait." Stan sounded almost gleeful as he hung up.

For a moment Ken found himself envying his partner's carefree attitude. The whole thing was just a big lark to him, not, as it was to Ken, the battle of a lifetime. And Ken wouldn't have it any other way. The strident hum of the dial tone finally penetrated his bemused thoughts, and he dropped the receiver back into its cradle. The weekend of waiting stretched interminably before him.

The deal went right down to the wire. It was not until a breakfast meeting on Tuesday morning in Alec's Calgary hotel suite that the four conspirators finally reached agreement.

"The way I see it, gentlemen, is this." Lee wiped his lips and dropped the napkin beside the plate. "We're faced with a situation where a man of undoubted ability — a man we all admire and respect — has set out on a course that threatens to destroy a company in which we all have a very substantial interest. He's got the bit in his teeth, and there's no turning him. I figure we have a responsibility to use the power we have, while we still have it, to bring an end to this madness of his." Lee's tone was more in sorrow than in anger, but the malice was unmistakable.

"So what do we do?" Alec wanted it spelled out so that there would be no confusion or misunderstandings at the crucial moment.

"We vote to retain Steve as president and to terminate Bill as chairman."

"What about a replacement for Crawford?" asked Adrian breathlessly, seeing the coveted prize almost within his grasp. He was crestfallen when Lee curtly replied that there was no need to worry about that now; unseating Crawford was all that mattered.

The Venture Tower was within easy walking distance of the hotel. It was agreed that they should avoid arriving in a group, and Alec stood at the door of his suite while his three fellow directors filed out. There was just enough time for him to place a hurried call to Vancouver and tell a sleepy but elated Winters that all systems were go.

30

The seven directors were grouped at one end of the long conference table, which could have comfortably accommodated four times the number. The only others present were Chester Martin who, as the corporate lawyer, attended all board meetings, and a stenographer to make notes of the proceedings. The atmosphere was subdued, and the friendly bantering that usually preceded a Venture board meeting was conspicuously absent.

In an attempt to open the meeting on a positive note, Bill said, "As you all know, gentlemen, no ship can make it through to the Beaufort Sea until the ice pack retreats from Point Barrow at the northernmost tip of Alaska. Our goal has always been to have *Polarex* in position off the coast of Alaska when the ice starts to move. The latest forecast shows the ice going out in early July, less than six weeks from now, and I can confirm that she will be there, ready and waiting. A week later she should be drilling ahead at the Inukshuk location, in plenty of time to complete and test the well before the end of this drilling season!"

This announcement was greeted with a stony silence that was broken only when Dave Wilson said, "That's good news, Bill."

"What about our other operations?" asked Adrian with an air of bright innocence. "Can Steve give us a report on those?"

"There are no other operations," Steve replied tersely.

"Steve exaggerates. As always. And in the most negative fashion possible." Bill's lips were compressed in the telltale straight line that betrayed his controlled fury. "Which is the main reason why I have been forced to seek his termination."

"Is there a motion before the meeting?" asked Alec mildly.

"You're right, Alec. I should have waited until there was a motion on the floor before making any editorial comments." Bill consulted a typewritten sheet of paper. "I hereby move that Steven H. Miller be removed from the offices of president and director; that he be offered severance pay equal to two years' annual salary; and that the price under his option agreement be adjusted downward to reflect the price of Venture shares at the close of trading yesterday. Do I have a seconder for the motion?"

There was another awkward pause before Dave said quietly, "I second the motion."

"Since it's my motion, I guess I'd better speak to it," began Bill slowly. "It really comes down to disloyalty to the company and a total inability to work with me as your CEO. You are all aware that Steve has made comments in public that have been extremely damaging to the company. This is cause enough, but what is worse — much worse — is the divisiveness he is deliberately creating within the company itself. No company can function properly when it is being pulled in different directions. It's as simple as that." Bill stopped talking and Alec, who seemed to be acting as ex officio chairman, looked enquiringly at Steve Miller.

"The real reason Bill wants me fired is that I refuse to fall in with this polar passion of his. I freely admit that I have fought him every foot of the way on that. In doing so, however, I have been loyal, not disloyal, to the company. I have prepared a table that sets out the impact of the Arctic project on our financial viability." Steve passed out copies of a single sheet of paper.

Bill glanced at his copy with an air of indifference, but inwardly he was dismayed. Steve was adroitly turning the issue into a debate over the Arctic, a debate that Bill could not win, given the present mood of the board. It was also a classic illustration of the old business maxim that he who brings a piece of paper to a meeting controls the meeting.

"I think we're straying from the point here," Bill protested. "We can talk about the Arctic later if you like, but right now the issue before us is Steve's fitness to continue as president and director."

"It strikes me that he is doing nothing more than trying to prove that he was acting in the best interests of the company," Lee drawled. "Right, Steven?"

Steve nodded eager assent, and Lee leaned back in his chair. "I think we should hear what the man's got to say."

Bill shrugged, and Steve led them through the table. "The figures tell the story, gentlemen. The cost of 'Crawford's navy,' as it is called on the street, is now estimated at $165-million. With the cost overruns we've been experiencing, it will likely come in even higher. The operating costs for this fleet of ships are estimated to be nearly a quarter of a million dollars a day ..." There was a sharp intake of breath around the table, and Steve smiled grimly as he continued.

"Now, if you will look under the column headed 'Source of Funds,' you will see bank loans at one hundred million, which, I might add, used up the last dollar of our available credit. Internally generated funds account for another forty million. This figure would have been higher except for the heavy interest burden of the bank loans. As you can see from the fourth column, this leaves quite a shortfall, which can only be made up by selling off our producing properties. You have heard me refer to it as 'dismantling the company,' and that's exactly what it is." Steve lifted his gaze from the paper. "And that, gentlemen, is what I have been fighting against."

Bill frowned down at the note Ches had just passed him. It read, "Maybe you should withdraw the motion." To hell with that. This was his company. When it came down to the nut-cutting, his board would support him. They always did. He glanced around the table. "Anyone else care to speak on the motion?"

"I think we're ready for the vote," said Alec. He turned to Steve. "I believe you should abstain, Steve, since you have a personal interest in the outcome."

"You have heard the motion. All those in favour?" Bill raised his right hand as he spoke. So did Dave Wilson. And that was all.

"Against?" said Bill in a voice that had gone suddenly dry. Four hands went up. "Motion defeated." Bill glanced in the direction of the stenographer who was bending over her shorthand with downcast eyes.

"I believe that amounts to a vote of non-confidence, Bill," said Alec as Bill sat, stunned into silence.

"It does no such thing," snapped Chester Martin.

"Legally, you may be correct," Alec replied. "However, it is clear that Bill no longer enjoys the support of this board. I think the proper thing is for him to resign as chairman."

Bill had thrown off his state of shock. "I have no intention whatsoever of doing that. I have made this company what it is today, and I'm not finished yet. Not by a long shot!"

"In that case, I move that William Crawford be dismissed from the offices of chairman of the board and chief executive officer."

"The motion is out of order!" Chester barked.

Shaken, Alec rounded on the lawyer. "What do you mean?"

"This is a special meeting, called to deal with one specific matter, proper notice of which was duly given. It cannot deal with any other item of business of which notice has not been given."

Like most executives who chaired meetings as a regular part of their duties, Alec had a working knowledge of the rules of procedure, but looked to his legal advisers whenever anything out of the ordinary arose. When it came to the intricacies of conducting a meeting, Alec was no match for the highly respected corporate lawyer, who was clicking his briefcase closed as if the meeting was already over.

"Since the meeting has dealt with all the business properly before it, I suggest you declare it adjourned," Martin calmly instructed Bill.

"The meeting is adjourned," Bill repeated immediately. White-faced with fury, he rose from his set and said in a strangled voice, "I bid you good day, gentlemen." Then he strode out into the passageway leading to his private office, closely followed by Chester. Dave Wilson started to come with them, but Bill signalled him with a slight jerk of his head to stay with the others.

"Just what the hell was going on in there, Ches?" demanded Bill when the office door closed behind them.

"An old-fashioned railway job, running right on time."

"They were all in on it together? I find that hard to believe."

"It had to be. Alec would never have exposed himself like that unless the fix was in."

"Thank God you came up with that point about lack of notice. I've never run into that one before."

"For the very good reason that it doesn't exist."

Bill stared at his lawyer, an incredulous grin slowly spreading across his face. "You mean it was all a bluff on your part?"

Chester nodded happily, and Bill laughed outright. "Beautiful! You stickhandled them right out of their socks. They'll be climbing the walls when they find out!"

"So what can they do? Lawyers have been wrong before. Meanwhile, the meeting is over."

Bill sobered. "They won't let it rest there. We've got to come up with some way to head them off."

"Here's the drill. We call a special meeting of the shareholders as soon as possible to elect a new slate of directors. You can elect whoever you want since you have voting control."

"How soon can we do that?"

"The bylaws of the company require a minimum of two weeks' notice."

"Won't they try and hold another board meeting and vote me out before then?"

"They might, but I'm confident we can get a court injunction preventing that. It would be easy to prove that you would suffer irreparable harm and prejudice if such a meeting were to take place. No, they had their chance, and they blew it."

"You mean you blew it for them. It was your finest hour, you old legal eagle!"

Chester acknowledged the accolade with a self-deprecating grin, then said, "I'm fairly sure we can win the battle for control, if we make all the right moves. However, there's another problem, every bit as serious, that's not going to be solved so easily."

"What's that? The Arctic, I suppose." Bill was defensive.

"To be more precise, minority shareholder lawsuits arising out of the Arctic. I doubt if the gang in there," Chester flicked a hand in the direction of the boardroom, "will start any, because they could be liable themselves. But if, as you seem to think, somebody's pulling Alton Grant's strings, it would be logical to have him round up some disgruntled shareholders and start a legal action. That's what I would do if I were acting for the other side."

"So they bring a lawsuit. What does that do for them?"

"They'll seek damages, of course. But the real threat is that they might succeed in having the court appoint a receiver to manage the company."

"Are you serious?"

"Absolutely. These attacks aren't going to go away, Bill. Not until you find an answer to the Arctic."

"That's precisely what I've been trying to do for the past twelve months."

"I know that. But those who are out to take over the company won't give you credit for good intentions." The lawyer shivered as if suddenly brushed by a cold wind. "I must be getting old, but I almost sense a presence behind all this. Not just

Lee and his preoccupation with the bottom-line, something more. More ... well, malevolent."

"You mean to say they let themselves be outwitted by a goddamn lawyer?" Ken almost shouted with frustration.

"Chester Martin isn't just *any* lawyer," protested Stan. "He's one of the best in the business. Our guys were all under strain, keyed up to dethrone the king, and this hotshot lawyer comes in out of nowhere, spouting legal technicalities, and pulls the rug out from underneath them." He spread his hands in a gesture of resignation. "What could they do?"

Shaken by Ken's look of utter dejection, Stan had another try at persuading him to abandon his futile assault on Venture. "This whole thing is getting a little out of hand. Why don't we sell our shares and go short on a bunch more. There's got to be a downside of at least two points as a result of this. That would get us out even, and then we could move on to something a little less nerve-wracking."

Ken didn't seem to hear him. "I want you to get onto our own lawyers, Stan. Give them a hypothetical case and see if there's anything that can be done."

"Ken, knowing when to quit is a very important part of our business." Ken stared stonily back at him, and Stan sighed and got to his feet. "You really want to press on with this?"

"We have just begun to fight," snarled Ken, reaching for the phone.

He hadn't seen or talked to Margo for several weeks, but the warm camaraderie was there the instant she came on the line. The sound of her voice reminded Ken that there was another world, a human and exciting world, outside his secret and losing battle with Crawford. "Your paper goes out tomorrow, doesn't it?" he asked.

"Yes." He could almost hear her listening.

"I have a blockbuster of a scoop for you."

"You know how I feel about scoops. One more blows up in my face and I'm finished. Period."

"This is legit. My God, you don't think I'm trying to pull a Debbie on you?"

"I didn't mean that the way it sounded, Ken. I know you would never give me a bum steer. It's just that I have a knee-jerk reaction when I hear the word scoop."

"Perfectly understandable. But you're going to love this one. At least I think you will. It involves an old friend of yours. Bill Crawford."

"Oh?" Her tone became more guarded. "Let's hear it."

He told her about Bill's unsuccessful attempt to fire Steve Miller and how he had barely missed getting the axe himself.

"It fits!" she cried with the excitement of a journalist watching a story take shape. "Just before you called I picked up a rumour floating around about a special meeting of Venture shareholders. I owe you for this one, Ken."

"Just keep in touch as this thing develops. Okay?"

"What I know, you know. It's a promise."

"Good." Ken was reluctant to end the conversation. He was surprised to hear himself say that he was going to be in Toronto the following week, though — until that very moment — he had had no such intention. They arranged to have dinner together.

Even before he put down the phone Ken was mentally factoring the new data into the Venture puzzle. Margo's item about the special meeting of Venture shareholders could only mean that Crawford was going on the attack. Clever bastard. No, he's not the bastard, I'm the bastard. Ken's lips twisted as he walked over to the computer terminal and entered the code word for Plan B — the one in which Alton Grant figured so largely.

At the Toronto end of the conversation, Margo also had food for thought. That information of Ken's was deep insider stuff. Could it be that he had a pipeline to the board of directors?

31

In recent months the energy department had been moved across the Ottawa River to help fill the immense office complexes erected in Hull by the federal government in an attempt to bind Quebec to the rest of Canada with dollars and jobs. Hilary was walking along the echoing concrete concourse of Place du Portage when she saw Bill. He was alone, moving toward the bank of elevators with a purposeful stride. He hadn't spotted her; she could still avoid an encounter by ducking into the fast-food outlet on her right.

Without realizing it, she had come to a standstill. With a muffled *"merde,"* someone caromed into her from behind. It was a civil servant who had been ambling peacefully along sipping coffee from a Styrofoam cup. Unfortunately, the cup was full, and he stood there doing a slow burn while coffee dripped from his plump chins and soaked through his shirt. Hilary spun around and was horrified when she saw the damage she had caused. Her apology, in fluent French, was so sincere, and she was so obviously contrite, that the man's resentment melted. He would have none of her offer to pay the cleaning bill and was so blown away by her beauty that he blamed the mishap entirely on his own failure to watch where he was going. What with one thing and another, it turned into quite a little scene and, as Hilary said goodbye to her damp new admirer, she saw Bill staring in her direction.

He was too far away to hear her, but her lips formed his name, her feet seemed to be moving of their own volition and then she saw him start toward her. When Bill saw the look of love on her face, his own face lit up with a joy that was almost incandescent. He opened his arms, and she ran the last few steps to him, murmuring, "Darling, oh my darling," over and over again. They clung together, mouth against mouth, breaking apart only to whisper each other's names as if they were the most precious words in the English language.

"Oh, Bill, I've missed you so terribly."

"Nothing like the way I've missed you. We won't let it happen again, will we?" His eyes searched hers.

"Never again," she promised, and he held her tightly, knowing a feeling of happiness beyond anything he had ever experienced.

Gradually, they became aware of the titters and amused glances of the other pedestrians in the indoor mall. She gave him a final hug and stepped back. "Were you on your way to see Harold?"

"Good Lord, yes." He flicked a quick glance at his watch. "Together with the minister. And I'm late. Call you around six?"

"Wonderful."

Harold Trotter was seated in the anteroom of the minister's office when Bill breezed in. "You're in luck," he said, "the minister's first appointment is running a trifle behind schedule." He studied Bill curiously for a few moments. "I must say you look uncommonly cheerful for someone who's in the bind you're in."

"All's for the best in this best of all possible worlds," Bill assured him blithely.

"Oh, sure. Your directors are after your blood; Alton Grant is organizing the dissident shareholders to put your company into receivership and shut down the Arctic project; the minister is bombarded daily in the House with unanswerable questions about the Venture mess; and my own political neck is out a mile."

"As a loyal civil servant, you should make that a kilometre, Harold. Remember that your government in its wisdom has decreed that everything goes better in metric." Bill beamed at the bureaucrat. "You and I are about to say the magic word and watch all our problems vanish into thin air."

"And just what is that magic word?"

"Two words, actually — super depletion," replied Bill just as a secretary announced that the minister would see them.

"I hope you have good news for me, Mr. Crawford." Gilles Vachon folded his hands over a thickening midriff and regarded Bill with mournful brown eyes. "Always in the House I must say 'Be patient — everything will be all right.' It rings, how do you say, hollow in my own ears."

"Harold and I think we may have the answer," Bill said smoothly. Trotter made as if to protest the casual way in which Bill was turning his idea into a joint proposal, but subsided when he saw the look of hope that had suddenly gleamed in Vachon's eyes. Any civil servant who could claim the credit for extricating the government from its embarrassing Arctic predicament would have it made. If it became obvious that Bill's scheme wasn't going to fly, any civil servant worth his salt could also find a way to dissociate himself from it.

"It all boils down to incentive," Bill was saying. "If we can get some of the big players to deal themselves in, our problems are over. The trick is to find a way to do that."

The hopeful look was fading from Vachon's countenance. "If you are talking about grants to the multinationals, forget it, Mr. Crawford. My government is not interested in subsidizing Big Oil."

Bill held up his hand. "No grants. No subsidies. Word of honour."

"Go on, Mr. Crawford." Vachon shot a questioning look at Trotter, as if to ask whether he should believe what he was hearing, but the bureaucrat only smiled enigmatically.

"It's called super depletion. The way it works is that for every dollar a company spends in the Arctic, it can write off, say, a dollar-sixty against its taxable income." Bill smiled. "No grants, no subsidies. But a powerful incentive to spend money in the Arctic."

Once again, Vachon's gaze sought out his advisor. "I can hear the NDP now with all that crap about corporate welfare bums."

Trotter looked judicious. "True. But you're going to get flak from them no matter what you do. Nothing short of total government ownership will satisfy that lot. On the other hand, the Tories would almost certainly have to support us, since the concept is completely in keeping with their political beliefs."

"They will be — how do you say ...?"

"Hoisted with their own petard?" suggested Trotter.

"Exactly." Vachon paused for a moment to enjoy the mental picture of his political enemies dangling from whatever in hell a petard was. When he continued, a note of doubt crept into his voice. "I am not sure what my confreres will think. This business of giving more tax credits than the amount spent ..." The politician in him recoiled at this heresy, and he shook his head. "Very strange."

"It's really not that unusual. Or radical," Bill hastily assured him. "For example, the Germans have used it extensively. After OPEC disrupted the world supply of crude, West Germany, which has no potential of its own, decided it would be in its best interest to develop supplies in other parts of the world not controlled by OPEC. The government also wanted to cool down the Deutsche mark, which was rising too rapidly against other currencies. So they set up the system I'm talking about, and German companies, regardless of what business they were in, were allowed to deduct a dollar-sixty for every dollar they spent looking for oil throughout the free world. When you think about it for a minute, it was a neat way of killing two birds with one stone — they not only encouraged the search for oil, they also created a demand for the currencies of the countries where the exploration took place. That was the rationale behind the German drilling funds that were so active in Canada a few years ago."

"Why are the Germans not drilling in the Arctic, then?" asked Vachon shrewdly.

"Because they terminated the program when it had served its purpose. The world oil supply has gone from a shortage to a glut, and the Deutsche mark is stabilized. That's the beauty of it." Bill leaned forward to make his point. "It's not carved in stone. Once the objective has been achieved, the special allowance can be discontinued. You could make it clear that the measure is temporary when you announce it. If, of course, you announce it." Bill hastily added the amendment when he saw Vachon beginning to stir in his seat.

"One final point. Harold can correct me if I'm wrong, but my lawyers tell me that the change can be made by order-in-council, since it only involves alterations to the depletion rate in one of the schedules of the existing regulations. I gather it does not require legislation."

"You agree, Harold?"

The civil servant pondered. Bill was intrigued by the fact that not once had Trotter sharpened a pencil in the minister's presence. Finally Harold said, "Yes. I believe that's how it would work."

A blissful look crossed the politician's face at the thought of not having to pilot the controversial measure through a stormy House of Commons. He would simply rise and loftily inform his fellow members that it had been done. Provided it got past the cabinet, of course. Granting concessions to multinational oil companies would be anathema to his colleagues — Max Bedard, for one, would be outraged, and Johnson and his cabal of Red Liberals would be bitterly opposed to the idea as well. But the PM prided himself on his pragmatism, and the government desperately needed a solution to the Arctic problem. And to think that he, Gilles Vachon, *le petit gars* from Lachute, might be the one to come up with that solution!

"Do we have any more questions for Mr. Crawford?" Vachon glanced at Trotter as he spoke.

"I don't, Minister."

"Then we can excuse you, Mr. Crawford. I think I can say this has been a useful discussion."

By God, he's going for it, Bill told himself exultantly as he took his leave. Of course, Vachon wouldn't say anything until he announced it in Parliament, but it sure looked as though he'd bought it.

Bill's way out of the complex took him past the spot where he and Hilary had embraced. Never would he forget the moment when he saw her take the first step toward him. And he would be with her again in a few hours.

The flower-seller's booth was just outside the main entrance. She smiled as she expertly wrapped tissue paper around the stems and handed the bouquet to Bill. "M'sieu looks *très content* today!"

"Why not?" He paid for the flowers and tipped her lavishly. "The sun is shining, and I'm in love with the most beautiful girl in the world!"

As usual, the message light was flashing when Bill returned to his hotel suite, although the calls now were mostly from the press rather than from other oilmen wanting to do business with Venture. This time there was only one message when he phoned down to the desk. It was to phone his secretary, and the clerk told him it was marked urgent.

"We've received notice of a directors' meeting for Thursday afternoon," Lisa informed him. "It's been called by Mr. Davies and Adrian. I checked with Mr. Martin immediately, and he said any two directors were empowered to call a meeting under the company's bylaws. However, he's going to apply to the court to block it. He says he's already discussed this with you."

"That's right. He figured they might try and pull something like this. What does he want from me?"

"To return here as soon as possible. Apparently you've got to swear an affidavit for this court thing."

"Tell him I'll be there late this afternoon."

Praying that Hilary wouldn't be tied up in some interminable meeting where she couldn't be disturbed, Bill phoned the energy department. Mercifully, he got through to her on the first try. "Look," he said, "I don't know how to tell you this, but I have to leave for Calgary right away. Some of my fellow directors are trying to call a meeting for the express purpose of removing me from office, and my lawyers are going to court in an attempt to block them. I've got to swear affidavits and things like that."

"Of course you must go, Bill. I understand perfectly. We'll have lots of time together after you've beaten them."

A great wave of relief washed over Bill. "Bless you for understanding, my darling. I love you."

"I love you."

His glance fell on the bouquet. "I bought you some flowers. Would you like to pick them up if I leave them at the desk?"

"Yes, please."

"By the way, will you marry me?"

"Yes, please."

How lucky can a guy get? Bill was humming to himself as he hastily packed his suitcase.

32

"It really pisses me off!" said Debbie.

"What does?" His daughter's language struck a discordant note with Bill. She could swear with the best of them when the situation called for it, but this kind of vulgarity was out of character.

"The Petroleum Club. You're the most prominent oilman in all of Canada and I'm the head of my own independent oil company, yet we can't have lunch at the club! Why? Because I'm a woman."

"It's a bummer, I agree. It's completely out of step with the times. Maybe you should do something about it?"

"Maybe I will. But right now I'm going to have a lovely lunch with my favourite man. Where are we going?"

"Well," he gave her an amused look, "the Ranchmen's Club does have one dining room where women are allowed. Why don't we go there?"

"Grr. This place. It's so chauvinistic. And I'm not even a women's libber!" Suddenly she laughed and took his arm. "Let's go. I'm parked in a towaway zone."

"You look very pleased with yourself," she said as the Mustang rolled down the ramp to the club's underground parking. "That must mean things went well in court this morning?"

"We got our injunction, thank God. The judge listened to the lawyers argue, recessed court for twenty minutes, then came back and granted us the injunction. He ruled that in the final analysis it's the shareholders, not the directors, who should govern. But that's not the only reason I'm pleased with myself."

"Tell me," she demanded as she skilfully backed into a parking slot.

"Wait till we've ordered our drinks." Bill was enjoying himself. This time he was the one with the stop-press news.

She surprised him by ordering a Virgin Caesar, but he filled out the chit with no comment. When it was placed before her, she said, "No more stalling. Out with it."

"I'm going to be married."

Debbie's drink stopped halfway to her mouth. She replaced it carefully on the table. "That's wonderful! I'm so happy for you."

"Aren't you going to ask who to?" he teased.

"Are you kidding? You've had the blind staggers ever since you met Hilary Marshall." She looked at him with suddenly narrowed eyes. "You're not going to tell me it's someone else, are you?"

He laughed. "No. It's Hilary. It couldn't be anyone else."

"I didn't think so. Still, you had me going for a minute there — man on the rebound and all that. You know, I've never met her. Seems incredible, but it's true. I hear she's absolutely stunning."

"She is. And I'm sure the two of you will get along famously," said Bill, although he was anything but.

"If she makes you happy, Dad, I'll think she's the greatest thing since the Pill."

"She has a young son, Jason. He's a likeable youngster." His grin was almost sheepish. "As you can see, there'll be some changes in your father's lifestyle."

"I think it's just super. Is she going to keep on working, or what?"

"If you knew her, you wouldn't have to ask that question. I can't see Hilary ever being just a housewife. We've talked about it, and she wants to take six months or so to get settled in, then she'll start to build herself a career. I think she has in mind some kind of economic consulting firm."

"In the private sector? I understood she is a hardline socialist."

"Her ideas on capitalism versus state ownership are not quite the same as ours, I grant you." Bill's smile was indulgent. "But I have an idea she's in the process of doing some rethinking."

"It should make for some stimulating family discussions." Debbie paused while the waitress cleared away the soup course. "When's the big day?"

"Soon. A week after the shareholders' meeting." Bill put a chunk of the club's special cheddar cheese on his bread and butter plate. "Speaking of the meeting, there's nothing I'd like better than to have you on the new Venture board, but Chester tells me that's a no-no."

"I think I know why. Venture and Pinnacle are in the same business, although," she wrinkled her nose at her father, "on a somewhat different scale. There could be conflicts of interest all over the place. Have you thought of Frank?"

"Yes. I've gone so far as to talk to him about it. You know how active he's become in these agricultural associations?"

"Well, I do know he's a vice-president of the Exotic Cattle Breeders and secretary of the Alberta Stockmen's Association. I hear he's very well thought of, and I'm not the least bit surprised. He gets along with people without even trying."

"That he does. Anyway, it seems he's come to the attention of the Conservatives, and the backroom boys are encouraging him to have a go at provincial politics."

"I get it," interjected Debbie. "Being on the board of a large oil company would not be too smart for a rising young politician."

"The kiss of death, apparently. And I tend to agree with him, although I don't think it should be that way."

"How do you feel about Frank going into politics?"

"I'm all for it, and I told him so. I think he would be a natural." Bill paused, then said, "I've persuaded Gavin Anderson to come back on the board."

"Super. He's a sweet man."

"That he is." He toyed with some bread crumbs. "Lee Travis is also going to be on the new board."

Debbie stared at him. "But he tried to vote you out of office."

"We'll never know that, will we?" Bill replied blandly. "Since it didn't come to a vote. Anyway, I asked him, and I was pleased when he accepted."

"The old smoothie strikes again," murmured Debbie.

"He realizes that he will be outnumbered by my other nominees," Bill went on imperturbably. "But I tell you who will not be on the board — and that's Alec Davies!"

"You blame him for the whole mess, don't you?"

"It fits the facts, Debbie. Frontenac is on the make for a big acquisition. Knock the hell out of the price of our shares and take us over. It's a textbook case."

"Maybe ... but it doesn't explain Alton Grant and his gang. I can't help feeling there's somebody we don't know about who is orchestrating this whole filthy business. It's almost as if it's directed at you, not the company. Do you have a mortal enemy lurking in your background?"

"Is there anyone who really knows the answer to that question about himself?" mused Bill. "But the answer is no, not to my knowledge. Over the years, I suppose I'm bound to have acquired some enemies — people who felt hard done by in a business transaction, for example, but nothing like you're talking about."

"Margo Jones?" suggested Debbie.

"You have been thinking, haven't you? No, not Margo. She's clever, but she just doesn't have the firepower to mount an operation like this. Besides, if she's mad at anybody, it's you, not me. Speaking of Margo ... do you remember saying that she was going to call me?"

Debbie nodded. "Did she?"

"Nope. Maybe she figured she didn't have to."

"Out-bluffed again." Debbie made a face. "But even if it isn't Margo, you can see what I mean. Someone with a personal motive. There's hate mixed up in this somewhere."

"Ches seems to feel the same way." Bill looked thoughtful for a moment, then went on with determined cheerfulness, "Once I get this shareholders' meeting safely behind me, it won't matter."

"Is that really true? I have it on good authority that Alton Grant is coming to the meeting armed with a statement of claim against both you and the company."

"I've heard that, too. However, if everything breaks just right, I may have a surprise for that self-righteous ass."

"You mean it?" cried Debbie, lowering her voice when several of the diners glanced in their direction. "You're incredible! Just when everybody figures you're painted into a corner, you pop up in the middle of the floor, all debonair and suave like a magician. How are you going to pull it off this time?"

"I'm not at all sure I'm going to pull it off. I think we'll both just have to wait and see if it works."

"It will. Whatever it is. Oh, you have no idea how much better I feel!"

Driving back downtown, she wanted to know if Bill's engagement was to be public knowledge, and he told her it was being kept quiet until after the meeting. "But I can call her, can't I? Let her know how thrilled I am, and stuff like that?"

"She'd love it." They drew up to a stoplight a block south of the Venture Tower, and Bill gave her an affectionate peck on the cheek and got out of the car, saying he would walk the rest of the way. Although he wouldn't admit it even to himself, he had been a little apprehensive about how Debbie would react to the news that he was going to be married. Her enthusiastic response was everything he could have hoped for.

It was odd how she had picked up on the same thing Ches had about there being some kind of sinister mastermind behind all the corporate turmoil. They both seemed to feel there was something almost evil about the whole business. Bill was still inclined to blame Alec Davies. Davies had the most cogent of all motives — greed. That was much easier to cope with than the possibility that there might be a crazy out there gunning for him. But who? Bill spent the next half-hour ransacking his memory all the way back to Consolidated Pete days, and drew a blank. Finally, wearying of this unprofitable activity, he turned his mind to the more concrete problems that confronted him.

Now that the court had prevented the rebel directors from holding their trump meeting, Ches Martin seemed to believe that nothing could stop Bill from electing his chosen board of directors. That, plus the fact that he and Lee seemed to have arrived at another uneasy truce, should effectively spike the directors' guns. The lawsuit by the minority shareholders, however, was a clear and present danger and would remain so until he came up with some way of stanching the company's cash hemorrhage.

And he wouldn't be able to do that unless the government came through. The oil business was supposed to be one of the last bastions of free enterprise, but time after time it had had to go cap in hand to the politicians. Oil and water might not mix, but oil and politics sure as hell did. Bill checked the time — it would be four-thirty in Ottawa, and all the government switchboards would be closed. That was no problem; he had the number of Trotter's private night-line, and the ambitious bureaucrat undoubtedly would still be at his desk. Bill pressed the intercom button and asked Lisa to see if she could reach Trotter.

The bureaucrat's greeting was reserved, which came as no surprise to Bill. High-ranking civil servants quickly became wary of the pressure exerted by private interests seeking to advance their own cause. Knowing that Trotter would only stonewall him if he asked for a hint as to the government's plans, he kept the conversation short.

"All I really wanted to say," he told Trotter, "was that if the government intends to do anything constructive about our situation, it will have to happen before the shareholders' meeting. After that, it may be too late."

"I hear what you're saying. But there's really nothing I can tell you at this point in time."

"I appreciate your position. Just remember the meeting is set for Friday morning."

There was nothing more to be done. It was the kind of situation Bill had lived with all his life — you gave it your best shot, examined the seismic data, worked up the geological interpretations, assembled a land position, started the drilling bit turning to the right, and then sat back to wait for the verdict.

33

At five minutes after three on Thursday afternoon, Gilles Vachon, Minister of Energy, rose in the House of Commons to make an announcement. Speaking in his accented English, he described the importance of the Arctic to Canada's energy balance and the vital necessity of finding out whether significant reserves of oil underlay all that ice. After going on in this vein for some ten minutes, he stated that in order to provide the necessary incentive to ensure an adequate level of exploration, the government had decided to permit a write-off of 150 per cent of expenditures made north of the sixtieth parallel. He emphasized that it was a temporary measure and would be reviewed annually to see if it should be continued. Favouring the Opposition with a smug smile, he sat down amid a thunderous chorus of approval from the government benches.

Bill got the news in a phone call from Jim Goulder; the story was coming in over the wire at the brokerage house. Within minutes, the switchboard was jammed with incoming calls, mostly from the media. With some help from Chester Martin, he prepared a press release welcoming the announcement, praising the enlightened attitude of the government, and expressing confidence that the riches of the Arctic would soon be tapped. Lisa, separating the wheat from the chaff in her usual fashion, put through calls from the presidents of both Esso Resources and Shell Canada, each wanting to talk about participation in the Arctic play. Bill expressed a willingness to listen to their proposals and warned that a fundamental term of any deal would be a large amount of cash up front.

"You want to know something?" Bill asked Martin and Dave Wilson, who were in the office with him when he took the call from Esso. "We have just recovered our entire investment in the Arctic project."

"Does that mean our conventional exploration program is alive and well?" asked Wilson.

"That's precisely what it means."

"Hallelujah!" breathed the exploration manager.

That night was the eve of the shareholders' meeting, and Bill had laid on a dinner for the proposed new slate of directors. It turned out to be a much more gala affair than anyone could have anticipated. The move by the government would surely restore Venture's fortunes and undermine, if not entirely eliminate, any revolt by dissident shareholders in the morning.

Ches, who, despite his misgivings about the propriety of lawyers serving on corporate boards and had agreed to become a director on a pro tem emergency basis, confirmed to Bill that Alton Grant had filed a statement of claim at the courthouse. "But that doesn't mean too much by itself," he explained. "It's only when it's actually served on the defendant that it becomes effective, and my hunch is that they will hold back in light of today's developments."

Alton Grant, surrounded by a coterie of supporters, was front and centre when the meeting commenced at 10:00 a.m. If there was going to be trouble, it would come from that quarter. He had proxies from several hundred of the smaller shareholders plus the Frontenac block. However, the scrutineers reported that a number of his proxies had been withdrawn at the last minute, which was an encouraging sign. Since Bill had voting control, he wasn't worried on that score, but he was positive Grant's black briefcase contained a statement of claim ready to be served.

Bill opened the meeting with a summary of what the new depletion rules would mean to the company. The shares had advanced nearly four dollars since the market opened that morning, and Bill's remarks were interrupted on three occasions with applause, while the scowl on Grant's face darkened.

Then, in accordance with the script Chester had prepared, a shareholder read out a motion that the present board of directors be removed from office. It passed easily, and Bill was heartened to note that the votes cast in favour of the motion included several thousand in addition to his own group. When the result was announced, Alton Grant rose dramatically to his feet, and Bill braced himself for what was to come. But instead of brandishing a statement of claim, he thundered, "I will take no further part in this farce!" and flounced out of the meeting accompanied by some but by no means all of his followers. A couple of reporters dashed after him to grab a quick quote, but the rest stayed in the crowded auditorium waiting for the next development.

When Bill called for nominations for the new board, a shareholder stood up and read off a list of seven names. In addition to Bill, Chester, Dave, Gavin Anderson, and Travis, there were a retired banker and a retired oil executive, both of whom had jumped at Bill's invitation to join Venture's board. When there were no further nominations, the new slate was declared elected. It was over. Bill exhaled a sigh of relief while his glance sought out Chester and Dave.

The final touches were added at the meeting of the new board of directors immediately afterward. Bill was elected chairman of the board and chief executive officer, and Gavin Anderson was named president.

The headline in Saturday's *Calgary Herald* said it all: "Oil Industry's Golden Boy Does It Again!"

The next few days were crammed with activity on both the business and social fronts. Unable to absent himself from the negotiations with Esso, which were down to the final strokes, Bill sent the Lear with Tim Connors at the controls to Ottawa to pick up Hilary and Jason. Connors had the look of a man who had been granted a last-minute reprieve. Every corporate pilot is aware that when a company falls on bad times, the executive jet is the first "frill" to go. But with the dramatic improvement in Venture's fortunes, Crawford knew he would still have an airplane to drive.

Debbie accompanied her father to the Calgary airport to meet the incoming plane. "She's lovely, Dad," she said as Hilary, hand lifted to shade her eyes from the rays of the late-afternoon sun, emerged from the aircraft.

Hilary and Bill wanted a small civil ceremony, with only family and a few intimate friends present. Debbie went along with that, but insisted that it be followed by a large reception at the country club. "You're both going to live in this town, and your friends are dying to meet Hilary. Besides," she hugged Hilary's arm, "I want to show my gorgeous stepmother off! Although," she added, "I really feel more as if I've acquired a wonderful new sister."

Debbie also arranged two ladies' lunches in Hilary's honour. Despite the short notice, the turnout was nearly 100 per cent; a number of guests who were out of town flew back especially for the occasion. Everyone was avid to meet the beauty who had captured the eligible Bill Crawford's heart. Debbie was in her element as she introduced her protégé, who invariably was the most attractive female present. Watching them chattering away to each other like two giddy schoolgirls after one of these functions, Bill realized with deep contentment that they were going to be friends — honest-to-God friends. It could so easily have gone the other way. The friendship was sealed one night when the three of them were alone at the Circle C and Hilary, who had not planned on having any attendants, asked Debbie to be her bridesmaid.

"I'd love to! I don't know about the maid part, though. I'm going to have a baby!"

Bill, accustomed to his headstrong daughter's ways, received this piece of information with a marginal lift of an eyebrow. "That's odd. I didn't even know you were married."

"You will have your little joke, won't you, Father? I'm not married and I have no intention of getting married. I simply decided that if I was ever going to have a child, I'd better do it now before I get too old. For the first time, I mean," she added with a quick glance at Hilary.

"How does the father feel?"

"He doesn't feel anything, because he doesn't know anything. I just selected a partner with all the right qualities: brains, great bod, and a sense of humour, and went off the pill."

Bill grinned across the room at Hilary. "I told you that you're marrying into an interesting family."

Hilary had recovered from her shock. "I think it's wonderful. And terribly exciting." She gave Debbie a quick hug.

"So do I." Bill wrapped his arms around both of them. "Leave it to Debbie to do things her own way!"

On Wednesday of the week following the meeting, Bill inked a "memorandum of understanding" with Esso Resources whereby Esso acquired a fifty-per-cent interest in the Arctic play for one hundred and seventy-five million in cash and the assumption of all the costs of completing and testing the Inukshuk well, plus a second exploratory hole. Venture was to remain as operator, and *Polarex* and her support vessels were leased out to the joint operation at rates that would return a handsome profit. Venture stock went up another three points when the deal was announced. As Dave Wilson said, they "had it made in the shade."

34

Ken deliberately left his Toronto hotel room a few minutes early for his luncheon date with Margo. He wanted to give himself the pleasure of watching her walk across the lobby, turning heads as she went, and knowing that he had been with her last night and would be again tonight. At precisely twelve-thirty, punctual as always, she came through the revolving door. She was every inch the successful career woman in her tailored suit, carrying a briefcase, and a folded newspaper under her arm. Crossing the lobby to intercept her, Ken felt a rush of excitement at the thought of the sleek, supple body underneath that conservative attire.

He ordered Dubonnet on the rocks instead of his usual Perrier and chuckled at her expression. "Don't looked so shocked. I just happen to feel like celebrating."

"Terrific. What are we drinking to?"

"How about you and me?"

"I'll drink to that." She leaned across the table to touch his cheek with the tips of her fingers.

"Have you seen today's paper yet?" she asked when they had finished the main course and were waiting for coffee.

He looked slightly abashed and shook his head. "Would you believe I haven't? See what you do to me?"

"There's an interesting item in the society section." Deftly, she turned to the right page, folded it neatly and handed it to him. "Oilman Weds" was the caption over a three-column photo of a beaming Bill Crawford standing beside a woman of extraordinary beauty. The writeup mentioned that the newlyweds were postponing their honeymoon until the Arctic drilling season was over.

"He's got it all," Margo murmured. "Wealth, power, and a gorgeous young wife."

"Some people have all the luck." It was said lightly, but the hint of a sneer did not escape Margo, nor did the sudden, involuntary thinning of the lips. For a person of Ken's self-control, his reaction was almost an outburst. It would be fascinating to know just what he had against Bill Crawford.

The lover's mood that had enveloped them in its warm glow throughout the lunch was broken, and it was an abstracted Ken Kwasny who put Margo in a taxi for her next appointment, promising to call her at six. His message light was flashing when he let himself into his hotel room and he found himself welcoming the summons back to the real world of business and deals. Except that the message marked "urgent" to call Stan Winters in Vancouver wasn't about business.

"I'm afraid I have some bad news for you, Ken," he said without preamble. "Your father passed away this morning. He suffered a massive coronary, and I understand it would have been mercifully quick."

For a moment, Ken thought he was talking about Bill Crawford, then he collected himself and said, "I'll catch the next flight to Edmonton. How did you hear about it, Stan?"

"A phone call to the office from the Edmonton police. Apparently one of your father's construction buddies found him when he went round to the house this morning."

Before ringing off, Ken listened while Stan uttered the customary soothing banality about that being the best way to go if you had to go. Thinking about it, Ken realized his father was a prime candidate for a heart attack, with that stocky, overweight physique and his heavy drinking.

He called Margo from the airport just before his flight left. She surprised him by asking if he wanted her to fly out to be with him at the funeral. Somewhat brusquely he told her it wasn't necessary and then found himself regretting his too quick refusal.

The numbness began to wear off on the long flight west, and Ken reflected on the nature of the man who had brought him up. He suspected that his "father" — the mental quotation marks were always there now — hadn't really wanted to go on living without his wife. And then to be confronted with the question of his son's paternity. Rose hadn't meant to hurt him; she was just desperately anxious that Ken know the truth. Probably blamed herself for not having told him before. But it couldn't have been easy for the man who had devoted his life to her.

Ken was grateful that he could sincerely mourn the tough little pipeliner. The rapport that should exist between father and son had never been there, and Ken was aware that his own personality lacked something as a result. It was understandable, though; the poor devil must have thought of Rose making love with another man every time he laid eyes on Ken. When you looked at it that way, he had acted pretty damn honourably.

The small chapel in the funeral home was filled with a respectable number of mourners, mostly pipeline and construction types and their wives. The funeral director checked to see that the pallbearers were in position on either side of the casket and nodded at Ken to go in. Ken was taken aback to see Margo sitting in one of the rear pews, smiling sympathetically at him. His face lit up with one of his sudden smiles that told her she had been right to come. It also reminded her of someone, but she couldn't place who it was.

The funeral service was brief and perfunctory. Kwasny senior had been no churchgoer, and the clergyman went through the ritual mechanically, having to refer to his notes every now and then for the name of the deceased. When it was over, Ken asked Margo to come with him to the house while he went through his father's papers. The Kwasny home was a modest frame bungalow in a working-class district, but the glistening fresh paint and the neatly tended front garden made it stand out from its neighbours. Everything gleamed and sparkled in the sunlight streaming through spotless windows.

"There's a lot of love in this house. You can feel it," she said.

"Dad turned it into a shrine for my mother. He worshipped her."

"That's beautiful."

"Yeah. He wasn't a bad guy."

If Margo thought this was a remarkably offhand way to refer to one's recently deceased parent, she kept it to herself.

Ken crossed over to the cabinet with a pulldown desk and pigeonhole shelves. His mother, who did what little bookkeeping the household required, had always sat there to make out cheques for the mortgage and groceries. A long, official-looking envelope had a pigeonhole all to itself. Ken fished it out and saw that it was labelled "The Last Will and Testament of Kenneth George Kwasny." Inside there was a brief letter from a one-man law firm in a nearby shopping mall confirming that they were enclosing a copy of the will and were holding the original at their office for safe keeping. Ken noted with some surprise that the letter was dated less than two months ago. The will consisted of a single sheet of legal-sized paper. He was jolted to discover that he wasn't named as executor; the lawyer was the sole executor and trustee. The will recited that the testator's beloved wife, Rose, had predeceased him and that his "well loved" son was financially independent and in no need of further assistance. It then went on to bequeath the entire estate to a scholarship fund established by the pipeline workers' union.

"I've been disinherited!" said Ken with a shaky laugh. "He's left everything to some scholarship trust fund."

"That's awful! But he can't have had all that ..." Margo gazed around the modest home and left the sentence unfinished.

"I know, he didn't leave very much, and I don't give a damn about that part. But he inherited my mother's things when she passed away, and this means I'll have nothing of hers. Not even this desk."

Margo was appalled. "Why in God's name would he do a thing like that?"

"Because he wasn't my real father. That's why!" Ken slammed the desk shut. The look of utter desolation on his face brought her flying over to him. She half expected him to pull away, but he held on to her with a desperate fervour that was totally unlike him.

His blurted admission stirred up all her journalistic instincts, and she desperately wanted to ask if he knew who his real father was, but she realized it would be useless. Chances were he was already regretting the momentary indiscretion.

Disengaging herself, she said, "Let's get some air. Go for a drive or something."

He managed a smile. "I have a better idea. Let's go to my hotel and make love."

This time his lovemaking was different from their usual, half-competitive, half-playful routine. Mostly he seemed to want to hold and be held. He was asking for an emotional response, and Margo was uncomfortable in the role, although she lovingly brushed back the lock of hair that perpetually fell over his forehead and murmured soothing endearments. Once, he lifted his head and gazed down at her with an intense, searching look. Sensing he was about to say something she didn't want to hear, she swung herself out of bed and, when he rather peevishly asked what she was doing, she laughed and said she had to go to the bathroom.

The hotel where she was staying was only two blocks away on Jasper Avenue, and he walked her there shortly after ten. She pretended fatigue, but her thoughts were restlessly probing the mystery of Ken's true parentage. She longed to stay in Edmonton and conduct the investigation right on the spot, but that would be much too risky. Her Toronto flight left at nine in the morning and she would be on it.

Two days went by before he called her. He was back in Vancouver and reported that the trustees of the scholarship fund had volunteered to let him have whatever personal belongings of his parents' he wanted.

"That must make you feel better."

"It takes a lot of the sting out of it," he agreed. "In fact, I'm thinking of establishing a scholarship fund myself in memory of my mother."

He was anxious to see her and wanted to come to Toronto that weekend, but she demurred, saying that they should have a cooling-off period while they both did some serious thinking. The implication that she might be emotionally involved as well seemed to satisfy him, and he didn't insist on coming.

Almost as if his call had been a signal to go into action, Margo put through a long-distance call to a firm of Edmonton solicitors. She had decided to act through lawyers because the privileged solicitor-client relationship meant they couldn't be forced to disclose information about their clients. The lawyer agreed that it would be a simple matter to obtain Ken Kwasny's birth certificate, particularly since she knew his exact age, and then, once they knew his mother's maiden name, they could readily procure his parents' marriage certificate. With luck, both documents should be on their way to her by courier the following day.

Mundell. Both Ken's parents were from the same small town in northern Alberta. And they had been married only five months before Ken was born. It was amazing how easy it was to find out things when you had that first vital clue that alerted you to the fact that there was something to look for. Rose Andrichuk had been only twenty-one when she had given birth to Ken.

Mundell was the key. It was probably not much more than a Go Slow zone on the highway, so it shouldn't be too difficult to get a line on the love life of young Rose

Andrichuk even after all this time. Margo pulled the phone toward her and dialled the number of the Edmonton law firm.

Yes, they did employ a firm of private investigators who were both competent and discreet. There was no need to worry about a cover story; there was one operator in particular who was ideally suited for investigations with a rural background. He was kind of a country boy himself, and they had found it best to leave him to his own devices. The lawyer promised to be in touch as soon as there was anything to report.

"I do have some information for you, but I'm afraid it's not as conclusive as one might wish," the lawyer said in his rather affected voice. "Young Rose seems to have been highly thought of in Mundell."

"Her baby was born five months after she was married," Margo reminded him.

"Ah, yes. Our agent reports that that caused a great deal of talk at the time. No one seems to believe that she was in love with that local boy she married."

"That fits."

"The only thing at all out of the ordinary that summer was the fact there were a number of drilling rigs operating in the area. Rose had a job as a cook's helper on one of them."

"That's probably what happened." Margo could see the story slipping from her grasp. "What you're saying is that we have a cast of thousands."

"We can narrow it down a bit more than that. The rig where she was employed would have had a crew of no more than eighteen men. One of them still lives in the area; he was a local farm boy hired on as a roughneck." He paused as if expecting Margo to say something. When she didn't, he continued, and now there was a hint of excitement in his voice. "Our agent spent last night in the Mundell tavern buying beers for this former roughneck."

"I've done that a time or two myself," Margo chuckled sympathetically, recalling the glory days of her oil-patch stories. "What did he find out?"

"Nothing definite. Certainly nothing that you could prove in a court of law. But it appears Bill Crawford, the Bill Crawford, was a young geologist assigned to that well. The roughneck believes that Crawford and Rose might have been — to use his words — getting it on together. Our agent is sure the man's recollection is accurate, because it's obvious he was jealous as hell. One gathers Rose was quite a looker."

Bill Crawford! Somehow Margo managed to keep her excitement under control as she thanked the lawyer for his report, told him to forward his account and listened patiently to his repeated warning that it was all supposition and that it would never stand up in court. But you don't know what I know, she thought triumphantly when the conversation was finished.

Now she remembered who Ken's rare smile reminded her of. It was identical to Crawford's, except that the oilman used his like a weapon while Ken smiled so seldom you really never thought of him as smiling. She wondered whether the two men were aware of the relationship between them. Surely they must be. That would account for Ken's jealous reaction whenever Crawford's name came up. She was really winging it now — Ken, the whiz kid with a genius for corporate manoeuvres and takeovers. Could there be a connection between him and the repeated runs against Venture? The first thing was to find out if there was any possible link between him and Alec Davies.

She had her answer within twenty-four hours. Davies and Stan Winters, Ken's mentor, were old buddies and were known to have done deals together in the past. Moreover, there was a rumour that Sterling Investments had recently disposed of a large block of Venture shares through a number of jitney accounts.

Okay, so now she had the ingredients. What was she going to do with them? She was involved in an affair with Ken, she genuinely liked him, and Bill had handed her career and her self-respect back to her. Well, it couldn't do any harm to see how the story would shape up. She began to tap the keys on her word processor. Like most journalists, she didn't really believe anything until she saw it in print, and as soon as she punched in "30" on the screen, she instructed the printer to type out a copy.

Now that was a story. As that creepie-crawlie, Lou Reznik, would say, it sang, it danced, it flew. And it was her story, one that she had built step by step from the very beginning; not one that had been foisted on her by a scheming bitch. A Crawford bitch at that.

Sooner or later some other investigative reporter would stumble over the story and rush into print with it. She couldn't let that happen. There, it was out in the open — she was going to go public with the story. The only question was how. There was nothing to prevent her from running an item in *Update*, but then the big dailies would pick it up and run with it, and Margo Jones would be lost in the shuffle. A story like this deserved big black headlines right across the nation. It could be her ticket back to journalistic respectability ... but none of the big newspaper chains would give her the time of day. Except — except for Norbert Reynolds, the publisher of a tabloid heavy on bathing beauties and gossip columnists and light on hard news. Reynolds was fond of boasting that the *Record* had been sued so often for libel and defamation that it was "fireproof."

"I've been wondering when we would get together. I'm a dedicated fan of yours." Reynolds, with his preppie looks and private-school background, seemed to be totally out of character as the publisher of a rag like the *Record*. Yet he performed his task with enormous zest and an instinctive grasp of what the downscale market wanted to read. Seating himself behind his polished bare desk, he gazed at her with bright-eyed anticipation. Wordlessly, she handed her article across.

"A mega-blockbuster!" he said in awestruck tones when he came to the end. "You have some corroboration, I assume?"

She handed him the two plastic certificates. He examined them and remarked,

"What used to be called a shotgun wedding. What else do we have?"

Margo swallowed and drew a deep breath. "A statement made to me by Ken Kwasny that Kwasny senior was not his real father. The fact that Bill Crawford was in the Mundell area as a geologist on a well the summer before Ken was born and was known to be friendly with Rose Andrichuk. Plus the connection between Alec Davies and Stan Winters, who is Ken's mentor, and Sterling's secret dealings in Venture shares."

"You believe in what you've written, Margo?"

"Yes, I do."

"Well, I have to clear it with our libel lawyer to keep our insurance company happy, but I can almost guarantee we'll run it. We've printed worse with a lot less proof." He sounded vaguely regretful as he added. "People seem to think twice before they sue me these days. We've bloodied quite a few noses in the courts. Still, it does take some of the fun out of it."

At the door, he held her hand a little longer than necessary. "I, for one, think it will be great to see your name back up there in the headlines, where it belongs!"

35

As always, the first thing Bill did on arriving at his office was to buzz for Lisa to arrange his agenda for the day. On the surface, she was her usual imperturbable self, but he knew the little signs that betrayed her agitation. She had a mother in Winnipeg who was very frail; maybe that was it.

"Something the matter?" he enquired.

"I guess you haven't seen the *Record* today?"

"I've got better things to do with my time than to read that rag." Even as he spoke, Bill braced himself for what was to come, in the manner of one who is a favourite target of the media.

"I'm afraid you'll have to see it." Lisa ducked back into her adjoining office and returned with a copy. "Margo Jones is at it again," she sighed as she laid it on the desk.

Bill was prepared for almost anything, but not this. He read feverishly, names from the past leaping out of the page at him: Rose Andrichuk, Mundell, even Consolidated Petroleum, the company that had first sent him to Canada. A close-up of his own face smiled back at him from the centre of the page, and there was another photo of a rather uptight-looking young man. There was something elusively familiar about the man in the photo, but Bill couldn't pin it down. Incredibly, this stranger seemed to be claiming to be Bill's son. No, that wasn't fair; he wasn't the one making the claim. It was Margo Jones who was making that assertion.

Dear God, it looked like she was right. Ken Kwasny had been born in an Edmonton hospital in early May of the year following the summer he had spent sitting wells in the Mundell area. They had all been dry holes, so there hadn't been much for a geologist — whose job was to examine the cores and monitor any tests — to do. Rose had been a virgin when he met her. Granddad Lathrop! That's who this Kwasny reminded him of. The old man had that same be-damned-to-you look. Bright as hell, too.

Rose must have decided not to have the abortion and instead married some local suitor to give the child a father. When that unforgettable letter informing him she was pregnant had arrived at his office in Houston, abortion seemed to be the only way out. He had never heard from her again after he sent her the money; he remembered having to take out a bank loan to raise part of the three hundred dollars. He had always just assumed that she had gone through with it.

Hilary! He had to talk to her before she had this mess thrown in her face. It might be too late already; the media would be onto this like a pack of ravenous wolves, thirsting for blood. They probably had already phoned the house seeking his reaction to the story. Finding him not there, they would do their best to pry a revealing statement from his new bride.

"Get my wife on the phone," he told Lisa. "I've got to warn her."

"I hope you don't mind, but I phoned Chong and told him to take the phone off the hook as soon as I saw the paper."

"Good thinking. I suppose the press has been calling here?"

"The switchboard's been jammed with calls for the last half hour. The operator has been instructed to say you are not available for comment."

Bill knew the respite was only temporary, but at least it provided a breathing space. He quickly scanned the second article — the one that linked Kwasny to the attempts to wrest control of Venture from him and was staggered by what he read. Words like "hatred," "illegitimate offspring," and "bitterness" resonated inside his head. Once again he had to admit to himself that the story had an aura of plausibility. Sterling Investments, Kwasny, Stan Winters, and Alec Davies were all meticulously linked together. There was no denying that the theory of a personal vendetta against him explained a lot of the things that had been happening around Venture. He stuffed the offending newspaper in his briefcase, hurried along a rear corridor that bypassed the reception area, and took the elevator down to the underground parking lot.

He stayed in the passing lane as he sent the silver Mercedes barrelling south along MacLeod Trail. He had been so pleased with himself over being able to bring Hilary to the new house that had no unhappy associations with Marianne. That was almost laughable in light of the morning's developments.

He slowed for the interchange and headed west on Highway 22X, swearing under his breath as he came in sight of his acreage. There were at least six cars and vans parked in front. A press photographer balanced himself on the bars of the Texas gate and aimed his telephoto lens up at the house. Bill slowed down and beeped the horn politely. He was too old a hand at the PR game to alienate the press needlessly. The reporters crowded around, holding out microphones and shouting questions. They would have been a lot more aggressive if it hadn't been for a recent case where a television cameraman had been convicted of assault because of his conduct at the funeral of a slain mobster. Bill kept the windows closed and gave the reporters a friendly wave as he headed up the long driveway.

Hilary was waiting for him in the doorway that connected with the garage. She looked anxious but composed. "What in the world is going on?" she asked. "The house is under siege by the press, the phone is off the hook, and all I could get out of Lisa when I called your office was that you were okay. Which, come to think of it," she put her arms around him, "is all that really matters. What have you been up to, darling?"

"It's all in here." He handed her the paper. "You'd better sit down while you read it."

She read through both articles without comment, then dropped the paper on the floor. "This is pretty wild. How do you feel about it?"

"It's not how I feel about it. It's how you feel! Here we are barely married, and you're faced with this garbage!"

"Bill, listen to me." She reached up and kissed him firmly on the mouth. "It doesn't matter to me. Honestly. This all happened so far in the past that it's in a totally different world so far as I'm concerned. The question is, my love, what are you going to do about it? You can't just ignore it and hope it will go away."

"I know." He kissed her again. Fervently. "I can't tell you how grateful I am that you're taking it so well. Good Lord," he exclaimed. "I was so worried about you, I forgot about the kids. I'd better get hold of them."

"Invite them over for a family council-of-war."

Debbie was waiting for his call. She subscribed to the *Record* and had called Frank at the ranch after one horrified look at what Margo had written. They had decided to do nothing until their father got in touch with them. Her main worry was the effect it might have on Hilary. Once she was assured that was all right, she seemed to find the whole thing rather entertaining. Bill warned her about the reporters staked out at the gate, and Debbie said that she and Frank would run the gauntlet together.

Frank was considerably more restrained than the insouciant Debbie, and Bill knew why. He would be thinking of his mother and how hurt she would have been. There was no point in telling him that, while she undoubtedly would have created a drunken scene, her emotions would not have been involved. For years before her death, the bottle had been the only thing she really cared about. Bill was confident he could rely on Frank's remarkable understanding of people and what made them tick to get him over this sticky patch. He apologized to his son for any negative effect the episode might have on his political ambitions.

Frank brushed it aside. "Don't give that another thought, Dad. The way things are today, it could even work to my advantage."

Then Debbie stunned them all by announcing that she knew Ken Kwasny. She didn't think it was necessary to add that she had even considered him a potential candidate to father her child, finally eliminating him on the grounds that he lacked a jock physique. At least, that was the reason she gave herself, although the possibility that he might reject her advances could have had something to do with her decision. Now, of course, she realized that he would have been aware of the blood relationship between them, which explained why he had been so cool and distant that night. All of a sudden, she felt more kindly disposed toward the aloof young man. Glancing at the newspaper photograph she said, "He's a lot more attractive than that in person. If you go for the intellectual type, that is."

"What's your impression of him?" asked Bill. "Is he the kind of person you can talk to?"

Debbie wasn't sure whether her father was seeking reassurance that she hadn't unknowingly had an affair with her half-brother, but she gave it to him anyway. "I just met him once and that was in a crowd of people, so I have no way of knowing."

"Well, team." Bill glanced at each of them in turn. "What's the game plan?"

"You'll have to issue some kind of public statement." It was Frank the fledgling politician speaking. "The sooner the better, and preferably joint."

"Joint? You mean me and this Kwasny?"

"'This Kwasny' also happens to be your son," Hilary chided him gently.

"Touché. But just how am I supposed to set up something like a joint press release?"

"There's a phone in your study," Hilary observed mildly. "You could always pick it up and call him."

"Way to go, Hilary," Debbie applauded.

Bill gave them both a look of affectionate exasperation as he walked across to his study.

The switchboard operator told him that Mr. Kwasny was not accepting calls. From the tone of her voice it was obvious that she had repeated the same message many times already that morning. He heard her give a small gasp when he asked her to let Mr. Kwasny know it was Bill Crawford calling. She put him on hold, and Bill sat in his sumptuously furnished study wondering what to say and half hoping Ken would refuse to take the call. The operator came back on the line to say she was putting the call through.

"Mr. Kwasny? Bill Crawford here. I thought we should talk."

"We have nothing to talk about."

"I think we have. For one thing, we've both been subjected to the tender mercies of Margo Jones." Did he hear an appreciative grunt at the other end? "She has the facts right, doesn't she?"

"Yes," replied Ken.

"I thought it had to be. Your mother and I were very fond of each other, Ken." That was greeted with silence, and Bill struggled on. "I want you to know that I had absolutely no idea of the connection between us until today."

"I know that."

Then why all this talk of hatred? Bill was tempted to ask, but contented himself with saying, "I don't know how you feel about it, but I would sure like to get the press off my back. The only way they're ever going to drop it is if you and I defuse it somehow. Otherwise they'll just keep building it up. I speak from bitter experience."

The guy was disarming, no question about that. He had neatly linked them as joint victims of Margo Jones and now was proposing a common front against the media. No wonder he had the government eating out of his hand. Seeing through his tactics somehow made him less intimidating. What the hell, there was nothing to lose by seeing the man.

"I can meet you after lunch tomorrow. Say two o'clock at my office. We're on the twenty-third floor."

"I'll be there." Bill was going to add the usual polite bit about looking forward to meeting him, but decided to leave well enough alone.

That night Bill and Hilary sat out on the terrace watching lightning flicker in the distance while thunder rolled down the sky and tumbled over the horizon.

"I want to go to Vancouver with you, tomorrow. Oh, I don't mean for your meeting with Ken," she hastily added when he showed signs of protesting. "I would just feel better being on the scene in case you need me."

"I would like that," replied Bill simply. And it was true. He could hack it alone — he knew himself well enough to know he could face anything alone. But it was wonderful that he no longer had to.

"I can't get over how well you're taking all this, Hilary. Are you sure it doesn't bother you?"

She got to her feet and held out her hands. "Why don't you come to bed and find out?"

36

The Lear had been wheeled out from the hangar and sat, gleaming and needle-like, on the tarmac. Tim Connors, professionally crisp and cheerful, introduced the new co-pilot who had just signed on with Venture. His predecessor had elected to go north and fly as captain on a Twin Otter in support of the drill ship operation.

Connors told Bill that air traffic control had routed their flight plan well to the south and that they would have to approach Vancouver from the sea. It appeared that a Yukon high was creating a severe weather disturbance in the interior of British Columbia, and the disturbance was playing hell with normal flight patterns. "We'll be delayed getting into Vancouver. Maybe a half-hour or more. Does that matter, boss? If it does, I might be able to persuade the tower to assign us a more direct route."

Bill told him he would like to arrive in Vancouver in time to grab a quick lunch before his afternoon meeting.

"No sweat. We'll be on the ground by eleven."

"I don't know what it is," said Hilary as they buckled up, "but all the Venture people I've met are so impressive. They're always pleasant and so obviously dedicated to what they're doing."

Bill had the good sense not to make a smart remark about her former associates in the civil service. In any case, some of them were altogether too dedicated for his liking.

"Well, our chief pilot is sure as hell dedicated," he said dryly. "There was a brochure on the Trijet Falcon on my desk the other day, with a little note from Tim: 'You'd gladly pay $10-million for that third engine if you lost one over the Atlantic.'"

"I trust you are going to give that serious thought?"

"I am, as a matter of fact. Especially since we're going international in a big way. I hope you like travel, partner."

"Love it. But won't that depend on what happens up in the Arctic?"

"I've already got that covered off. Venture will make money no matter what. If we happen to find an ocean of oil up there, there will be all kinds of fascinating technological and logistical problems, but that's for the experts, not a plain old wildcatter like me."

Bill's eagerness to talk surprised Hilary, who had expected him to be preoccupied with the coming encounter. When she mentioned this, saying that he didn't have to force himself to make conversation if he didn't feel like it, he replied that so much would depend on Ken's reaction and on the whole emotional atmosphere that the only thing to do was to wing it.

"That doesn't mean I'm not worried about it, however," he added. "This could turn out to be the toughest assignment I've ever tackled. Especially if Margo's right about him hating my guts. That's the point I really don't understand."

"Oh, I think it's only human. A feeling that you rejected him, or worse, that you rejected his mother, would do it."

"I guess you're right. You know," Bill's expression brightened with that eager, alive look she loved. "I'm sort of looking forward to it. Did I tell you that he reminds me of my grandfather?"

"That's the way to look at it," she approved. "It could turn out to be a very positive thing — for both of you."

"That's what I want. But I don't know about him. I gather he's a pretty cool cat. Anyway, we'll soon know."

He reached across the aisle for her hand and they flew on in silence. As time passed with no change in their course, Bill muttered, "I know Tim said there'd be a delay, but this is too much. We must be halfway to Hawaii by now." He craned his neck to peer back to where the coastline should be, but there was only the cobalt blue of the Pacific Ocean. He was reaching for the intercom when Tim's voice came over the cabin speaker telling them to look ahead of the port wing and they'd see one of the prettiest sights in the world.

"What is it?" asked Hilary who was on the wrong side of the cabin. She got up and leaned over Bill's shoulder.

"It's *Polarex*!" he exclaimed as he spotted the slender silhouette of the drilling mast on the horizon. "And she's got company," he added, as the Lear rapidly closed in on its target. The two icebreaking workboats must have sailed out from Victoria and taken up station on either side of the drill ship. The little flotilla was a stirring sight as it steamed north to meet the ice.

Bill pressed the intercom switch. "So much for you and your Yukon highs and weather disturbances!"

The pilot's chuckle rattled in the speaker. "We figured you could use a little morale booster."

The Lear was circling a few hundred feet above the ships, wheels and flaps lowered to reduce flying speed. There had been so many occasions when it seemed as if the Arctic project would never become a reality. But those three ships with their blunt bows smashing through the rolling whitecaps were plenty real.

"Do they know who we are?" asked Bill.

"They sure do. We're in radio contact. The captain presents his compliments and says they appreciate the welcome to Venture country. Do you want to send anything back?"

"Tell them they're looking great, and that we'll be up to visit them as soon as they start making hole at Inukshuk." Bill looked up at Hilary. "Want to come?"

"Yes, please."

The jet, wheels and flaps up, screamed across *Polarex*'s bow in a final pass, dipping its wings in salute. Bill twisted in his seat to keep the ships in view as they dwindled in the distance. Then he spoke over the intercom. "That was a great moment, Tim. Thanks."

"It's a great moment for all of us at Venture, boss. Thanks to you."

Bill and Hilary dropped into a nondescript downtown cafe for a light lunch of soup and sandwiches. It was almost one-thirty when they were ready to leave, and Bill used a pay phone to call ahead to Ken's office. He introduced himself and asked to speak to Mr. Kwasny's secretary. As soon as Karen came on the line, Bill knew he was dealing with a bright and efficient executive secretary. It always made things so much easier. He enquired if the press had the Sterling offices staked out, and she told him no, they were still getting dozens of phone calls, but there were no signs of reporters lurking about the premises. When she found out he would be arriving by taxi, she told him there was an underground parking ramp just off West Hastings Street and the cab could drive down to the loading dock to let him off. A shuttle elevator would bring him up to ground level.

In the back seat of the cab, Hilary pressed herself against Bill and whispered, "No matter what happens this afternoon, darling, remember there are people who love you very, very much."

They arranged to meet later in the lobby of the airport Hyatt. Depending on how things went with Ken, they might stay in Vancouver overnight.

Bill approved of Sterling's taste in receptionists — she was immaculately groomed and sexily attractive in an understated way. It seemed Ken was not yet back from lunch, although he was expected any minute. Jesus, was he going to pull a no-show? Bill smilingly declined her offer of coffee and settled himself in one of the quilted leather chairs. The receptionist kept her eye on the elevators. "Here he is now, Mr. Crawford," she announced as the doors slid open.

Bill peered over the top of the *Fortune* magazine he was holding. It was like looking at a younger version of his grandfather. The photograph hadn't shown it, but a lock of hair fell over Kwasny's forehead, just like Granddad's used to.

When Ken saw his visitor, his hand automatically went up to brush the hair from his forehead. Bill had seen his grandfather make the identical gesture times without number. Neither man made a move to shake hands, and Bill had the distinct feeling that if he offered to he would be cut dead.

"We'd better go to my office," Ken muttered and led the way down a broadloomed hallway.

"Now, what can I do for you, Mr. Crawford?" Ken was at his iciest as he closed the door behind him.

"You remind me very much of my grandfather," Bill remarked conversationally.

"He would be your great-grandfather. He was a whiz with figures."

"Oh?" Despite himself, Ken felt an urge to know more. "What was his name?"

"Lathrop. He was my mother's father. He was an accountant-bookkeeper, I guess they called them back then — and lived most of his life in Dallas." Bill paused. "It must be kind of strange to hear things about your background that you knew nothing of."

"What I know about my background is that you abandoned my mother and tried to kill me!"

Bill felt as if he had been slashed across the face with a whip. At least it was out in the open, though. The festering sore was exposed to view. But how did Ken know about the abortion? Had his mother told him? Bill just couldn't believe Rose would do a cruel thing like that. When he recovered from the initial shock of Ken's accusation, he protested, "That's unfair."

"It's an accurate, factual statement of what occurred."

"If you would just let me explain, I'm sure you wouldn't be so bitter."

"There's nothing to explain. The facts speak for themselves."

"You know as well as I do that events can only be understood against the background in which they occurred," Bill retorted and got a slight nod of acknowledgement from Ken. It appeared that this new-found son of his possessed a certain intellectual honesty. Bill found himself beginning to like this prickly young man.

"The facts were that when I learned your mother was pregnant I was back home in Texas with a young wife and infant daughter. I was locked into a marriage that was already turning sour, but in those days divorce was damn near unthinkable. At least, that's the way it seemed to me at the time. I was about your age then, but a great deal less experienced and worldly wise than you are."

The sneer on Ken's face infuriated Bill, and he burst out, "What the hell have you got to complain about anyway? You've already achieved more than most men do in a lifetime. And you've done it completely on your own. As far as I can make out, life has treated you pretty damn well."

"That doesn't change the fact that you tried to murder me."

"Come off it. The two things aren't even remotely the same. You're supposed to be intelligent, so why don't you start acting like it. Don't think you're going to lay a guilt trip on me, because I'm not going to accept it." Bill was on his feet. "If this is going to be your attitude, there's nothing more I can say to you."

He turned toward the door as if to leave, but Ken held up his hand. "I'm curious about why you're doing this. What do you have to gain?"

"I had the naive idea that we could have been friends. And I'd like to see you get out from under this burden of hate you've been carrying around. It's you it will destroy, not me."

There was no change in Ken's expression, but Bill's words had struck home. Ken's experience with Margo, painful as it had turned out to be, had opened his eyes to how rewarding relationships between people who cared for each other could be. Somehow it didn't matter that in the end she had betrayed him. She had shown him what was possible.

"I'll go this far with you. I'll co-operate in some kind of release. Anything to get rid of the bloody press."

Bill nodded in sympathy. The newspaper chains were feasting on the story. At first they had been careful to use exculpatory phrases like, "as reported in the *Record*," and "the alleged illegitimate son of," but as time passed with no denial or explanation from the principals, the references were becoming bolder and more direct.

Ken called Karen into his office, and they dictated a two-paragraph press release. It confirmed that Bill was Ken's natural father, that Bill had not been aware of the relationship until the story appeared in the *Record*, and that Ken would always regard Ken Kwasny, senior, as his true father.

They found it impossible to draft anything mutually acceptable about the Venture situation. There was no way of putting it down in black and white without admitting too much. But they both knew that this was the story the press was really after. A personal vendetta had "juice" and wouldn't go away by itself. It had to be put to rest.

"Why don't we call a press conference?" Ken finally suggested. "That way we can deal with it in the form of answers to questions."

"That's it! What answer will you give, Ken?"

"That it wasn't a vendetta at all, but just an attempt to take over an inviting corporate target. A straightforward business transaction."

"They're sure to ask you about your future intentions."

"I'll tell them that you have succeeded in making the company impregnable and that I've got my eye on some more accessible targets. Which happens to be true, by the way."

When they parted, it took all Bill's self-discipline to keep his hands at his sides. He desperately wanted some contact — a handshake, a clasp on the shoulder. Anything. But Ken's defences were firmly in place.

Ken closed his office door and locked it from the inside. He needed time to get his act together. He was astonished to find his hands trembling slightly. That had never happened before in his entire life. Well, he had been exposed to the famous Crawford charm and survived. The guy was likeable, no question about that. Undoubtedly it was because he came across as being sincerely interested in other people. Probably as phony as a three-dollar bill, but he gave you the impression that he cared. Crawford was a very impressive package indeed. Once again, Ken experienced a sense of elation that he had inherited this man's genes. Not shabby at all.

And he, Ken Kwasny, had the plausible son of a bitch at his mercy. All he had to do was to let it slip at the press conference how wounded he felt because his father had tried to have him aborted, and Bill Crawford would be finished. It would be a much more deadly revenge than taking Crawford's company away from him. This time the man himself would be the target, not his corporate entity.

Ken unlocked the door and asked Karen to come in. He would demonstrate his self-control by dictating a long memorandum on his plan to launch a "greenmail" campaign against a BC lumber company.

The hastily summoned press conference was set for ten-thirty the following morning in Sterling's boardroom. Despite the short notice it was well attended; the Crawford-Kwasny connection was the hot news of the day. Bill and Ken sat side by side at the head of the T-shaped conference table, and Karen handed out copies of the terse press release. Outwardly Bill was his usual smiling and relaxed self, but he was sweating inside. The press conference had been Ken's idea, and for all he knew Ken might be setting him up to be sandbagged by dragging in that abortion bit. The public would readily condone an illegitimate offspring resulting from a youthful love affair, but abortion carried its own indelible stigma that would cling to Bill forever. It could be Ken's ultimate revenge. But there was no going back now.

The assembled reporters read the brief press release with something close to disappointment. Long-lost illegitimate children reunited with their natural parents with everybody exuding sweetness and light was pretty humdrum stuff in this day and age, and the glamour of the Crawford name could only do so much for it. The financial reporters weighed in with a barrage of prepared questions about the raids on Venture, but they couldn't shake Ken's stand that the whole thing was a straight business proposition. Joan Murray, a nationally syndicated columnist who specialized in human interest, questioned Ken at length about his feelings toward his own family and was visibly moved when he assured her that the Kwasnys would always be his only real family.

Then someone asked how they felt about Margo Jones.

"Speaking for myself," Bill said with a sideways glance at Ken, "I am deeply grateful to her for making it possible for me to get to know this gifted young man who is my natural son."

A photographer asked for a picture of them shaking hands, and Bill thought to himself, Uh-oh. Here's where we blow it. He got to his feet and tentatively held out his hand, hardly daring to look at Ken as he mumbled under his breath, "I suppose we'd better go through the motions."

"It's not just the motions as far as I'm concerned," said Ken and grasped Bill's hand warmly in his own.

In her column for the evening editions, Joan Murray gushed over how Ken had inherited the "famous Crawford smile."

Death Spiral

I

This was living! Debbie Crawford exulted with sheer animal high spirits as her new horse, High Command, cantered smoothly up the gently sloping hillside. Debbie and her two male riding companions were keeping well in front of the main body of horses and riders that made up the hunt.

The Beaver Creek Hunt Club bore little resemblance to the formal fox hunts of England. In the first place, there was no fox, that species not being exactly thick on the ground in Alberta. With no fox to chase, there was no need for hounds, so the hunt became a casual and undisciplined cross-country scramble over low, but solid, fences. To Debbie, a champion show rider, it was a zoo, with the riders bunched too close together, making it impossible to avoid a pileup if anyone went down.

She reined in at the crest of the hill to take in a view that never failed to thrill her. A golden carpet of harvested grain fields rolled across the foothills to the massive ramparts of the Rocky Mountains looming on the distant horizon. Their sharp peaks were already dusted with a light mantle of snow. Down below, at the base of the hill, a mixed stand of poplars and spruce trees followed the winding course of the little creek that gave the club its name.

While Debbie gazed at the breathtaking panorama, Jerry Gillespie, who had reined in just behind her, was enjoying his own favourite view — the exciting contours of Debbie herself.

The trim fit of her riding jacket accentuated her slim waist and full bustline. Her blonde hair, so bright it barely missed being brassy, was tied in a neat ponytail beneath her black riding cap.

Whooping with excitement, the pack was catching up to them, the riders spreading out in line abreast of each other as they galloped up the hillside. Throwing a quick glance over his shoulder, Jerry shouted, "Let's get out of here!" and touched his horse's flank with a spur. High Command, a green and excitable thoroughbred, fought for the bit as Jerry's horse took off. Expertly, Debbie kept him up to the bit with strong leg pressure, but his hindquarters danced sideways and he threw his head.

Sliding sideways down a steep, rock-strewn slope on the back of an overexcited horse holds little charm for the experienced rider, and Debbie was forced to give High Command his head. She was pleased that the young gelding made only a half-hearted attempt to bolt, but he was still much too flattened out. With all his weight up front, he would be in a poor position to negotiate the log jump that waited for them a short distance down the trail.

Glen Urquhart, riding behind her, was holding his well-schooled Hanoverian back in order to give her room to manoeuvre. The rocky slope ended abruptly at the point where the trees began. As soon as they were on level ground, Debbie tried to make High Command collect himself and shift some of the weight off his forelegs. She heard a loud thump up ahead as Jerry's horse struck the top log with a hoof. Her horse heard it too, and his ears flicked back and forth uneasily. She clucked encouragingly and his ears pricked forward again. But he was still too much on the forehand and now the jump was right in front of them.

Debbie did the only thing left to her: she threw the reins at High Command, leaving him to jump them out of trouble. A trained horse could have done it — jumping off his hocks and scrambling over the obstacle somehow. But High Command charged blindly at the jump, barely getting his front legs off the ground. He crashed into the heavy logs and upended himself — hurtling Debbie through the air.

As Debbie waited for the ground to come up and meet her, one thought flashed through her mind: "My baby! What have I done to my baby?"

Instinctively, she attempted to curl into a ball to protect the child she was carrying. She hit the hard-packed path with a bone-jarring force that knocked her momentarily unconscious. Driven by a desperate anxiety, she regained consciousness almost immediately, and cried out as she felt the sticky wetness below her pelvis. Gingerly, fearful that her neck might have been broken, she lifted her head and stared in horror at the red flood that was staining her beige riding breeches. The trees above her swayed and dipped dizzily, and she passed out.

Gradually she became aware of voices, murmuring words she couldn't understand. Then she heard an authoritative voice say, "She's losing too much blood. We have to get her to a hospital." Opening her eyes, she saw the concerned, middle-aged face of Dr. Bruce Robertson looking down at her. Mounted on his big, sway-backed pinto, he was a regular member of the hunt.

"My ba ..." she whispered, but he shushed her and said, "Don't try to say anything. We're going to get you to a hospital."

Then strong hands were picking her up and she felt herself being carried by four men with their hands linked together to form a human stretcher. Jerry Gillespie, looking as if he might faint himself, was holding up her head.

"Is the horse all right?" asked Debbie in a croaky voice.

"He's fine," Jerry assured her. "Tom Wilson said he would trailer him back to Blue Meadows.

She screamed as a sudden stab of pain raced through her abdomen. Unnerved, Jerry almost let her head drop. The thought that it might have been her baby's death throes filled her with a sick nausea. The pain was constant now, ebbing and flowing in waves that made her want to cry out, but she clamped her teeth down hard on her lower lip, making it bleed.

Debbie was dimly aware of being bundled in blankets and lifted into a station wagon that took off with a furious spinning of wheels and rattle of loose gravel.

She heard Dr. Robertson speak sharply to the driver just before she drifted into a state of semi-consciousness. Then she was being rushed down a brightly lit corridor with white-clad figures trotting alongside the stretcher. A door opened, a bright light shone down on her and she was enveloped in a welcome oblivion.

"Dr. Robertson is expecting you," the floor nurse told Bill Crawford. "He would like you and Mrs. Crawford to wait in the solarium," she pointed down the hall. "He'll join you in a few minutes."

Bill thanked her and wordlessly reached for his wife's hand. They had the solarium, a cheerless lounge with cracked plastic furniture and a few tired plants, all to themselves.

Bill opened his arms and he and Hilary clung together. "She'll be all right, Bill," she whispered against his shoulder.

"Of course she will," he replied with an air of confidence that was totally unconvincing. Over the years he had seen his daughter take some nasty spills, but never one that had sent her to hospital. Ever since Jerry Gillespie's almost incoherent phone call, Bill had been tortured with visions of his vibrant Debbie condemned to spend the rest of her life in a wheelchair.

Hilary was about to whisper some additional words of comfort when Dr. Robertson, a white gown thrown over his riding clothes, came striding in. He and Bill were slightly acquainted since the Beaver Creek Hunt Club occasionally hunted over Circle C lands.

"Debbie will be fine, Bill," the physician said as the two men shook hands. "She and that young horse took a real 'purler,' but nothing's broken and she should be out of here tomorrow."

"Thank God for that." Bill sagged with relief.

"She's pregnant," said Hilary. "What about the baby?"

Dr. Robertson looked slightly taken aback. "I wasn't sure you would know about that — she couldn't have been more than three months along." Hilary wondered if the doctor would even have mentioned the fact that Debbie was pregnant if she hadn't brought it up. Probably not. She winced when Robertson said, "She lost it, I'm afraid. It was all over the moment she fell. The horse must have hit the fence all wrong."

"She never should have been riding a green horse in her condition," said Bill, still light-headed with relief that his beloved daughter was all right. He added with a wry, forgiving smile, "However, as we all know, Debbie has a mind of her own. The important thing is that she's okay."

"Will she be able to get pregnant again?" asked Hilary.

"I don't see any reason why not. They did a D-and-C on her as soon as she arrived and gave her a transfusion to replace the blood she lost. She should be feeling fine in a few days with no residual trauma."

Easy for you to say, thought Hilary with a trace of bitterness. Reminding herself of what the doctor had done for Debbie, she brushed the thought aside and favoured him with a dazzling smile. The doctor blinked under its impact. Some people seemed destined to get the most out of life, thought Robertson. Bill Crawford was almost his own age and yet here he was with a gorgeous young wife who, according to the gossip, was madly in love with him. He had to admit, though, that Bill still looked like a goddamned movie star. And all those oil millions didn't hurt, either. Putting these unprofessional musings aside, he agreed it would be all right for them to see Debbie for a few minutes.

Bill shook him warmly by the hand. "It's a blessing you were there, Bruce. We're extremely grateful."

"I was happy to do what I could to help her. I'm very fond of that daughter of yours, Bill. She sits a horse like an angel. Remember, ten minutes — no more."

"I feel like such a fool." Debbie smiled wanly up at them.

"Dr. Robertson says you'll be out of here tomorrow," said Bill cheerfully.

"And you'll stay with us for a few days," added Hilary. "Just until you're completely back on your feet."

"Did they tell you I lost the baby."

"Dr. Robertson did," replied her father. "We know how badly you must feel."

"I feel like a murderer."

"Debbie! Hilary was shocked. "You mustn't say that. It was an accident."

"It was an accident that should never have happened. I shouldn't have been on the back of that horse."

Deeply concerned by Debbie's attitude, Bill tried to reassure her. "The doctor says there's nothing to prevent you from having another baby."

Tears welled into Debbie's eyes and she turned her face into the pillow. A nurse, carrying a hypodermic syringe on a tray, bustled in and shooed the dismayed Crawfords out of the room.

"Breakfast in bed! You sure know how to spoil a girl." Debbie sat up as Hilary put the breakfast tray down on a bedside table and touched the button that opened the drapes. Debbie stretched as if she had just wakened from a deep sleep, but in reality she had been awake since five-thirty, racked with guilt over the unborn child she had lost.

If only she hadn't been so arrogantly sure of her own ability as a horsewoman! Granted, the jumps were laughably small compared to the ones she was used to in the horse-show ring, but she had been riding an unschooled horse. Somewhere in the dark reaches of the night, she had found herself wondering if maybe the real reason she had gone on the hunt was because a man wouldn't have had his pleasures interrupted by the inconvenience of having a baby. Taking the cup of coffee Hilary handed her, Debbie told herself that tonight when she was back in her own apartment, she would take a sleeping pill to make sure she got a good night's sleep.

The two women spent a companionable morning together in the Crawford's modern and spacious home, just south of Calgary's city limits. They had treated each other like favourite sisters from the moment Hilary had arrived in Calgary to marry Debbie's father.

Although she would never admit it, even to herself, Debbie was still slightly in awe of her stepmother, even though Hilary was only six years her senior.

Hilary had a regal beauty and a cool poise that could be somewhat daunting until you became aware of the warmth and humour that lay just beneath the surface. Sipping coffee in the kitchen, Debbie smiled fondly as she watched Hilary confer with Chong, the Chinese manservant from Bill's bachelor days, over the menu for a dinner party she and Bill were giving the following night. The hostess and major domo smiled approvingly at each other as they agreed on a raspberry mousse for dessert. The menu settled, Hilary left the pantry and joined Debbie in the sunlit kitchen.

"You're the picture of domestic bliss!" marvelled Debbie while Hilary poured herself a cup of coffee.

Hilary laughed somewhat self-consciously. "I guess I am at that. It will probably wear off one of these days, but at the moment I absolutely revel in it. Come on, I'll run you into town."

The light was against them at the junction with Macleod Trail. While they waited for it to change, Hilary asked casually, "Morale okay?"

"I'm not going to slash my wrists, or do anything stupid like that, if that's what you mean," replied Debbie. "But I'm furious with myself for pulling off a dumb stunt like that."

"You could always get pregnant again," murmured Hilary as she steered the Seville onto the six-lane highway.

"I think I've had that scene. For the moment anyway. It was kind of hare-brained, when you think about it; my picking out the father like he was some kind of a prize stud. You and Dad must have thought I was a complete idiot."

"Whatever you want is all right with your father. You know that. And the same goes for me."

"That helps. Really and truly helps." They fell into a comfortable silence as the Cadillac sped north toward the city. Debbie finally broke it as she said musingly, "I think the best therapy for me would be to take Pinnacle Petroleums out of mothballs and try to build it into something."

"It's almost uncanny, Debbie — the way you and your father think so much alike. He doesn't talk about it, but I know that work has always been the stabilizing force in his life."

2

The head office of Pinnacle Petroleums was a small suite of rooms on the fifteenth floor of one of the office towers that were springing up almost overnight to accommodate Calgary's oil-fuelled boom. From her corner-office windows Debbie could count six construction cranes, Calgary's "national bird," reaching skyward.

Marie Johnson, the part-time receptionist/typist, was opening the morning mail when Debbie came in. Marie, married with two young children, worked three mornings a week. The rest of the time, any calls were taken by the answering service.

In addition to the reception area where Marie presided, there were just two offices — Debbie's on the northwest corner, and one that Tim Burdon had used on a sporadic basis during the brief time he had served as Pinnacle's president. That arrangement hadn't worked out. The hectic pace of exploration created a tremendous demand for petroleum consultants like Tom, and he quickly discovered that being the president of an oil company, even one as small and relatively inactive as Pinnacle, was harming him professionally. Oil companies are not comfortable with the idea of disclosing confidential information to a potential competitor.

Besides, Debbie admitted to herself as she sat down at her desk, things hadn't gone quite as planned with Pinnacle. The fourth well in the Black Diamond field, a quarter-mile step-out on the southern flank of the reservoir, had come in dry, and production from the first three wells was declining at an alarming rate. The wells should still pay out in less than three years, but the big question was how much of a revenue stream would be left after that?

Marie interrupted Debbie's musings by bringing in the mail. "How are you feeling, Debbie?" she asked. "I heard it was a really bad fall," she continued as she added the few pieces of mail to the small stack already accumulated on Debbie's desk.

"Some nasty bruises here and there, but otherwise fine," Debbie assured her with a bright smile, wondering if she knew about her miscarriage. Of course she would. The whole damn town would know about it — except that everyone would figure that she had become careless about the Pill and been caught. It would never occur to them that a single woman would deliberately get herself pregnant and plan to raise the child herself as well.

The mail was pretty uninspiring, mostly advertising circulars and trade journals. There was one cheque, covering Pinnacle's share of the August production from the Provost gas well. It was frighteningly small, primarily because of the reduced demand for gas in the summer months, but Debbie also knew that the decline curve of production from the well was much too steep for comfort. You couldn't stand still in the oil business. If you didn't keep adding to your reserve base, sooner or later you'd end up out in the street.

While these depressing thoughts occupied her mind, Debbie continued to peruse the mail. The current issue of *Update*, Margo Jones's financial newsletter, was near the bottom of the pile. She thought of the time Margo had interviewed her in the first flush of excitement over the Black Diamond discovery.

Debbie would never forget what Margo had said — that Debbie was the first woman to really make it in the oil patch, the first one to have created her own company and not just hold down a token position in a large corporation.

Well, that might have been true enough back then, but not now. Somehow she had gotten twisted off into female things: her father's wedding — not that she begrudged a moment of that happy time — and getting pregnant.

She ignored the twinge of pain that the thought of her miscarriage always seemed to bring, and smiled at the thought of her father's happiness. No need to worry about him.

Debbie went to the little kitchenette and poured two cups of coffee. She carried them both out to the reception area, gave the one with Coffee-mate to Marie and sat down on the leather settee.

"Marie, I've decided to put this company on a full-time basis." Debbie paused for a sip of coffee. "When I hired you, you made it very clear that you only wanted to work part-time."

"That's right. I was mainly interested in getting out of the house. My little boy is a pre-schooler and goes to play school in the morning. This way I get to be with him when he's home." Marie put down her coffee cup and said, "It's no big deal, Debbie. I won't have any trouble finding another part-time job as a receptionist. Not the way things are booming in this town."

"That's for sure." Relieved, Debbie got to her feet and said, "I'll be happy to give you a letter of recommendation, and if there's anything else I can do to help, just let me know."

"Drilling funds are the in thing at the moment." Fred Fullerton smiled beatifically as the waiter placed his second double martini in front of him.

"I have a general idea of how they work." Debbie was still on her first glass of white wine. "But I wish you would fill me in on the details. They're some sort of tax dodge, aren't they?"

Fred shot her a reproving look. "They're not dodges at all. They're perfectly legal and above board. The government in its — ahem — infinite wisdom has decided it wants to encourage exploration for oil and gas in Canada. So it allows the taxpayer to write off exploration expenses against his ordinary income. For instance, a medical doctor can invest in a drilling fund and deduct the cost from his income as a physician. Of course," he paused to take an appreciative sip of his martini, "a doctor wouldn't have the faintest idea of how to go about exploring for oil. That's where the promoter comes in."

"He puts together an exploration play and sells it to your doctor friend," said Debbie, leaning back slightly to allow the waiter to serve her salad. Fred had ordered a steak sandwich, rare. "If a good veterinarian can't cure it, I won't eat it," he had warned the bored waiter, who smiled tolerantly.

"That's right," affirmed Fred, cutting into the almost raw meat.

"But he does more than that. He runs the play on behalf of the investors and charges a hefty management fee for doing it. Plus, of course, he gets an interest on the land when the investors have recovered their money."

He paused to wipe a drop of grease off his chin with his napkin and then asked, "You got a play you want us to underwrite? This is a great time to do it; the end of the taxation year is coming up fast, and there's a shortage of product."

"I wish I had," sighed Debbie. "But that takes geologists and a land position, and I don't have either one. I'm just casting around for a way to get my company back into the action. Maybe I can get geared up to get into the drilling-fund business next year."

"It'd be a shame to miss this market. They're really crying for product out there. There might be something I could do to help."

"I'm all ears."

"In my business we're great believers in the old quid pro quo. Know what I mean?"

Here it comes, thought Debbie to herself. The old proposition. But I'm not going to sleep with this overweight slob, no matter what. "How about if I give you first crack at the underwriting when Pinnacle goes public?" His expression told her it wasn't what he had in mind, but she could tell he was thinking about it. A business connection, no matter how small, with the Crawford family interests would be a real feather in the cap of any investment dealer.

"I'll call in a few markers and see if I can come up with anything," he agreed finally. Debbie was pretty sure that he already had something in mind, but if he wanted to make a big production out of it, so be it.

She was slightly appalled when he ordered a cognac to go with his coffee. Fred had started his career as a trader on the stock exchange floor and still tended to believe his working day was over when the stock market closed at one p.m. Calgary time.

Debbie couldn't help contrasting the self-indulgent Fullerton with Jim Goulder, her father's financial advisor, who thought nothing of working around the clock whenever there was a deal to be closed. Still, Fred had a reputation among the yuppie crowd of knowing where it was at.

She signalled for the check before her guest decided to have a second brandy, and extracted his promise to call her in the morning, regardless of whether or not he had come up with something.

"I think I've found a way for you to get in on the drilling-fund scene this year," Fred announced as soon as Debbie came on the phone. "There's a guy I know who's got the makings of a deal — he's selected the land and worked up the geology, but he needs upfront money to lease the mineral rights, obtain an independent engineering study, and clear the offering with the securities commission."

"That sounds as if it's going to cost an awful lot of money."

"It sounds worse than it is," Fred assured her blithely. "The mineral rights will be the big item, but this guy swears he can pick up oil and gas leases in the area for ten bucks an acre. Anyway, he'll spell it all out for you. I asked him to give you a call at two o'clock this afternoon. Okay?"

"Okay. What's his name?"

"Graves. Dick Graves. He's just getting started, but I have a feeling the lad's going to make it big. He's a good-looking son of a bitch, too. Watch yourself, Debbie."

"I'm a big girl, Fred."

"So I've noticed." Debbie could picture the look on Fred's fat, unhealthy face on the other end of the telephone conversation. "Let's have lunch real soon," he was saying. "My turn to buy."

"Anytime, Fred," replied Debbie with a marked lack of enthusiasm.

Dear God, is this guy for real? Debbie asked herself after about fifteen minutes of conversation with Dick Graves. It wasn't that he was coming on strong. If anything he was too diffident, almost deferential. Debbie was uncomfortably aware that she was somewhat older than her visitor; he looked to be twenty-seven or twenty-eight, which made her two or three years his senior. Not enough to justify his treating her like a goddamn matron, for Chrissake. What a salesman he would make! He looked like the all-American boy. Except that he was Canadian — born in Standard, Alberta, of all places. Is there such a thing as an all-Canadian boy? wondered Debbie. Annoyed with herself for woolgathering, she concentrated on what Dick Graves was saying.

"The program will consist of three drilling prospects, each one of which stands on its own feet. Two of the wells are gas prospects which means each one will require 640 acres to form a spacing unit for the drilling of a well. The third prospect is a potential oil play, so we need 160 acres for the drilling unit, and I want to tie up an adjoining quarter-section for a follow-up well. That's a grand total of 1,600 acres and I'm pretty sure we can lease the land for an average price of ten dollars an acre. If we act fast that is."

Sixteen thousand dollars: no sweat. Debbie pondered. "You'll need to pay a fee to the lease hound," she pointed out.

"Oh no I won't." He jerked a thumb at his chest. "You're looking at the lease hound. I'll do all the negotiating with the farmers myself. I'll make out okay."

I just bet you will, Debbie thought to herself. "What are those wells going to cost?" she asked.

"For the gas wells, $190,000 each, dry and abandoned; $265,000 completed for production. The oil well is deeper and more expensive — $250,000 if it's dry, and $325,000 if it's a producer. But you don't have to worry about that; the limited partners pay for the cost of drilling and completing."

"Where do I come in?"

"You provide the seed money. $16,000 to acquire the lease; another $4,000 for the evaluation study and security commission clearances."

"And what do I get for my $20,000?"

"One half of my back-in rights. The drilling-fund agreement will provide that I receive a forty per cent interest in the lands after the investors have recovered their money. You get half of my forty per cent."

"What about your management fee?"

"Mine. All of it. Remember I'm the one who will be managing the program — I have to get the leases, deal with the drilling contractors, arrange for the drilling licenses — all that kind of stuff. That's a sweet deal."

He was right, and both of them knew it. "You've got yourself a partner," Debbie said briskly and held out her hand.

He seemed a bit taken aback by the gesture, but he recovered quickly and shook hands in a businesslike fashion. "Terrific! Now if you'll just make me out a cheque, I'll head out to the field and start sweet-talking those mineral owners."

Within a week Dick Graves had put it all together. Eager to add whatever she could to her knowledge of the industry that was to be her life's work, Debbie carefully scrutinized the engineering report that described the three drilling prospects. It basically consisted of computer printouts that set out the anticipated revenue streams, described the payout periods, and calculated the present worth of the future revenues. She was disconcerted to find that the impressive-looking tables with their columns of figures were headed Typical Basal Quartz Gas Well and Evaluation of a Typical Cardium B Oil Well.

When she queried Graves about this, pointing out that the evaluation didn't deal with the specific properties to be drilled, he shrugged off her concerns. "It's good enough for the Securities Commission," he said. "It tells the participants in the drilling fund what they can expect from a successful well."

"Yes, but it doesn't tell them what the chances are of these particular wells being successful," she protested.

He pointed to the first page of the offering memorandum. There, in bold face type, were the words: "Exploring for oil and gas is a high-risk enterprise, with no guarantee of success."

"People who invest in drilling funds are sophisticated investors." There was a slightly patronizing tone to Dick's voice that set Debbie's teeth on edge. "They know the risks are high. What they're really interested in is the tax relief."

Fred Fullerton had certainly been right about there being a demand for product, as he liked to call it. All twenty units of the drilling fund were snapped up within the week. Debbie couldn't help but be impressed by Dick's energy and hustle. Faced with the necessity of getting all three wells drilled by the end of the year so that the investors could enjoy the maximum tax advantage, he was either in the field expediting operations, or on the phone cajoling drilling contractors and a variety of sub-trades.

This was the part of the oil game that Debbie really enjoyed, in a masochistic kind of way. The commitment had been made, the drilling bit was turning to the right, and all one could do was wait for the verdict. It was at times like this that she felt especially close to her father whose entire life had been dedicated to seeking the elusive black gold. His biggest exploration project was on hold until next summer when the short Arctic drilling season would open up once more. The ice pack had moved in early this year, forcing the drill ship, *Polarex*, to move off location in mid-September and retreat to its winter anchorage. There was almost 4,500 feet still to be drilled before the target formation was reached. Still, the long delay wouldn't be nearly as stressful for him as it would have been if he hadn't managed to lay off the enormous cost of drilling in the Beaufort Sea by farming out part of his interest to one of the multinationals. It would be terribly disappointing if the new well came in dry, of course, but at least his company was no longer exposed financially.

The worst part of waiting for the results from her own wells was that Debbie had altogether too much time to think. It would be different when Pinnacle was bigger and had a number of exploration projects on the go. But right now, Dick's drilling-fund operation was the only game in town for her and, with time on her hands, her thoughts relentlessly turned inward to the life that no longer grew inside her. It was worse at night when she would wake from a dream in which she was holding her newborn son — it was always a boy in her dreams — in her arms. She would fight to stay asleep and remain safely inside the dream but inevitably she drifted upward to the surface of consciousness and painful reality would engulf her. After the first couple of times she gave up trying to get back to sleep and stood at the living room windows of her apartment looking out at the darkened city. Directly below her was the Calgary Tower, ablaze with Christmas lights. Here and there, lights burned in the downtown office towers as geologists waited for reports to come in from the field, and lawyers and underwriters toiled over the prospectus for some new share issue. One afternoon, when she was feeling really strung out, Debbie had purchased a pack of cigarettes that lay unopened in the top drawer of her dresser. On a particularly bad night she got as far as peeling off the cellophane wrapping before hastily stuffing the still-unopened pack in the garbage compactor.

The next day she put High Command back in training. The physical exercise might help her sleep, and he was just too good a prospect to waste. If he developed properly she would be able to sell him for a big price, as she had with her champion hunter, Imperial Way, and use the money to finance some exploration work for Pinnacle. A groom had exercised High Command by circling him on a long line for an hour every day, but he was still full of himself after not having been ridden for more than a month, so it was not until their third session that Debbie reintroduced him to jumping. She began with the basics — trotting him over cavaletti: evenly-spaced wooden poles raised some six inches off the ground — and, as soon as he was trotting over the poles with his neck nicely flexed, she raised the height of the last pole to make him arch his back and jump.

It was while she was cooling High Command after a jumping lesson that Debbie felt the stirrings of her libido, suppressed since the accident by the trauma of her miscarriage. Dick Graves. Now *there* was a challenge. Almost too good-looking to be true, and with a cool air of detachment that was strangely exciting. But he was so wrapped up in his drilling program that he seemed totally oblivious of her as a woman. And the last thing she wanted was to distract him from his work in which she herself had so much at stake. She decided to put Dick Graves on hold for a more opportune time. Meanwhile, Ray Nielsen had been pestering her for a date. He was pretty good in bed and, best of all, he knew how to get her off. Debbie's cheeks were flushed as she handed the reins over to a stable hand.

3

Debbie made Ray wait outside in the hallway while she punched in the code that turned off the alarm system. When the red warning light changed to green she closed the folding closet doors and invited him in. The shoulders of his overcoat were still damp with melted snowflakes and she hastily backed away when he reached for her. "Let's not rush things, darling. We have all the time in the world. Hang up your coat and I'll fix us a drink."

Draping her black mink over a chair in the entrance hall, Debbie walked across the sunken living room toward the bar trolley over by the far window. As she passed the archway that led into her study she saw that the answering machine on her desk was blinking. Telling Ray to help himself to a drink, she went into the study and waited until he was busy at the drinks trolley before she played the tape back. She also took the precaution of turning the volume down — when some of her male friends got into the booze they had the not so endearing habit of leaving highly suggestive messages. But it was Dick Graves, and not an amorous suitor, whose voice came over the speaker. "The first gas well was a duster, Debbie. We're moving the rig over to the second location."

The glow from the wine Debbie had drunk during dinner evaporated instantly in the wake of Dick's disheartening report. Along with the disappointment came a faint resentment over the laconic way he had chosen to break the news. She told herself it didn't matter how the news was broken, the result was the same. There was no appeal from a dry hole. Still, the resentment was there.

Ray Nielsen had seated himself on the curved chesterfield and was perfunctorily examining one of the figures from Debbie's collection of Haida argillite carvings. She called out to him, "Something's come up. Bear with me a sec," and flipped through the telephone directory for Dick's home number.

She got his answering machine. It probably wasn't deliberate on his part, but, one way or another, Mr. Dick Graves had managed very effectively to distance himself from the bad news he brought. She couldn't help but compare his attitude with the helpful way Tom Burdon always kept her informed. Controlling her irritation, she waited for the beep and then said into the mouthpiece, "Debbie here, Dick. I'd like to know more about that dry hole. Call me as soon as possible."

Ray scrambled eagerly to his feet when she walked back into the living room. The way he hastily plunked the fragile totem pole down on the glass tabletop made

Debbie wince with apprehension but, to her relief, the delicate figure didn't shatter.

She held up her hand as he advanced toward her. "I've just had some rather bad news, Ray. I'll have to ask you to leave after this drink."

She cut off his protests with a flat, "Don't be tiresome, Ray," and he knew he was licked. "There'll be other times," she added by way of a sop.

"Is that a promise?"

"That's a promise."

"Okay. I'll go quietly."

Dick Graves sounded mildly exasperated when he returned her call the next morning. "What more can I tell you?" he asked plaintively. "The Basal Quartz just wasn't there. It's that simple."

"But you sounded so optimistic."

"Explorationists are optimists by definition," he replied with a laugh. "Don't forget we've still got two more wells to go."

"I'd like to come out and see the one that's drilling now."

"Sure, if you want to," he replied without enthusiasm. "But if I were you, I'd wait until we drill the oil well. That's where the real excitement is."

Fortunately for her nervous system, Debbie was given little opportunity to brood over the drilling program. The Christmas social season was in full swing and, as the daughter of one of the city's most prominent families, she was completely caught up in it.

One of the biggest social events was the skating party her brother Frank had decided to throw at the Circle C, the Crawford family ranch some forty miles southwest of Calgary, in honour of his glamorous new stepmother. Thanks to an overly ambitious mother, Hilary was a superb skater. When Frank discovered this, he set to work to convert the slough in the south pasture into a skating rink by scraping off the snow and trucking in additional quantities of water to produce an even surface.

The party got under way at two p.m. on a Saturday afternoon, early enough to get in a couple of hours of outdoor activity before the winter sun slipped behind the mountains. Like Bill Crawford, many of the guests had been raised in the southwestern United States and were totally helpless on skates. Frank had laid on sleigh rides to keep the non-skaters occupied, along with some well-broken saddle horses for the more adventurous. Small poplar logs soaked in kerosene burned briskly in two oil drums placed at the edge of the slough for the red-cheeked skaters to warm themselves by, and a makeshift bar dispensed hot toddies and eggnog for the grown-ups, with hot chocolate and soft drinks for the kids.

Frank, with his inborn talent for people and organizational ability, made a wonderful host. He had obviously given the guest list a great deal of thought. Most of the guests were family friends with their children and, in some cases, grandchildren, but he had also included a number of local political heavyweights. Frank had informed his father and Debbie a couple of nights ago that he had definitely made up his mind to seek the Conservative nomination for the riding in which the Circle C was located. A nomination meeting had been called for the end of January, after the incumbent had announced that he was retiring from politics in order to devote more time to his feed business. At twenty-six, Frank was very young to be launching a political career, but his good-natured competence gave him an air of maturity beyond his years.

Somewhat to Debbie's surprise, her father had been warmly supportive of Frank's plans. As president of a large oil company, Bill Crawford had to deal with politicians from time to time; in fact, he had helped his company by playing the political card with consummate skill on more than one occasion. Despite this, or possibly because of it, he had, with a few notable exceptions, a low regard for politicians and their works. When Debbie questioned him about this after their conversation with Frank, he replied, "I think Frank may turn out to be one of those rare individuals who is ideally suited to public life. It's more than just an ego trip for him. He truly wants to help people, and in politics you have the power to do that. The crap a politician has to put up with would drive me right up the wall, but Frank has just the right temperament for it."

Lacing up her skates, Debbie watched Frank talking animatedly with Jan Carruthers over by the unused barbecue pit. Was he about to make himself more politically acceptable by becoming a family man? The look on Jan's face made it abundantly clear that all he had to do was ask. Debbie found Jan's 4-H brand of fresh wholesomeness rather boring, but there was no doubt she would make a perfect helpmate for an ambitious politician. As far as Debbie knew, she and Frank had never dated and were just casual friends. She certainly wasn't Frank's date this afternoon, for she had arrived with a whole carload of young people from nearby ranches. But there was no doubt about her being smitten. *She's the type who'll put on weight when she starts having babies.* Unbidden, the spiteful thought flashed through Debbie's mind, bringing in its wake the familiar sense of loss. She tightened the laces with a fierce tug and straightened up.

Debbie hadn't been on skates since high school, but after a few tentative steps it all came back to her and she picked up speed with increasing assurance. After a few laps around the rink she even attempted some of the elementary figures she had been taught as a youngster at the Glencoe Club.

"Bravo, Debbie! I had no idea you could skate like that," applauded Hilary as Debbie made a rather wobbly recovery from a backspin. Hilary was holding her young son, Jason, by the hand. She skated along with him for a few short strides, then stopped and let him go on his own. He managed to stay upright for almost half the length of the rink before falling. His well-padded snowsuit cushioned his fall and he was beaming with self-satisfaction as Hilary and Debbie skated up to him.

Smiling, Debbie helped him to his feet and brushed him off. "How about you and me taking a couple of whirls around the rink, partner?" He grinned cheerful assent and put his mittened hand in hers. As they moved off, Debbie said over her shoulder to Hilary, "Enjoy yourself."

Hilary, breathtaking in her abbreviated skating costume, glided through the crowd of skaters with long, smooth strides, throwing in a dazzling spiral or loop whenever she came to a clear space.

"Your mom's a terrific skater, isn't she, Jason?" said Debbie as Hilary flashed past them, skating backwards with flawless style.

"We used to skate on the canal in Ottawa," the five-year-old told her proudly. "Nobody else was near as good as Mommy. We always had hot chocolate afterwards," he added with an innocent smile.

Debbie laughed down at his eager, upturned face. "I can take a hint. Tell you what. Once more around the rink and we'll go find Frank and ask him for some." It had been decided within the family that, despite the age difference, Jason should call his new stepbrother and stepsister by their first names.

"Isn't she something?" marvelled Frank as Debbie and Jason joined him at one of the fires. Like many others he had stopped what he was doing to admire Hilary's performance.

"She's fantastic," agreed Jan Carruthers who was standing beside him. "I bet I know what this young man wants." Jason thanked her politely as she ladled out a mug of hot chocolate and handed it to him.

Waiting for it to cool, he watched his mother skate with a connoisseur's eye and said matter-of-factly, "She can do better than that."

He was right. Hilary, conscious of the attention she was attracting, was holding herself in. Even so, she cut a spectacular figure. Then she saw her husband standing on the bank near Debbie and Jason. He was beaming proudly and gave her the high sign as she flashed past. Encouraged, she opened up, and bounded across the ice in a series of twirling leaps and spins. "That was fun," she glowed as she slid to a stop in front of Bill. He kissed her and whispered in her ear, "Just like that wonderful Sunday afternoon on the Rideau Canal."

Jerry Gillespie and a group of his friends were applauding enthusiastically. "Fabulous, Mrs. C! Just fabulous," he said as they skated over. Bill, grateful for what the young man had done to help Debbie at the time of her accident, greeted him cordially, and soon the whole group was mixing companionably around the fire.

"What's the matter, Frank?" asked Debbie, puzzled by the strange look on her brother's face. Following the direction of his glance, she muttered, "Oh, oh" under her breath. Jan Carruthers had seen it, too. Debbie caught her dejected look before she turned away and busied herself with the pot of hot chocolate. The girl was a stunner. Blonde hair, worn long and straight, framed a face that would have graced the cover of any fashion magazine. Debbie, who had no reason to complain of her own appearance but had always resented the fact that she was only five-foot-four, envied her long-legged height.

The beautiful stranger, whoever she was, was certainly not thrusting herself forward. She was smiling politely and rather diffidently at no one in particular. Debbie saw with a small shock of surprise that she had metal braces on her teeth. Oddly enough, the imperfection, possibly because it was temporary, did nothing to lessen her appeal.

"Who's the looker, Jerry?" asked Debbie as she saw her brother making his way toward the blonde.

"Her name is Linda Shepherd." Jerry frowned as he saw Frank introduce himself to her. "She's from Toronto and she's out here on a skiing holiday. We met up with her on the slopes at Lake Louise yesterday. There's a whiteout today and the skiing is the pits, so we invited her to drive down from Banff with us and come to this super party of yours." Jerry's frown turned into a scowl as he saw Frank fall into easy conversation with Linda Shepherd.

"Jerry said this was your ranch. Is that true?" Linda looked fairly incredulous at the thought of anyone as young as Frank owning a spread like the Circle C.

"It's a family business, but I run it."

"How big is it, anyway? It seemed like we were driving forever after we turned in the gate."

"Two thousand acres deeded land with another 640 under lease. Not all that big by local standards but I'm trying to make it into an efficient operation." As he spoke, Frank was hurriedly putting on his skates. Out of the corner of his eye he saw Jerry start toward them, but then Debbie took Jerry by the arm and laughingly skated off with him. Frank couldn't be absolutely sure, but it looked as if his sister had just done a beautiful job of running interference for him. He bowed low and offered his arm to the lovely newcomer.

She took it with a self-conscious little laugh and said, "This is the first time I've been on skates for years, so I'm kinda rusty."

Frank was appalled to hear himself saying, "You're in good hands. I'm an old hockey player."

If she thought he was being overly boastful, she gave no sign of it as she asked, "You mean professionally?"

"No. Just high school and university." He refrained from telling her that he had turned down a draft from two NHL farm clubs.

As it turned out, she needed very little help from him. After a few moments of adjusting their strides, they skated along smoothly together, happily engrossed in what each other had to say. Once or twice as she laughed, she raised her free hand to hide the braces on her teeth. They also impaired her speech somewhat, imparting a slight lisp to some of her words. Frank found it totally captivating.

Immediately following the outdoor activities, a hearty ranch-style supper was served in the main house. Bill and Hilary ate together, standing beside the immense fireplace made from river stones. Hilary put her plate down on the mantel to cut her steak and looked over at the leather settee where Frank and the young blonde were sitting together. "I think our boy Frank has it bad," she murmured under her breath.

"He's got good taste, I'll give him that." Bill took an appreciative glance at his son's companion. "But how about Debbie and Jerry Gillespie? They're inseparable. I've never seen Debbie give him a tumble before. It must be because of the way he helped her when she took that fall."

Hilary gave her husband a commiserating look. "What your daughter is doing, my love, is taking young Mr. Gillespie out of the play so that Frank can make his move."

"Women! What chance do we mere mortal men have against them?" Bill shook his head in mock helplessness. Then he said, "You know, I'm kind of relieved that's all it is. Jerry's a fine young man, but he just doesn't have the ... the right stuff, I guess ... to handle Debbie."

"Who does?" asked Hilary with a thoughtful smile.

As planned, the party was breaking up early. Parents held drowsy children in their arms as they said goodnight and headed for their cars and the long drive back to town. As the last few guests were taking their leave, Frank appeared in the front hallway with his ski equipment and announced that he was driving Linda up to Banff.

"Harvey can run the place for a couple of days," he said to his father rather defensively.

"Of course," Bill agreed, tactfully refraining from adding that the ranch foreman had been doing it for ten years before Frank came back from college and took over.

"It'll do you good to get in some skiing. We'll probably drive back over here tomorrow and go for a ride. Jason," Bill looked down at his young stepson who was valiantly trying to keep his eyes open, "is turning into a real little horseman."

Jerry Gillespie and his friends were the last to leave. Bill, somewhat concerned that young Gillespie might have had one drink too many for the drive to Banff, stared hard at him, then decided he was okay.

Jerry was wound up all right but that seemed to be because he was finally making time with Debbie.

As he went out the door, he shouted back at her, "Remember, eight o'clock sharp at the bottom of the Larch chairlift."

"The things I do for you, little brother," muttered Debbie in an aside to Frank while she waved gaily as Jerry and the couple who had driven down from Banff with him piled into his BMW.

"My transportation is a lot more basic than Jerry's," said Frank as he led Linda across the yard to his Dodge pickup, its motor already turning over. "It's a rancher's version of the yuppie-mobile."

"It's fine with me." Linda waited for him to stow his skis in the back, then climbed cheerfully into the warm cab.

Frank drove slowly on the way to Banff, stretching out the precious time he and Linda spent alone in the easy intimacy of the cab, shut away from the outside world. Normally reticent about himself, Frank talked freely about his plans for the ranch and his decision to give politics a try. From time to time he stole a sideways glance at her lovely face, shadowy in the light from the dash, to see if he was boring her, but her eyes were bright and her smile was warm and unforced. It was that most magical of times when everything about a person who was a complete stranger only hours before is suddenly of absorbing interest.

Linda was an expert and dedicated skier, determined to get in as many runs as the lift lineups would allow. Knowing that Jerry and Debbie and the other couple planned to ski Larch, Frank elected to ski the backside of the mountain, and it wasn't until they skied down to Temple Lodge for lunch that they joined up with the others. Debbie, with her customary combination of iron will and female guile, had managed to hang onto two empty chairs on the crowded wooden deck and Frank lowered himself into one with a grateful sigh. "You know how many runs we did this morning?" he demanded. "Ten! It got so that the longer the lineup the better I liked it. My legs are spaghetti!"

"She's a tiger, all right," agreed Jerry. "I didn't even try to keep up with her on Saturday." He gave Linda a rueful look. Debbie had just told him that she was driving back to Calgary after the last run that afternoon, and it was clear that Frank had the inside track with the beauteous Linda. The worst part was that he couldn't be absolutely sure whether Debbie was finally showing some interest in him, or whether she was just throwing a block for Frank — the famous Crawford one-two. Morosely he looked around the crowded sundeck. In the spring, skiers would strip down to their shorts and soak up the rays on "Temple beach," but in mid-December the best they could do was to unzip their parkas. There was plenty of talent but most of it seemed to be paired off. However, there was bound to be some action in the après-ski scene.

As soon as the last sandwich was eaten Linda was on her feet. Groaning, Frank pushed himself up from the chair and followed her over to the ski rack. "You know, the runs will still be there a half-hour from now," he remarked conversationally as he stepped into the bindings.

"You've got the mountains right in your own backyard," she replied. "But I'm lucky to get out here once a year, so I've got to make the most of it."

"I take your point," Frank waved his pole in the direction of the lift. "Lead on."

By the end of the third run that afternoon the muscles in Frank's thighs were on fire with fatigue. He marvelled at Linda's stamina, although he noticed she was getting a little sloppy around the moguls. Unsure of her reaction, but knowing he should say something, he turned to her as they stood in the lineup and said, "We're overcooking it. And that's when you get hurt."

To his surprise, she agreed and said, "We'll make this the last run."

She came off a mogul too fast and barely had time to recover before hitting the next one. Frank waited for her to throw in a turn to check her speed but she couldn't seem to bring her skis around in time. She tried to go around the next bump but it was too close and she zoomed over it and "took air." Badly off-balance, she fell hard, cartwheeled once, then rolled and slid down the steep, hard-packed slope. Appalled, Frank raced down to where the crumpled figure lay motionless on the snow. He knelt beside her, almost afraid to touch her.

"Linda, are you all right? Darling, are you okay?"

"I think so," came a muffled voice. "But it's too early to tell." Carefully she rolled over and looked up at him. The force of the fall had pushed her goggles up on her forehead and he was gazing directly into those dark-fringed blue eyes. She smiled at him reassuringly and he gathered her in his arms. Her lips were cool and firm against his and Frank knew he was in love.

"I've never talked so much about myself in my entire life." Frank polished off the last of his beef Wellington and took a swallow of burgundy. "I admit I've enjoyed it but I know next to nothing about you. Give, pretty lady."

Linda smiled faintly and turned her head to gaze out the window of the second-floor restaurant on Bear Avenue. The light from the street lamps was blurred with a curtain of large, fat snowflakes. "You know more about me than you think," she said teasingly. "You know I'm twenty-two and that I live in Toronto and that I love to ski. I'm five-foot-eight and weigh one hundred and thirty pounds. I am wearing braces to correct an overbite and they come off in six months. Then I'll be able to speak better. How's that?"

"It'll do for starters. But I need to know more. Much more. For instance, what do you do? Are you still in university?"

She shook her head, setting her long blonde hair swinging. "I'm a working girl."

"Let me guess. You're a secretary in a large law firm."

Again she shook her head. "Nope. I'm in PR — public relations."

"What's the name of the firm you're with?" When she looked a little startled, he added, "So I can call you, dummy. You don't think for one moment that I'm going to let you just disappear from my life, do you?"

"Look, Frank, I'm not ready for anything heavy. Not yet."

"Okay, we'll keep it light. Now, what public relations firm are you with?"

"I freelance. I'll give you the number of my apartment. You'll probably get the answering service, but I'll call you back."

Snow was still falling when they left the restaurant. "The powder will be perfect tomorrow. Let's get up real early and catch the first gondola into Sunshine so we can get in some powder skiing before it's all packed down."

"Fabulous!" She raised her face to catch a snowflake on her tongue. Other flakes fell on her eyelashes where they sparkled like diamonds. Frank couldn't decide which he wanted to do more — kiss her, or just go on looking at her.

To Frank's considerable gratification, Linda was not accustomed to skiing powder, so he had the pleasure of teaching her how to turn, and the importance of keeping her weight back on her skis. At the end of the third run, when the powder began to show the effects of traffic, Linda spotted Jerry waiting in the lineup of the lift they were headed for. She waved a pole at him but, instead of responding, he said something to the girl he was with and they left the lineup and skied off together.

"I'm almost positive that was Jerry." Linda frowned behind her goggles. "But then everybody looks so much alike in ski clothes."

"It was him all right," Frank told her. "He just doesn't want me to see him with that chick for fear I'll tell Debbie."

"Would it bother her?"

"Not a bit. She thinks he's a wimp."

"I wondered about that. But she was sure leading him around on a string at your party."

"Debbie's good at that."

They shut down their skiing shortly after lunch so Frank could run Linda down to Calgary in time to catch her flight to Toronto. As the airport terminal came into view, she became visibly tense. Probably a nervous flier. Frank kept up a flow of light banter to distract her, but by the time they were inside the terminal building she seemed even more uneasy, stealing quick, furtive glances around the crowded concourse.

"What are you afraid of?" asked Frank, only partly in jest. "A jealous lover?"

"Wha ...? Oh ... no, nothing like that. It's just that I'm a white-knuckle passenger."

She appeared to relax once she had been checked in. Frank held her hand as they walked toward the security counter.

"When would be a good time for me to come to Toronto?"

"What?" The idea seemed to take her aback. "I dunno. When were you thinking of?"

"Soon."

"Not till after Christmas, that's for sure. I'm spending it with my family in Peterborough."

"What about between Christmas and the New Year?"

"I guess so. Except that I do have a date for New Year's Eve. But what about this political campaign of yours?"

"Nothing will happen until after the holidays. So I'll see you in two weeks. Just saying that makes me feel better."

"Next please," said the security guard with mild exasperation, holding out her hand for Linda's boarding pass.

4

"It's for you, Debbie," said Hilary.

Debbie carefully picked her way through the welter of torn Christmas wrappings and opened packages and took the phone from Hilary. It was Dick Graves and he was telling her that if she wanted to be there when the well reached total depth they'd have to leave for the wellsite within the hour.

"Don't you know what day this is?" wailed Debbie. "It's Christmas, for Christ's sake!" Realizing how incongruous that sounded, she continued in a calmer tone, "I thought there was no chance of reaching total depth until tomorrow?"

"That's because the drilling superintendent figured they'd have to make a trip out of the hole to change the bit. But now he's decided to drill to bottom with the one they've got on. You don't have to come, of course. Your being there isn't going to change anything, and I can understand why you'd want to be with your family at Christmas."

"I'm coming. Where do you want to meet me?"

"Why don't I wait for you outside the main entrance to your office building. You can leave your car in the indoor parking. How long is it going to take you to get in from the ranch?"

"I'll have to pull some clothes on. I'm still lazing about in my dressing gown. I'll see you there in an hour and a half. Okay?"

"No later. They're within 150 feet of where the formation should be."

Debbie put down the receiver and looked apologetically at Hilary. "I hate to do this but I've got to go out to that well. Can you manage?"

"Of course I can manage. Chong's out in the kitchen working on the Christmas dinner right now. Look at your father!" Laughingly she pointed at Bill who was crossing the room to join them. "You can tell by the look on his face that there's nothing he'd rather do than go with you."

"It's not my show." Bill shook his head and smiled at his daughter. "I've had to visit wells at some of the damnedest times over the years, but never on Christmas day."

"Just shows you how dedicated an oilman I am," laughed Debbie as she tore off to change. Five minutes later she returned, zipping up her parka. "Tell dear Ken how sorry I will be to miss him."

At Hilary's prompting, Bill had invited the young man who was his natural son to fly over from Vancouver and spend Christmas with them. To Bill's delight he had agreed to join them for Christmas dinner. "And tell him he's not to go back to Vancouver without seeing me," Debbie added as she bent down to kiss Jason, busy with his Star Wars set. Then she kissed Frank on the cheek. "And I expect you'll be calling Toronto later today?"

"Peterborough," he corrected her happily. "Linda's spending Christmas with her folks."

A Christmas Chinook had blown in, raising the temperature to a balmy forty degrees Fahrenheit, and throwing a dramatic arch of cloud over the mountains. The paved highway was clear of ice and Dick kept the Cherokee well above the speed limit as they sped past the little farming communities that dotted the southern Alberta landscape. "Our turn should be just over the next hill," he told Debbie. "Then we head west for twelve miles and that should bring us to the lease road."

This was the moment that oilmen become addicted to — when the waiting is almost over and the drill bit is about to tell its tale of success or failure. Debbie hugged herself as if to contain the rush of pleasurable excitement. She was also acutely conscious of the attractive and enigmatic man beside her, although he seemed, as always, politely indifferent to her presence.

"This isn't exactly what you would call oil country, is it?" Debbie muttered as she peered through the window in the rapidly failing light. "I mean, I haven't seen a drilling rig or a pump jack since we passed Cremona."

"It's a rank wildcat all right," Dick agreed. "That way the investors get to write off one hundred per cent of the cost this year. It's what they want."

"It's not what I want," snapped Debbie. "Especially with both those gas wells coming in dry."

"You're a big girl, Debbie. What the financial community calls a sophisticated investor. You're getting a look at three wells for your seed money, so you've got no complaints. Besides, if this one hits pay dirt, it will more than make up for the two dry holes."

Debbie felt better. What Dick had just said was what the oil industry was all about. But you had to make that strike before you went broke. Dick had turned the headlights on and soon they were reflecting off a crudely painted metal sign with an arrow pointing to Rimrock 3.

"That's us," said Dick as he braked for the turn. "And those lights over there will be the rig."

The Cherokee pitched and rocked over the rough road, deeply rutted with the passage of heavy vehicles. The island of light that was the drilling rig grew steadily brighter, and they could see its mast festooned with lights and its base partially obscured with clouds of steam. With a final axle-wrenching jolt from an unseen crater, they drove into the yard. The bottom part of the tower was shrouded in dirty tarpaulin and unpainted plywood, and racks of heavy drill collars and rusty drill pipe were strung out below the slipway, ready to be hauled up to the drill floor. The slowly rotating pipe in the derrick showed they were drilling ahead — turning to the right, in oil-patch parlance.

"It's not exactly the Cadillac of the drilling industry," admitted Dick as he gratefully switched off the ignition. "But it's all that was available with this drilling frenzy that's going on. As a matter of fact, the contractor paid a bonus to the crew to get them to work over the holidays so he can move onto another location and start drilling before the end of the year."

The drilling superintendent stepped out of his trailer and walked across the lease to meet them. He was an independent consultant hired by the owners of the well to oversee the drilling operation. In addition to being an expert on drilling and the daily problems and emergencies that go with it, the superintendent has to be adept at public relations, ready to give conducted tours of the rig to the owners and assorted VIPs.

"How long before we reach target depth, Don?" asked Dick after he had introduced Debbie to the visibly impressed superintendent.

"Another three hours should do it. That bit's getting pretty dull and it's slowing us down considerable but it's still faster than making a trip. Come on over to the trailer. The cook's serving a turkey dinner to the boys who just came off tour," he said, pronouncing it *tower*.

The trailer that served as the dining hall was overheated and redolent with the smell of roast turkey. The men, most of them in their early twenties, ate silently and ravenously, speaking only to ask for something to be passed to them. From time to time they cast surreptitious sideways glances at Debbie and muttered lewd asides under their breath. The young man — hardly more than a boy, thought Debbie — sitting next to her was missing three fingers of his left hand, a common injury among the roughnecks who work on the drill floor amid the tongs and flying chains. The accident must have happened fairly recently, for the skin covering the stumps was still pink and raw.

The Chinook hadn't reached this far north and the night was chilly and clear as they trudged across the frozen ground to the rig. Looking up at the brightly lighted tower, Debbie fancied to herself that it was her Christmas tree. They climbed the metal steps, treacherous with grease and drilling mud, to the doghouse where all the dials and gauges that monitored and controlled the functioning of the rig were located. The driller was examining a slowly revolving cylinder that recorded the depth in two wavy lines of blue ink. He looked up as they clattered in and told Don that they should get the drilling break within the hour.

"This drilling break. What does it signify?" demanded Debbie. She could tell from the expression on Dick's face that it was important.

But it was the drilling superintendent, accustomed to playing the show-and-tell role, who explained, "Right now we're drilling at the rate of six-and-a-half feet per hour. When that rate suddenly increases to fifteen or twenty feet we know we're in the conglomerate that's right on top of the formation."

He led her over to the cylinder with its wavy blue lines. "This tells us that we're at 7,620 feet sub-surface. According to the seismic, the Cardium formation should come in at 7,624 and that's when we should start looking for the drilling break."

"And if this drilling break doesn't occur?"

Don pulled a face. "It means the formation isn't there. We're chasing a sandbar along the shoreline of an ancient sea and it's full of curves and indentations just like our modern-day coastlines."

"I understand." The idea fascinated Debbie. Transfixed, she stared at the graph paper as the blue lines crept almost imperceptibly down its tiny squares. The tension steadily mounted in the cramped doghouse as the minutes ticked by. Debbie held her breath as the stylographs reached the line that marked 7,624 feet on the graph paper. Slowly, they crept past, their pace unchanged. She looked back over her shoulder at Don. "When should it start to happen?"

"Anytime now. In fact, we should have seen a difference already."

The lines moved on. When they reached 7,630 feet, Don muttered, "It don't look good, folks. Not good at all."

The members of the drill crew who were in the doghouse with them stared out its grease-smeared windows as if expecting the Three Wise Men to appear. Their job was to drive the iron; they had no stake in the outcome of the well. Still, it was uncomfortable being around the owners when a well turned out to be a duster.

At 7,632 feet Don glanced at Dick Graves and asked, "What do you think?"

"I think we should keep on going for a while yet."

"Okay. We'll wear out the bit on her."

The cook sent over a pot of coffee and they drank it while staring morosely at the depth recorder. By the time it had reached 7,650 feet the lines had almost come to a standstill.

"All that bit is doing now is polishing the rock," Don said with an air of finality.

"You're right," agreed Dick. "If the formation was there, we would have hit it by now." He looked at Debbie and shrugged. "I'm sorry. What more can I say?"

"There's no need to say anything," she told him. The long wait had given her time to recover from the crushing disappointment. "You win some and you lose some."

The drilling superintendent looked at her approvingly. "You reminded me of your father when you said that. It's the only way to stay sane in this game."

"What happens now?" she asked.

"We run a log to satisfy the Conservation Board requirements and then we plug and abandon," replied Dick with renewed briskness. "That's the big advantage to drilling funds as compared to other tax shelters. If you drill a dry hole you walk away from it and it doesn't keep draining your cash the way a real estate shelter can do."

"I'm sure your investors will be very happy," said Debbie wryly. Dick had collected a cool $80,000 in management fees, so he was laughing. He could use part of that as up-front money for his next deal and had no further need for someone like her. Come to think of it, a promoter like Dick could make a handsome living from the management fees alone, regardless of what happened with the wells.

Dick looked at his wristwatch. "One o'clock in the morning and all is not well." He looked at Debbie. "I suggest we get a few hours sleep before we drive back to Calgary."

Debbie agreed that this made sense and the dispirited trio trudged back across the lease to the trailers. Debbie looked up at the dark sky hung with glittering stars and muttered, "This is one Christmas I won't forget in a hurry."

"Drilling for oil is doing it the hard way," said Ken Kwasny.

Debbie peered at her half-brother's narrow, intelligent face. "Now just what is that supposed to mean?"

"Exactly what I said. There's a much safer and less expensive way to acquire reserves of oil than punching holes in the ground."

"And what might that be?" asked Debbie, although she already had a pretty good idea where Ken was headed.

"By taking over a company that already has established reserves."

"Sure. But that requires big bucks and that I don't have."

"Not necessarily." Ken, the financial wizard who had almost succeeded in capturing control of Venture Oils, Bill Crawford's corporate flagship, was enjoying himself as he worked his way through the problem. "The target doesn't have to be big. There must be lots of small-time operators around who have built up a little company with assets of one or two million and want to cash in. As far as the cash is concerned, you could always do a leveraged buyout."

"Which is?"

"You simply use the assets of the company to buy it out; you go to the bank and borrow the money using the assets of the target company as security and you pay back the loan from the revenues generated by those same assets."

"Does it really work that way, Ken?"

"Yes. But you have to be very careful that all the pieces fit — especially that the reserves are sufficient to retire the loan over a reasonable period of time. But there are experts you can hire to crunch the numbers."

Debbie gazed at her illegitimate half-brother with affection. "I'm glad we found you. You make life interesting."

5

Frank made sure he arrived at the restaurant five minutes ahead of the appointed time. When the door opened and Linda, her face glowing from the cold, came in with a gust of snow-laden air, he was almost frightened by the strength of his emotions. She seemed glad to see him, although when he went to kiss her, she gracefully turned her face aside so that his lips brushed her cheek. She carried herself with a sense of style that had not been so apparent in the casual holiday environs of Banff.

"The public relations business must be booming," he said as he helped her out of a luxurious fur coat with lustrous grey overtones that were a perfect complement to her blonde beauty.

"It's just a fun fur, I'm afraid," she replied as they followed an obsequious maitre d' to their table. Frank was grateful that she was still wearing braces. If it hadn't been for that, he would have been more than a little intimidated by the change in her.

"I think I'm going to be almost sorry when they go," he said.

"What? Oh, my braces? Well, I won't be. It's not much fun wondering whether you've got a great gob of lettuce stuck in your front teeth and having to use a water pick every time you eat."

Conversation about their respective Christmases carried them most of the way through the main course. She shed some of her air of sophistication as she talked about her family. There were just her parents — her father was branch manager of an automotive parts distribution company — and a married sister who lived in Vancouver but had come home with her husband and baby to spend Christmas.

"I don't have to ask about your family," she said at one point. "The whole country must know about how Ken Kwasny tried to take over your father's company and turned out to be his own illegitimate son."

"We got a lot of ink over that," Frank admitted ruefully. "Ken's quite a guy."

"Do you like him?"

"It's a little early to tell," replied Frank cautiously. "I find it rather hard to forget that he did his best to ruin my father. He and Debbie sure hit it off, though. They're on the same wavelength — business deals and that sort of stuff."

Over coffee he asked how she would like to spend the day, adding that anything was okay with him as long as they were together.

"You have the rest of the afternoon off," she replied. "I have an important client — my biggest account — who insists that I attend a meeting at three. I don't know how you feel about the theatre, but there's a super musical on — original Broadway cast and everything — and I was given a couple of tickets for tonight. I thought we could go to that and have supper afterward. How does that sound?"

"Fine with me," Frank concealed his disappointment that they wouldn't have the afternoon together. The last thing he wanted was to give the impression that he didn't think her work was important.

The musical was a lighthearted piece of froth that perfectly suited the mood of two young people on the verge of falling in love. Linda laughed delightedly at all the right places and sat with shining eyes through the dance numbers. When the tenor and the soprano sang their duet, Frank reached for her hand and she turned to smile at him.

The romantic, almost magical mood lasted all evening and she responded ardently when Frank kissed her in the taxi that was taking them to her apartment building. When the taxi arrived at its destination, however, she said, "I'm afraid I can't ask you to come up. I share the apartment with a girlfriend and two of her friends from out of town are staying with us. They're bunked down in the front room."

"No problem. It's been a wonderful evening. The very best."

"For me, too."

Frank was in a daze of euphoria as he climbed back into the cab.

As if by common, unspoken consent, they kept it light for the remainder of Frank's visit. The only serious moment came at dinner on the following night when she suddenly blurted, "Your family is so darn prominent. And you're going into politics. You'll spend your whole life in the spotlight."

"Not all the time, Linda," he said gently, while his pulse quickened with the implications of what she had said. "Even a politician is entitled to some privacy."

The delicate question of how far to go in the early stages of their relationship was solved by the lack of a suitable venue. Linda's apartment was apparently still out of bounds and she looked so shocked — almost frightened — when Frank mumbled something about going back to his hotel that he quickly and apologetically withdrew the suggestion.

His plane left early in the morning and once again they said goodnight in the foyer of her apartment building.

"I'll come to see you again right after the nomination meeting is over."

"Okay. And be sure to call me when you've won."

"If I win."

"You'll win." She kissed him. With high heels on, she was almost eye-level with him.

"I like you, Linda," he whispered.

"I like you, too. A lot."

As the elevator doors closed behind her, she blew him a kiss and said, "Good luck at the nomination meeting."

Frank won the nomination on the second ballot. As soon as he decently could, he slipped away from the congratulatory hugs and handshakes of his family and other well-wishers and made his way to the pay phone in the corridor outside the high school auditorium. Tonight he wouldn't get the answering service. Linda had promised to switch it off and take the call herself. The way she used her answering service nearly doubled the long-distance charges, and Frank had tried to persuade her to call collect when she returned his calls. She did about fifty per cent of the time. Probably her idea of being fair about sharing the extra expense.

She seemed genuinely thrilled for him when he told her about his victory. "You'll make a wonderful MLA, Frank," she enthused. In their long talks about his future he had carefully explained to her the difference between a member of a provincial legislature and a Member of Parliament.

"Hold on," he protested laughingly, "there's still an election to be won." But within himself, he knew she was right. In Alberta, winning the Conservative nomination was tantamount to getting elected.

"It'll take me about a week to get the chores done around here. You know, writing thank-you letters to my supporters, appointing a couple of committees. Things like that. Then I'll hop a plane for Toronto. Okay?"

"Okay by me," she responded gaily. "But be sure and let me know exactly when you're arriving. And there's a brand new hotel that has just opened a few blocks away from my apartment. It looks exciting and it's got bargain introductory rates so it's much cheaper than the Four Seasons. Why don't you give it a try? I can make the reservation if you like."

"Terrific! I've got to go now and get back to pressing the flesh."

Her face looking up at him from the pillow was the most beautiful sight Frank had ever seen. How he wished this moment would last forever. Neither spoke. She seemed to sense his desire to go on gazing at her. Finally she shifted slightly and he, instantly contrite, rolled off her. "Sorry. I was somewhere on cloud nine and completely forgot that all of my weight was on top of you."

"I didn't mind. It was just that I was getting a kink in my legs," she smiled as she headed for the bathroom. She had obviously made up her mind that they would make love that night and had accepted readily when Frank had once again hesitatingly suggested a nightcap in his hotel room. He would have been perfectly content if she had refused, but now that vision of her face with her hair fanning out on the pillow would be his forever.

Linda, blonde and leggy, was the embodiment of every woman he had ever fantasized about. "I want to memorize every single thing about you," he murmured into her neck as he stood behind her and looked at her naked loveliness in the mirror. A bedside lamp provided just the right amount of illumination. Gently, he followed the firm contours of her exquisite breasts, lightly squeezing the pale pink nipples, then cupping the lush globes in his hands. He felt a faint ridge of scar tissue under each breast.

Her eyes were watching him in the mirror. "You wouldn't have liked me if I hadn't had that done," she whispered.

"Oh, yes I would," he whispered back, his hands gliding along the curve of her hips. "But I have to admit you're perfect the way you are now. When did you have the operation?"

"Almost three years ago. As soon as I made some money of my own. I guess the scars will never disappear completely."

"That doesn't matter. Not in the least. It only makes you more you."

She grinned suddenly, in the enchanting girlish way she sometimes had. "Implants in my tits and braces on my teeth. I'm a real self-improvement project, I am."

Holding her by the arms he turned her around and kissed her. "You also keep yourself in great physical shape. Those are real muscles I'm feeling."

"That's because I lift weights."

"Honest?"

"Sure. Lots of women do."

"Just don't overdo it. We wouldn't want you to get muscle-bound."

"Don't worry. I only lift up to a certain level. Just enough to maintain muscle tone."

"You're quite the athlete, aren't you? God, I'll never forget the way you crashed and burned on that ski hill."

She laughed. "It was pretty spectacular, wasn't it? I was too greedy about trying to cram in as many runs as I could."

"You know something? We're building up a data bank of memories we can share. Just like an old married couple."

She gave his penis a playful tweak. "Let's go make some more of those memories."

The long flight back to Calgary gave Frank ample time to sort out his feelings. He'd marry Linda like a shot if she'd have him, but she had made it all too clear that marriage was not for her. Not at the moment, anyway. His only strategy was to hang in there and hope that she'd come around eventually. At least she liked him, and enjoyed being in his company. And the physical chemistry was there. In spades. His face grew warm as he thought of their lovemaking. It was obvious that she'd had some previous experience in that department, but then who hadn't? He took comfort from the occasional little hints of shyness in the way she made love that showed her experience couldn't be all that extensive. Just in time, he managed to stifle a groan at the thought of her making love with other men. No point in trying to kid himself that it wasn't a likely possibility. With looks like hers she was bound to have other lovers. If only he lived in Toronto he could try to monopolize her time but, as things were, he'd just have to grin and bear it. It would be a long campaign, with a high risk of heartbreak for him, but he had no choice.

The flight attendant arrived with a hot meal on a tray and Frank began to chat politely with his seat companion. It turned out the man lived in Calgary, had recognized Frank as the newly elected Conservative candidate from Highview and was busting to talk politics, but had held back because Frank was so engrossed with his own thoughts. By the time the plane landed in Calgary, Frank had acquired an enthusiastic new supporter.

6

"I want people to know I'm in the market, Dick," said Debbie. "I'm looking for a tiny little oil company that somebody's built up and wants to cash in on. I'd like you to spread the word."

"Be glad to. What size were you thinking of?"

"Small. Purchase price not to exceed one million dollars. And with some producing properties."

Graves looked doubtful. "There aren't many that small around. You might have to raise your sights a little."

"That may be possible. If the deal is right."

They were sitting on a leather couch in Debbie's office. Her skirt was hiked just above her knees, offering an enticing view of her shapely legs. If Dick was aware of the display, he gave no sign. Someday she would find out what made this guy tick.

I assume there's a finder's fee?" Dick carefully placed his empty coffee cup on the glass-topped table.

Debbie was tempted to tell him that he owed her because of the drilling fund fiasco, but Dick got around and he could be useful. "The usual five per cent once the deal is complete. Non-exclusive."

Dick looked as if he might balk at the non-exclusivity bit, but then he shrugged and said, "Okay. You're on. I guess I'll just have to find the target faster than the other guy."

"I'm counting on you to do that. How's the drilling fund business?"

"Thriving, thank you very much. I'm just about to hit the street with a new one. Twice the size of the first. It's a fantastic way to raise money. You shouldn't overlook it."

"Oh, I won't. But right now I'm on a different tack."

"I know," he replied shrewdly. "Exploring for oil in the corporate boardrooms. Right?"

"Something like that," she agreed, letting herself brush against him as they walked through the door. He politely stepped aside and opened the door for her.

True to his word, Dick Graves was the first to come up with a takeover prospect. He placed a black ring binder on her desk and said, "It's all in there. The complete package: reserve evaluations, cash-flow progressions, and land holdings. It's tailor-made for you, Debbie. And we're dealing with a willing seller — he's just had his second heart attack and wants to get his estate in order."

Debbie glanced down at the thick binder. It had Maple Ridge Petroleums Ltd. embossed in gold on the cover.

"What's the purchase price?" she asked suspiciously.

"Two and a quarter million. We can probably get it for two. At that price it should pay out in four and a half years. If I could bank it, I'd grab it myself."

"It's too rich for my blood."

"You only *think* it is. It'll carry itself. At least let your consultants take a look at it."

The consultants were enthusiastic, but the major bank she had dealt with ever since she had incorporated Pinnacle, turned her down flat. "Not enough collateral," the manager of energy loans declared.

"You're asking us to lend you the entire purchase price, and that's completely against our policy."

Debbie was surprised at how disappointed she felt. The geological consulting firm had been really high on the potential of some of the unexplored properties and the economic evaluation showed a four-and-a-half year payout just as Dick had predicted. Back in her own office she placed a call to her half-brother in Vancouver. Ken was supposed to be a financial whiz and the whole thing was his idea in the first place.

"Why not give the Westfirst Bank a try?" he suggested when she explained the situation. "They're just getting started and they'll be going all out to get business. They might jump at this deal of yours."

"The man to talk to is their president, Steve Morrison. He's young and aggressive, and knows he's got to be very competitive if he's going to make a dent in the loan market. Just make sure it's a non-recourse loan."

"That means they can't come after me personally if the loan isn't paid, doesn't it?"

"Exactly!"

Even for Calgary, where lavish executive offices are the rule, Steve Morrison's office was audaciously ostentatious. The banker looked to be in his late thirties and had a pleasant, rather rounded face. He waded through about a half-acre of deep-pile white carpet to shake her hand. His desk was a slab of black marble mounted on two clear lucite pediments. The art was Native Canadian and it was magnificent. An enormous dancing bear, that Debbie knew could only have been carved by Pauta of Cape Dorset, stood on a pedestal near a corner window. She was drawn irresistibly to a spectacular argillite totem pole, more than two feet high. "That's a Yeltatzie," she said. "It's gorgeous."

The bank president almost squirmed with pleasure. "It is a superb piece, isn't it? I understand you're quite a collector of argillite carvings yourself. The only trouble is that I've never been able to pronounce the name of the carver. How did you say it?"

"He once told me that if I say, 'Yell Taxi,' I'd have his name right."

"Charming. And very helpful. Visitors almost always ask about it and now I'll really be able to impress them." He smiled at Debbie as if a bond had been established between them. "Now, how can I help you?"

Debbie opened her briefcase and took out the black binder and the reports of her own consultants. "I want to purchase this company and I want to borrow two and a quarter million dollars using it as security." Dick had told her that the owner of Maple Ridge Petroleums had just turned down an offer of two million and that if she wanted to buy the company she'd have to meet the full asking price. "And I have very little time," she added. "I don't have an option or anything like that, and there are other people interested in the company."

Steve Morrison looked up from his perusal of the Maple Ridge financial statements. "That's our big advantage over our competitors. We don't have to go running to Toronto for approval. With our head office right here in Calgary we can make decisions on the spot." He closed the binder and rose to his feet. "I'll have a little chat with our loans department and give you a call right after lunch. Fast enough for you?"

"Super. In fact, you almost take my breath away."

"Yell Taxi," Morrison murmured with a pleased smile as he escorted Debbie back across the vast expanse of carpet. "I can hardly wait for the next person to ask me who carved that totem."

At two o'clock he called to say the loan had been approved, adding that he hoped it marked the beginning of a long and profitable relationship between her and the bank. By two-thirty Dick had advised the owner of Maple Ridge that his client was prepared to meet his price and Debbie had herself a new oil company.

Somewhat to her consternation, she also inherited a full-time employee. Maple Ridge sublet its office space, and hired secretarial and receptionist services from a small accounting firm, but it did have a geologist on its own payroll. He offered to resign, knowing he would have no difficulty in finding other employment, but Debbie asked him to stay on, at least until they saw how things were working out. His name was Stan Petersen and, according to his personnel file, he was thirty-six years old, had a B.Sc. in geology from the University of Alberta and was married with three children.

Debbie instructed her lawyers to merge her two companies, with Pinnacle being the surviving entity. The impact of the acquisition on Pinnacle's reserves and production gave her a thrill of accomplishment and convinced her that the acquisition route was the way to go. The only problem was the scarcity of suitable candidates for acquisition.

It was Morrison, the banker, who set up the next one for her. Two customers of Westfirst were major stockholders in Sovereign Oils, a private oil company, and were anxious to sell. They had incurred a substantial operating loss on a mountain resort they jointly owned and could use that loss to shelter the profit from the sale of the oil company shares. The other two shareholders, while not enthusiastic about selling, were prepared to do so if the price was right.

The price gave Debbie pause. It was just under five million dollars. But the bank was prepared to lend her the money on the security of the assets owned by the company. Once again, the newly acquired company was folded into Pinnacle Petroleums.

"The street has it that you've pulled off a couple of real coups, Debbie. Congratulations." Fred Fullerton took a sip of his martini and sighed with contentment.

"I feel pretty good about them," Debbie admitted.

"People are calling you the poor man's Wayne Shaw."

Miffed, Debbie snapped, "I'm not the poor man's anything." But her curiosity was piqued. "I keep hearing about this Wayne Shaw but I've never met him. Do you know him?"

"I've shaken hands with him once or twice, that's all. But I know about him. I've made it my business to ..."

Debbie put down her fork. "Give."

Fred looked a little fretful at being asked to share his hard-won information but the temptation to parade his knowledge before his toothsome luncheon companion was irresistible. "He's called the 'Yankee Raider,'" he began, "and the nickname is accurate on both counts. He's a true blue Yankee, born and raised in New England, and he's a corporate raider par excellence.

"He's forty-five years old and came to Calgary right after he resigned his commission with the US Marine Air Corps. He was a major when he left, and served with distinction, as they say, in Vietnam. He has the Air Force Cross so he must have been pretty good. He was a jet fighter pilot, which may be the reason he named his company Pursuit Enterprises Inc., but there are many who think that the name is appropriate for a very different reason."

He paused for a sip of his second martini and Debbie murmured encouragingly, "This is fascinating. What about his family?"

"Divorced. Seven or eight years ago. His ex remarried and lives here in Calgary. Her husband is a small-time real estate developer who is showing signs of wanting to make it into the big time."

"What's her name?"

"Norma Clarkson. Mean anything to you?"

Debbie shook her head. "Never heard of her. Were there any children?"

"No." Fred thought for a moment. "I'm almost sure I read something in the background materials about a baby being stillborn. Anyway, he has no living issue as my lawyer friends like to say. God, I wonder who he's going to leave all that money to!"

A brief spasm of pain twisted inside Debbie at the memory of her own lost infant. After a pause she asked, "What does this Shaw look like? You know, I don't think I've ever seen a picture of him."

"Not surprising when you consider that he spends a small fortune to avoid publicity. In some ways, he's a typical Yankee type — he's got the craggy facial features, and speaks with that sort of nasal twang they have. But he's not the tall, lean type. He's only about five-foot-ten and more stocky than slim. Just right for a fighter pilot, I expect." Fred signalled the attentive waiter and asked for a carafe of red wine.

"The guy's as elusive as the Scarlet Pimpernel," he continued as the waiter filled his glass, "doesn't attend social gatherings and seems to spend most of his time flying around in his Lear jet. Pilots it himself, of course."

"And taking over companies," added Debbie.

"And how!" agreed Fred fervently. "When the Yankee Raider sets his sights on a company, it's like the kiss of death."

"Tri-Star Resources managed to fend him off," observed Debbie, referring to a takeover battle that had been in the news a few months earlier.

"Yeah. By committing corporate suicide. They used the scorched-earth ploy and sold off the asset that made them attractive in the first place. In Tri-Star's case that was their interest in the Morningside oilfield." He paused and looked curiously at Debbie. "I gather you don't know the sequel to that story?"

She gave a negative shake of her head and he chortled, "Shaw took over the company that bought the Morningside property!"

He took a moment to enjoy the expression on Debbie's face then said, only half facetiously, "I intend to write this lunch off as a business expense, and that means you and I have to talk business. Have you given any thought about going public? You're big enough now and the market is bullish on oil stocks."

"I don't need the hassle. Shareholders wanting to know why you're not paying dividends, securities commissions poking their noses into your affairs. Not for this girl. As a matter of fact, I've got more hassle than I really need from this latest acquisition."

"How's that? It was a privately owned company."

"Staff. I can use the clerical and stenographic people but I sure don't need two geologists."

"So what are you going to do?"

"Keep the one I acquired with Maple Ridge. I've worked with him now for a while and he's good. The other one gets a golden handshake and will laugh all the way to the bank, because he knows he can find another position just by picking up the phone."

"Hassle or not, selling shares to the public is a cheap way of raising money," Fred pointed out.

"I seem to be able to borrow all the money I need from Westfirst."

"I know. Steve Morrison is always bragging about you being a client of the bank. But your equity-to-debt ratio must be way out of whack. I bet your balance sheet would show something like ninety per cent debt and only ten per cent equity."

"That will sort itself out," replied Debbie with a touch of defiance. She knew Pinnacle was badly over-leveraged, but the steadily rising oil prices would take care of that.

"If you say so. But don't say I didn't warn you." Fred signed the credit-card slip and noted on his receipt that he had lunch with D. Crawford, president of Pinnacle Petroleums, to discuss a possible share underwriting.

Driving out to the Circle C on the following Sunday, Debbie saw her first gopher of the year. To the residents of southern Alberta it's the appearance of the cheeky little rodent, not the robin, that is the first true sign of spring. She was looking forward to the family outing. She hadn't seen her father for weeks. With the drill ship operation shut down for the long Arctic winter, the restless oilman had spent much of his time overseas, acquiring additional properties in the North Sea and participating in a drilling venture off the coast of Spain. Hilary accompanied him whenever she felt she could, but she was reluctant to leave Jason alone too much of the time. And Debbie's own hectic schedule had kept her from seeing as much of her family as she wanted, although she and Hilary kept in touch by phone. It would be great to have them all together and catch up on things. Besides, her father knew the mysterious Wayne Shaw and she intended to pump him for all he was worth.

"Wayne Shaw?" Bill Crawford bent down to touch a match to the gas jet that ignited the birch logs in the fireplace. He adjusted the flame and shot Debbie a quizzical glance as he straightened up. "Why the interest in him?"

"His name keeps cropping up. Fred Fullerton was telling me about him the other day. I got the impression he and I are thinking along the same lines."

"Exploring for oil on the stock-exchange floor?" asked her father in a tone that did not quite conceal the distaste of the true explorationist for someone who finds oil by corporate takeovers.

"I suppose I could be tarred with the same brush," replied Debbie with a touch of defiance.

"Your acquisitions have been friendly, while I sometimes think that with Shaw the more hostile they are, the better he likes it." Bill went over to the bar to mix some pre-dinner drinks. With the exception of Hilary, who would never feel comfortable around horses, the entire family had just returned from a horseback ride and, for the moment, he and Debbie were alone in the huge living room. "To be fair, however," he added as he handed her a Bloody Caesar, "Shaw claims that the corporate raider plays a useful and valid role in business. Gets rid of inefficient management, gives the shareholder a better price for his stock, and often produces a more efficient economic unit. That may be true enough as far as it goes, but, still, Wayne has spilled a lot of corporate blood since he came to Calgary."

"How would you feel if he zeroed in on Venture?"

"Good God! Are you trying to tell me something?"

"No. Nothing like that. I didn't mean to alarm you." Debbie was taken aback by the violence of her father's reaction. Anyone who could provoke that kind of response from Bill Crawford was formidable indeed. "Anyway," she added, "Venture's far too big for him to take on."

"Tell that to the Yankee Raider," her father snorted. "To answer your question — I like to think I have a pretty firm hold on Venture, but if I ever heard that Shaw was sniffing around, I'd be nervous. Mighty nervous."

"I've finally got the place bedded down for the night," Frank said cheerfully as he came in and helped himself to a beer from the bar.

Bill winked at Debbie. "Wouldn't you say things were getting pretty serious when a girl takes a fellow home to meet her parents?"

"I can hear the church bells now," grinned Debbie. She turned to Frank. "How did the visit go, by the way? You and I haven't really talked since you got back."

"Couldn't have gone better. Her parents are good people and we got along just fine."

On Frank's second visit to Toronto, Linda had surprised him by suggesting they drive up to Peterborough to visit her parents. Interpreting this as an encouraging sign, Frank readily agreed. The Shepherds lived in a modest brick house on a quiet street lined with huge old oaks whose bare branches were just beginning to show traces of green. Linda had inherited the best features of both her parents: she had her mother's fair coloration and her father's height and slim build. They had welcomed Frank cordially, and they obviously doted on their talented young daughter. Driving back to Toronto in her baby-blue Corvette, Frank felt that his campaign to win her had taken a major step forward. The expensive sports car had given him a bit of a jolt the first time she showed up in it. She blithely explained that she had bought it second-hand at a real bargain price, but even so it was another indication of her success, and reminded a glum Frank of what he would be asking her to give up.

Hilary and Jason walked into the living room to complete the family circle. Without asking, Frank poured Hilary a Dubonnet on the rocks, a drink she had taken up recently, while Jason got himself a Coke from the refrigerator and went over to sit beside Bill on the couch. Bill and his stepson grinned companionably at one another.

"In addition to meeting her parents," Frank announced when everyone was settled, "I have just persuaded her to fly out here for some spring skiing."

"Super," enthused Debbie. "Maybe we should throw a party for her?"

"I'd cool the party bit," warned Frank. "At least until I check it out with her. I have a feeling she's not all that fond of being in a crowd."

"She'll have to get over that if she's going to be a politician's wife," observed Hilary knowingly, thinking of the endless round of receptions and dinners that went on in Ottawa.

"Hey, not so fast," protested Frank with an embarrassed laugh. "And whatever you do, don't even joke about being a politician's wife, or any kind of a wife for that matter, or she'll be on the next plane back east. The lovely lady is mighty gun-shy when it comes to talk about marriage."

The chair rocked slightly as Linda flung out her arm to encompass the view. "We're on top of the world!" she crowed. "I just can't get enough of this."

"I know how you feel," agreed Frank, his eyes fixed not on the towering mountain peaks, but on the gorgeous creature sitting beside him on the chairlift.

She wrinkled her nose at him and pulled her goggles down over her eyes. The pulleys clicked over a splice in the cable and the level area where they would step off the lift was fast approaching. Both he and Linda were skiing in abbreviated shorts; she was wearing a matching halter while he was stripped to the waist. Yesterday had been cloudy but today the sun beamed down from an immaculate Alberta-blue sky. They had slathered themselves with sunscreen but Frank could feel the heat in his shoulders, and he could see where Linda's fairer skin was beginning to turn pink in places.

"We better make this the last run. Before we fry ourselves," he suggested. "The snow is getting pretty soft and slushy anyway."

She glanced down at the telltale patches of red on her bare midriff. "You're right. But I want to stand here for a couple of minutes and take in that incredible scenery."

"Help yourself." Frank stole a casual glance around the top of the ski run. As he expected, a number of men, normally gung-ho to get in as many runs as possible, had decided to linger and meditate on the beauties of nature. There were times when Frank found himself wishing that Linda weren't so devastatingly attractive. Even the way other men looked at her made him jealous. He kept telling himself that his attitude was childish and that he would have to learn to live with the way men reacted to her, but that didn't seem to help much.

"Had enough?" he inquired brusquely. She gave a rather puzzled nod and followed him as he pushed off down the hill.

Linda went through her familiar little routine as they waited to be shown to a table in the combined bar and restaurant. She stood slightly behind Frank while her eyes surreptitiously searched out every corner of the room. Sometimes Frank wondered if she had a mortal enemy — perhaps a rejected lover. Christ, he was getting paranoid. If you came right down to it, he wasn't acting all that rationally himself: deliberately seeking out a place where he was unlikely to encounter anyone he knew, where he would have Linda all to himself.

"I hope your sister didn't mind me turning down the party she wanted to throw," said Linda after the waiter had taken their drink order. "It was sweet of her, but I just couldn't see giving up a day's skiing to attend some old cocktail party."

"You've got your priorities right. As usual. We can do it the next time you're out."

Linda blinked. "Yeah, I guess we can." She took a sip of white wine. "These have been two of the best days of my entire life. Spring skiing in the Rockies is even better than I dreamed it would be."

"Amen to that," responded a delighted Frank. "Now, tomorrow I thought we'd start out on Larch, then ski over to ..." Linda's blonde head leaned closer to him as he outlined his plans for the following day. But they never got the chance to carry out those plans. An urgent message to call the president of his constituency association was waiting for Frank when they arrived back at the lodge.

"I've got to go back," said Frank dully as he replaced the receiver. "The premier is going to call an election sometime tomorrow."

"When do you have to leave? Tonight?"

"First thing in the morning. Of all the rotten breaks — right in the middle of your stay."

"You can't help it."

"What will you do?"

"Me?" She looked surprised. "Ski, of course. But don't you worry about me. I'll rent a car and drive myself to Lake Louise. I'll make out just fine on my own."

The thought of her out there on the ski slopes with every male lusting after her made Frank almost sick with jealousy. Linda pressed herself against him. "Don't look so blue, darling. We still have tonight." Her hand tugged at his shirt. "Don't you think we better make the most of it?"

7

The feeler from Caravan Resources Inc. came through Dick Graves, who the Caravan management knew had cut a couple of deals with Debbie. Caravan was the unwilling target of a hostile takeover bid by Wayne Shaw, a fact that had resulted in a bitterly fought battle that involved court injunctions and threatened lawsuits.

Both sides had taken out full-page advertisements in *The Globe and Mail*. Shaw's ad charged the directors with mismanagement and acting in their own self-interest, to the detriment of the ordinary shareholders, while the directors claimed that Shaw would suck the company dry if he got control. Shaw had upped his offer to the Caravan shareholders twice and the board of directors, panicked by his relentless attack, were desperately casting about for a "white knight."

"They want me to take on Wayne Shaw? The Wayne Shaw?" asked Debbie incredulously.

"Not only take him on, but beat him at his own game." Dick smiled his salesman's smile. "You'll have the support of the directors and senior management. The shareholders of Caravan are a loyal bunch — the board of directors has always been very good about declaring dividends. Much too generous, in fact — according to Shaw. Anyway, the only reason a majority of the shareholders hasn't accepted Shaw's offer is because the management is so opposed to it."

"They're opposed because he would turf them all out if he took over. Right?"

"Exactly! As soon as they got wind of his plans, the top management cut themselves a sweetheart deal binding the company to employ them for another five years, with hefty annual increases and fat stock options. No flies on those boys!" Dick's guileless countenance quickened with admiration at this self-serving manoeuvre, and Debbie felt a quick stirring of interest. He was an attractive rascal and his seeming indifference to her as a woman only made him more intriguing.

Debbie had been following the extensive press coverage of the takeover battle, and what Graves was saying wasn't new to her. "Shaw seems pretty confident that he can get the courts to overturn those contracts," she remarked.

"A classic case of conflict of interest," agreed Dick. "He would be almost certain to win. Which is where you and Pinnacle come in. As a white knight brought in by management, you would agree to honour those contracts if you acquired control. You would then make an offer just slightly above Shaw's and the management and board of directors would immediately tender their own shares and recommend in the strongest possible terms that the other shareholders do likewise."

"We're talking big dollars, Dick."

"Thirteen million, six hundred thousand, to be exact," he agreed equably. "There are one million six hundred thousand shares outstanding and we feel that you should offer at least fifty cents a share more than Shaw, which means $8.50 a share."

Debbie shook her head. "That's way out of my league."

"Aw, c'mon Debbie! Your pal over at Westfirst would jump at the chance to lend you the money. And Caravan's worth every penny. You can bet that if Wayne Shaw is willing to pay eight bucks a share, it'll be a steal at $8.50."

"Doesn't Shaw already own something like ten per cent of the shares? Shares he bought on the open market before he made his offer?"

"That's right. He picked up a bunch in the $6.50 to $7.00 range before the stock exchange rules forced him to disclose that he was after control. But top management and the directors, who are the same except for two outside directors by the way, own or control something like twenty-two per cent, which gives you a big edge over Shaw."

Despite herself, Debbie was impressed. Anyone who had the support of a block of shares of that size had a leg up on the competition.

Almost half-heartedly, she voiced another objection. "Caravan's a public company. It's listed on the TSE. I've always said I don't need that kind of hassle."

"That's a plus, for God's sake! If you're going to keep on growing and taking over companies, you've got to have shares that trade on the stock exchange. That way you can offer shares instead of cash. There's a limit to how much cash even you can raise."

Debbie knew that he was right. The time had come for her to go public, and the acquisition of Caravan would be a painless way to achieve it. "How much time do I have to think about this?" she asked.

"It's on a real short fuse. Some of the shareholders are getting restless and feel they should grab Shaw's offer. The Caravan people want a firm commitment from you within twenty-four hours."

"But that's impossible!"

Graves gently shook his head. "I don't think you realize the stroke you've got, Debbie. Why don't you have a little chat with Steve Morrison?"

"I can do that much, at least."

"Great." Dick got to his feet. "Call me later this afternoon and let me know how you made out."

"One minute, Dick. You know I don't like surprises. Where do you fit into all this?"

"Oh, I'll be looked after. But it won't come out of your pocket. You're the one who will be the big winner in this deal."

"I don't see why we can't accommodate you, Debbie," Steve Morrison astonished her by saying, after she had outlined the situation. He had put on weight and kept tugging at his collar.

She managed to hide her surprise. "The company does have some good properties," she murmured, realizing that he was already sold on the deal.

"Of course it does, or Wayne Shaw wouldn't be interested in it," he chortled. "He banks with the Merchants," he added, in what Debbie realized was not an irrelevant afterthought.

"Still, it makes me a little nervous to finance the entire acquisition with a loan," she objected mildly. Strange, it should be the banker and not her who was raising this point.

"Ah," said Steve knowledgeably. "You're overlooking how much the assets you already own have increased in value because of rising energy prices. The two oil companies you acquired are worth much more than what you paid for them only a few months ago."

He smiled benignly. "Inflation is creating equity for you. That's how the system works for those who understand it. And that's why I'm prepared to approve the loan."

Well, there it was. The decision was entirely up to her. Back in her own office, Debbie thought of calling her father and talking it over with him. But she was a big girl now, capable of making her own business decisions. The thought of being able to buy a company worth almost fourteen million dollars sent a shiver of excitement through her. This truly was life in the fast lane! And it had all happened almost overnight. Like Steve Morrison said, you had to understand how the system worked. Taking a deep breath, she picked up the phone and dialed Dick's number. There was only a faint tremor in her voice as she told him she didn't need the twenty-four hours; she was prepared to commit right away.

They put the shortest limit on their offer that the Securities Commission would allow — three weeks — but that still left plenty of time for Wayne Shaw to outbid them. As agreed, top management and the board of directors tendered their shares and circulated a letter to the shareholders endorsing Pinnacle's offer. The other shareholders, many acting on the advice of their brokers, held back, waiting to see if Shaw would come in with a better price. Three days after Debbie's offer hit the street, Shaw's flagship company, Pursuit Enterprises, announced it was raising its offer to $9.00. Still the shareholders held back, waiting for Debbie's next move. Caravan shares were trading at $9.25, indicating that the market felt the bidding war wasn't over yet. Debbie conferred with the top management of Caravan who urged her to top Shaw's offer, supporting their arguments with an independent consultant's report that showed Caravan had a break-up value of $12.50 per share. It was like bidding at an auction; you got caught up in the excitement and the urge to win at any cost. Besides, a fifty-cent increase wasn't much when you were already talking $9.00. And the price of oil had just gone up another dollar a barrel. When a quick phone call to Steve Morrison confirmed that the money was available, she authorized a new bid at $9.50. What she didn't tell the Caravan people was that she had decided this was her absolute ceiling. If word of that got back to Shaw, he could counter her offer with a stink bid of $9.60 and pick up all the chips.

After a week went by with nothing but a deafening silence from the Shaw camp, the shares began to trickle in. Debbie was seated at her desk, checking an updated list of the shares that had been tendered, when Diane, her secretary, buzzed her on the intercom to say that Mr. Wayne Shaw was calling. Debbie's stomach contracted; what kind of a bombshell was about to explode in her face?

"Ms. Crawford? Wayne Shaw here." His voice with its slight nasal twang was clear and pleasant. "I would very much like to have the pleasure of meeting you and I wondered if sometime this afternoon might be convenient. Sorry for the short notice," he added perfunctorily.

"That's perfectly all right." Debbie was pleased with how cool she sounded. "Would three o'clock be okay?"

"See you then," he replied breezily, and rang off.

Diane knocked discreetly on the connecting door between their offices before opening it. "You did arrange a working lunch with the department heads, Debbie, but," she glanced in the direction of the phone, "if something more important has come up, I can easily cancel it."

"No. Tell them I'll be right in. Just give me a moment to freshen up."

The meeting with the department heads wasn't quite as impressive as it sounded; Pinnacle had precisely two of them: Stan Petersen, the geologist she had acquired with the Maple Ridge takeover, and Janet Evens, who was in charge of administration. Debbie had been determined that the administration post would be filled by a woman, but she had to go outside the oil patch to find one who was qualified. Janet Evans had been the office manager for a large law firm before Debbie persuaded her to come and grow with Pinnacle. Acting on her father's advice, she had refrained from making them vice-presidents. "If you keep on making takeovers," he had said, "you are bound to pick up some highly qualified people, so you should keep your options open."

How right he was, thought Debbie to herself. If the Caravan deal came through, she's be overloaded with high-priced executives. That is, if Wayne Shaw didn't blow it out of the tub when he came calling this afternoon. With a guilty start she realized that Petersen had stopped talking and was looking at her as if expecting a response.

"I'm sorry, Stan. I'm afraid my mind was somewhere else. Would you mind running that by me again?"

"No problem. We know you've got a lot on your plate right now." He looked down at the contour map spread out on the conference room table. "This is the Beaumont play, one of the Maple Ridge properties. I'm kinda high on it. As you can see," his pencil followed the curving lines, "it's got good closure and it's on trend."

Debbie squinted at the map, pretending to understand. Next fall she'd enrol in a night class in geology for sure, so she'd have some idea of what these little squiggles and lines were all about. She could get by without it; there were always experts like Stan to work up the plays, leaving her free to do the wheeling and dealing. But she felt so damn foolish not being able to follow what they were saying and afraid to ask questions for fear of betraying the extent of her ignorance.

They took a break after Debbie had approved the drilling of an exploratory well in the Beaumont area, and the three of them munched on gloopy deli sandwiches, washed down with Diet Coke. Then Stan presented a draft of Pinnacle's exploration budget for the next six months. Including the Beaumont well, it called for a total expenditure of one and a half million dollars. As they worked their way through it, item by item, with Stan giving a well thought-out justification for each one, Debbie felt a glow of pride. Now they couldn't accuse her of doing all her exploring for oil in corporate boardrooms. She was still absorbed in the discussion when her secretary rang through on the intercom to remind her that she had another appointment in fifteen minutes.

"That's good, Stan. Very good," she said as she got up from the table. "I think you can put it in final form and run with it."

Debbie was smiling to herself as she walked down the short hallway to her office. She had been so caught up in discussing Pinnacle's operations that she hadn't had a chance to brood about what nasty surprises Wayne Shaw might have in store for her. And it didn't seem to matter that much, either. She would still have Pinnacle and it could stand on its own feet, with or without Caravan.

Debbie went out to the small reception area to greet her famous visitor. She half expected him to be accompanied by a retinue of lawyers and advisers, but he was alone. Fred Fullerton's description of him was accurate as far as it went, but it left out the man's presence, the energy that seemed to emanate from him in waves. Maybe it was the dark brown eyes — weren't fighter pilots supposed to have blue eyes, which danced with intelligence and curiosity. Laugh lines — or were they lines from squinting into the sun — crinkled around his eyes when he smiled. As he held out his hand, he leaned back slightly with his feet placed well apart, like a boxer ready to dance away from a punch.

They made polite small talk until Diane brought them coffee — as much a ritual in oil industry dealings as mint tea is to the Arab. "It's your nickel, Wayne," said Debbie as she took a careful sip of the steaming brew.

"Straight to the point, eh?" Shaw had obviously picked up on the Canadian idiom that turns a statement into a question. "I like that." He leaned back in his chair and smiled at Debbie. "I thought I would tell you in person that I'm going to tender my shares. Caravan is yours. Congratulations!"

"Well ..." Debbie exhaled a long breath. "I was prepared for almost anything, but not this. May I ask why?"

"Two reasons. The price was getting into the marginal range and I decided I simply did not want to spend my time and energy fighting management over those out-rageous contracts. I have more productive things to do." He paused before adding, "You're paying a lot more for this company than you realize."

Oh, oh, here it comes, thought Debbie. "What do you mean?" she demanded.

"Just that you'll end up buying those mossbacks off. They're empty chairs, take my word for it. Except for one, possibly. And those golden handshakes will add a couple of million to the price, making it more than the company is worth."

"I have no intention of buying up their contracts. They're experienced executives and I've got plenty of work for them to do."

"They're experienced all right. At looking after themselves. They run that com-pany like a private fiefdom, throwing the shareholders a few crumbs of dividends to keep them quiet. Anyway, you'll find out for yourself." He got to his feet and held out his hand.

As she took it, Debbie said, "Caravan is small potatoes to you. I have a feeling that if the target had been more your size, things would be very different."

Laughter danced in the brown eyes. "Maybe we'll find out someday."

Debbie waited until the shares held by Pursuit Enterprises came in before deciding that a victory celebration was in order. When Fred Fullerton, whose underwriting firm was handling the offer for her, called to say that all 130,000 shares of the Caravan shares that were owned by Pursuit had been tendered to the depository trust company, Debbie had Janet Evans arrange a small dinner party in an enter-tainment suite at the Westin. Watching the Caravan executives lapping up the booze and wolfing down hors d'oeuvres, while slapping each other on the back for having defeated the Yankee Raider, Debbie knew with a sinking heart that Shaw was right — this bunch didn't belong on her team. She was pretty sure she had identified the one exception he had mentioned — Ted Reimer, the ascetic-looking vice-president of finance, who reminded her a little bit of her half-brother, Ken Kwasny. But there was nothing that could be done about it now. Debbie smiled vivaciously up at the chair-man of the board, who seemed to be flirting with her in an avuncular sort of way.

Dick Graves was in tremendous form, as he had every right to be. God only knew how much he had been paid for his role in the successful takeover, but it would be substantial. Knowing the Caravan crowd, Debbie was prepared to bet that somehow his fee would be charged against the company. To pay it out of their own pockets would violate everything they stood for. She made a mental note to watch for it, her excitement rising as she realized it might be a lever to pry them out of the company. That would show Mr. Wayne Shaw!

Dick was on his feet, proposing a toast. His clear skin was slightly flushed with liquor and excitement and he seemed to have shed his customary air of aloofness in the glow of the moment. Taking him to bed would be the perfect way to cap the Caravan caper.

Debbie had deliberately left her car at home. Toward the end of the evening, an inebriated Fred Fullerton blundered up to where she was standing with Dick and offered her a lift home. She thanked him but said she had already accepted a ride from Dick, and he, with his con-man's quick smoothness, immediately confirmed that she had.

Debbie gave a low whistle of admiration as Dick led the way across the underground parkade to a Mercedes roadster, its golden-brown finish gleaming with newness. "What a set of wheels! When did you get this, Dick?"

"This afternoon." He grinned somewhat sheepishly as he unlocked the door. "I bought it off the showroom floor."

"It's gorgeous!" Debbie inhaled the intoxicating smell of a brand-new automobile.

"I can understand why you didn't want Fred to drive you home," said Dick as the Mercedes purred along 4th Avenue. "He was hammered out of his skull."

"He usually is, poor thing. But it was you I wanted to drive me home, anyway. I want you to come in and have a nightcap. And I won't take no for an answer. I haven't thanked you properly for bringing me the Caravan deal."

In the dim light of the dash she saw what might have been a look of alarm flit across his face ... then his easy smile flashed on and he said, "Sounds great."

"It's no use. It's just not going to work." Dick rolled over and sat on the edge of the bed. "Shit."

"It's probably because you had too much to drink tonight," Debbie consoled him.

"I better get dressed." The bleak despair in his voice shocked Debbie, but she couldn't think of any way to comfort him. She slipped into a bathrobe while he, refusing to look at her, climbed into his clothes in the softly lit bedroom.

"Dick?" she called after him as he headed toward the front door. He paused with his hand on the knob and looked back. "I want you to know that I don't talk," she assured him.

He nodded a curt acknowledgement, mumbled, "Good night, Debbie," and left.

8

The Highview riding was so staunchly Conservative that Frank could have spent the entire campaign sunning himself on a beach in Hawaii and still have been elected. But that wasn't Frank's style. He campaigned hard, knocking on doors in the two small communities in the riding, driving in his pickup to visit every ranch, attending coffee parties, and making speeches to service clubs and any other group that would provide an audience. He came across beautifully, mainly because people were attracted to his youth and sensed his sincerity and dedication. They told themselves approvingly that even though he was a Crawford and had all that oil money behind him, he didn't put on airs. And look at what he had done with the Circle C. The boy was a real honest-to-God rancher, the ideal choice to represent them in the legislature.

On the fifteenth day of the twenty-eight-day campaign Frank was addressing a luncheon meeting of the White River Rotary Club. He was telling them what they wanted to hear: that agriculture was every bit as important as the oil industry to the province. "That's the message I will take to Edmonton!" he declared to a round of applause.

Sitting in the audience, Dale Young, Frank's campaign manager, leaned over to his neighbour and whispered, "You're looking at a future premier of Alberta."

The man nodded enthusiastic agreement and got to his feet to join in the standing ovation that greeted the end of Frank's speech. Frank remained on the platform, shaking hands with well-wishers and answering questions about his stand on specific issues. A campaign worker elbowed his way through the crush of people and tapped Frank on the shoulder. "Dale wants to see you, Frank. Right away."

Puzzled, Frank glanced over to where Dale Young was standing in the middle of a small knot of people, just inside the entrance to the banquet hall. He raised his arm and urgently beckoned to Frank. Even at a distance Frank could see that the rancher's normally ruddy countenance was ashen. What in hell was the matter? Filled with a rising sense of foreboding, Frank hurriedly excused himself and strode over to the entrance. As he drew closer, he saw that Dale was holding a magazine, *The Prairie Voice*, a weekly newsmagazine that prided itself on "telling it like it is."

"It's bad, Frank. Real bad." Dale's hand shook as he gave the magazine to Frank.

The cover was innocuous enough — a colour photo of Alberta's champion woman diver doing her thing in mid-air — but a yellow banner across the top screamed:

"Conservative Candidate Consorts with Call Girl! See Page 5."

Dale's hand was on his elbow. "We better step outside, Frank. You'll want to be alone when you read that piece of garbage. Harold showed it to me just after you finished your speech. The bastards! Printing crap like that!"

Crap or not, the magazine seemed awfully sure of its facts. The story was headed: "The candidate and the $1,000-a-night call girl." There was a photograph of Frank and Linda standing together in a ski-lift lineup and another of a stylishly attired Linda walking into the Hallmark, one of Toronto's poshest hotels. The page swam before Frank's eyes as he finished the last paragraph and he thought he was going to pass out. Dale silently steered him to a chair and waved away a group of supporters who wanted to shake the candidate's hand. Frank swallowed the bile in his throat and forced himself to read on.

According to the magazine, Linda Shepherd worked for an agency so exclusive it had no name and could only be contacted through an unlisted telephone number. She used the pseudonym "Flair," and the fee for her favours was a cool $1,000 per night. The story stopped short of claiming that Frank had been a paying customer, but mentioned that she had been a guest at the Crawford ranch and that she and Frank were an item on the ski hills around Banff.

Dale Young, seeing the sick misery in Frank's face, muttered, "You poor bastard," under his breath. Becoming aware of a mounting buzz of excitement, he took a quick glance around the hotel lobby. Copies of the magazine were circulating among the crowd; small groups clustered around every person who had a copy, exclaiming under their breath as the story was read out to them. From time to time the murmurs were punctuated with snickers and the occasional loud guffaw.

Dale reached down and grabbed the benumbed Frank by the shoulder. "We've got to get out of here. Get on your feet."

The murmurs and whispers fell silent as Frank allowed himself to be led out through the revolving front door. He blinked in the strong sunlight, shook himself, and began to walk toward his Dodge pickup, his campaign manager trailing along beside him.

"We got some heavy thinking to do." Dale cringed with apprehension at the thought of how the media would eat this up. Frank, moving like an automaton, said nothing until he had unlocked the truck and climbed into the cab. When Dale made as if to climb into the passenger seat, Frank stopped him with a gesture. "I have to be alone for a while, Dale. I've got to talk to her."

Reluctantly, the campaign manager stepped back down from the cab. "We've got to decide how to handle this. You can't just run and hide."

"I don't intend to," replied Frank stiffly. "Just give me a couple of hours. Then you can meet me at the ranch."

"You're not going to do anything rash, are you?" Dale peered anxiously through the open window at Frank.

Frank smiled wanly and shook his head. Then he gunned the engine and sped out of the parking lot with a screech of tortured tires. Campaign posters, with blown-up photos of his own confident, smiling face, mocked him on all sides as he drove through the town and out into the open country, heading for the Circle C.

The story just couldn't be true. Linda, his Linda, couldn't be ... what the magazine said she was. Surely to God he would have sensed something. Wouldn't he have? From some corner of his mind came the memory of how she would seem to freeze whenever they walked into any public place like a restaurant or an airport terminal, relaxing only when she had checked it out. Then there was her refusal to go with him when he was staying at the Four Seasons.

Was she afraid of being recognized by someone? The staff maybe? And the fact that she could only be reached through an answering service. He had put that down to the demands of her public relations job. Public relations! A bitter grimace twisted a corner of Frank's mouth.

The ranch foreman was in the yard, doctoring a wire cut on a horse's leg, when Frank drove in. "How did the big speech go?" he called out as Frank headed straight for the house.

"Great, Harvey," replied Frank with perfect truth. Everything had been great up to the moment his world had come crashing down around him. The spacious living room was cool and shadowy, its drapes drawn to keep out the afternoon sun. Frank sucked in several lungfuls of air before picking up the phone.

"Tell her I have to talk to her right away. Make sure she understands it's urgent," Frank instructed the answering service.

"We expect her to call one hour from now. I'll tell her then."

She probably reports in when she's finished a ... a ... Frank groaned under his breath, and refused to let his mind complete the thought. He got through the next hour by playing back on his mental screen all the pleasant memories of Linda: her eyelashes sparkling with snowflakes in the light cast by a street lamp; her face, alive with anticipation, as they stepped off a ski lift; and her lying quietly beside him in bed while he stroked that golden hair.

He gave a violent, galvanized start, nearly knocking over a lamp with his arm, when the sudden shrilling of the phone interrupted his reverie. The knot in his stomach pressed against his diaphragm, making it almost impossible for him to breath.

"Something's come up out here," he said, making a pathetic attempt to sound casual, desperately hoping that she would turn his world right side up again by laughing the story to scorn. "A local magazine has come out with some crazy nonsense about you ..."

Linda interrupted him. "I know, Frank. I just heard about it when I checked in with the agency."

The agency? "Then it's true? You're a ..." stammered Frank.

"A call girl? Yes, I am. And I'm not ashamed of it, either. But I'm sick about the way it's hurting you. I knew I shouldn't have let myself get involved in a normal relationship. But I liked being with you and I kidded myself into believing it wouldn't do any harm. I'll never forgive myself for that."

"That doesn't matter. What matters is me and you. Linda, I still love you. Can't we put all this behind us and just be together?"

"Impossible," she replied with a finality that chilled him. "You must forget me, Frank. Forget everything, except that I never meant to hurt you like this. Goodbye ... Fr...." He was sure he heard her choking back a sob before the line went dead.

The phone rang again almost as soon as he replaced the receiver and he eagerly scooped it up. Linda had had second thoughts, he figured. But it was a newspaper reporter wanting to know if he had a statement to make about the magazine article. Frank referred him to Dale Young and left the receiver off the hook.

He was still sitting beside the phone when Bill and Hilary arrived. With his instinctive good manners, he got to his feet. "Hello Dad, Hilary. Hell of a mess, isn't it?"

"Reasonably spectacular," agreed his father calmly, and continued, "I suppose the first thing to determine is whether it's true or not!"

"It's true. I just talked with her." That answered one question that had been running through Bill's mind — whether Frank had any prior knowledge of Linda's true occupation.

Hilary kissed her stepson on the cheek and murmured, "I'm so terribly sorry, Frank. I know how it must hurt."

He gave her arm a grateful squeeze.

"By the way," Bill said, "the media are camping out at the gate." He grinned suddenly. "Kinda reminds me of the old days. I don't know what it is about us Crawfords but we do seem to draw the media like wasps around a jar of honey."

Frank knew what his father was doing — reminding him that this, too, would pass. He looked at his watch. "Dale will run smack into them. He's due to arrive any minute now."

The campaign manager looked almost shell-shocked when Bill answered the door and let him in. "The press are howling like a pack of wolves," he muttered dazedly. Looking at Frank, he said, "We're going to have to make a statement. Can we deny anything?"

Miserably, Frank shook his head. "It's true. I'm going to resign. That ought to satisfy them."

"Let's not be too hasty about this," protested Bill. "You can ride this out and still get yourself elected. It's not your fault, after all. The voters will understand that." He turned to Dale Young. "Don't you agree?"

"It's out of our hands, I'm afraid. The premier has been in touch with me. He's deeply concerned, to put it mildly."

"Naturally, he was hoping that we could issue a complete denial and back it up with facts. If we can't do that, he feels very strongly that the proper course is for Frank to withdraw. I'm glad that Frank sees it the same way."

"It's less than two weeks to the election," said Bill. "Does that give you enough time to field a new candidate?"

"Nominations closed at two p.m. yesterday," the campaign manager replied grimly. "Fourteen days after the election writ was dropped. The riding will go to the Socreds by default, and I don't need to tell you how I feel about that. It doesn't sit any too well with the premier, either. But he knows that he's going to sweep the province, so he's prepared to sacrifice Highview."

"I'm sorry, Dale. Sorry as hell," Frank said miserably.

"Like your father says, Frank, it's not your fault. I don't have any hard feelings. Believe that. It's just too damn bad that you had to meet that bitch."

"She's not a bitch, and I don't appreciate your calling her that," snapped Frank.

"Well, pardon me all to hell."

"I'm sorry, Dale. I guess we're all a little strung out." Frank, who had been pacing back and forth, stopped and looked inquiringly at Dale. "I suppose I ought to talk to the premier before I make a public announcement?"

"I understand he's waiting for your call. I'll get him on the line for you." Dale glanced around the room. "Is there someplace where you can talk privately?"

"There's a phone in the study," Frank told him. "This way."

"Well?" inquired Bill when Frank returned.

"He didn't exactly try to talk me out of it," answered Frank dryly.

Bill, relieved that his son could find a saving touch of humour in the situation, raised a sardonic eyebrow.

Hilary could see how much Bill's laid-back attitude was helping Frank get through the crisis, but she also saw the bewildered hurt in Frank's eyes. He had loved that girl so terribly much.

"There's no point in you telling me you don't have that phone number, because I won't believe you." Frank hitched his chair closer to Dennis Fletcher's imposing desk. Fletcher had the impressive title of vice-president of public relations with Argosy Oil Ltd., but everyone in the oil patch knew that his real job was to make sure that his alcoholic boss never lacked for booze or party girls.

"Don't forget that if I hadn't talked you out of investing in that cattle transplant tax shelter you'd be in big trouble with your bank today. I'm calling in that marker, Dennis."

Leather squeaked as the executive shifted uncomfortably in his chair. "I just don't understand why you want that number, Frank. I'd think after what's happened you would steer clear of that chick." He glared at his visitor with sudden suspicion. "You plan on killing her, or something?"

"Jesus Christ, no! Look, I already told you. All I want is to talk to her."

"I bet." Fletcher smirked, making Frank wonder if he had ever used Linda's services. He swallowed. Hard. "I want that number, Dennis."

"I have your guarantee that you're not going to do anything stupid?"

"You do."

"Okay. Hang on a sec." Fletcher left his office by a side door that looked just like another section of panelling. He returned almost immediately and handed Frank a slip of paper. "It may not be as easy as you think," he added, as Frank took a quick glance at the paper and slipped it into his pocket.

"What do you mean?"

"That agency is a high-class operation and they do their best to protect their girls. You'll have to give your name and you can be sure that they will check with the front desk to see it's the same one you're registered under. Give them a phony name and nothing happens. So I ask you, is this love chick likely to show up if she knows her customer is a guy named Frank Crawford?"

Dennis's warning was proof positive that he and his boss had used the agency Linda worked for, but nonetheless Frank was grateful for it. "You've been a big help, Dennis, and I want you to know I appreciate it."

"Anything happens to that girl, Frank, and I go to the police. Remember that."

"How can we help you?" Frank was mildly surprised to hear a male voice answer the phone.

Frank had carefully rehearsed what he was going to say.

"This is Cam. I'm calling from the Hallmark Hotel. Room 1226. I'd like to have some female companionship tonight."

"What's your last name, Cam?"

"That doesn't matter," Frank protested. "I gave you my room number."

"I'm afraid that's not good enough, Cam. We have to look after our young ladies. I need your last name and it better be the same as the one you're registered under."

Frank hesitated, as if thinking. As soon as Dennis Fletcher had warned him about the name business, Frank had known what to do and whom to turn to. The next day he had taken a Western Airlines flight to Denver. Cam Brooker was the head of the Denver Cattle Corp., one of the biggest dealers in exotic cattle in North America. He and Frank had cut a number of deals, sealed only by a handshake. Cam prided himself on being a man of honour — his word was as good as his bond. It was a reputation that served him well in the volatile cattle business, where prices fluctuated wildly from one day to the next.

"Cam, I need to borrow one of your credit cards for a few days. I'll keep you whole."

If the cattle dealer was surprised by this unusual request, he hid it well. "No questions asked?" he said mildly.

"That's right."

"Amex Gold okay?"

"Perfect. I'll send it back by registered mail."

Frank had also taken the precaution of calling from Denver to reserve a room for a Mr. Brooker at the Hallmark.

When he checked in, he used Brooker's credit card. Now he sighed into the mouthpiece, "You're a hard man to deal with, mister. My name is Brooker. Cam Brooker."

"Where are you from, Mr. Brooker?"

"Denver, Colorado."

"That's fine, Cam. Stay in your room and I'll get right back to you."

He called back within five minutes. "You're in business, Cam. Now, you wanted to see one of our lovely young ladies tonight?"

"Yes. But not just anyone. A friend of mine was telling me about the one called Flair. She sounds like my type."

"Yes, Flair is one of our most popular ladies. Unfortunately, she is booked for tonight. However, we have several other girls who are every bit as attractive."

He began to describe them but Frank cut him off. "I pretty well made up my mind that it's Flair or no one. My friend told me about your rates and for that kind of money a guy should get what he wants, I reckon."

"I see. How long are you going to be in town, Cam?"

"Just a couple of days."

"Would tomorrow night be convenient? Flair could be available then."

Christ. It was going to happen. Frank struggled to keep the tremor out of his voice as he replied, "Tomorrow night's okay with me."

"Good. Be in your room at seven o'clock in the evening. You can expect a call from her then."

The phone call came at precisely seven o'clock. Flair, her voice low and seductive, said she was calling from the lobby and would be right up. All Frank had to do was grunt, "Okay." Her smile congealed into something close to terror when Frank opened the door. It had never occurred to him that she might actually be frightened of him, and it took him a moment to realize that she was about to flee. Quickly, he grabbed her arm and pulled her into the room. "For God's sake, Linda, I'm not going to hurt you. I just want to talk to you. Here," he handed her an envelope which she slipped into her handbag with a smooth, automatic motion. "That's your fee. Doesn't that buy me some of your time?"

Her blue eyes were fever bright as they darted around the room. Distressed at seeing her so agitated, Frank again assured her that he meant her no harm. This time the message seemed to get through; her rapid breathing slowed and her eyes ceased their restless darting. But they still shone with that bright fevered light.

"Linda, I love you and I want you to marry me." Ignoring her incredulous look,

Frank plowed on. "We can wipe out the past and start from tonight."

"Oh, God, I didn't need this." Linda sat on the edge of the bed and crossed her long, shapely legs. "Frank, I'm a call girl and I have been for more than three years. I couldn't begin to count how many men have made love to me."

Frank winced and held up his hand. "That's in the past. I'm talking about the future."

"You make it sound as if you're rescuing me from a fate worse than death. Frank, I like my life. It's exciting, I live the way I want to, and I'm good at what I do." She was idly swinging her leg and a shoe dropped on the carpet. "Want me to stay, Frank?"

Miserably, he shook his head.

She picked up her handbag. "I'll have to keep the money, Frank. Otherwise we'll both be in trouble."

He spread his hands in a gesture that said it didn't matter. After a few moments of silence, she sighed and got to her feet. "You're a nice man, Frank. It won't take long for you to realize that it could never work for us. Take good care of yourself."

The flight attendant, pert and attractive, leaned over Frank's seat. "Can I get you something to drink, sir?"

Frank looked up from the *Enroute* magazine he was pretending to read. Oblivious to the interested look on her smiling face, he said, "Vodka and tonic please. A double."

9

"I always thought that brother of yours was a real straight arrow, but ..." Fred Fullerton began. Debbie cut him off. "I've had it up to here with smart-ass remarks about Frank and that girl, and I don't need any from you."

The broker looked injured. "I wasn't talking about that," he protested. "Marge and I went to a party a couple of nights ago at Mike Thornton's. You know what they're like!" Debbie nodded; the thrice-divorced playboy was notorious for his swinging parties. "Frank was there, and he was making mighty big tracks. The girls were falling all over him." Fred chuckled. "I don't think it went over too well with our host. You know, Frank's young, good-looking and a Crawford. He could cut quite a swath if he decides to let himself go."

"I'm glad to hear he had a good time," Debbie replied noncommittally. Not wishing to discuss her brother any further, she picked up the underwriting proposal that had been prepared by Duff, Cooper & Company, the investment firm Fullerton worked for. "I still don't really believe this. I end up with $4-million cash in my own hot little fist?"

Fred beamed. "It's a natural. As things are now, you've got a publicly listed company in which you personally own nearly all the stock. That's a no-no since it means there are no shares for the public to buy and sell and, if something isn't done about it, the company will be delisted. So, we issue new stock from the treasury and at the same time you dispose of some of your shares in a secondary offering. You end up with four million dollars cash, additional funds for the company to work with, and you still have control."

"Sounds almost too good to be true, but I like it." Debbie looked at the broker. "Your head office thinks this will fly?"

"They're prepared to underwrite the whole issue. A bought deal. That's how comfortable they feel about it."

"Tell you what. My half-brother, Ken Kwasny — you know him?" Fred nodded and said, "Everyone in the financial community knows Kwasny. He's good."

"The best, in my opinion. Well, he's in town, giving a speech somewhere, and he's going to drop in later. I'd like to run this by him and see what he thinks. You don't mind, do you?"

Fred looked slightly miffed, but he shrugged. "Fine with me. I'm sure he'll tell you to go ahead with it."

When a somewhat deflated Fred had taken his leave, Debbie wandered into the staff lounge to pour herself a cup of coffee. Ken wasn't due for another half-hour. A copy of the *Calgary Sun* lay open on the table and she flipped idly through it as she drank her coffee. Her eye fell on a photo of four paramedics carrying an ominous-looking plastic bag, with a policeman standing in the background. The accompanying story stated that the partially decomposed body of a young woman had been found by two girls out horseback riding. One of the horses had been spooked by the grisly sight and had thrown its rider, who was reported to be in good condition, with a mild concussion, at the Rockyview Hospital. The victim, who had been identified as a prostitute who worked a stroll on 3rd Avenue, had been repeatedly stabbed in the genital area. "Whoever killed her," an unidentified police officer was quoted as saying, "must have been in a frenzy. I haven't seen anything as bad as this in my fifteen years of police work."

It suddenly occurred to Debbie that Linda must live with this kind of danger every day of her working life. Every time she knocked on a hotel room door she could be walking into the arms of a fiend like the one who had mutilated the young streetwalker. Debbie found the idea strangely exciting.

She had often thought that she wouldn't mind being a high-class call girl for a spell; it would be a rush never knowing who or what was waiting on the other side of that door. Except that now they would tell her she was too old — the sudden realization shook her. She took a quick glance at the bare-chested torso of today's "sunshine boy" and returned to her office, feeling rather subdued.

"How did your talk go?" asked Debbie, giving her half-brother an affectionate hug.

Ken shrugged. "I don't think they really wanted to hear what I had to say."

"You never have been bullish on the oils, have you!"

"Too many loose cannons rolling around the decks for my taste. At least in the long term. If OPEC loses control of the world price, or interest rates start to climb — look out below!"

"You make it sound like we're living in a house of cards." Debbie shivered. "Ken, there's something I'd like to run by you. Duff, Cooper want to underwrite a share issue for Pinnacle and they also want me to sell some of my shares in a secondary offering."

"Sounds like a good move to me. What kind of an issue-price are they talking about?"

"Ten dollars a share. I would get a cool four million dollars for the shares I sell. It all sounds a little too good to be true. I mean, I haven't really done anything...."

Kwasny grinned. "We call it 'smoke and mirrors' in the trade. But you've built your company up into something that has value, something the public is willing to pay hard cash for. The way I see it, you can step up to the pay window with a clear conscience."

"That does make me feel better. It's just that I haven't actually gone out and found that oil. All I've done is use bank credit to buy up a bunch of companies."

"That smoke and mirrors stuff gets to a lot of people in my business. They start thinking that they spend all their time trading bits of paper and never do anything useful. At least you've made Pinnacle into what it is today."

They talked shop for another hour. Debbie loved to watch Ken's mind in action. He was so objective, so global, about things. It didn't seem to matter to him whether his analysis led him to predict a disaster scenario, or a buoyant economy. What was important to him was that he understood what was going on in the marketplace. Debbie knew that she could never be that detached; she would always lean toward the way she wanted things to happen. Almost sheepishly, Ken admitted that he was taking a long position on a few selected oil stocks. He was banking that the new federal energy policy that gave Canadian-controlled oil companies a competitive advantage over their foreign-owned counterparts would unleash a takeover frenzy.

Brushing back a lock of hair from his forehead, he said, "You're going to find pools of eastern Canadian capital that up until now would have nothing to do with the oil industry heading west looking for bird's nests on the ground. But my foray into the oil stocks is strictly a short-term proposition for me. Buy shares in an array of companies that look like potential takeover targets and then sell out fast when the Bay Street boys come calling."

"That's all very well for you, but I want to build an oil company. I always have."

"I realize that. My advice to you is to act fast before the eastern money moves in. Look for companies that need to increase their Canadian blood count so they can qualify for exploration grants."

"If the Yankee Raider doesn't grab them all first."

Ken's face lit up as the idea struck him. "Do you realize that his company won't qualify for the full exploration grants because he's not a Canadian citizen? My God, the Yankee Raider has had his wings clipped! How about that?"

"Wayne Shaw became a naturalized Canadian citizen last week," Debbie informed him.

"Beautiful!" Ken gave a low whistle of admiration. "You've got to hand it to the guy — he's got all the right moves."

"What do you think of him, Ken?"

"Shaw? He likes to go on about how he's good for free enterprise and how he represents the constituency of the forgotten shareholder, but basically he's a predator."

The Pinnacle share issue was oversubscribed and the price swiftly climbed to twelve dollars after just a few days of trading. On the following weekend, Debbie attended a large cocktail party and immediately became the centre of attention. For the first time the oil patch seemed prepared to acknowledge that she was achieving success on her own, and not because she was Bill Crawford's daughter. Her operations had grown too large for that easy explanation to hold water.

She was flattered by the number of people who came up and confided they had purchased Pinnacle shares. Her pride became tinged with apprehension, however, when she realized that all these people were expecting her to make money for them. In a sense, they owned a part of her, and, if the price of the shares ever started to fall, they would turn on her. Debbie took a sip of her drink and smiled when Jim Goulder, her father's long-time financial adviser, told her he was proud to be one of her shareholders. Jim had been a key player in Bill Crawford's successful defence of Venture Oils when Ken made a run at it, and Debbie often wished she could turn to him for advice. But, like Chester Martin, the corporate lawyer, he was closely associated in the public's eye with her father, and she was stubbornly determined to build her own team.

Speaking of teams, she had decided to do a little bench clearing of her own. Ever since that victory dinner, she had known that the Caravan executives, except for Ted Reimer, would have to go. God only knew how the stock market would react when the news broke that three of her top executives had been told to open their golden parachutes and bail out. Debbie had briefly toyed with the idea of trying to break their contracts because of their poor performance, or at least negotiating a reduction in their severance pay, but had finally decided to buy out their contracts in full. If she reneged on the deal she would sacrifice her status as a white knight.

Debbie was so engrossed in these corporate musings, it took her a moment to realize that someone was speaking to her. She blinked and beheld the formidable presence of Miss Johnson who years ago had been one of her instructors at Pony Club. "I never thought I would go to the Calgary Horse Show and not see Debbie Crawford flying over the jumps," trumpeted Miss Johnson, mannish in a tweedy suit.

"I know," said Debbie apologetically, "it's just that I've been so tied up with business that I couldn't find the time. I really miss it."

The horsewoman raised an admonishing finger but Debbie was spared the lecture when Wayne Shaw suddenly appeared at her side. He must have just arrived, for she hadn't spotted him before, and Wayne Shaw was definitely not the type one overlooked in a crowd. He confirmed this when he said, "I only came because I was pretty sure you would be here and I wanted to congratulate you on the share issue. The investing public obviously has a great deal of confidence in you."

"To tell the truth, I find that a little unnerving," replied Debbie, then added, with a hint of alarm in her voice, "You didn't happen to buy any, did you?"

He laughed. "No. I only buy shares in companies that I expect to end up owning."

Debbie became aware that the buzz of party chatter had died down. It was as if the other guests were trying to overhear what she and Shaw were saying to each other. A waiter came up and handed Wayne a glass of clear effervescent liquid that looked suspiciously like Perrier water. Debbie placed her empty glass on the tray and asked for another Caesar. The surreptitious scrutiny of the crowd was starting to get to her.

"You'll get used to it after a while," murmured Shaw.

"Used to what?"

"To having people stare at you as if you might bite."

"It's you they're looking at, not me," snapped Debbie, sounding more irritable than she intended.

"Oh, they're interested in you as well," he replied mildly.

"You're a full-fledged member of the raiders' club, whether you know it or not." Then to her considerable disappointment, he swallowed the last of his drink and said, "Well, I'm off. Congratulations once again."

Watching him move briskly through the crowd toward the exit, Debbie wondered whether she was slipping. She seduced one guy and he couldn't get it up, and now the most interesting man in the room, a man who she had been hoping would take her to dinner, walked away and left her flat. Her glance fell on Jerry Gillespie. He was standing near the bar talking to another man, but, as always, he was looking at her out of the corner of his eye. Debbie smiled and started toward him. Jerry didn't know it yet, but tonight was his lucky night.

Mike Thornton's bachelor pad was playboy kitsch — white shag rug and low, oversized, white armchairs and couches. The only touches of colour were the bar, made from an enormous lacquered Oriental chest, and a life-size painting of a nude, standing on a beach with the sea and sky behind her. Tonight the fortyish Thornton was hosting an informal party that had begun earlier in the evening when a few of his cronies had dropped in for drinks. As the party picked up speed, Mike got on the phone and invited some of his stable of willing young ladies to come over and enjoy the fun.

Mike was flattered to have Frank as a new recruit for his high-living circle. He was enough of a snob to enjoy being on familiar terms with a Crawford, and, in this peer group at least, the notoriety over the call-girl affair also gave Frank an undeniable cachet. Mike had even come to terms with the fact that Frank was the star attraction where the women were concerned. God knew there were enough to go around. But Floyd Ericson wasn't so philosophical. Floyd, the assistant manager of a drilling company, had recently been divorced by his wife, who had finally had enough of his drunken coarseness. The heavy-set Floyd stood alone in front of the unlit white marble fireplace, belting back Scotch and glowering across the room at Frank and the three young lovelies who were vying for his attention. Then he smirked to himself, put his empty glass on the mantel and lurched over to Frank.

"How's Flair these days, Frankie boy? I hear she gives great head." "Floyd spoke loudly enough to be heard by everyone in the room. One of the women standing beside Frank gasped, and over by the bar someone gave a nervous bark of laughter. Frank, who detested Floyd, had started to turn away, before the enormity of what he had said hit him. He stood stock-still as if paralyzed, then felt a red rush of blood to his head. Spinning around, he lunged at Floyd, nailing him with a hard right. He was

620 / JOHN BALLEM

no brawler, but there were times during his hockey career when he had had to mix it up, something that Floyd had obviously overlooked. There was a bone-crunching splat as Frank caught his tormentor with a crisp left jab, breaking his nose. A blow to his midsection and Floyd began to topple forward. Frank stepped back and straightened him with a right uppercut that snapped his head back. Frank's fury drained away when he realized that his opponent was no longer capable of defending himself. He dropped his arms and let Floyd fall to the floor where the blood pouring from his nose and mouth made a spreading crimson stain on the white rug.

Looking down at the unconscious Floyd, Frank was assailed with sudden panic. Had he done the guy permanent damage? Someone brushed by him and he saw Tommy Fraser kneel beside the fallen Floyd. Tommy was due to graduate from med school the following year and came in for a good deal of razzing over the ever-present stethoscope sticking out of his rear pants-pocket. Now that stethoscope was pressed against Floyd's chest. Holy Jesus, was the son of a bitch going to die? Maybe he had a wonky heart.

The drilling manager's eyelids flickered and the medical student grunted with relief and straightened up. Groggily, Floyd began to sit up. He gagged, and spit out a mouthful of blood and white fragments of teeth.

"Sorry to spoil your party," Frank said to Mike as they both helped Floyd to his feet.

"He asked for it."

"I'll pay to have the rug cleaned."

"Don't worry about it." Inwardly, Mike was squirming with delight. News of the fight would spread through Calgary like a brushfire, adding to the growing legend of the wild parties he threw.

Debbie debated with herself before picking up the phone. She knew that it was just an excuse to make contact with Wayne, but would he see through her ruse? He might suspect her motive, but, on the other hand, it would be just common courtesy for her to tell him that he had been right about the Caravan top brass. She nodded to herself and began to dial.

"You paid them off in full?" He sounded incredulous.

"Yes. I was tempted not to, and God knows I would have been justified, but then I decided it would not be too smart to suddenly change from a white knight to a black hat."

"Good thinking." Wayne was impressed. "Anyway oil went up a dollar a barrel this morning, so Caravan still ends up being worth every penny you paid for it. Good old OPEC to the rescue again."

"Ken Kwasny thinks the oil industry is mad to rely so much on that cartel. According to him, they could blow apart anytime."

"They've got too much to gain by working together. It's amazing how unifying a hundred billion or so dollars a year can be. You know something? I'd really like to meet that half-brother of yours."

"That's easy to arrange," replied Debbie quickly. "I know he's planning to come to Calgary sometime soon." Ken had no such plans but that was a mere detail. "Maybe we could all get together for lunch."

"Terrific. I'll buy. Let me know when he'll be in town."

Debbie was well-satisfied as she put down the receiver. It was a bit of a blow to her ego that it was Ken Kwasny and not herself that Shaw was interested in seeing, but the important thing was that the lines of communication were open. Her secretary came in with a message that Jerry Gillespie had called and wanted her to call back. Impatiently, Debbie crumpled the slip of paper and threw it in the wastepaper basket. Jerry seemed incapable of accepting the fact that what had happened was strictly a one-night stand. The next thing she knew, the poor fool would be proposing marriage.

The scowl disappeared from her brow as she became absorbed in an evaluation report on Liberty Energy Corporation. With the share issue safely put to bed, Pinnacle was poised to make a large acquisition. Debbie had prepared a menu of takeover targets and after much study, had finally settled on Liberty as her first choice. Liberty was the Canadian branch of a large American oil company headquartered in Shreveport, Louisiana. While it might be just a branch operation, Liberty was nonetheless a pretty impressive package. The report placed the value of its assets at just under $75-million.

It always pleased Debbie whenever she could see a parallel between her career and her father's, and this, on a slightly smaller scale, would be like his acquisition of Hampton Resources. Her father was having a pretty lean time of it at the moment. The Beaufort Sea well had been drilled to total depth and come in dry, which meant that the Arctic project had yet to turn up anything worthwhile. It was true that Venture was earning revenue from its Arctic drilling operations, but the name of the game was to find oil, not generate drilling money. And Venture had also participated in two costly dry holes in the North Sea. If her father was perturbed, he gave no outward sign of it. The one thing that really seemed to concern him was the way Frank was behaving. Her staid younger brother had fallen in with Mike Thornton's crowd and seemed determined to win Calgary's playboy-of-the-year award.

She had heard rumours that her father had taken steps to prevent Floyd Ericson from bringing assault charges against Frank. She didn't know exactly what he had done, but the CEO of a giant oil company like Venture would have adequate clout with the management of a drilling company. Jesus, what a rotten, filthy thing Ericson had said to Frank! She didn't blame her brother for taking him apart. That drunken slob of an Ericson had drooled on her — actually drooled on her — one night at a dance. Debbie gave a shudder of distaste and turned her attention back to the report on Liberty Energy.

The next morning she placed a call to the company's Shreveport head office. After she had identified herself, she was put through to the president with an ease she found a little surprising. And interesting. When the president came on the line, she went right to the point, telling him that she was prepared to make an offer and that she hoped the takeover would be friendly.

"It will have to be, won't it?" he replied softly. "Since we own all the shares."

Annoyed with herself, Debbie said, "I realize that. What I meant was that I hoped we could arrive at a deal that was satisfactory to both parties."

"Amen to that. Although from what I know of your company, it would seem to be a case of Jonah swallowing the whale."

"I have adequate financial resources," Debbie replied stiffly, while recognizing that the Liberty executive had let something slip. If he knew about Pinnacle, that meant they must have been looking at possible purchasers for their Canadian operation and that meant she was dealing with a willing seller.

"Can you give me a ballpark idea of the price you have in mind?" the Liberty executive was asking.

"I think it would be better if I put my offer down in writing. I'll have it couriered down to you. You should have it the day after tomorrow."

"We'll be happy to take a look at it, but remember that's all we're agreeing to do, nothing more."

"I understand perfectly. One more thing. As soon as I make the offer, I will have to disclose it to the securities people because it could be a material change in the affairs of Pinnacle."

"No harm in that. In fact, it might scare up some other offers for us. I look forward to receiving your offer, Ms. Crawford, and we'll get back to you promptly."

News items concerning Pinnacle's offer to acquire the Liberty assets for a combination of cash and treasury shares had appeared in the financial pages of all the leading newspapers by the time Debbie and Ken met Wayne Shaw for lunch. As Debbie expected, Ken had been more than willing to come to Calgary to meet the Yankee Raider. He also agreed to go along with the little white lie that he had planned the visit for other business reasons, although he had raised a speculative eyebrow in a way that reminded her of her father.

The two men ordered Perrier, making Debbie feel almost debauched as she asked for her usual Caesar. It quickly became apparent that the lunch was going to be a success; all three shared a common fascination with the world of corporate wheeling and dealing. Debbie was resigned to the fact that she had not yet mastered the jargon of this highly specialized field and probably would never attain the grasp of the intricacies that the other two had at their fingertips. More disturbing was the growing realization that she didn't seem to be able to think creatively on the subject;

she could understand the most complex plan when it was explained to her, but she couldn't see herself creating one on her own. She suspected she was like her father in this regard. Maybe he was right when he said they were both explorationists, not acquisitors. Still, as long as she could identify the prospects and come up with the necessary financing, she could afford to let the specialists do their thing.

It was Wayne who brought up the subject of Debbie's offer to acquire Liberty. He was complimentary, congratulating her on being fast off the mark and telling her that if she got it for her price, she would have done a fabulous job for her shareholders.

Debbie decided to go for broke. "If you think it's such a bargain, does that mean you're going to come in with a higher offer?"

"That would be telling, wouldn't it?" he replied with a teasing grin. Then he unexpectedly added, "You won't have any competition from me on this one. I've got a couple of other targets in my sights."

Debbie sensed, rather than heard, the intake of Ken's breath. The Yankee Raider had just made her a present of a vital piece of information — something that was almost unheard of in the dog-eat-dog world of corporate takeovers.

"That's useful to know. Thank you," she said quietly. "But I'm sure there will be others pounding on their doors with better offers."

"I'm inclined to doubt that," replied Shaw. "There really hasn't been enough time for the eastern pools of capital to get their act together, let alone evaluate potential candidates for acquisition. I have a hunch you're going to pull this one out of the fire, almost by default."

Shaw's hunch proved to be correct. The Liberty management yelped with pain, and immediately labelled Pinnacle's $68-million offer a stink bid, but Debbie refused to budge, despite the anguished bleating of Fred Fullerton whose firm stood to earn a sizeable adviser's fee if the deal went through. The only concession she made was to agree to increase the portion of the purchase price represented by Pinnacle shares from $7.5-million to $10-million. For some complicated tax reason she didn't fully comprehend, the US investors were better off taking shares instead of cash. She made the concession reluctantly and only after she assured herself that it would not give Liberty voting control. But the Liberty people still held back, hoping for a better offer to materialize. Debbie gave them a week, then coolly informed them they had forty-eight hours to accept, or the offer would be withdrawn. The call from Shreveport accepting the offer came exactly one half-hour before the deadline.

To her own considerable bemusement, Debbie found that her first reaction was an urge to call Wayne and tell him the news. After all, she reasoned with herself, he had practically handed Liberty to her on a platter. But how much better it would be if he called her instead. She decided to wait until news of the deal hit the street and see what happened.

She didn't have to wait that long. She was still at her desk, working on a joint press release announcing the deal, when Wayne called to congratulate her.

"I have spies everywhere," he assured her blithely when she expressed astonishment at his finding out so quickly. He spoke jokingly, but she believed him.

"I feel like celebrating. How about joining me for a champagne supper when I get finished here?"

"Nothing I'd like better," he replied, "but unfortunately, I have a breakfast meeting in Houston. I was just about to leave for the airport when I heard that you had cut your deal with Liberty. By the way, they've got a corporate jet attached to their Canadian operations."

"I know. I was thinking of disposing of it."

"That would be a mistake, in my opinion. You'll be amazed when you find out how much time it can save you. Try it for a couple of months before you do anything drastic."

Deflated, Debbie thanked him for the advice. It was becoming depressingly clear that Wayne saw himself in the role of her business mentor, and that really wasn't what she had in mind.

10

A wildcat well drilled by Argosy Oils, the company that Dennis Fletcher toiled for as vice-president of public relations, had found what promised to be a prolific, new oil-field in northern Alberta. Ross Edwards, Fletcher's flamboyant boss and a man with a genius for self-promotion, had decided to celebrate the victory — and boost the Argosy stock — by throwing a party at his Mount Royal mansion.

Frank hadn't been surprised when the invitation arrived in the mail. Despite his alcoholism and wildly self-indulgent lifestyle, Edwards was a prominent member of the Calgary establishment and his family and the Crawfords travelled in the same social circles. Frank's first reaction was to find an excuse not to go; he had every reason to suspect that Edwards might have been one of Linda's — he corrected himself immediately — Flair's ... clients. But he couldn't be sure; all he really knew for sure was that Edwards patronized the agency Flair worked for. Even if he had been with her, it would have been on a strictly professional basis. When things got really bad, Frank found it helped some to try to separate Flair and Linda in his mind. That way, he could think only of the good times he and Linda had shared, and the other part — well, that wasn't Linda, that was someone called Flair. What finally convinced Frank that he should attend the party was that Ross Edwards offered a comparatively painless way of beginning to face up to his problem. In the first place he could tell himself that Edwards hadn't been intimate with Flair and, even if he had, that middle-aged, dissipated body could only have filled her with revulsion.

Frank drove in from the country in his red Trans Am, a vehicle much more suited to his new lifestyle than the ranch pickup. He had purchased the flashy automobile with the proceeds from the last sale of cattle. With cattle prices having fallen right out of bed, there was no point in spending money buying new stock. They lost money on every animal they raised, so Frank had cut back the size of the herd to just a small nucleus of the best breeding stock. Harvey, the ranch foreman, could run the reduced operation with one hand tied behind his back, and they both knew it. The knowledge that he was serving no useful purpose only added to Frank's discontent.

The party was well underway by the time Frank finally found a parking spot three blocks away from the Edwards's place, and walked up the long flight of flagstone steps to the front door. Dennis Fletcher, in his ironically self-described role of Argosy's "vice-president in charge of parties," stood at his boss's elbow, unobtrusively monitoring his alcohol intake. Ross Edwards, who was reputed to be terrified of his formidable wife, was on his best behaviour and greeted Frank in a voice that was only slightly slurred. His watery eyes took on a sudden gleam of amusement and Frank had the feeling that he had made the older man's day. The scandal that had befallen Frank was exactly the sort of thing that the notorious oil tycoon could relate to. But there was something else besides amusement in those ruined eyes; there was understanding, even a kind of comradeship. Warmed by the touch of humanity from this unexpected source, Frank moved on into the living room.

Denizens of the oil patch tend to live it up for as long as their physical constitutions can stand it, so large Calgary social gatherings cut across a wide spectrum of age groups. Over in the far corner of the immense room, a group of dark-suited and heavily fleshed men, whisky glasses in hand, stood talking among themselves like dominant males in a sea-lion colony. Frank was pleased to see that his father was having nothing to do with his peer group. Instead, Bill Crawford, lean and elegant in a fawn-coloured silk suit, with a regal looking Hilary at his side, was standing on the patio bathed in the mellow light of the late-setting sun, chatting easily with a group of respectful young oil executives and their wives. What a class act those two were!

Catching sight of Frank, Bill gave a casual wave and, with a murmured word of excuse to the others, came over to join him. "Are you planning on going back to the ranch tonight?"

"Yes. I was. Why?"

"Somebody was just telling me that the Mounties are out in force tonight. Check-stops all over the place."

Frank grinned. "I'll use the back way."

"You've got to make it to the turn-off before you can do that. If they set up a checkpoint on the south highway, you're sunk." Bill fished in his pocket for a key.

"Tell you what. Hilary and I aren't staying in town tonight, so why don't you use the apartment if things get a little ... ah, hairy, later on?"

"Thanks, Dad." Frank pocketed the key. His father was something else — no lectures, no recriminations, just practical help.

The circle of dominant bulls began to break up as some of them caught sight of Bill Crawford and crossed the room to pay their respects. Behind his back they might make snide remarks about the publicity he received and his Golden Boy image, but Bill Crawford was at the very apex of the oil patch hierarchy. To the outside world, he was the embodiment of all that was glamorous and exciting about the oil industry, but, more importantly to industry insiders, he was an oil finder who had brought his company into the international big league where it competed head-on with the multinationals.

As the group broke up, Frank was not surprised to see that Henry Purvis had been one of them. Henry was Frank's age, which made him a generation removed from his companions, but he was as solemn and pompous as the best of them. Purvis's career was another of those dramatic, overnight success stories that have become part of the mythology of the oil industry. He had arrived from Montreal three years ago with a small stake from his father and had rapidly put together a company that was now one of the leading suppliers of oil-field equipment. He shook hands with Frank with a stiff formality that was oddly boyish.

"Oh, you men! Standing around talking dull old business all night." A young woman with a head of close-cropped, orangey-red curls came up and linked her arm through Henry's. "And you, darling, are the worst of the bunch. I'm very cross with you."

Henry patted her hand in a gesture that was almost paternal.

Before he could say anything, she turned to Frank. "You don't remember me, do you? I'm Janice Parsons. You played hockey with my older brother in high school."

"Doug Parsons? Sure, I remember him."

"Janice is my fiancée," Henry informed him solemnly.

"Really? Well, congratulations," replied Frank, taking the hand that Janice held out to him. He was startled to feel her finger pressing against the inside of his wrist. What the hell was going on?

"C'mon, you two," she cried gaily, looping her other arm through Frank's. "The real party is down by the pool!"

Her small breast pressed against Frank's arm and her hip brushed his as they walked. The lady was definitely on the make, but what kind of screwy deal was this, with her fiancé right there? You'd think she'd at least wait until they'd been married for a while before starting to play around. With a sense of shock, he saw that she was very young, scarcely out of her teens. Her face, lightly scattered with freckles, was flushed and her hazel eyes glittered with excitement.

Drinks in hand, the three of them stood chatting in the crush of people around the poolside bar. Janice was obviously enjoying herself; she seemed filled with a secret amusement, and Frank was pretty sure he knew what was behind it. For a guy who once had a reputation of being a bit on the square side, he had picked up more than his share of notoriety recently. It sure didn't seem to bother the women, though. An image of Linda floated across his mental screen and he almost groaned aloud. He drained his vodka and tonic and turned back to the bar for a refill. Henry spotted another cluster of executives and, with a muttered word of excuse, hurried over to join them. Frank couldn't help noticing how much more at ease he seemed to be with them than with his lively young fiancée.

The tempo of the party was steadily building, fuelled by the flow of liquor and by the excitement and overall feeling of well-being generated by the new oil discovery. Suddenly, a medley of wolf whistles, catcalls, and scattered applause broke out as a shapely blonde woman in her early forties, stood teetering on the springboard. "Oh, God, Louise is going to do her thing," a woman standing next to Frank groaned.

"You'd think Larry would put a stop to it," another woman muttered.

"He's passed out in one of the upstairs bedrooms," someone else said.

The woman on the springboard was beginning a striptease, her pelvis moving in a passable bump and grind as she kicked off her shoes and let them fall into the pool. With a coquettish smile, she lifted her long skirt and slowly peeled off her stockings, her performance nearly coming to an untimely end as she lost her balance and teetered precariously on the diving board. Next she held her silk panties aloft to a renewed burst of applause and then a strapless bra was floating in the pool. The lady had obviously dressed for the party with her performance in mind. Now her dress was down over her shoulders and she smiled demurely as men in the audience obliged with cries of "Take it off! Take it off!"

Suddenly her evening gown lay in folds at her feet, and she posed for a moment with arms upraised before diving cleanly into the pool. She swam slowly to the side of the pool in a smooth backstroke, the raunchiness of the striptease suddenly transformed into a graceful water ballet. Two of her women friends, armed with beach towels, waited for her to emerge.

Someone shrieked and Frank spun around, sloshing some of his drink over his hand. On the far side of the pool two young men were swinging a girl between them. On the count of three they let go and she splashed, fully clothed, into the pool. Suddenly Frank was pushed hard from behind. He threw up his arms, sending his drink flying, and took a half-step forward in an attempt to maintain his balance. Another push and he was in the pool, treading water as he looked around for his attacker. Janice stood at the edge of the pool, laughing down at him, teasingly extending a sandaled foot for him to grab. Figuring it was the only gentlemanly thing for him to do, he pulled her in. She surfaced beside him, spitting a mouthful of water in his face and rubbing her long length against him in a way that removed all doubt about what she had in mind.

In his new-found role as a carefree playboy, Frank would have followed through without missing a beat. Janice was definitely on the weirdo side, but she was also one foxy chick. But carrying on like a mink in heat in front of her fiancé? He wanted no part of that deal. Besides, he kinda liked Purvis. The guy acted like an apprentice undertaker, but there was no mistaking the intelligence underneath that earnestly anxious manner of his.

Frank back-pedalled, but Janice grabbed him by the ankles and pulled him under. Her hand brushed his private parts and it wasn't by accident. She fought to keep his head underwater, wrapping her agile body around him like an amorous eel. When his feet touched the tiled bottom of the pool he flexed his knees and thrust upward, grabbing her by the thighs and throwing her off his shoulders. Gratefully, he drew a lungful of air. Spluttering and laughing, she came for him again. He turned aside and saw Purvis standing on the edge of the pool, a pained look on his narrow face. Frank gave a sheepish grin as if to say no harm intended, then his head disappeared under the water as Janice jumped on him from behind.

When he surfaced there was a girl standing beside Purvis. There was nothing flamboyant about her — if anything, her beauty was understated, the kind that crept up on you. Elegant cheekbones, a nose that was ever so slightly and delightfully aquiline, framed by a sleek helmet of shining brown-gold hair. All this registered on Frank before his shrieking tormentor returned to the attack. Janice must have sensed something because this time her fingernails really scratched and the playful pinches hurt. Frank squeezed her arm hard enough to attract her attention and said, "Time to go ashore, little girl. Henry's looking a mite put out."

"Screw Henry," she muttered rebelliously, but she splashed obediently after Frank as he swam over to the side where Henry and the young woman were standing. By the time he swung himself out of the pool, Frank had come to a decision. He would not — repeat not — make a play for the attractive stranger. He would be much better off sticking with the nubile young things who were so readily available in Mike Thornton's crowd. Henry was doing his best not to see Janice whose thin dress was moulded to her long-waisted, small-breasted body. It seemed Henry's approach to her wilful antics was to simply ignore them. He blinked gratefully when the brown-haired girl handed her a towel.

"I guess the party's over for me." Frank squeezed a dribble of water from his shirt-tails, then gave it up as a bad job. "I'll have to go home and change out of these clothes."

"Oh, I don't think you'll have to do anything quite as drastic as that." The girl looked amused. "We're pretty well prepared for little emergencies like this."

She pointed to the cabana. "There are all kinds of spare bathing suits in there and I'm sure one of them will fit you. And there's a clothes dryer in the changing room."

"Great. You must be, ah ..."

"Fiona Prentiss." She held out her hand. "There's no need to apologize for not recognizing me," she interrupted smoothly when Frank began to stammer something. "I would have been a schoolgirl with braces on my teeth the last time you saw me." She broke off at the look on Frank's face. "What is it? Did I say something wrong?"

"No. Just some water trickling down my back made me jump."

Changing out of his sodden clothes, Frank tried to recall what he knew about Fiona Prentiss. She acted as if she belonged here. He remembered now: she was the Edwards's adopted daughter. There was something about her parents being killed in a car accident when she was a small child. Her parents were friends of the Edwards; they had adopted her legally but she had kept her own name. She attended university somewhere in the States and she mustn't have come home very often because she was right about his not having seen her for years. He had forgotten she even existed, as a matter of fact. You sure couldn't blame her for not wanting to spend much time around the Edwards's household, what with old Ross drinking himself blind every night and Mrs. Edwards taking to her bed for days on end. They fought all the time, too. Frank's own mother had been an alcoholic and he knew from experience just how traumatic that could be. If there was anything Frank resented about his father, it was the way he had conveniently absented himself on constant business trips while his wife sank deeper and deeper into alcoholism.

Just as Frank was ready to leave the changing room, it was invaded by a crowd of half-inebriated young males hurrying to change into swimsuits and get into the pool where the action was. Frank stood aside as they trooped in, then he worked his way through the throng of guests and dove cleanly into the deep end. Floating on his back, he caught a glimpse of Janice, wrapped in a terrycloth bathrobe, her orangey curls now dark with damp, standing beside an uncomfortable-looking Henry Purvis. Frank wondered if the poor bastard realized what he was letting himself in for. Henry was just the type who would regard divorce as an admission of defeat and would hang in there with grim determination. There was no sign of Fiona. Frank flinched as two overweight young bucks jumped clumsily into the pool, almost landing on top of him. The springboard boinged and thumped as others, more expert, made running dives into the increasingly crowded pool. Frank swam out of range and then felt the soft fullness of breasts as he was hugged from behind and pulled under. Since it seemed to be expected of him, he grabbed a few handfuls of firm flesh as he and the unknown female engaged in a mock underwater battle. As they both surfaced for air, he saw the homely face of Helga Smith, her small eyes glinting with invitation. Frank smiled at her amiably, pushed her head under the water and swam to the far end of the pool.

The noise and splashing suddenly died away and Frank wondered if they were to be favoured with another aquatic striptease. It was Fiona they were gawking at, as she, stunning in a black one-piece suit, stood poised on the diving board. Like everything else about the lady, her figure was exquisitely proportioned. She was, if anything, on the small side, but the way everything fitted together made her a breathtaking package. Frank suddenly realized she was looking at him. She gave a small wave of her hand, ran lightly down the board, dove into the water and swam over to him with an effortless crawl.

"Your sister has just arrived," she told him.

"Oh. She did say she would probably be late. She's kinda busy these days." Was giving him that message the reason Fiona had sought him out?

"I think what she is doing is just terrific. She's taking on the whole chauvinistic oil patch and winning."

Frank mumbled something noncommittal and cast a wary eye at his delectable companion. Was he about to be subjected to a feminist harangue? Then a laughing Jerry Gillespie splashed water over Fiona's face and she good-naturedly gave chase as he raced back to the middle of the pool. Gillespie popping up out of nowhere like that filled Frank with a feeling of cold desolation. Was he to be reminded of his lost love at every turn?

As soon as Debbie spotted Dick Graves standing on the patio, she zeroed in on him. She hadn't seen him since the disastrous night of the Caravan dinner and she was anxious to reassure him that everything was okay between them. He looked startled, and more than a little alarmed, when she appeared at his elbow, but relaxed visibly as she breezily chatted away.

"Plotting another corporate coup, are we?" said a voice from behind with that crisp twang that sent shivers up Debbie's spine.

"Would you believe we were just discussing Pursuit Enterprises?" laughed Debbie as she turned around. Was she imagining it, or did those brown eyes suddenly narrow?

Dick greeted Wayne Shaw with a deference that bordered on the obsequious.

He remained talking with them just long enough to make sure that everyone saw him in this illustrious company, then flashed his salesman's smile and said, "Well, I better go and do some rubbing and stroking."

Wayne watched him approach a group of oilmen with outstretched hands. "I remember you once mentioning living in a house of cards," he remarked to Debbie. "That gentleman has built himself a castle of sand that could collapse on him any-time."

"You mean his drilling-fund deals?"

"And incentive grants. His backers are primarily interested in the tax consequences, so the drilling results don't matter that much. Did you know he almost never tests a well? Just completes it for production, at added cost of course, and then boasts about all the gas reserves he has 'behind pipe.' He has no production revenue to speak of."

"So if the drilling funds ever dry up, he has nothing to fall back on." Debbie shivered. "I hate to think of what that would do to him. He has so much pride and he worries so much about what people think of him."

"Well, I personally don't believe that these government handouts can go on forever. This business of rewarding effort rather than success is madness.

"Ken calls it voodoo economics."

Wayne laughed. "That's exactly what it is. I like that brother ..." he raised an inquiring eyebrow, "half-brother? of yours."

"He's my brother," Debbie said firmly. "I don't go in for percentages when it comes to family."

"Well said." Wayne glanced at the terrace where white-jacketed chefs and servers had stationed themselves behind a long row of trestle tables covered with red- and white-checkered cloths. He looked at his watch and shook his head. "Eleven o'clock and they finally get around to serving the food! Only in Calgary!" Offering his arm, he said, "Will you sit with me?"

"Love to."

"Frank is with the Prentiss girl," said Hilary. "Do you see them, right at the end of the lineup?" She leaned forward and peered more closely at her stepson. "What in the world's happened to him? He looks like he slept in his clothes."

"Impromptu dunkings in the pool are a standard feature of an Edwards's party," said Bill dryly. "I saw the two of them together in the pool a little while ago. The girl's a real beauty. You have to look twice, but it's there."

"She seems very nice."

"Maybe she'll take Frank's mind off Linda."

Hilary looked at her husband with a fond smile. Anyone else would have sneered, "that call girl" or "that blonde." But Bill was reluctant to pass judgment on people. He could always come up with some explanation for why they acted as they did. He and Frank were alike in that respect. Hilary looked down at Fiona smiling up at Frank and murmured, "I just hope he doesn't break her heart."

"I've had a super time." Frank was surprised at how sincere the polite words were. He had enjoyed himself. It made him feel almost guilty.

"So did I."

They were standing at the top of a long flight of stone steps that led down to the street. They remained there for a moment, saying nothing, while departing guests flowed around them, calling out jovial goodnights. Finally, Frank added, "Are you going to be here for the rest of the summer?"

"Yes. I've got a summer job as a lifeguard at the Glencoe."

"Great. We'll see you around then."

"I'd like that."

Frank sat behind the wheel of the Trans Am, debating whether to drive home to the ranch instead of dropping in on the mini-orgy that was laid on at Mike Thornton's pad. He'd had relatively little to drink and wasn't worried by the check-stops. A sudden memory of Linda, trying hard not to laugh, and failing completely, her hand coming up to hide the braces, hit him like a physical blow. He switched on the engine and steered the Trans Am in the direction of Mike's apartment block.

II

"We're going fishing!" Wayne announced as he entered Debbie's office suite. "Very nice," he added in an appreciative murmur as he took in the light teak panelling and the sumptuous furnishings. "Of course, the Liberty boys always did go first class."

"There'll be some changes made," said Debbie, "and those will be the first to go." She pointed to a row of colourful oil paintings lining one panelled wall. Each one depicted scenes of the American west: Indians in brightly coloured blankets standing in front of adobe huts, and mounted cowboys atop a sandy butte gazing out over a desert filled with purple shadows.

Wayne waded through the grass-high carpet to inspect them. "Not exactly my line of country, if you'll excuse the pun. But I'm sure you'll find art galleries in Phoenix or Santa Fe that would be happy to take them off your hands. Nothing but the best would do for old Charlie," he added, referring to the executive who had managed Liberty's Canadian operations.

"Anyway, you can leave such mundane matters far behind you while I show you some of the best fly-fishing in the world."

"I can't go fishing!" Debbie almost wailed. "I've got too much to do. I've just taken over a rather large oil company, in case it's slipped your mind."

"You've got a staff to handle the details. That's what they're for."

When Wayne Shaw decided to make a move, he really made a move. He and Debbie had had dinner together twice that week, and while their lovemaking hadn't gone beyond some increasingly urgent necking, they both knew it was only a matter of time. "When do we leave?" asked Debbie in a voice that suddenly had a breathless catch.

"Noon tomorrow. I'll pick you up at your apartment and we can grab a sandwich at the airport."

With Wayne at the controls of the Lear, they flew in a northeasterly direction for just under two hours. Shortly after takeoff, Debbie changed seats with the co-pilot and sat beside Wayne as the sweeping prairies covered with a patchwork quilt of grain fields gave way to lake-splattered evergreen forests. "I'd like to let you drive," Wayne said at one point, "but this model has a very critical range between cruising and stall speeds."

Debbie placed her hands firmly in her lap and unconsciously pressed against the back of her seat. "I can assure you that my feelings are not hurt. Not in the slightest. Please carry on."

As the radio traffic began to pick up, the co-pilot returned to the cockpit. They put down on a long, paved runway that had been carved out of the forest and was miles from any visible sign of human habitation. The only buildings were the control tower and a small wooden shed that did double duty as a passenger terminal and weather office. Once on the ground, Wayne led the way over to a single-engine floatplane with wheels fixed to its pontoons, its white paint and red trim gleaming in the sunlight. With its stubby nose, it looked vaguely familiar to Debbie and she asked, "What kind is it?"

Wayne was stowing their gear in the space behind the seats. "It's a de Havilland Beaver," he replied as he snapped the restraining straps in place. "The best bush plane that was ever built. She's kind of a pet of mine."

"She's yours, then?"

"Yep. I had her flown over yesterday. A float plane is the only way to get into the fishing camp."

Wayne flew low over the water, checking it out for floating logs and other debris, before he set the Beaver down on the breeze-ruffled surface of the lake. A middle-aged man, wearing a plaid shirt and stiff new jeans, walked out to the end of the dock to grab the rope as they taxied up. It was not until she was standing on the dock that Debbie could see the lodge, set in a clearing well back from the edge of the lake. She was surprised at how small it was. "It doesn't look as if they have room for many guests," she said under her breath to Wayne. "I wonder how they make it pay?"

"It's private."

"Oh? I might have guessed."

They were welcomed by the plump, smiling wife of the guide who was bringing up the rear with their two soft-sided suitcases. Debbie wondered to herself about what Wayne had in mind for the sleeping arrangements, but the woman led her to her own room, sparse and rustic with its log walls and plain wooden furniture, but spotlessly clean and comfortable.

Wayne was waiting for her in the living room. "I thought we'd take the canoe and have a look around. We'll have lots of time to fish in the next couple of days." He picked up an ice bucket with a bottle of champagne and folded a car rug over his arm. The brown eyes were dancing.

"Let me carry something." A pulse began to throb in Debbie's throat as she reached for the ice bucket.

Her paddle stopped in mid-stroke when a burst of maniacal laughter came from somewhere out on the lake. A scrap of knowledge from her school days enabled her to say "loon," and continue paddling. It pleased her that she had managed to iden-tify the wild call before Wayne did it for her. They beached the canoe on a shingle of flinty stones and stood for a moment looking back over the lake. They had sprayed themselves with insect repellent before setting out in the canoe but, even so, swarms of mosquitoes that Wayne claimed were trophy size, converged hungrily on them.

"They won't bother us once we get away from the water." Wayne took her hand and led the way along a narrow path, slippery with its carpet of pine needles. There was almost no undergrowth, the dense stand of pine effectively filtering out all but a few rays of sunshine. He helped her climb over a deadfall and spread the rug on the ground in the small open space that had been created by the fallen trees. Then he took her in his arms and kissed her hungrily. Thrilled to find him so reassuringly aggressive, Debbie let him take the initiative, smiling almost tenderly as he pulled her shirt down over her shoulders and buried his face between her full breasts.

Moaning softly, murmuring low words of endearment, they undressed each other and sank slowly down to the rug. When it was over, Debbie smiled languorously up at his flushed face. "I'll never smell insect repellent again without thinking of this moment," she murmured.

"I'll buy you a case of the stuff." He grinned and lightly kissed the tip of her nose. "Time for some champagne."

They had the lake to themselves throughout their stay, and they devoted considerably more time to making love and finding out about each other than they did to fishing. In any case, the walleye, trout and grayling were so plentiful that they could have filled the boat whenever they felt like it. Wayne gently removed the hook and released nearly all the fish that they caught, keeping only enough grayling for their evening meals. By an unspoken agreement, they only made love when they were outdoors, under the fragrant pines, and slept in separate rooms at night. It wasn't for fear of shocking the guide and his wife; the couple retired to their own cabin as soon as the supper dishes were done; and anyway, Wayne was hardly the type to worry about what others might think.

The sex was the most fulfilling she had ever experienced in a lifetime of seeking out sexual pleasure, and she knew it wasn't just because of the idyllic setting. Wayne was a self-confident male and she responded to his maleness with a deep passion that felt totally right. But there was also no doubt that the remote northern woods with the breeze soughing through the pine trees made a spectacularly romantic backdrop. She and Wayne joked about it being Nelson Eddy country. So strong was its spell that on the second afternoon when Debbie, relaxed and dreamy with lovemaking and wine, heard the haunting strains of "Indian Love Call" echoing through the forest, it seemed so natural that it took a moment before she reacted. She sat up and wrapped the rug around her bare shoulders as a laughing Wayne stepped out from behind a tree trunk with a small tape player in his hand.

Wayne was intensely curious about Debbie's brilliant half-brother, Ken Kwasny, and peppered her with questions about the financial wizard. "It's a shame that guy doesn't hire himself out as a consultant," he remarked at one point. "I would sure pay top dollar for advice from someone like that." He nodded thoughtful agreement when Debbie replied that there might be situations where the two of them could find common cause. And it turned out that he was well acquainted with Margo Jones. He told Debbie that at first he hadn't wanted to grant Margo an interview, but gave in when she said she was going ahead with a profile of him whether he co-operated or not. A dashing mover and shaker like Wayne would be irresistible to Margo, both as a journalist and as a woman; and instinctively Debbie knew that Margo wouldn't have settled for just an interview, if it had been up to her. Debbie scolded herself for the feeling of jealousy that suddenly flared somewhere deep inside her — after all, she and Wayne were both adults weren't they. But there was no denying that she felt immeasurably better when he went on to say, "Remembering the way she trashed your father in that damn magazine article, I treated her with kid gloves. That's one dangerous lady."

"Margo would cheerfully sell her soul for a good story," agreed Debbie. "But in many ways I admire her for what she has achieved. By the way, she and Ken still see each other occasionally."

"Now that does surprise me." Wayne was intrigued. "I don't know the details of course, but I had the impression that she double-crossed him when she broke the story that he was your father's natural son."

"To be fair to her, I think that was a case of good investigative journalism on her part. Anyway, Ken doesn't hold it against her. In a very real sense, she did all of us a big favour. Ken has been one of the most rewarding things that's ever happened to our family, and I think he feels the same way about us. He enjoys Margo's company, and they're both attracted to each other, but I don't believe he would ever let himself trust her again."

They were sitting out on the screened veranda of the lodge, having after-dinner coffee and liqueurs. A loon, wakeful in the bright moonlight, yodelled its tremolo call.

The night was so still that even at this distance from the lake they could hear fish jumping as they fed on surface insects. Debbie held out her cup for a refill and said, "the member of the family that I'm really worried about is Frank. Ever since that call-girl thing blew up in his face, he's changed so much I hardly know him."

"That would be a pretty traumatic experience, all right," agreed Wayne. "Costing him the election, the way it did."

"That's not what's bothering Frank, if I'm reading him right. He was madly in love with that girl."

"Tough. Mighty tough. But he's young, and he'll get over it."

"I certainly hope so," replied Debbie dubiously. "But he's always been such an idealist ... I just don't know." She put down her empty coffee cup and asked in a brisker tone, "What's on the agenda for tomorrow?"

"I thought we'd do a little fishing in the morning and then leave for Calgary in the early afternoon, so we'll be in good shape to get on with our empire building on Monday."

"I need to digest what I've already bitten off before I do any more empire building. You know, Wayne, sometimes I'm scared half to death by the speed with which everything has happened. Don't you ever feel that way?"

"Never look back. That's the secret." He glanced at his watch and drained the dregs of his brandy. "That's it for me. The pilot's golden rule calls for eight hours between bottle and throttle, but I've always felt that wasn't long enough."

Debbie wasn't sure what to expect from Wayne once their brief northern sojourn was over. After politely ignoring her for months, he had come on to her like gangbusters, and she warned herself that he was perfectly capable of dropping her just as abruptly. So she played it cool, which wasn't always easy since the corporate buccaneer was far and away the most exciting man she had ever met. She needn't have worried — he was just as committed to their relationship as she was. They made a point of not seeing each other during the week — he was mostly out of town anyway, laying the groundwork for his next raid, and she was left free to concentrate on integrating her collection of oil companies under the umbrella of Pinnacle Petroleums. However, they seldom missed spending a weekend together — sometimes in Calgary; occasionally, she would travel to meet him in whatever city he happened to be in that week; and other times they would fly to some remote fishing spot on Vancouver Island or the Queen Charlottes.

Never before had Debbie felt so alive, so challenged. Not even when she was campaigning full time in the horse-show circuit. At work her task was to fashion an effective and unified team from the personnel of the various corporate entities that now made up Pinnacle Petroleums. Because Liberty formed by far the largest component, its employees filled most of the positions, but she was able to insert several standouts from the old Pinnacle group into the lineup. She appointed Stan Petersen as the chief geologist, thereby causing two Liberty geologists to resign. Ted Reimer, the sole survivor of the Caravan executives, she made vice-president of finance. To Debbie's complete lack of surprise, there was not one woman holding anything other than a secretarial job in the entire Liberty organization. It was completely typical of the male-oriented oil patch, but now she was in a position to do something about it. She instructed Stan Petersen that at least one of the two geologists who would fill the vacancies created by the resignations had to be a woman. He came up with Wilma Gretsinger, a junior geologist in the employ of the Energy Resources Conservation Board. Wilma, a muscular six-footer with a plain, good-humoured face, looked as if she could more than hold her own with any mere man out in the field, but she was, as Stan triumphantly pointed out, unquestionably female.

Debbie selected the next female employee herself. A young lawyer who was part of the legal team from MacMillan & Andrews, the firm that did the documentation on the Liberty acquisition, had impressed her. As a junior member of the team, Caroline Underwood was careful not to assert herself too forcibly, but Debbie noticed that when she did make a comment in her soft, low-pitched voice, the other, more senior lawyers listened attentively. Debbie had also made a mental note when one of the partners in the law firm remarked during a coffee break that "Caroline has the knack of cutting right through to the core of a problem." It made economic sense for a company the size of Pinnacle to have its own in-house law department. Its day-to-day activities would generate enough paperwork to keep one or more lawyers profitably employed, and there was the added advantage of having legal advice readily at hand.

Recruiting Caroline turned out to be more difficult than Debbie had anticipated. She sensed a resistance in the dark-eyed young lawyer that baffled her until Chester Martin explained that there was an attitude in the legal profession that in-house lawyers were somehow second-rate and not on the same professional level as those in private practice. "She's probably too polite to come right out and say it, but I bet that's the reason," said Chester, the senior partner of his own highly successful law firm.

"How do I convince her then?" asked Debbie. "I am absolutely determined to fill some of the top positions in the company with women and the law department is a natural. I've already offered her quite a bit more than she's making at MacMillan & Andrews.

"You might take the approach that the move doesn't have to be permanent. Tell her she can try it for a while and, if she doesn't feel comfortable, she can return to private practice. I take it from what you have said she's primarily interested in corporate law?" The lawyer waited for Debbie's affirmative nod, then continued, "You can also tell her that she would be picking up corporate experience that would be invaluable if she returns to private practice. I've known cases where that approach has worked."

Debbie could tell that this argument had an impact on the quiet young lawyer, who also admitted to being impressed by Debbie's resolve to give their gender entry into the higher echelons of the oil industry. But it wasn't until Debbie had sweetened the offer with an option on 2,000 shares of Pinnacle stock that she finally accepted. MacMillan & Andrews was resignedly co-operative, although Debbie was pleased to see that they were visibly upset at losing Caroline. Still, they knew that Pinnacle would generate a great deal of work that would require the services of an outside law firm and it was always useful to have a friend at court.

Debbie pressed the switch and waited while the drapes swished gently open. Wayne, champagne glass in either hand, followed her out onto the balcony of the penthouse suite. Fifty stories below, Central Park was an island of darkness in a sea of light. A small breeze had sprung up, cooling and freshening the oppressively sultry air. The catchy title tune from the Broadway musical they had just attended hummed happily along inside Debbie's head. Wayne lifted his glass in a silent toast to the glittering skyline.

"You like being up high, don't you?" asked Debbie.

He laughed. "I guess I do, at that. Gives one the right perspective, don't you think?" He paused, then went on as if speaking mainly to himself. "Someday, not too long from now, I'm going to build the tallest office tower in Calgary. I've already started to assemble the land. On the q.t., of course."

"CanOil won't like that."

"That's one of the reasons why I'm going to do it. It burns my ass that the tallest building in the heart of the oil patch is owned by a goddamn state oil company."

12

"Saved many lives today?" Frank craned his neck to look up at Fiona in her lifeguard's chair.

"Not so far." She waved her hand at the outdoor pool, crowded with hyperactive youngsters. "This is one of those days when I feel more like a glorified babysitter than a lifeguard." She climbed down from her perch to join Frank at poolside. It had been a week since the Edwards's party and, until now, Frank had made no attempt to get in touch with her. If this bothered Fiona, she gave no sign of it as she smiled up at him.

"I've been meaning to give you a call, but I've been kinda busy," Frank said lamely, not troubling to explain that what had kept him busy was some heavy partying with Mike Charlton's set. In fact he had made up his mind to stay away from the delectable Ms. Prentiss for reasons which he carefully did not articulate to himself, but which stemmed from his awareness that she could get hurt. He, himself, was fireproof. But Fiona was simply too attractive to be ignored, especially when compared to some of the slightly shop-worn specimens in Mike's stable. Frank was still debating with himself even when he was in the locker room changing into his swim trunks, but his first glimpse of Fiona in her lifeguard's swimsuit put an end to his doubts. She was even better looking than he remembered.

It was quickly apparent to Frank that Fiona was a favourite of her young charges. They all wanted her to watch as they slid down the water slide, or, holding their noses, bravely jumped into the water from the side of the pool.

"Were you planning on going for a swim?" asked Fiona with a glint of amusement in her eyes.

"Not in there, that's for sure," he said hastily. "I'll do a few laps in the indoor pool. Anyway, the real reason I came here was to see you. What time do you get off work?"

"My shift doesn't end until eight. And I'm afraid I'm not free for the next few nights."

Frank felt like several kinds of a fool for blandly assuming that she would jump at the chance to go out with him. You couldn't expect someone with her looks to stay on the shelf for very long. But he took some comfort from the genuine regret in her voice, especially when she said she was free on Saturday night, if that suited him.

"It's a deal," he said quickly, wincing in sympathy as a plump young girl smacked the water in a colossal belly flop. "Well, I better let you get back to work. See you Saturday."

"Nothing more for me, thanks." Fiona placed a hand over her glass. Frank shrugged and ordered himself another Scotch and soda. The second band, the one they liked, returned to the stage and they got up to dance. Frank was having a good time. He was more than slightly buzzed but that was all right — it kept the mental image of Linda slightly out of focus and made it easier to concentrate on his date. Fiona was a fun date — she was a good listener and a good talker with a sense of humour that had an unexpected, and highly entertaining, tinge of irony. Because of her adopted parents' lifestyle, her upbringing had been mostly entrusted to expensive private schools, which had made her socially secure — at least outwardly. No furtive peering into corners for her. "Oops. Sorry," apologized Frank as he missed a beat and bumped clumsily against her, throwing her off-balance. She forgave him with a smile and they slipped back into the smooth synchronization that seemed to come so naturally to them.

The up-tempo piece came to an end, and the band leader made a suggestive joke about the pleasures of slow dancing to introduce a ballad that had been on top of the charts all the previous spring. It had been Frank and Linda's favourite song, or at least it had been his — he would never know how she had really felt about it.

He stopped dancing after a few bars and muttered, "Let's go back to the table. I see my drink has arrived."

"Whatever you like." Fiona gave him a curious look that was disconcertingly knowing, but made no comment as she followed him back to the table. He took a stiff pull of his drink as the slow, sensuous beat of the love song tugged at his emotions. He knew he was behaving childishly, but there was no way he could stay on the dance floor while they were playing that tune. He managed a weak smile and began to make conversation, which was never a problem with Fiona who smoothly picked up the conversational ball and ran with it. But the mood had been broken, and they were both rather subdued as they left the night club and walked along the Stephen Avenue Mall and down a side street to where Frank had stashed the Trans Am in a parkade.

"You were thinking about her back there, weren't you?" asked Fiona as they tooled along the almost deserted streets. "When they played that piece."

"Was I that obvious?" Frank shifted down for the steep hill that led to Mount Royal. "Sorry about that."

"I don't mind. I can understand how you feel."

"Meaning you've been through it yourself?" Frank parked in front of the Edwards's residence and pulled on the handbrake.

She smiled, the soft glow of the instrument lights doing marvellous things with the enticing hollows under her cheekbones. "No. Not for real. But I can imagine what it must be like."

"Like the world all of a sudden dropped out from under your feet," replied Frank grimly. "But I'll live."

"I'm glad to hear that. You're fun to be with."

"So are you. Do you ride?"

"I'm no Debbie Crawford, but I can stay on a horse."

"Great. When's your next day off?"

"I don't have to work on Tuesday."

"How would you like a horseback tour of the Circle C?"

"Love it."

"Just give Poco his head and lean forward in the saddle," said Frank as Fiona gazed apprehensively at the narrow, rock-strewn path cut into the face of the cliff. "Remember the horse doesn't want to fall any more than you do. Okay?"

Fiona swallowed and nodded silently. She felt the horse gathering his powerful hindquarters under him as he followed after Frank's mount. Frank turned around in the saddle to watch her. "Hang on to the pommel," he told her as the path grew steeper.

Fiona's heart thudded uncomfortably when Poco slipped on the rocky slope. He stumbled, but recovered quickly and kept on climbing with a sturdy, scrambling gait. The path was so narrow that she was afraid of her right leg being scraped against the cliff, but the well-trained quarter horse always managed to give her the necessary few inches of clearance. A final scramble and they were over the top. She gave the sweating horse a grateful pat on the neck and declared, "He gets a whole bunch of carrots when we get back to the corral."

Frank smiled indulgently but his attention was on a small herd of giant white cattle that grazed in the adjoining field.

"They're huge!" breathed Fiona. "I know they're exotics, but what kind are they?"

"A bit of a mixture. I've got some ideas about producing a sort of super cow, but with the cattle market in the shape it's in, it hardly seems worth the effort. Still, I'm going to maintain the nucleus of a herd in case things turn around."

"That explains why we've seen so few cattle. I didn't want to say anything, but it did surprise me."

"It doesn't make a whole lot of sense to keep breeding when every cow you raise costs you about twice what you get for it." Frank's voice was bitter. "We've sent all our herds to market except for the top breeding stock, and turned most of the pastures into hay. It's strictly a holding operation and the foreman can run the spread with one hand tied behind his back."

And that's why you're feeling at loose ends and are so much at odds with yourself, thought Fiona.

While they talked, a marsh hawk flapped low over the meadow, made a sudden pounce into the tall grass and flew off with a field mouse in its talons. High overhead, a circling red-tailed hawk screamed its harsh hunting cry. The horses began to toss their heads impatiently. "The nose flies are getting to them," said Frank. "We better move on."

"I don't think I'll ever be able to walk again," Fiona groaned as their horses, ears pricked forward, stepped eagerly into the ranch house yard and stopped beside the corral gate. "My hips feel like they're permanently locked in place."

"I guess we did overdo it," said Frank contritely. "You ride so well that I forgot it's been a long time since you've been on the back of a horse."

He dismounted and reached up to help her down, steadying her as her feet touched the ground. Fiona held on to his arms for support and smiled up at him, "I'll have my sea legs in a minute."

Their eyes met and held, and, wordlessly, they came together in a lingering and tender kiss.

Frank stood for a moment on the porch before pressing the doorbell. Framed by the bay window, Fiona, bathed in the warm glow of a table lamp, was seated at the piano. It was a scene of upscale domesticity, and, once again, Frank was assailed with doubt. Shaking his head, he thumbed the button and Fiona rose smoothly from the bench and walked toward the door. They were going to take in a movie they both wanted to see. It was the kind of date that was utterly different from party time at Mike Charlton's. Mike would have hooted with derision if he had known about it. No, Frank corrected himself, Mike would have been envious as hell. Fiona was what the ageing playboy called a "class act" in a tone of voice that unconsciously betrayed his knowledge that such a woman was beyond his reach.

After the show they drove to a fast-food outlet. "I feel like I'm back in high school," Frank muttered as he edged the Trans Am forward in the line and placed his order for cheeseburgers and chocolate malts. "But I like it," he added hastily, and with perfect truth. Fiona made a face at him.

"Are we going any place in particular?" she asked as Frank pulled out of the parking lot and headed south on Macleod Trail.

He grinned. "I thought we should maintain the high school theme." Still grinning, he turned the car radio to an easy-listening station and turned west on Heritage Drive. Inside the Heritage Park grounds he found a slot in the row of parked cars and quickly doused the lights in response to enraged bellows from all sides. In the nearby cars, heads drew apart momentarily then settled back to the business at hand.

Frank flipped his hand at the parked cars. "Lovers' lane. The classic ending to a high-school date."

"What could be more appropriate?" murmured Fiona as she flowed willingly into his arms.

Chopin was definitely too blithe and sunny for the mood she was in. Fiona lifted her hands from the keyboard, looked yet again at her wristwatch, muttered something unladylike under her breath, and launched herself into the thunderous opening of a Rachmaninoff prelude. There was no need to worry that her playing would disturb anyone in the vast house. Her mother was in her upstairs bedroom, completely out of it with Seconal and gin, and the maid was in the downstairs playroom, engrossed in a TV game show. Her father hadn't been home for days; he was in New York on business, with no one to control his drinking. The captain of Argosy's corporate jet would have the unenviable task of putting him to bed every night.

Fiona realized that she was making a hash of the prelude, but it didn't matter — it was just a means of venting her feelings. Frank was already more than an hour late. On their last date two nights ago he had also showed up late and more than a little high. That had turned out all right; they had stayed at home and ended up having a warm, relaxed time together. But tonight they were due at an apartment-warming party for one of her newly married girlfriends and her husband. Fiona had already called to say that Frank was held up and that they would be late. She could only hope that he wouldn't arrive plastered and make an ass of himself at Steve and Janey's place. She hit a wrong note and, exasperated with herself, stopped playing just as the doorbell rang.

"Sitting at the piano like that, you look like a photo in one of those glossy society magazines," Frank informed her as she let him in.

"Well, I don't feel like high society at the moment. We're inexcusably late." Her heart sank as she smelled the liquor on his breath. "Let's take my car," she suggested.

"There's nothing wrong with mine," he replied belligerently, and then added with a flash of his innate good nature, "But you can drive if you like."

Somewhat mollified by this unexpected capitulation, Fiona picked up the house-warming present she had so carefully wrapped and swept out the door.

"You forgot to release the handbrake," Frank pointed out. "It's under the dash-board," he added helpfully as she groped around in search of it.

"Who ever uses a handbrake?" she demanded as she finally got the car underway.

"I do when I'm parked on a hill as steep as this one." Frank's good humour was totally restored by this minor victory. "Will I know anyone there?" he asked.

"Oh, I imagine so. Of course," her lips twitched mischievously, "it will be mostly a younger crowd but there should be a few of your contemporaries you can chat about old times with."

"Don't be impudent, child. Five years difference isn't exactly a generation gap, you know."

"The place will be swarming with football players." Fiona didn't sound exactly thrilled by the prospect. "Steve's a real football junkie. Youngest member on the board of directors of the Stampeders — that sort of thing."

The party had overflowed the apartment and spilled out into the hallway. Frank recognized a few faces, but most were strangers to him. It was a phenomenon that he, as a native Calgarian, had long since grown accustomed to. Exponential growth was the norm in this city and the boom times had returned with a vengeance now that the government had decided to back off and give the oil industry some room. The men in the crowd were much younger than the members of the Charlton set, and there was another subtle difference, one which took Frank a few minutes to pin down. The women were different from the sexual playthings that hung out at Mike's parties. They were definitely the take-home-to-mother type, and most of the couples had an air of permanence. They were young professionals on the way up, many of them already married.

You didn't need a program to pick out the football players. Frank counted six of them, including two huge blacks. Frank's game was hockey and he took little more than a passing interest in football, but still he had no trouble recognizing a couple of them from their constant appearances in the sports section of the local press. Easiest of all to identify was Garth Thorblen, widely touted as one of the new breed of big quarterbacks — rugged enough to stand up to quarterback sacks by defensive head-hunters, and tall enough to spot his receivers over the wall of advancing linemen. While the Stamps, with six losses and two wins, were not exactly having a vintage year with Thorblen at the helm, there was no doubt that he was a magnificent physical specimen. The guy had to stand at least six-foot-four or five and probably weighed in at better than 230 pounds. With his own well-muscled, five-foot-eleven frame, Frank had never had any reason to feel physically inadequate, but now he was strangely uncomfortable and even somewhat intimidated. It didn't help matters that Thorblen was also strikingly handsome, if your taste ran to blonde Viking gods. His eyes were too pale, though.

The party was a bring-your-own-bottle affair and a makeshift bar had been set up in the kitchen. Frank was fixing a couple of vodka and tonics when he heard a voice from behind say, "How's the pimping business these days, Frankie boy?"

At first Frank couldn't be sure he had heard correctly, or maybe he just didn't want to hear, and he busied himself squeezing lime slices into the drinks. The voice came again, this time much too loud and clear to ignore. "I'm asking you, pimp, how's business these days? We're playing in Toronto this Sunday and maybe you'd like to give me and the boys the little lady's phone number."

Someone breathed, "Right on, man!"

Frank, cheeks flaming, turned to face his tormentor. It was obvious that Thorblen was out to pick a fight. And it was equally obvious that Frank would be no match for the hulking quarterback. Somewhat desperately, he looked around, hoping someone would intervene, but all he could see were the other Stampeders who had crowded into the kitchen to watch the action.

In a voice loaded with contempt, Thorblen sneered, "I guess there's no way you can insult a guy who pays for it."

He blinked as Frank nailed him with a hard right-cross and followed up with a pretty good left. The smaller man was going to be more of a handful than he had bargained for, but that only served to increase Thorblen's pleasure. A triumphant smile spread across his face and he grunted, "You just made my day, little man," and launched a long looping right.

Frank stepped inside and pounded the giant's solar plexus. It was like punching the side of a cliff. Thorblen grinned ferociously and deliberately dropped his hands to let Frank pound away. Still grinning, he hit Frank with a vicious rabbit punch that almost dropped him. Frank tried to hang on but Thorblen easily pushed him away and this time the looping right connected. The man's power was awesome; it was like being cuffed by a bear. Frank shook his head in an attempt to clear it and barely managed to duck a thundering blow that would have shattered his nose if it had landed. Thorblen chuckled evilly and moved in closer, not even troubling to fend off Frank's body blows. He wrapped Frank in a bear hug and leaned heavily on him while pummelling him in the kidneys. It dawned on Frank that his opponent had no intention of finishing him off quickly; he was out to work him over and do some serious damage. Someone was screaming and pounding ineffectively on Thorblen's massive biceps. The terrible constriction on Frank's ribs eased; he tottered backwards and would have crashed into the bar if the black fullback hadn't grabbed him. As his vision began to clear he saw Fiona, crouching and spitting like an enraged tigress as she faced down a cowed Thorblen.

"You're despicable, Garth Thorblen, and I hate you! You're nothing but a bully and a coward." Seeing that Thorblen had lost his steam, she rushed over to Frank who, by hanging onto the bar, was managing to stand on his own feet.

"Are you all right, darling?" she asked anxiously, her fingertips gently exploring his face.

"I'm kinda bent out of shape." Unconsciously, Frank lapsed into cowboy jargon. "But, like I said once before, I think I'll live."

Fiona smiled with relief, then glared reproachfully at the fullback. "Why did you let this happen, Jim? Why didn't you stop it?"

He looked abashed. "I figured it was Garth's play. Something he wanted to do. But I wasn't goin' to let it go on much longer."

Jim looked down at Frank who was gently probing his aching ribs. "Pound for pound, this guy is worth two of Garth." He stepped out to the middle of the floor. "Okay, guys. Curfew. Let's move it."

"I don't think very much of your choice of playmates," Frank grunted as he eased himself painfully into the Trans Am's passenger seat. "Next time you might warn me before I run into one of your jealous boyfriends."

"I only went out with him a few times." No point in adding that she had told Garth she wasn't going to see him again after she had started dating Frank.

"It never occurred to me that he would pull a stunt like that. I still don't believe it." She drew up to a stop sign. "Look, are you sure you won't let me take you to the hospital so they can check you over?"

"I'm okay. At worst, I may have a couple of cracked ribs, and if they don't start to feel better in a few days, I'll get an X-ray."

She drove up the long driveway to her house and parked in front of the three-car garage, making a big production out of setting the handbrake. "You can sleep here tonight. You can't possibly drive out to the ranch. There are all kinds of spare bedrooms."

When he protested, she said, "Okay. Be a hero. Put your hands on the steering wheel. Go ahead and try." Gingerly, he tried to lift his arms, then groaned at the sudden stab of pain in his left side. "You win. Sure your parents won't mind?"

"Who's to mind?" she asked matter-of-factly.

Frank decided that he deserved a brandy — a large one. She brought it over to him as he sat on the softest sofa in the room.

"You can kiss me, if you're very, very careful," he informed her as she handed him the snifter. As she leaned over, her dress fell away, revealing the smooth tanned skin of her breasts. Instinctively, Frank reached up to touch them, then cried out with pain.

"You'll never manage," Fiona murmured. She unhooked her bra and let her dress slide down from her shoulders.

"Beautiful," breathed Frank as he gazed at her exquisite breasts. "Everything about you is so perfect." She leaned down further to let him touch them with his lips. Gently stroking his hair, she whispered to herself, "Oh, Frank, what am I going to do with you?"

13

"Jason really gets along with that little chestnut mare," said Frank, watching the youngster sit tight in the saddle as the mare loped easily down the trail in front of them. "If it's all right with you, Dad, I'd like to give her to him."

"Say, that would be great," Bill Crawford enthused. "I was thinking just last week that he's outgrown that pony of his."

"Yeah, he needs a real horse."

That matter satisfactorily resolved, Frank reined back to fall in beside Fiona whose mount was stepping out briskly, ears pricked forward. Debbie and Wayne Shaw were way out in front. Debbie's thoroughbred had hardly been ridden all summer and was giving her a hard time, prancing sideways and fighting the bit, much to the amusement of Wayne Shaw who was mounted on one of the ranch's well-broken quarter horses. Debbie had secretly been looking forward to this day, convinced that it would be one occasion where she would have the advantage over the versatile Wayne Shaw. She should have known better. He turned out to be an accomplished Western rider; not, he explained, because he particularly enjoyed the sport but because many of the remote hunting and fishing areas he favoured could only be reached on horseback. The only one missing was Hilary. Although the family outing had been her idea, she couldn't bring herself to trust even the gentlest of horses and had elected to remain behind and preside over preparations for dinner. She was standing in the doorway of the Circle C ranch house, waiting to greet them as they trooped in from the corral.

Drinks in hand, Bill and Wayne stood in front of the unlit fireplace, talking oil. Bill had recently returned home from a fact-finding swing through the Middle East where he had been signally honoured by having been granted an audience with the king of Saudi Arabia. What he learned had convinced him to take some radical steps to eliminate Venture's exposure to the expensive North Sea exploration play. While he was still in the Middle East, he had called London to notify his drilling partners that Venture would not be participating in the next exploratory hole. And now he was just about to complete the sale of his interest in the North Sea properties for $90-million to those same partners.

He did not, of course, mention any of this to Wayne but he did tell him that "the Saudis have really had it with always being the ones who have to keep cutting back their oil production while all the other OPEC and non-OPEC countries flood the market. They're down to three and a half million barrels a day, even though they're capable of producing three times that amount."

"But they have no viable alternative. If they were to increase production the world price of oil would plummet. That's got to be the last thing the Saudis want. Christ, it would reduce the value of their reserves by," Wayne paused for a fast mental calculation, "something like a trillion US dollars."

"That's the conventional wisdom, I agree. But don't forget it only costs them about ten cents to produce a barrel of oil."

"Which means that with oil selling at $32 US a barrel, they make an unholy profit on every barrel they produce. It's in their best interest to protect that profit at all costs."

There wasn't any point in prolonging the argument. People believed what they wanted to believe. Bill shrugged and said neutrally, "I sure hope you're right," as Hilary announced that dinner was served.

"Getting everybody together like that was a positive inspiration on your part," Bill told Hilary as they drove back to their own place.

Jason, worn out with the day's activity and the excitement of owning a real horse, was asleep in the rear seat of the Mercedes. "We haven't seen enough of the family this summer and you forget what great fun they are."

"I really like Fiona. She and Frank are wonderful together."

"I get a charge out of the way they spar with each other. I've never seen Frank carry on like that with anyone else."

"She's in love with him. Wouldn't it be super if they got together?"

"You mean as in married?" Bill looked dubious when she nodded vigorously. "I wouldn't hold my breath. He was truly and deeply in love with Linda Shepherd, and Crawford men," he reached for her hand, "don't fall out of love easily."

She smiled and they drove the next few miles in silence until she murmured musingly, "I don't know quite what to make of Wayne Shaw. He's very attractive, of course, but still ..."

"He's a hunter. That's what you're reacting to."

Driving at night with a couple of Scotches under his belt put Bill in an expansive mood. "Shaw's not a real oilman. Not in the way I like to think that I am. For me, the search for oil is where it's at. Not, you understand, that I'm turning up my nose at the money and all that goes with it. However, if I have one ambition left in life, it would be to make a world-scale discovery. A real elephant of a find. I get the impression with Shaw that his companies could just as well be manufacturing widgets as producing oil. It's the corporate takeover game that turns his crank."

"You seem remarkably pleased with yourself," murmured Debbie, smiling sleepily up at her lover. As always, sex with Wayne left her in a state of blissful lassitude.

"Who wouldn't be after a session like that?"

"The love was great, thank you very much. But it's more than that. I know you, Wayne Shaw. You're up to something."

He laughed and handed her a terrycloth bathrobe. "Let's take our champagne out on the balcony."

His Calgary residence was a luxury two-story penthouse condominium a few blocks north of the downtown core with a view of both the Bow River and the city skyline. He inhaled deeply and declared, "This air is just like wine! Absolutely exhilarating."

"You're exhilarated by something more than fresh air," said Debbie, her sleepiness replaced by curiosity. "Give."

Wayne stared intently at her for a long moment, took a swallow of champagne, and turned his gaze to the brightly lit office towers. "I've got big plans, Debbie. And you're part of them."

What was this — a proposal? Debbie had sometimes wondered just what she would do if one day Wayne asked her to marry him. She had never bothered to think it through since she was positive it would never happen. Now she was filled with apprehension. He was the most exciting man she had ever known, but she wasn't at all sure that she could handle the personal compromises and adjustments that marriage would bring. He was talking again. What was he saying?

"I'm going to make you a rich woman, Debbie. A very rich woman."

"I already am." What kind of marriage proposal was this?

"I'm going to make an offer for Pinnacle you can't refuse."

"You're not serious." Debbie peered at his shadowed face which, as usual, wasn't giving much away. "You are serious, though. Aren't you?"

"Perfectly."

"Wayne, listen to me." Debbie strove to keep her voice from cracking. "Give up this idea. I'm begging you. If I mean anything to you at all, don't make a move on Pinnacle."

"You don't seem to understand. You and all your shareholders will be big winners, Debbie. All of you will walk away from the table with bulging pockets."

"I'm not interested in walking away from the table."

"You can start all over again. The very next day. With an enormous stake to play with. Although if I were you, I wouldn't put it all at risk."

"Why are you doing this, Wayne? And if you say, 'because it's there,' I'll hit you."

"Well, that's as good a reason as any."

"Doesn't our ... relationship ... mean anything to you?"

Wayne looked puzzled, or more likely, pretended to look puzzled. "Why should it affect our relationship? After all, it's only a business deal. A deal which, moreover, is exceedingly generous to you."

"If I tell you that we're through if you go ahead with this ... this insane scheme ... will that have any effect?"

"I have a feeling that after tonight we're through anyway." He paused to look keenly at her expression, clearly visible in the bright glow of the city sky. "I'm right, aren't I?"

"Yes. Damn you to hell! I'll fight you every inch of the way."

"You don't have the necessary fire power. You forfeited personal control when you made that share issue to finance the Liberty acquisition."

"The shareholders are loyal to me. They'll listen when I tell them to reject the offer."

"Grow up, Debbie. Money talks."

"You bastard!" Debbie flung the contents of her glass in his face and stormed back into the living room, shedding her robe as she went. The champagne dribbled stickily down Wayne's chin and onto his terrycloth robe. When he heard Debbie turn on the shower, he nipped up to his own bathroom to wash himself off.

He was back in the living room with a towel clipped around his waist when Debbie emerged naked from the bathroom, and, without so much as a glance in his direction, headed for the master bedroom where her clothes were. Realizing with dismay that it would be his last opportunity, Wayne imprinted a picture of that spectacular figure in his memory bank. Her breasts were so firm and full that at first he had mistakenly assumed they had been surgically enhanced. When he saw that saucy bottom disappearing up the stairs, he almost groaned aloud. It was a good thing he had drained himself in her before telling her about his plans. He had expected her reaction to be pretty negative but her being so absolutely shattered had taken him a little by surprise.

She hadn't even asked what price he had in mind for the stock, and he had been counting on the generosity of his offer to help reconcile her. Instead, she had carried on as if he were trying to wrest her only child from her arms. Women. He had thought Debbie was different — more objective — yet when push came to shove, she ran true to form.

Impulsively, he decided to lower his bid price; although not by too much since he wanted to scare off any possible competition right from the start. He needed Pinnacle and meant to have it at all costs. He had carried out an exhaustive search for an alternate target, but independent oil companies with an asset base in the $100-million range that were also vulnerable to a quick, clean takeover were not all that easy to find. In fact, his research had turned up precisely one — Pinnacle Petroleums. With Pinnacle safely in his corporate portfolio he would be able to present the banks with a financial statement that would convince them to support his next corporate move — the deal that would finally make him one of the big boys.

The sudden slamming of a door shocked Wayne out of these not entirely unpleasant ruminations. Debbie, dressed in designer jeans and a silk shirt, was coming down the stairs. Her face wore a look of abject misery, which brought out the slight hint of coarseness that people said she had inherited from her dead mother. But her blue-grey eyes were stormy.

"I had no idea it would hit you like this, Debbie. Won't you at least stay for a nightcap?"

"You know what you can do with your nightcap," snapped Debbie, using anger to fight back the tears. "What I can't understand is how you could do a thing like this. I thought we meant something to each other."

"Of course we did, Debbie. We still do. This is just business. Can't you see that?"

"What I can see is that you're enjoying this. It's there in your eyes."

"It's called empire building, Debbie. It gives me a kick like nothing else in the world."

"Regardless of who gets in the way. You're sick, Wayne, and I hope your damn empire crashes to the ground and takes you with it!"

14

The offer from Pursuit Enterprises hit the wires the next morning, minutes after the stock markets opened across the country. Trading in Pinnacle shares was immediately suspended. The terms of the offer were squeaky clean — $21.50 per share, payable entirely in cash. That was $4.50 above the price at which the stock was currently trading, a premium designed to be irresistible to a shareholder looking for a profit on his investment. It was made even more attractive by the fact that the offer was for all the shares, not just those required for effective control.

The Pinnacle switchboard immediately lit up with incoming calls. Debbie instructed that no calls were to be put through to her, and punched number 1 on her private memory phone. Her father was in his office and had just heard the news.

"Well," he chortled, "you two sure know how to keep a secret. No one had the least clue about what you were up to."

"Daddy, listen carefully. This is a hostile takeover bid. I want no part of it, and I'm going to fight it with everything I've got. Wayne sprang it on me last night. Right out of the blue."

"I'll be damned. I must say it seems to be a very generous offer, some might say overly generous. That's why I figured the two of you were in on it together." Bill paused. "In fact it's so attractive that maybe you should have second thoughts about fighting it."

"You didn't feel that way when they were trying to take Venture away from you."

"Touché. Okay, let's see if we can come up with a game plan. Right off the bat, I'd suggest that Pinnacle retain Jim Goulder as its financial adviser on the takeover bid. And I realize you have a thing and I respect that, but Chester Martin is a master of corporate law."

"I'll get in touch with Jim right away, but I think I'll hold Mr. Martin in reserve for the moment. We've got a bright young lawyer on staff and I'd like to see what she can come up with."

"Fair enough. Let's meet for a council-of-war in your boardroom in what — a half-hour?"

"The first thing we need to find out is where the Liberty people fit." Jim Goulder was slumped in a chair, looking as always as if he were about to expire from sheer fatigue. "If they've committed their block of shares to Shaw, then ..." he paused to brush ineffectually at the cigarette ash spilling down the front of his jacket, "it's game over, I'm afraid."

"Why do you say that?" demanded Debbie. "They don't have the control block."

"That's true. But their holdings are so substantial that if they tender their shares, the other shareholders will follow suit."

"Why don't I place a call to Mac McEnroy and ask him point-blank?" Debbie suggested. "I think he'll level with me.

"I've got you on the speaker phone, Mac. I hope you don't mind," she said when the Liberty CEO came on the line. "I have my father with me ..." she paused as the American executive broke in to exchange warm greetings with Bill, then continued "and Mr. Goulder who is acting as Pinnacle's financial adviser in this matter and our general counsel, Caroline Underwood."

"Quite an impressive gathering. You are celebrating, no doubt!"

"Not exactly. We're still trying to evaluate the offer. I'm going to ask you right up front, Mac, has Liberty agreed to tender its shares?"

McEnroy was silent for a moment before replying, "The answer is no. We haven't even been approached, which I find a little surprising. Maybe this Shaw fellow figures his offer is so good he doesn't need to do anything to help it. He could be right, too."

"You're not going to tender your shares, are you?"

"Well, not right away at least. As I understand it, the offer is open for four weeks. I'm bound to say, however, that it's mighty tempting. It would just about make up for the way you stole our Canadian operation.

"But if anyone comes up with a better offer — we're always prepared to listen. Hey," he added as the thought suddenly struck him, "you all don't happen to know something we don't, do you?"

"Not a thing," Debbie assured him. "There's absolutely nothing about the company that you, as a member of the board of directors, aren't already fully aware of."

"Then I'd sure as hell like to know how he justifies that $21.50 a share."

"Inflation, most likely," put in Bill.

"That's probably it, all right. It's made some of these corporate raiders look pretty good in the past."

"That helps," said Debbie when the telephone conversation was over. "Doesn't it?" she asked, looking directly at Jim Goulder.

"It keeps us alive," the stockbroker agreed. "But McEnroy zeroed right into the problem that's facing us — the price seems to be right at the upper limit. That means it will be virtually impossible to come up with a white knight. Unless ..." He glanced questioningly in Bill's direction.

"That's out," Debbie interrupted. "Completely. All I will accept from Daddy is his advice and counsel. A white knight isn't the answer anyway. That would only mean that someone other than Wayne Shaw would end up owning Pinnacle. Not that I wouldn't love to see that son of a bitch beaten at his own game," she added fiercely, bringing a raised eyebrow from her father. "What I really need," she went on, "is to become my own white knight." Turning to Caroline Underwood, she asked, "Is there anything illegal about a major shareholder of a company making an offer to buy its shares?"

"I'm pretty sure the answer is that it's perfectly legal, but I'd like a few hours to come up with the definitive answer."

"Let's adjourn until after lunch." Jim got to his feet with a sigh of weariness. "That will give our counsel," he inclined his head toward Caroline, "time to prepare her opinion and I'll work the phones to see if I can come up with anything."

But when the meeting reconvened, all he could report was that the story on the street was that Shaw simply wanted to add the company to his collection and was prepared to pay top dollar for it. The brokers he had spoken to were inclined to recommend that their clients accept the offer and were only holding back to see which way the directors would jump. He looked at Debbie. "You'll be calling a meeting of the board to consider the offer, I presume?"

"Of course. However, Caroline tells me we can put that off for at least a week, particularly since some of the directors live so far away. It will buy us some much-needed time." She turned to Caroline. "Well, can I be my own white knight?"

"Yes. There is nothing to prevent a shareholder or an officer from making a bid for its shares. You cannot, of course, use the company assets to finance or otherwise facilitate that bid."

"I'm not sure I understand that one," said Debbie. "Can you unpack it for me?"

"What it means is that, for example, you couldn't use company properties as collateral for a loan to pay for the shares, or sell off some of its assets to finance their purchase."

"But I could still pledge the shares themselves as collateral?"

"Yes."

"Jesus, Debbie," whispered her father, "you'd be putting yourself in hock for $100-million."

"More like $60-million," she corrected him. "The rest of the company's capitalization is debt."

He shrugged to indicate it didn't make any difference, and settled back in his chair with a worried frown on his face.

"There's one other point," Caroline broke the stunned silence that filled the room. "If you do go ahead with an offer, you'll have to retain your own legal counsel and financial advisers.

"It wouldn't be proper for the company to pay the cost of management fighting a takeover bid, especially one that could be beneficial to the shareholders."

Bill Crawford and Jim Goulder exchanged glances. Back when Bill was engaged in a life-and-death struggle to retain control of Venture, the company had paid all the professional fees of all the lawyers and advisers, including Jim. Until this moment he had never given it a second thought; he realized now that he had automatically identified the company's interests with his own. However, the young lady lawyer had a point. The natural desire of management to remain in control might not be consistent with the best interests of the shareholders who owned the company.

After a moment's reflection, Debbie nodded agreement. She looked at the financial adviser. "Jim, I retained you on behalf of the company, so I guess it wouldn't be ethical for you to act for me. I guess that means you'll end up advising the company. I hope we don't find ourselves opposing each other."

Jim was on his feet, smiling benignly. "I would never let that happen, Debbie. The best thing is for me to withdraw completely and that's what I'm doing."

After his departure, Bill gave his daughter a quizzical look and said, "Ken?"

"Right. I'm going to call him now."

"It's wonderful of you to drop everything and fly to my rescue." Debbie hugged her half-brother.

"I wouldn't have thought you were in need of rescue." Ken kept his arm around her shoulders while they came to the escalator. His luggage was a briefcase and a carry-on bag so they proceeded directly outside. He stared in some astonishment at the chauffeured limousine. "What happened to the white Mustang?"

"I've still got it," replied Debbie. "But I find I get more work done by using the limo."

Ken settled himself in the rear seat and Debbie sat facing him across a foldout table. A thick glass partition separated them from the uniformed driver. "Is this one of the perks that came from the Liberty acquisition?"

"No. We don't own it. We hire it when we need it, which I admit is pretty often. It probably would be cheaper for the company to own it outright, but I don't think it would look good to the shareholders."

"Your shareholders should be erecting statues to you and establishing scholarships in your honour. You've done handsomely by them." Ken leaned back in the seat and adjusted the crease of his pants. "The first thing I need to know is whether Pinnacle has made a major oil find, or discovered a gold mine, or something equally dramatic!"

Debbie shook her head. "There's nothing like that. It's strictly business as usual. We're having a good year, better than we budgeted for, but then so is everybody else in the oil patch."

"In that case, my advice to you is very simple — tender your shares." He paused to look at her, then added gently, "But that's not what you want to hear, is it?"

"That's exactly what I don't want to hear."

"What is it about you Crawfords that makes you fight for your companies like a she-bear with cubs?"

"Maybe because we built them." The thrust brought a cheerfully rueful smile from

Ken. His parent company, Sterling Investments, was notorious for green mailing, buying up shares in a company in the hope that a nervous management would arrange to have them bought back at a profit. The last thing Sterling wanted was to end up actually owning a company.

The limousine glided down a long, curving overpass and entered the perimeter of the city centre. Ken peered out through the tinted windows with lively interest. "This is the damnedest city. They no sooner put up a building than they knock it down to build a bigger one in its place."

"It makes for a great place to work; everything's so close together you don't waste time travelling from one meeting to another."

"It's a work-oriented city, all right," Ken observed approvingly. The Cadillac drew up in front of the building that housed the Pinnacle offices and he alighted eagerly. "Speaking of work, I need to look at your latest financials. I need data. I positively lust for data!"

"If you ask me, I think Shaw must have been smoking his own pipe." Ken switched off his calculator and looked up from the reports and financial statements spread out on the boardroom table.

"Dad thinks he's banking on inflation and the rising world price of oil."

"He's got to be. Debbie, why don't you just take the money and run?"

"That's what Dad wants me to do. He keeps saying that this is a good time to be on the sidelines for a while. But Pinnacle is my company. Wayne isn't the only one who can gamble on oil prices. Aren't oilmen supposed to be risk-takers?"

Ken pushed back the lock of hair from his forehead. "One comfort is that there's an even chance Shaw will top any bid you come in with. He's not the type to let a few bucks per share stand in his way."

"If he does end up with Pinnacle, I want to make him pay through the nose."

"I'm with you there." Ken took off his glasses and rubbed his eyes. "If you're determined to be your own white knight, you will have to come up with a staggering amount of money. What about Bill? The sale of those North Sea properties has improved Venture's liquidity. Is he going to be your 'white squire'?"

"White squire? Oh, I get it. Someone who puts up the funds for the white knight's campaign but doesn't want control of the company. No, I've already ruled out any financial involvement on his part. For one thing, it wouldn't be fair to ask him to make another sizeable investment in the oil industry when he's taking steps to reduce his own exposure."

"Contra investment," Ken murmured. "Investing against the popular perception of the future. Selling when everyone else is buying. I think it's a shrewd move on his part. I can only assume that you have some ideas about how you're going to raise the money."

"You assume correctly," Debbie told him.

"Let's talk strategy for a minute. I think the company should get out some kind of statement to the effect that a directors' meeting has been summoned to consider the offer and that other offers may be forthcoming. If nothing else, that will discourage people from tendering their shares to the Shaw offer."

"If it's going to be a company statement, then you should work with our general counsel. I'll ask her to join us."

When the comely young lawyer entered through the massive carved doors, Ken smiled the devastating smile he had inherited from Bill and held out his hand. Caroline listened attentively to his proposal and thought it over for a few minutes before deciding that it was something the company could properly do. Debbie left them conferring on the wording of the release and went back to her own office. She wanted to catch Steve Morrison before he left for the day, and to set up a meeting with him for the morning.

Debbie dressed with great care for her appointment with the bank president. Discreetly sexy, yet businesslike, was the effect she was after. Steve Morrison himself came out to the reception area to greet her and escort her back to his office. Fairly wriggling with excitement, he told her to be prepared for a surprise.

"Oh Steve, this is unbelievable!" There was no need for Debbie to put on an act; the collection of argillite carvings was stunning. Inside the display cabinet tiny spotlights illuminated totem poles, mortuary poles, bird dancers and other human and mythical figures, together with intricately carved platters and bowls.

"You were the one who got me interested in argillite art," the banker said as he unlocked the cabinet and invited her to examine his treasures. Virtually all of the big-name carvers were represented: the Collinsons, Reg Davidson, Bill Reid.

"That's a 'Yell Taxi,'" Steve told her with a reminiscent chuckle when she picked up a superbly carved pole.

"I think I know who carved this beauty," she said reverently as she picked up another carving, a stylized raven, and read the name on the base. "Rufus Moody. Dear God, this piece is featured in everything that's ever been written about the Haidas!"

"Take a look at the pole on the shelf below."

Debbie gazed at the slender pole. To the uninitiated the figures all flowed together, but her expert eye had no difficulty in picking out the bear seated on four potlatch rings and an eagle perched on the rings. Below the eagle, the bear motif was repeated with the lowermost bear holding a fish in its arms. Unlike most of the other pieces, the pole had a look of great age. "That can't be a Charlie Edenshaw!" she exclaimed.

"But it is," she whispered with awe, holding the carving as if it might fall apart in her hands. "I never expected to see one of his major works outside a museum." She carefully replaced the pole and turned to the banker. "I sincerely congratulate you, Steve. Assembling a collection like this is a real achievement, and to do it in such a short time."

"It's amazing what can be accomplished when you have the resources of a bank behind you."

"That's exactly what I wanted to talk to you about — getting the resources of the bank behind me." Debbie gave him a little cleavage as she seated herself and crossed her shapely legs.

His pink face turned a shade redder, but his tone was calmly professional as he told her to proceed.

"Wayne Shaw is out to steal my company and I don't want him to get away with it."

Steve Morrison was fascinated. Like everyone else connected with the oil patch, he was aware that Shaw and Debbie had been having an affair and, until this very moment, he had assumed that the takeover was something they had both agreed to. "My information is that the offer is a very favourable one," he murmured.

"Well, it's not. It doesn't even begin to take into account the value of our unexplored lands."

"I see. And what do you propose to do about it, if I may ask?"

"Of course you can ask." Debbie leaned forward confidentially. "I intend to make a counter-offer for the shares and I want your bank to lend me the necessary funds."

"You're talking about a great deal of money."

"I know I am. But Westfirst has always granted my requests for loans and we've done well together." The banker nodded acknowledgement of this undeniable fact.

"Shaw doesn't use your bank and if he takes over Pinnacle, you lose the account. If I acquire it, you keep the company account plus the loan to me. And don't forget ...," she paused for effect, "if Wayne Shaw is prepared to offer $21.50 a share, it's got to be worth a lot more."

He agreed to have the bank's staff and professional accountants take a look at Pinnacle's records. It was all Debbie could hope for at this stage. She was counting on the fact that the president of the young and growing bank had been known on occasion to ride roughshod over the recommendations of his staff in his eagerness to obtain a market share of oil-industry loans.

Debbie and the banker spent a few more pleasant minutes admiring the carvings before she left. She was confident that if it were up to him, the loan was hers.

"I hate to sound like a broken record, but there's got to be more to this than whether the price is right," declared Debbie stubbornly. Ken raised a sceptical eyebrow. It was another of his mannerisms that reminded Debbie of her father.

"What I'm trying to say is that Wayne Shaw is not right for this company. In fact, he will merge it with Pursuit Enterprises and it will pass into oblivion. Am I making any sense at all?"

"I think you are." Caroline Underwood frowned thoughtfully. "What you're suggesting is that the company, the organization itself, has an interest that should be protected."

"That's it exactly," Debbie agreed eagerly.

Caroline thumbed through the pages of a thick book of statutes, scanning the pages with practical ease. "You may be on to something," she murmured. "Listen to this. According to the Business Corporations Act, directors must act 'honestly, in good faith and in the best interests of the corporation.' You could certainly argue that allowing a going concern to be eliminated by a merger is not necessarily in its best interests."

"But surely the corporation and the shareholders are one and the same," argued Ken.

"In a general sense, that's true. But the interests of a group of shareholders could diverge from that of the company itself. And then there's the question of the directors' responsibilities." Caroline found what she was looking for in a legal textbook. "There's a Supreme Court case, Torbeck Mines versus Fraser, where it was held that the directors ought to be allowed to consider who is seeking control and why. That would seem to justify them looking at the person who is making the offer and what his motives are."

"Where are we going with this, Debbie?" Ken asked.

"The directors could vote to reject the offer as not being in the best interests of the company."

"That wouldn't prevent the shareholders from tendering their shares. They're not bound by what the directors say."

"I realize that. But it should at least make them think twice."

"Next question. Do you think the directors can be persuaded to vote against acceptance of the offer? I'm thinking of McEnroy, for instance. The Liberty people must be dancing in the streets over this chance to unload their shares at a handsome profit."

Like many chief executives, Debbie was inclined to take her board of directors for granted. This was the first time she had been faced with the possibility that they might not automatically endorse her recommendations. Feeling almost disloyal, she mentally ran through Pinnacle's roster of directors. Surely she could count on the support of the inside directors — directors who were also employees of the company. Including herself, there were three full-time employees of the company on the board: Stan Petersen, the Vice-President of Exploration, and Ted Reimer, the Vice-President of Finance. Ken was probably right in thinking that McEnroy would want the board to approve the offer, but there was no way of knowing which way the remaining director, Marvin Peltzer, would jump. Marvin was a retired banker who was only too happy to supplement his not overly generous pension with corporate directors' fees. As a director of Pinnacle, he had an option to purchase 5,000 shares at $10 per share. Shaw's cash offer was bound to look awfully attractive to someone like Marvin. If only the loan from Westfirst would come through before the meeting, her hand would be strengthened immeasurably. But Morrison had told her there was no chance of meeting that deadline.

"Surely you can confide in your fellow directors." McEnroy was seated next to Debbie at the round conference table. "Do you intend to top Shaw's offer? If you don't, then I am going to move we recommend to the shareholders that they accept it."

Debbie took a deep breath. "That is my intention. Subject to obtaining the necessary bank financing, of course."

It was precisely what McEnroy wanted to hear. There was nothing like a bidding war to drive up the price of a stock. "In that case, I move that the board of directors reject the offer as not recognizing the true potential of the company and recommend that the shareholders do not tender their shares at this time."

The other outside director, Marvin Peltzer, seconded the motion and it was carried unanimously.

15

"I just don't understand how Wayne could do that to her." Fiona bit Frank gently on the neck and sat up. She was naked above the waist. "You saw what they were like that day at the ranch. They were great together."

"It beats me." Frank pulled her back down for another deep, tonguing kiss. "Debbie's made up her mind to fight him," he added when they came up for air. "Dad's worried sick about it."

"Could you do something like that to someone you cared for?" Fiona looked at Frank's open face and answered her own question. "Not you. It's not your style. Oh God, Frank, I ..."

"You what?" Frank gently played with her erect nipples.

"Touch me, Frank. Down there."

He looked at her for a moment, then slid his hand under her skirt. He was almost shocked at how wet she was.

"I want you to make love to me, darling," she whispered in his ear.

Frank said nothing for a moment. As the summer wore on and they saw more and more of each other, they had begun to indulge in some fairly serious petting and Frank had known for some time that she wouldn't stop him if he wanted to go all the way. He had held back, partly out of respect for her as a person, and partly because he realized her commitment was much greater than his. But now her fingers were tugging at his zipper. It was more than any man could stand. "Where?" he whispered urgently.

"Upstairs. In my room. Mother took a bottle to bed and we won't hear from her until noon."

"That was extreme," he murmured as the last delicious throbbing ebbed. "To the max."

"It feels so right to have you inside me. I'm so glad it was you."

Jesus Christ! Was she telling him she was a virgin? He had wondered about that at the start. He had entered her without too much difficulty but that was because she was so excitingly moist. Anyway, who could tell? He decided not to pursue the subject.

Fiona was in love with the heady, obsessive intoxication of a young woman engaged in her first serious affair of the heart. She longed to say it out loud, to whisper it to Frank and to shout it to the world.

But she had to keep it bottled up inside herself; she would not speak the word *love* until he did. She was sure that wonderful moment would come; if not this summer, then sometime soon. He was still emotionally scarred by that bizarre call-girl incident but at some point in time he would have to acknowledge to himself that it was a dead end. In the meantime, she had Frank for herself: the hard muscular maleness of him; the gentle expression that sometimes settled on his troubled face; and the good-humoured bantering that came so easily to them. If it wasn't everything, it was at least a great deal.

Frank's feelings were more complex than Fiona imagined. His obsession with Linda had not abated with the passage of time. There were moments when a sudden memory of something about her would make him clench his teeth to keep from crying out, and when the thought of living the rest of his life without her filled him with black despair. More than once that summer he had come close to booking a flight to Toronto, resisting the temptation only because he knew she would greet his arrival with faintly disguised scorn. There was no place for sentiment or romantic love in the world she inhabited.

After the first night Frank used condoms. When Fiona said nothing, he knew she was not on the pill. For Fiona, their lovemaking took on an exquisite bitter-sweet quality as the opening day of her college term inexorably drew closer.

"That's a real harvest moon, Frank." They were driving back from a swimming party at Bill and Hilary's.

The huge orange orb, rising majestically above the horizon, shone through the windshield. "Summer's almost over. Do you realize I leave for school exactly ten days from now?" She sighed. "It doesn't bear thinking about."

"I thought you liked Smith?" Frank deadpanned.

She shot him a dirty look. "As a matter of fact, I do. It's a super school. It's just that I don't want this summer to end, and you know perfectly well why."

"There's always the Christmas holidays."

"Christmas holidays?" exclaimed Fiona. "Are you telling me that we're not going to see each other till then?"

"On second thought, I guess I'm not," replied Frank with a grin.

Frank had only been teasing, Fiona realized, but to her the upcoming separation was nothing to joke about.

Nor did she much care for his being so lighthearted over the thought of their not seeing each other until Christmas.

They found Fiona's adoptive father passed out in the living room.

"What do we do?" asked Frank. "Drag him upstairs and put him to bed?"

She shook her head. "It's best to leave him here. I'll get his shoes off and cover him with a blanket. When he comes home it usually means the binge is over."

They left the snoring oilman in possession of the living room and went out to the patio. Frank had poured a vodka tonic for himself and a Diet Coke for her.

"What's he trying to do? Kill himself?" asked Frank.

"No. That's not it," replied Fiona wearily. "It's just that he gets so bored. That's also why he takes such wild gambles in business. He's extremely intelligent, you know."

"I've heard it said that he's a better oilman drunk than most men are sober."

"He likes that one." Fiona's smile was fond. "And the fact that he and mother have detested each other for years doesn't help matters, either."

"It can't have been a very happy home for you to grow up in."

"It's not as bad as you might think. They're both very loving to me and they've always been good to me in their own way.

"But there are times when I feel like they're the children and I'm the parent."

"If they hate each other so much, why haven't they gotten a divorce?"

"Mother wouldn't hear of it. I know it sounds funny when you think about how she goes around most of the time with a skinful, but she's a real stickler for the proprieties. She abhors scandal, poor thing, and here's good old Dad, out on the town, falling down drunk, and getting into God knows what kind of scrapes. It's kind of comical, in a sad sort of way."

Gazing down at her lovely young face, pensive in the moonlight, Frank felt a sudden attack of self-loathing. If all he wanted was a summer diversion, an antidote to the loss of Linda, he should have stuck with the girls in Mike's crowd. If Fiona's feelings for him were anything like the way he felt for Linda — dear God, he wouldn't wish that burden on his worst enemy, let alone her. They were both subdued as they said goodnight.

If nothing else, the long indolent summer had done wonders for Frank's golf. He holed out on the eighteenth, carding a respectable eighty-two to jubilant congratulations from his partner and disgruntled mutterings from the losers. Pocketing his winnings, Frank led the way to the Spike Lounge for the nineteenth hole.

The foursome included one of the oil patch's most celebrated raconteurs. Dave Green was in good form as he regaled his audience with the exploits of some of the more colourful members of the oil patch. Not surprisingly, the drunken antics of Ross Edwards figured largely in his repertoire. After recounting one particularly scandalous but hilarious escapade involving Edwards, he glanced a trifle anxiously at Frank and said, "I hope I'm not out of line. After all, the guy could be your father-in-law one of these days."

"He's not going to be my father-in-law," Frank replied tersely. "Anyway, he's so notorious that he's become public property."

The stories flowed on and so did the liquor. Frank was enjoying himself enormously. At some point he realized that he was already late for his date with Fiona, but it didn't seem to matter. He felt a kind of anger toward her almost as if she was to blame for his own feeling of guilt. It was almost an hour later when a tiny Oriental waitress approached the table and told Frank he was wanted on the phone.

Fiona was icily furious. "Are you coming or not?" she demanded.

"If you put it that way, I'm not."

She could tell from his voice that he'd been drinking. "Why don't you come over, Frank, and I'll put on some coffee."

But Frank, his judgment skewed by alcohol, felt righteously aggrieved that she had dared to call him at the club, and told her he'd take a rain check.

The foursome stayed in the bar until it closed at midnight. Somewhere along the line they had ordered steak sandwiches which helped to absorb some of the alcohol, but Frank was unsteady on his feet as he walked across the almost deserted parking lot. He toyed with the idea of driving over to Fiona's but that would be treating her like one of Charlton's girls and she sure didn't deserve that. Charlton. He's check out the action at good old Mike's.

The security guard at Mike's condo recognized Frank through the glass door and pressed a button to admit him into the main foyer. The guard, long accustomed to the constant parade of swingers in and out of Mike's pad, looked unwontedly grave as he lumbered out from behind the security desk.

"I guess you haven't heard yet, sir, but Mr. Charlton suffered a serious heart attack a few hours ago. He's in intensive care at the Foothills."

"Jesus!" was all Frank could say.

"It comes as a shock, sir, don't it? Him being so full of life and all. It looks like Mr. Charlton's party days are over." This last was said with a certain grim satisfaction. The guard hesitated as if having some sort of inner struggle with himself, but the temptation proved too strong, and he added with a malicious smirk, "He was in the saddle when it happened, sir. With Sophie, you remember her — the redhead with the big tits. What a way to go, eh? It scared the living shit out of her. She was screaming and having hysterics all over the place. The doc had to give her a needle to quiet her down."

A badly shaken Frank went back outside to his car. He was having trouble focusing and had to hold the ignition key with both hands before he managed to get it in the slot. He wondered whether Mike would make it and whether the playboy would even want to pull through. The story about how Mike was putting the blocks to a woman when he had the attack would spread like wildfire, but Mike wouldn't give a shit about that. If anything, he'd revel in it. The story was eerily reminiscent of one Dave had told earlier that night about Peter Edwards, Ross's father. He was the one who started Argosy Oil — Fiona had once said that was part of Ross's problem, the fact that he had inherited the company and that, despite all his success, he could never claim to have built it from the grassroots. Old man Edwards was a notable boozer, like his son, and was also partial to the ladies. He had expired in bed with some dolly who had the presence of mind to call his lawyer. The lawyer and one of Edwards's drinking buddies came down to the hotel, dressed the corpse, and supported it between them across the lobby and into the lawyer's car. And so it was that Peter Edwards died peaceably and respectably in his own bed.

Frank suddenly realized he was on the wrong side of the white line. He cursed and over-corrected, almost hitting the curb. If he ran into a checkstop tonight, he'd blow the needle right off the dial. But it was still the middle of the week, when the police weren't likely to be on the lookout for impaired drivers, so he decided to chance it.

He breathed easier when he finally turned onto the gravelled back road that, in a very roundabout way, would eventually take him to the Circle C. It wouldn't be worth the RCMP's while to set up a check point on this road; the traffic was almost non-existent. Confident that he was home and dry, Frank accelerated. The other car came around the curve at high speed, its lights on bright. Dazzled, Frank wrenched the wheel to the right and the other car sped by. He was on the soft shoulder, fighting desperately for control. But the wheels refused to straighten out in the heavy going and the Trans Am plowed ahead, then tilted and plunged over the bank and into the trees. Frank clung to the wheel, hearing the snapping of branches and small tree trunks. He could feel the car rolling over on its side but he was held in place by his seat belt. Then the onrushing vehicle smashed into something solid, there was a flash of light inside Frank's skull and he blacked out.

He couldn't have been unconscious for very long because the noises of the crash were still going on around him when he came to. The hot metal was pinging and cracking and the ominous sound of leaking fluid penetrated his dazed consciousness. If that was gasoline and if it came in contact with any part of the hot engine, the car would go up like a bomb. Frank forced himself not to panic and took stock of his situation. Holding his breath, he flexed his fingers and shuffled his feet on the floorboards. Miraculously, it seemed that the bang on his head was the only injury he had suffered. It was the seat belt that had saved him.

Now to find a way of getting out of the wrecked car. It had rolled partway over. The roof on the passenger side — where Fiona would have been sitting — had been caved in until it was almost level with the dashboard. There was no way she would have survived. The steering wheel had been driven back by force of the impact. That's what he must have banged his head on. Another few inches and it would have crushed him. Frank undid the seat belt and tried the door handle, but the car's frame had buckled and the door refused to open. Fear raced through him at the thought of being trapped inside the car. It could burst into flames any instant. Broken glass tinkled and the car shifted ominously with Frank's movements. The headlights had gone out but he suddenly realized the tape deck was still playing. That meant the battery was functioning. Quickly he pressed the power-window switch and sighed with relief as the glass slid smoothly down. He eased himself out, fearful that the car would roll completely over and crush him. It moved a few degrees, then settled back in its cradle of severed tree trunks as he dropped lightly to the ground, almost turning an ankle on a rock.

When he regained the road after a stiff scramble there was no sign of the other car. It had obviously kept on going, unaware of the havoc it had left in its wake. The moon shed enough light so Frank could pinpoint where he was — approximately six miles from the ranch. He set off, keeping to the fields and away from the road; he had no wish to be picked up by a helpful motorist or, God forbid, the RCMP. His head had pretty well cleared by the time he reached the ranch but he was still in no shape to face a Breathalyzer test. One of the ranch dogs barked in the distance. That would be Becky; she was always the first to sound the alarm. It was just a preliminary, questioning bark, not the furious snarling that would signify an intruder at close range and bring the ranch foreman out to investigate. He would just as soon not run into Harvey, although the taciturn foreman would never snitch on him. Becky barked again and this time Fritz joined in. Frank whistled and the two German Shepherds, bushy tails wagging a frantic welcome, raced up the road to meet him.

Inside the house Frank went immediately to the bathroom and swallowed two extra-strength Tylenol tablets. What with hangovers and fights, he had taken more pain killers in the last few months than in the entire rest of his life. His head was pounding and there was a large lump in the centre of his forehead. Incautiously he touched it and winced with pain. His right eye was turning an interesting shade of purple as well. But he was lucky, very lucky. And if Fiona had been with him ...!

He slowly stripped to his undershorts and climbed carefully between the cool and inviting sheets. A soothing breeze blew in through the open window. For a few moments he stared at the ceiling, almost sick with remorse and self-recrimination. The next thing he heard was the scared voice of Marion, the housekeeper, who drove over five days a week from a neighbouring ranch. "The police want to see you, Frank. My God, what did you do to yourself."

"I parked the car in the middle of some trees." He groaned as he sat up too quickly. The room swayed dizzily. When it finally stopped, he slowly swung his legs over the edge of the bed. "Tell them I'll be with them as soon as I clean up a bit."

The digital clock on the bedside table read 9:30 a.m.; the alcohol should be pretty well out of his system. His mouth tasted like a gorilla's armpit and brushing his teeth didn't help much. A youthful uniformed constable was waiting for him in the living room. Frank admitted that he was the registered owner of the Trans Am and that he had been driving it at the time of the accident. The Mountie's attitude changed perceptibly when he discovered that no one else had been in the car and that it was a single vehicle accident. After a few more questions he closed his notebook and asked Frank to come round to the station to fill out an accident report. "But you better see a doctor first," he added as he left. "That's a nasty-looking lump."

The phone rang just as Frank closed the door behind the Mountie. "Thank God." Fiona's voice was shaky with relief. "Frank, are you all right?"

"I've felt better. But all things considered I don't have much to complain about."

"Janice just called. She was in an absolute state. Henry picked up some wild story about you being in a car accident and me being killed."

"Jesus Christ. Look, Fiona, I did prang the car last night and I did get banged around some. But it's nothing serious. Hang on a sec, Dad's just arrived."

Relief swept through Bill when he saw his son on his feet and talking on the phone. The sergeant in charge of the local RCMP detachment had phoned him to let him know that Frank's car had been found wrecked on the back road but there was no sign of anyone at the crash-site. Leaving Hilary to check out the hospitals, he jumped into the Mercedes and raced to the ranch.

"You're having yourself quite a summer," Bill observed dryly, grimacing at the sight of Frank's swollen face.

"I guess this just isn't my year," rejoined Frank with a weak grin. "I'll tell Fiona I'll call her back."

"Have the police been here?" Bill asked when Frank turned away from the phone.

"Yep. No sweat. They want me to fill out an accident report."

"I'll drive you into town and we'll have Doctor Jamieson look you over."

"Okay. Let me give Fiona a call first, though."

"You're thinking about Billy, aren't you?" asked Frank. Billy, his older brother, had been killed as a teenager when the car he was driving missed a turn on a mountain road. Billy's best friend and the two high-school girls who were with them were also killed in the tragedy. All four were stark naked and stoned on hash.

Bill pulled out to pass a cattle-liner en route to the stockyard. "I was. I don't particularly care for the thought of losing both my boys in some stupid automobile accident. You were drinking, I expect?"

"That's about all I seem to do these days."

"As you know, Frank, I've never gone in for the heavy father bit. I realize you were badly hurt over Linda, but don't you really think it's time you cleaned up your act?"

"That's just what I intend to do."

As arranged, Fiona picked him up at the hospital where the doctor had sent him for X-rays. Her expression was a mixture of relief, concern and exasperation. "I don't know what this town would do for gossip without you, Frank," she said as he eased himself into the passenger seat. His head was throbbing abominably.

"The stories are pretty wild, huh?" Frank lowered his window to get some air, thinking once again that Fiona was a class act. In addition to all her other qualities she was a good sport. He wished he loved her.

"You would not believe the number of calls I've had. I finally left a message on the answering machine thanking them for their concern and saying that the rumours of my demise were greatly exaggerated. Where would you like to go?"

"Let's stop at a drugstore so I can get this prescription for 292s filled, and then would you mind running me back out to the ranch?"

"Mind?" Fiona stared at him. "Of course I don't mind."

"Let's take the back road," he said as they pulled away from the drugstore. The druggist had given him a glass of water and he had swallowed two of the potent painkillers. "I better bite the bullet and take a look at the Trans Am, although it's probably been towed away by now."

"Oh, oh," muttered Frank as they rounded a curve and saw the tow truck on the edge of the bank, its spinning yellow lights reflected off several parked cars, including Bill's silver Mercedes.

Fiona pulled over to the side and they walked up to join the small throng of onlookers watching two men cutting down the snapped tree trunks to clear the way for the wreck. Bill's eyes brightened when he saw Fiona and he kissed her on the cheek. Whispers rustled through the crowd at the sight of Frank.

"You was damn lucky to walk away from that wreck," a rancher, who had once been a chuckwagon driver and thus was a connoisseur of wrecks, observed quietly.

Frank nodded grim agreement. He felt Fiona's grip on his hand tighten involuntarily as she stared down at where the car's roof had been crushed in. The once sporty automobile was a pathetic sight, its wheels, two of the tires flat, sticking up in the air like a helpless turtle, its chassis twisted out of alignment and the front end crumpled against the large pine tree that had finally stopped its plunging progress.

The driver started the tow-truck's motor and his assistant began to play out the wire cable. Bill turned to Frank.

"Maybe you should leave now. The insurance people have been here and written it off as a total loss and I'm not sure you want to be around when they drag it out."

"You're right." Frank's stomach was already a little queasy at the thought of the Trans Am being ignominiously hauled out of the woods. There wasn't much to be proud of in last night's work.

"I think I'll hit the sack." Frank was practically out on his feet by the time they reached the ranch.

"That's the place for you, all right. But you've got a concussion and you aren't supposed to sleep for long. I'll wake you in two hours."

She woke him with a cup of tea. It was the perfect choice for the way he felt and he sipped it appreciatively while she plumped out the pillows behind his head. If it had only been Linda fussing over him like this he would have been ecstatic.

Later that afternoon Bill, Hilary, and Debbie descended on the ranch, bringing with them the supper that Chong had prepared.

Debbie's eyes were damp as she hugged her brother. "I'd like to crack some joke about it, but I can't seem to."

"I know. It's Billy. I've been thinking about him ever since it happened."

Bill was behind the bar mixing drinks. He fixed a vodka tonic for Hilary, a Caesar for Debbie, and poured a glass of white wine for Fiona. "What's yours, Frank?" he asked.

"Diet Coke, please."

Bill carefully kept his face expressionless as he handed the glass to his son.

"The chemistry between us is terrific but I'm not in love with you, Fiona."

"There's nothing more to be said then, is there?"

"I guess not." Frank got up from his chair and gazed around the richly appointed living room. His summer seemed to have revolved around the Edwards's huge old mansion. Fiona never called it anything but house, yet it was a mansion in every sense of the word.

"Tell me one thing, Frank. Are you doing all these things as a way of punishing yourself? Some form of atonement? You've given up drinking, you're breaking up with me, and now you've signed on as a roughneck on a drilling rig. Not what you would call a cushy job."

"The last thing I want is a cushy job. Besides, it's a good way of getting in shape, and I'm just a fifth wheel around the ranch these days. I stopped drinking because of what it was doing to me. And I said what I did because I didn't want there to be any misunderstanding between us."

"All very logical. Goodbye, Frank, and thanks for a fun summer."

16

Waiting for his senior loans officer to arrive, Steve Morrison rapidly scanned the *Daily Oil Bulletin*. There was a brief item on page two that the price of West Texas Intermediate, the benchmark US crude, had gone up $1.25 to $33.25 per barrel. That would give him just the ammunition he needed to deal with that old mossback, Gerlitz.

"The numbers just won't go around it." Art Gerlitz realized he wasn't telling his boss what he wanted to hear. Until he was hired by the newly organized Westfirst Bank two years ago, Art had spent his entire career with one of the major banks. Steeped in the tradition that every loan had to be backed by gilt-edged security, his conservative soul was scandalized by what was currently going on in Calgary banking circles, where astronomical loans were made in the expectation that ever-increasing oil prices would bail out even the shakiest of them. Westfirst was among the worst offenders, but it was by no means alone. Steve never tired of reminding his subordinate that the majors were out there soliciting loans like there was no tomorrow, wining and dining prospective borrowers, and practically shoving multi-million dollar loans down the throat of anyone who would stand still. "Market share" was the battle cry as the banks gleefully financed drilling rigs on the strength of a three-martini lunch, capitalized interest payments, and made new loans to pay off those that had come due.

Scarcely paying attention, Steve fidgeted in his chair as his loans officer droned through the numbers.

When Art's monotone finally ceased, Steve frowned impatiently. "I keep telling you, Art, we're dealing with a moving target. Your numbers are already out of date. Look at this." He pushed the *Bulletin* across the desk and leaned back in his chair with a triumphant smile.

"I'm going to approve this loan, Art." Gerlitz started to protest, but Steve cut him off. "If we don't make the loan you can bet that others will. Including," he shook an admonishing finger at Art, "your former employers. There's nothing they'd like better than to take the Pinnacle account away from me."

The jump in the price of crude also gave some comfort to Ken Kwasny when Debbie announced that she was going to make an offer of $22.50 per share.

"Maybe you oil people know something that is beyond the understanding of us mere mortals, but I'm still from Missouri on this one."

One unexpected result of Debbie's offer was a phone call from Wayne. Debbie hesitated a few moments before telling her secretary to put it through.

"You realize you're way out on a limb and I've got a saw in my hand," was Wayne's way of opening the conversation.

"Start sawing. That's exactly what I want you to do."

"I know you've got Ken Kwasny advising you, but this doesn't look like Kwasny strategy to me."

"He's sitting here in the office with me. Would you like to talk to him?"

"No. Just give him my regards. Debbie, I never intended this thing to turn into a personal vendetta between us. I'd like to see you.

"Get lost, Wayne."

As Ken had predicted, virtually no shares were tendered to Debbie's offer.

The shareholders were holding back, anticipating a counteroffer from Shaw. After a temporary halt on the day of Shaw's offer, Pinnacle shares had resumed trading and the price hovered around $22.50 as speculators gambled on a better offer being made.

"I kinda expected Frank to come back for the funeral," Debbie said. Mike Charlton had suffered a second heart attack and died while still in the hospital.

"He wanted to, but the well is in such a remote location that he couldn't get out in time. I offered to send the jet up for him but he wanted no part of that. He was right, of course. The other members of the crew would give him a hard time about being chauffeured around in his daddy's jet."

"That well must be way the hell and gone out in the boondocks."

Bill smiled. "Let's go into the study and I'll show you."

He pressed a switch on the panelled wall and a map of the world rolled down from the ceiling. "It's right about there." He placed his fingertip on an unmarked spot in the Yukon Territory, just north of the British Columbia border.

"Are you hoping that hiring on as a roughneck is the first step in Frank going back into the oil patch?"

Bill shrugged. "You've got to admit it's a vast improvement over what he was doing this past summer."

Hilary joined them in time to hear the last part. "I still haven't forgiven him for the way he treated Fiona. I'm told she was badly hurt."

"I don't think Frank has forgiven himself, if it comes to that," Bill murmured.

"You never know, they may still get together," said Debbie.

"Do you really think so? Wouldn't that be wonderful?" Hilary glanced at her watch. "Ken should be arriving any time now. He asked if he could bring a friend."

"Did he, now?" Debbie breathed. "This I want to see."

She didn't have long to wait. Ken showed up a few minutes later with Caroline Underwood, taking Debbie completely by surprise. Around the office, the two of them hadn't shown the slightest sign of being interested in each other. But when you thought about it, it was a natural matchup. Both of them were brainy as hell and Caroline was a real looker in her own quiet, dark-eyed way. It would serve Margo Jones right, too.

Caroline was a very self-possessed young lady, but Debbie could see that she was a little unsure of her reception. After Bill and Hilary had welcomed her with their usual effortless hospitality, she turned to Debbie and said, "I hope you don't mind."

"Of course I don't mind. Why on earth should I?" Debbie held out both her hands. "You two can sure keep a secret."

"Don't go jumping to conclusions, Debbie," laughed Ken. "We're just good friends."

"That's a good place to start," she replied innocently.

The evening was a great success. Caroline fitted in beautifully and Debbie was amused to see Hilary's matchmaking instinct, thwarted by Frank's intransigence, coming to the fore once again.

Jason was won over when Caroline went with him to the stable to admire his horse, and told him stories about the pet gerbils she had kept as a child.

"He's a charmer," Caroline told Hilary after dinner, when Jason had gravely wished the grownups goodnight and gone to bed.

Hilary thanked her and said with an indulgent smile, "He's also in danger of becoming thoroughly spoiled."

"Not Jason." Bill came to the defence of his stepson. "The little guy's got too much common sense."

Out of respect for a possible conflict of interest on Caroline's part, they avoided any talk of the battle for control of Pinnacle. When the lawyer excused herself to go to the washroom, Ken took advantage of her absence to ask Debbie if she had heard anything about a possible counter-offer from the Shaw camp.

"Not a word. But I'm sure he'll make a move."

"He could also pick up his winnings and leave."

"Not a chance. Wayne doesn't give up that easily."

Debbie's hunch proved to be correct, although Wayne waited a full week before improving his offer to $23.75. "It's a pre-emptive strike," Ken whispered when he heard about the new bid. "He wants you out of the way."

Steve Morrison was on the phone almost immediately, to assure Debbie of the bank's continued support if she wanted to continue the bidding war. He didn't think it necessary to tell her that he had personally acquired 10,000 shares of Pinnacle in a dummy account. On the other hand, Ken was appalled at the thought she might top Shaw's offer.

"You think I'm practising voodoo economics, don't you?" smiled Debbie with an air that seemed oddly preoccupied.

"It's worse than voodoo economics. It's kamikaze economics. You make the wrong move at this stage and you're ruined for life."

"At least, we don't have to make any final decisions just yet."

On her way home that night Debbie stopped in at a drugstore and purchased a home pregnancy test. The next morning she carefully added three drops of urine to the reddish chemical powder in the test tube and then mixed in two drops of a liquid chemical from the vial that came with the kit. She stoppered the test tube and put it aside for the prescribed one hour. At first when she missed her period she had put it down to the strain of the takeover battle. Stress had done that to her before. But as the days went by she had become more and more convinced that she might be pregnant.

The red chemical in the bottom of the test tube had coagulated. The test was positive. A soft little smile played around the corners of Debbie's mouth as she tossed the test tube and the rest of the kit into the trash compactor.

"I'm going to tender my shares," she announced as soon as she arrived at the office.

"Hallelujah!" Ken almost shouted his relief.

Once the acquisition of Pinnacle was put to bed, Wayne moved swiftly to mend his fences and consolidate his position. A memo was circulated to all Pinnacle employees assuring them of a place in the rapidly expanding Pursuit organization. Many, including Caroline Underwood and Stan Petersen, sought advice from Debbie, wanting to know what her future plans were and indicating they would prefer to remain in her employ if she was going to start anew.

In fairness, she had to discourage them since she had decided to take time out to have the baby and to find out what she wanted to do with the rest of her life. She was pretty sure she would return to the ever-fascinating oil game, but this time around she would build her enterprise through exploration rather than by acquisitions. The corporate takeover approach still left her with a bad taste in her mouth, as if she were capitalizing on other people's efforts.

A handwritten note from Wayne accompanied the awesome check that paid for the shares she had tendered. The numbers on the cheque were almost unreal — $16,978,080, payable to her personally. The taxman would take a ferocious bite, but with what was left plus the proceeds from the initial share underwriting, she was an extremely wealthy woman, free to follow whatever whim might strike her fancy. Not quite, she reminded herself, placing a hand on her abdomen, feeling for a bulge that was still non-existent.

Holding the cheque by the edge as if it might disintegrate in front of her eyes, she placed it back on her desk and picked up Wayne's note. He congratulated her on achieving such a terrific deal for her shareholders and offered to provide the necessary corporate consents so she could get the Pinnacle Petroleums name back. She hated to accept any favours from the man who had taken her company from her, but she badly wanted the original name, so she would swallow her pride and accept. His invitation to lunch she would ignore.

Wayne made a point of taking Steve Morrison to lunch and assuring the bank president that Westfirst would retain the Pinnacle business. He explained that Pinnacle as such would be merged into Pursuit and thus would disappear as a corporate entity, but he promised Morrison that he could count on an equivalent share of Pursuit's business. The dazzled banker listened avidly when Wayne hinted at future plans for a truly spectacular deal, and nodded eager agreement when Wayne expressed the hope Westfirst would be one of the leaders in the banking consortium that would be required to raise the necessary financing.

To the astonishment of his public relations department, whose standing instructions for years had been to keep his public exposure to the absolute minimum, Wayne began to make himself available to the media. He gave in-depth interviews and, for the first time, photographs of his striking, rather hawkish features began to appear in the press. He even made speeches to service clubs and industry associations, where he quickly gained a reputation as an effective, controversial speaker with some interesting things to say. Not only did he defend the role of the corporate raider, he championed it as a necessary method of rationalizing and streamlining an industry that had grown inefficient with far too many chiefs and too few Indians. He paraded horror stories of how highly paid professionals often supervised as few as four or five employees and how countless small exploration departments endlessly and needlessly duplicated each other's efforts.

Bill Crawford watched his performance with sardonic amusement. When Wayne declared that the North American oil industry had to become lean and mean or go the way of the dinosaurs, Bill, watching him at home on television, muttered to Hilary, "He's doing his best to transform himself from the Yankee Raider into the saviour of the oil industry."

There was enough truth in what he was saying that Wayne began to develop a following in the media. Astutely, he also set about broadening his contacts in political circles, ensconcing himself in a palatial suite at the Westin hotel in Ottawa where he held court to a wide spectrum of MPs and cabinet ministers. His recently acquired Canadian citizenship made him very much *persona grata* to the politicians, and many saw him as an effective ally in the struggle to impose federal energy policies on a rebellious west.

The bankers he courted most assiduously of all, although it was a toss-up as to who was romancing whom. The banks were in a feeding frenzy and Wayne, whose company loans by now amounted to several hundreds of millions of dollars and who held out the tantalizing promise of much more to come, was the darling of the banking world.

With his groundwork carefully laid, Wayne began to close in on his target. He was about to make his first move when his plans received an unexpected setback. He was seated at the head table at a luncheon sponsored by the Canadian Petroleum Association, when it happened. The speaker was Otis Newhouse, chairman of the giant multinational, Fordex Oil Inc., whose head office was in Chicago. Fordex's wholly owned Canadian subsidiary, Fordex Canada Ltd., with its vast reserves of oil and gas, was a jewel in the multinational's crown and the highly partisan audience expected the American executive to bitterly denounce the detested Canadian government policies that discriminated against foreign-controlled oil companies. He didn't disappoint them as he condemned the confiscatory taxes, and the government grants that were weighted so heavily against foreign oil companies. "And in the context of the oil industry in Canada, foreign equates to American — don't forget that," he thundered into the microphone. "It's the very same people who created the great oil industry of this country who now are the targets of this unwise and discriminatory legislation!" The audience, many of whom were employed by American-owned companies, applauded vigorously. Wayne, aware that the Canadian government policies worked very much in his favour, was careful not to show too much enthusiasm.

Newhouse waited for the applause to subside before continuing in a calmer, almost philosophical tone.

"We all know that many American companies, some of which have been here since the days of the Leduc discovery, have decided that you can't fight city hall and have pulled back across the border. Some have sold off their Canadian assets at fire-sale prices; others have put a hold on any further investment in Canada. Many analysts and other experts expect us to follow suit." He paused for emphasis. "But I'm here to tell you, ladies and gentlemen, Fordex Canada is not for sale!" Another round of applause greeted this announcement, but Wayne was too stunned to join in.

"The reason we are not going to walk away from our Canadian operation," Newhouse went on, "is because we are confident that Canadians will soon come to realize that these discriminatory practices are not in their own best interest. We believe that common sense and fair dealing will shortly put an end to these short-sighted measures and allow all of us to once again compete on a level playing field!"

It was only a few blocks from the Palliser Hotel where the luncheon had been held to Wayne's office and he would have enjoyed the walk, but instead he obediently climbed into the waiting limousine. Wealthy oilmen had become high-risk targets for kidnappings, and the security specialists retained by Pursuit insisted that he travel within the city in a car with a chauffeur trained in defensive driving techniques. For the same reason he carried a set of his own fingerprints in his wallet so the kidnappers wouldn't have to cut off one of his fingers to prove they had him. Telling the chauffeur to drive around for a while because he had some thinking to do, Wayne leaned back in the seat and gazed blankly out through the one-way, bulletproof windows at the dreary brown landscape of late fall.

For months he had schemed and manoeuvred to put himself in a position where he could make a run at Fordex Canada. Acquiring Fordex Canada would catapult him into the ranks of the major oil companies. He had even sacrificed his relationship with Debbie, and that was turning out to be a much stiffer price than he had expected. Only recently had he come to fully realize just how good they had been together. And now the target had been snatched away like an enemy aircraft abruptly disappearing from the radar screen. Its US parent held all the shares of Fordex Canada, and if management decided against selling the subsidiary, that was the way it was going to be. You couldn't do an end run around them by making a public offer because there was only one shareholder — Fordex Oil Inc.

As he had so often in the past, Wayne brooded over the fact that the top management of a company like Fordex wielded almost unlimited power and for all practical purposes was accountable to no one. The millions of Fordex shares were widely held by the public, with the result that there was no significant shareholder, or group of shareholders, to exert influence over management decisions. Good Lord, he had found the Achilles heel! The unsuspecting target was suddenly back in his sights. Telling the driver to head for the office, Wayne picked up the car phone and began to issue a rapid series of instructions to his executive assistant.

Even *The Wall Street Journal* took notice when Pursuit Enterprises filed documents with the US Securities and Exchange Commission disclosing that it had acquired fifteen per cent of the outstanding shares of Fordex Oil Inc. There was an air of incredulity in the *Journal*'s write-up, as if it was almost unthinkable that an unknown Canadian corporation now owned a sizeable chunk of one of the largest US oil companies. Wayne's bold move was headline news in Canada, with the accompanying stories heavily slanted along nationalistic lines. "Canadian venture capital successfully invades the US," and "Wayne Shaw proves he can mix it up with the big boys" were the recurring themes.

The big question was whether Shaw would go after control of the US giant. Pursuit's filing with the SEC was tantalizingly vague on the point. It simply declared that the company had no intention of adding to its share holding "at the present time." It soon became common knowledge on the street that Shaw had been supported with massive loans from a consortium of Canadian banks, and this led many analysts to conclude that he had the necessary financial backing to go after an absolute majority, if that was his game plan. Even with his present holdings, the pundits pointed out, he was by far the largest single shareholder of the company and, as such, was in a position to exert considerable clout.

This fact was only too obvious to the thunderstruck executives at Fordex's Chicago head office. Dazedly they asked themselves how it could have happened. They were to find out it was disturbingly simple. Acting on Shaw's behalf, a leading New York financial house had assembled a network of brokers throughout the country and, through a multiplicity of small, unremarkable purchases, they quietly accumulated the specified number of shares within the ten-day period the SEC allowed before Shaw had to declare himself.

Executives and directors gathered at hastily convened meetings to develop a defensive strategy. Hired financial specialists outlined possible countermoves ranging from shark repellents to the issue of new treasury shares in order to dilute Shaw's interest. The Fordex top brass waited with trepidation for the second shoe to drop, and for Shaw to announce his intention to take over the company. An ashen-faced aide interrupted a directors' meeting to tell Otis Newhouse that Mr. Shaw was calling from Calgary, Canada.

Otis left the boardroom like a man expecting to hear the worst from his doctor, but he had regained his normal air of overbearing self-assurance when he returned from taking the call. "Mr. Shaw has shown his hand, gentlemen, and I think we may be able to live with it. He wants to trade his fifteen per cent of our shares for our Canadian subsidiary. He claims they are of equal value, and I expect he's right."

The directors, the majority of whom were full-time employees of the company, exchanged relieved glances. One of them asked, "What happens if we refuse the deal?"

"He intends to take a run at the company. According to him he has the necessary financial resources."

The vice-president of production looked at each one of his fellow directors in turn, then said, "I move that we open negotiations with Mr. Shaw." The motion was carried unanimously.

Wayne's "repatriation" of Fordex Canada was hailed in Ottawa as a complete vindication of the federal energy policies. The energy minister came out to Calgary, ostensibly to deliver a speech but really to share a photographic opportunity with Wayne, whom he described as the kind of business leader who would win back for Canada control over its oil industry and set the country on the path toward energy self-sufficiency. The political posturing made the oilmen fume, but they gave Wayne full marks for the spectacular coup he had pulled off, although some wondered why he hadn't tried for the whole ball of wax and gone after the US parent company.

Wayne was back in the news when he announced an immediate start on the construction of Pursuit Towers. The *Sun* splashed an architect's drawing of the new building across its front page and the *Calgary Herald* noted with satisfaction that it would be ten stories taller than the CanOil Building. "Thanks to Mr. Shaw," an editorial crowed, "Calgarians will no longer suffer the indignity of the tallest building in town being a symbol of the detested federal government's presence in the oil patch."

17

Bill checked the Arrivals screen. "Debbie's flight is on time and it's coming in at Gate 14."

"I keep wondering what she meant when she said she has a surprise for us," Hilary said as they headed for the gate.

Bill rolled his eyes heavenward. "With Debbie it could be anything. She's been away for more than three months. Maybe she picked up a husband in her travels."

But Debbie was unaccompanied when she, gloriously tanned, bright blonde hair set off by a lustrous black mink coat, walked through the gate. Embracing her, Bill felt the soft fullness beneath the coat. "Oh, oh," he said, "I think I know what the surprise is."

"I hope you're pleased." Debbie looked up at her father a little anxiously.

"You obviously are, so I am too."

"How far along are you?" asked Hilary while they waited for the luggage.

"Five months."

Bill did a bit of mental arithmetic. "Wayne?"

"I ain't telling."

"Debbie!" Hilary was shocked.

Debbie shrugged. "That's the way it's going to be."

They drove directly to the Crawford's place in the country where Debbie would spend the night. Bill eyed her figure as she slipped out of her coat and said dryly, "You're sure going to create a sensation at the wedding. Poor Janice will be completely upstaged."

"I hadn't even thought about that. Do you suppose I ought to stay home?" Debbie answered her own question. "To hell with that. I've got nothing to be ashamed of." She accepted a Virgin Caesar from her father and asked, "When does Frank arrive? I can hardly wait to see him, but I'm a little surprised he's going to all this trouble to attend the wedding. I never thought he and Henry Purvis were all that close."

"They get along. Henry helped him get a job with Spartacus Drilling, which was the company Frank wanted to work for, and the last time Frank was in town Henry made a special point of asking if he planned to attend. Henry's the kind of guy who was born old and I don't think he's got too many friends his own age."

"Will Fiona be there?"

"She's the maid of honour," replied Hilary. "I've met her at several of the bridal parties, looking absolutely lovely." She frowned disapprovingly. "According to the ladies at my book club, the reason the Edwards spent Christmas in Hawaii was because Fiona didn't want to take a chance of running into Frank here in Calgary."

"The poor kid. She'll be front and centre tomorrow, so they won't be able to avoid each other." Debbie's eyes gleamed with sudden mischief. "It promises to be an interesting wedding."

The city had been in the benevolent grip of a Chinook for the past week and the streets were bare and gritty with sand left behind when the ice melted. The cloud cover that accompanies a Chinook had thinned out, allowing a brilliant winter sun to shine down on the wedding guests thronging into Christ Church. The Crawford party arrived together in the Mercedes. Walking up the hill from where they had finally found a place to park, Frank, looking almost impossibly fit, was greeted warmly on all sides. Everyone seemed genuinely pleased to see him, and he responded with the easy charm that was part of his nature. He was touched and a little taken aback, since he believed that the escapades he had starred in during the last year had indelibly branded him as an uncaring playboy.

Debbie was treated more circumspectly; people were somewhat in awe of her for what she had accomplished in the business world. Being Debbie, her first inclination had been to flaunt her condition, but she had finally elected to play it cool and wore a loose-fitting dress. It would be all right in the church where she could keep her coat on until she got to her seat, but her secret would never survive the reception. To hell with it. She smiled at Janice's younger brother, who was one of the ushers, and took his arm as they walked up the aisle.

Low murmurs of appreciation rippled through the vaulted nave as the bridal procession came down the aisle. Fiona, directly in front of the bride and behind the four bridesmaids, drew all eyes. Some of the guests, familiar with the events of last summer, stole surreptitious glances in Frank's direction. If they hoped for some reaction on his part, they were disappointed — his bland, pleasant smile never wavered. Fiona bestowed smiles on both sides of the aisle and, whether by accident or otherwise, her gaze was on the opposite side when she passed the Crawfords' pew. The same thing happened during the recessional at the end of the service when she, smiling radiantly, swept down the aisle on the arm of the best man. The bride, however, had an especially warm smile for Frank.

For all her outward insouciance, Debbie was on edge as she hung up her coat in the ladies' cloakroom.

Looking in the mirror to freshen her lipstick, she saw Mavis Anderson do a double take. The startled look in Mavis's eyes had changed to one of delighted malice by the time Debbie swept past to join her family in the foyer of the country club. The reception line was drawn up at the top of the staircase.

Fiona, standing next to the best man, greeted Bill and Hilary with open affection. "You look lovely, Fiona," Frank said when his turn came.

"You look marvellously fit, yourself." She averted her head slightly so that his kiss landed awkwardly on her cheek. "You haven't met Jim Huntley, have you?"

It was typical of Henry Purvis that he had had to recruit one of his old schoolmates from a Toronto private school to act as best man. Huntley was tall and good-looking and it was obvious he could scarcely credit his good fortune in finding someone like Fiona in the wedding party. He greeted Frank stiffly as though he was fully aware of his past relationship with her.

"Still on the wagon, Frank?" asked Jerry Gillespie as Frank ordered a cola.

"I have the occasional beer with the boys in the crew, but that's about it."

The reception line had disbanded and the wedding party was mingling with the guests. Watching Fiona laughing flirtatiously with the best man, Frank wondered why it bothered him so much. He wanted her to have a good time and forget about him, didn't he?

"Jesus Christ!" Jerry almost choked on his drink as he caught his first sight of Debbie. "Is that sister of yours pregnant?"

"Kinda looks that way, doesn't it?"

A visibly agitated Wayne Shaw came up to Debbie as she chatted with some of her former horse-show friends, and took her by the elbow. "We have to talk, Debbie."

"What's there to talk about?" But she let him lead her away.

"You're going to have a baby."

"How clever of you to notice."

"It's mine, isn't it?"

"Don't ask me."

"Debbie, this is important. I have to know. I'm begging you. Tell me, for God's sake."

"You're making a scene, Wayne. People are staring."

"Marry me, Debbie."

"Are you trying to make an honest woman out of me, Wayne? How delightfully old-fashioned."

"Damn it, Debbie," he said in an urgent whisper, "you know I have no children of my own. This could be the most important thing that's ever happened to me."

"If it's happened to you," she replied sweetly. "Sssh," she raised a finger to her lips, "they're about to give the toast to the bride."

Janice had asked Ross Edwards, who had known her ever since he and his wife had brought Fiona to Calgary and the two young girls had started to play together, to give the toast.

Anxious to do her credit, he had cut back on his drinking and a public-relations type at Argosy had written a witty and tender speech for him. Fiona blinked back tears of pride and joy as he completed the toast and raised his glass to Janice.

Debbie slipped away from Wayne's side while everyone had their glasses raised and joined a group of her married friends who welcomed her with almost breathless titillation. Standing in their midst, she threw a mocking glance over her shoulder at Wayne, alone and seething in the middle of the floor.

"It's just like old times, isn't it, Tom?" Debbie was so excited she was almost gushing.

"Seems like," was the petroleum engineer's noncommittal answer.

"Don't go looking at me all cross-eyed because I'm pregnant. I feel great, I can't drink, and I'm bored out of my tree. I'm ready to go back to work, Tom."

He nodded acceptance of this, and then muttered, "There are some real rinky-dink deals out there."

"That's why I need you. I've got a pretty good stake and I don't want to blow it."

"It's been known to happen."

"What I want are good solid geological prospects, backed up with seismic wherever possible. You get your consulting fee plus a piece of the action." She broke off to look keenly at Tom. "You must be a very wealthy man by now."

"I reckon they won't have to hold a tag day for me."

"How come you're still consulting and working on deals?"

"It's what I know."

"That's the way it is with me. Oh Tom, I want to make a discovery that'll knock everyone's eyes out. I know, I know ..." She laughed at the look on his face. "We'll start out small before we go elephant hunting."

"Get real, Dick. You didn't even run drillstem tests on these wells."

Within a week of her opening up shop, Dick Graves had come round flogging a gas production play.

"Besides," she added more kindly as she saw the pained look on his face, "I'm not after production deals."

"The price is right."

"Sorry, Dick, it's not for me." She rolled up the geological map dotted with gas-well symbols, and handed it back to him."

There was something almost forlorn about Dick's smile as he took the map. "Are you okay, Dick? Financially, I mean."

"I am a trifle overextended at the moment. But it's no big deal. All I have to do is unload a few properties and I'll be back onside with the banks."

If the properties weren't of any better quality than the one he had just shown her, Dick had one hell of a selling job ahead of him, thought Debbie to herself as they said goodbye. She tried to soften her brusque reaction to his deal by asking him to keep her in mind if he came up with any good exploratory plays.

Ted Reimer gave his boss a puzzled look. Normally, Wayne absorbed information like a sponge, instantly grasping all its implications. But today he didn't seem to be listening to what Ted was telling him, and it was important. Damn important.

Ted cleared his throat and tried a different tack. "You realize that every time the bank interest rate goes up a point it costs you $7-million a year?"

That got through to Wayne and snapped him out of his daydreaming about Debbie being pregnant.

"What are you trying to tell me, Ted?"

"That the prime rate has gone up two points in the last three weeks. That costs us an additional fourteen mil a year in interest charges. I've done some projections that show if it goes up another point we begin to slip into a loss position. If it keeps on like this, the interest rates on the bank loans will be higher than the junk bonds."

The mention of junk bonds made Wayne's lips compress into a thin line. The goddamn banks had balked at lending the final $100-million to pay for the Fordex shares and he had had to sell junk bonds in the US at the usurious rate of sixteen per cent. It had been the banks getting cold feet at the last minute that prevented him from going all the way and taking over the Fordex parent company itself.

"What's the prime rate at now?"

"Thirteen per cent," Ted told him. "An all-time record high."

"Surely it can't stay up there. The whole economy will grind to a halt."

Ted looked doubtful. "If the Ottawa mandarins decide to keep propping up the Canadian dollar, there's no telling how high it might go."

"Never mind. The sheikhs of Araby will come riding to our rescue once more." As Wayne spoke he experienced a sudden chill of apprehension at the thought of how much depended on the ability of that fractious cartel to continue to work together.

Two weeks later the prime rate had climbed another two points, and since Pinnacle's rate was one point above prime, Ted's prediction that the bank interest rates would equal those on the unsecured junk bonds had come true. Cliff Barton, the regional vice-president of Merchants Canada, the lead bank in the Fordex acquisition, took Wayne to lunch at the Ranchmen's Club. Wayne, accustomed to being fawned upon by bankers, was quick to notice a disturbing change in the bank executive's attitude. Over the consommé, Cliff muttered something about Pursuit not being able to service its debt.

"If that's so," Wayne retorted, "it's only because the banks have gone completely overboard with the rates they're charging. This deal was structured on interest at ten per cent and now it's more than fifty per cent higher. You can't blame me for that."

"No one is blaming anyone. It's just a fact of life." The banker paused while the waiter served them their toasted lobster sandwiches. "We think you should consider selling some of your assets and paying down the loans to a more manageable level."

Wayne stared at him. "Let me get this straight. Are you telling me how to run my business."

"It was just a suggestion, that's all."

"Look, you run your bank and I'll run my oil company. Okay?"

Cliff shrugged and dropped the subject. Wayne was still fuming when he arrived back at the office. Where in the hell did these bankers get off, thinking they had a right to stick their noses into his business.

"Even if I wanted to help you — and I'm by no means sure that I do — there's literally nothing I can do," Bill told Wayne. "Debbie's her own woman. Always has been."

"God, Bill, it's driving me right up the wall. Knowing she's carrying my child and I'm on the outside looking in."

"To my knowledge, she has never put a name to the father."

"It's mine, Bill. I know it is."

"I think you should face up to the possibility that you may never know, Wayne." Bill got up from his desk, walked over to the floor-to-ceiling windows and gazed out at the spring snowfall that was covering the city with a soft white blanket. He'd better call Hilary and tell her he'd be staying in town tonight. "You probably know she had a miscarriage as a result of a riding accident ..."

"But she's not riding now, is she?" Wayne interrupted anxiously.

Bill turned to stare at him. "You really are in bad shape, aren't you? The point I'm trying to make is that when she was pregnant before she had no intention of ever telling the father anything. She fully intended to raise the child entirely on her own. That's what you may find yourself up against."

Going back to his office along the Plus 15 walkway, his bodyguard a few paces to the rear, Wayne admitted to himself that it had been a mistake to have asked Crawford for help. All he had achieved was to put the guy in an impossible position and make himself look like an overwrought fool. That really didn't matter, though. He was desperate enough to try anything. What Bill had told him about Debbie's attitude in her previous pregnancy was a real shocker. She wouldn't get away with it this time, however. She'd find out that he was no anonymous stud.

The situation that confronted him at the office did nothing to improve his mood. It was getting so he hated to see Ted Reimer and his damn cash-flow projections. Pursuit's revenue from its oil and gas production averaged close to $14-million a month, which wasn't exactly shabby. The trouble was that virtually all of that now went to pay interest on debt. "Do you realize what we're really doing, Ted? We're just taking all that oil and gas out of the ground and converting it into interest for the goddamn banks."

"It's a vicious circle, I agree. What's worse is that we have no available cash for our operations. The way things are, we couldn't even afford to connect a new oilfield to a pipeline."

"What do we do about it?"

"The only thing I can suggest is to persuade the banks to let us capitalize some of the interest, say thirty per cent, and add it to the debt. That way we would retain some cash to work with."

"I hate the thought of asking favours from those bastards," Wayne grumbled. "But I'll do it."

It was only the undeniable fact that Pursuit's asset base would start to erode unless some cash were freed up that finally persuaded the banks to agree to Wayne's proposal. Steve Morrison was very helpful in the negotiations, arguing that the interest rates were bound to fall, which would permit Pursuit to once more fully service its debt and still have enough cash to operate with. The banks exacted their pound of flesh, however, by demanding the right to purchase common shares of Pursuit at a price that was well below market. The total amount was not significant, only two per cent of the outstanding shares, but to Wayne it was heresy. Banks were lenders, not owners. However, he had no choice but to acquiesce.

Margo Jones was the first to break the story that all was not well with Wayne Shaw and his company. The lead article in the most recent issue of *Update* posed the question: "Is the high-flying Yankee Raider headed for a crash landing?" The article suggested that Shaw might have bitten off more than he could chew in his highly leveraged purchase of Fordex Canada. "With interest rates skyrocketing," Margo wrote, "Pursuit Enterprises is strapped for cash and Wayne Shaw had to go cap in hand to the bankers. The banks are reported to have ended up holding some common shares of the company. Are we witnessing the start of a new trend, with the banks suddenly cast in the role of owners? Stay tuned."

A week after Margo's scoop, Pursuit's cash flow problems became public knowledge when the company announced it was letting one hundred employees go. Layoffs were virtually unknown in the oil patch and the news hit the street like a thunderclap. The layoffs came because of the insistence of the banks that operating costs had to be reduced. Wayne called Lloyd Chernak, who rejoiced in the title "director of human resources," into his office and bluntly told him he had to lose one hundred employees over the next six weeks.

The assignment staggered Lloyd. He had long been accustomed to benignly announcing pay raises, increases in pension plan benefits, improved company dental plan coverage, and similar goodies. Privately, Wayne thought Lloyd was a bit of a wimp, but he had been inherited from Fordex and there had been no real reason to replace him.

"One other thing," Wayne said as the shaken personnel officer was leaving. "Make sure that each one of them is out the door within one hour of getting the news and that you're there when they clean out their desks. We don't want them making off with some of our best plays when they go."

Lloyd gulped and returned to his office to try and organize his hateful task. He had encouraged the employees to regard him as their friend and intermediary, and now he had to tell one hundred of them that they were terminated.

While Wayne wrestled with his intractable corporate problems, he was tormented and frustrated by his inability to make any progress with Debbie.

It wasn't that he couldn't see her; she was highly visible — attending parties and receptions, glowing with good health. She was active on the business scene as well — the Pinnacle name was once again showing up on the drilling reports. But she kept Wayne at arm's-length, moving away after the briefest of greetings and refusing to return his phone calls.

He was distraught enough at one point to consult a lawyer who specialized in family law. She told him that, yes, the law was beginning to recognize that a putative father had some rights, but counselled him to do nothing until the child was born. Then, with blood tests and other corroborative evidence, he might be able to establish his paternity. "But it could turn out to be pretty messy," she warned, "particularly for a high-profile person like yourself."

Debbie gave birth to a full-term baby boy at the Foothills hospital. She named him William, after her father, and decreed that he would be called Billy. When she left the hospital, she and the baby went directly to her spacious new condominium where an English nanny awaited them. The condo was only a few blocks from Debbie's office so she could commute back and forth at feeding times. She was determined to breast-feed the baby and she was also determined to go back to work as soon as possible.

18

Standing on the monkey board ninety feet up in the derrick, Frank watched Sammy Bornecki, who was on the breakout tongs, walk the last string of heavy drill collars across the rig floor. When the top end of the collars came within reach, Frank looped a rope around it and guided the string into the racks. The trip out of the hole was finished. So was his twelve-hour tour of duty. The next crew would attach a new bit and start back down the hole with the 10,000 feet of drill pipe. Frank unsnapped his safety harness, clambered swiftly down the ladder and headed for the change house. He was stripping off his coveralls, caked and stiff with drilling mud, when Sammy stumbled in and collapsed onto a bench. "Eight hours trippin' out of the hole! My fuckin' arms are going to drop off," he groaned.

"Hey, you looked pretty good on those tongs, old buddy," Frank encouraged the exhausted roughneck.

Sammy brightened. "You think so, Frank? I gotta admit it seems to get a little easier each time."

Pulling his T-shirt over his head, Frank grinned at Sammy, who had overcome his weariness enough to start undoing the buttons of his work clothes. The pudgy Sammy was an unlikely-looking specimen to find on a drilling rig. He fancied himself to be the poor man's Ralph Nader of the drilling industry and invariably turned up at every inquiry into drilling accidents and fatalities. His comments were exaggerated and wildly inaccurate, but that didn't stop the press from quoting him extensively. At one official inquiry his testimony so exasperated the lawyer for the drilling company that he asked him why he didn't go out into the field and get some hands-on experience. Stroking his beard as though it were a pet cat, Sammy smiled humbly and asked, "Who would hire me?"

During the coffee break, the manager of Spartacus Drilling came over to him and said, "You want a job, Sammy? I'll give you one." As he later explained to his peers, "If the little son of a bitch is going to bad-mouth us, he should at least know what in hell he's talking about."

Feeling as if he had blundered into a trap, Sammy had no choice but to accept the challenge. He insisted on a condition that he wouldn't be muzzled, half-hoping that this would get him off the hook. The drilling manager had merely shrugged and said, "You can shoot your mouth off all you like. But we're going to make a Christian out of you, boy."

Thus it was that Sammy Bornecki, a minor thorn in the side of the drilling industry, came to be on Spartacus No. 4 in the middle of a vast muskeg area in northern
British Columbia. Sammy was determined to stick it out, but he wouldn't have lasted
the first week on the drill floor if he hadn't been on the same tour as Frank, who took
pity on him and carried out the toughest roughnecking chores himself.

Two days later, the well having been drilled to total depth and having turned out
to be a million dollar dry hole, they came out of the hole laying down — placing
the drill pipe in horizontal rows on a platform instead of stacking it vertically in
the derrick. Frank worked on the floor, manning the tongs that unscrewed the
individual joints of pipe. Sammy walked each thirty-foot joint suspended from the
travelling block over to the ramp leading down to the catwalk and pipe rack. The
next tour would tear out the rig, breaking it down into its component parts, which
could be transported on low-boy trailers. This time, however, the rig would be
stacked on the gravel-drilling pad until the quaking muskeg froze hard next winter.

As soon as each crew finished its last tour, they hurriedly packed and left the camp
— a group of modular, Atco-type buildings mounted on skids. The drivers of the
four-wheeled vehicles that would take them out wanted to get on the road before
the cement truck that had brought in the cement to plug the well set out on its return
journey. The truck, towed by a huge caterpillar tractor over the bad spots, would take
bloody forever to navigate the rutted quagmire that constituted the lease road.
Wedged between Sammy and the driller in the back seat of the pickup, Frank had
nothing to do but endure the bouncing and jostling as the vehicle, its four wheels
equipped with chains, laboured in low gear along the almost impassable road. As
usual, the taciturn driller had little to say, and Sammy looked as if he was going to be
carsick, so Frank was free to let his thoughts wander.

What a knockout Fiona had been at Henry's wedding! She sure had that best man
drooling. The guy lived in Toronto so he had probably travelled down to Smith to see
her on the weekends. Frank wondered if she had returned to Calgary for the
summer. If she had, he was almost certain to run into her. He had three weeks off
before joining another Spartacus rig that was contracted to drill a Nisku test in the
Drayton Valley area. Sammy was also going to work on the same rig. The toolpush
must have had a bird when he found out the notorious Sammy Bornecki was to be
a roughneck on his crew. He wouldn't have been able to do a damn thing about
it though; turning Sammy into an honest-to-God driller had become one of the
manager's pet projects.

Frank didn't know whether he felt more disappointed or relieved when he heard
Fiona was spending the summer at Smith to take some additional courses. She was
an A student and used to talk about going on to take a master's degree. On his
second day home, Frank strolled along the Mall on his way to meet Henry Purvis for
lunch, feeling almost intimidated by the noonday crush of people after his long
sojourn in the northern bush. "Hi, Frank," a soft voice called out as he was passing

the colonnaded facade of The Bay. Turning his head, he saw a petite and curvaceous brunette waving at him. He remembered seeing her at some of Charlton's parties but he couldn't for the life of him recall her name. She solved the problem for him. "I'm Nan Chisholm. We met last summer." She was obviously pleased to see him, and he was suddenly just as pleased to see her. She was a toothsome little package and, having once belonged to Charlton's set, would be highly beddable.

"I'd really like to get together," Frank said. She nodded enthusiastic agreement and gave him her number.

Promising to call her after she finished work, he went off to keep his luncheon appointment with a pleasant tingling of excitement in his veins.

"You've changed a lot since last year." Nan trailed the back of a painted fingernail along the faint line of hair that extended from his groin to his navel.

"For the better I hope."

"Definitely. I used to wonder about you last summer. I thought you were terribly attractive but I was afraid you were going to self-destruct. But you really have your act together now."

"What's happened to Mike's old crowd?"

"Pretty much scattered to the four winds." Her fingers continued to explore. "Mike dying like that kinda sobered everyone up. Do you like this?" she murmured as her lips followed the path traced by her fingers.

Nan was the perfect playmate to while away the summer with. She worked as a secretary with an oil company and was free to be with Frank every night.

He wondered about this but figured that he had probably caught her between boyfriends. She was easy, undemanding company and a good, no strings, lay. She shared an apartment with another girl who seemed to spend most of her nights at her boyfriend's place so the logistics of the affair worked out perfectly.

Propped up with pillows against the headboard, Frank took a sip from his can of beer and said, "I promised Dad I'd go with him on a business trip to Toronto the day after tomorrow. I'll only be gone three or four days and I'll call you as soon as I get back."

"I don't want you to."

"What?" Frank sat up and stared down at her face, indistinct in the shadow of the partly open bedroom door.

"It's over, Frank. It's been great fun and you're a very attractive man. But I know I can't have you, so I'm booking off. In fact, I think I'll get married."

"Do you have anyone particular in mind?"

"A fellow who's been after me to marry him for months. He's a geologist with Norpet. A nice guy. Not Frank Crawford, but a nice guy."

"And where have you parked this nice guy for the past week?"

"He's been out in the field, sitting a well. Don't look at me like that. I saw a chance to have a piece of you, and I grabbed it. No harm done." Her nipples brushed against the hairs of his chest as she leaned over to kiss him. "Make love to me. For the road."

"How are things with Venture, Dad?"

"I'm putting it into a survival mode as fast as I can. We still owe the banks somewhat more than I feel comfortable with, but by cutting back we've managed to maintain enough discretionary cash flow to keep operating."

Frank let his gaze travel innocently around the luxurious interior of the Falcon Tri-Jet. "Yeah, I can see where you've really been cutting back."

Bill laughed. "This may also have to go at some point in time. But right now, while I'm trying to extricate Venture from the majority of its overseas operations, the jet more than earns its keep."

"It's hard for a simple roughneck like me to understand how so many oil companies can be in deep trouble when the price of oil keeps going up and up. From what you read in the papers companies like Pursuit and Globe are basket cases, but the price of oil is ...?"

"Thirty-six dollars US a barrel, as of this morning." Bill supplied the answer. "But that balloon's got to burst, sooner or later." He opened the panelled bar. "Would you like something to drink?"

"Just a Diet Coke, thanks. I've had more than my share of beer since I've been back in civilization."

Bill settled back in his seat with a vodka tonic. "The reason why companies like Pursuit and Globe are in trouble is very simple. Interest. You remember what interest rates did to our cattle operation?" Frank shuddered, and his father continued. "That was at a time when interest rates were at ten per cent. Now they're nearly double that. A company like Globe with a debt load of $5 billion would have to come up with one billion dollars of interest a year. Pursuit's in precisely the same box, except on a smaller scale. They're still around only because the banks have decided to keep them on life-support systems. It must be sheer hell for a guy with Shaw's temperament."

"I bet he wishes he'd never made a move against Debbie's company. I guess the baby is his, huh?"

"Debbie's attitude is that the baby is hers. Period." Bill's lips twitched. "Knowing your sister, however, I very much doubt that we're dealing with a case of immaculate conception!"

He took a thoughtful sip of his drink. "Let's talk about Frank for a bit. Life on the drilling rigs certainly seems to agree with you. And you must be damn good at it to have made derrickman in less than a year."

"That was a fluke really. The regular derrickman lost most of his left hand to the tongs and head office didn't have a replacement right on tap, so the toolpush decided to go with me." Frank paused. "Working in the field has turned out to be the best thing in the world for me, but I don't plan on spending the rest of my life at it."

"Have you given any thought to starting up your own drilling company? I might be of some help with the financing."

"That's not for me, either. Now that politics is out of the question, I'll have to find something else I really want to do. Maybe I'll get back into exotic cattle if the market ever turns around."

"Politics is what really turns you on though, isn't it?" asked Bill with a faint air of incredulity that any sensible person would willingly opt for that existence.

"I guess that's right," admitted Frank. "But I sure blew it!"

"I wouldn't be so sure about that. Anyway, you'll be interested in meeting Senator Garvey. We're having lunch with him tomorrow." Garvey, a retired Toronto stock-broker who had recently been appointed to the Senate, had been for years the chief fundraiser and backroom strategist for the national Conservative Party.

"Jesus, Dad. I'm not sure I want to face him. He's got to think I'm the world's prize idiot."

"He seems very interested in meeting you," observed Bill mildly.

"A generation ago, and I agree that you could never recover from a pratfall like that." The florid-faced Garvey signalled the waiter to pour another glass of Gevrey-Chambertin. "But today's voter is a great deal more tolerant of human foibles."

"The opposition candidates would have a field day with my past." Frank grimaced. "You wouldn't believe the crap I've had to put up with!"

"You haven't always put up with it," Bill reminded him dryly. "I seem to recall a few wars being fought over the subject." Bill was well-pleased with the way the meeting was going.

"You might get some mud thrown at you," the political rainmaker conceded. "But any politician knows that mud slinging can be a two-edged sword. Voters have been known to turn on the person who's throwing it. Anyway," he added as he reluctantly passed up the dessert tray, "don't be in too much of a hurry to write yourself off."

"I never knew you had been under so much pressure to be a federal candidate for the Conservatives," Frank said as he and his father took a taxi back to the hotel. "You could tell that Garvey is still kinda upset with you."

"People like the senator just can't understand why anyone wouldn't jump at the chance to run for office. To them, politics is the most exciting game there is." Bill chuckled. "He used to stare at me like I was an alien from some other planet when I told him I felt the same way about finding oil. Anyway, it's all in the past. I expect he'll come knocking on your door one of these days."

"There won't be anybody home when he does. I'd be laughed right off the platform."

"Garvey doesn't seem to think so. And he's the pro."

At ten o'clock that night Frank gazed in astonishment out the open rear window as the taxi pulled up in front of a seedy-looking bar. "We're going in there?"

"Don't judge a book by its cover," Bill murmured as he paid the fare. "There's an act in here that I want you to catch."

"You sure are full of surprises." Frank shook his head, as he followed his father into the recessed doorway under the neon sign that spelled out Nicki's Bar. Neon lights advertising similar establishments glowed and blinked on both sides of the block. The interior of the bar was so dimly lit that the hostess, clad in a black satin bunny costume and fishnet stockings, used a penlight to guide them to a table.

Bill was uncharacteristically fussy about the location of their table. He rejected the first one and handed a ten-spot to the astonished waitress — the patrons of Nicki's Bar not being given to lavish tipping — to give them one over by the far wall.

After the waiter brought them their drinks — beer for Frank and Scotch with soda on the side for Bill — Frank looked around and asked, "Where's this famous act of yours? I don't even see a stage."

Ignoring the soda, Bill downed the whisky straight and said, "I hope to God I'm doing the right thing, Frank. Turn around slowly and look over at the far end of the bar."

Mystified, Frank did as he was told. Light from behind the array of bottles provided a certain amount of illumination. About half the bar stools were occupied, some with solitary men staring morosely into their drinks and others with customers who were being chatted up by flashily dressed hookers.

"The two stools at the end," Bill whispered. A frazzled-looking blonde, her heavily made-up face garish even in the soft lighting, was propositioning a male customer, her hand sliding up his thick, trousered thigh. Frank glanced over at his father with a puzzled frown.

"Take a closer look," Bill whispered. "You can go over by the rail and she won't see you."

It couldn't be. Frank gripped the brass rail to steady himself. That raddled face, those mascaraed, lifeless eyes — that couldn't be Linda. But it was. What in God's name had she done to herself? The customer she had been working on finished his drink, removed her hand from his leg and left. Her shoulders slumped, then she picked up her glass, pasted a grotesquely false smile on her face and moved along the bar to where another man was sitting alone.

Tasting the bile in the back of his throat, Frank went back to the table and whispered tersely, "Let's get out of here!" Outside the bar, Frank, his face greenish in the neon light, drew in a long shuddering breath. "What's happened to her?"

"She's heavily into the drug scene. To my knowledge she's been hospitalized twice in the last six months. The escort agency dropped her as soon as she started to lose her looks." Bill hailed one of the many cabs that cruised the strip, ready to transport hookers and their johns to nearby hotels where rooms were rented by the hour.

"You've been keeping track of her." Frank rested his head against the seat as if exhausted.

"I first learned she was on the skids by accident. Then I hired a private detective agency to give me periodic reports. I knew how deeply you loved her, Frank, and I just couldn't stand by and watch you go through life chained to a dream that could never be."

In the hotel lobby Bill gazed anxiously at his son. "Are you okay, Frank? Would you like to go in the bar and have a drink?"

Frank shook his head. "I think I'd better be alone now."

"I understand. Why don't we meet for breakfast in my suite at seven-thirty?"

Bill tipped the room-service waiter and poured himself a cup of coffee. Frank was five minutes late. Maybe he was wrong to have left him on his own last night; he was obviously deeply traumatized. But what else could he have done? Frank was a grown man. Bill took another nervous glance at his watch. Seven-forty. Had Frank done something desperate? My God, had he gone back to that bar? The buzzer sounded, making Bill slosh coffee into the saucer. Flinging open the door, he exhaled a sigh of relief when he saw Frank standing there.

"Sorry I'm late, Dad. I didn't sleep too well last night."

"I can understand that." Bill's hands were still shaking so he said, "Help yourself to coffee. How do you feel, son?"

"Like I've just had major surgery. Kind of weak and hollow inside. But also like I've been cured of something that was eating away at me."

"I'm glad to hear that, Frank. Very, very glad."

"You must have felt you were taking a hell of a chance." Frank's smile was affectionate. "But then you've been a risk-taker all your life."

"If it has helped set you free, Frank, it's the best return on risk I've ever had. Now," Bill said briskly, "how about some bacon and eggs?"

As the Falcon bucked a hundred-knot headwind on its way west, Frank asked, "Isn't there some way you can help her, Dad?"

"I can certainly try, and I will. But people in her situation very often don't want to be helped."

19

Wayne scowled at the papers the lawyer acting for the banks placed in front of him. He glanced down the long conference table at Caroline Underwood who gave an almost imperceptible shrug as if to say there was nothing that could be done. Wayne sighed and scrawled his name on the pages flagged with red clips. The banks thought they were being magnanimous as hell, converting a portion of Pursuit's debt into equity in order to provide some relief from the crippling interest charges. But they had arbitrarily fixed a value on the shares that Wayne felt to be outrageously low. Worse, his ownership position was seriously diluted. Pretty soon he'd be working for the damn banks.

"We've done our part, Wayne," said Cliff Barton, the vice-president of Merchants Canada, in his raspy voice. "Now it's up to you to do your part by cutting operating costs to the bone."

"We've already done that," Wayne replied curtly. Cliff had been the smarmiest of all the bankers when it came to soliciting loans. And now the son of a bitch was lecturing him like a schoolteacher.

"We think ..." Cliff paused to collect nods of approval from the other banking representatives, "that there is much that could still be done. Especially since you are now running what is essentially a caretaker operation."

"We could start with the jet," the representative from the Federal National chimed in.

Wayne felt a rush of furious anger. It was his airplane they were talking about, and, by God, they weren't going to take it away from him. "We've already disposed of the Gulfstream III that came with the Fordex deal," he protested.

"There's still the Lear," the Federal National man pointed out.

"The Lear is absolutely essential. I have to travel constantly: meeting with creditors, underwriters, stock analysts, you name it. There are a lot of brush fires out there, gentlemen, and somebody has to put them out."

"Well," Cliff reluctantly retreated from the touchy issue of the jet, "we want to see a ten per cent reduction in staff within the next month." When Wayne started to protest, he banged the table with the flat of his hand. "We want blood on the floor, mister!"

"Sometimes I feel like packing it in," Wayne told Caroline as they trudged back to their office building. The bodyguards were a thing of the past; the security experts had been one of the first items to be eliminated. "No criminal in his right mind would bother kidnapping me now," Wayne had joked at the time.

"I guess it's a matter of hanging in there until things turn around," Caroline replied. "The interest rates do seem to have peaked. And if it's any comfort, we're not alone. Practically every company in town is cutting back and letting people go."

"Things will have to improve one hell of a lot before we're out of the glue," Wayne muttered. As the elevator swiftly rose to the executive floor, he sighed, "I better have Chernak in and tell him to sharpen his axe."

"The layoffs are taking a terrible toll on the poor guy," said Caroline as the elevator doors slid open. "He takes it all so personally."

"Have you heard about Syl Dubek?" Lloyd's voice was tremulous as he seated himself in front of Wayne's desk. Dark-brown circles under his eyes gave him the look of a frightened racoon.

"Who's Syl Dubek?"

"One of the geologists we let go. He's charged with wife-beating." Lloyd shook his head dolefully. "I still can't believe it. He was with Fordex for ten years and was about as well-adjusted a person as you could want to meet. I guess he just couldn't take the stigma of being unemployed."

"I know there's a lot of trauma out there, and I realize you're in the front lines. But you've got to stop letting it get to you, Lloyd. You look like a candidate for the intensive-care ward."

"Do you know what the employees call me? Doctor Death. When they see me coming they stop talking and run away. It's like I have the plague."

"Look, if you don't feel up to it, just say so."

"No, no, that's not what I meant," Lloyd backtracked hastily, terrified at the prospect of losing his own job. "I realize somebody's got to do it."

"We have to make another cut. Ten per cent this time," Wayne told the director of human resources, whose high-sounding title had become a hollow mockery. "Look," Wayne added defensively, "we're not the only company cutting back on staff. Everybody's doing it."

"That only makes it worse. There's no place for these people to go." Lloyd shifted in his chair as if trying to rid himself of an intolerable burden. He cleared his throat and went on, "I've been giving a lot of thought to our termination procedure, Wayne. That pack-your-stuff-and-out-you-go works okay when you're firing an individual employee, but it's not the answer when you're laying off hordes of people through no fault of their own. I've been reading about a new kind of specialist. They call themselves career-transition consultants. They take over after the employee has been terminated and help him adjust and find other employment."

Wayne gave a mirthless snort of laughter. "Now that's bound to be a growth industry in this city. Do you know any of these outfits?"

696 / JOHN BALLEM

Lloyd brightened slightly. "Of course. There are at least three firms that I could recommend."

Wayne sighed. "Get on it then. The banks will squawk at the added expense, but I can square it. You better have Caroline eyeball whatever arrangement you make with the consultants. And Lloyd," Wayne added as Chernak stood up to leave, "I want the cut made by the end of the month."

The new Graves Building was a modern six-storey office building several blocks south of the downtown core. It couldn't begin to compare with Pursuit Tower though, whose rapidly rising steel skeleton already dominated Calgary's crowded skyline. Nonetheless, it deserved a gala opening, at least in the opinion of the owner. The building was to have been a symbol of Dick Graves's success, confirming that he had finally made his mark in the oil patch. The fact that the building had more than a million dollars worth of builders' liens registered against it, and was mortgaged to the Westfirst bank for an amount that was considerably higher than its current market value, did tend to dim the lustre somewhat. However, Dick was determined to put on a show regardless.

Watching him circulate among the guests, exuding his preppy charm, Debbie marvelled at his sang-froid. Just last week he had paid her a second visit with a shopping list of potentially productive properties he wanted to sell. Tom Burdon had rejected them all out of hand.

"Put those wells on stream and maybe you'd have enough gas to heat a chicken coop," he snorted.

Debbie saw a beaming Steve Morrison bearing down on her, a glass of champagne in either hand. They had developed a very good working rapport. She did all her financing through Westfirst and the account was greatly prized by the bank since Pinnacle was one of the few oil companies that still boasted a healthy balance sheet. She accepted the glass of champagne but didn't raise it to her lips.

"Have you added any more argillite pieces to your collection?" she asked by way of making conversation.

Steve's lips turned down at the corners. "In this economy the bank is more likely to sell the collection than add to it. How about you?"

"Nothing recently. But I've bought a display cabinet for my pieces. Billy will be starting to crawl in another few months. Nice party, isn't it?"

"If your taste runs to death watches, yes." Steve drained his glass and Debbie handed him hers. "I'm still nursing," she explained.

"Ah, yes, quite so," muttered the flustered banker. "Are you and Dick still pretty thick?"

"He's called on me at the office a couple of times flogging some properties, but apart from that I haven't seen him in ages."

"The guy's got chutzpah, I'll give him that. Hosting a reception like this when he could be in receivership tomorrow."

"That would just about kill Dick. He's got so much pride. Won't the drop in interest rates help?"

"His problem is far worse than simply defaulting on interest payments. When we got around to taking a hard look at the assets securing his loans, we got one hell of a shock, I can tell you. His loans are so far underwater, you'd need a submarine to find them."

Although he was grateful for Steve's support in his rancorous dealings with the banking consortium, Wayne was not particularly eager to make small talk with him when Pursuit owed Westfirst $100-million in non-performing loans. He waited until Steve and Debbie had finished their conversation and drifted apart before approaching her. "How's Billy?" he asked.

"Just fine, thank you." She made to move away but he detained her with a hand on her arm. "Debbie, if it's revenge you're after, you've succeeded beyond your wildest dreams. But it's gone far enough. I'm pleading with you to let me see my son."

"Your son? Whatever gave you that idea?" Debbie was disdainful, but inwardly she felt a sudden flutter of alarm. Wayne looked like a desperate man.

"I have rights too, you know," he muttered.

Debbie turned on him like a she-bear protecting her cub. "Don't give me that, Wayne. You have no rights. And you stay away from us, or you'll find yourself in big trouble."

Debbie's baby proved to be an almost irresistible attraction for Hilary, who began to drive into town with Bill once or twice a week to spend the morning shopping, followed by lunch with friends, and then dropping in at Debbie's place to see the baby and wait for Bill. Debbie was always there at four o'clock since that was one of the baby's feeding times.

After having breast-fed him faithfully for the first four months, she was weaning him to the bottle to free herself from the tyranny of the every-three-hours feeding schedule.

"That grandson of yours is a handsome little devil," Hilary said as the Mercedes purred south on Macleod Trail. "I can't spot any family resemblance yet, except that he's got the Crawford eyes. Does that work out genetically, what with Wayne's being dark brown?"

"Wayne's eyes obviously made quite an impression on you."

She gave him a playful punch in the ribs. "Jealous, darling? I'd love it if you were. The truth is that Debbie used to go on about them in our girlish get-togethers."

"Give me a moment to think that one through. Yes, it does fit genetically. I read a few textbooks on genetics when I was playing around with cattle breeding and I remember that brown eyes are dominant and can mask a recessive blue gene. So, Wayne could be carrying a recessive blue gene which could combine with the same gene in Debbie to produce a blue-eyed offspring."

"I wonder what colour you and I would produce."

"Blue, or grey. Never brown. That is a purely academic discussion we are having, I presume?"

"I would love to have your child, Bill. And Jason would adore having a baby brother or sister. He absolutely dotes on young Billy."

"Too risky. Sperm can turn out to be highly unreliable when men get to be my age."

"There's a test they do to find out whether the baby's normal or not. Amn ... something."

"Amniocentesis," Bill supplied the word.

"That's a gotcha!" exclaimed Hilary gleefully. "If you know the name, you've been looking into it." She leaned back against the headrest with a contented little smile and let the music from Bill's "bridge mix" tape wash over her. Bored with listening to the same performer for an entire tape, he made up his own with a variety of artists on each one.

"Have you been able to do anything for Linda Shepherd?" Hilary asked as he changed tapes.

"I'm trying, but with total lack of success so far."

"Maybe she's too proud to accept help from you."

"She doesn't know it's me. I got hold of a guy who used to be a steady customer of hers and persuaded him to look her up and make out like he was concerned about her and was anxious to help. Pay for her to stay in a detoxification clinic and anything else that would break her drug habit. So far she's given him nothing but abuse."

"Does she still call herself Flair?"

"Yes. In fact she tries to capitalize on it to impress the johns. It's pathetic in a way. She can't possibly be making enough money to support her habit. She's into cocaine and heroin speedballs and they come expensive."

"I have this private nightmare that she'll go to one of those clinics and get cured and come out looking gorgeous and Frank will fall madly in love with her all over again."

"You can stop worrying about that." Bill slowed down for the exit to the secondary highway. "I have the feeling Frank saw her naked soul that night in the bar and he'll never be able to get that image of her out of his mind. I know I'll never forget it."

"Bernice Dawson was saying the other day that Fiona is still carrying a torch for Frank."

"I'm sorry to hear that. Our boy Frank didn't exactly cover himself with glory that summer. Is she still going to college in the States?"

"Yes. She's at Princeton this year, taking a master's in something. Don't ask me what."

"You always seem remarkably well-informed about that girl."

"Some of my friends are close to the Edwards so I hear things. And I've always liked her, right from the start. Much as I love Frank, I can't help feeling he behaved badly toward her. I've told him so, too."

"It's too bad those two met when they did. If Frank had been himself, I have an idea things would have turned out differently. By the way, that well he's on must be pretty close to total depth by now."

"It's in a sour-gas area, isn't it? Not too far from that Lodgepole well that blew out a few years ago."

Bill chuckled. "I keep forgetting that you were a big wheel in the Energy Department until you say something that reminds me. Ever miss that world, darling?"

"I'm astonished at how little I actually do. And if we carry through with that little project we were discussing a few minutes ago, I wouldn't give it another thought. But you haven't answered my question about the well."

"The operator doesn't expect to encounter sour gas. It's a Nisku pinnacle reef test and there's no H_2s in the Nisku, just sweet crude oil. These fringe reefs contain natural gas with a high concentration of H_2s. That's what caused all the trouble in the Lodgepole well. But even if they do encounter the Meekwap rather than the Nisku, it's no big deal. There have been hundreds of sour-gas wells drilled in this province without any problem."

He drove the Mercedes into the four-car garage and switched off the ignition. Gathering her parcels together, Hilary said, "One of the parts I like best about living out here in the country is driving home with you. It gives us a chance to really talk."

20

The oil company representative bent over the core lying on the rig floor. It was the second core they had pulled; it was vuggy, with large holes like a piece of Swiss cheese, and gave off the rotten egg smell of H_2s. Like the first core, it had jammed in the barrel and had broken off short of the specified fifty-foot length.

"We'd have a better chance of pulling a complete core if we add a pup joint to the barrel," the driller suggested and the company rep nodded agreement. While the workers on the floor coupled a ten-foot extension to the core barrel, Frank scrambled up the ladder to the monkey board and buckled on his safety harness. It was his job to latch the drill pipe elevators on to each ninety-foot section of pipe, which was then swung into position over the rotary table and connected to a section of pipe already in the hole. Since the well was some 9,000 feet deep, it was ten o'clock at night before they finished the trip and Frank could descend to the brightly lit drill floor. The driller engaged the drawworks and the hollow, diamond-studded bit began to bite into the formation. Instead of chewing up the rock, the special bit was designed to cut out a circular core that would be retained in the barrel and eventually brought to the surface.

Underneath the drill floor Sammy Bornecki was hosing down the blowout preventer, a bulbous, steel assembly of hydraulic and mechanical rams that controlled the flow of fluids from the hole and could seal them off in the event of an emergency. He cursed as a gout of mud splashed out of the flow nipple and spilled down over the blowout preventer. He hosed that mess off but then another larger flow of mud erupted from the nipple and over the BOP. Sammy turned off the steam hose and stomped up the metal stairs to the drill floor.

"How the fuck do you expect me to keep the goddamn BOP clean when mud keeps spilling out of the nipple," he demanded of the driller.

The driller stiffened, then turned to tell Frank to check the level in the mud tanks but Frank was already running along the catwalk.

"We've got a mud gain," he reported back.

"Any sign of gas?" asked the driller.

"Not yet."

"Shit, we got a kick." If the toolpush had been on the lease, he would have taken over, but he was off duty and logging some sacktime at the motel where the crew was billeted in the little town of Lundell, two miles away. The driller told Sammy to call the motel and alert the toolpush, then he went about the business of controlling the kick before it turned into a full-fledged blowout.

He closed the annulus preventer to seal off the space between the wall of the hole and the drill pipe, then took a pressure reading. The gauge indicated 400 psi, which meant he was dealing with a pretty fair-sized kick. No sweat. He'd circulate it out through the BOP. But first he ordered barites to be added to the drilling mud to increase its weight to fifteen pounds per gallon. It was the hydrostatic pressure created by the column of drilling mud that counterbalanced the formation pressure. They had been using the mud weight specified in the drilling program, which had been calculated to create a hydrostatic pressure marginally higher than the pressure in the formation. Selecting the appropriate mud weight was always a delicate balancing act — too light a mixture would allow fluids, especially gas, to flow from the formation, while mud that was too heavy and viscous slowed down the drilling. The driller reasoned that the trips in and out of the hole with the core assembly must have had a swabbing effect that reduced the density of the mud column enough to allow the gas to start to flow.

The gas bubble expanded with frightening rapidity as it climbed up the wellbore, displacing the denser mud as it rose. The drop in pressure allowed more gas to flow from the formation and, although the driller had no way of knowing it, he now had a second kick on his hands. The gas hadn't reached the surface yet; there were no telltale bubbles in the mud tanks, but there was a faint smell of H_2S seeping up around the drill floor. As little as a four per cent concentration of H_2S paralyzes the brain and kills in seconds. The driller told Frank to run over to the toolpush's shack, located some 150 feet from the rig, and fetch the breathing equipment. With the annulus preventer still closed, the driller engaged the pump and circulated the weighted-up mud through the Kelly hose down through the Kelly and the swivel and into the drill pipe. The mud returning up the annulus from the bottom of the hole was diverted by the BOP through a de-gasser to cleanse it of the poisonous gas before it flowed over the shale shaker and into the mud tanks.

The first bubble of gas, now enormously expanded, arrived at the surface with a sudden rush that sent a surge of mud and gas through the de-gasser, jamming the float down and wedging it into its seat. With the de-gasser out of action, the combined stream of mud and poisonous gas surged into the mud tanks. On the drill floor, the crew heard the ominous hiss of escaping gas and caught a whiff of H_2S. Even a second's delay could spell death.

Frank, air bottles and mask in place, and lugging as many air-paks as he could carry, stepped out of the toolpush's shack just as the second kick hit. He saw the panic-stricken crew fleeing the rig and then he saw the Kelly hose split wide open, spewing mud, condensate, and poisonous gas into the atmosphere. She was going up! With all the back pressure escaping through the tear in the Kelly hose, the gas would race up the hole with an irresistible force and hurl the entire 9,000 feet of drill pipe and drill collars into orbit. The lethal H_2s, being heavier than air, would cling close to the ground as a cloud of the gas drifted over the sleeping countryside, killing everything in its path.

While these chilling thoughts raced through his mind, Frank dropped his load of air-paks and was running toward the rig. Bursting into the doghouse, he grabbed the Kelly-cock wrench from its special place on the wall and dashed out to the drill floor. The roar of escaping gas was appalling, and everything was coated with layers of drilling mud. Any second now something would tear loose under the terrible pressure, a spark would be struck as metal hit metal and the gas would ignite, turning the rig into a raging inferno. Frank, drenched with drilling mud and pummelled with rock cuttings and other debris from the well, fought his way across the slippery floor. Thank God there was no gas escaping around the drill pipe or rotary table; the rip in the hose was enough to bleed it off. Until, of course, the whole damn formation came roaring up the hole at them, taking everything with it.

He climbed up the derrick ladder until he was level with the Kelly cock, a ball-type valve mounted directly on top of the Kelly joint. The ruptured Kelly hose was jumping and swaying like an aroused python from the force of the fluid gushing out of it. Hanging onto the ladder, he leaned out over the floor, trying to reach the swaying valve. If he could manage to insert the wrench in the aperture on the side of the valve and close it, the stream of deadly gas would be shut off. The trouble was that the valve was leaping about like a live thing and he couldn't risk missing the hole and letting the wrench strike the side of the valve. Any resulting spark would incinerate him instantaneously. At least he would never know what hit him. He made a pass at the valve and missed, the wrench clanging against its metal casing. Frank cringed behind his face-mask and waited for the explosion that would snuff out his life, but his luck held and there was no spark. Now the valve was swinging back toward him. Timing his move, he made a desperate stab at it. The wrench slid and scraped around the edge of the opening, then dropped into the slot. One twist and the ear-splitting roar was replaced by a sudden, eerie silence.

Dreading what he might find, Frank looked down at the rotary table. His mask momentarily clouded up as he exhaled a sigh of relief when he saw no sign of escaping mud or gas. The drill pipe had held, and with the Kelly cock closed and the annulus sealed shut, the situation was under control.

He clambered down the ladder and picked his way across the mud-coated floor to the edge of the platform. His co-workers, all wearing air-paks and standing at a safe distance from the rig, stared up at him. In a gesture that came straight out of his days as a hockey star, Frank raised the wrench and waved it triumphantly over his head.

If it hadn't been for Sammy Bornecki, the near-disaster would have gone unnoticed by the general public. To Sammy it was a complete vindication of what he had been saying all along about the appalling risk to the public from sour-gas wells. The media ate it up. The story had everything — a potential disaster of frightening proportions, and a hero who was not only a member of the prominent Crawford family but also carried with him a fascinating aura of scandal and disgrace.

"Canadian Bhopal A Near Thing!" screamed one headline; the accompanying story asserting that if the poisonous cloud had been allowed to escape it would have claimed as many victims as the Indian catastrophe where 20,000 died when a chemical plant developed a deadly leak.

The Conservation Board immediately convened a public inquiry, which bore out every detail of Sammy's account and was widely reported on across the nation. The Board found that the oil company operator had shown bad judgment in coring into a potentially productive zone with only marginally adequate mud density, and recommended that breathing equipment be kept on the drill floor whenever there was a possibility of encountering a formation containing sour gas. The Board's report was unstinting in its praise of Frank's conduct and found that if it had not been for his resolute action a blowout would have been inevitable.

Frank downplayed any suggestion of heroism on his part, saying repeatedly that he just happened to be the person wearing a breathing apparatus at the critical moment. This also very neatly took the other crew members off the hook, although no sane person would have faulted them for not going back to a rig that was on the verge of blowing up. The Board expressly exonerated them from any blame in this regard.

Despite his modest disclaimers, Frank was a hero to the people of Lundell, who knew only too well what a close call they had had. The mayor and town council insisted on hosting a dinner in Frank's honour in the high school auditorium. They were so sincere that it was impossible to turn them down. The local inhabitants who filled the hall were under no illusions about the danger they lived with every time a well was spudded, but they, knowing how vital the industry was to the province, accepted the risk with a stoicism that was astonishing. "It goes with the territory," they told each other as they took their places at the long trestle tables. When Sammy got up to harangue them and parade the horrors about how easy it was to lose control of a dangerous well, they gave him a good hand, but it was more because he was a member of the crew than for his message.

Frank made a gracious little speech, praising the local residents for their responsible attitude toward drilling in their area, while at the same time acknowledging that more could and should be done to avoid sour-gas well accidents. His attempts to minimize his own role were met with politely disbelieving smiles. Many of the men in the audience supplemented their farming income by working on the rigs and they knew how much guts it had taken to single-handedly tackle that well. The standing ovation when he finished lasted for five minutes.

In his closing remarks the mayor said, "I don't know if Frank intends to go back into politics, but if he was going to run in the Lundell riding, he'd win in a landslide!"

"The mayor of that little town called it right. You're a hot political property." Dale Young, Frank's erstwhile campaign manager, spoke casually but there was a speculative gleam in his eye.

"You really think so?" asked Frank. "After that fiasco the last time around?"

"Ancient history. Just proves you're human." Dale turned to Bill for support. The three of them were sitting in the rustic comfort of the Circle C ranch house on a Sunday afternoon in early December. "How do you see it?"

"In my opinion, Frank could win any riding in Alberta, either federal or provincial, in a walk. Senator Garvey is of the same view, I might add."

"You thinking of running federally, Frank?" Dale looked a little disappointed, but was fair enough to add, "The new elections act gave the Calgary area three new seats. Any one of them would be yours for the asking."

"If I do run, it won't be federally. Not at first, anyway. The problems I know about, and feel I could do something about, are local."

"We've never gotten around to holding a nomination meeting in Highview to replace you. How about it, Frank?"

Frank looked at his father who said, "You know that's what you really want to do."

Taking a deep breath, Frank said, "All right. Let's go for it!"

"Terrific! When do we hold the nomination meeting?"

"Not till the spring breakup. I've signed on with Spartacus for another deephole."

21

High over the foothills, a Lear 24, looking remarkably like the Swedish fighter plane from which its design was derived, performed an aerial ballet. Diving out of a split S, it pulled up in a loop, rolling off the top into another split S that flowed into a graceful chandelle, side-slipping from the chandelle into a shallow dive and then zooming heavenward in a spectacular series of steep-climbing rolls. Levelling off at 45,000 feet, Wayne dipped a wing and flew a tight circle to make sure there was no traffic in the practice area. Then he popped the air brakes and sent the jet, which was stressed for seven Gs, hurtling earthward. The altimeter unwound like a berserk clock and the high-pitched buzz of the ailerons filled the cockpit. The control yoke bucked and shook in his grip with the buffeting of the wind on the elevators. As the speed increased the windshield began to vibrate and hum, obscuring his view of the ground rushing up to meet him. Pressing the yoke forward he kept the Lear in a screaming power dive.

The airspeed indicator climbed to 600 knots and the cockpit thrummed and shook with the scream of tortured metal. He was close enough to the ground now that, even with his view distorted by the vibrating windshield, he could make out individual trees. He saw a car that had come to a halt on the road, and the tiny figures of the driver and passengers jumping out to watch his terrifying descent. At the last possible moment, Wayne pulled back on the yoke. A red film came down over his eyes and he was pressed deep into the seat, his stomach feeling as if it had split in two and was running down his legs. As soon as the effects of pulling all those Gs had worn off, he spent a very satisfying twenty minutes screaming along the country roads at treetop level before climbing back to cruising altitude and leaving the practice area.

Wringing out the Lear had been therapeutic but the anxiety that now always seemed to be with him began to gnaw at his guts as soon as he climbed out of the cockpit.

When the interest rates had peaked, and then declined precipitously, Wayne had hoped for a respite from the grinding pressure of trying to keep Pursuit afloat. It was not to be, for no sooner had the burden of interest payments eased, than the world price of oil began an alarming downward spiral.

He dreaded the directors' meeting scheduled for tomorrow. The bank nominees on the board would be bound to bring up their favourite topic — the lunacy of a company that was fast going down the tubes continuing to operate a corporate jet. Eventually, Wayne acknowledged to himself, they would have their way since it was basically the banks' money that Pursuit was spending. He grinned briefly as he pictured their horror if they knew what he had just been doing with their million-dollar asset. Especially since his flying it single-handedly would have annulled the insurance coverage.

Oddly enough, the fall in the price of oil did take some of the pressure off Wayne. No longer was it possible to pinpoint his ill-timed purchase of Fordex as the sole cause of Pursuit's disastrous situation. Cliff Barton sounded almost conciliatory as he asked Wayne for his views on how deep the price cut might turn out to be and how long it would last.

"Who knows?" Wayne shrugged. "The members of OPEC are fed up with being the ones who always have to cut back production in order to maintain the price. Their production ceiling was sixteen million barrels a day and now they're up over seventeen and still rising. You gentlemen don't need me to tell you what that over-supply will do to the price." Wayne's lips twisted in a rueful grimace as he remembered how he had airily dismissed Bill Crawford's gloomy predictions.

"What's the price today?" one of the directors asked.

"Twenty-six fifty a barrel on the spot market," Wayne replied.

"Christ. That wipes out any hope of floating an equity issue," Rupert French, a retired stockbroker who was one of Wayne's tame directors, muttered.

"It does for a fact," Wayne replied stonily, not bothering to remind the meeting that every underwriter they had consulted had advised against trying a share issue ever since the Fordex deal had started to turn sour. Until the advent of the bankers, Wayne had enjoyed complete dominance over his board of directors, who could be counted on to rubber stamp his every decision. The one exception had occurred at the time of the Fordex acquisition when some of them, including Rupert French, had urged that a substantial part of the purchase price should be raised by share issue. Wayne, unwilling to have his control diluted, had overruled them, insisting that the market price did not reflect the true value of the Pursuit stock. By bemoaning the fact that it was no longer possible to make a public share offering, French was reminding Wayne that if he had taken their advice the company wouldn't have been brought to its knees by a crippling debt load.

Wayne consulted the agenda and informed the meeting that the next item was a proposed fifteen per cent cut in all executive salaries and directors' remuneration.

It was passed with a minimum of debate, everyone recognizing the need for some symbolic gesture in the face of the layoffs that were decimating the ranks of the employees.

"A lot of those who were laid off last spring have exhausted their severance pay and have had to apply for welfare." Rupert French shook his head dolefully. "Can you imagine ten- and fifteen-year veterans of the oil patch on welfare? It must just about kill them."

"It *is* killing them. Literally," Steve Morrison said. "The wife of one of my vice-presidents is a trained psychologist and she's a volunteer at the suicide hotline. They had to upgrade their switchboard to handle the calls."

The remaining items on the agenda dealt with operating results and financial forecasts. The operating statistics were outstanding; the company ran like a Swiss clock, but to no avail; it was slowly suffocating under the combined effect of its debt and depressed oil prices. Barton looked up from his perusal of the damning figures and peered over his half-moon reading glasses. "We have to face reality, gentlemen. The bank's auditors have been after us to write down the value of our loans by a third and, in the light of these forecasts, I don't see how we can avoid it."

"Let's not be too hasty, Cliff," pleaded Steve, whose own auditors had been growing restive over Westfirst's shaky loan portfolio. "Once we start writing down our energy loans, God knows where it will end. It could trigger a run on the banks that would wreck the entire banking system."

"Well, I guess I can hold the auditors off until the next quarter," Cliff agreed reluctantly. "But the shit is going to hit the fan sooner or later."

As they reached the item headed "Other Business," Wayne heard Peter Gunther, the Federal National representative on the board, clear his throat, and knew he was going to bring up the matter of the Lear. Wayne, bludgeoned by the implacable numbers on the financial statements, was almost beyond caring.

"Corporate jets are a glut on the market," he observed by way of a token defence. "In today's market, there's no way of telling what the Lear will bring, but it will be a damn sight less than a million dollars."

"It would have been twice that if we had sold it when we should have," Peter snapped. "The important thing is to get rid of it. If you have to, fly it down to one of those auctions in Arizona and put it on the block with no reserve bid. Just get rid of it!"

Wayne looked at the faces around the table. Only Cliff and Peter met his gaze, the latter defiantly while Cliff's expression was that of a man left with no choice. "All right, gentlemen," Wayne said crisply. "There's no need to have a vote. I'll start making arrangements to dispose of the Lear first thing tomorrow."

Long after the meeting had broken up, Wayne remained at the conference table, staring at the financial statements. Their message was unequivocal: unbelievably, he, Wayne Shaw, the Yankee Raider, was insolvent.

A few blocks away, Debbie was giving the same message to a distraught owner of a junior oil company.

He was the latest in a parade of small-time promoters who called on Debbie to inquire, with seeming casualness, how much she was prepared to pay for the shares of their individual companies.

Most of them were known to her, and she felt obliged to hear them out. If nothing else, she was becoming expert at evaluating balance sheets. Rapidly scanning the one before her, she punched some figures into her pocket calculator and looked across the desk at her visitor. "According to this, you should pay me a million dollars to take over your position. At least."

"Aw, come on, Debbie," the shaken owner protested. "That's a good little company."

"A good little company that owes the bank a million dollars more than its assets are worth. Next week its loans will probably be even more underwater than they are now. It's what's known as negative equity, Eric."

"Damn it, Debbie," there was a quaver in Eric's voice. "I was offered $4-million for that company a year ago."

"The sun was shining every day back then. I'm truly sorry, Eric, but that's the way it is."

When the crestfallen owner had crammed his papers into his briefcase and departed, Debbie walked over to the window and looked up at the framework of Pursuit Tower. A climbing crane lifted a steel beam, dull-red with its coating of anti-corrosion paint, into position. Sparks flew as the construction workers welded it into place. A lowering winter sky sent fine particles of snow swirling around them as they worked. The office tower, climbing arrogantly skyward as it neared its projected height of sixty-two storeys, was a challenge flung in the face of the depressed economy. She was surprised that it was still going ahead, but then, how does one go about shutting down a huge project like that, especially when it was so far along? Maybe Wayne figured the economy would have turned around by the time the building was ready for occupancy. Except that it wouldn't be Wayne who would be making the decisions; he no longer called the shots over at Pursuit. God, it must be galling for the eagle to have his wings clipped so late in his career. She wondered if he would stick it out. According to Ken, there was virtually no chance of the creditors ever receiving one hundred cents on the dollar, which meant there would be nothing left for the shareholders. Negative equity, just like Eric's little company, except on a much vaster scale. Maybe Wayne felt honour-bound to try and work the company out of the mess he had led it into. If so, he was making a mistake. He wasn't psychologically suited to running a salvage operation. He was all attack: not for him the day-to-day slogging through a hopeless situation. Would Billy inherit his restless, driving personality?

With Billy happily propped up in the shopping cart, Debbie was standing in the checkout line at Fenton's, an upscale food emporium, when Bernice Dawson descended on her with glad cries. "Isn't he just the little man, though?" she cooed, clucking Billy under the chin. He accepted the attention with his customary equanimity, offering a faint, polite smile while his cool Crawford eyes inspected the shrill-voiced woman wearing the large floppy hat.

"Hello Billy," a deep male voice said and Debbie looked up in alarm. Wayne was staring down at the infant, as if trying to memorize every detail of his appearance. Billy, used to being spoiled by his male relatives, responded with a gurgling laugh.

"He's a beautiful baby." Wayne reached out a finger, which Billy immediately grasped.

"He's just gorgeous," Bernice gushed, scarcely crediting her good fortune at being in on the dramatic encounter.

"Next, please," the cashier called out, and Debbie, grateful for the chance to escape, nudged her cart up to the register. Wayne stayed behind the cart, making a fuss over Billy, while the cashier rang up Debbie's purchases.

"Let me help you with your packages," he offered.

"I can manage just fine, thank you." Billy laughed with gleeful delight as Debbie almost ran out of the store, pushing the cart ahead of her. Hastily, she pitched the groceries into the rear seat of her new Jaguar and locked the doors from inside even before fastening Billy into his car seat. Gripping the steering wheel with both hands, she took several deep breaths to steady herself before turning on the ignition. She told herself that Wayne had every right to be in the store and that there was nothing sinister about the chance meeting. She wished to God that it hadn't happened, though.

The annual Christmas bash that Katie and Bob Creighton threw in their spacious Mount Royal home was a fixture on the Calgary social calendar. It was well under-way when Debbie and Frank arrived; they had come together so Frank could try out the new Jag. The hostess blew him a kiss from where she was standing hemmed in by the crush of people at the bottom of the circular staircase. Dick Graves came up to kiss Debbie on both cheeks. "Let's do lunch sometime soon," he murmured.

"I'd be delighted to have lunch with you, but I'm damned if I'm going to 'do' lunch with you," Debbie replied.

Dick laughed light-heartedly, congratulated Frank on his heroics at the well, and was carried off by a young thing who couldn't have been more than twenty.

"You don't look at all like Dad," Frank was watching his sister's expression as she gazed after the departing couple, "but whenever you do that raised eyebrow routine you sure remind me of him."

Pleased, Debbie smiled. "Speaking of Dad, he should be here somewhere. There he is, over by the fireplace. Talking to Jim Goulder and Chester Martin. Now that's interesting. I wonder what they're up to?" While she was speaking, Debbie was working her way through the crowd to where her father and his two cronies were standing. "The Three Musketeers!" she cried, kissing each one in turn. "What diabolical coup are we plotting now?"

"Just reminiscing," her father replied blandly.

"Oh, sure," scoffed Debbie, looking around for Frank. He had been waylaid by the prettier of the Fraser twins; catching Debbie's eye, he excused himself and came over to greet his father's friends, both of whom had known him since childhood. Like everyone else, they showered congratulations on him.

"You must be mighty proud of this boy of yours," Ross Edwards boomed as he barged up to the group, hand outstretched. It was obvious that he had been drinking, but he was still in reasonably good shape.

"I am. Very," replied Bill quietly. In reality, he was fairly bursting with pride over Frank's feat. What Frank had done was right at the heart of the oil patch, something that commanded instant respect from roughnecks and company presidents alike.

If Ross Edwards was here then Fiona might be as well. Frank's heart was pounding as he shook the tycoon's hand. There she was, over by the grand piano, standing beside her mother who looked to be hammered out of her skull. Some guy with wavy blonde hair and a fabulous tan was handing drinks to Fiona and her mother. At first, Frank thought it was Jim Huntley, the fellow who had been the best man at Henry's wedding. If Jim was still on the scene after all this time, chances were that he would have the situation pretty well locked up. The stranger turned toward Frank as he headed back to the bar and Frank felt a surge of relief. It wasn't Jim after all; the two men were just the same physical type. God, but Fiona was beautiful!

Beatrice Edwards watched with extreme disfavour while her husband made a big fuss over Frank Crawford. She had come to detest the Crawford boy ever since he had callously broken her little girl's heart. She managed to smother an unexpected hiccup and battened it down with a hasty swallow of rye. She was pissed and she knew it; somehow she had to get her act together.

Frank was coming over to speak to them; the half-longing, half-fearful look in Fiona's eyes was heart-rending. Fiona's cool poise fooled a lot of people, but she couldn't fool her mother. Just before Frank reached them, Henry Purvis intercepted him and struck up a conversation. Beatrice sucked in a lungful of air.

"I'm surprised at Katie having a man who consorts with prostitutes as a guest in her home," she announced in a loud stage-voice calculated to reach every corner of the room.

Frank heard every hateful word, but pretended not to. He kept on talking to Henry whose eyebrows had shot up like a window blind. He heard Fiona's horrified, "Mother!" but carefully avoided looking in her direction. A few nervous titters broke the stunned silence, and then Debbie was at Frank's elbow, chattering away to a flustered Henry. "We don't leave," she hissed in an undertone to Frank. "We stick it out."

The hum of conversation resumed as the party closed over the awkward moment. Both host and hostess made a point of wandering over to Frank and engaging him in conversation, while Janice Purvis helped a mortified Fiona lead her mother outside to the car. Ross Edwards, vaguely aware that his wife had once more disgraced herself in some fashion, shrugged indifferently and took up station at the bar. Beatrice's drunken remark would be a delicious piece of gossip in the clubs and living rooms tomorrow but, for the moment, it was as if it had never happened.

"I just get to thinking all that is behind me and somebody throws it in my face," Frank said bitterly.

"It's old news. People will be talking about what a fool Mrs. Edwards made of herself, not about you," Debbie told him. "It's Fiona I'm sorry for. She looked absolutely devastated."

"Damn."

"What are you going to do about her, Frank?"

"What do you mean? What's there to do?"

"You're in love with each other."

"We haven't seen each other for nearly sixteen months."

"And how many days and hours? You're priceless, Frank." Debbie fished in her purse for her car keys and held them out. "Here. I'm sure I can find some nice man to give me a lift home."

"I really gave him what for, didn't I, dear?" Beatrice belched contentedly and laid her head back on the pillow.

Fiona gazed down at the veined, raddled face and sighed, "You most certainly did." Gently, she brushed back a wisp of hair from her mother's forehead, damp with perspiration. Beatrice smiled drowsily, gave Fiona's hand a loving pat, and fell into oblivion with a stupendous snore. Leaving a hall light burning, Fiona slowly descended the carved oak staircase. The lights of the Christmas tree she had spent all day decorating seemed to mock her with their cheerful glow. Realizing that there was a good chance Frank would be at the Creightons', she had prepared herself for the encounter while she trimmed the tree. First, she would congratulate him on his bravery at the well — that wouldn't be hard, she had thrilled to the stories in the newspapers Janice had sent to her at Princeton — and say, while smiling brightly, how nice it was to see him again. If she managed to carry it off, he would never know she was breaking up inside. And then, to have her mother come out with that outrageous, hurtful remark! Frank must wonder if that's what was going through everyone's mind when they saw him. Beatrice had really outdone herself tonight, but there was no point in being angry with her. Fiona knew the reason behind the outburst was that her mother loved her so much, and resented the shabby way Frank had treated her. And the poor old dear had been drunk enough to let it all come pouring out. After tonight, Frank would turn and flee at the sight of the Edwards family.

The door chimes pealed melodiously and Fiona hurried over to the intercom in the front hall. It was probably somebody bringing her father home, although it seemed a little early for that. She pressed a button and asked, "Yes? Who is it?"

"It's me. Frank."

"Just a minute," Fiona said, then realized she had forgotten to press the talk button. Her heart was lodged somewhere in her throat as she unlatched the massive front door and swung it open. Frank, his coat collar turned up and his breath condensing in the chilly air, asked uncertainly, "Is it all right if I come in? I mean, is there anyone with you?"

"There's no one here except mother, and she's passed out upstairs." Fiona stood aside to let him enter. "You must be terribly upset, I'm ..."

Frank interrupted her, "I'm not upset. I'm in love."

"What did you say?"

"I'm in love. With you."

"Say it again. Please."

"I love you."

Then Fiona was in his arms, whispering as their lips met, "I love you, too. Oh, Frank, darling, how I do love you!"

22

Suddenly, almost overnight, the worrisome decline in the world price of oil turned into a free fall to disaster — West Texas Intermediate selling at less than $20.00 US per barrel. Unthinkable! Wayne shook his head in disbelief.

"The Merchants Bank has agreed to postpone the next interest payment so we can clear up our trade payables," Ted Reimer was saying. "Some of our suppliers are threatening to cut us off."

"That'll buy us some time," Wayne approved. Inwardly, he wondered if it was worth the bother. If the price of crude kept dropping, the company would fall deeper and deeper into its death spiral. The banks were in complete control; Ted had to go cap in hand to them for authority to spend every dollar. Just before Ted had arrived, Wayne had been reading the drilling report. Drilling report! That was a laugh. Pursuit was participating in precisely one well, and that was only because the lease was about to expire. Even a few months ago, the report would have listed at least twenty wells in which Pursuit was involved. As the vice-president of finance, Ted had replaced the heads of the exploration and production departments as the most important man in the company. He was the one who had to deal with the banks, and that's all they did these days — deal with the bloody banks. Pursuit was no longer an oil company; it was just a collector of revenues for the lenders.

Ted looked exhausted. There were unhealthy blue smudges under his eyes as if he hadn't had a decent night's sleep for weeks. Ted had a personal stake in the continued existence of the company. If it went into receivership, he'd be out on the street along with everyone else, with no way of supporting the expensive lifestyle he and his family presently enjoyed. To make matters worse, his stock options that once were so lucrative had turned into a liability that could ruin him if the receiver called on him to pay for the shares at the option price.

Barely pausing to knock, an agitated Caroline Underwood burst into Wayne's office. "Something's terribly wrong with Lloyd Chernak," she announced breathlessly. "He was talking to a group of employees who had just been let go, telling them about the career-counselling program, when he suddenly stopped talking and started to yell. It was awful, just this blood-curdling scream, as if he was going to explode right there in front of us. Then he flung his papers in the air and ran out of the room. He was hitting and bumping into things. He ran right into a filing cabinet. I thought he had knocked himself out, but he just shook his head and kept on going. A couple of engineers from the production department finally tackled him and held him down until the ambulance arrived."

"Where is he now?" demanded Wayne.

"On his way to the General Hospital. One of the psychologists from the consulting firm was at the meeting and according to him, Lloyd was having a complete nervous breakdown. He says they should be able to treat it with tranquillizers and counselling. It was a pretty wild scene, I can tell you. The poor man."

"The employees called him Doctor Death," Wayne said. "It just about finished him when he found out. I never should have let him keep on with the job of terminating people. He just didn't have a thick enough hide. But he insisted he was okay."

"He needed the job," Ted murmured.

"It's funny, in a gruesome kind of way," said Caroline, "but now he'll be able to draw disability pay under the insurance policy. He'll be a lot better off than the other people we've let go."

Wayne looked at his watch and sighed, "We're going to be late. Our lords and masters will not be pleased."

"Our apologies, gentlemen," Wayne said as he and Ted followed Caroline into the boardroom on the fortieth floor of the Merchants Canada building. There were sympathetic murmurs around the table when he told them what had happened, but only Steve Morrison seemed genuinely upset. Cliff Barton even looked a trifle smug as he glanced in the direction of the two representatives from Merchants's Toronto head office. The bank had long since given up the pretence that the Pursuit loan was being handled by its western regional office, and the "goon squad," as Wayne called them, now flew out to attend all the meetings. For the most part they let Cliff do the talking.

"We've cut a deal with the builders," he announced after a few gloomy remarks about the drop in oil prices had been exchanged. "All work on the building will cease on Monday. It's no longer safe to assume that the recession will be over by the time the tower would be ready for occupancy."

Caroline drew in a sharp breath. It was an intolerable insult to Wayne to spring it on him like that without even bothering to consult him beforehand. But his expression was impassive. "That must have cost an arm and a leg," was all he said.

"They were remarkably reasonable." Cliff's smile was thin. "They realized they couldn't expect to recover much from a bankrupt company with a long list of secured creditors."

"Is there anything else, gentlemen?" asked Wayne.

"I don't believe so." Cliff looked around the rectangular table. Steve Morrison was the only one who spoke. "We're sorry it had to come to this, Wayne."

Wayne nodded, but said nothing.

"Maybe Caroline could stay behind and help us with the press release," suggested Cliff. "We will emphasize that it's only a temporary suspension."

"The mayor and city council are going to love having that steel skeleton looming over Calgary like a spectre of hard times." Wayne's smile was sardonic as he took his leave.

Arriving back at his own office, he went directly to the conference room that looked out on Pursuit Tower, the edifice that in his blind arrogance he had meant to be his monument.

It would be a monument all right — a monument to failure on a colossal scale. That stark framework thrusting into the sky would become a landmark; hell, it would probably turn into a tourist attraction. It wasn't exactly the claim to fame that he had intended for himself when he first set about building his empire. But what the hell.

Everything, good or bad, that had happened since the day he had ejected over the Gulf of Tonkin and the pilot of the MiG had dipped his wings in salute instead of shooting him out of the sky, was a kind of bonus. The receptionist came through on the intercom to tell him that a Ms. Crawford was there to see him.

"I was just telling myself that nothing good happens anymore and then you ..." Wayne's enthusiastic welcome died on his lips as her accusing glare finally registered on him. "We better go to my office," he muttered and led the way down the carpeted hallway.

"What have I done now?" he asked with a resigned shrug as he closed the door behind them. He frowned uneasily as she continued to stare fixedly at him, as if trying to probe his innermost being. "What is it, Debbie?"

"Billy's been kidnapped."

"Jesus. When did it happen?"

"About an hour ago."

"And you came to me for help. I'm fl ...Wait a minute ... you think ... you think I had something to do with it?"

"Did you, Wayne? Fathers do that sometimes. Abduct their children." Her tormented eyes searched his face, and she gave a small despairing sigh, "You didn't, I can see that. I was almost hoping it was you. Then I would at least know he'd be looked after."

Wayne grabbed her by the arm and hustled her down the hall toward the elevators. "We've got to get back to your place, Debbie. That's where the kidnappers will make contact.

"I'll drive. You talk." Wayne held out his hand for the car keys as they descended to the underground parkade.

Debbie felt a flash of resentment at the way he was taking charge, but, realizing how much she would need his support to get her through this ordeal, she handed over the keys. Fighting to keep her voice under control, she began to tell him what had happened as he gunned the Jag up the ramp."

"His nanny was taking Billy for a walk, like she does every afternoon if it's not too cold. Then this car pulled up to the curb, and a man jumped out. He had a gun and he had one of those woollen ski masks pulled down over his face. He held the gun on her while he picked Billy up out of the carriage and drove off."

"Did she get the license number?"

"The car didn't have any plates."

"What about the make?"

"She's not very good on cars. She thinks it was one of the Japanese models, but she's not sure."

"Probably stolen, anyway. I take it you haven't notified the police?"

"No. And I don't intend to. All I care about is getting Billy back."

"You had a phone call," Nancy Jenkins, the distraught-looking nanny, said as soon as Debbie told her it was all right to talk in front of Wayne. "He was very upset that you weren't here to take the call. He said for you to be sure to be here when he called back."

"He? It was a man, then?" asked Wayne.

"Oh, yes. He had a really deep voice. He was speaking funny and it was hard to make him out." Nancy's eyes filled with tears. "I feel awful about little Billy."

Distractedly, Debbie patted her shoulder. "Why don't you go into the kitchen and make us some tea?"

Debbie's hand flew to her throat when the phone suddenly shattered the silence. Wayne nodded, and she picked up the receiver. "Yes?" she managed to croak.

"Debbie Crawford?" The voice sounded strained, pitched so low it was almost guttural. There was a muffled quality to it as if coming through several layers of cloth.

"Yes."

"Listen good, lady. You do exactly like we say and you get your son back. You didn't contact the cops while you was out, did you?"

"No. No. I swear."

"You do and your baby dies. What's his name?"

"Billy. Please don't hurt him. Listen. He needs his formula — he likes Similac — six times a day and a little bit of Pablum three times a day."

"We'll take good care of him, don't you worry about that. He's our ticket to $2-million in ransom money. How long will it take you to come up with that kind of cash? Don't try to tell me you can't raise that much, because we know you can."

"I'll do my best. But you've got to realize it all depends on how long it will take the bank to come up with that amount of currency. I'm sure it won't be until tomorrow at the earliest." Resolutely she pushed aside the thought of Billy having to spend the night in the hands of the kidnappers. The best thing she could do for her baby was to keep calm and do everything his captors asked.

"We'll call you in the morning. Remember, you go near the cops and you'll never see Billy again."

"They want two million. In cash," she said to Wayne as she replaced the receiver.

He whistled. "What are you going to do?"

"Give it to them."

"I wish I could contribute. But as my accountants keep reminding me, I'm stony-broke. Are you going to bring your father into this?"

"No. I can manage on my own. But I would like you to help me see it through. Would you?"

"Of course." Wayne paused. "Debbie, I know in my heart that Billy is my son, but I want to hear it from your lips."

"He is your son, Wayne. And once we have him back you two can get to know each other." Debbie picked up the phone. "I've got to get hold of Steve Morrison. I only hope he hasn't left the office already."

She caught the banker just as he was about to leave for the day. He promised to wait for her and told her he would make arrangements with the security desk to let her through. On the way to the bank she dropped Wayne off so he could pick up his car. They were to get together after her meeting with Morrison.

"Steve, I need $2-million in cash. How soon can you get it?"

The banker pursed his lips. "That's an awful lot of cash. Wouldn't a certified cheque do as well?"

"No. It has to be cash. Be an angel, Steve, and do this for me without asking questions. You know I'm good for it."

Morrison shrugged and reached for a desk pad and pocket calculator. "Let's see. We can get some from the armoured car people and the instabank centres." He scribbled down some figures and said, "We might, and I emphasize might, be able to do it by sometime tomorrow morning."

"Wonderful."

"You realize this amount of cash will be extremely bulky."

"I hadn't thought of that. Will I be able to carry it?"

"Good Lord, no. We're talking about ten blocks of $100 bills, ten blocks of $50 bills and twenty-five blocks of twenties. That will fill a body bag and it takes a damn strong man to handle one of those. The problem is that most of the money will have to be in denominations of $100 and less. There just aren't enough big denomination bills around."

"It's got to fit into a briefcase. One of those big Samsonite cases."

Morrison divided some numbers on his calculator. "We could do it if we had enough $1000 bills. Maybe I can arrange to borrow them from the Bank of Canada. It would mean chartering a jet." He looked questioningly at Debbie and, when she nodded, went on, "if everything works perfectly, we could have the funds here sometime tomorrow afternoon."

"I'm counting on you, Steve."

Morrison got up from his desk. "Wait here while I start some wheels in motion."

When he returned, he said, "So much for the mechanics of this transaction. How do you intend to pay for it — a loan?"

"Yes. I've got more than enough collateral." Debbie unsnapped her briefcase. "Here's my stock portfolio. They're all blue chips and have a market value of almost six million. The certificates are in street form and they're in my safety deposit box. I can deliver them whenever you give the word."

Steve studied the list approvingly. "I'm glad to see you didn't jump right back into the oil patch with the proceeds from the Pinnacle sale."

"It was Dad who urged me to go slow. He's been bearish on the near-term future of oil and gas for almost a year."

"A very astute man. His timing in reducing Venture's financial exposure was superb. His shareholders have much to be grateful for." As he talked, the banker studied his attractive visitor. She was putting on a good act, but she sure as hell was upset about something. He glanced again at the list of stocks, noting with wry amusement that his own bank was not listed among the financial institutions. Too risky for that gilt-edged portfolio. As long as she pledged the certificates as security for the loan, his ass was well covered.

"Well, I guess that does it," he said. "I'll call you in the morning and let you know how we're making out." He walked her across the expanse of carpet to the door. "Is something the matter, Debbie? Anything I can help with?"

"No, everything's fine. It's just a business deal I'm involved in. Like they say, I received an offer I can't refuse. Anyway, you are helping. Tremendously. But it's all very hush-hush, so I have to ask you to keep it confidential."

"There'll be paperwork to go through; you understand that, don't you?"

"I realize that. But this can't get out on the street."

"The only person from the bank who will know about it apart from myself, will be the senior loans officer. Compared to him, the sphinx is a blabbermouth."

"Under different circumstances I would really be enjoying this." Wayne stood in the doorway of the kitchen watching Debbie grill the steaks. He was about to add something when the phone rang, making her drop the fork.

It was the kidnapper and he was agitated. "Who's that guy wit' you? I tol' you no cops."

"He's not a cop. He's a friend. I need someone with me at a time like this."

He seemed to accept that and asked about the money. She heard a grunt of what could have been surprise when she explained the problem posed by its bulk, and he gave another grunt, this time of approval, when she told him about the $1000 bills in one briefcase. Then he became agitated again over the possibility that the serial numbers of the bills might be recorded. She did her best to reassure him, telling him that so far as the bank knew, she needed the cash for a business deal. "In any case," she added, "I'll make sure there are no records. I want to do everything exactly right so I'll get my baby back."

"That's what we like to hear."

Emboldened by his approval, she pleaded, "Tell me how Billy is. Has he had his formula?"

"He just finished his bottle," the disguised voice said. "We burped him and he's sound asleep."

"Oh God, I wish I could believe him," Debbie whispered as she relayed to Wayne what the kidnapper had said.

"He's probably telling the truth. You're co-operating, and he must know that things will go a lot harder for him if the baby isn't returned alive." Debbie shivered, and Wayne continued, "They must be watching the entrance to the parkade since he knows I'm here."

"He doesn't seem to worry about his phone calls being traced."

"He'll be calling from a different pay phone every time. As long as he doesn't hang around long enough for the police to close in, he knows he's got nothing to worry about. He was cutting it pretty fine, though, with all that talk about the bills."

"You know something? When he got excited, his grammar suddenly improved. His voice still sounded weird, but he forgot about the dises and dats."

"Interesting. But it doesn't help us much."

There were two more phone calls that night, but neither was from the kidnapper. One was a man, wanting to take Debbie out to dinner the following night. She told him to call her next week. The second call was from Hilary, wanting to chat. She rang off hurriedly when Debbie said she was entertaining company.

"She probably thinks she interrupted me in the middle of making love," murmured Debbie with a fleeting grin.

To distract themselves, they talked. Wayne told her about Chernak's nervous breakdown and about the banks' shutting down construction of the office tower.

"My God, Wayne," she said, momentarily shocked out of her misery. "You mean it's going to just stand there like a giant Meccano set?"

"Exactly. It will probably become known as Shaw's Folly. The eighth, or is it the ninth, wonder of the world."

"That's incredible!"

"Incredible, but true. I'm beginning to think it's funny, in a sick sort of way."

"I guess the banks are calling all the shots, huh?"

"About the only thing I can do without their permission is go to the bathroom."

"That doesn't seem like your style."

"It isn't, I assure you. I think I'll pack it in one of these days."

"Serious?"

"Dead serious. There's no upside as far as I'm concerned. Even if things were to improve dramatically, there's still nothing left for the shareholders. The assets of the company will be exhausted long before we pay off the banks. It's what they call the 'death spiral.' It's like getting into an inverted spin you can't pull out of. The only thing left is to hit the eject button. Besides," he went on after a pause, "who needs the wear and tear? There was a demonstration outside the office the other afternoon. About 200 ex-employees waving placards and shouting. They had an effigy of me with a rope around my neck."

"That's awful, Wayne. You don't deserve that."

"They seem to think I do."

"What about Caroline Underwood? Is she still with the company?"

"Definitely. She's busy as hell. There's no shortage of work for lawyers and accountants when everything's turning into rat-shit."

"I used to think she and Ken were going to get it on together."

"I asked her about that once. Probably shouldn't have, but I did. She looked like she was going to tell me to mind my own business, but then she said she didn't care for the idea of sharing him with Margo Jones."

"So that's what happened. It doesn't surprise me. I sometimes think Margo has cast some sort of spell over Ken." The spark of interest in Debbie's eyes flickered out and she whispered, "Poor Billy. What are we going to do, Wayne?"

He looked at his watch. "It's late. The best thing we can do for him is to get some sleep. We have to be sharp tomorrow when we get him back."

"Are we going to get him back, Wayne? Do you honestly think so?"

"Absolutely," he assured her with a confidence he was far from feeling. "Now, let's get some rest."

Lying on the converted studio couch in her study, Wayne heard Debbie moving about in the living room. Then she was standing in the doorway. "Are you awake, Wayne?"

When he half sat up in bed, she crawled in beside him. "Hold me, Wayne. Just hold me. I'm so frightened."

Steve Morrison phoned while they were forcing themselves to swallow some breakfast. "The package is on its way," he told Debbie. "It should be in my office by two o'clock."

"I'll be there. And Steve ... bless you. You're a true friend."

The next call from the growly voiced kidnapper came shortly after ten. He instructed Debbie to return home as soon as she had the money and await further instructions. Then he said, "The guy with you. I want him out. Now. You and me are going to take it from here on our own. You been doin' real good, lady. Keep it up and you'll have your baby back by suppertime."

Wayne didn't bother to make even a token protest when she told him he had to leave. Billy's life depended on following the kidnapper's instructions to the letter.

The formalities at the bank took less than fifteen minutes. Art Gerlitz, who Steve had used to help round up the money, was aghast when Debbie walked out of the office with the cash in her briefcase. "She should have an armed escort," he protested.

"The little lady doesn't want one, Art. I agree she's acting damned mysterious, but I've never seen her yet when she didn't know exactly what she was doing."

Debbie was barely back inside her condominium when the phone rang. The grating voice became almost breathless with excitement when she informed him she had the ransom money.

"Here's what you do," he instructed. "Get in your car — make sure you take the Jag — and drive west on 17th Avenue. Keep going past the city limits. You know the road I'm talking about?"

"Yes."

"Okay. Keep on driving 'til you see a pickup truck comin' the other way. It will flick its lights three times. You stop your car and hold the briefcase out the window."

"But when do I get my baby back?" Debbie cried.

"As soon as we's sure everything's cool."

As always at this stage, the advantage lay with the kidnappers. There was nothing to prevent them from making off with the ransom and simply disposing of their tiny victim. In fact, that probably would be their safest course. Maybe Billy was already dead. As the Jag threaded its way through the westbound traffic, Debbie desperately tried to convince herself that the odds were in her favour. Surely the kidnappers would realize that if they didn't return Billy alive she would go to the police and they would track the child-killers down relentlessly. And there was always the possibility that the kidnappers would hope that if she got her child back unharmed, she would be so overjoyed she wouldn't report it to the police. They seemed to know she could well afford to pay the ransom, and maybe they figured she would just accept the loss of the two million and keep quiet.

West of Sarcee Trail, 17th Avenue turned into a two-lane paved country road that followed the ups and downs of the rolling foothills countryside. A huge Chinook arch framed the distant mountain peaks, glistening with a fresh fall of snow. The mid-afternoon traffic on the narrow road was almost non-existent. Debbie slowed to a crawl to let a pickup loaded with hay bales get well ahead of her. It turned off at an intersection at the foot of the last hill and the road stretched empty and straight in front of her. She saw another pickup turn off the main road and head toward her. As it drew closer, its lights flashed three times. Taking a quick glance in the rear-view mirror to make sure the road was clear, Debbie braked to a stop and lowered her window. It took both hands to lift the briefcase from the seat beside her.

The driver wore a flesh-coloured ski mask and his eyes were hidden behind yellow-tinted ski goggles. Without looking at Debbie, he reached for the case with a gloved hand and pulled it into the truck's cab. Dear God, if he wore that get-up around Billy, the child would have nightmares for months. Debbie watched in the rear-view mirror as the truck accelerated and disappeared over the hill. She put the Jag in gear and turned left on the main road, heading back to town. She had done her part; now she could only pray the kidnappers would keep their word.

The nanny was waiting for her with a cup of tea. Debbie would have much preferred a stiff drink but she didn't care. Not until she had Billy safely back in her arms.

She told Nancy that the ransom exchange had gone off successfully and now there was nothing to do but wait. Wayne was suspicious of Nancy and thought there was a distinct possibility she could be involved in the kidnapping, but Debbie didn't go along with his theory. Nancy's distress was too genuine. Unless, of course, she was a superb actress. And even if she were a party to the plot, it was still the wisest course to treat her as if she were innocent.

The two women avoided each other's eyes as the minutes dragged by and the phone remained silent. "I can't stand this!" Debbie finally burst out, and began to pace up and down the Oriental rug.

Nancy tried to comfort her. "They'll need time to count the money and see that it's all there. Then they'll call."

Debbie looked at her watch for what must have been the twentieth time. "I've been home for more than an hour. They should have called by now, if they are ever going to."

"Don't …" Whatever Nancy was going to say was lost with the sudden ringing of the phone. Debbie snatched up the receiver. The kidnapper's harsh, grating voice was the most welcome sound she had ever heard."

"You know the Heritage LRT station?"

"Yes. Yes."

"Look for a green Pontiac in the parking lot. License number LKT 726. Got that?"

"Yes. Yes. I've written it down."

"Billy's in the trunk."

"The trunk? He'll suffocate!"

"Nah. But I wouldn't waste no time if I was you. The keys are on top of the front tire on the driver's side. Unnerstan'?"

"Yes. Thank you. Thank you." Debbie was disconcerted to find herself babbling words of gratitude to the kidnapper.

Macleod Trail was still choked with rush-hour traffic and Debbie almost wept with frustration as she was held up at every light. Fortunately for her sanity, she had remembered a recent news story about a young boy who had managed to lock himself in the trunk of a car and was still alive when he was discovered three days later. Long lines of homeward-bound automobiles blocked the exits of the rapid transit parking area, but the entrances were clear. Almost dreading what she might find, Debbie swung into the nearest one. The lot was well-lit and she had no difficulty in locating the green Pontiac, standing almost alone in the last row. There was no sound from the trunk but the keys were where the kidnapper had said they would be. Her hand shook so badly that she had difficulty in inserting the key. Finally it turned and the trunk lid swung open.

Billy was covered with blankets in a large wicker hamper. He stared up at her for a long moment, then began to cry. Sobbing with relief, Debbie picked him up and crooned soothing endearments in his ear. Still holding him in her arms, she placed the wicker basket in the back seat of the Jag, closed the Pontiac's trunk, and replaced the keys where she had found them. On the way home, she drove with one hand, holding Billy close to her with the other. Comforted by her nearness, his crying gradually subsided and, blissfully, she heard his familiar gurgling chuckle as his little hands reached up to pat her face.

"You say you paid the ransom. How much was it?" asked Detective Sergeant Loewen.

"Two million dollars," replied Debbie.

The detective gave an audible gulp. "When word of that payoff gets around, we could end up with a rash of kidnappings on our hands."

"It was the price I had to pay for my child's life."

"You were lucky. The way these things usually work, you'd be out $2-million and never see your baby again."

Debbie was growing restive with the implied criticism, but she said evenly, "Apparently I was dealing with criminals who had a sense of honour."

"You keep referring to 'them.' Did you ever deal with more than one person?"

"No, I didn't, now that you mention it. I just assumed there had to be more than one."

"From what you've told me, one person could have carried it off." Loewen closed the ring binder he had been making notes in. "Well, we don't have a lot to go on, but we'll do our best, Ms. Crawford. You'll leave the basket and blankets with us?"

"Certainly. What about the license number? Won't that help?"

"The car is almost sure to have been stolen. However, the first thing I'm going to do is check it out with our stolen-vehicles branch. It looks like our kidnapper just helped himself to a vehicle whenever he needed one. Smart."

"Is it that easy? Stealing a car, I mean."

"Child's play."

Loewen held the door of the interview room for Debbie and smiled for the first time. "I'm sure glad you got your son back, Ms. Crawford. If you think of anything that might help, give me a call."

Debbie drove directly to her condominium to be with Billy. She would call the office from there and tell them she was feeling better and would be in sometime tomorrow. She was so euphoric about having Billy back that, if it had been up to her, she probably wouldn't have bothered with the police. But Wayne had been horrified. He told her she had a public duty to report the crime, adding, "besides you might recover the money, or some of it, at least." But Sergeant Loewen had made it abundantly clear that he thought the chances of nailing the kidnapper at this stage were pretty slim. "Unless he does something downright stupid, like throwing his money around, he's home and dry."

23

Alone in the windowless map room, Bill experienced the excitement of a hunter catching his first glimpse of the elusive quarry. The digital filter program was the key to deciphering the seismic information. And now they had proof that the program worked. The seismic data, unmasked and redefined by the filters developed by Venture's geophysical department, had indicated the presence of a large Devonian reef on a Crown petroleum and natural gas lease held by the company. Venture had spent a million dollars drilling a well to find out whether the reef was there. It was there all right. Bill looked at the long squiggly lines of the electric log that showed 350 feet of reservoir rock. The only problem was that the giant reef was filled with salt water from an ancient sea rather than oil.

Nonetheless, the well proved that the new interpretation of seismic data could be relied on. If it indicated there was a reef present under a certain location, the chances were that an exploratory well would find one. Of course you could never be sure what would be in that reef — it would take an expensive wildcat to answer that all-important question — but the knowledge of the probable existence of the geological structure was tremendously valuable in itself. With something close to awe, Bill examined the contour map derived from the enhanced seismic. Its curving lines indicated three huge geological anomalies on a southeast-northwest trend. Moreover, the Precambrian basement rock on which the reefs stood tilted upward as it extended north. The fact that the basement trended updip was a very positive factor, since oil and gas tend to migrate toward the surface. Thus the water in the reef they had already discovered might well be replaced by hydrocarbons in the higher reservoirs. Bill's gaze was riveted on the middle anomaly — if that mother was really there, it could contain as much as 150 million barrels of recoverable oil. Even at today's depressed prices, which were as sure to rise as the sun in the morning, you were talking $2 billion. A true elephant, in the industry's vernacular for a giant new field. Making a discovery of this magnitude was the one thing that had eluded Bill in his long career as an explorationist.

The only problem was that these magnificent structures, which any oilman would kill for, were not on Venture lands. All three of them were located on a Crown petroleum and natural gas license now owned by Pursuit as a result of the Fordex acquisition.

Two years ago — in winter, when tracked vehicles could move across the frozen muskeg — Venture had shot seismic lines over a vast area in northern Alberta. The seismic program included the lands on which the water-filled reef had been encountered and lands owned by what was then Fordex Canada. But it also included hundreds of square miles of other lands, a lot of which was "moose pasture" that was shot for the sole purpose of preventing industry scouts from identifying the area of real interest to Venture. It was this seismic data that had been massaged and enhanced by the digital filter program to uncover the giant reefs.

It was ironical that, if Shaw only knew it, the solution to all the seemingly insuperable problems that faced him and his beleaguered company could be right there on his own lands. He could explore his way out of the death spiral, and turn himself overnight from a bum into a hero. But Shaw didn't have the key to the puzzle. Without the enhanced seismic, his exploration department wouldn't recognize the anomalies; and he had no way of knowing that the Venture wildcat had found a reef. The well could keep all the information confidential for a year. All the outside world would know was that it had come in dry and had been abandoned.

Deep in thought, Bill removed the small magnets that held the contour map to the wall, rolled up the map and seismic section and carried them back to his office. In the oil patch, when someone has information or a theory that leads him to believe there might be oil or gas on another company's land, the normal practice is for him to try and negotiate a farm-in of the lands — an offer to drill a well to earn a fifty per cent interest. But that wouldn't work in this case; not with a prospect like this. If Venture, after having drilled an exploratory well in the area, approached Pursuit with a farm-in proposal, it would alert Pursuit to the possibility of having a reef play on their property. Shaw might not tumble to it — he had other things on his mind and he wasn't much of an oilman anyway — but Stan Petersen sure as hell would. Strapped as they were for cash, Pursuit would still be able to come up with a million dollars to drill the well. If need be, the banks would put up the money themselves. You just don't walk away from a potential Devonian reef. Besides, Bill told himself, as he locked the map and seismic section away, the reefs were his — the discovery that would cap his career as an oilman. He had found them and he was damned if he would share them with anyone.

Bill knew he would have to act fast. In its last quarterly report to the shareholders, Pursuit disclosed that negotiations were underway with the banks for a restructuring of its debt. Once a restructuring agreement was in place, Pursuit would be allowed to carry on for a considerable period of time to give things a chance to work themselves out.

If he was going to acquire that license, it would have to be before the restructuring agreement was finalized.

Coming to a decision, Bill pressed a button on the intercom and asked Dave Wilson, Venture's exploration vice-president, to join him.

Dave Wilson had spent virtually his entire career working for Bill and was the perfect number-two man. Dedicated, intensely loyal, and with no ambition to run the show himself, he had ridden shotgun for Bill on many high-risk plays over the years.

"Dave, how long will it take your people to come up with a ballpark evaluation of Pursuit's assets?"

"Assigning a purely nominal value to that P&NG license, I assume?"

"Correct."

"On a crash basis — about a week. If you're thinking what I think you're thinking, Bill, you may not have all that much time. Rumour has it that the banks are starting to flog Pursuit's assets to see if any of the big boys are interested. They want an alternative if the restructuring falls through."

"Damn. I hadn't heard that. It was the restructuring agreement that I was worrying about. But I think I can guess why the banks might be interested in selling. The chairman of Merchants has just retired and his successor might be tempted to take a big hit on the bad loan, which he can conveniently blame on his predecessor, and put the whole mess behind him. Has there been any interest?"

"A few tire-kickers have been poking around, according to the rumour factory. I gather the only firm bid was an offer of 300 million by Intercontinental, and they were sent packing." Wilson paused. "Bill, I know you've done wonders to protect the financial integrity of the company — laying off the Beaufort project, selling our interests in the North Sea at the top of the market, and so on — but can we really handle something this big?"

"Depends on how far we have to reach. But, yes, I think so. With a little help from our friendly bankers."

"Bet the company, eh, Bill?"

"Not if we do our homework properly. In your evaluation, I want to use a price projection of $17 Canadian. That's conservative enough so that the assets should be able to carry themselves regardless of what OPEC does. Then, if necessary, we can assign a premium to that license."

Wilson was whistling a tune under his breath as he left. It took Bill a moment to recognize it — Mancini's "Baby Elephant Walk."

The newspaper item was headed, "Ex-millionaire's wife fined for theft." Intrigued, and feeling a certain empathy, Wayne scanned the story. The opening paragraph read: "The wife of a one-time millionaire, who turned to shoplifting when times got tough, was fined $1,000 for her offences." Wayne blinked as the name leaped out at him from the second paragraph. "Norma Clarkson, 44, admitted stealing from three different stores in December and January."

Her lawyer told the court that his client was the wife of a real estate developer who a few months ago had assets valued in the millions. But the real estate business had gone bankrupt and Mrs. Clarkson had been treated for stress. The prosecutor argued that her financial problems shouldn't have turned her into a thief and caused her to be so unco-operative with the security personnel who had apprehended her. Despite himself, Wayne grinned as he read that she had bitten two security officers. Norma always was a hellcat when aroused. The judge had offered to give her time to pay the fine, but she declined, saying she could come up with the money that same day. The story ended by noting that Clarkson had once been married to Wayne Shaw, head of Pursuit Enterprises, who was also rumoured to be having financial difficulties.

Poor Norma. That was twice her world had turned sour on her. He wondered if he should call her, but quickly discarded the notion. She would think he was patronizing her, or worse, gloating over her misfortune. Saddened by the humiliation his former wife would be suffering, Wayne rinsed out his coffee cup and stacked the breakfast dishes on the counter. This was one of the days for his twice-weekly maid service.

As always, the rear-view of the unfinished office tower was the first thing Wayne saw when he started out on the five-block walk to his office. Its top floors highlighted and bronzed by the early morning sun, the tower looked not unlike a gigantic outdoor sculpture. *Time* magazine had run a colour photo of it as a symbol of the plight of the oil industry in North America. Although the press coverage had been extensive, the general tone was curiously restrained. Instead of thundering on about the overreaching folly of vainglorious corporate leaders, the media seemed to accept the outlandish structure as a reflection of the times. "Grotesque as it may be," the *Herald* editorialized, "the abandoned tower is nothing compared to the loss of 70,000 jobs in the oil industry." Calgary's irrepressible mayor saw it as a barometer of the economy and declared, "When the construction cranes return to work on Pursuit Tower, the world will know that we're on the way back."

After weeks of negotiation, the restructuring agreement was scheduled to be signed that afternoon. Wayne spent the morning going over it with Caroline, his gloom deepening as they worked. Its terms were no surprise to him, of course, but their implications almost overwhelmed him as the hour of final commitment drew near. Basically, the proposal was simple. Pursuit's $900-million of bank debt would be divided into $250-million of hard debt on which interest had to be paid, with the balance being soft debt on which interest would be paid only if the company's financial results justified it. The rub was that the interest on the soft debt wasn't forgiven outright; it was merely postponed, with the unpaid interest being added to the principal amount of the soft debt. It was like trying to dig your way out of a sandpit when the sides kept falling in faster than you could shovel.

"It's receivership in everything but name," he sighed as his secretary brought in the sandwiches and milk.

"Of course," shrugged Caroline, biting into a chicken sandwich. "It's what the banks call a soft receivership. The only thing you can say for it is that it allows the company to continue operating."

"Yeah. But for whose benefit?" asked Wayne morosely.

"This is the pen I reserve for signing only the most important documents." With some ceremony, Cliff Barton uncapped a fat Mont Blanc fountain pen and began to sign the eight copies of the agreement. The lawyer acting for the banking consortium waited for the ink to dry before passing each copy on to Wayne. Wayne made no move to pick up his pen as the copies were spread out before him. Caroline, sitting beside him with the corporate seal in her hand, shot him a speculative sideways glance.

"Don't keep us in suspense, Wayne," joked Cliff with an uneasy laugh.

"I can't sign this document."

"What do you mean you can't sign it," the banker blustered. "The board of directors specifically authorized you to."

"I'm still the chief executive officer of this company and I'm not going to sign. There's nothing in it for the shareholders."

"The shareholders still have to approve it," Caroline reminded Wayne.

"I know that, and I'm sure they will rubber-stamp it, however reluctantly, because they can still kid themselves there might be something in it for them someday. And," he added, looking directly at Caroline and Ted Reimer, "if individual members of management want to stay on and run things for the banks, I have no problem with that. It's just that I don't intend to, and I'm damned if I can bring myself to sign this unconditional surrender."

"You're not fighting a war, Major," Steve Morrison interjected with a smile. He was intrigued, but not unduly disturbed, by Wayne's reaction. The banks, after all, held all the cards.

Cliff brushed the interruption aside. "If you won't sign it, Wayne, we'll damn well find someone who will!"

"You can't do anything here," Caroline told him. "This isn't a directors' meeting."

"I realize that," the furious banker snapped. "But what Mr. Shaw seems to overlook is that his shares are pledged to my bank to cover his personal indebtedness. Which, I might add, is totally underwater."

Wayne winced. "I'm only too well aware of that. And I'm sure my token protest will be no more than a temporary glitch in your plans. What I suggest is that we sleep on it and then," with a meaningful glance at Cliff, "see what we can work out."

"I've burned some significant bridges today and what I would really like to do is to see Billy and then take you out to dinner."

At the other end of the phone conversation, Debbie hesitated. Wayne seeing Billy was no problem; he had visited his son on a regular basis in the weeks since the kidnapping and the two got along beautifully. But those brief visits were the only contact she and Wayne had and now he was asking her to go out with him. "I'd like that," she said finally.

"I've never screamed like that before in my entire life. I hope the walls are soundproof."

"Solid concrete," Wayne assured her as they untangled themselves.

"Fine date you are," Debbie scolded playfully as she emerged from the bathroom, wrapped in his terrycloth robe. "Invite a woman to dinner and then rush her straight into bed. Is there any food in the fridge?"

"The old standby — bacon and eggs. And, if I remember correctly, you beat me to the bed."

Debbie grinned wickedly and headed for the stairs. "Did you resign officially?" she asked as she searched the cupboards for a frying pan.

"It's under the sink. And I haven't resigned officially, but what I did amounted to a resignation. At the last moment, I balked at signing the restructuring agreement. I'll talk to Cliff Barton tomorrow and strike some sort of deal."

"What kind of a deal."

"Oh, I'll tender my resignation and sign over my shares in return for a release from my personal indebtedness. Barton's let it be known for some time that if I resigned, the bank would let me off the hook."

"Which leaves you with what?"

"This condo, which in today's market is worth a lot less than I paid for it; one Pitts aerobatic biplane stored in a hangar in Phoenix. That's pretty much it."

"What about the Beaver float plane we used to go fishing in? Didn't you own it personally?"

"Oh, I sold it months ago. Along with a whole bunch of other toys."

"My God, Wayne, what are you going to do?"

"Move to New York and start over. Nothing to do with oil though. I've had that scene. An old wingman of mine is head of one of the big financial houses and he's got some ideas. I've lost my citizenship which is a nuisance, but he can get me a green card while I'm waiting to get it back."

"Are Billy and I ever going to see you?"

"You bet. I'll fly up here every couple of months. And the two of you can visit me in the Big Apple." He lifted her head to look into her eyes. "I think that's just about right for us, isn't it, Debbie?"

She smiled and kissed him. "Friends and lovers and the parents of a beautiful child. I'd say that's just about perfect for two people like us."

24

Jason had trotted on ahead to put his horse over some low jumps that had been set up in one of the fields. Each time she saw him, Debbie agonized over whether she should tell her father about Billy's kidnapping. She had compromised by warning him that Jason would be a tempting target for kidnappers.

His reply had been that in his opinion that particular danger was mostly past, and that oil tycoons and their families were no longer the prime targets for criminals looking for the big score. "And that may be the only good thing that's come out of this economic holocaust."

After a thoughtful pause, he had continued, "I don't want you to think I'm dismissing the risk out of hand. It's always there with high-profile people like us, but the problem is that if the protective measures were to be truly effective, they'd have to be so tough that they would prevent Jason from leading anything like a normal life for a young boy. And that I do not want."

As they rode along, side by side, Debbie and her father were having one of the conversations about business they both enjoyed so much. "What do you really think is the future of companies like Global and Pursuit?" she asked.

"If the banks refuse to put them out of their misery, they'll turn into corporate zombies, lurching around the oil patch like the living dead. They're already a drag on the industry because they don't have the cash to participate with their partners in ongoing operations. And both of them are so big they're involved in joint ventures all over the place."

"Wayne has decided to pack it in."

"Oh?" Her father was interested. "That doesn't surprise me all that much. He's not the sort of person you can keep on a tight rein. Did he and the banks have a falling-out?"

"I'll say. He refused to sign the restructuring agreement."

Bill stared at her for a long moment, then said, "Look. You stay with Jason. I've got to go back to town." Without giving her a chance to reply, he wheeled Big Country around and headed for the home ranch in a fast, ground-eating lope.

Debbie and Jason arrived back at the stables in time to see the silver Mercedes streaking down the driveway. Inside the house they were greeted by a perplexed Hilary. "What in the world did you say to your father? He came tearing in here, called his secretary at home and told her to round up Ches, Jim, and Dave Wilson and have them meet him at the office. Then he said he couldn't wait for dinner and took off!"

Chester Martin, Jim Goulder and Dave Wilson. The old team! It was pretty obvious that her father was working on something that involved Pursuit Enterprises, but just why had Wayne's refusal to sign the restructuring agreement galvanized him into such furious action on a Sunday evening?

Debbie's unspoken question was answered when Bill told his top advisers, "I knew they were working on a restructuring deal, but I had no idea they were this close. It was only Shaw's last-minute change of heart that's kept a window of time open for us."

"That window won't stay open very long," Chester Martin, the corporate lawyer, observed. "All they have to do is call a directors' meeting to either accept Shaw's resignation, or vote him out and appoint a new president who is prepared to sign the agreement. That can be done in a matter of days."

Bill was thumbing through the telephone directory. "I'm going to try and reach Barton at home and ask him to hold his fire for a few days to give us time to see if we can come up with a proposal."

Cliff Barton's unpleasant voice was even hoarser than usual, and it was obvious from his careful way of speaking that he had been into the martini pitcher, but he agreed with alacrity when Bill asked him not to do anything precipitately. His stalled career would be right back on track if he was instrumental in removing the Pursuit albatross from around the bank's neck.

"Now all we have to do," said Bill as he replaced the receiver, "is to come up with a proposal that will fly."

"And not turn Venture into another Pursuit," cautioned Jim. "I'm not entirely clear in my own mind why you've suddenly got the hots for a stretcher case like Pursuit, Bill. Thanks to some remarkable farsightedness on your part, Venture is in good financial shape, with a debt equity ratio that is almost indecently healthy in these troubled times. But, no matter how you go about acquiring Pursuit, you will have to take on very significant debt." The investment dealer paused to look speculatively at Bill. "Are you thinking of some approach that doesn't put Venture at risk? Maybe take over Pursuit's operations in return for a piece of the action?"

Bill shook his head. "No. I'm after outright ownership." The dubious look on Jim Goulder's face made him pause. "Look," he explained, "there's nothing complicated about it. Pursuit's oil and gas assets are immensely valuable and all I'm trying to do is use my company's credit-worthiness to pick them up at an attractive price."

"If you're thinking of a fire sale, don't hold your breath," advised Jim as he began jotting down some notes. "The banks have already made it clear that they're prepared to wait it out in the hope that the next economic upswing will bail them out." He glanced at the determined set of Bill's mouth, and continued with a slight shrug,

"Anyway, enough of that. I assume you see a share issue as a means of raising a good part of the purchase price?"

"Not if I can possibly help it. The market is so soft for oil stocks right now that we'd have to come out with an unacceptably low price that would seriously dilute the shareholders' equity."

"You're talking about one hundred per cent debt financing?" Jim was unable to completely hide his astonishment.

"That's about it."

Jim turned to Dave Wilson. "What kind of numbers are we talking about?"

"At $300-million, it's rape and pillage. From $400-million up, it begins to get real iffy."

"We already know the banks have turned down one offer of $300 million," Bill told Goulder. "But I think that should be our starting position."

"Where do we get the $300-million?"

"We borrow it from the banks, of course."

Cliff Barton didn't throw them out of his office when Bill came out with the $300-million offer, but he made it abundantly clear that they were wasting his valuable time. Before going into the meeting, Bill and Jim Goulder had agreed not to sweeten the offer at this preliminary stage, but, instead, to try and judge from Cliff's reaction how much more might be required to swing the deal.

Goulder was pessimistic as they left the bank's office tower. "The trouble is the banks financed that loan at $25 US per barrel and we're trying to buy it for less than $17 Canadian. That's one hell of a gap to try and bridge."

"I'm confident you'll find a way," Bill told him blandly, drawing a derisive snort from his financial adviser. "I'd be prepared to consider some arrangement where the purchase price would escalate with an increase in the price of crude, for example."

"That could make it more palatable to them," Jim conceded. "The only trouble is that the banks have their own price-projections which I know are very pessimistic. They're not likely to agree to a scheme that may never result in them getting more than the floor price."

"We'll just have to come up with the right bells and whistles," said Bill, slowing his walking pace to accommodate the chronically out-of-shape Goulder.

"You really want this deal, don't you, Bill? There must be more to it than appears on the surface."

"You going to Frank's engagement party tonight?" Bill abruptly changed the subject.

"Wouldn't miss it," replied Jim with a wry grin.

The Edwards were hosting a lavish reception at the country club to announce Frank's and Fiona's engagement. It was also by way of being a victory celebration because two nights ago Frank had won the Highview Conservative nomination on the first ballot over a token opponent. Beatrice Edwards never mentioned her drunken outburst against Frank, and it was easier for everyone to operate on the basis that she simply had no recollection of it. Ever since the incident, however, she had treated him with a cordiality that at first seemed forced but by now had turned into genuine affection. She had also begun to drink noticeably less on public occasions, and was almost sober as she stood in the receiving line.

Once again, Debbie found herself standing beside Steve Morrison, watching Dick Graves circulate among the guests. "Daddy says that if you only owe the banks a couple of million, they'll close you down without a second thought, but if you owe them a billion, they keep you on a life-support system forever. That's what I can't understand about Dick. His loans aren't all that large and yet the banks let him live on. He must have a charmed life."

Steve took a swallow of his Scotch and soda. "Graves is very much a white-haired boy with the banks at the moment. He's paid down his loans and brought them nicely on side."

"Where in the world did he get the money to do that?" asked Debbie, not liking the direction her thoughts were taking.

"He sold off some properties. I know that for a fact because we had to discharge the security we held against some of them. In return for full payment of our loan, of course. And he was into the Merchants for a million, and they got paid off in full. No need to worry about your friend — he will be one of the survivors."

From her own evaluations of the oil and gas properties Dick's company owned, Debbie knew they couldn't possibly bring much more than a half-million from any reasonably prudent buyer. Maybe he had some others that he didn't know about. Praying that this was so, she asked Morrison if he could remember the area where the properties his bank had a lien on were located.

"As it happens, I can. Cessford."

Dick's interest in the Cessford area consisted of a small percentage of two untested gas wells that Tom Burdon had said would fizzle out as soon as the valves were opened.

"Do you know how much he got for them?"

Morrison looked at her a little oddly, but said, "All I know is that we had a half-million loan out on them and the loan was discharged in full. That was the only loan Dick had with us, so you can see why he's A-OK with the Westfirst." He gave a little cough to clear his throat. "Don't get me wrong, Debbie, but I kinda had you pegged as the mysterious buyer of those properties. You know, because of our hush-hush operation raising all that cash."

"No. That was altogether different. It had nothing to do with oil."

Out of the corner of her eye, Debbie saw a smiling Dick Graves advancing on them. Hastily, she excused herself, saying that she wanted to give Fiona her best wishes, and moved away.

When Debbie got to the part about Dick suddenly being able to pay down his loans, Loewen interrupted her. "I better bring someone from the commercial crime division into this. Be right back."

He returned with a thin, intense-looking man, somewhere in his late thirties, whom he introduced as Detective Sergeant Guillo. Loewen rapidly briefed his brother officer on the case, explaining how up until now they hadn't had even the vaguest hint of a lead. "But," he turned to Debbie sitting across the table from him, "Ms. Crawford has a friend who seems to have suddenly come into possession of a large sum of money. Maybe you could take it from there, ma'am."

Debbie repeated what she had learned from Steve Morrison: that Dick had suddenly come up with what she figured was close to $2-million to reduce his bank indebtedness and stave off receivership. She told them that from what she knew of Dick's character, he would have felt utterly disgraced if he had been forced to declare bankruptcy. "Success is very important to him. He has a very low self-image."

"Does he have an explanation for this sudden wealth?" asked Guillo.

"The story is that he sold off some of his oil and gas properties."

"And you don't believe the sale took place?"

"It took place all right. I know that at least one of the banks had to release some security on one of the properties. Presumably, other banks did the same."

"That seems straightforward enough."

"The only thing wrong with it is that those properties aren't worth anything like that amount of money."

Guillo looked dubious. "Beauty is in the eye of the beholder. From what little I know of oil and gas properties, their value can fluctuate all over the place. Maybe this Graves found a purchaser who thought they had real potential."

"That's possible, of course. Nothing would please me more than if it turned out to be true. I'm fond of Dick Graves. But I know those properties, and I just can't see anyone paying $2-million for them."

"Except Graves himself?"

"Exactly! Couldn't he have worked some kind of a sham transaction?"

"Happens all the time," Guillo agreed. "It would be a simple matter to set up a dummy corporation as the purchaser, fund it with the ransom money — that would take a little doing. But he probably used a number of bank accounts established in the name of the dummy corporation — and then went ahead with the phony sale. The motive's a little screwy though. You'd think the guy would just take the money and run. But you say he's the kind of person who hates to lose face?"

"It would kill him. Literally, I think." Debbie picked up her purse and prepared to leave. "You will follow up on this, then?"

"Absolutely," Loewen assured her. "Finding someone who's suddenly come into a lot of money is the best possible lead in a kidnap case."

"What will you do?"

"First," replied Guillo, "we'll find out the name of the company that bought the properties, then we'll check out who owns it in the provincial companies branch. Maybe it'll turn out to be Graves himself, or maybe some lawyer holding it in trust for him. Then we'll check with the banks to see how the company came into possession of the funds. If things don't check out, we'll have your friend in for a little talk."

The thought of what that interview would do to Dick made Debbie almost wish she had kept her suspicions to herself. But if he was the one who had kidnapped Billy, he deserved everything he got.

"He's bound to find out that you're making inquiries," she said.

"Word will probably get back to him at some point," Guillo agreed. "We'll warn people to say nothing, but there's always someone who'll tip him off. One good thing, though, is that he'll have no reason to link our inquiries with the kidnapping. He'll just think we're investigating the deal as a possible commercial crime."

"Not for long, he won't. He's too clever for that," replied Debbie as she said goodbye to the two detectives.

Dick wanted to stop his ears, to wipe out the terrible words that Steve had just uttered. His heart jumped like a wounded bird in his chest, and Steve's beefy, anxious face slipped in and out of focus.

"Dammit, Dick, didn't you hear me?" The agitated banker was almost shouting. "I said the police spent all morning in the bank, asking questions about Phoenix Oil, the company that bought your properties. They seem to think that you own it in some way. And I got a call from the regional manager of the Central; the police have been over there, interviewing tellers and asking questions about how funds were deposited in the Phoenix account."

It was all over. Once the police got hold of one end of the string and gave it a pull, the whole elaborate plot would unravel. Its success depended on no one looking beneath the surface. And there was no reason for anyone to question the deal. No one got taken, and the banks got their money. What had gone wrong? As if from a great distance, Dick was aware of the banker demanding to know if the money that had paid the loan was tainted, and would the bank be forced to give it back?

"Don't worry about a thing, Steve. Everything's going to be just fine."

Steve started to make an angry retort, but the look on Dick's face silenced him. The man looked ghastly, with a fixed little smile and a vacant, empty look in his eyes.

A light tapping on the window made the elderly commissionaire look up from the paperback Western he was reading. An apparition in a flesh-coloured ski mask was looking in at him, signalling with his revolver for the commissionaire to open the door of the security shack.

"We're going for a little elevator ride," the masked figure said as he stepped inside. "Do exactly as I say and you won't get hurt. Where's the key for the elevator?"

"Right here." The terrified guard picked up a key from a row of hooks on the wall.

"All the way to the top?" he asked in a quavering voice as he worked the lever of the freight elevator that ran up the side of Pursuit Tower.

"All sixty-two stories," the masked man replied with a grim little chuckle. Apparently satisfied that the commissionaire had no intention of making any fool-hardy moves, he turned to gaze out the window at the lights of the city unfolding beneath them. The elevator whooshed to a smooth stop at the top floor and he motioned with the gun, in a gesture that seemed strangely polite, for the guard to open the door and precede him onto the small work platform. The top of the tower was harshly lit by the glare of floodlights installed to warn off low-flying aircraft. A night wind keened mournfully among the steel girders. The masked man grabbed the railing and seemed to be struggling for breath. Then he squared his shoulders, and handed the black, snub-nosed revolver to the astonished commissionaire with a polite little bow. "I won't be needing this anymore. The safety catch is on, by the way."

While the horror-stricken commissionaire watched helplessly, the man climbed over the protective railing and began to walk along the narrow steel beams, eight hundred and forty feet above the ground. He walked with the easy confidence of one to whom nothing matters any longer. Incredibly, he made his way without mishap to the front of the building, overlooking 6th Avenue. He paused there, one hand holding onto a vertical girder, before continuing his terrifying journey, stopping only when he reached a point directly above where the entrance would have been. Moving his feet a few degrees at a time, he turned until he was facing the street, hundreds of feet below. "Come back. Come back, man. Don't jump for God's sake!" the commissionaire shouted through cupped hands. The man half-raised his arm as if in acknowledgement of the guard's concern, then flexed his knees and launched himself into space. At some point in his long fall, he started to scream. When the scream was abruptly cut off, the commissionaire's stomach heaved and he vomited half-digested meat loaf over the platform.

"What I don't understand," Detective Loewen muttered, "is why Graves bothered with a mask. What did he care if the commissionaire could recognize him?"

"If I'm right," Debbie said slowly, "it may be his confession to the kidnapping. Dick didn't leave a note, did he?"

"If he did, we haven't found it, and when suicides leave notes behind they tend to put them where they'll be seen." Loewen was on his way out of the room. "I'll get the mask so you can have a look at it."

"It's not a pretty sight," Guillo warned her while they waited.

"I realize that. But I have to know. He must have been pretty badly smashed up, huh?"

"Strawberry jam."

The mask was stained with dark patches of dried blood and splattered with flecks of lighter-coloured matter that Debbie realized could only be brain tissue.

"That's it," Debbie said. "That's the mask the kidnapper was wearing when he collected the ransom money. You bastard, Dick Graves, you scheming, cowardly bastard!"

"At least he didn't harm your child," Detective Guillo murmured.

"That helps. Thank you for reminding me." Debbie averted her eyes from the gruesome mask. "Look, it won't be necessary to go public with the kidnapping, will it?"

"If you want to get your two million back, it will be," replied Guillo. "I don't know all the legal ins and outs, of course, but it strikes me that you could claim the money that paid off the banks was obtained as the result of the commission of a crime and you might be able to recover it."

"Forget the two million. I already have."

"Just like that, huh?" Guillo shook his head.

"It's a price I'm willing to pay for Billy's never knowing what happened to him. The story would haunt him for the rest of his life, and set him apart from other people."

"I take your point." Guillo looked at the other detective. "It's your case, Jim, but it seems to me that we could close the file on the kidnapping. You've always felt it was a one-man operation. We can satisfy the press about Graves's suicide if we let it be known that he was under investigation for possible fraud in connection with a commercial transaction, but that the investigation will be closed because of his death."

"That would be wonderful." Carefully not looking at the mask, Debbie shook hands with the two police officers. "Thank you both for being so helpful and understanding. I'm going to close my own personal file on the whole business as of right now."

25

The banking consortium had finally come up with a figure. They wanted $500-million for the oil and gas assets of Pursuit. The assets did not include the skeletal office tower that stood out on the Calgary skyline as a grim reminder of the dreams it had once been possible to dream. Two months ago the banks had bought it off the holders of the junk bonds for fifty cents on the dollar and they had let the company keep current on its trade accounts, so they were in a position to give clear title to the properties. But half a billion dollars!

The decision was solely up to Bill. Oddly enough, when you were selling the assets of a company, you required the approval of three-quarters of the shareholders, but when you were purchasing assets, which, if the transaction was large enough, could be even riskier, the most you needed was the support of the directors. And Bill had a majority of the directors comfortably in his pocket. They might ask questions and express doubts, but when push came to shove, they would vote with him. Lee Travis, the Texas multi-millionaire who was unquestionably the most independent member of the board, had already given him carte blanche. Preoccupied with the havoc that falling oil prices were wreaking on his vast family fortune, he had told Bill to cut the best deal he could and he would back him. He even apologized for being too busy with the alligator in his own hands to be of any help to Bill in coming to a decision. Bill hadn't told any of the directors about the reefs; all he had said were that some of the Pursuit lands were "highly prospective."

He salivated over those Devonian reefs. They filled his thoughts in the daytime and he was beginning to dream about them at night. He and Dave Wilson spent hours behind closed doors, poring over the seismic data and lovingly tracing and retracing the awesome contours of the middle reef that would be their primary target.

"I assign a probability of nine to one of that mother being there," Dave finally announced.

Bill put down his pencil and smiled wearily. "But what's in it? That's the billion-dollar question."

"Tickets to that lottery come pretty high."

"At these figures it's getting damn close to betting the company, Dave. Just like you said it would."

"I'm glad it's your decision, and not mine."

"Thanks a bunch," murmured Bill. "At least we've got some time. They've put the restructuring deal on hold because of our negotiations and I'm sure we must be the only potential buyer with a reason to even consider paying that kind of price. Or the wherewithal to pay it, for that matter," he added after a pause.

"I wouldn't be too sure of that." Dave frowned thoughtfully. "I didn't make the connection until you said that, and I may be totally out to lunch, but your old buddy Mark Hunter was back in town last week."

"Mark? I haven't seen him in years," Bill muttered, while his thoughts raced to assess the implications of Hunter's presence in Calgary. There was no doubt that Mark had the financial muscle to swing the deal. Hell, he could probably pay for it out of petty cash. After his big-inch pipeline to California was completed, Mark Hunter had left Calgary and moved to San Francisco — my God, it must have been at least twenty-five years ago. Over the years he had acquired a large stake in Norcal Gas & Electric Co., the huge utility that supplied gas and electricity to northern California. While he was in Calgary as a young geologist trying to make it on his own, Mark had discovered the famous Claymore field which, after a quarter-century of production, still kicked out a respectable fifty million cubic feet of gas per day.

If Mark, either personally or on behalf of Norcal, wanted to get back into the upstream exploration and production end of the oil business, Pursuit would be the perfect vehicle. Jesus. It would be unbelievably ironical if Mark, by acquiring Pursuit, accidentally stumbled upon another elephant, one that would dwarf his Claymore find. Well, that wasn't going to happen, by God! He liked Mark, but he was damned if he would let those irregularities fall into his lap like so many ripe plums!

Now that he was back in politics, Frank made a point of watching the news on TV at least once a day. His twelve-hour tour began at midnight, which gave him time to catch both the late night national and local newscasts. He was sitting with the driller and a couple of roughnecks in the trailer that served as the camp's recreation room when the commercials that followed the national news finally came to an end and the local news began.

The announcer wore a solemn expression as he reported that the minuscule opposition party in the provincial legislature had lost one of its leading members. "Arthur Crossan, the member for Highview, was killed earlier tonight in a single-car accident southwest of the city. Mr. Crossan had attended a constituency meeting earlier in the evening and was being driven home by his executive assistant, Norman Littler. Mr. Littler is listed as being in critical condition in the Rockyview Hospital. It is believed that Mr. Littler, who was driving, lost control of the car on a curve and it went into the ditch and overturned. Mr. Crossan was elected when his Conservative opponent, Frank Crawford, who had been heavily favoured to win, suddenly withdrew. Mr. Crawford recently won the Conservative nomination in the Highview riding and will be a candidate in the by-election to fill the vacancy caused by Mr. Crossan's demise."

"Seems like your drilling days are about over," the driller drawled.

A shaken Frank could only nod.

"Did you know the guy?"

"Barely. Shared the same platform with him a couple of times, that's all. He was okay. He had a young family."

"Tough. But it's a big break for you."

"Not the kind of break I want." Frank got up. "I'm going down to the change house. We're due to make a trip out of the hole on this tour."

The change house was filled with the sounds of a drilling rig at work — the pulsing roar of diesel engines, the slam of a steel door, the hum of the mud pumps, the scrape of hobnailed boots on corrugated metal steps, and the clang of chains on the drill floor. The unholy din was part of Frank's daily working life and usually he was barely conscious of it. Tonight, however, each individual sound was sharp and distinct. Working the rigs was a life of danger and long hours of unremitting physical labour under the severest of conditions, but it had been good to him and he was going to miss it. The other members of his crew came stomping into the change house, and Frank slowly pulled on his mud-encrusted overalls.

As usual, Cliff Barton was doing the talking but it was the two members of the goon squad from the bank's Toronto head office who were calling the shots. Representatives of the other leading banks were also present, but in the course of negotiations they had come to rely primarily on the Merchants, by far the largest lender, to carry the ball. The meeting had been called to discuss Bill's latest offer. He had raised the initial purchase price to $350-million and had thrown in a sweetener that would give the sellers an additional $50-million if the price of crude rose to $20 US per barrel and remained there for sixty consecutive days in the next twelve months.

"I keep telling you, gentlemen," Cliff's reference to gentlemen was meant to include Jim Goulder, but the banker's gaze remained fixed on Bill. "Our price is five hundred million. Firm. No linkage with the price of oil, or any fancy gimmicks like that. We've made up our mind that we're not going to take any more of a hit than that."

Out of the corner of his eye, Bill saw one of the head-office men give an almost imperceptible nod of agreement. It could have been a negotiating tactic, but Bill was almost positive it had been done unconsciously. If so, it meant the Merchants had come to a bottom-line decision and he had run out of negotiating room.

"Bill," Cliff was still talking, "we've told you that we would lend Venture the necessary funds."

"Which would improve your security position enormously since the loan would be backed by the assets of both companies."

"True. That's why we're willing to do the deal. It would change the loan into something we can carry on our books at full face value."

"And I would have turned Venture into the same kind of over-leveraged corporate cripple as Pursuit."

"Our figures show the combined assets can service a loan of this magnitude," Cliff replied.

"Not if the price of oil keeps falling through the floor."

"That's a risk you'll have to take." The banker's voice, which had been almost reasonable in tone, hardened. "Bill, nobody's twisting your arm to make this deal. It's entirely up to you. But I'm telling you that if you want the oil and gas properties of Pursuit Enterprises, the price tag is $500-million."

"You've got yourself a deal," Bill said tersely.

"Wha ...?" Cliff quickly recovered from his surprise and reached across the table with his hand outstretched. "Terrific, Bill. Congratulations."

"Bill," Jim Goulder said almost pleadingly as they went through the revolving doors and began to walk along the Mall, "Tell me there's something I don't know that makes sense out of what you just did."

"In a few months we'll know whether I just made the deal of the century, or blew it. Suffice it to say that there are some lands in the package that I just had to get my hands on. And that's all I'm going to say to anyone until title to the properties has been transferred to Venture and all the legal *i*'s and *t*'s have been duly dotted and crossed. The lawyers tell me that will take upwards of a month. Then we still have to wait for freeze-up."

"Northern muskeg country, huh? Well, you make me feel a little better but it still boils down to one hell of a gamble."

"That's what the oil business is all about, isn't it?"

Frank's campaign was already well underway by the time the premier called a by-election to fill the vacancy caused by Crossan's death. Dale Young had put together an enthusiastic team of workers, and stacks of signs and placards were stored in the warehouse of a Calgary printing plant. Dale was predicting a tough fight. The Socreds, desperate to maintain their toehold in the legislature and sensing a lingering vulnerability in Frank because of the call-girl scandal, had put aside their predilection for staid schoolteachers and rawboned farmers, and nominated a charismatic young lawyer who had built up a flourishing rural law practice. There was also the by-election factor to contend with. By-elections afford the voters an opportunity to rap the government's knuckles without running the risk of turfing them out of office. While most people realized that the collapse in oil prices and the depressed state of the agricultural industry were caused by international forces over which the provincial government had no control, there was still that human tendency to blame the government, regardless.

Realizing all this, Dale Young fashioned the campaign around Frank himself: emphasizing his lifelong connection with the riding, his agricultural background and, to an extent much greater than Frank was comfortable with, the heroic role he had played in averting the sour-gas well disaster. Frank campaigned hard and effectively — he really wanted a political career, and he realized if he lost again this time, he might as well pack it in. Fiona had put aside work on her master's thesis to campaign with him, and the press inevitably began to refer to them as "the golden couple." Frank and Fiona had set a wedding date for early December, by which time she would have completed her thesis and defended it before the examining board.

The notorious call-girl episode babbled along just underneath the surface of the campaign. Frank's opponent wisely took the high road and refrained from mentioning it in public. Some of his supporters were not so high-minded, however, and slipped snide remarks about it into their speeches and private conversations.

The only course open to Frank was to ignore the issue entirely and hope that it wouldn't influence too many voters.

A poll taken three-quarters of the way through the campaign gave the Crawford camp reason to cheer. It showed Frank holding a five-point lead among the decided voters with only thirty-five per cent terming themselves undecided. "Not bad for a by-election. Not bad at all," was Dale's reaction, adding for the benefit of the campaign workers who were in the office at the time, "We'll improve that lead by election day, with Frank coming on stronger and stronger the way he is. That talk to the Ladies' Horticultural Guild this afternoon was a masterpiece, Frank. I reckon you can count on every vote in the room."

He clapped his hands together. "All right, troops, we've got half an hour to grab some sandwiches and then it's off to the Oddfellows Hall. You've only got that one appearance tonight, Frank, so give 'em hell."

Buoyed by the results of the poll, Frank gave a rousing talk that was warmly received. The meeting was over by nine o'clock and he was looking forward to a restorative night's sleep as his elated campaign manager dropped him off at the Circle C. He could hear the phone ringing as he inserted the key in the front door. Damn. It was probably a voter who wanted to harangue him about some pet peeve, or a newspaper reporter looking for a quick quote, or a radio station wanting to patch him into a hotline show. Frank was tempted to delay until the phone stopped ringing, but his conscience made him rush across the living room and snatch up the receiver.

"Frank? Is that you?" It was a woman's voice. A woman with a sore-throat kind of voice.

"Yes, it is."

"This is Linda, Frank. Linda Shepherd."

Jesus. He didn't need this; not now. Maybe it wasn't Linda. That hoarse, almost croaking, voice certainly didn't sound like her. It could be someone playing a cruel trick on him, or trying to trip him up politically.

"How do I know it's you, Linda?" he asked carefully, praying that the caller would realize her bluff had been called and hang up. "Can you tell me something to identify yourself?"

"We met at a skating party at your family ranch."

"True. But a lot of people would know that."

"You found out I had implants when you felt the scars under my tits."

Frank was ready to concede, but he asked one further question. "Where did this happen?"

"In a hotel room in Toronto. The first night we made love. We were standing naked in front of a mirror." As she spoke of those happier times, Linda's voice lightened into something like the clear, youthful one Frank remembered.

"Why are you calling, Linda? It's been a long time. And where," this with rising alarm, "are you calling from?"

"I'm in Calgary. I have to see you, Frank. I'm in a jam, and you're involved."

"What kind of a jam?" Frank's voice was steady, but his knuckles were white from gripping the phone.

Linda went into a spasm of coughing. "It's the press," she said between racking coughs. "They're hounding me for a story about you and me. What you're like in bed. Stuff like that."

Frank cursed under his breath. Was Linda Shepherd fated to be his nemesis? To rise out of his past and haul him down whenever he got in sight of the goal? "You don't have to talk to them, Linda. They can't make you."

"It's the money, Frank. They're offering me a lot of bread. And I need it. Bad. Business hasn't been too good lately, and I got an expensive habit to support. I guess you know about that, huh?"

"How much money are we talking about?"

"Ten thousand dollars. I was thinking, Frank, if you could come up with the ten thou, I could get out of the country till the election's over."

So that was it. Linda had seen a chance to shake him down and was taking it. There probably wasn't any interest on the part of the press; she could have made that up.

"That's an awful lot of money," he said slowly. "Who is this 'press' that's putting all this pressure on you for a story?"

"Just reporters, you know."

Her vague answer did much to convince Frank that she was acting on her own initiative. Still, she could do a lot of damage if she was on the scene in Calgary and began selling interviews. Frank knew he should be furiously angry at her, but for some reason, he wasn't. He didn't even mind giving her the money. It sounded like she needed it desperately. He could raise the cash without any trouble; he had been able to bank a good part of the top wages he earned working on the rigs. The real problem was how to find a chance to get it to her.

"Where are you staying?"

"The Silver Spur Inn; it's in Motel Village. The manager says it's on the North Hill. You know where it is?"

"I can find it."

"I'm in room 127. It's on the first floor." Motels and hotels were her natural habitat and a seductive note crept into her ruined voice. It was as if Flair was beginning to emerge. Frank shuddered.

"Listen," he said urgently, "I want you to stay in your room. Don't leave it, even for meals. You can't be seen in Calgary. You understand that, don't you?"

"I'll be good. But what about the money?"

"I'll give it to you. I have to campaign most of the day, but I've got a break between four and six-thirty in the afternoon. I'll call you at the motel and we can arrange to meet."

Frank cursed helplessly as he hung up the receiver. But he was convinced he had done the right thing. The only thing, in fact. And only he could do it. He couldn't bring Dale into this. And he for sure wasn't about to upset Fiona with the news that Linda had surfaced once more. God, how would he ever be able to sleep tonight? And he had to get some sleep — there was so much on the line tomorrow. He went to the kitchen and poured himself the first drink of hard liquor he had had since he totalled the Trans Am.

"Linda?" Somewhat sheepishly, Frank added, "This is you know who."

His feeble attempt at anonymity fell through when she said, "Frank? Have you got the money?" Her open greed put him off, but he answered, "I have it. Where do we meet?"

"My room is real comfortable. It's even got a king-sized bed. Why don't we meet here?" She must have taken a shot of whatever drug she was on, for she sounded relaxed, almost playful.

There was no way he would meet her in a motel room. But there was so little time. "Let's meet in the motel parking lot. Outside your room. It'll take me fifteen minutes to get there."

Linda had obviously taken a lot of trouble to cover up the ravages of her lifestyle, but Frank was appalled by her appearance. Thin to the point of emaciation, she was wearing long sleeves to hide her arms; below the buttoned cuffs, her hands were like brittle claws. But it was her face that was most unsettling — mask-like under layers of makeup. The watery, unfocused eyes were ringed with mascara. Even a newspaper photo of this apparition linked with him would be enough to finish him politically.

"It's all there," he said stiffly as he handed her the brown envelope.

"Knowing you, I'm sure it is."

"No talking to the media, right?"

"Right. I've got a flight out of here tonight and I think I'll just keep on going. I've never seen London."

"I'm sure you'll enjoy it," Frank said ironically. "Look, Linda, if you want to get some treatment, maybe get yourself straightened out, I'd be happy to help."

"You're almost unbelievable, Frank, you know that! But it's the real you. I was real proud when I read about what you did at that well." She blinked hard several times and her lips turned down with self-disgust. Then she snapped, "I don't need your help, Frank. I don't need anyone's goddamn help. I know fucking well what I'm doing and I don't want to change anything. Not one damn thing! You understand?"

"I understand. Well, have a nice time in Europe." Frank raised his hand in farewell and began to walk to the car he had rented.

"Good luck in the election, Frank," she called out softly. Then she sobbed, "Oh, God!" and ran blindly back into the motel room.

The Record broke the story two days later under a headline that screamed: "Candidate Pays Blackmail to Hooker." The tabloid had it all: Linda's motel phone had been bugged, and she had been wired for her meeting with Frank. The sensation-mongering newspaper also had a cameraman hidden in one of the cars in the motel's parking lot and he had taken telephoto shots of Frank handing the envelope to Linda. There was also a repellent close-up of her looking so haggard it was almost frightening.

"Those bastards!" Frank, in an agony of despair, repeated over and over. *The Record* was the same rag that had run Margo Jones's explosive story revealing that Ken Kwasny was Bill Crawford's natural son. And now they had deliberately set him up, and destroyed his career. Linda had been part of the sting all along. Wonder how much they paid her. He hoped it was enough to keep her going till she reached the end of the road she had chosen to travel down.

Frank immediately came under enormous pressure to withdraw from the election. He came closest to buckling under when a disgusted Dale Young told him he should quit, that he didn't stand a chance of winning. Aware of how badly he had let his supporters down, Frank was on the verge of throwing in the towel, when he suddenly rebelled.

"I didn't do anything to be ashamed of," he told his stricken quartet of top advisers. "All I did was help out someone who once was a friend of mine."

"Come off it, Frank," Dale said wearily. "The voters will see you as a weakling who gave in to blackmail. The best course for both you and the party is for you to resign. Personally, I don't see how you can have the gall to get up on a platform and face the public."

Frank winced and looked over their heads to where Fiona was standing, a little apart from the group. "Stay with it," she mouthed.

"I'm not resigning," he declared. "I still think I have a chance, and if I'm beaten,

I'll at least have gone down fighting. Needless to say, none of you are under any obligation to stay on-board. We were running a great campaign and I screwed up. You'll never know how badly I feel about that."

"Well, you can count me out." Dale Young got to his feet. "I'm going to publicly dissociate myself from the campaign, Frank. It's turned into another goddamn fiasco and I want no part of it."

Two others stood up to join him but the fourth remained sitting. "I got a brother who farms in the Lundell area and I owe this young man something."

"We can do it," Fiona said briskly when the three of them were alone in the campaign trailer. "It's only five more days and the arrangements for all your appearances are already made."

Within the hour, an icily furious premier was on the phone to Frank, demanding that he resign. Frank politely refused, although he realized that even if by some miracle he won the election, he was forever doomed to remain a backbencher.

The premier then called Bill, pleading with him to prevail on his son to do the honourable thing and withdraw from the race. Bill turned him down flat, saying that Frank was his own man, and that he personally agreed with his decision to fight on. "After all," he pointed out, "what Frank did isn't a crime."

"He has committed the crime of disgracing the party on two occasions," the premier retorted angrily. "Relations between this government and the Crawford interests have always been cordial," he went on in a steely voice, "but if Frank persists in this folly, that will change. Radically."

"I'm sorry to hear that, Mr. Premier," Bill replied with cool indifference and hung up.

Frank's remaining public appearances attracted overflow crowds, including many from outside his riding, curious to see this star-crossed young man in person. The reaction of the crowds was strangely muted; for the most part they sat on their hands and studied Frank and Fiona, who always shared the platform with him, like actors in a fascinating real-life drama. The man with relatives in the Lundell area took on the job of introducing Frank. He reminded the audience of the lives that had been saved by Frank's refusal to run from the renegade well. "And he ain't running now, neither," he would say, ending on a note that never failed to bring a big hand.

Frank tried to concentrate on the issues, outlining the steps he felt should be taken to help the hard-pressed farmers. His ideas were received with many nods of approval but the moment would inevitably arrive when he had to face the issue of the payment to Linda. Taking a deep breath, and letting his voice drop, he told the hushed audience that he realized many were asking themselves why he had given money to a woman with a badly tarnished reputation. He refrained from mentioning the exact amount, knowing how shockingly large it must seem to most of them.

"That unfortunate woman was a friend of mine. At one time a good friend." It was impossible to get past this part without eliciting a few titters, but he used them to make the point. "When Linda Shepherd was my friend, I knew nothing of her other life. Nothing. And later, much later, when she appealed to me in desperation, needing help, I couldn't turn my back on her. In hindsight, I might be guilty of a mistake in judgment, but it was a human mistake."

"What about the press?" a heckler would invariably shout. "You paid her off so she wouldn't talk to the press."

"It was the press hounding her that she wanted to escape from. At least, so she led me to believe." It was the best he could do, and it was usually received with an embarrassed silence, mixed with a few jeers and catcalls.

"The poor boy," a middle-aged matron, who had been a political groupie all her life, whispered to the man sitting next to her. "He could have gone all the way."

His opponent capitalized on Frank's blunder brilliantly. In a television commercial that was broadcast almost hourly, and in his speeches, he took the line that up until now he had deliberately refrained from mentioning Frank's association with a notorious prostitute.

"The events of the last few days," he went on, seemingly more in sorrow than in anger, "have convinced me that in doing so, in attempting to keep this campaign on a high plane and to concentrate solely on the issues, I was unwittingly doing you, the voter, a great disservice. Events have shown just how vulnerable Mr. Crawford is to blackmail, and also the readiness with which he caves in to it. I say to you that such a man is unfit to represent the riding of Highview."

"That hurts," muttered Frank, staring glumly at the television screen. At Fiona's suggestion, he tried to counter the telling blow by claiming that he, having been through the fire, was now immune to further blackmail. The audience's reaction to this assertion was openly sceptical.

Voting on election day turned out to be exceptionally light, even for a by-election. Political pundits opined that many Conservatives, not wanting to vote for Frank and unable to bring themselves to vote for the Socreds, simply stayed away from the polls. When all the returns were in, Frank was defeated by the slim margin of 576 votes.

"I must say you look surprisingly chipper, all things considered," remarked Bill as they let their horses stretch their necks and settle into a loose-reined walk. It was two days after the election and father and son had gone out for a pre-breakfast ride together at the Circle C.

"In a strange sort of way, I feel almost purged," replied Frank thoughtfully, his expert eye checking the condition of the Herefords grazing in an adjoining field. "As though I've come through some kind of ordeal and am stronger for it."

"What's next for you?" Bill put Big Country into a collected trot as they approached a small rise.

"Go back to working on the rigs. It's a great way of dropping out of sight when you need to."

"You going back with Spartacus?"

"Yep. I figure they're the class act of the drilling industry."

"I agree. They're the outfit I want to drill the well."

"The well?" asked Frank as they trotted up to the top of the knoll and then dropped back into a walk. "After all the hundreds of wells you've drilled, you call this one the well. How come?"

"Because," his father replied soberly, "there's more riding on this one than on any other well I've ever drilled."

Frank whistled. "Coming from you, that's something! Just make sure you insist on rig Number 4. That's the best iron they've got, and, besides, it's my rig. I want to be there when that mother goes down!"

26

To Bill's chagrin, that fall turned out to be unseasonably warm in northwestern Canada. With growing frustration, he watched the nightly weather forecasts on television where a perpetually smiling woman cheerfully reported temperatures running ten to fifteen degrees higher than normal in the far north. There was no sign of the intense, grinding cold that was required to freeze the muskeg solid so that it could be traversed by heavy drilling equipment. Normally, Bill took the delays caused by the vagaries of natural forces in his stride. A lifetime spent in the oil industry, and especially his experience drilling in the Arctic, had taught him that when Mother Nature turned capricious, the only course was to wait her out. But this philosophical approach began to wear thin as the days dragged by, leaving him altogether too much time to think about the predicament he had created for himself and his company.

With the onset of the winter-heating season, the price of crude had stabilized. The only problem was that it had stabilized at a level that was too low to service Venture's new debt. If Bill hadn't involved the company in the costly acquisition of the Pursuit assets, Venture would have been in good shape to ride out the storm until the economic situation righted itself. As things were, however, the interest on Venture's huge debt was draining off all its cash flow. That would cease to matter, of course, if the well discovered anything like the kind of reserves he was hoping for. On the other hand, if it came in dry, he would have turned the successful company he had built and watched over for a lifetime into yet another corporate zombie. And there was no escaping the knowledge that he had paid the $200-million premium for the Pursuit properties so that he, Bill Crawford, could have a crack at making a spectacular oil find. The Pursuit acquisition had been ego driven and he began to ask himself the hard question as to whether he had the right to put the shareholders at risk just so that Bill Crawford could have a chance at glory. These uneasy musings were put aside with the arrival of an Arctic front that extended as far south as Peace River. Temperatures plunged to thirty and forty degrees below freezing and the winter drilling season was finally underway.

When the wildcat, Venture 6-24-114-6 w6m, appeared in the *Daily Oil Bulletin*'s list of new locations (pathetically shrunken since the glory days of two years ago when 475 rigs were active in Alberta), the oil patch snapped to attention. Last winter, Venture had drilled a dry hole just a few miles south of there, and that could have given Crawford the geological clue he needed to justify another exploratory hole in the area. That must be the reason, they speculated over drinks at the Pete Club, why he had paid the moon for the Pursuit properties. The new Venture well was in reef country, and it could be that Crawford was out hunting himself an elephant. God knew, it would take an elephant to turn the Pursuit purchase around.

Spartacus No. 4, rigged and ready to spud, was an insignificant blemish on the vast white expanse of frozen land.

The whickering clatter of a low-flying helicopter overrode the sound of the rig's idling diesels, making Frank and the toolpush who was standing beside him on the drill floor, look up at the immaculately-blue sky. The chopper banked to the right as it closed in on the rig and began to fly around it in shallow circles. Frank and the toolpush could see someone peering down at them through high-powered binoculars. The toolpush gave a snort of disgust. "We're being scouted already, and we haven't even spudded in yet, for Christ's sake!"

"I have a feeling we're going to be mighty popular while this hole is going down," grinned Frank. "Everybody knows this is a reef test and half the companies in the oil patch will be hiring scouts to keep tabs on it."

The toolpush squinted up at the helicopter as it rapidly gained altitude and turned away from the rig. Working a pinch of snuff under his upper lip, he said, "They say your old man's bet the farm on this one, Frank."

"I don't know about that, but I do know he's pretty excited about it. But he's been around long enough to know that drilling a rank wildcat is playing against the odds."

"If there's anybody who knows that, it's Bill Crawford." The toolpush made no effort to hide his admiration. "He's an oilman's oilman, that guy." Adjusting the tilt of his hard hat, he said, "Okay, Frank, get yourself up on that monkey board and let's start this son of a bitch turning to the right."